KU-072-921

Louise Penny is the number one *New York Times* bestselling author of the bestselling Chief Inspector Gamache series, including *Still Life*, which won the CWA John Creasey Dagger in 2006. Recipient of virtually every existing award for crime fiction, Louise was also granted the Order of Canada in 2014 and received an honorary doctorate of literature from Carleton University and the Ordre Nationale du Québec in 2017. She lives in a small village south of Montreal.

LOUISE PENNY

KINGDOM
OF
THE BLIND

sphere

SPHERE

First published in the United States in 2018 by Minotaur,
a division of St Martin's Press
First published in Great Britain in 2018 by Sphere

Copyright © Three Pines Creations, Inc 2018

The moral right of the author has been asserted.

A CIP catalogue record for this book
is available from the British Library.

Hardback ISBN 978-0-7515-6661-1
Trade Paperback ISBN 978-0-7515-6659-8

Printed and bound in Great Britain by
Clays Ltd, Elcograf S.p.A.

Papers used by Sphere are from well-managed forests
and other responsible sources.

Sphere
An imprint of
Little, Brown Book Group
Carmelite House
50 Victoria Embankment
London EC4Y 0DZ

An Hachette UK Company
www.hachette.co.uk

www.littlebrown.co.uk

For Hope Dellon, my editor and friend.
Whale oil beef hooked.

CHAPTER 1

—

Armand Gamache slowed his car to a crawl, then stopped on the snow-covered secondary road.

This was it, he supposed. Pulling in, he drove between the tall pine trees until he reached the clearing.

There he parked the car and sat in the warm vehicle looking out at the cold day. Snow flurries were hitting the windshield and dissolving. They were coming down with more force now, slightly obscuring what he saw outside. Turning away, he stared at the letter he'd received the day before, lying open on the passenger seat.

Putting on his reading glasses, he rubbed his face. And read it again. It was an invitation of sorts, to this desolate place.

He turned off the car. But didn't get out.

There was no particular anxiety. It was more puzzling than worrisome.

But still, it was just odd enough to raise a small alarm. Not a siren, yet. But he was alert.

Armand Gamache was not by nature timid, but he was a cautious man. How else could he have survived in the top echelons of the Sûreté du Québec? Though it was far from certain that he had survived.

He relied on, and trusted, both his rational mind and his instincts. And what were they telling him now?

They were certainly telling him this was strange. But then, he thought with a grin, his grandchildren could have told him that.

Bringing out his cell phone, he listened as the number he called rang once, twice, and then was answered.

"*Salut, ma belle*. I'm here," he said.

It was an agreement between Armand and his wife, Reine-Marie, that in winter, in snow, they called each other when they'd arrived at a destination.

"How was the drive? The snow seems to be getting worse in Three Pines."

"Here too. Drive was easy."

"So where are you? What is the place, Armand?"

"It's sort of hard to describe."

But he tried.

What he saw had once been a home. Then a house. And was now simply a building. And not even that for much longer.

"It's an old farmhouse," he said. "But it looks abandoned."

"Are you sure you're at the right place? Remember when you came to get me at my brother's home and you went to the wrong brother? Insisting I was there."

"That was years ago," he said. "And all the houses look alike in Ste.-Angélique, and, honestly, all your hundred and fifty-seven brothers look alike. Besides, he didn't like me, and I was fairly sure he just wanted me to go away and leave you alone."

"Can you blame him? You were at the wrong house. Some detective."

Armand laughed. That had been decades ago, when they were first courting. Her family had since warmed to him, once they saw how much she loved him and, more important to them, how much he loved Reine-Marie.

"I'm at the right place. There's another car here."

Light snow covered the other vehicle. It had been there, he guessed, for about half an hour. Not more. Then his eyes returned to the farm-house.

"It's been a while since anyone lived here."

It took a long time to fall into such a state. Lack of care, over the years, would do that.

It was now little more than a collection of materials.

The shutters were askew, the wooden handrail had rotted and gone its separate way from the sloping steps. One of the upper windows was boarded up, so that it looked like the place was winking at him. As though it knew something he did not.

He cocked his head. Was there a slight lean to the house? Or was his imagination turning this into one of Honoré's nursery rhymes?

> *There was a crooked man, and he walked a crooked mile,*
> *He found a crooked sixpence against a crooked stile;*
> *He bought a crooked cat, which caught a crooked mouse,*
> *And they all lived together in a little crooked house.*

This was a crooked house. And Armand Gamache wondered if, inside, he'd find a crooked man.

After saying goodbye to Reine-Marie, he looked again at the other car in the yard, and the license plate with the motto of Québec stamped on it: JE ME SOUVIENS.

I remember.

When he closed his eyes, as he did now, images appeared uninvited. As vivid, as intense as the moment they'd happened. And not only the day last summer, with the slanting shafts of cheerful sunlight hitting the blood on his hands.

He saw all the days. All the nights. All the blood. His own, and others'. People whose lives he'd saved. And those he'd taken.

But to keep his sanity, his humanity, his equilibrium, he needed to recall the wonderful events as well.

Finding Reine-Marie. Having their son and daughter. Now grandchildren.

Finding their refuge in Three Pines. The quiet moments with friends. The joyful celebrations.

The father of a good friend had developed dementia and died recently. For the last year or so of his life, he no longer recognized family and friends. He was kindly to all, but he beamed at some. They were the ones he loved. He knew them instinctively and kept them safe, not in his wounded head but in his heart.

The memory of the heart was far stronger than whatever was kept in the mind. The question was, what did people keep in their heart?

Chief Superintendent Gamache had known more than a few people whose heart had been consumed by hate.

He looked at the crooked house in front of him and wondered what memory was consuming it.

3

After instinctively committing the license-plate number to memory, he scanned the yard.

It was dotted with large mounds of snow, under which, Gamache guessed, were rusted vehicles. A pickup picked apart. An old tractor now scrap. And something that looked like a tank but was probably an old oil tank and not a tank tank.

He hoped.

Gamache put on his tuque and was about to put on gloves when he hesitated and picked up the letter yet again. There wasn't much to it. Just a couple of clipped sentences.

Far from being threatening, they were almost comical and would've been had they not been written by a dead man.

It was from a notary, asking, almost demanding, that Gamache present himself at this remote farmhouse at 10:00 a.m. Sharp. Please. Don't be late. *Merci.*

He'd looked up the notary in the Chambre des Notaires du Québec.

Maître Laurence Mercier.

He'd died of cancer six months earlier.

And yet— Here was a letter from him.

There was no email or return address, but there was a phone number, which Armand had called but no one had answered.

He'd been tempted to look up Maître Mercier in the Sûreté database but decided against it. It wasn't that Gamache was persona non grata at the Sûreté du Québec. Not exactly, anyway. Now on suspension pending the outcome of an investigation into events last summer, he felt he needed to be judicious in the favors he asked of colleagues. Even Jean-Guy Beauvoir. His second-in-command. His son-in-law.

Gamache looked again at the once-strong house and smiled. Feeling a kinship toward it.

Things sometimes fell apart unexpectedly. It was not necessarily a reflection of how much they were valued.

He folded the letter and placed it in his breast pocket. Just as he was leaving the car, his cell phone rang.

Gamache looked at the number. Stared at the number. Any sign of amusement wiped from his face.

Dare he take it?

Dare he not?

As the ringing continued, he stared out the windshield, his view obscured by the now-heavy snow, so that he saw the world imperfectly.

He wondered if, in future, whenever he saw an old farmhouse, or heard the soft tapping of snowflakes, or smelled damp wool, this moment would be conjured and, if so, would it be with a sense of relief or horror?

"Oui, allô?"

The man stood by the window, straining to see out.

It was distorted by frost, but he had seen the car arrive and had watched, with impatience, as the man parked, then just sat there.

After a minute or so, the new arrival got out but didn't come toward the house. He was standing beside his car, a cell phone to his ear.

This was the first of *les invités*.

The man recognized this first guest, of course. Who wouldn't? He'd seen him often enough, but only in news reports. Never in person.

And he'd been far from convinced this guest would show up.

Armand Gamache. The former head of homicide. The current Chief Superintendent of the Sûreté du Québec, on suspension.

He felt a slight frisson of excitement. Here was a celebrity of sorts. A man both highly respected and reviled. Some in the press held him up as a hero. Others as a villain. Representing the worst aspects of policing. Or the best. The abuse of power. Or a daring leader, willing to sacrifice his own reputation, and perhaps more, for the greater good.

To do what no one else wanted to do. Or could do.

Through the distorted glass, through the snow, he saw a man in his late fifties. Tall, six feet at least. And substantial. The parka made him look heavy, but parkas made everyone look heavy. The face, not pudgy, was, however, worn. With lines from his eyes, and, as he watched, two deep furrows formed between Gamache's brows.

He was not good at understanding the faces faces made. He saw the lines but couldn't read them. He thought Gamache was angry, but it could have been simply concentration. Or surprise. He supposed it could even have been joy.

But he doubted that.

5

It was snowing more heavily now, but Gamache had not put on his gloves. They'd fallen to the ground when he'd gotten out of the car. It was how most Québécois lost mitts and gloves and even hats. They rested on laps in the car and were forgotten when it came time to get out. In spring the land was littered with dog shit, worms, and sodden mitts and gloves and tuques.

Armand Gamache stood in the falling snow, his bare hand to his ear. Gripping a phone and listening.

And when it was his turn to talk, Gamache bowed his head, his knuckles white as he tightened his hold on the phone, or from incipient frostbite. Then, taking a few steps away from his car, he turned his back to the wind and snow, and he spoke.

The man couldn't hear what was being said, but then one phrase caught a gust and made its way across the snowy yard, past possessions once prized. And into the house. Once prized.

"You'll regret this."

And then some other movement caught his attention. Another car was pulling in to the yard.

The second of *les invités*.

CHAPTER 2

—

"Armand?"

The smile of recognition and slight relief froze on her face as she took in his expression.

His movement as he'd turned to face her had been almost violent. His body tense, prepared. As though bracing for a possible attack.

While she was adept at reading faces and understood body language, she could not quite get the expression on his face. Except for the most obvious.

Surprise.

But there was more there. Far more.

And then it was gone. His body relaxed, and as she watched, Armand spoke a single word into his phone, tapped on it, then put it into his pocket.

The last expression to leave that familiar face, before the veneer of civility covered it completely, was something that surprised her even more.

Guilt.

And then the smile appeared.

"For God's sake, Myrna. What're you doing here?"

Armand tried to modulate his smile, though it was difficult. His face was numb, almost frozen.

He didn't want to look like a grinning fool, overdoing it. Giving himself away to this very astute woman. Who was also a neighbor.

A retired psychologist, Myrna Landers owned the bookstore in Three Pines and had become good friends with Reine-Marie and Armand.

He suspected she'd seen, and understood, his initial reaction. Though he also suspected she would not grasp the depth of it. Or ever guess who he'd been speaking with.

He had been so engrossed in his conversation. In choosing his words. In listening so closely to the words being spoken to him. And the tone. And modulating his own tone. That he'd allowed someone to sneak up on him.

Granted, it was a friend. But it could just as easily have not been a friend.

As a cadet, as a Sûreté agent. As an inspector. As head of homicide, then head of the whole force, he'd had to be alert. Trained himself to be alert, so that it became second nature. First nature.

It's not that he walked through life expecting something bad to happen. His vigilance had simply become part of who he was, like his eye color. Like his scars.

Part DNA, part a consequence of his life.

Armand knew that the problem wasn't that he'd let his guard down just now. Just the opposite. It had been up so high, so thick, that for a few crucial minutes nothing else penetrated. He'd missed hearing the car approach. He'd missed the soft tread of boots on snow.

Gamache, not a fearful man, felt a small lick of concern. This time the consequences were benign. But next?

The threat didn't have to be monumental. If it were, it wouldn't be missed. It was almost always something tiny.

A signal missed or misunderstood. A blind spot. A moment of distraction. A focus so sharp that everything around it blurred. A false assumption mistaken for fact.

And then—

"You okay?" Myrna Landers asked as Armand approached and kissed her on both cheeks.

"I'm fine."

She could feel the cold on his face and the damp from the snow that had hit and melted. And she could feel the tension in the man, rumbling below the cheerful surface.

His smile created deep lines from the corners of his eyes. But it did not actually reach those brown eyes. They remained sharp, wary. Watchful. Though the warmth was still there.

"Fine," he'd said, and despite her disquiet she smiled.

They both understood that code. It was a reference to their neighbor in the village of Three Pines. Ruth Zardo. A gifted poet. One of the most distinguished in the nation. But that gift had come wrapped in more than a dollop of crazy. The name Ruth Zardo was uttered with equal parts admiration and dread. Like conjuring a magical creature that was both creative and destructive.

Ruth's last book of poetry was called *I'm FINE*. Which sounded good until you realized, often too late, that "F.I.N.E." stood for "Fucked-Up, Insecure, Neurotic, and Egotistical."

Yes, Ruth Zardo was many things. Fortunately for them, one of the things she was not was there.

Armand stooped and picked up the mitts that had fallen off Myrna's substantial lap, into the snow. He whacked them against his parka before handing them back to her. Then, realizing he was also missing his own, he went to his car and found them almost buried in the new snow.

The man watched all this from the questionable protection of the house.

He'd never met the woman who'd just arrived, but already he didn't like her. She was large and black and a "she." None of those things he found attractive. But worse still, Myrna Landers had arrived five minutes late, and instead of hurrying inside, spouting apologies, she was standing around chatting. As though he weren't waiting for them. As though he hadn't been clear about the time of the appointment.

Which he had.

Though his annoyance was slightly mitigated by relief that she'd shown up at all.

He watched the two of them closely. It was a game he played. Watching. Trying to guess what people might do next.

He was almost always wrong.

Both Myrna and Armand pulled the letters from their pockets.

They compared them. Exactly the same.

"This is"—she looked around—"a bit odd, don't you think?"

He nodded and followed her eyes to the ramshackle house.

"Do you know these people?" he asked.

"What people?"

"Well, whoever lives here. Lived here."

"No. You?"

"*Non*. I haven't a clue who they are or why we're here."

"I called the number," said Myrna. "But there was no answer. No way to get in touch with this Laurence Mercier. He's a notary. Do you know him?"

"*Non*. But I do know one thing."

"What?" Myrna could tell that something unpleasant was about to come her way.

"He died six months ago. Cancer."

"Then what—"

She had no idea how to continue, and so stopped. She looked over at the house, then turned to Armand. She was almost his height, and while her parka made her look heavy, in her case it was no illusion.

"You knew that the guy who sent you the letter died months ago, and still you came," she said. "Why?"

"Curiosity," he said. "You?"

"Well, I didn't know he was dead."

"But you did know it was strange. So why did you come?"

"Same. Curiosity. What's the worst that could happen?"

It was, even Myrna recognized, a fairly stupid thing to say.

"If we start hearing organ music, Armand, we run. Right?"

He laughed. He, of course, knew the worst that could happen. He'd knelt beside it hundreds of times.

Myrna tipped her head back to stare at the roof, sagging under the weight of months of snow. She saw the cracked and missing windows and blinked as snowflakes, large and gentle and relentless, landed on her face and fell into her eyes.

"It's not really dangerous, is it?" she asked.

"I doubt it."

"Doubt?" Her eyes widened slightly. "There is a chance?"

"I think the only danger will come from the building itself," he nodded to the slumping roof and sloping walls, "and not from who- ever is inside."

They'd walked over, and now he put his foot on the first step and it broke. He raised his brows at her, and she smiled.

"I think that's more the amount of croissants than the amount of wood rot," she said, and he laughed.

"I agree."

He paused for a moment, looking at the steps, then the house.

"You're not sure if it's dangerous, are you?" she said. "Either the house or whoever's inside."

"*Non*," he admitted. "I'm not sure. Would you prefer to wait out here?"

Yes, she thought.

"No," she said, and followed him in.

"Maître Mercier." The man introduced himself, walking forward, his hand extended.

"*Bonjour*," said Gamache, who'd gone in first. "Armand Gamache."

He swiftly took in his surroundings, beginning with the man.

Short, slight, white. In his mid-forties.

Alive.

The electricity had been turned off in the house and with it the heat, leaving the air cold and stale. Like a walk-in freezer.

The notary had kept his coat on, and Armand could see it was smudged with dirt. Though Armand's was too. It was near impossible to get into and out of a vehicle in a Québec winter without getting smeared by dirt and salt.

But Maître Mercier's coat wasn't just dirty, it was stained. And worn.

There was an air of neglect about him. The man, like his clothing, appeared threadbare. But there was also a dignity there, bordering on haughtiness.

"Myrna Landers," said Myrna, stepping forward and offering her hand.

Maître Mercier took it but dropped it quickly. More a touch than a handshake.

Gamache noticed that Myrna's attitude had changed slightly. No longer fearful, she looked at their host with what appeared to be pity.

There were some creatures who naturally evoked that reaction. Not given armor, or a poison bite, or the ability to fly or even run, what they had was equally powerful.

The ability to look so helpless, so pathetic, that they could not possibly be a threat. Some even adopted them. Protected them. Nurtured them. Took them in.

And almost always regretted it.

It was far too early to tell if Maître Mercier was just such a creature, but he did have that immediate effect, even on someone as experienced and astute as Myrna Landers.

Even on himself, Gamache realized. He could feel his defenses lowering in the presence of this sad little man.

Though they did not drop completely.

Gamache took off his tuque and, smoothing his graying hair, he looked around.

The outside door opened directly into the kitchen, as they often did in farmhouses. It looked unchanged since the sixties. Maybe even fifties. The cabinets were made of plywood painted a cheery blue the color of cornflowers, the counters of chipped yellow laminate and the floors of scuffed linoleum.

Anything of value had been taken. The appliances were gone, the walls were stripped clean except for a mint-green clock above the sink, that had long since stopped.

For a moment he imagined the room as it might once have been. Shiny, not new but clean and cared for. People moving about, preparing a Thanksgiving or Christmas dinner. Children chasing one another around like wild colts, with parents trying to tame them. Then giving up.

He noticed lines on the doorjamb. Marking heights. Before time had stopped.

Yes, he thought, this room, this home, was happy once. Cheerful once.

He looked again at their host. The notary who did and did not exist.

12

Had this been his home? Had he been happy, cheerful, once? If so, there was no sign of it. It had all been stripped away.

Maître Mercier motioned to the kitchen table, inviting them to sit. Which they did.

"Before we begin, I'd like you to sign this."

Mercier pushed a piece of paper toward Gamache.

Armand leaned back in his chair, away from the paper. "Before we begin," he said, "I'd like to know who you are and why we're here."

"So would I," said Myrna.

"In due course," said Mercier.

It was such a strange thing to say, both as a formal and dated turn of phrase and in its complete dismissal of their request. A not-unreasonable request either, from people who didn't have to be there.

Mercier looked and sounded like a character from Dickens. And not the hero. Gamache wondered if Myrna felt the same way.

The notary placed a pen on the paper and nodded to Gamache, who did not pick it up.

"Listen," said Myrna, laying a large hand on Mercier's and feeling him spasm. "Dear." Her voice was calm, warm, clear. "You tell us now or I'm leaving. And I'm assuming you don't want that."

Gamache pushed the paper back across the table toward the notary.

Myrna patted Mercier's hand, and Mercier stared back at her.

"Now," she said. "How did you rise from the dead?"

Mercier looked at her like she was the crazy one, then his eyes shifted, and both Gamache and Myrna turned to follow his gaze out the window.

Another vehicle had pulled up. A pickup truck. And out hopped a young man, his mitts falling into the snow. But he swiftly stooped and picked them up.

Armand caught Myrna's eye.

The newest arrival wore a long red-and-white-striped hat. So long that it tapered to a pom-pommed tail that trailed down his back and dragged in the snow as he stepped away from his truck.

Noticing this, the young man lifted the end of the tuque and wrapped it once around his neck like a scarf before tossing it over his shoulder in a move so rakish that Myrna found herself smiling.

Whoever this was, he was as vibrant as their dead host was desiccated.

13

Dr. Seuss meets Charles Dickens.

The Cat in the Hat was about to enter Bleak House.

There was a knock on the door, then he walked in. Looking around, his eyes fell on Gamache, who'd gotten to his feet.

"*Allô, bonjour,*" said the cheerful young man. "Monsieur Mercier?"

He put out his hand. Gamache took it.

"*Non.* Armand Gamache."

They shook hands. The newcomer's hand was callused, strong. His grip was firm and friendly. A confident handshake without being forced.

"Benedict Pouliot. *Salut.* Hope I'm not late. Traffic over the bridge was awful."

"This is Maître Mercier," said Armand, stepping aside to reveal the notary.

"Hello, sir," said the young man, shaking the notary's hand.

"And I'm Myrna Landers," said Myrna, shaking his hand and smiling, Armand thought, just a little too broadly.

Though it was hard not to smile at the handsome young man. Not that he was laughable. But he was affable and almost completely without affectation. His eyes were thoughtful and bright.

Benedict took off his hat and smoothed his blond hair, which was cut in a fashion Myrna had never seen before and hoped never to see again. It was buzz-cut short on the top then, at his ears, it became long. Very long.

"So," he said, rubbing his hands together in anticipation and perhaps because it was so cold. "Where do we begin?"

They all looked at Mercier, who continued to stare at Benedict.

"It's the haircut, isn't it?" said the young man. "My girlfriend did it. She's taking a stylist course, and the final exam is to create a new cut. What do you think?"

He ran his hands through it as the others remained silent.

"Looks great," said Myrna, confirming for Armand that love, or infatuation, was indeed blind.

"Did she also make your hat?" Armand asked, pointing to what was now a large red-and-white lump of wet wool at the end of the table.

"Yes. Final marks in her design class. Do you like it?"

Armand gave what he hoped might be a noncommittal grunt.

"You sent the letter, didn't you, sir?" Benedict said to Mercier. "Now, do you want to show me around first, or should we look at plans? Is this your house?" he asked Armand and Myrna. "To be honest, I'm not sure it can be saved. It's in pretty rough shape."

Gamache and Myrna looked at each other and realized what he was saying.

"We're not together," said Myrna, laughing. "Like you, we were invited here by Maître Mercier."

She brought out her letter, as did Armand, and they placed them on the table.

Benedict bent over, then straightened up. "I'm confused. I thought I was here to bid on a job."

He put his own letter on the table. It was, except for his name and address, identical to the other two.

"What do you do?" Myrna asked, and Benedict handed her one of his cards.

It was bloodred and diamond shaped, with something unreadable embossed.

"Your girlfriend?" asked Myrna.

"Yes. Her business class."

"Final marks?"

"*Oui.*"

Myrna handed it to Gamache, who had to put on his reading glasses and tip the card toward the window to have any hope of reading the bumps.

"'Benedict Pouliot. Builder,'" he read out loud, then turned it over. "There's no phone number or email."

"No. Marks were deducted. So am I here to bid on a job?"

"No," said Mercier. "Sit."

Benedict sat.

More like a puppy than a cat, really, thought Gamache as he took the seat next to Benedict.

"Then why am I here?" Benedict asked.

"We want to know too," said Myrna, ripping her eyes off Benedict and directing them back to the notary.

CHAPTER 3

———

"State your name, please."

"You know my name, Marie," said Jean-Guy. "We've worked together for years."

"Please, sir," she said, her voice pleasant but firm.

Jean-Guy stared at her, then at the two other officers assembled in the boardroom.

"Jean-Guy Beauvoir."

"Rank?"

He gave her a filthy look now, but she just held his stare.

"Acting head of homicide for the Sûreté du Québec."

"*Merci.*"

The inspector gazed at the laptop in front of her, then back at him.

"This isn't about you, you'll be happy to hear." She smiled, but he did not. "Your suspension was lifted several months ago. But we still have serious questions about the decisions and actions of Monsieur Gamache."

"Chief Superintendent Gamache," said Beauvoir. "And how can you still have questions? You've asked, and he's answered, every possible question. You must've cleared him by now? It's been almost six months. Come on. Enough."

Again he looked at who he thought were his colleagues. Then back at her. His gaze becoming less hostile and more baffled.

"What is this?"

Jean-Guy had been in many such interviews and had felt confident he could control the situation, knowing they were all on the same side.

But as they stared at him from the other side of the table, he realized his mistake.

He'd entered the room expecting this would just be a formality. A last interview before, like him, the Chief was exonerated and returned to work.

The atmosphere had indeed been convivial, almost jovial. At first.

Beauvoir was sure they'd tell him that a sternly worded statement was being drafted, explaining that a rigorous investigation had been held. It would lament the fact that the covert Sûreté operation in the summer had ended with such bloodshed.

But it would, ultimately, voice support for the unconventional and bold decisions taken by Chief Superintendent Gamache. And unwavering support for the Sûreté team involved in what turned out to be a wildly successful action. A commendation would be given to Isabelle Lacoste, the head of homicide, whose actions had saved so many lives but who'd paid so high a price.

It would end there.

Chief Superintendent Gamache would go back to work, and all would return to normal.

Though the fact an investigation that had begun in the summer was still going on in the depth of the Québec winter was disconcerting.

"You were second-in-command to your father-in-law when decisions were taken leading to the action we're investigating?" the inspector asked.

"I was with Chief Superintendent Gamache, yes. You know that."

"*Oui*. Your father-in-law."

"My boss."

"Yes. The person responsible for what happened. We all know that, Chief Inspector, but thank you for clarifying."

The others nodded. Sympathetically. Understanding the delicate position Beauvoir found himself in.

They were, Beauvoir realized with some surprise, inviting him to distance himself from Gamache.

It would be easier to distance himself from his hands and feet. His position was not at all delicate. It was, in fact, firm. He stood with Gamache.

But he was beginning to get a sick feeling deep in his gut.

"Neither of us is guilty, *mon vieux*," Gamache had said months earlier, when the inevitable investigation had begun. "You know that. These are just questions that need to be asked after what happened. There's nothing to worry about."

Not guilty, his father-in-law had said. What he didn't say was that they were innocent. Which, of course, they were not.

Jean-Guy Beauvoir had been cleared and had accepted the post as acting head of homicide.

But Chief Superintendent Gamache remained on suspension. Though Beauvoir had been confident that was about to end.

"One last meeting," he'd said to his wife that morning as they fed their son, "and your father will be cleared."

"Uh-huh," said Annie.

"What?"

He knew his wife well. Despite the fact she was a lawyer, a less cynical person would be hard to find. And yet he could tell there was doubt there.

"It's taken so long. I'm just worried it's become political. They need a scapegoat. Dad let a ton of opioids through his hands. Drugs he could've stopped. Someone has to be blamed."

"But he's got most of it back. And he had no choice. Really." He stood up and kissed her. "And it wasn't quite a ton."

A clump of oatmeal Honoré had flung hit Jean-Guy's cheek, then dropped onto the top of Annie's head.

Picking the glop out of her hair, Jean-Guy looked at it, then put it into his mouth.

"You'd have made a great gorilla," said Annie.

Jean-Guy started searching her scalp, aping a gorilla grooming its mate, while Annie laughed and Honoré flung more oatmeal.

Jean-Guy supposed he knew that Annie would never be the most beautiful woman in any room. A stranger wouldn't look at her twice.

But if one did, he might discover something it had taken Jean-Guy many years and one failed marriage to see. How very beautiful happiness was. And Annie Gamache radiated happiness.

She would always be, he knew with certainty, not just the most intelligent person in any room but also the most beautiful. And if anyone didn't see it, it was their loss.

He unbuckled Honoré and walked to the door with him in his arms.

"Have fun today," he said, kissing both of them.

"Just a moment," said Annie.

She took off Jean-Guy's bib, wiped his face, and said, "Be careful. I think this might be a two-holer."

"Deep *merde*?" Jean-Guy shook his head. "*Non*. This's the last of it. I think they just have to make it clear that there was a thorough investigation. And there was. But believe me, after looking at the facts, they'll be thanking your father for what he did. They'll understand that he faced a shitty choice and did what had to be done."

"Please, no swearing in front of the kid. You'd hate his first word to be 'shit,'" she said. "I agree with you. Dad had no choice. But they might not see it that way."

"Then they're blind."

"Then they're human," said Annie, taking Honoré. "And humans need a place to hide. I think they're hiding behind him. And preparing to shove Dad to the predators."

Beauvoir walked briskly to the subway and what he knew would be the final internal-affairs interview before all returned to normal.

His head was down, and he concentrated on the sidewalk and the soft, light snow hiding the ice below.

One misstep and bad things happened. A turned ankle. A wrist broken trying to break the fall. Or a fractured skull.

It was always what you couldn't see that hurt you.

And now, sitting in the interview room, Jean-Guy Beauvoir was wondering if Annie had been right and he had, in fact, missed something.

CHAPTER 4

———

"Who are you?" Gamache asked, leaning forward and staring at the man at the head of the table.

"We already know, sir," said Benedict.

He spoke slowly. Patiently. Myrna had to drop her head to hide her amusement and delight.

"He's. A. Notary." The young man all but patted Armand's hand.

"*Oui, merci,*" said Armand. "I did just get that. But Laurence Mercier died six months ago. So who are you?"

"It says it right there," said Mercier. He pointed to the illegible signature. "Lucien Mercier. Laurence was my father."

"And are you a notary?"

"I am. I've taken over my father's practice."

In Québec, Gamache knew, notaries were more like solicitors than clerks. Doing everything from land transactions to marriage contracts.

"Why're you using his stationery?" asked Myrna. "It's misleading."

"It's economical and environmental. I hate waste. I use my father's letterhead when I'm doing business that was his. Less confusing for the clients."

"Can't say that's true," muttered Myrna.

Lucien brought four file folders from his briefcase and handed them around. "You're here because you're named in the last will of Bertha Baumgartner."

There was silence as they absorbed that, then Benedict said, "Really?" at the same time both Armand and Myrna said, "Who?"

"Bertha Baumgartner," the notary repeated. And then said the name a third time when the two older *invités* continued to stare at him.

"But I've never heard of her," said Myrna. "Have you?"

Armand thought for a moment. He met a lot of people and felt fairly certain he'd remember that name. But he was drawing a blank. It meant absolutely nothing.

Armand and Myrna turned to Benedict, whose handsome face was curious, but not more.

"You?" Myrna prompted, and he shook his head.

"Did she leave us money?" Benedict asked.

It wasn't said with greed, Gamache thought. More amazement. And yes, perhaps some hope.

"No," Mercier was happy to report, and then unhappy to see that the young man didn't seem at all disappointed.

"So why're we here?" asked Myrna.

"You're the liquidators of her estate."

"What?" said Myrna. "You're kidding."

"Liquidator? What's that?" asked Benedict.

"It's called 'executor' in most places," Mercier explained.

When Benedict continued to look confused, Armand explained. "It means Bertha Baumgartner wants us to oversee her will. Make sure her wishes are carried out."

"So she's dead?" asked Benedict.

Armand was about to say yes. That much seemed obvious. But "dead" had already proved less than obvious that day, so perhaps Madame Baumgartner . . .

He turned to the notary for confirmation.

"*Oui*. She died just over a month ago."

"And she was living here until then?" asked Myrna, looking up at the sagging ceiling and calculating how long it would take to get out the door if the sag became a collapse. Or maybe she could just fling herself through the window.

Between the new snow and the fact she was made almost entirely of gummy bears, it would probably be a soft landing.

"No, she was in a seniors' home," said Mercier.

"So is it like jury duty?" asked Benedict.

"*Pardon?*" asked the notary.

"You know, people whose names just come up. Our civic duty, that sort of thing. To be . . . what did you call it?"

"A liquidator," said Mercier. "No. It's not at all like jury duty. She chose you specifically."

"But why us?" asked Armand. "We didn't even know her."

"I have no idea, and, sadly, we can't ask her," said Mercier, who did not look at all sad.

"Your father didn't say anything?" asked Myrna.

"He never spoke about his clients."

Gamache looked down at the brick of papers in front of him and noticed the red stamp in the upper left corner. He was familiar with wills. You didn't generally get into your late fifties without having read a few. And Gamache had read a few, including his own.

This was indeed a legitimate, registered will.

Scanning the top page quickly, he noted that it had been written two years earlier.

"Turn to page two, please," said the notary. "You'll see your names in section four."

"But wait a minute," said Myrna. "Who was Bertha Baumgartner? You have to know something."

"All I know is that she's dead and my father looked after the estate. And now I have it. And now it's yours. Page two, please."

And sure enough, there they were. Myrna Landers of Three Pines, Québec. Armand Gamache of Three Pines, Québec. Benedict Pouliot of 267 rue Taillon, Montréal, Québec.

"This is you?" Mercier watched as each of them nodded. He cleared his throat and prepared to read.

"Wait a minute," said Myrna. "This's crazy. Some stranger picks us at random and makes us liquidators? Can she do that?"

"Oh yes," said the notary. "You can name the pope if you want."

"Really? That's pretty cool," said Benedict, his mind whirring at the possibilities.

Gamache didn't completely agree with Myrna. He doubted it was random. He looked down at the names in Bertha Baumgartner's will.

Their names. Very clear. There for a reason, he suspected. Though that reason was anything but clear.

A cop, a bookstore owner, a builder. Two men, one woman. Different ages. Two lived in the country, one in the city.

There was no pattern. They had nothing in common except their names on this document. And the fact none of them knew Bertha Baumgartner.

"And whoever is named has to do it?" asked Myrna. "We have to do it?"

"Of course not," said Mercier. "Can you imagine the Holy Father liquidating this estate?"

They tried. Only Benedict seemed, by the smile on his face, to be succeeding.

"So we can refuse?" asked Myrna.

"*Oui*. Would you like to refuse?"

"Well, I don't know. I mean, I haven't had a chance to think about it. I had no idea why you wanted me here."

"What did you think?" asked Mercier.

Myrna sat back in her chair, trying to remember.

She'd been in her bookstore the morning before when the mail arrived.

She'd poured a mug of strong tea and sat in the comfortable armchair with the indentation that fit her body like a mold.

The woodstove was on, and beyond her window was a brilliant winter day. The sky was a deep perfect blue, and the sun bounced off the snow-covered lawns, the road, the ice rink, and the snowmen on the village green. The whole village gleamed.

It was the sort of day that drew you outside. Even though you knew better. And once you were outside, the cold gripped you, burning your lungs, soldering your nostrils together with every breath. It brought tears to your eyes. Freezing the lashes so that you had to pry your lids apart.

And yet, gasping for breath, you still stood there. Just a little longer. To be part of such a day. Before retreating back inside to the hearth and hot chocolate, or tea, or strong, rich café au lait.

And the mail.

She'd read and reread the letter, then called the number to ask why this notary wanted to meet her.

Getting no answer, she took the letter with her to meet her friends and neighbors, Clara Morrow and Gabri Dubeau, for lunch in the bistro.

As Clara and Gabri discussed the snow-sculpture themes, the ball-hockey tournament, the tuque judging, and the refreshments for the upcoming winter carnival, Myrna found her attention wandering.

"Hello," said Gabri. "Anybody home?"

"Huh?"

"We need your help," said Clara. "The snowshoe race around the village green. Should it be one circuit or two?"

"One for the under-eights," said Myrna. "One and a half for the under-twelves, and two for everyone else."

"Well, that was decisive," said Gabri. "Now, teams for the snowball fight . . ."

Myrna's mind drifted again. She vaguely noted Gabri getting up and tossing more logs onto the fires in the open hearths at either end of the bistro. He paused to chat with customers as more villagers came in from the cold, stamping their feet and rubbing their freezing hands.

They were met with warmth and the scent of maplewood smoke, tourtières just out of the oven, and the permanent aroma of coffee embedded into the beams and wide-plank floors.

"I have something I need to show you," Myrna whispered to Clara while Gabri was occupied.

"Why're you whispering?" Clara also lowered her voice. "Is it dirty?"

"Of course not."

"Of course?" said Clara, raising her brows. "I know you too well for the 'of course.'"

Myrna laughed. Clara did know her. But then she also knew Clara.

Her friend's brown hair stuck out from her head, as though she'd had a mild shock. She looked a little like a middle-aged Sputnik. Which would also explain her art.

Clara Morrow's paintings were otherworldly. And yet they were also achingly, profoundly human.

She painted what appeared to be portraits, but that was only on the surface. The beautifully rendered flesh stretched, and sometimes sagged, over wounds, over celebrations. Over chasms of loss and rushes of joy. She painted peace and despair. All in one portrait.

With brush and canvas and oils, Clara both captured and freed her subject.

She also managed to get paint all over herself. On her cheeks, in her hair, under her nails. She was herself a work in progress.

"I'll show you later," said Myrna as Gabri arrived back at their table.

"Better be dirty, after that buildup," said Clara.

"Dirty?" said Gabri. "Spill."

"Myrna thinks the adults should do their snowshoe race naked."

"Naked?" asked Gabri, looking at Myrna. "Not that I'm a prude, but the children . . ."

"Oh for God's sake," said Myrna. "I didn't say that at all. Clara's making it up."

"Of course, if we held it at night, after the kids were asleep," said Gabri. "Put torches around the village green, it could work. We'd certainly set some speed records."

Myrna glared at Clara. Gabri, the president of the Carnaval d'hiver, was taking it seriously.

"Or maybe, instead of naked, because—" Gabri looked around at the bistro crowd, imagining them without clothing. "Maybe they have to wear bathing suits."

Clara frowned, not in disapproval but in surprise. It actually wasn't a bad idea. Especially given that most of the conversation in the bistro through the long, long, dark, dark Québec winter was about escaping to the sun. Lying on some beach, roasting.

"We can call it Running Away to the Caribbean," she said.

Myrna let out a sigh.

Across the bistro an elderly woman saw this and thought the dismissive look had been directed at her.

Ruth Zardo glared back.

Myrna caught this and thought of the unfairness of nature, that the old poet should be wizened without being wise.

26

Though there was wisdom there, if you could get beyond the haze of scotch.

Ruth returned to her lunch of booze and potato chips. Her notebook, on the table, contained neither rhymes nor reason but held, between the worn pages, the lump in the throat.

She looked out the window, then wrote:

Sharp as thin ice
the clear cries of children pierce the sky . . .

Rosa, on the sofa beside Ruth, muttered, "Fuck, fuck, fuck." Or it might have been, "Duck, duck, duck." Though it seemed silly that a duck would actually say "duck." And those who knew Rosa felt that "fuck" was much more likely.

Rosa leaned her long neck over and delicately took a potato chip out of the bowl while Ruth watched the children tobogganing down from the chapel to the village green. She scribbled:

Or in the snow-lapped country church,
kneeling at last to pray
for what we could not have.

Lunch arrived. Clara and Myrna had both ordered the halibut, with mustard seeds, curry leaves, and grilled tomato. And for Gabri, his partner, Olivier, had made grouse with roasted figs and cauliflower puree.

"I'm going to invite the Prime Minister," said Gabri. "He could open the *carnaval*."

He invited Justin Trudeau every year. And never heard back.

"And maybe he could take part in the race?" asked Clara.

Gabri's eyes widened.

Justin Trudeau. Racing around the village green. In a Speedo.

From there the conversation went south.

Myrna's heart wasn't in it, and neither was her mind, though she had paused for a moment on the Trudeau image before her thoughts went back to the letter folded in her pocket.

What would happen if she didn't show up?

The sun was turning the snow outside pink and blue. Shrieks of children could be heard, giddy with that intoxicating mix of fun and fear as their toboggans plunged down the hill.

It looked so idyllic.

But.

But if, by chance or fate, you got caught too far from home as clouds rolled in, as a flurry blew into a blizzard, then all bets were off.

A Québec winter, so cheerful and peaceful, could turn on you. Could kill. And each winter did. Men, women, children alive in the autumn did not see the blizzard coming and never saw the spring.

In the countryside, winter was a gorgeous, glorious, luminous killer.

Québécois with gray in their hair and lines in their faces got there by being wise enough and sensible enough and prudent enough to get back home. And watch the blizzard from beside a cheery hearth, with a hot chocolate, or a glass of wine, and a good book.

While there were few things more terrifying than being outside in a blizzard, there were few things more comforting than being inside.

As with so much in life, it was, Myrna knew, a matter of inches between safe and sorry.

While Gabri and Clara debated the merits of all-inclusives versus other resorts versus cruises, Myrna thought about the letter and decided to leave it up to fate.

If it was snowing, she'd stay home. If it was clear, she'd go.

And now, as she sat in the off-kilter kitchen, with the off-kilter table, and the off-kilter notary, and the wacky young builder, Myrna looked out at the worsening snow and thought—

Fucking fate. Tricked again.

"Myrna's right," said Armand, laying a large hand on the will. "We need to decide if we even want to do it." He turned to the other two. "What do you think?"

"Can we read the thing first?" said Benedict, patting the will. "Then decide?"

"No," said the notary.

Myrna got up. "I think we should talk about it. In private."

Armand walked around the table and bent down beside Benedict, who was still sitting there, and whispered, "You're welcome to join us."

"Oh great, yes. Good idea."

CHAPTER 5

—

As Gamache passed from the kitchen into the dining room, he paused to look at the doorframe and the marks.

Bending closer, he noted faint names beside the lines.

Anthony, aged three, four, five, and so on up the doorjamb.

Caroline, at three, four, five . . .

And then there was Hugo, three, four, five, and so on. But his lines were denser. Like the rings of some old oak that wasn't growing very fast. Or very tall.

Hugo lagged far behind where his brother and sister were at the same age. But, uniquely, beside his name, at each faint line, there was a sticker. A horse. A dog. A teddy bear. So that while little Hugo might not stand tall, he did stand out.

Armand looked back into the kitchen, stripped bare. Then into the empty dining room, its wallpaper stained with moisture.

What happened here? he wondered.

What happened in Madame Baumgartner's life that she had to choose strangers to enact her will? Where were Anthony and Caroline and Hugo?

"Roof leaking," said Benedict, splaying his large hand on a stain on the dining-room wall. "It's getting between the walls. Rotting. A shame. Look at these floors."

They did. Old pine. Warping.

Benedict walked around, inspecting the room, staring up at the ceiling.

He'd unzipped his winter coat to reveal a sweater that was alternately fuzzy and tight-knit, and one section looked like it was made of steel wool.

Myrna could not believe it was comfortable, but she could believe it was made by his girlfriend.

He must love her, she thought. A lot. And she him. Everything she created was for him. The fact it was awful didn't take away from the thought. Unless, of course, she did it on purpose. To not only make him look foolish but to cause him actual pain, as the steel-wool sweater scratched and rubbed the young flesh beneath.

She either loved Benedict a lot or despised him. A lot.

And he either didn't see it or was drawn to pain, to abuse, as some people were.

"So," said Myrna. "Do you want to be a liquidator?"

"What's involved?" asked Benedict. "What do we have to do?"

"If the will's simple, not much," said Armand. "Just make sure the taxes and bills are paid and any bequests get to the right people. Then wrap up the estate. The notary helps with that. Liquidators are generally family members and friends. People who're trusted."

They looked at each other. They were none of those things to Bertha Baumgartner. And yet here they were.

Armand glanced around for a photograph left behind on the damp walls or fallen to the floor. Something that might tell them who this Bertha Baumgartner was. But there was nothing. Just the smudged lines on the door. And the horsey, doggy, teddy bear.

"That doesn't sound so bad," said Benedict.

"That's if it's simple," said Armand. "If it isn't, it could take a lot of time. A long time."

"Like days?" asked Benedict. When there was no answer, he added, "Weeks? Months?"

"Years," said Armand. "Some wills take years, especially if there're any arguments between the heirs."

"And there often are," said Myrna. She turned full circle. "Greed does that. But it looks like they've already stripped the place. And I can't imagine there's much left to divide."

Beside her, Armand made a noise like a rumble.

She looked at him and nodded. "I know. It might not seem like much to us, but to people who have little, a little more can seem a fortune."

He remained silent.

That wasn't exactly what he was thinking. A will, an estate, could become about more than money, property, possessions. Who was left the most could be interpreted as who was loved the most. There were different sorts of greed. Of need.

And wills were sometimes used as a final affront, the last insult delivered by a ghost.

"Do we get paid?" asked Benedict.

"Maybe a little. It's normally done as a favor," said Armand.

Benedict nodded. "So how do we know if this's simple?"

"We can't know until we read the will," said Myrna.

"But we can't read the will until we decide," Benedict pointed out.

"Catch-22," said Gamache, to the young man's blank face. "I think we have to assume the worst and decide if we still want to do it."

"And if we don't?" asked Myrna. "What happens?"

"The courts will appoint other liquidators."

"But she wanted us," said Benedict. "I wonder why. She must've had a reason." He stopped, deep in thought. They could almost hear the wheels grinding. Finally he shook his head. "Nope. Can't think what it would be. You two know each other, don't you?"

"We're neighbors," said Myrna. "Live in the same village about twenty minutes away."

"I live in Montréal with my girlfriend. I've never even been out this way. Maybe she meant another Benedict Pouliot."

"You live on rue Taillon in Montréal?" asked Armand, and when the young man nodded, he went on. "She meant you."

Benedict focused on Armand, as though really seeing him for the first time. He brought his hand up to his own temple, placing a finger there. "That looks nasty. What happened? An accident?"

Armand raised his hand and brushed it along the furrow of the scar. "*Non*. I was hurt once."

More than once, Myrna thought, but didn't say it.

"It was a while ago," Armand assured the young man. "I'm fine now."

"Must've really hurt."

"It did. But I think it hurt others more."

He obviously has no idea who Armand is, thought Myrna. And saw that Armand had no intention of telling him.

"Either way, we should decide," she said, walking over to the window. "Snow's getting heavier."

"You're right," said Armand. "We need to get going soon. So are we in or out?"

"You?" Myrna asked him.

He already had his answer. Had it from the moment the notary explained why they were there.

"I have no idea why Madame Baumgartner chose us, but she did. I don't see any reason to refuse. I'm in. Besides"—he smiled at Myrna—"I'm curious."

"You are that," she said, then looked at Benedict. "You?"

"Years, you say?" he asked.

"Worst case," said Gamache. "*Oui.*"

"So it could take years and we don't get paid," Benedict recapped. "Oh, what the hell. I'm in. How bad can it be?"

Myrna regarded the handsome young man with the grievous haircut and the steel-wool sweater. If he could put up with that, she thought, he could put up with irritating strangers fighting over a pittance.

"You?" Armand asked Myrna.

"Oh, I was always in," she said, smiling. And then there was a shudder and the rattle of windows as wind rocked the house. It gave a creak, then a sharp crack.

Myrna felt panic rise up. And spike. They weren't safe in the house. But neither were they safe outside.

And they still had the drive home to Three Pines.

"We need to leave."

Walking rapidly back into the kitchen, she looked out the window. She could barely see her car, now buried under blowing and drifting and eddying snow.

"We're in," she said to Lucien. "And we're leaving."

"What?" said Lucien, getting up.

"We're leaving," said Armand. "And you should too. Where's your office?"

"Sherbrooke."

It was an hour's drive away, at least.

They hadn't taken off their coats or boots, and now they grabbed their mitts and hats and made for the back door.

"Wait," said Lucien, sitting down again. "We have to read the will. Madame Baumgartner stipulated that it be done here."

"Madame Baumgartner's dead," said Myrna. "And I plan on living through the day."

She rammed a tuque onto her head and followed Benedict out of the house.

"Now, *monsieur*," said Armand. "We're leaving. And that means you."

Benedict and Myrna were wading through the snow, already knee-deep in places, toward her car. The young man had yanked a shovel from the snowbank and was starting to dig her car out.

Lucien leaned back in his chair and crossed his arms.

"Up," said Armand, and when the notary didn't move, he grabbed Lucien by the arm and pulled him to his feet.

"Put your things on," he ordered, and after a moment's shocked pause, Lucien did.

Armand checked his iPhone. There was no signal. The storm had knocked everything out.

He looked out at the blizzard, then around at the creaking, cracking, crooked home.

They had to leave.

He thrust the paperwork back into the briefcase, which he handed to the notary. "Come on."

When Gamache opened the door, the snow whacked him in the face, taking his breath away. He closed his eyes and winced against the pellets that all but blinded him.

The sound was deafening.

Howling, hitting, furious movement. It burst in on them and over them. The world unraveling. And them in the middle of it.

As the snow plastered itself against Gamache's face, he turned his head away and saw Benedict furiously shoveling, working to free Myrna's car from the snowdrifts that had formed around it. No sooner had the young man dug out one section than the wind picked up the snow and filled it back in.

The only thing not white in the landscape was Benedict's tuque, its long red-striped tail looking like lashes of blood on the snow.

Myrna was using her hands to scoop snow off the windshield.

Benedict's own truck, parked in the open, was already covered, and the notary's car had disappeared completely.

By the time he reached the others, Armand could feel snow down his boots, and down his collar, and up his sleeves, and under his tuque.

Myrna was trying to yank her car door open, but the snow, blown against it, was trapping it shut.

"It's too deep," Armand called into Myrna's ear. "Leave it." Then he trudged to the back of the car and grabbed Benedict's arm, stopping the shovel. "Even if we could dig everyone out, the roads are too bad. We need to stay together. Your truck's probably the best bet."

Benedict looked over at it, then back at Armand.

"What is it?" shouted Armand, sensing there was an "it."

"I don't have snow tires."

"You don't—" But he stopped himself. When the house was burning, it was not the best time to lay blame. "Okay." He turned to Myrna and Lucien. "My car is slightly protected by Myrna's. Hers is acting as a windbreak. We can probably get mine out."

"But I need to get back to Sherbrooke," said Lucien, waving behind him to his vehicle, which was now just another white lump in the yard.

"And you will," Myrna shouted. "Just not today."

"But—"

"Dig," said Myrna, waving toward Armand's Volvo.

"With what?"

Armand pointed to Lucien's briefcase.

"No," said the notary, hugging it to him like a teddy bear.

"Fine," said Myrna.

Yanking it away from him, she went to work, using the briefcase to push the snow from around the doors while Benedict shoveled and Armand ripped wooden planks from the front steps of the house and pushed them under the rear wheels, using his boots to kick them firmly into place.

And Lucien stood there.

Finally they managed to get the doors open.

Myrna all but rammed the notary into the backseat, then got in beside him.

"You drive," shouted Benedict to Armand, motioning to the driver's side. "I'll push."

36

"*Non.* When we get moving, we can't stop. We'll sink in again. Whoever pushes will be left behind."

Benedict paused.

My God, thought Armand. *He's actually considering it.*

"In," he commanded.

The young man stared at the older man, still undecided.

"This will work," said Gamache, softly this time, while the snow piled up around them again and the precious moments ticked by. "Get in."

Benedict reached for the driver's-side door, but Armand stopped him.

"In," he said, with a smile, and pointed to the passenger door.

Myrna double-checked her seat belt, then closed her eyes and breathed. Deeply. And prayed.

The car started to back up, and Gamache slowly, slowly, gently, gently pressed the gas.

There was a hesitation as the tires worked to mount the planks.

They caught and climbed the inch or so out of the snow and ice and onto the wood.

With traction now, the car moved. An inch. Six inches. A foot.

Benedict exhaled. Myrna exhaled. The notary hyperventilated.

Then Armand put it in gear and gently turned the wheel, so that they were headed back down the pine drive.

"Oh, *merde*," said Benedict.

Myrna leaned forward between the seats and saw what he saw.

A wall of snow blocked their way out. So high they couldn't see the road beyond.

"It's okay," said Gamache. "It means the plow's been by. This is good."

"Good?" asked Benedict.

"Look what it did," said the notary, finding his voice. Or someone's. It was unnaturally high and breathy. "We can't get through that."

The plow had pushed snow across the entrance to the driveway, creating a barrier. There was no way to tell how thick, how packed it would be. Or what was on the other side.

But they had no choice. There was only one way to do this.

"Hold on," said Armand, and pressed his foot on the gas.

"Are you sure?" said Benedict as they headed straight for the wall of snow.

"Oh shit," said Myrna, bracing herself.

And then they hit.

The snow exploded, plastering itself against the windshield and blinding them as the car skewed violently one way, then the other.

And then, to Benedict's horror, Armand leaned back in his seat.

"Hit the brake," Benedict screamed.

Benedict reached for the wheel, but Armand grabbed his wrist in a grip so tight the young man flinched.

A chunk of snow flew off the windshield, and they could see the forest—trees, trunks—heading toward them.

Benedict gasped and put his hands against the dashboard while Armand stared ahead, waiting. Waiting. And then, just when it appeared too late, he gently, gently, pumped the brakes.

The car slowed. Then stopped. Its nose just touching the other bank.

There was complete silence, then long exhales.

They were right across the road, blocking it. Armand quickly looked left and right, to see if there were any oncoming cars. But the road was empty.

Only fools would be out in a blizzard.

There was quiet, giddy laughter.

"Oh shit," sighed Myrna.

Armand backed the car up and pointed it toward home. Putting on the warning flashers, he got out to inspect for damage.

"What the fuck was that?" demanded Benedict, marching around the car to confront Armand. "You gave up. You almost killed us."

Armand gestured with both hands toward the car.

"Yeah," shouted Benedict. "Dumb luck."

"There was that." Had there been another vehicle coming or the plow returning—

"You froze," shouted Benedict as Armand began digging snow out of the grille of the car. "I saw you."

"What I did and what you saw seem to be two different things. Sometimes the best thing we can do is nothing."

"What sort of Zen bullshit is that?"

Snow whipped around Benedict, his fists clenched as he stared at Gamache.

"You want to know why I did what I did?"

"You panicked."

"Did no one teach you how to drive in snow?" Gamache shouted into the blizzard.

"I can do it better than you."

"Then you can give me a lesson. But perhaps not today."

They got back into the car, and Gamache put it in gear.

"And," he said, concentrating on the road, "just so you know. I never give up."

"Where're we going?" asked Lucien from the backseat.

"Home," said Myrna.

CHAPTER 6

$\sim$

"Are we there?" asked the notary. Again.

"*Oui.*"

"Really?"

The answer was so unexpected it silenced him. Lucien used his sleeve to wipe the condensation from the car window and peered out. And saw . . . nothing.

And then the blowing snow momentarily shifted, and for a split second, through a tear in the blizzard, he could see a house. A home.

It was made of fieldstone, and there was soft light coming through the mullioned windows.

And then it was gone, swallowed by the storm. The sighting was so brief, Lucien wondered if desperation and imagination had conjured a fairy-tale cottage.

"Are you sure?" he asked.

"Pretty sure."

Less than an hour later, Armand and his guests were showered and changed into clean, dry clothing. Except Lucien, who'd refused all offers.

They were seated at the long pine table in the kitchen while the woodstove pumped out heat at the far end of the room. Snow had piled up on the frames of the windows on either side of the fireplace, making it difficult to see out.

Benedict wore a borrowed T-shirt, sweater, and slacks and had calmed down since the drive. The hot shower and the promise of food had lulled him.

He looked around.

This place didn't shudder, the windows didn't rattle, despite the fury outside. It had been built to last, and lasted it had. He figured it was more than one hundred, perhaps even two hundred years old.

Even if he tried, if he really, really tried, he doubted he could build a home this solid.

He looked across the room, at Madame Gamache serving up soup and Armand cutting bread. Occasionally consulting. Their bodies just touching in an act both casual and intimate.

Benedict wondered if he tried, really, really tried, if he could build a relationship that solid.

He scratched his chest and winced.

A few minutes earlier, while standing under the hot stream of the shower, Armand had asked Reine-Marie, "Does the name Bertha Baumgartner mean anything to you?"

"Wasn't she a cartoon character?" said Reine-Marie. "No, that was Dagwood. Was she a villain in *Doonesbury*?"

He turned off the shower and stepped out, taking the towel she handed him.

"Merci." As he rubbed his hair dry, he looked at her, amused, but then saw she was serious. "No, she was a neighbor, sort of."

He put on cords, a clean shirt, and a sweater and told her why he'd been summoned to the remote farmhouse.

"A liquidator? But you must've known her, Armand. Why else would she choose you?"

"I have no idea."

"And Myrna doesn't know her?"

"Neither does the young fellow. Benedict."

"How do you explain that?" she asked.

"I can't."

"Huh," said Reine-Marie.

When they had their soups and sandwiches and beer, Reine-Marie left them at the kitchen table, taking her own lunch into the living room.

Sitting by the fireplace with Gracie, their little foundling, beside her, Reine-Marie stared into the flames and repeated:

Bertha Baumgartner. Bertha Baumgartner.

Still the name meant nothing.

"Now," said Lucien, adjusting his glasses. "You've all agreed to be liquidators of the estate of Bertha Baumgartner. Is that correct?"

What sounded like "Yes" came from Benedict, but his mouth was so full of roast-beef sandwich it came out as a muffled "Woof."

Henri, lying at Armand's feet, perked up his ears, his tail swishing slightly.

"That is correct," said Myrna, using the same tone as the notary, though he didn't seem to notice.

The chair creaked as she sat back, a warm mug of pea soup in her hands. She longed to reach for the beer, but the mug was so comforting she didn't want to let it go.

Armand had dropped her at the door into the bistro, her bookstore being snowed in, so she could have a hot shower and change before heading to their place.

"Oh for Christ's sake," said Clara as she hugged her friend. "We were so worried."

"I wasn't," said Gabri, though he also hugged her tight. "You okay?" he said. "You look like shit."

"Could be worse."

"Where were you?" asked Olivier.

Myrna saw no reason not to tell them.

"Bertha Baumgartner?" said Gabri. "Bertha Baumgartner? Really? There was someone around here named Bertha Baumgartner and I didn't know her? Who was she?"

"You don't know?" asked Myrna. Gabri and Olivier knew everyone.

"Don't you?" asked Clara, following her to the door connecting the bistro to the bookstore.

"No. Not a clue." She stopped and looked at their astonished faces.

"You say that Armand is also a liquidator?" asked Olivier. "He must know her."

43

"No. None of us do. Not even the notary."

"And she lived just down the road?" asked Clara.

"Well, about twenty minutes from here. You sure the name doesn't sound familiar?"

"Bertha Baumgartner," said Gabri again, clearly enjoying the sound of it.

"Don't you dare," said Olivier. He turned to Clara and Myrna. "He's been looking for another name to sign to the letter inviting Prime Minister Trudeau to the carnival. We suspect Gabri Dubeau is on the straight-to-garbage list."

"I have sent him a few letters," admitted Gabri. "And a couple photographs."

"And?" said Olivier.

"A lock of hair. In my defense," said Gabri, "it was Olivier's."

"What? You bastard." Olivier touched his head. Already thinning, each blond strand was precious.

When Myrna came back down from her loft twenty minutes later in warm dry clothes, she discovered that Gabri and Olivier were out clearing paths.

"They're not digging out Ruth?" Myrna said to Clara.

It was like releasing a chimera. Not something done lightly. And very hard to put back, once out.

"Afraid so. And feeding her too. They took over soup in a scotch bottle, hoping she won't notice the difference."

"Ruth might not, but Rosa will."

The duck was discerning.

"Where're you going?" asked Clara, following her to the door.

"To Armand's. We're going to read the will."

"Can I come?"

"Do you want to?"

"Yes, I'd far prefer to walk into a blizzard than sit by the fire with my book and a scotch."

"Thought so," said Myrna as she yanked open the door. Bending into the wind, she trudged through the thick snow.

She did not know Bertha but was growing to dislike her. Intensely.

Armand stood in the study, the phone to his ear.

He could just see, through gaps in the blowing snow, Myrna making her way around the village green to their home.

Reine-Marie had told him the phone was dead, but he thought he'd just check to see if the line had been restored.

It had not.

He looked at his watch. It was one thirty in the afternoon but felt like midnight.

Three and a half hours since he'd received the call while sitting in his car outside Bertha Baumgartner's home. Three and a half hours since the angry exchange of words.

Thinking of it conjured the smell of wet wool, the sound of snow tapping his car.

He'd said he'd get back to them. Made them promise not to do anything until they heard from him. And now this.

Reine-Marie greeted Myrna, and, after replacing the dead phone, Armand joined them in the warm kitchen, for soup, sandwiches, beer, and the reading of the will.

"Heard on the radio that the blizzard's all over southern Québec," said Myrna, trying to repair her hat head. "But should blow itself out sometime in the night."

"That widespread?" asked Armand.

Reine-Marie examined his face. Instead of concerned, he seemed relieved.

The lights of Annie and Jean-Guy's apartment in the Plateau *quartier* of Montréal flickered.

They stopped what they were doing to stare at the overhead light.

It wavered. Wavered.

Then held.

Annie and Jean-Guy exchanged glances and raised their brows, then went back to their conversation. Jean-Guy was telling her about his meeting that morning with the investigators.

"Did they ask you to sign anything?" asked Annie.

"How did you know about that?"

"So they did?"

45

He nodded.

"Did you?"

"No."

"Good."

Once again he saw the sheets of paper pushed across the table at him, and their expectant faces.

"You were right. They have an agenda. I think your father might be facing more than suspension or even being fired."

"Like what?"

"I don't really know. They didn't make any accusations, but they kept going back to the drugs. The ones he let through."

"They already knew about that," said Annie. "He told them right away. Alerted cops across the country and into the States. The DEA got back the junk that crossed the border, right?"

"With your father's help, yes."

"And yours."

"*Oui.* But there's a whole lot still missing. Kilos of it. Here. In Montréal. Somewhere. We've spent months looking. Using all our informants. And nothing. When that shit hits the streets . . ."

He left it hanging there, not sure how to finish the sentence.

"It's terrible stuff, Annie."

"I know."

He shook his head. "You think you do, but you don't. Think of the worst. The very worst."

She did.

"That would be the very best that could happen," he said.

Annie smiled, thinking he was kidding. Certainly exaggerating. And then her smile faded.

That bad.

"I think they know there's going to be a shitstorm once the stuff hits the streets. They need someone to blame."

"They?"

"Them." He lifted his hands. "I don't know. I'm not good at this political crap. That was your dad's job."

"But it is political?"

"I think so. No one seems particularly worried about the poor sons

46

of bitches who're going to take the stuff. They're all covering their own asses."

"Does Dad know?"

"I think he suspects. But he's still trying to get the stuff back. He isn't looking in that direction. I honestly thought when I walked in there this morning that they were going to tell me they were ending the investigation and reinstating your father."

"Now what?" asked Annie.

"I don't know," he said, leaning back heavily. "I'm tired of all this, Annie. I've had it."

"I know. It sucks. Thank you for sticking by Dad."

Jean-Guy nodded but didn't say anything.

He again heard Marie's reassuring voice. *All this will go away, Chief Inspector. Once you sign. Then you can get on with your life.*

CHAPTER 7

⌒

Benedict, Myrna, and Armand stared down at the page in front of them.

Then they looked up, and at each other.

Then, as one, they turned to Lucien.

"This's a joke, right?" asked Myrna while, beside her, Armand took off his reading glasses and watched the notary.

"I don't understand," said Benedict.

"It's all very clear," said Lucien.

"But it's nonsense," said Myrna. "It makes no sense."

Armand looked back down at the document in front of him. They'd finally reached the eighth section of the will, with the notary having read every preceding section, every clause, every word, in a sonorous voice. Given their exhaustion after the stresses of the morning, the meal they'd just had, the warmth from the woodstove, and now Lucien's voice droning on, it was all they could do to remain conscious.

Armand had noticed Benedict's eyelids fluttering and his head drooping more than once, and then the young man had fought his way back to them. Opening his eyes wide, before the heavy lids slowly lowered again.

But he was wide awake now. They all were.

"It says here," Myrna looked back down and put her finger under the line as she read, "'I bequeath to my three children the sum of five million dollars each.'"

She looked up again, hard, at Lucien.

"Five. Million. Dollars," she repeated. "And that makes sense to you?"

"Each," Benedict pointed out. "That's . . . fifteen million."

"Five million, fifteen million, a hundred million," said Myrna. "It's all the same. Nonsense."

"Maybe she meant Canadian Tire money," said Benedict, trying to be helpful.

It was not.

"What're we supposed to do with this?" Myrna asked.

She gestured toward the will, then appealed to Armand, who looked at the notary and raised his brows.

"Does she have it?" he asked.

"Bertha Baumgartner?" asked Myrna. "Were we in the same house this morning? That woman, while apparently rich in imagination, was obviously not a multimillionaire."

"She might've been a . . . what's the word?" said Benedict.

"Miser?" asked Armand.

"Lunatic," said Benedict.

"We haven't finished yet," said Lucien.

His voice droned on, but now they were alert, following closely, as bequest followed bequest.

Her home in Switzerland was to be sold, as was the building in Vienna. The proceeds to be divided among her children and grand-children. With a million dollars going to the local animal shelter.

"That's nice," said Benedict.

Section 8, thought Armand, scanning the figures on the page. In the U.S. military that was the section for the mentally unfit. Benedict might have found exactly the right word.

"'The title will, of course,'" the notary read, "'be passed to my eldest son, Anthony.'"

"Huh?" said Myrna.

By now words had failed her, and she could just make sounds.

"Title?" asked Benedict. "What's that?"

"Must be the title to the property," said Armand.

All the lights in the kitchen flickered.

All the people in the kitchen fell silent, staring up at the chandelier over the pine table. Willing it to stay on.

But willing something to happen, as they were discovering with

Madame Baumgartner, and having it happen were often two different things.

The lights wavered again, then came back to full brightness.

They looked at one another and breathed a sigh of relief.

Then the lights, all at once, went out.

No flicker this time. Just gone. And with it went all sound. No hum of the fridge, no rumble of the furnace. No tick of a clock. They sat at the kitchen table in silence.

Sunlight still struggled through the windows of the kitchen. But it was weak. As though it had fought long and hard to get that far.

Before it too died.

Armand struck a match and lit the storm lamps at either end of the table while Myrna lit the candles on the kitchen island. Put there in case.

"You okay?" Armand asked, going to the door between the kitchen and the living room.

There he saw the fire in the hearth and one lantern already lit.

"No worries," said Reine-Marie. "And no surprise."

"We're almost finished. Be with you in a few minutes."

He took two small logs off the neat pile in the kitchen and shoved them into the woodstove. It was now their main source of heat. There was no emergency, yet. But if this blackout lasted a long time, days even, and the temperature dropped still further, and the fire went out . . .

"Well, this's nice," said Benedict, looking around at the pools of light.

"Let's call it a day," said Armand, and when Lucien protested, Myrna hauled herself out of the chair and just left. Taking her beer into the living room to join Reine-Marie.

Benedict followed.

Armand held his arm out, inviting Lucien to join them. After a moment's hesitation, he grudgingly got up.

Once seated, Myrna asked, "How're we supposed to liquidate a will that makes no sense? We can't give away money that isn't there."

"Madame Baumgartner overestimated her estate?" asked Reine-Marie.

"By about twenty million," said Myrna.

Reine-Marie grimaced. "That is overshooting."

"We're all assuming she didn't have the money," said Lucien. "Maybe she did."

"You think so?" asked Armand.

"Conrad Cantzen."

"I beg your pardon?" said Armand.

"Conrad Cantzen," the notary repeated. "My father told me about him. Monsieur Cantzen was a bit actor on Broadway back in the 1920s. He'd beg for money and go through the garbage for food, and when he died, he left a quarter of a million dollars. It's a lot of money today. Back when he died, that was a fortune."

They were silent, absorbing this.

"You just never know," said Lucien.

CHAPTER 8

⁓

"Armand, are you awake?"

"Hmmmm."

He turned over so that he was on his side, facing Reine-Marie. The air was chilly, but the duvet was warm. He reached under the covers for her hand.

They'd moved their mattress down to the kitchen and were camped by the woodstove. So that they could get up in the night and feed more logs into it.

"This afternoon, when you heard that the blizzard covered most of Québec, you seemed pleased."

"Relieved," he admitted.

"Why?"

That, he thought, was harder to explain.

Henri and Gracie, curled on the floor beside them, stirred, and then, with reassuring pats from Armand and Reine-Marie, they went back to sleep.

"I needed to go to the Sûreté Academy yesterday afternoon, to a meeting," Armand whispered. "I told them not to do anything until I arrived. Then the storm hit and the phones went out, and I was worried that they'd proceed without me. But with the blizzard being so big, I knew nothing could happen. They were snowed in too."

And he could relax. Knowing for the next number of hours, as the blizzard howled, the world was on hold. Frozen in place.

In the hectic, often frantic pace of life, there was something deeply peaceful about not being able to do anything. No Internet, no phone, no TV. No lights.

Life became simple, primal: Heat. Water. Food. Companionship.

Armand crawled out of bed, feeling the chill immediately as the warmth of the duvet slid off and the cold took hold.

Stepping over the other mattress on the kitchen floor, he fed more split logs into the fire.

Before returning to the warm bed, Armand stared out the mullioned windows into the darkness. Then bent and tucked the duvet around Reine-Marie.

As he did that, a voice, sharp and unexpected, came to him out of the darkness.

The evening before, those who weren't snowed in dug out those who were, clearing paths from homes to the road.

Gabri and Olivier had been invited over to the Gamaches' after they'd finished but had declined.

"Want to keep the bistro open," Olivier explained.

"And we have unexpected guests at the B&B," Gabri shouted into the battering wind. "Can't get their cars out to drive home."

"Can't find their cars." Olivier used his shovel to point to the burial mounds around the village green.

"Do you think we can get kids to do it? Convince them that it's a game?" Gabri yelled into Olivier's tuque. "Whoever digs a car out first wins a prize?"

"The prize would have to be a brain," said Olivier.

A path had been shoveled to Ruth's home, and Reine-Marie had knocked, but the old woman had refused to open the door.

"Come to our place for dinner," Reine-Marie shouted through it. "Bring Rosa. We have plenty of food."

"And drink?"

"Yes."

"No, I don't want to leave."

"Ruth, please. You shouldn't be alone. Come over. We have scotch."

"I don't know. The last bottle I had tasted strange."

Reine-Marie could hear the fear in her voice. An old woman leaving her home to venture into a blizzard. Every survival instinct screamed no. While Ruth Zardo was not well endowed with survival instincts, she still had managed to claw her way into her eighties.

And not by walking into snowstorms.

One by one over the course of the early evening, they'd gone over to Ruth's, clearing the fresh snow ahead of them. And one by one they'd been rebuffed.

"Okay, enough of this," said Armand, getting up.

He grabbed a Hudson Bay blanket before heading to the door.

"What're you going to do?" asked Reine-Marie.

"I'm going to get Ruth here, if I have to break down her door."

"You're going to kidnap her?" asked Myrna.

"Isn't that against the law?" asked Reine-Marie.

"It is," said Lucien, who had no ear for sarcasm. "Who's this Ruth? Why's she so important?"

"She's a person," said Armand, his parka and boots now on.

"But is she really?" Myrna mouthed to Reine-Marie.

"You do know if you kidnap her, no one will pay the ransom," said Reine-Marie. "And we'll be stuck with her."

"Ruth's not so bad," said Myrna. "It's the duck that worries me."

"Duck?" asked Lucien.

"I'll go with you, sir," said Benedict.

"You don't think I can take her on my own?" asked Armand with some amusement.

"Her, yes," said Benedict. "But the duck?"

Armand looked at him for a moment, then laughed. Unlike Lucien, Benedict had slipped easily into the stream of conversation. Understanding what was banter and what was important.

Benedict got his boots, parka, tuque, and mitts on, and Gamache opened the door. Only to step back in surprise.

Ruth was standing there, covered in snow. Her heavy winter coat bulging and squirming.

"I hear there's scotch," she said, walking past them as though they were the guests and she the owner of the place.

As she walked, she dropped tuque, mitts, coat on the floor. And left puddles from her huge boots.

"Who're they?" Ruth used Rosa to indicate Lucien and Benedict.

Reine-Marie introduced them. "They're not drinking scotch," she said, rightly assuming that was all Ruth really wanted to know.

A buffet of bread, cheese, cold chicken, roast beef, and pastries had been set out on the dining table at the far end of the living room, with storm lanterns and candles placed on it.

"Does the name Bertha Baumgartner mean anything to you?" Armand asked Ruth as he handed her a plate he'd made for her and joined her on the sofa.

"No," said Ruth.

Myrna stepped from the buffet table long enough to whisper into Armand's ear. "Unless it's Johnnie Walker or Glenfiddich, she's not interested. Watch and learn."

Going back to the table, Myrna placed a chicken leg, some camembert, and a slice of baguette on her plate and said, "Bertha Baumgartner? Olivier just got a case in. Twenty-five years old. Slow-aged in oak. Very smooth."

"Bertha Baumgartner's booze?" asked Ruth, rejoining the conversation.

"No, she isn't, you old drunk," said Myrna. "But we wanted your attention, as wavering as it is."

"You're a cruel woman," said Ruth.

"We're liquidators of her estate," said Armand. "But we've never met her. She lived locally."

"An old farmhouse down Mansonville way," said Myrna.

"Bertha Baumgartner? Means nothing to me," said Ruth. "You the notary?"

"Me?" asked Benedict, his mouth full of bread. Again.

"No, not you." Ruth eyed him. And his hair. "I see Gabri has competition for village idiot. I meant him."

"Me?" asked Lucien.

"Yes, you. I knew a Laurence Mercier. He came to discuss my will. Your father?"

"Yes."

"I see the resemblance," she said. It did not sound like a compliment.

"You've made a will?" asked Reine-Marie, carrying her plate back to her seat by the fireplace.

"No," said Ruth. "Decided not to. Nothing to leave. But I have written instructions for my funeral. Flowers. Music. The parade. Tributes from dignitaries. The design of the postage stamp. The usual."

"Date?" asked Myrna.

"Just for that, I might not die," said Ruth.

"Unless we can find a wooden stake or a silver bullet."

"Those are just rumors." Ruth turned to Armand. "So this Bertha person made you her liquidators and you never even knew her. She sounds batty. Wish I'd met her."

"Though she wouldn't be the first person to leave something strange in a will," said Reine-Marie. "Wasn't there something in Shakespeare's?"

"*Oui*," said Lucien, finally on familiar ground. "It was fairly standard until the end, where he wrote, 'I give unto my wife my second best bed.'"

This brought laughter, then silence, as they tried to figure out, as scholars had for centuries, what that meant.

"How about Howard Hughes?" said Myrna. "Didn't he die without a will?"

"Yeah, well, he really was crazy," said Ruth.

"My favorite Hughes quote was when he said, 'I'm not a paranoid deranged millionaire. Goddamn it, I'm a billionaire,'" said Reine-Marie.

"Now, that sounds familiar," said Ruth.

"His will was finally settled," said Lucien.

"Yeah," said Ruth. "After about thirty years."

"Holy shit," said Benedict, turning to Armand. "Hope it doesn't take us that long."

"Well, it probably won't take me that long," said Armand, doing the math.

As the room grew colder, they leaned closer to the fire and listened as Lucien Mercier told them about the man who'd left a penny to every child who attended his funeral and about the husbands who punished wives and children from beyond the grave.

"'They fuck you up, your mum and dad. / They may not mean to, but they do,'" Ruth quoted.

"I know that poem," said Benedict, and all eyes swung to him. "But that's not the way it goes."

"Oh really?" said Ruth. "And you're a poetry expert?"

"No, not really. But I know that one," he said. If not oblivious to sarcasm, at least impervious to it. A useful trait, thought Armand.

"How do you think it goes?" asked Reine-Marie.

"'They tuck you up, your mum and dad,'" said the young man, reeling it off easily. "'They read you Peter Rabbit, too.'"

All around the hearth, eyebrows rose.

"'They fill you with the faults they had,'" said Ruth, squaring herself to Benedict, like a duelist. "'And add some extra, just for you.'"

"'They give you all the treats they had,'" he replied. "'And add some extra, just for you.'"

Ruth glared at him. While the others stared in open amazement.

"Go on," said Reine-Marie.

And Ruth did.

> "Man hands on misery to man.
> It deepens like a coastal shelf.
> Get out as early as you can,
> And don't have any kids yourself."

Their eyes swung back to Benedict.

> "Man hands on happiness to man.
> It deepens like a coastal shelf.
> So love your parents all you can,
> And have some cheerful kids yourself."

"Is he for real?" Ruth demanded, going back to her scotch.

The fire muttered in the hearth, and the wind howled outside, and the blizzard settled in, trapping everyone in their homes.

And Armand thought that was a pretty good question.

Was Benedict for real?

It had been decided that Lucien, Myrna, and Benedict would stay the night, as would Ruth. She and Rosa were put on the mattress closest to the woodstove in the kitchen.

In the early-morning hours, after stoking the fire, Armand bent down and tucked the duvet closer around Reine-Marie.

Man hands on happiness to man.
It deepens like a coastal shelf.

Oddly enough, Benedict's version of the famous poem now pushed the original to the back of his mind.

Then he heard a stirring in the other bed. And a voice came to him out of the darkness.

"I think I know who Bertha Baumgartner was," said Ruth.

CHAPTER 9

Reine-Marie, eyes half open, half asleep and half awake, slid her hand along the bedding toward Armand, feeling the curved ridges of the blow-up mattress.

But that side of the bed was cold. Not simply cooling. Cold.

She opened her eyes and saw soft early-morning light through the windows.

Flames were roiling in the woodstove. It had been stoked recently.

She got up onto one elbow. The kitchen was empty. Not even Ruth and Rosa. Or Henri and Gracie.

Putting on her dressing gown and slippers, she tried the light switch. The power was still out. Then she noticed a note on the pine kitchen table.

> *Ma Chère,*
> *Ruth, Rosa, Henri and Gracie and I have gone to the bistro to talk to Olivier and Gabri. Join us if you can.*
>
> *Love, Armand*
> *(6:50 a.m.)*

Reine-Marie looked at her watch. It was now 7:12.

She went over to the window. Snow had climbed halfway up, blocking most of the light and almost all the view. But Reine-Marie could see that the blizzard had blown itself out and left in its wake, as the worst storms often did, a luminous day.

Though it was, as any good Quebecker knew, an illusion. The sun was gleaming off its fangs.

"My God," Reine-Marie gasped as the warmth of the bistro enveloped her. "Why do we live here?"

Her cheeks were bright red and her eyes, tearing up, took time to adjust to the dim light. The short walk over to the bistro through the brilliant sunshine had rendered her almost snow-blind. It wasn't enough that the bitter winter wanted to kill them, first it had to blind.

"Minus thirty-five," said Olivier proudly, as though he were responsible.

"But it's a dry cold," said Gabri. "And no wind."

It was their refrain when trying to comfort themselves as they looked out on a day so inviting and so brutal.

"I smell something," said Reine-Marie after taking off her coat and hat and mitts.

"It's not me," said Ruth. But Rosa was looking a little sheepish. Though ducks often did.

"I was wondering why you two braved the cold to come here," said Reine-Marie, following her nose, and the aroma, to the table and the empty plates smeared with maple syrup.

Armand shrugged in an exaggerated Gallic manner. "Some things are worth risking life and limb."

Olivier came out of the kitchen with a plate of warm blueberry crêpes, sausages, and maple syrup, and a café au lait.

"We left some for you," said Gabri.

"Armand made us," said Ruth.

"Oh heaven," she said, sitting down and putting her hands around the mug. "*Merci.*" Then a thought struck her. "Do you have power?"

"*Non.* A generator."

"Hooked up to the espresso machine?"

"And the oven and fridge," said Gabri.

"But not the lights?"

"Priorities," said Olivier. "Are you complaining?"

"*Mon Dieu*, no," she said.

Her eyes settled on Armand. For all the kidding, she knew her husband would not bring an elderly woman into the bitter cold without a good reason.

"You came here with Ruth for more than crêpes."

"*Oui*," he said. "Ruth knows who Bertha Baumgartner was."

"Why didn't you tell us last night?"

"Because it only came to me this morning. But I wasn't really sure."

Reine-Marie raised her brows. It was unlike Ruth to be anything other than absolutely sure of herself. It was others she doubted.

"I needed to speak to Gabri and Olivier, to see what they thought," said Ruth.

"And?"

"Did you ever hear of the Baroness?" asked Gabri, taking a seat beside Reine-Marie.

It did sound vaguely familiar. Like a memory of a memory. But it was so removed that Reine-Marie knew she would never get it.

She shook her head.

"We were introduced to her when we first moved here," said Olivier. "Years ago. By Timmer Hadley."

"The woman who used to own the old Hadley house," said Reine-Marie.

She gestured in the direction of the fine house on the hill, overlooking the little village. The house where the "rich" family had once lived and had, a century ago, lorded it over the great unwashed below.

"I met the Baroness at Timmer's home," said Ruth.

"And she came to us too," said Gabri. "When we opened the B&B."

"A regular? A friend?" asked Reine-Marie.

"A cleaning woman."

"Hurry up," called Myrna, tugging at Benedict's arm.

Lucien was a few paces ahead, but Benedict had stopped and Myrna had had to backtrack to get to him.

It felt akin to running back into a flaming building.

The skin on her face was so cold it burned. It had even penetrated her thick mittens and was biting at her fingers. She squinted through the searing sunlight.

But Benedict, instead of hurrying to the bistro like any sensible

Québécois, had stopped. His back to the shops, his immense red-and-white tuque dragging on the ground, he was staring at the three huge pine trees, laden with snow, and the cottages that ringed the village green.

"It's beautiful."

His words came out in a puff, like a dialogue cloud in a cartoon.

"Yes, yes, beautiful, beautiful," said Myrna, pulling at his arm. "Now, hurry up before I kick you where it hurts."

They'd arrived in the blizzard, so this was Benedict's first look at Three Pines. The ring of homes. The smoke drifting out of the chimneys. The hills and forests.

He stood and looked at a view that hadn't changed in centuries.

And then he was tugged away.

A few minutes later, another table had been dragged over to the open fire, and they too were enjoying breakfast and coffee in the bistro.

Clara, having seen everyone running over, had joined them.

"If it's this cold for *carnaval*, I'm not taking my clothes off," she said, rubbing her arms.

"Excuse me?" said Armand.

"Nothing," said Gabri. "Never mind."

"What were you talking about when I came in?" asked Clara, accepting the mug of hot coffee. "You were all looking pretty shocked."

"Ruth figured out who Bertha Baumgartner was," said Armand.

"Who?"

"Do you remember the Baroness?" asked Gabri.

"Oh, yeah. Who could forget her?"

Clara lowered her fork and locked eyes with Ruth.

Then her gaze traveled across the bistro, to the windows. But she didn't see the sun hitting the frost-etched panes. She didn't see the village under the deep snow and the impossibly clear blue sky.

She saw a plump older woman, with small eyes, a big smile, and a mop she held like a North Pole explorer about to plant a flag.

"Her name was Bertha Baumgartner?" asked Clara.

"Well, you didn't think it was the 'Baroness,' did you?" asked Ruth.

Clara frowned. She'd actually given it no thought.

"Do you know why she was called the Baroness?" asked Armand.

They looked at Ruth.

"How the hell should I know? She never worked for me." She looked at Myrna. "You're the only cleaning woman I've ever had."

"I'm not—" Myrna began, then said, "Why bother?"

"Then why do you think this Bertha and the Baroness are the same person?" asked Armand.

"You said her home was down Mansonville way?" said Ruth, and he nodded. "An old farmhouse by the Glen?"

"*Oui.*"

"I dropped the Baroness off once, when her car broke down, years ago," said Ruth. "It sounds like the same place."

"What was it like? Can you remember?"

But, of course, Ruth remembered everything.

Every meal, every drink, every sight, every slight, real and imagined and manufactured. Every compliment. Every word spoken and unspoken.

She retained it all and rendered those memories into feelings and the feelings into poetry.

> *I prayed to be good and strong and wise,*
> *for my daily bread and deliverance*
> *from the sins I was told were mine from birth,*
> *and the Guilt of an old inheritance.*

Armand didn't have to think hard to know why that particular poem of Ruth's, a fairly obscure one, came to mind.

"Her house was small, sort of rambling. But inviting," said Ruth. "Window boxes planted with pansies and barrels of flowers on either side of the steps up to the porch. I could see a cat lying in the sun. There were all sorts of trucks and farm equipment in the yard, but there always are in these old farmhouses."

Once Armand stripped away the snow and straightened the crooked house, he could just about see it. As the home had been, once. On a warm summer day. With a younger Ruth and the Baroness.

"You haven't seen her lately?" he asked.

"Not for years," said Gabri. "She stopped working, and we lost contact. I didn't know she'd died. Did you?"

Clara shook her head and dropped her eyes.

"My mother was a cleaning lady," said Reine-Marie, rightly interpreting how Clara was feeling. "She grew close to the families she worked for, while she worked for them. But then she lost track of them. I'm sure many died and she had no idea."

Clara nodded, grateful to her for pointing out that it went both ways.

"Do you think if the Baroness Baumgartner wrote to Justin—" Gabri began.

"*Non.*"

"What was she like?" Armand asked.

"A strong personality," said Olivier. "Liked her own voice. Used to talk about her kids."

"Two boys and a girl," said Gabri. "The most wonderful children on earth. Handsome, beautiful. Smart and kind. Like their mother, she used to say, then laugh."

"And we were always expected to say, 'Don't laugh, it's true,'" said Olivier.

"And did you?" asked Reine-Marie.

"If we wanted our house cleaned, we did," said Gabri.

As they described the Baroness's personality, Clara could see her. Almost always with a smile. Sometimes warm and kind. Often with a touch of cunning. But never malicious.

A woman who was less like a baroness would be hard to find.

And yet Clara also remembered the Baroness really leaning into the mop or brush. Working hard.

There was a nobility in that.

Clara wondered why it had never occurred to her to paint the Baroness. Her small, bright eyes, at once kind and needy. Cunning, but also thoughtful. Her worn hands and face.

It was a remarkable face, filled with generosity and bile. Kindness and judgment.

"Why're you asking?" asked Gabri. "Does it matter?"

"Not really," said Armand. "It's just that the provisions of her will are a little odd."

"Oooh, odd," said Gabri. "I like that."

"You like queer," said Ruth. "You hate odd."

"That is true," he admitted. "So what was odd about the will?"

"The money," said Benedict.

"Money?" asked Olivier, leaning forward.

Lucien told them about the bequests.

Olivier's expressive face went from dumbfounded to amused and back to dumbfounded.

"Fifteen million? Dollars?" He looked at Gabri, who was also gaping. "We should've kept in touch."

"*Oui*," said Lucien, pleased with the reaction. "And a home in Switzerland."

"And one in Vienna," said Myrna.

"She was always a little loopy," said Gabri, "but she must've gone right around the bend."

"No. My father would never have allowed her to sign the will if he thought she wasn't clearheaded."

"Oh come on," said Ruth. "Even I can see it's madness. And not just the money, but choosing three people she didn't even know to be her liquidators? Why not one of us?"

Armand looked at Gabri, Olivier, Ruth, and Clara.

They'd known her. And hadn't known her.

They knew the Baroness. Not Bertha Baumgartner.

Is that why?

He and Myrna had no preconceptions. They saw her as a woman, not a cleaning woman, and certainly not a baroness.

But why would that matter?

Maybe it was their skill set. He was a cop, an investigator. Myrna was a psychologist. She could read people. They both could. But again, why would that matter to Madame Baumgartner in the execution of her will?

And how did she even know about them, when they didn't know her?

And what about . . . ? Armand turned to Benedict. How do you begin to explain him as liquidator?

"Who were the witnesses?" he asked, sitting forward again.

"Neighbors," said Lucien. "Though they wouldn't have seen the contents of the will."

Armand looked at his watch. It was coming on for eight thirty in the morning. The power hadn't yet been restored, but the tiny village of Three Pines was often among the last to be remembered by Hydro-Québec.

"You need to go?" asked Reine-Marie, remembering their conversation of the evening before.

"I'm afraid so."

"What about us?" asked Lucien.

"I'll drive you back to the farmhouse. We can dig your cars out together."

"The heirs need to be contacted," said Lucien. "I'll try to set something up for this afternoon. No use waiting."

"Sounds good to me," said Benedict.

Armand nodded. "Just let me know when and where."

The Guilt of an old inheritance," he thought as he walked toward his car, his boots squealing on the hard-packed snow.

Is that what was in the crumbling farmhouse? Guilt, and sins that were there from birth?

CHAPTER 10

—

"Come in, come in," said the neighbor, gesturing. "Get out of the cold."

She was young, in her mid-thirties, Gamache guessed. Only slightly older than his own daughter, Annie. And she probably shouldn't be letting complete strangers into her home.

But by the way she'd looked at him when she'd answered his knock, Gamache suspected he wasn't a complete stranger. And that was confirmed a moment later when he took off his gloves and offered his hand as they crowded into her vestibule.

"*Désolé*," he said. "Sorry to disturb you, especially on a day like this. My name is Armand Gamache. I live down the road, in Three Pines."

"Yes, I know who you are. I'm Patricia Houle."

She took his hand, then turned to Myrna. "I know you too. You run the bookstore."

"I do. You've been in quite a few times. Nonfiction. Gardening books. But also biography."

"That's me."

Lucien introduced himself, and then she turned to Benedict.

"Benedict Pouliot," he said. "Builder."

"Come in, get warm."

They followed her into the heart of the home, the kitchen, where a large woodstove was throbbing out heat.

As with her home, there was nothing pretentious about Madame Houle. She seemed to be someone without need to impress, who, because of that, was impressive. Like her strong, simple home.

"I have a pot of tea on. Would you like a cup?"

"Not for me, thank you," said Myrna. The others also declined.

"We won't take much of your time," said Armand. "We just have a couple of questions."

"*Oui?*" asked Patricia.

"Did you know the woman who lived next door?" Myrna asked.

"The Baroness? Oh yes, though not well. Why?"

She'd noticed her visitors exchanging glances but could not have known the significance of what she'd just said. Patricia Houle had just confirmed that Ruth was right. Bertha Baumgartner was the Baroness.

"Nothing," said Myrna. "Go on."

"Was it that I called her the Baroness?" asked Patricia, looking from one to the other. "It wasn't our nickname for her. Believe me, we wouldn't have chosen that one. She called herself that."

"How long have you known her?" Lucien asked.

"A few years. Is everything all right?" She looked at Armand. "You're not here officially, are you?"

"Not in the way you think," he said. "We're liquidators of her estate."

"She died?"

"Yes, just before Christmas," said Lucien.

"I hadn't heard," said Patricia. "I know she moved into a nursing home a couple of years ago, but I didn't know she'd passed away. I'm sorry. I'd have gone to the funeral."

"You witnessed her will?" asked Armand. When she nodded, he went on. "Did she strike you as competent?"

"Oh yes," said Patricia. "She was all there. She was a little odd, granted. She did insist on being called Baroness, but we all have our eccentricities."

"I bet I can guess yours," said Myrna.

"I bet you can," said Patricia.

"You like poisonous plants. Probably have a bed dedicated to them."

"I do," Patricia admitted with a laugh.

"How did you know that?" Benedict asked.

"The books she bought," said Myrna. "*The Poison Garden* was one, as I remember. Another was . . ." Myrna strained her memory.

"*Deadliest Garden Plants,*" said Patricia. She looked at Armand and cocked her head. "Bit of a clue, that."

Armand smiled.

"That's how I first got to know the Baroness and how I learned about poison gardens. She had one. Walked me through it and pointed out that foxglove is digitalis. Deadly. She also had monkshood, and lily-of-the-valley, and hydrangea. All toxic. Among other perennials, of course. But, strangely enough, the poisonous ones are the most beautiful."

Myrna nodded. She was also a keen gardener, though it had never occurred to her to dedicate a bed to plants that kill. But enough people did so that there were a number of books written about it. And Patricia Houle was right. The deadly flowers were among the most beautiful. And, perversely, the longest-lived.

"There're flowers that'll really kill someone?" asked Benedict.

"Supposedly," said Patricia, "though I wouldn't know how to get the poison out. You probably need a chemistry degree."

"And a desire," said Gamache.

His voice was pleasant, but his eyes took in Patricia Houle, and he amended his earlier impression. She gave off an aura not just of confidence but of competence.

He'd noticed her car parked outside, completely cleaned off. The snow around it shoveled with crisp, straight lines.

When she did a job, she did it well and she did it thoroughly.

He suspected if she needed to, she could figure out how to squeeze poison from a daffodil.

Thanking her for her help and hospitality, they left Madame Houle and headed next door.

Bertha Baumgartner's home seemed to be tilting even further under the weight of the new snow. It would be folly to go anywhere near it, and Gamache made a note to call the local town hall and get warning tape put up. And, as soon as possible, a bulldozer should be brought in.

They dug out Myrna's and Lucien's cars, but when they'd cleared off Benedict's pickup truck, Armand stopped the young man from getting in.

"You can't drive without winter tires."

"But I have to. I'll be fine."

Those were, Gamache knew, the last words of too many young people.

"Yes, you will be fine," he said. "Because you're not going anywhere in that."

"And if I do drive?" asked Benedict. "What're you going to do? Call the cops?"

"He wouldn't need to call," said Lucien, and saw that Benedict still didn't get it. "You really don't know who he is?"

Benedict shook his head.

"I'm the head of the Sûreté du Québec," said Armand.

"Chief Superintendent Gamache," said Lucien.

Benedict said either "Oh shit" or "No shit." Either way, *merde* was involved.

"Really?"

Gamache nodded. *"C'est la vérité."*

Benedict looked behind him, to his pickup, and mumbled something that sounded like "What fucking luck."

Gamache grinned. He'd had luck like this too, when he was Benedict's age. Took a long time before he realized it was, in fact, good luck.

"I guess I have no choice," said Benedict.

"Bon. Call the CAA when the phones come back. Have it towed to a garage and decent winter tires put on. Not the cheap ones. *D'accord?"*

"Got it," Benedict mumbled to the snow on his boots.

"It's all right," said Gamache quietly. "We'll pay for the tires."

"I'll pay you back."

"Just give me that lesson in driving on snow you promised. We'll call it even."

"Merci."

"Good." Gamache turned to Lucien. "Let me know about the meeting with Madame Baumgartner's children."

"I will," said Lucien.

As she drove Benedict back to Three Pines, Myrna looked at the thick snow in the yard. And thought of the poisonous plants buried there. Frozen, but not dead. Just waiting.

Though the real threat, Myrna knew, didn't come from the poison flowers. Those you could see. Those you knew about. And besides, they at least were pretty.

No. The real danger in a garden came from the bindweed. That moved underground, then surfaced and took hold. Strangling plant after healthy plant. Killing them all, slowly. And for no apparent reason, except that it was its nature.

And then it disappeared underground again.

Yes, the real danger always came from the thing you couldn't see.

CHAPTER 11

—

"So what's the problem?"

"What makes you think there's a problem?" Armand asked.

"You aren't eating your . . . éclair."

Each of her words was carefully enunciated, though they were still muffled, as though wrapped in too much care and cotton batting.

And her movements, as her hand brought her own pastry to her mouth, were also considered. Deliberate. Precise. Slow.

Gamache visited Isabelle Lacoste at least once a week at her home in Montréal. When the weather was good, they'd go for a short walk, but mostly, like today, they sat in her kitchen and talked. He'd gotten into the habit of discussing events with her. Getting her take on things. Her opinions and advice.

She was one of his senior officers.

He looked now, as he always did, for any sign of improvement. Real was best, but he'd even settle for imagined. He thought perhaps her hands were steadier. Her words clearer. Her vocabulary richer.

Yes. Without a doubt. Maybe.

"Is it the internal investigation?" she asked, and took a bite of the mille-feuille that Armand had brought her from Sarah's Boulangerie, knowing it was her favorite.

"No. That's just about over."

"Still, they're taking their sweet time. What's the problem?"

"We both know the problem," he said.

"Yes. The drugs. Nothing more there?"

75

She studied him. Looking for signs of improvement. Of reason to hope this really would all go away soon.

The Chief looked relaxed. Confident. But then he almost always did. It was what he hid that worried her.

Isabelle's brow furrowed in concentration.

"I'm tiring you out," he said, and made to get up. "I'm sorry."

"No, no, please." She waved him back down. "I need . . . stimulation. The kids are off school because of the storm and have decided I need to learn to count to a . . . hundred. We did that all morning before I kicked them outside. I tried to explain that I can count. Have been able to for . . . months, but still, they insisted." She looked into Armand's eyes. "Help me."

It was said with a comically pathetic inflection, intentionally exaggerated. But still, it broke his heart.

"I'm kidding, *patron*," she said, sensing more than seeing his sorrow. "More coffee?"

"Please."

He followed her to the counter. Her gait was slow. Halting. Deliberate. And so much better than anyone, including her doctors, had dared hope.

Isabelle's son and daughter were outside, building snow forts with the neighborhood children. Through the windows Armand and Isabelle could hear shrieks as one "army" attacked those who held the fort.

Playing the same games Armand had played as a child. The same ones Isabelle, twenty-five years later, had played. Games of domination and war.

"Let's hope they never know . . . what . . . it's really like," said Isabelle, standing by the window, next to her boss and mentor.

He nodded.

The explosions. The chaos. The acrid stink of gun smoke. The blinding grit as stone and cement and brick were pulverized. Choking the air.

The screams. Choking the air.

The pain.

His grip tightened on the counter as it washed over him. Sweeping him up. Tossing and spinning. Drowning him.

76

"Does your hand still tremble?" she asked quietly.

He gathered himself and nodded.

"Sometimes. When I'm tired or particularly stressed. But not like it used to."

"And the limp?"

"Again, mostly when I'm tired. I barely notice it anymore. It was years ago." Unlike Isabelle's wounds, which were mere months old. He marveled at that. It seemed both ages ago and yesterday.

"Do you think about it?" she asked.

"What happened when you were hurt?"

He turned to look at her. That face, so familiar from across so many bodies. So many desks, conference tables. So many hastily set-up incident rooms in basements and barns and cabins across Québec. As they'd investigated murders. Isabelle. Jean-Guy. Himself.

Isabelle Lacoste had come to him as a young agent, barely twenty-five. Rejected by her own department for not being brutal enough, cynical enough, malleable enough to know what was right and to do wrong.

He'd been the head of homicide then and given her a job in his department, the most prestigious within the Sûreté du Québec. To the astonishment of her former colleagues.

And Isabelle Lacoste had risen through the ranks, eventually taking over from Gamache himself when he'd become head of the academy and then head of the whole Sûreté. As he was now.

Sort of.

She'd aged, of course. Faster than she should have, would have, had he not brought her on board. Had he not made her Chief Inspector. And had that last action against the cartels not taken place. Mere months ago.

"Yes," he said. "I think about it."

Isabelle hitting the floor. Shot in the head. What had seemed her last act had given them a chance. Had, in fact, saved them all. But still, it had been a bloody nightmare.

He remembered that, the most recent action. But he also remembered, equally vividly, all the raids, the assaults, the arrests. The investigations over the years. The victims.

All the sightless, staring eyes. Of men, women, children whose murder he'd investigated. Over the years. Whose murderer he'd hunted down.

All the agents he'd sent, often led, into the gun smoke.

And he remembered his hand raised, ready to knock on the closed door. The rapping of the Grim Reaper. To do murder himself. Not physically, but Armand Gamache was realistic enough to know this was a killing nevertheless. He carried with him always the faces of fathers, mothers, wives, and husbands. Inquisitive. Curious. Politely they opened the door and looked at this stranger.

And then, as he spoke the fateful words, their faces changed. And he watched their world collapse. Pinning them under the rubble. Crushed under a grief so profound most never emerged. And those who did came out dazed into a world forever changed.

The person they were before his arrival was dead. Gone.

When a murder was committed, more than one person died.

Yes. He remembered.

"But I try not to dwell on it," he said to Isabelle.

Or, worse, dwell in it. Take up residence in the tragedies, the pain. The hurt. To make a home in hell.

But leaving was hard. Especially his agents, men and women whose lives were lost because they'd followed his orders. Followed him. He'd felt, for a long time, that he owed it to them to not leave that place of sorrow. To keep them company there.

His friends and therapists had helped him to see that that was doing them a disservice. Their lives could not be defined by their deaths. They belonged not in perpetual pain but in the beauty of their short lives.

His inability to move on would trap them forever in those final horrific moments.

Armand watched as Isabelle carefully lowered her mug to the kitchen table. When it was just an inch away from the surface, her grip slipped and the coffee spilled. Not much, but he could see her anger. Frustration. Embarrassment.

He offered her his handkerchief to sop it up.

"*Merci.*" She grabbed it from him and wiped. He put out his hand to take it back, but she kept it. "I'll w-w-w . . . wash it and get it back to you," she snapped.

"Isabelle," he said, his voice calm but firm. "Look at me."

She lifted her eyes from the soiled handkerchief to his face.

"I hated it too."

"What?"

"My body. I hated it for letting me down. For letting this happen." He ran his finger along the scar at his temple. "For not moving fast enough. For not seeing it coming. For being on the ground, not being able to get up to protect my agents. I hated it for not healing fast enough. I hated when I stumbled. When Reine-Marie had to hold my hand to keep me steady. I could see people staring at me with pity as I limped or searched for a word."

Isabelle nodded.

"I wanted my old body back," said Armand. "The strong and healthy one."

"Before," she said.

"Before," he nodded.

They sat in silence, except for the far-off laughter of the children.

"That's how I feel," she said. "I hate my . . . body. I hate that I can't pick up my kids or play with them, or if I do get onto the floor with them, they have to help me up. I hate it. I hate that I can't . . . read them to sleep, and that I get tired so easily, and lose my train of thought. I hate that some days I can't add and some days I can't . . . subtract. And some days—"

Isabelle paused, gathering herself. She looked into his eyes.

"I forget their names, *patron*," she whispered. "My own children."

It was no use telling her he understood. Or that it was all right. She'd earned the right to no easy answer.

"And what do you love, Isabelle?"

"Pardon?"

Gamache closed his eyes and raised his face to the ceiling. "'White plates and cups, clean-gleaming, / Ringed with blue lines; and feathery, faery dust; / Wet roofs, beneath the lamp-light; the strong crust / Of friendly bread.'"

He opened his eyes, looked at Isabelle, and smiled, deep lines forming at his eyes and down his worn face.

"There's more, but I won't go on. It's a poem by Rupert Brooke. He was a soldier in the First World War. It helped him in the hellhole of the trenches to think of the things he loved. It helped me too. I made mental lists and followed the things I love, the people I love, back to sanity. I still do."

He could see her thinking.

What he was suggesting wasn't a magic cure for a bullet to the brain. A huge amount of work, of pain, physical and emotional, lay ahead. But it might as well be done in the sunlight.

"I'm stronger, healthier now than I was before any of that happened," said Gamache. "Physically. Emotionally. Because I've had to be. And you will be too."

"Things are strongest where they're broken," said Lacoste. "Agent Morin said that."

Things are strongest where they're broken.

Armand heard again the impossibly and eternally youthful voice of Paul Morin. As though he were standing right there, in Isabelle's sunny kitchen with them.

And Agent Morin had been right. But oh the pain of mending.

"I'm lucky in a way," Isabelle said after a few moments. "I can't remember anything about that day. Nothing. I think that helps."

"I think it does."

"My kids keep wanting to read me . . . Pinocchio. Something to do with what happened, but damned if it makes sense to me. Pinocchio, *patron*?"

"Sometimes being shot in the head is a blessing."

She laughed. "How do you do it?"

"Remember?"

"Forget."

He took a breath, looked down at his feet, then back up, into her eyes.

"I had a mentor once—" he said.

"Oh Jesus, not the one who taught you poetry," she said in mock panic. He had that "poetry" look about him.

"No, but just for that." He cleared his throat. "'The Wreck of the Hesperus,'" he announced, and opened his mouth as though to launch into the epic verse. But instead he smiled and saw Isabelle beaming with amusement.

"What I was going to say is that my mentor had this theory that our lives are like an aboriginal longhouse. Just one huge room." He swept one arm out to illustrate scope. "He said that if we thought we could compartmentalize things, we were deluding ourselves. Everyone we meet, every word we speak, every action taken or not taken lives in our longhouse. With us. Always. Never to be expelled or locked away."

"That's a pretty scary thought," said Isabelle.

"*Absolument*. My mentor, my first chief inspector, said to me, 'Armand, if you don't want your longhouse to smell like *merde*, you have to do two things—'"

"Not let Ruth Zardo in?" asked Isabelle.

Armand laughed. "Too late for that. For both of us."

In a flash he was back there. Running toward the ambulance. Isabelle on the gurney, unconscious. The old poet's bony hands holding Isabelle's. Her voice unwavering as she whispered to Isabelle over and over again the only thing that mattered.

That she was loved.

Isabelle would never remember that, and Armand would never forget it.

"*Non*. He said, 'Be very, very careful who you let into your life. And learn to make peace with whatever happens. You can't erase the past. It's trapped in there with you. But you can make peace with it. If you don't,' he said, 'you'll be at perpetual war.'"

Armand smiled at the memory.

"I think he knew what an idiot he was dealing with. He could see I was getting ready to tell him my own theory of life. At twenty-three. He showed me the door. But just as I was leaving, he said, 'And the enemy you'll be fighting is yourself.'"

Gamache hadn't thought of that encounter for years. But he had thought of his life, from that moment forward, as a longhouse.

And in his longhouse, as he glanced back down it now, he saw all the young agents, all the men and women, boys and girls, whose lives he'd affected.

He could also see, standing there, the people who'd hurt him. Badly. Almost killed him.

They all lived there.

And while he would never be friends with many of those memories, those ghosts, he had worked very hard to make peace with them. With what he'd done and what had been done to him.

"And are the opioids there, *patron*? In your longhouse?"

Her question brought him back with a jolt, to her comfortable home.

"Have you found them?"

"Not all, *non*. The last of it, here in Montréal, has disappeared," he admitted.

"How much?"

"Enough to produce hundreds of thousands of hits."

She was silent. Not saying what he knew better than anyone.

Each one of those hits could kill.

"*Merde*," she whispered, then immediately apologized to him. "*Désolé*."

She rarely swore and almost never in front of the Chief. But this one escaped, riding the wave of revulsion.

"There's more," she said, studying the man she'd gotten to know so well. Better than her own father. "Something else is bothering you."

Weighing on him, was more like it, but she could not quite come up with that word.

"*Oui*. It's about the academy."

"The Sûreté Academy?"

"Yes. There's a problem. They want to expel one of the cadets."

"It happens," said Isabelle. "I'm sorry, *patron*, but why is it your concern?"

"The one the Commander called me about, and wants to expel, is Amelia Choquet."

Isabelle Lacoste settled back in her chair and considered him closely. "And? Why would he call you about this? You're no longer head of the academy."

"True."

And she saw that this wasn't just a weight on Gamache. It was close to crushing.

"What is it, *patron*?"

"They found opioids in her possession."

"Christ." And this time she didn't apologize. "How much?"

"It seems to be too much for personal consumption."

"She's trafficking? At the academy?"

82

"It would appear so."

Now Isabelle was quiet. Absorbing. Thinking.

Armand gave her time.

"Is it from your shipment?" she asked. She hadn't meant to give him ownership, but that was the way it came out. And they both knew he did have ownership, if not of the actual drugs then of the situation.

"They haven't been sent to the lab yet, but it's possible, yes." He looked down at his hands, one clasping the other. "I have a decision to make."

"About Cadet Choquet."

"*Oui*. And frankly, I don't know what to do."

She wished with all her heart she could help him.

"I'm sorry, Chief, but surely this is up to the Commander. Not you."

Watching Chief Superintendent Gamache, Lacoste couldn't fathom what he was thinking. He seemed to be asking for her help and yet keeping some information from her.

"There's something you're not telling me."

"Let me ask you this, Isabelle," he said, ignoring her statement. "What would you do if you were me?"

"And a cadet was found with drugs in her possession? I'd leave that up to the Commander of the academy. It's not your business, *patron*."

"Oh, but it is, Isabelle. If it's my opioids, as you put it, in her possession."

"Where did she get the drugs from?" Isabelle asked. "Has she told you?"

"The Commander hasn't interviewed her yet. As far as he knows, Cadet Choquet doesn't even realize they've been found. I'm going there now. If he expels her, she'll die. I know that much."

Lacoste nodded. She knew it too. What most didn't know was why Gamache had let Amelia Choquet into the academy in the first place. Why that messed-up young woman, with the history of drug abuse and prostitution, had been given a coveted place at the Sûreté school.

But Isabelle knew. Or thought she knew.

The same reason he'd reached down into the bowels of her own career and given her a job.

Had reached down and dragged Jean-Guy up, a moment from being fired himself.

It was the same reason Chief Superintendent Gamache was now considering convincing the current Commander to keep Cadet Choquet.

This was a man who profoundly believed in second chances.

Except this wouldn't be Amelia Choquet's second chance. It would be her third.

And that was, in Lacoste's view, one too many.

There was grace in second chances and foolishness in third. And perhaps worse than foolishness.

There was, or could be, outright danger. Believing a person capable of redemption when they'd proven they were not.

Amelia Choquet hadn't been caught cheating on an exam or stealing some trinket from a fellow cadet. She'd been caught with a drug so potent, so dangerous, it eventually killed almost everyone who took it. Amelia Choquet knew that. Knew she was trafficking in death.

Chief Inspector Lacoste regarded the steady man in front of her, who believed everyone could be saved. Believed he could save them.

It was both his saving grace and his blind spot. And few knew better than Isabelle Lacoste what that meant. Some things hurtled. Some slithered. But nothing good ever came out of a blind spot.

Isabelle noticed that Gamache's right hand wasn't trembling. But it was clenched into a fist.

CHAPTER 12

⁓

"Sit."

The Commander of the Sûreté Academy did not stand when Cadet Choquet entered the office, and neither did Chief Superintendent Gamache.

Amelia waited at the door, defiant as ever, then walked across the room and dropped into the chair indicated, crossing her arms tight over her chest. Glaring straight ahead.

She looked exactly as Gamache remembered her.

Hair jet-black and spiky. Though perhaps not quite as belligerent in its cut. She was not, he suspected, softening so much as maturing. Or perhaps he was just getting used to it.

Cadet Choquet was in the final year of her training. Within months of graduation.

She was small but powerful. Not in her build but in her presence. She radiated aggression.

Fuck off.

The words fairly pulsed off her, a spiky aura.

Was a time, when Gamache first met her, that she'd actually say it. To his face. To anyone's and everyone's face. But now she simply thought it. Such was the force of the petite woman, though, that she might as well be screaming it.

Still, thought Gamache, it was progress. Of sorts.

She gave him one curt nod.

Fuck off.

He didn't respond. Simply watched her.

The piercings were still in place. Through her eyebrow, her nose and cheek. Along the gristle of her ears.

And . . . ? Yes. There it was.

The click, click, click as she moved the post in her tongue up and down, knocking it against her teeth.

In poker it would be considered a "tell."

Click, click, click. Amelia's unconscious Morse code.

One day he might tell her about her tell. But not just yet. Right now it served a purpose. His purpose.

Click. Click. Click.

SOS.

Clean sheets, thought Gamache. *The scent of wood smoke. Feeling Henri's head on my slippers.* He went through his own private code. A sort of rosary.

Flaky croissants.

"Do you know why you're here?" the Commander asked the cadet.

When Gamache had left the academy to take up the job of chief superintendent of the Sûreté, he'd had long discussions with his successor about the cadets. Including the suggestion that the students be allowed to be individuals. Amelia Choquet was certainly that. And more.

"No, I do not know why you wanted to see me." Pause. "Sir."

The Commander picked up an envelope from his desk, and from it he took a baggie.

"Recognize this?"

"No."

The answer came too quickly for her to be surprised. She knew exactly why she was there. And she knew exactly what was in that little plastic bag.

Gamache knew Amelia well enough to know she'd prepared for this encounter. Perhaps a little too much. She wasn't showing the natural curiosity, even astonishment, of the innocent.

Instead she displayed the rehearsed answers of the guilty.

He glanced at the Commander to see if he'd picked up on the same thing and saw that he of course had.

Gamache felt his heart speed up as he saw the point of no return approaching. He'd made up his mind what had to be done, though it seemed his heart remained unconvinced. But he knew he had to see this through.

Amelia Choquet's breathing had changed. Shorter, more rapid.

She too could see the point of no return. Just there. On the horizon. Getting closer. Fast.

The clicking had stopped. She was alert. An animal who, after living with smaller creatures, suddenly discovered a world of giants. Suddenly discovered it was tinier than it realized. More vulnerable than it thought. More threatened than it believed possible. A creature looking for escape and finding only a cliff.

"It was in your room, under your mattress," said the Commander.

"You searched my room?" She sounded indignant, and Gamache almost admired her rally.

Almost.

"That's not exactly the lede, is it, Cadet Choquet?" The Commander lowered the baggie to his desk. "This is a narcotic. Enough to traffic."

"It's not mine. I have no idea where it came from. If I was going to do something as stupid as having shit in the academy, I'd find a better hiding place. Like maybe someone else's room."

"Are you suggesting someone planted it?" asked Gamache.

She shrugged.

"Intentionally?" he persisted. "Trying to set you up? Or just wanting to get it out of their own room?"

"Take your pick. All I know is, it isn't mine."

"The bag has been fingerprinted—"

"Clever."

The Commander stared at her. Amelia, Gamache knew, had a rare ability to get up people's noses. Though why she'd want to be there was anyone's guess.

"—and we'll have the results soon. Where did you get it from?"

"It's. Not. Mine."

The clicking had begun again. A rat-a-tat-tat now, designed to annoy.

Gamache could see the Commander struggling not to claw his way across his desk and reach for her throat.

And Cadet Choquet was doing nothing to save herself. In fact, just the opposite. She was taunting them. Arrogant, smug, almost certainly deceitful, she was demanding to be doubted. And worse.

An innocent cadet, when a Schedule 1 drug was discovered in her room, would protest innocence and try to work with them to find out whose it was.

A guilty cadet would almost certainly at least pretend to do the same.

But she was doing neither.

She'd gone from a vulnerable creature, trapped and frightened, to an aggressor, throwing out ridiculous and obvious lies.

Amelia Choquet was a senior cadet. She'd matured into a natural leader, not the bully Gamache feared she'd become.

She was quick-witted, alert. Someone others instinctively wanted to follow.

Which made Cadet Choquet as trafficker in narcotics all the more dangerous. But not, with her background, completely unbelievable.

Leaning closer to her, he saw the tattoos on her wrists and forearms, where the sleeves of her uniform had ridden up. Then his sharp gaze traveled to her face, and he saw something else. Something that might explain her lack of judgment, her self-destructive, erratic behavior in this meeting.

Her reactions had been wild. Unpredictable. The reactions of a junkie.

She hadn't . . . ?

His own eyes widened a little.

"You foolish, foolish woman." His voice was practically a snarl. Then he turned to the Commander. "We need a blood test. She's high."

"Fuck you."

He glared at her. "When did you last use?"

"I've taken nothing."

"Look at her," Gamache said to the Commander before turning back to Amelia. "Your pupils are dilated. You think I don't know what that means? Search her room again," he said, and the Commander placed a call.

"I have a mind to end it right now," Gamache said, turning back to Amelia.

"Don't you dare. I've come too far. We're so close. I can do this."

"You can't. You've messed up. You're messed up. You've gone too far."

"No, no. These are eyedrops. Only eyedrops." She was almost begging. "It looks like I'm stoned, but I'm not."

"Tell the agents searching her room to look for eyedrops," said Gamache, who wanted, was almost desperate, to believe her. To believe she hadn't taken any of the drug herself.

"They won't find any," said Amelia. "I threw them away."

There was silence as Gamache stared deep into the dilated eyes of the cadet.

Seeing the look on Gamache's face, she turned away from him and spoke to the Commander. "If you think I'd deal in that shit, you're a worse judge of character than I thought."

"Drugs change people," said the Commander. "Addiction changes people. As I think you know."

"I've been clean for years," she said. "I'm not stoned. Why the fuck would I enroll in the Sûreté, for God's sake, if I was still a junkie?"

Gamache started to laugh. "You're kidding, right? You get a gun and access to any amount of drugs. Most dirty agents at least have the sense to wait until they've graduated and are on the street before they turn. But then most don't arrive as addicts."

"I was never an addict, and you know it." She was all but screaming at him now. "I used, yes. But I was never addicted. I quit. In time."

Her own words seemed to give her pause as she remembered how and why she quit. In time.

It was because of this man. Who'd given her a home here. A purpose and a direction. A chance.

"I'm not trafficking," she said. Her voice quieter. "I'm not using."

Gamache examined her. Studied her. So much was riding on this.

He'd known, when he'd let her into the academy, that if she succeeded, she had the makings of a remarkable Sûreté officer. A street kid, a junkie turned cop.

It had given her a huge advantage. She knew things other agents never could. She knew them not just in her intellect but deep in her gut. She had contacts, credibility, the language of the streets etched into her very skin. She could get to places and people no one else could reach.

And she knew the despair of the streets. The cold, lonely deaths of opioid addicts.

Gamache had hoped Amelia Choquet shared his profound desire to stop that plague. But now he wondered just how big a misjudgment he'd made. And how big a mistake he was about to make.

While in the gutter, Amelia Choquet had read the poets, the philosophers. She was an autodidact, who'd taught herself Latin and Greek. Literature. Poetry.

Yes, if she succeeded, she'd go far. In the Sûreté. In life.

But he'd also known if she failed, it would be equally spectacular.

And it seemed, so close to the finish line, Amelia Choquet had failed. Spectacularly.

She knew, of course, when she walked in that they'd found the drugs. Having them there was an act of self-destruction.

Gamache closed his eyes. A decision had to be made. No, he realized, that was wrong. The decision he'd already made had to be carried out. No matter how distasteful.

Sitting in the Commander's office, he could smell wet wool and hear the tapping of snow as it fell.

Opening his eyes, he turned to the Commander. "We need a blood test, to confirm and to build the case against Cadet Choquet."

"Look, give me another chance," she said. "It was a mistake."

"A mistake?" said Gamache. "Is that what you call it? A parking ticket is a mistake. This is . . ." He searched for the word. "Ruinous. You've ruined your life, and this time there'll be no more chances. You'll be arrested and you'll be charged. Like anyone else."

"Please," she said.

Gamache looked at the Commander, who made a subtle gesture. It was the Chief Superintendent's call.

"Where did you get the stuff?" Gamache asked.

"I can't tell you that."

"Oh, I think you can, and you will. Tell us that and we might go easier on you."

There was a pause, as everything hung in the balance.

And then Amelia Choquet tipped that balance.

"I got it from you."

Gamache's eyes widened just a little as he glared at her. Warning her. Go no further.

The scent of fresh croissants. Holding Reine-Marie in my arms, in bed, on

a rainy morning. Driving across the Champlain Bridge and seeing the Mon-
tréal skyline.

"What do—" began the Commander.

"You don't even know, do you?" she said to Gamache, cutting off the Commander. "You don't know if this's the shit you let in. You've lost track of it, haven't you?" Now she leaned toward Gamache, her pupils dilated. "What the fuck did you think would happen when you made that choice? Is that why you're so angry? Is that why you want to punish me? For your own mistake?"

"This isn't a punishment, Cadet, it's a consequence. Do I want to find the drugs? Absolutely. But I never thought it would start with you."

"Save it. You knew who I was when you let me in."

"We should consider ourselves lucky, I suppose, that you didn't burn the place down."

"How do you know I haven't?"

Her words froze him for a moment.

"Where did you get it from? Who sold it to you?" he asked, menace in his voice now.

"What a fucking shitshow you've made of being Chief Superintendent."

"Cadet," warned the Commander.

"Why're you even consulting him?" she asked the Commander, acknowledging him again, jabbing her finger at Gamache. "He's on suspension. You're nobody now, *patron.*"

The last word was spit out. And in the silence the clicking began again. This time metronome-slow. Counting the passing moments. While Gamache sat perfectly still.

"If I'm going down, I'm just following you," Amelia said, leaning even further forward. "You're a ruin, old man."

She must be out of her mind, thought the Commander. Stoned. Suicidal. Insane.

"Feel better?" asked Gamache, his voice steady. "Getting the bile out? Spewing over someone else?"

"At least I chose someone my own size," said Amelia.

"Good. And now we can talk reasonably."

While Chief Superintendent Gamache's voice was calm, the Commander felt the force of his personality. So much stronger than the young cadet's. If he wanted to, the Commander knew, Gamache could crush her.

But what he felt vibrating off the Chief Superintendent wasn't what he expected. He expected anger, rage.

There was, certainly, some of that, but there was something else. Something even more powerful.

Concern. Far greater than Gamache's anger was his caring.

Good God, thought the Commander. *He's going to try to talk sense into a junkie.*

But the Commander was wrong.

"We will take a blood test," said Gamache.

"You don't have my permission," said Amelia. "And unless you're willing to tie me down, you won't get anything out of me. And I'll sue your ass."

Gamache nodded. "I see." He turned to the Commander. "I suggest Cadet Choquet wait outside, supervised, while we talk."

Myrna set down her ham sandwich on croissant as the phone rang.

From deep in the armchair in her bookstore, she looked over at it. Hauling herself up with a grunt, she went to the counter.

"*Oui, allô.*"

"I spoke to the oldest son. Anthony Baumgartner. He's arranged for his brother and sister to be at his place today at three o'clock."

"Who is this?" asked Myrna pleasantly, though she knew perfectly well who it was.

"It's Lucien Mercier. The notary."

Out the bay window of her shop, Myrna Landers saw puffs of snow being lifted, then falling onto the massive banks that now circled the village green. They were so high, Myrna could no longer see who was doing the shoveling. Just the bright red shovel and the cloud of snow.

It felt as though she was ringed in by a newly formed mountain range.

"Three o'clock," repeated Myrna, writing it down. She glanced at the clock. It was now one thirty. "Give me the address." She wrote it too. "I'll let Armand know to meet us there."

Myrna replaced the phone and turned to look out the window again, watching the small eruptions all around the village green.

Then she put in a quick call to Armand, giving him the time and place of the meeting with the Baroness's family. After wolfing down the last of her sandwich, she headed back outside.

"My turn," said Myrna, taking the shovel from Benedict, who was both sweating and freezing.

"My God," said Clara, leaning on her shovel and surveying the amount still left to be cleared. "Why do we live here?"

The day sparkled and their noses dripped and their feet froze, and their inner layer of clothing clung to their bodies in perspiration while their outer layer froze brittle. As they dug the village out.

Beside her, Myrna heard Clara muttering. Each word contained in a puff, accompanied by a shovelful of snow.

"Barbados."

"St. Lucia," said Myrna.

"Jamaica," came the response.

"Antigua," both women said, leaning into their job.

When they'd run out of Caribbean islands, they went on to food. Mille-feuilles.

Lobster. Lemon posset.

These things they loved.

Armand hung up just as the Commander returned to his office.

"She's sitting on the bench in the anteroom. My assistant is watching her."

"Does your assistant have a Taser?"

The Commander gave one brief laugh and pulled a chair up to face Gamache.

"So what're we going to do with her?"

"What would you suggest?" asked Gamache. "This is your academy. She's one of your cadets."

The Commander paused for a moment, watching the Chief Super-intendent.

"Is she, Armand? She seems yours."

Gamache smiled. "Do you think it was a mistake, letting her in?"

"A stoned former prostitute junkie who's dealing opioids in the academy? Are you kidding? She's a delight."

Armand gave one, not altogether amused, chuckle.

"And yet not everyone sees it that way," he said before his face grew serious again.

"You know, the truth is," said the Commander, "until this happened, Cadet Choquet was a standout. Unconventional. Annoying as hell. But brilliant. And not given to deceit. I thought."

The Commander looked at the door and imagined the once-promising young woman sitting on the other side.

Once again the fate of reckless youth was being decided by old men behind closed doors. Though neither man was old, they were probably, he thought, older than she would ever be.

Cadet Choquet hadn't been just reckless. Chief Superintendent Gamache was right. Her actions had been ruinous. But ruins could, with great effort, be restored. Or they could collapse entirely, hurting everyone trying to help.

"What're you thinking?" the Commander asked.

For Gamache was thinking something. Considering something.

"What would happen," Gamache asked, "if we cut her loose?"

"Expel her, you mean."

It was certainly one of the few options open to them.

He went through the possibilities. They could give Cadet Choquet a warning and forget this ever happened. Sweep it under an already fairly lumpy academy carpet.

Kids made mistakes and should not be handicapped the rest of their lives for them. Though this seemed considerably more than a "mistake."

Or they could kick her out of the academy.

Or they could have her arrested and tried for possession and trafficking.

Chief Superintendent Gamache was considering the middle option. What would be, with any other cadet, a reasonable, even kind response.

It would be punishment, a consequence, but it would not blight the rest of their life.

Except they were talking about Amelia Choquet. A young woman with a history of prostitution. Of drug abuse. Who had fallen back into old habits.

The Commander reflected. "I've begun researching rehabs. Whichever route we choose, that'll be necessary."

When there was no response, he looked over at the Chief Superintendent, who was staring at him.

The Commander's eyes widened.

"*Non?* But if we don't—"

His mind retreated, back to the fork in the road. And then he took the other route.

His face flattened, all expression sliding from it, as he stared into Cadet Choquet's future. If they took that road.

"You'd do that?" he asked, quietly. "Not even try to get her help?"

"I helped once, and look where it got us. If she wants help, she has to come to it herself. It's more effective. We both know that."

"No we don't. What we know is that she's a junkie who's slipped. She's our responsibility, Armand. We have to help her up."

"She isn't ready. You can see that. It would be wasting a precious rehab place. A place another kid could use. A kid who is ready."

"Are you kidding me?" It was all the Commander could do to get the words out. "Are you trying to convince me, or yourself, that this is some big favor you're doing?"

"Carrying her is no favor."

"Seems to me when you were hurt, you were carried to safety. No one expected you to crawl to the emergency ward."

Gamache sat there, his entire body tingling. With the truth of it. But he needed to remain firm. Resolute.

"She's wounded, Armand. Deep down. As surely as if she'd been shot. She needs our help."

"She needs to know she can do this herself. If she can, there'll be no more slips. That's the help we give her now."

"For God's sake, Armand, if you cut her loose, you kill her. You know that."

"No. If I cut her loose, I allow her to own her own life. She can do it. I know she can."

"You came to that conclusion sipping scotch beside your fireplace, did you?"

The two men stared at each other. What the Commander said wasn't far from the truth. Armand had sat in his living room, Henri's head on his feet, Reine-Marie reading archive files across from him. While outside, snow gently fell. And Chief Superintendent Gamache considered the fate of reckless youth.

Amelia. And thousands of others. Maybe hundreds of thousands of others.

He'd weighed the options. In front of the hearth.

Safe and sound. Warm and loved. He'd considered his options and the atrocity he was about to commit.

Twenty minutes later they stood in the long hallway by the entrance, and exit, to the Sûreté Academy.

Amelia Choquet, no longer in her uniform, walked toward them, a member of staff on either side of her. A large knapsack was slung over her shoulder, bulging not with clothes, Gamache suspected by the sharp angles of the canvas bag, but with the only things Amelia considered worth keeping.

Books.

He watched her progress, and as she passed him, neither said a word.

She'd return to the streets, of course. To the gutter. To the drugs and prostitution necessary to pay for the next hit. And the next.

A few paces from them, Amelia stopped. She reached into her bag, then in one fluid motion she turned and threw something at them. It spun through the air with such speed the Commander, standing next to Gamache, barely had time to duck away.

But Gamache's instincts were different.

He didn't flinch. Instead his right hand shot up, and just before the object struck him in the face, he caught it.

The last he saw of Amelia Choquet was a sneer as she turned her back on him and, lifting her middle finger, she walked into her new life. Her old life.

Gamache stood there contemplating the empty rectangle of light, until the door closed and the place fell dark. Only then did he look down at the book in his hand. It was the small book he had offered her that first day at the academy. A lifetime ago.

His own copy. Marcus Aurelius. *Meditations.*

She'd turned it down, sneering at the offer. But now he looked at the slim volume. Amelia had gone out and bought her own. And hurled it in his face.

"*Excusez-moi*," he said to the Commander, who was staring at him with something close to loathing. "May I use your office? Privately?"

"Of course."

Gamache placed a call, though the door wasn't quite closed and the Commander heard. Because he was listening.

"She's left. Follow her."

The Commander understood then what Gamache had done. What he was doing. What had almost certainly been the plan all along.

Chief Superintendent Gamache was releasing the young woman into the wild. And where would she go? Back to the gutter, certainly. And there, amid the filth, she would search out more dope.

She would lead them to the trafficker. And perhaps the rest of the opioids that the head of the Sûreté du Québec had allowed into the country.

Chief Superintendent Gamache would recover the drugs and save any number of lives. But he would have to step over the body of Amelia Choquet to do it.

As he watched Gamache leave the academy, the Commander didn't know if he admired the head of the Sûreté more. Or less.

He also harbored an unworthy thought. And as much as he tried to dismiss it, the idea refused to leave.

The Commander wondered if the Chief Superintendent had planted the drugs himself. Knowing this would happen.

In his car, before heading to the rendezvous with Myrna and the others, Armand took off his gloves, put on his reading glasses, and held the book between his large hands.

Then he opened it, revisiting the familiar passages. An old friend.

As he flipped through the dog-eared pages, he found lines she'd underlined.

"It is not death that a man should fear, but he should fear never beginning to live."

And he thought of the click, click, clicking he'd heard as Amelia had passed him in the hallway. Her tell.

Save Our Souls.

CHAPTER 13

⁓

"Armand, you need to hear this."

Gamache had barely arrived at the home of Bertha Baumgartner's eldest son when Myrna dragged him into the living room, where they'd all assembled.

He'd taken off his coat, tuque, mitts, and boots and now stood in stocking feet quickly taking in the room. Bookshelves were built along the far wall, with books and framed photos and the mementos people accumulate. There was art on the other walls. None of it avant-garde, but some decent watercolors, a few oil paintings, some numbered prints. Windows looked onto the backyard, with mature trees and lawn covered in deep, bright snow. A fire was in the grate.

The room was done in muted, slightly masculine shades of beiges and blues. It was a room, a home, that whispered comfort and success.

"Armand Gamache," he said, extending his hand to the three Baumgartner siblings. "I'm so sorry for your loss."

There was a slight hesitation as they stared at him. That now-familiar look of surprise as someone they saw in their living rooms on TV appeared unexpectedly in their living room in person. In three dimensions.

Walking and talking.

They shook hands.

Anthony, Caroline, and Hugo.

Tall, fine boned. The healthy complexions of people who ate well and looked after themselves.

Except Hugo.

He seemed to take after his mother. He was short, round, ruddy. A duckling among swans. Though, really, he more resembled a toad.

At fifty-two, Anthony Baumgartner was the oldest, followed by Caroline, and finally Hugo. Although Hugo seemed much older than the others, with features that looked like they'd been worn down by the elements. A sandstone statue left out too long. His hair was iron-gray. Not the distinguished gray-at-the-temples of Anthony or the soft dyed-blond of Caroline.

Anthony held himself with ease and even a certain grace. But it was Caroline who'd moved forward first, her hand extended.

"Welcome, Chief Superintendent," she said, using his rank though he himself had not. Her voice was warm, almost musical. "We didn't realize my mother knew you. She never mentioned it."

"Which was strange, for her," said Hugo. His voice was unexpectedly deep, rich. If a trench in the earth could speak, it might sound like this man.

"We never actually met," said Armand. "None of us knew your mother."

"Really?" said Anthony, looking from one to the other. "Then why are you liquidators?"

"We were hoping you could tell us," said Myrna.

The siblings consulted one another, perplexed.

"To be honest," said Anthony, "we thought we were the liquidators. Came as a surprise when Maître Mercier here called."

"Well, the Baroness must've had her reasons," said Caroline. "She always did. There must be a connection."

"Madame Landers and I live in a village called Three Pines," said Gamache. "I believe your mother worked there."

"That's right," said Hugo. "She said it was a funny little village in a sort of divot in the ground."

He cupped his hand as he spoke.

While the word "divot" didn't make it sound attractive, the actual gesture did. His strong hand cupped was suggestive not of emptiness but of holding something precious. Water in a drought. Wine at a celebration. Or some creature, near extinction, that needed protection.

And it struck Armand how very expressive this rough man was. With a small, common gesture, he'd conjured a world of meaning.

Like Armand, Myrna was watching these people closely. Not with any suspicion, more a professional interest in dynamics. Of groups. Of families. And what happened when strangers came into their midst.

These three seemed comfortable with one another. Though there was a hierarchy, with Anthony clearly at the top.

"Would you like something to drink?" Caroline asked their guests. "Coffee, tea? Something stronger perhaps."

"I think we should get started," said Lucien.

"I'll take a beer," said Hugo, and went into the kitchen.

"A tea would be nice," said Myrna, and Armand agreed.

"I'll take a beer too, if you're offering," said Benedict.

Caroline and Anthony followed Hugo into the kitchen while Armand joined Myrna at the bookcase.

"You said there was something I need to hear. What is it?"

"It's about the Baroness. Why she's called that."

"Yes?"

Myrna gave him such a pained expression he wondered if she wasn't in some sudden acute agony. Which, it turned out, she was, though not the physical kind.

"I can't tell you."

"Why not? You just said I had to hear it."

"You do, but you have to hear it from them." She tilted her head toward the kitchen. "It's kinda amazing. I wonder if it's true."

"Oh come on," said Armand. "Now you're just being annoying."

"Sorry, but actually, they didn't get to the full story before you arrived." She looked toward the kitchen again. "What do you make of them?"

"The Baumgartners?" He glanced over there too. "I have no real opinion yet. They seem nice enough. You?"

"I'm always looking for psychoses," Myrna admitted. "Too many years digging around people's brains. If you search long enough and deep enough, you're sure to find something. Even in the most well balanced of people."

She gave him a meaningful look and he grinned.

"I'm glad it's their turn now. And? Have you unearthed any psychoses in these nice people?"

"None. Which I find quite unsettling."

He laughed. "Not to worry. If anything can expose craziness, it's a will."

"We already have plenty of that," she agreed. "Do you think they're upset that we're the liquidators?"

"I'm not sure. They were certainly surprised. I wonder why their mother didn't tell them they'd been replaced."

"I wonder why she did it," said Myrna, glancing through the open door into the kitchen. "Do you think one of them's a little off?" She lifted her hand to her temple and rotated it. "But she felt she couldn't just drop him, so she replaced them all?"

"Him? Do you have someone in mind? Hugo, maybe?"

"Because he looks the part? Poor fellow, imagine being raised with two gorgeous siblings. It could warp a person. But my money's on Anthony."

Armand watched the three Baumgartners prepare the refreshments. Caroline and Anthony together making the tea and putting out cookies. Hugo alone, farther down the counter, pouring two beers.

On the surface, friendly. And yet they barely said a word to one another.

"Why Anthony?" he asked.

"Because he doesn't look the part. I'm always suspicious of people who seem too well balanced."

"Sometimes a cigar . . ." said Armand, to Myrna's laugh.

He noticed something behind her, on the bookcase, and reached to pick it up.

It was a small photo. The silver frame was tarnished, and the black-and-white snapshot had faded, but he knew who they were and where it was taken.

The three Baumgartner children, two skinny, one plump, arms lazily slung over one another's shoulders, stood in front of the farmhouse. It was summer, and they wore sagging bathing suits and huge, toothy grins.

Behind them, in the garden, he saw tall spires of foxglove and the easily identified monkshood.

"What's that?" He pointed to another clump.

"Huh," said Myrna. "The Baroness must've been quite a gardener. I didn't think that would grow here, but I guess the house protects it.

Or maybe she planted it as an annual. That's deadly nightshade. Also known as belladonna."

Armand replaced the photo of the three kids, growing like weeds amid the poisonous plants.

"Here you go," said Caroline as Anthony carried in a tray with tea things and Hugo followed with the beers.

It did seem his natural place, Gamache was beginning to see. A few steps behind his brother and sister. Separated from them. Just a little. Close enough to see their closeness but far enough away not to be included.

"Can we continue?" asked Lucien, who'd refused all offer of refreshments.

"I think we need to back up a bit, now that Armand is here," said Myrna. "He didn't hear what Caroline said just before he arrived."

"It's not pertinent," said Lucien. "We're here to read the will and that's all."

"You were telling us why your mother liked to be called Baroness," Myrna prompted Caroline.

"Liked?" Anthony threw another log on the fire. "She didn't 'like' to be called Baroness, she insisted."

He settled back into his chair.

Caroline turned to face their guests, tucking her skirt in. Her knees together, her ankles crossed. The doyenne entertaining.

"Our mother called herself Baroness because she was one."

Armand stared at her, then at the others. His mouth didn't exactly drop open, but his eyes certainly widened.

Myrna turned to him. She was beaming. If she could have combusted with pleasure, she would have. What had started as a chore, accepting to be the liquidator of a stranger's will, was quickly becoming not just entertaining but kind of wonderful.

A baroness, her glowing eyes said. A noble cleaning woman. Does it get better than this?

Across from them the Baumgartner siblings had their own reactions. Anthony seemed to share the joke and had raised his brows in a *Parents. What can you do?* expression.

Caroline was composed, but her complexion betrayed her. Little pink patches had appeared on her cheeks.

And Hugo—

"She might be," he said. "We don't know."

"I think we do," said Anthony. "Some things just have to be faced, Hug. No matter how unpleasant."

He pronounced it as "Oog" and was staring at his brother.

"I've never met a real baroness," said Benedict. "This's kinda cool."

"And you still haven't," Myrna pointed out.

"Why would she think she's a baroness?" asked Armand.

"Well, among other things, there's the family name," said Anthony.

"Baumgartner?" asked Benedict.

"No," said Caroline. "That was our father's name. Her maiden name was Bauer. But her grandfather, our great-grandfather, was a Kinderoth."

She looked at them intently, apparently expecting something.

"Kinderoth," Hugo repeated.

"We heard," Myrna said. "Is there something you're trying to say?"

Benedict's eyes were narrowed, and his lips moved as he lifted his fingers. Obviously trying to work out the relationship.

"Kinderoth," he finally said. "Child roth."

"Child roth," Armand repeated, then paused. "Roth child? Roth-schild?"

Hugo nodded.

"That's ludicrous," said Lucien with a snort. Then he looked at the Baumgartner siblings. "You're not saying that Bertha Baumgartner was a Rothschild?"

Anthony leaned back in his chair, apparently distancing himself from the claim.

Caroline looked politely defiant, as though daring them to challenge it. And Hugo looked triumphant.

"Yes."

"The Rothschilds?" asked Myrna. "The banking family? Worth billions?"

"Well, a branch of the family," said Caroline. "The one that came to Canada in the 1920s and decided to invest everything in the stock market."

"They were the lucky ones," said Anthony. "They at least got out."

"And there was no 'everything,'" said Hugo. "They came here because it'd all been stolen from them. Us."

"Enough," said Anthony, lifting his hand. "We've been through this all our lives. It hounded our parents, our grandparents. It drove them near mad with resentment. Let's just stop."

"Anthony's right," said Caroline. "Even if it's true, there's nothing we can do about it."

"Maman said—" Hugo began.

"Maman was an embittered old woman who made things up to make her feel better about cleaning other people's toilets," she said. "She raised us with love and bile and made us promise to continue the fight. But we were children when we made that promise."

"*Kinder*," said Benedict.

Caroline looked at him with some annoyance.

"How do you know that word?" asked Myrna.

"*Kinder?*" said Benedict. "My girlfriend's family is German. Besides, I went to kindergarten. Didn't everyone?"

Kindergarten, thought Gamache, and glanced over at the bookshelf where the tarnished frame sat. The photo of children in a deadly garden.

"We're not German," said Hugo. "Austrian."

"Ahh," said Benedict, then he lowered his voice. "Were they convicts?"

"Of course not," said Caroline.

They stared at him for a moment before Myrna got it.

"Not Australian. Austrian. Like the von Trapp family." When he looked blank, she went on. "*The Sound of Music? 'The hills are alive'?* Help me, Armand."

"Oh, I think you're doing just fine."

From off to his left, he heard the thin strains of a voice singing, "'*Edelweiss, Edelweiss . . .*'" before it petered out.

They looked over, and Hugo dropped his head, apparently studying his hands.

"Maman used to sing it to us," Anthony explained. "We must have watched that movie a hundred times."

Armand had seen the movie too. More times than he could count, with his children. And now his grandchildren. And he'd sung that haunting song to them as they fell asleep.

Edelweiss. Their heavy lids would close. *Edelweiss.*

"Can we continue?" asked Lucien. He handed around copies of Bertha Baumgartner's will to her children, while the liquidators brought out their own copies.

"Please turn to page fifteen," said Lucien. "I'll go over the highlights. She leaves each of her three children five million dollars, as well as buildings in Geneva and Vienna."

"And the title goes to the eldest son," said Lucien, speaking earnestly, as though the title actually existed. He looked at Anthony. "To you."

"Merci," he said.

It could have come out as sarcastic, but instead he just sounded sad. And he wasn't alone. Armand looked at the others. Their sorrow was palpable.

The Baroness might've been delusional. Might've even been bitter. But she loved these three, and they loved her.

Lucien read the rest of the document, and when he'd finished, he looked at them.

"Any questions?"

Benedict raised his hand.

"From the family," said Lucien.

"How does this work?" Caroline asked. "Given that none of this exists?"

"And what about what does exist?" asked Anthony. "She had some small investments, a little in the bank. The home? We didn't sell it while she was alive. Out of respect. She always hoped maybe she'd return."

"I'm glad you mentioned the farmhouse," said Gamache. "We were there yesterday. It's in pretty bad shape and should probably be torn down."

"No," said Hugo. "I'm sure it can be saved."

Armand shook his head. "It's too dangerous. Especially with the weight of this snow. I'm afraid I'm going to have to make a call to have it inspected and possibly condemned."

"That's fine with me," said Caroline. "We can just sell the land.

Maman hadn't lived there for a couple of years. I have no sentimental attachment."

"You grew up there?" asked Myrna.

It was rare that kids, no matter how old they were, held absolutely no attachment to their childhood home. Unless it had been an unhappy place.

"Your father—" she began.

"What about him?" asked Anthony.

"Your mother was widowed, it says in the will."

"Yes, he died thirty years ago."

"Thirty-six," said Hugo.

"Accident on the farm," said Caroline. "He was run over by the combine while haying."

Myrna winced, and while Armand's professional face held, his mind conjured the image.

"Tony found him," said Hugo. "Went out looking when he didn't come in for lunch. He died right away. Probably didn't feel a thing."

"Probably not," said Armand, and hoped his tone didn't betray what he really thought.

"That's when the Baroness went out to work," said Caroline. "Had to support us."

"I got a job bagging groceries at the IGA," said Anthony. "And, Caroline, you went out babysitting."

"Remember when that couple hired you to look after their goats?" asked Hugo with a laugh.

"Oh Jesus, yeah," said Anthony, also laughing, as was Caroline. "You'd put up a notice in the church hall saying you loved kids and would like to look after them."

"Hey, those kids were way better behaved than the human ones," said Caroline. Relaxing back in her seat, her smile wide, her eyes gleaming.

"Except when they kicked," said Hugo. "I remember going with you a few times to help."

He rubbed his shins.

"They just didn't like you."

Armand listened as the brothers and their sister went over clearly familiar ground. Part of the family liturgy. The same stories, told over and over. They looked, for a moment, like the children in the photo.

For his part, Armand kept his eyes on Anthony Baumgartner.

He must have been all of sixteen when he found his father in the field.

That was a sight that could never be unseen. A memory that would take up more than its fair share of Anthony's longhouse. Squeezing other, happy childhood memories into corners.

Armand's own parents had died, in a car accident, when he was a child. And to this day he could remember every moment of when the police arrived at the door.

That day, that moment, had affected every moment of the rest of his life.

And he hadn't found his parents. Had not seen their bodies. He remembered the scent of the peanut-butter cookies that had been baking, and to this day it made him nauseous.

This man remembered the mangled, bloody body of his father.

"I think we should try to save the place," Hugo was saying.

"Why don't you stay behind after everyone leaves," said Anthony. "We can discuss it then."

"As for the rest of her assets," said Lucien, "we'll do an inventory, and you can sign off."

"Do you have any photographs of your mother?" Armand asked.

He followed Anthony to the fireplace, where there was a framed picture on the mantel.

"May I?" When Anthony nodded, he picked it up.

"That was taken last Christmas," said Caroline, who'd joined them.

Armand recognized the hearth he was standing in front of. In the picture it was decorated with garlands of pine and bright red bows, and in the background stood a Christmas tree heavy with baubles and strings of popcorn and candy canes. Brightly wrapped gifts tumbled out from beneath the tree. But the focal point of the photo, the point of the photo, was the elderly woman in the large chair. Children were festooned over it and around her, and her own three stood behind the chair. Everyone was smiling. Some were laughing.

The Baroness wore a paper crown from a Christmas cracker and a beaming smile and looked not unlike Margaret Rutherford.

White hair. Jowls. Bright blue eyes sagging like a bloodhound's. Huge bosom and trunk, made for wiping off flour-caked hands and hugging grandchildren.

Looking at it, Armand could almost smell the vanilla extract.

He found himself smiling, then handed it to Myrna.

"Grand Duchess Gloriana," he suggested, and her smile grew all the broader as she nodded.

"*The Mouse on the Moon.*" Then Myrna's expression became wistful as she studied the photo that had pride of place in her son's living room. "Or *Harvey.*"

"You'll take them, right," said Lucien a few minutes later, when they were about to leave.

It was a statement, not a question. "Them" being Myrna and Benedict. Like bags of salt. Only less useful.

"I have a few more things to go over with Anthony Baumgartner," said the notary.

"*Oui,*" said Armand.

Caroline was leaving with them, but Hugo had stayed behind with Anthony, to talk about the future of the farmhouse.

A little while later, Myrna, Benedict, and Armand sat with Reine-Marie by the fire in the bistro. Clara, Ruth, and Gabri joined them, and drinks were ordered.

The power was back on, and the phones repaired.

"They can't come until tomorrow afternoon," Benedict reported, returning from the phone on the bistro bar.

"Who?" asked Clara.

"The garage," said Benedict. "My pickup's still at Madame Baumgartner's farmhouse. It needs towing. And new tires."

He shot a look at Armand, who nodded approval.

"I've called the township and strongly suggested they send inspectors to her home," said Armand. "I think it needs to be condemned."

"It might be savable," said Benedict. "If the Baumgartners would like me to try."

"Don't even think about it," said Armand. "Caroline was right. They should just tear it down and sell the land."

109

The sun was setting, the sky a soft blue before fading to black.

"You'll stay with us another night," Reine-Marie said to Benedict.

"But I don't have any clothes."

"We'll give you some," said Gabri, assessing the young man. "I think you're about Ruth's size. Though she is a bit more masculine."

Over drinks they told the others about the meeting with the Baroness's family and the fact she seemed to think she was an actual baroness. Descended from the Rothschilds.

"Quite a descent," said Ruth.

"But even if it is true," said Reine-Marie, "that wouldn't necessarily mean there was a title and money."

"Or maybe it does," said Clara. "How do you find out?"

"Lucien's checking into it," said Myrna.

"Sounds strange to hear her called 'Madame Baumgartner,'" said Clara. "I know the Baroness, but this Bertha Baumgartner's a stranger."

"I liked what you said." Myrna turned to Armand. "She did look like Margaret Rutherford."

Ruth snorted scotch back into her glass and laughed. "Yes, that's it. That's who she reminded me of."

"But still," Armand said to Myrna, "I think you were closer to the heart of the matter. Not her looks but her personality."

"How so?" asked Gabri.

"*Harvey*," said Myrna. "The whole meeting with the family reminded me of that movie."

Clara smiled. "Elwood P. Dowd."

"That's just stupid," said Ruth. "The Baroness looked nothing like Jimmy Stewart."

On seeing Benedict's blank expression, Reine-Marie explained. "*Harvey* is an old movie. It's about a man—"

"Elwood P. Dowd," said Myrna.

"—whose best friend is a six-foot rabbit," continued Reine-Marie.

"Harvey," said Myrna.

"They go everywhere together," continued Reine-Marie. "But no one else can see him."

"Obviously," said Ruth. "He's a six-foot white rabbit."

"They try to convince Elwood that Harvey doesn't exist," said Clara.

"They think he's crazy," said Ruth, stroking Rosa. "Try to have him committed."

"It's a reminder that if someone's happy, maybe that's the only reality that matters," said Reine-Marie. "What harm is there in believing in a giant white rabbit?"

"Or a title," said Clara, raising her glass. "The Baroness."

"The Baroness," they said.

"But it's not just the title, is it," said Benedict. "It's the money too. Millions. I wonder if there's harm in believing in a fortune that doesn't exist."

"'You have a lot to learn,' young man," said Ruth, quoting the movie. "'And I hope you never learn it.'"

CHAPTER 14

———

"So what're you going to do?" asked Annie as their car crept carefully down the hill into Three Pines. "Are you going to tell him?"

"Which part?" asked Jean-Guy. "The investigation or—"

He could feel the rear of the vehicle begin to slide sideways on the snow and ice, and he stopped talking to concentrate. His eyes sharp on the road, his focus complete. His hands gentle on the steering wheel.

He glanced swiftly into the rearview mirror and saw Honoré buckled into his car seat, looking out the window.

"I think it's up to us to decide first, don't you?" he finally said as the car made it safely down the hill, and they drove around the village green.

Walls of snow mounted on either side so that nothing beyond was visible except the glow of hidden homes.

Jean-Guy had never seen anything like it. It was both beautiful and alarming. Comforting and ominous. As though nature were trying to decide whether to protect or consume the little village.

He pulled the car up to the opening chiseled into the banks, a snow tunnel leading to the Gamache home. But instead of getting out, Annie sat there, her face lit by the headlights bouncing back from the snow.

"It'll be all right," she said, and, leaning over, she kissed him on the cheek.

It was an act of such simplicity it would have been easy for Jean-Guy to overlook the glory of it.

To be kissed. For no reason.

For a man of reason, it was staggering.

"How did the meeting go yesterday?" asked Gamache as he and Jean-Guy settled into the study.

They'd had their dinner. Shepherd's pie and chocolate cake. Honoré was asleep in his room.

The Gamaches' unexpected guest, the young man with the weird hair, Benedict, had gone off to the bistro for a few drinks. He'd spent much of the time, after being introduced to Annie and Jean-Guy, playing with Honoré. Once Honoré was put to bed for the night and they'd had dinner, Benedict asked if they'd mind if he went out for a beer.

"Nice kid," said Jean-Guy.

"Yes," said Armand.

"What do you know about him?" Jean-Guy's voice was casual, but Armand knew him too well to be fooled.

"You mean, is he likely to kill us in our sleep?"

"Just wondering," said Jean-Guy.

It wasn't as though this Benedict had been found hitchhiking, wearing a ski mask and carrying a machete. But really, what did Armand know about him?

"I did a quick check," said his father-in-law. "He is who he says he is. A builder. Lives in Montréal, apparently with a girlfriend."

"Apparently?"

"Well, that is a little odd," admitted Armand as they took their seats. "When the power and phones were out, Benedict didn't seem at all stressed about not being able to contact his girlfriend to tell her where he was and that he was safe. Or in making sure she was okay. If it was me, cut off from Reine-Marie in a storm, I'd move heaven and earth to make sure she was safe."

Jean-Guy nodded. The same for him and Annie. It wasn't even a choice, it was instinctive.

"Maybe they're not in love," he said. "You think it's something else?"

"I think she might be a convenient fabrication," said Armand with a smile. "I think he's a handsome kid who needs a way to get out of uncomfortable situations."

"So he created a fictional girlfriend?" He looked at his father-in-law closely. "Don't tell me you once had one?"

Armand laughed. "When I was young, I had quite a few. Getting a real one was the problem."

"I can see why you'd have trouble, but why would this kid make up a girlfriend? I doubt he has any problem getting girls."

"And that might be why. This way he can fend off unwanted advances."

"The fictional lover. Clever."

He wished he'd thought of that, back in the day. Invitations to social events he didn't want to attend, declined. Blamed on the girlfriend.

Damn. If it was true, that Benedict was smarter than he looked. Though that would not be difficult.

"Well, if she doesn't exist, how do you explain that haircut?" Jean-Guy asked. "She did it, didn't she?"

"It is hard to explain. You didn't see the sweater he was wearing yesterday. She'd made it out of steel wool."

"Then she must exist. What a young man will do for sex. I remember—" Just in time he realized who he was speaking to. And stopped.

"Do you want me to check him out, *patron*?"

"No, don't bother. It's none of our business."

"Of course, the other question is why he was chosen to be a liquidator of the woman's will," said Jean-Guy. "Why any of you were. Do you think she really was a baroness?"

"No," said Armand. "I don't. I think her daughter was right. She made it up to comfort herself. We all have fantasies, especially when we're children. But most grow out of it. I think Madame Baumgartner never did."

"And she passed it along to her own children."

"I'm not so sure about that. I think the daughter might've let it go, and the eldest son, Anthony, seemed amused by it, but the youngest son? Hugo? I don't know."

"Maybe that's why she chose you and Myrna. In a moment of sanity, she got that she'd really messed them up with her fantasies. Can you imagine the fighting if her kids were in charge of the will?"

"But that doesn't explain why us specifically," said Armand. "And it sure doesn't explain Benedict."

"No." Jean-Guy thought for a moment. "Honoré likes him."

It seemed a non sequitur, but Armand knew it wasn't. He'd noticed that too. It would be folly to trust the instincts of a baby. But it would also be a mistake to completely dismiss them.

Armand shifted in his chair and then asked the question. "How did the meeting go yesterday?"

"The one with the investigators?"

There was a pause, and Jean-Guy immediately understood his mistake. In asking that question, he'd let drop that there'd been another meeting.

Beauvoir waited for his father-in-law to ask.

Had there been another meeting?

But Gamache did not ask. Instead he crossed his legs and waited.

"It went okay."

"Now, don't forget who you're speaking to."

It was said calmly, conversationally. But the warning was clear.

Do not lie.

Through the closed door, they could hear voices in the next room. Annie and Reine-Marie.

There were few things more soothing, Jean-Guy thought, than hearing people you love talking softly in another room.

Instead of a white-noise machine, or recordings of rain or the ocean, if he ever needed help falling asleep, he wanted the sound of these two women. He'd drift off, the unintelligible murmurs on a loop. Reminding him he was no longer alone.

And the truth was, he hadn't slept well the night before. He had a decision to make and was worried.

Beauvoir cast his mind back to his meeting with the Sûreté investigators the day before. Wanting to be accurate. "They were friendly," he said, his voice slow, careful. "But they seemed to be offering me an out. A lifeboat."

"And you didn't realize the ship was sinking?"

Beauvoir nodded. "I thought it was over. I really did. I expected to walk into the meeting and be told it was all cleared up. You'd be reinstated."

"Do you really expect that?"

"Don't you?"

Gamache considered. Maybe, at first, he'd thought that was a possibility.

Then, as more and more questions were asked, as he'd explained what happened and why, over and over again, he could see their minds working. And he could hear it, from their point of view.

This whole thing had given him an interesting perspective on being a suspect. Trying to explain something that, in the cold light of day, seemed inexplicable.

Though his thinking had been clear at the time.

"I think, at this stage, anything is possible," he said to Jean-Guy.

Through the door the voices continued. They could hear soft laughter as one or the other said something amusing.

There was silence in the small room. A silence like Jean-Guy had rarely experienced, though it reminded him a little of their time in the remote monastery. Saint-Gilbert-Entre-les-Loups. Where the quiet had been so profound he'd found it disquieting.

He wanted to break this silence but knew instinctively that it was not his to break.

And so he waited.

Gamache sat in the familiar chair, and yet everything, for a moment, felt unfamiliar. And he realized he had, in fact, harbored a hope that he'd be exonerated.

That Jean-Guy would call yesterday after his meeting with the investigators to tell him it was over. And then he'd get a call from the Premier Ministre, telling him he'd been cleared and would be reinstated.

The call hadn't come. But then the phones had been down, allowing this phantom hope to remain alive.

Gamache smiled to himself and understood Madame Baumgartner a little better. We all had our delusions.

He could see now how wrong he'd been.

Someone had to be blamed. If the drugs hit the streets, as they surely would any day now, they'd throw the book at him. And why not? The blame was, after all, his. Alone.

That much was a comfort. When the ship did sink, he'd take no one else down with him. It would be a result of his own decisions. And friendly fire.

He saw his mother kneeling beside him, adjusting his mitts and cap. Tying his huge scarf at his neck and patting it as he headed out into the bitter-cold Montréal morning, to school. She looked at him and said, "Remember, Armand. If you're ever in trouble, you find a police officer."

She'd held his eyes, as serious as he'd ever seen her, and didn't smile again until he'd solemnly agreed.

Cross my heart and hope to die.

And now, fifty years later, he sat in his own home and smelled a slight scent of peanut-butter cookies.

Then he heard, through the door, the soft laughter of his wife and daughter. He thought of his grandson, asleep. He thought of his son, Daniel, and daughter-in-law and two granddaughters in Paris.

He looked into the eyes of his son-in-law. His second-in-command. His friend.

Safe. And he had no regrets.

Then Armand glanced at his desk and the book sitting there. The one that had, literally, been thrown at him earlier in the day.

It is not death that a man should fear, but he should fear never beginning to live.

"Your old room," said the landlady.

Her pudgy hand with its nicotine-yellowed fingers was splayed on the door as it swung open, releasing a stale odor.

Despite the bitter-cold night, the place was stifling, the old iron radiators unregulated. Pumping out heat that only hurried the decay. It smelled like something decomposing.

In the time since Amelia had lived in the rooming house in East End Montréal, very little had changed.

There was still the reek of urine. Still the moans, groans, of men. As their lives slipped away. Through their fingers and down the drain.

The landlady had grown fatter, softer. A single tooth hung by a thread of gum, waving as she chortled. Her breath like a slaughterhouse.

The door closed, and Amelia could hear her shuffling back down the hallway.

Amelia breathed through her mouth, and clicked the stud against her teeth, and tossed the book-laden knapsack onto the single bed.

Regretting throwing that book at Gamache. Not the act of violence. That had felt good. But she regretted not having Marcus Aurelius to keep her company.

When she opened the door to leave, Amelia almost tripped over the mop and pail. The landlady must've left it there. Her job, in exchange for a room, was to clean. A place that had not, it appeared, been cleaned since she'd last lived there.

"Fuck it," she said, kicking the bucket over and watching the suds rush down the hallway.

That would wait. She had far more pressing things to do than hang around this shithole.

"Walk with me," said Gamache, and to Jean-Guy's surprise, and disappointment, he saw that Armand did not mean walk into the kitchen for more chocolate cake.

Instead Armand went to the front door and took his parka off the hook.

"Going somewhere?" asked Reine-Marie, turning in her seat to watch them.

"Just a stroll."

"To the bistro?" asked Annie, getting up to join them.

"No. Around the village green."

She plunked back down onto the sofa. "Bye."

Henri and Gracie raced to the front door, expecting yet another walk, but Armand explained it was too cold for them.

"But not for us?" asked Jean-Guy. Yet followed him anyway.

Once outside, they walked down the snow tunnel to the road. There was no need of a flashlight. It was a clear night, and quiet. Just the squeal and crunch and munch of their heavy winter boots on the snow.

The Chief often said that everything could be solved by walking. For himself, Beauvoir was pretty sure everything could be solved in the kitchen with a piece of cake.

"Ready yet?"

"Huh?"

"You do know we're going to go round and around until you tell me the other thing on your mind."

"You—"

"Ahhh," warned Armand.

"Ahhh nothing," said Beauvoir. "I can't feel my feet, my fingers are numb. My nose is frozen shut, and my eyes are watering from the pain in my sinuses."

"Then you're probably ready to talk."

"This is torture," said Jean-Guy.

"I'm not very good at it, then," said Armand, his voice friendly. "Since I'm out here too."

Squeak. Squeak. Squeak.

Gamache's pace was measured. His mittened hands clasped each other behind his back as he walked. As though it weren't minus a thousand. As though the cold weren't scraping his face as it was Jean-Guy's.

"There's something else, isn't there? There was another meeting."

"Just with our bank. We're thinking of buying a home."

Squeak. Squeak. Squeak.

"Well, that's exciting."

Squeak.

"I didn't want to tell you until all the finances were in place," said Jean-Guy. Willing himself to stop talking. To stop lying.

"I see."

Armand had stopped and tilted his head back. "Look at that, Jean-Guy."

And he did.

What he saw were northern lights. The aurora borealis. Otherworldly green light, flowing across the night sky.

Then Jean-Guy lowered his gaze and saw that Armand was looking at him. The older man's face clear in the remarkable dancing light.

In those gentle eyes, he saw himself reflected.

And he knew that what his father-in-law saw, when he looked at him, was a man in a lifeboat. Getting further and further away.

120

CHAPTER 15

—

"Can someone go and wake up Benedict?" asked Jean-Guy as he pushed the bacon around the cast-iron skillet with a fork.

The kitchen smelled of maple-smoked bacon and fresh-perked coffee. The eggs were ready to go on.

It was eight fifteen in the morning, and the sun was up. But Benedict was not.

"I'll go," said Armand.

He'd just emerged from his study, having made a private call. He looked slightly distracted, his attention elsewhere, as he walked up the stairs.

They heard a knocking on the bedroom door and Armand calling, "Benedict. Breakfast's ready."

Then more knocking. "Up and at 'em."

Reine-Marie smiled. How often had she heard Armand saying the same thing? *Up and at 'em.* Outside their son Daniel's door?

Though the final few months Daniel had been at home had been less than amusing, given the reason he was passed out at ten in the morning. And she remembered the rage their son had felt when his father entered his room to wake him up.

It had verged on violence.

But still Reine-Marie smiled. It had started out as normal, and natural, for a young fellow to sleep in. And had been that way for a long while. Before it all changed.

"Can you come here, please?" Armand called down.

They looked at one another, then Annie gathered Honoré in her arms and they all walked upstairs.

"He's not here," said Armand, stepping aside so they could look through the open door.

They peered in. Not only was he not there but the bed hadn't been slept in. Armand stepped into the room and looked around.

"His things?" asked Jean-Guy.

"Still here."

Sure enough, the room was exactly as Benedict had left it the night before.

"I'll make some calls," said Reine-Marie, heading down the stairs and into the living room, picking up the phone while Armand and Jean-Guy put on their coats, tuques, mitts, and boots.

Armand had already been outside once that morning, walking around the village green with Henri and Gracie. But the sun had been barely up, and it was possible Armand had missed something. Someone. In a snowbank.

The bitter-cold snap had broken, and now it was merely cold. Once outside, Gamache glanced at the thermometer on the verandah. Minus six Celsius.

Cold enough.

The men broke into a trot, Armand pointing clockwise while he went counterclockwise around the village green.

He forced himself to slow to a rapid walk. He didn't want to miss anything.

His eyes were sharp, scanning. His mind on the search. Trying to divorce action from emotion. Trying not to imagine Benedict curled up by the side of the road.

If that was the case, then there was no hurry, and yet they hurried. In case.

Jean-Guy came around the bend. "Nothing, *patron*."

They went around again, slower this time. The snowbanks were steep, but Jean-Guy managed to scramble, with Armand's help, to the top and walk, like a man on a tightrope, across the jagged ridge. Peering on either side.

Clara came out of her cottage, soon joined by Myrna from her bookshop. Even Ruth appeared.

"Reine-Marie called," said the old poet. "Anything?"

"Nothing."

Reine-Marie joined them. "I just spoke to Olivier. Benedict was in the bistro last night. He had a few beers but wasn't drunk."

She knew as well as Armand that sometimes people got disoriented in the cold and dark. Often helped along by drink and drugs.

"Nothing here," said Jean-Guy, sliding off the snowbank.

"We need to split up," said Armand. "Check the roads in and out of town."

"I'll take the Old Stage Road," said Clara, not waiting for a response but heading in that direction.

They divvied up the paths while Ruth went into the bistro to talk to Olivier.

A few minutes later, they heard a sharp whistle. Ruth was calling them back to the bistro.

Their skin tingled and ached as they stepped into the warmth.

"He was here last night," Olivier confirmed. "I didn't see him leave—"

"But I did," said Gabri, wiping his hands on his apron. "He left with Billy Williams. They'd been talking, and the two went out together."

"Where did they go?"

"I have no idea, but I did see Billy's truck drive away. I don't know if the kid was with him."

Gabri picked up the phone on the bistro bar and called. They saw him nod, listen, then hang up.

"Billy says he gave Benedict a lift to Madame Baumgartner's farmhouse."

Myrna stopped rubbing her hands by the fire and turned to him. "Why would he do that?"

"Benedict asked to go," said Gabri. "Something about the kid's truck. It's on Billy's way home, so he drove him over."

"And just left him there?" asked Clara.

"I guess so," said Gabri. Though it didn't sound like Billy Williams. He maintained the roads and did odd jobs around the area, and he was well aware that the cold kills. "That's all Billy knows."

"Benedict must've driven back to Montréal," said Olivier.

"Maybe," said Armand.

"What is it?" asked Clara as Myrna went into her shop to get the papers from the notary, with Benedict's phone number.

"He promised he wouldn't drive his truck," said Armand. "That's why we left it behind. It doesn't have winter tires."

"Don't tell me someone lied to you?" Ruth thrust out her lower lip and made a sad face.

"Did he cross his heart?"

And hope to die?

But she stopped short of saying that, to Armand's surprise. Seemed Ruth had a filter after all.

"Wouldn't he have told us if he'd returned to Montréal?" asked Reine-Marie.

"He's probably still asleep in his apartment," said Clara. "You'll get a call when he wakes up."

"Well, I'm not waiting," said Myrna, waving the papers she'd retrieved and going to the phone. "I'm calling his cell."

She placed the call. They watched. And waited. And waited.

She spoke into the receiver, then hung up.

"It clicked over to voice mail. I told him to call here."

"There's just the one number for him?" asked Jean-Guy, looking over Myrna's shoulder at the papers. "No home phone?"

"Kids today don't have home phones, numbnuts," Ruth explained to Jean-Guy. "You're old, so you wouldn't know that."

"We have to go to the farmhouse," said Armand, heading to the door. "And make sure."

"I'll come with you," said Myrna. "We're a team. Liquidators stick together." She returned Armand's stare. "What? It's a thing."

"It's a nothing," said Ruth.

"I know," said Myrna, responding more to Armand's eyes than Ruth's words.

He nodded. They both knew what they might find. And of the group, he and Myrna were closest to Benedict. The young man invited a kind of intimacy, a near-immediate affection. And Myrna was right. They did feel like an odd little team.

"I'm coming too," said Beauvoir, walking to the car with them.

"So am I," said Reine-Marie.

"Can you stay at home?" Armand asked her. "In case he calls there?"

"Let me know," she said as they got into the car.

"Oh Christ," said Myrna, straining forward in her seat belt as they turned the corner and saw the farmhouse.

"I'll call 911," said Jean-Guy.

Armand grabbed the shovel from the trunk of his car.

Benedict's truck was parked where they'd left it. Armand walked quickly over and looked into the cab.

Empty. The keys were in the ignition, and it had been turned on but must've run out of gas. He pulled the keys out and pocketed them.

"Rescue team's on its way," said Beauvoir, catching up.

"No one here," called Myrna. She was standing next to the other vehicle in the yard. Not one Armand recognized. "This wasn't here when we left yesterday, was it?"

"*Non,*" said Armand.

Beauvoir had pulled a shovel out of the snowbank by the front steps and now held it like a weapon.

Myrna joined them, and all three stared.

Madame Baumgartner's home had collapsed.

The roof and second floor had caved in, part of it crushing the main floor, part of it hanging loose, barely holding together.

"Call back. Tell them to bring the dogs," said Gamache as he advanced, slowly.

Beauvoir made the call.

"Is he inside?" Myrna whispered.

"I think so." Gamache glanced behind him, at the other car. "And he's not alone."

He took off his tuque and cocked his head toward the farmhouse.

"Did you hear that?"

Jean-Guy and Myrna took off their hats and listened.

Nothing.

Gamache strode over to his car and hit the horn. Two quick blasts, then stopped. And listened.

125

But there was only grim silence.

Nothing. Nothing.

Something.

A knock. A crack?

They looked at one another.

"It could be a beam breaking, *patron*."

"Or it could be Benedict," said Myrna. "Or someone else, trying to signal. What do we do? We can't just stand here."

Help was on the way, but it could be twenty or thirty minutes before it arrived. The difference, in this cold, between life and death. If someone had survived this long through the bitter night, they must be close to the end.

"We have to make sure that someone's alive in there before we decide what to do," said Armand. He cupped his hands around his mouth and shouted, "Benedict!"

"Allô!" called Beauvoir.

They fell silent. Listening.

There was a knock. Definite this time. Then another. A rat-a-tat. No mistaking it. Someone was alive. And afraid.

It reminded Gamache, just for a moment, of someone else. Amelia and her tongue stud. Rat-a-tat. Her tell.

Save Our Souls.

"He has to stop," said Myrna, her eyes wide, her breathing rapid. "He'll bring the whole place down." She shouted, "Stop it."

"We hear you," Gamache called. "We're coming. Stop knocking."

He turned to them and saw the fear in their faces.

"We have to go in, don't we?" said Beauvoir.

Armand nodded. Their fear, and one he shared, was that the place they were about to enter would collapse completely. But while he and Myrna were afraid, Jean-Guy was terrified.

He had claustrophobia. This was, quite literally, his nightmare.

Beauvoir gave a curt nod, gripped the shovel even tighter, and took a step toward the ruin.

"I think you should—" Gamache began, but stopped when he heard a sound.

They turned to look back down the drive. A pickup truck had arrived. Jean-Guy lowered his shovel and almost wept.

Help. Rescuers. Who actually knew what they were doing. Who could go in instead of them.

The truck stopped, and a single man got out. And Beauvoir could have wept again.

It wasn't help. It was Billy Williams.

"Heard the boy was missing. Came to see if I could help." He stood beside his vehicle and stared at the house. Then said something else that sounded to Gamache like "Whale oil beef hooked."

Gamache turned to Myrna. "What did he say?"

For reasons that baffled Gamache, he seemed the only person on earth who could not understand a word Billy Williams said. Not a word. Not even close.

"Not important," she said.

"Boy alive in there?"

"We think so," said Myrna. "Someone is. Either Benedict or some-one else. Was that here when you dropped him off last night?" She pointed to the car, parked off to the side.

"Not so's I noticed." He turned to the house again. "But it were dark. Right. I should go in and get him. My fault he's here."

Gamache, trying to follow this exchange, looked at Myrna. "Ask if he has any training. In rescuing people out of buildings. Does he know what he's doing?"

Now Billy turned to Gamache. "You think I don't understand you? I understand perfectly."

Billy's face was so weathered and worn that it was impossible to say if he was thirty-five or seventy-five. His body was cord-thin, and even through the heavy winter clothing there was a sense of taut muscle and sinew.

But his eyes were soft as he looked at Armand, with an expression of tenderness. Billy smiled.

"One day, old son, you'll understand me."

But Gamache did understand.

What he understood, and had from the first moment he'd met the man, was that Billy Williams had more than the average measure of the divine.

Billy's face grew grim as he studied the heap of house, and then he turned back to Armand.

"When this is over," he said, picking up a huge tire iron from his truck, "you owe me a lemon meringue pie."

Myrna didn't bother to translate that.

Billy took a step forward, and Gamache reached out to stop him, but Billy shook him off.

"I dropped the kid here last night. Boosted his truck to get it going. Then I left. I should never have left him. So I've come back. To get him. To bring him home."

Gamache didn't need Myrna this time to translate. It didn't matter what Billy said—all that mattered now were actions.

"You can't go in alone. You need help. I'll come with you." Armand turned to Jean-Guy and Myrna. "Wait for the emergency team. They should be here soon. Let them know what's happening."

"If you're going, so am I," said Myrna.

"No you're not."

"There're two people trapped in there," she said. "You need more help." When Armand still hesitated, she said, "This isn't your decision, Armand. It's mine. Besides, I'm stronger than I look."

His brows rose. She looked pretty strong.

Gamache nodded. She was right. They would need her. And it wasn't his decision.

"*Patron?*" said Jean-Guy. He looked in torment.

"You get the heights, *mon vieux*," said Armand quietly. "And I get the holes. Remember? That's the deal."

"Are you coming?" called Billy, already at the front steps. "Hurry up."

Beauvoir stepped back.

"He says be careful," said Jean-Guy, but Armand had already squeezed into the semicollapsed doorway behind Billy and Myrna.

It was darker in there, though shafts of sunlight from openings above them were hitting the floor. Snow trickled down in drifts as it slid off the roof and through the jagged holes.

It was quiet too. Except for their breathing and the sound of their footfalls as they made their way forward, squeezing along narrow, debris-clogged passages.

They moved as quickly and quietly as possible.

And then came to a halt.

A bathroom above had fallen into what had been the kitchen. The debris, including a claw-foot tub, blocked their way forward.

Gamache tapped his shovel, softly, on the tub and waited.

There was silence, and just as Armand's heart was sinking, there was a knock. Then another.

Billy pointed in the direction of the sound.

Exactly where the debris blocked their path.

Billy muttered something that Gamache completely understood. Some oaths needed no translation.

Then Gamache watched in surprise as Billy dropped to his knees. Catching Myrna's eyes, Armand saw she was thinking the same thing.

Was the man praying? Armand was all for that, but now might not be the time. Besides, he suspected that God knew exactly how they felt and how they wanted this to go.

But he also knew praying was more to steady the person than inform the deity.

Then he noticed that Billy had shoved his tire iron under the tub and was trying to get leverage. He put down his shovel and went to help. The two men leaned. Armand straining, pushing down with all his might.

The cast-iron tub moved, but only slightly.

"Wait, hold it," said Armand, stepping back and catching his breath. Then he nodded to Billy, and the two of them went at it again.

But the tub, crushed under tons of debris, barely budged.

"Can you help over here?" asked Myrna.

"Just. A. Moment," said Armand, through gritted teeth. Pushing. Pushing. Before staggering back. Defeated. Staring at the solid barrier between them and whoever was alive behind it.

There was a creaking, groaning sound. The wall of rubble was moving. Shifting.

Gamache took a half step back, sweeping Billy back with him.

He turned to warn Myrna. But stopped. His face opening in astonishment. It looked as though Myrna was single-handedly lifting the debris. Then he looked more closely.

Where he'd grabbed a shovel and Billy a tire iron, Myrna had quietly picked up the jack from Armand's car and now had it wedged under a beam. And was leaning on the arm.

The beam was lifting, inch by precarious inch.

"I need help," she called.

The two men joined her and leaned into the arm of the jack. One. Two pumps. More snow drifted down, and they paused. Three.

There was a cracking as rafters and crossbeams shifted.

Gamache, his breathing shallow, his eyes sharp, his hearing keen, waited. For it to either collapse or stabilize.

Then he heard, through the shifting debris, more tapping. Increasingly frantic.

"Stop," he called. One sharp word. And the tapping stopped.

Myrna, with their help, had jacked up the beam as high as they dared. The opening was about eighteen inches.

Gamache stared at it, then at Myrna.

"You're not leaving me behind," she said, reading his thoughts.

"You won't make it through."

"And you will?"

Armand was taking off his heavy parka. "I will."

"Then so will I. We go together." She took off her coat and hugged it to her.

"Ego?" asked Armand.

"Practicality," she said. "You need me."

"If I have a choice, I'd take her over you any day," said Billy, smiling at Myrna. "Mighty fine woman."

"What did he say?" asked Armand.

She told him.

"You must've misheard," said Armand. But he was smiling.

"Oh for fook's sake," said Billy. "Let's try again. Another coupla inches should do it."

He grabbed the lever and pushed. Armand and Myrna joined him.

More groaning. Some from the house. Most from them.

But it shifted. Just enough. They figured. They hoped.

"I'll go first," said Armand.

He glanced behind him, down the narrow, rubble-strewn passage they'd just come through. They were, he knew, in what had been the kitchen. Heading, it seemed, toward the dining room. Via the second-floor bathroom.

He turned again toward the opening. It looked like a mouth, ready to clamp shut. Every survival instinct cried out for him not to do it.

Getting onto his back, faceup, he pushed himself into the opening. His eyes within centimeters of shards of wood and rusted nails, like teeth. Turning his head, closing his eyes, exhaling to make himself as flat as possible. He inched forward.

The scent of fresh-cut grass. Walking along the Seine, holding the little hands of Flora and Zora. Reine-Marie in his arms on a lazy Sunday morning.

His face was through. Then his neck. He twisted his shoulders. His chest made it through.

And then his progress stopped. His shirt was snagged on the nails.

He was too far in for Myrna or Billy to be able to help.

The place shifted again, and he felt it drop. The nails now touched his chest every time he took a shallow breath.

"Armand?" called Myrna.

"Just a moment," he said.

Closing his eyes again, he steadied his breathing. Steadied his mind.

Laundry on the line. The scent of Honoré. Sitting in the garden with an iced tea. Reine-Marie. Reine-Marie. Reine-Marie.

He pushed again and felt the nails ripping his shirt.

Tiny pieces of rubble fell onto his face, peppering his lids and lips. As he breathed, they went into his nose, and he could feel himself on the verge of a cough. Smothering it, fighting it, he pushed harder, more frantically.

The ripping stopped, and he broke free.

Scrambling to his knees, Armand bent double, hacking and coughing.

"Armand?" called Myrna, more insistent.

"I'm okay," he said, his voice raspy. "Don't come yet."

He looked around, and, finding a piece of concrete, he reached into the opening and used it to flatten the nails.

"It should be okay now."

With some effort, Myrna also made it through, then Billy, who pushed their parkas in ahead of himself.

"What's that?" asked Myrna. Her head was lifted, nose in the air.

Armand had just caught it too. A whiff of something acrid. It was familiar. Comforting, even. Except—

Wood, charred. Charring.

He and Myrna locked eyes, then over to Billy, who looked genuinely alarmed for the first time.

Gamache felt the hairs go up on his neck.

The place was on fire.

"We need to move."

"Come on, come on," said Jean-Guy, staring at the farmhouse.

His focus was so complete he barely breathed. Didn't blink. Didn't hear the vehicles arrive.

Nothing existed except the house.

The time for caution was past.

"Hello," Myrna shouted. "Where are you?"

"Here, I'm here" came the reply. The voice hoarse. Unfamiliar.

They looked in the direction of the shout. There was another barrier of debris between them and the voice.

Scrabbling with their hands, they cleared chunks of concrete and wood until they'd made a hole. Armand lay on his stomach and peered through.

And saw the long, thin tail of a tuque.

And then a familiar face.

"It's Benedict," he called to the others.

"Oh thank God," said Myrna, and hugged Billy.

Benedict had his back against a doorway. His eyes were wide, barely daring to believe that what he'd prayed for, cried out for, had actually happened.

The young man brought his hand up to his face, not able to hold back tears.

"You came. You came."

Billy enlarged the opening, and when Armand crawled through, Benedict gripped him in a tight embrace, sobbing.

Armand held him for a moment, then stepped back so he could see Benedict's face. His body. He seemed unhurt.

"There's someone else here," said Gamache. "Where is he?"

"There is?" asked Benedict. "I don't think so. I can't believe you came—"

"There's another car in the drive," said Myrna, who'd joined them, as had Billy.

"Yes, I saw that, but when I came in, I called and no one answered."

Armand noticed a small circle of smoldering wood on the floor. Benedict had survived the bitter-cold night by burning whatever wood he could lay his hands on.

That had been the smell. The house wasn't on fire after all.

He began to point it out to Myrna, just as Billy touched Armand's arm. For quiet. Billy's face was tilted up, his head cocked to one side. Listening.

"Is it the rescuers?" Myrna asked.

"Rescuers?" asked Benedict. "Aren't you the—"

"Shh," hissed Billy, and they hushed.

Billy stared at the ceiling. Then Armand saw his eyes widen, at the same moment he heard a great rending. Like a scream. The house was shrieking.

"No," Jean-Guy shouted.

He started forward, but hands held him. He twisted and bucked, struggling to break free.

Members of the local Sûreté rescue team dragged him back, as the farmhouse disappeared into a cloud of snow.

"Holy hell," whispered one of the agents.

As the structure fell, Benedict pulled Armand toward him.

"Get into the doorway," the young man shouted.

Billy grabbed Myrna and just managed to leap in there before there was an almighty splitting sound.

They sank to their knees, eyes screwed shut. Clinging to each other.

133

The violence was overwhelming. The din deafening. Disorienting. Banging, booming. Scraping. Screaming. From the house. From them. As the house came crashing down on top of them.

Rubble fell against Armand, pushing him sideways, but there was nowhere to go. Debris, wreckage, was closing in on both sides of them now. Pinning them there. Crushing them there.

Benedict pulled him closer, and he heard the sobbing of the boy, whose body was folded over his. Protecting him from the inevitable.

He could barely breathe now. There was room for only one thought. One feeling.

Reine-Marie. Reine-Marie.

And then the unholy shrieking died down. There were thumps and thuds as rafters fell. And settled. But the great rending sound, the crashing, had slowed.

Armand opened his eyes, squinting against the grit stinging them. He lifted his head, coughing.

And looked right into Benedict's face.

There was blood on Benedict's forehead, making its way through the plaster and concrete dust. So that the handsome young man looked like a statue that had cracked.

But his eyes were bright. And blinking.

"Myrna?" Armand rasped, barely recognizing his own voice.

"Here." He felt her move against his back but couldn't turn around. They were pinned there.

"Billy?"

There was a word Armand didn't recognize, in a voice he did.

They'd all survived.

Benedict closed his eyes, shutting out the grit in the air. But Armand kept his eyes open. Staring. Peering beyond the boy who still hugged him. Through eyes, watering and burning, he could see the doorjamb that had saved their lives and the familiar marks made on it decades ago. Height charts.

Anthony. Caroline. Shooting up with each measurement. And Hugo, who was not.

But Armand was staring beyond the marks on the wood. At a gray hand thrust up through the rubble.

CHAPTER 16

—

Amelia woke up, clawing her way to the surface, to the sunlight. Her head throbbed, and her mind was numb. And her eyes refused to focus.

She looked around, blinking, until she could make out what she was seeing. And not seeing.

This wasn't her bedroom. Certainly not the small, neat room at the academy that she'd called home for the past two years.

But neither was it the shithole in the rooming house.

This was a whole other shithole.

And then she remembered. Sinking back into the grimy sheets, her face going slack, and she closed her eyes.

"What have I done?"

"What did you do, Sweet Pea?"

Marc sat on the edge of the bed in his underwear gray and sagging. His eyes were bright in their sunken sockets. Like a gleam from some deep well.

She and Marc had been toddlers in the same village. Playing in the same playgrounds, schoolyards. Streets.

Marc had come to Montréal first. Young, gay, fresh, and alive. Fit and handsome. Excited to be out. He'd made a life for himself. A male prostitute, to be sure. But clean and careful. With his own tiny place.

His dream was to find some rich old queen and settle down.

She'd followed Marc to Montréal. He'd guided her. To the best dealers. The ones who didn't cut their shit with worse shit. When she'd sunk low enough, he guided her to the best street corners. And protected her. He was like a big brother to her.

He was careful himself, teetering on the edge of addiction but not quite tipping over. Keeping himself presentable. For the nice restaurants, the private clubs, the international travel he knew was in the next car. On the next corner.

When Gamache kicked her out of the academy, Amelia had gone to the only person she knew could help her find what she needed.

They'd stared at each other, on either side of the threshold of his apartment. Barely recognizing each other. Marc's hair wasn't just greasy, it was falling out. His scabbed scalp visible in patches. His lips chapped, his skin mottled.

When he smiled, she could see gaps where teeth had once been.

"Am I so bad?" he asked, reading the look on her face.

"No, no. Am I?"

She could see herself in his eyes. A stranger. Repulsive in her cleanliness. Jet-black hair shiny. Complexion smooth.

They were no longer brother and sister. They were barely of the same species.

"Why're you here?" he asked, barring the door.

"I need your help. I got kicked out of the academy."

"Why?"

"Possession. Maybe trafficking."

He'd laughed then, relieved. "Maybe?"

Amelia might look like another species, but they shared some DNA after all. She'd come home. To him. To the gutter. Where she belonged.

"What?" he'd asked, dropping his arm and letting her in. "Hell dust? Percs?"

"Fen."

"The good stuff."

She nodded.

"Do you have it on you now?"

He reached filthy hands toward her. She backed up, tripping over a pile of clothes on the floor but quickly righting herself.

"Of course not. They took it all. I need to find some more. But there's even better shit. It's not out yet, but it will be. That's what I really want. You heard of it?"

"Yeah, I've heard the rumors, but it's bullshit. There's nothing." Marc stared at his unexpected guest. "What do you know, Sweet Pea?"

"I know it's not bullshit. Some cop let it through his fingers. And it's good, Marc."

"Really?"

"Really good. Way better than fen. Whoever has it will make a fortune. Will have everything they've ever wanted. Forever."

"Everything?"

She nodded.

"Forever?"

She nodded. "No more shitholes. No more turning tricks. No more wondering where the next hit's coming from. We'll have lots of everything."

"We?"

"I need your help. Look, I learned things in the academy. Useful things, like how to organize, how to fight. The cartels are gone. Everyone's scrambling, right?"

He nodded.

"I can take over."

"You?" He looked at the small girl and laughed.

"It's not the size of the dog in the fight . . ." she said. It was, she knew, his favorite saying.

"It's the size of the fight in the dog." He studied her for a moment. "You are quite a bitch."

She laughed. "You'll help?"

He looked at her with both hope and suspicion.

"You know people, Marc. I've been gone too long."

"Not just gone. You were a cop."

"Not quite," said Amelia. "And since when can't a cop also deal drugs? Not exactly a stretch. Will you help?"

He looked out the window, then back at her. "The streets aren't what you remember."

She needed no proof beyond what she saw in front of her. He wasn't what she remembered.

"You don't want to mess with what's out there, Amelia."

He opened his arms in display. What happened. When a tipping point was reached—and exceeded.

"Go home, Sweet Pea."

"I am home."

Marc looked at her. And his weary brain considered. "Everything?"

"Everything," she said. "All we have to do is find the shit."

He nodded, coming to a decision. "What the fuck. I have nothing to lose. Maybe that should be our motto."

Amelia grunted. "Maybe."

Thanks to Gamache, she too now had nothing to lose. It was, she realized, a very powerful place to be.

"Come with me," he said.

Marc hadn't lied. The streets of inner-city Montréal had changed. Never safe. Never clean. Never fun, now they were many degrees worse. Darker, filthier. Clogged with excrement, puke.

The faces that met her were gray. But the looks were canny. She was a stranger to them, even with Marc to vouch for her.

"Don't tell anyone where you've been," he whispered.

"No shit," she said.

"If anyone asks, I'm going to say you were in Vancouver, living on the streets."

They approached a loose knot of dealers, who stared at her.

She still had some meat on her bones. Pink in her cheeks. Clothes that hadn't hardened with a crust of frozen puke. And piss. And cum.

"If she was in Vancouver," a dealer asked Marc, as though Amelia weren't standing right in front of him, "why'd she come back?"

"I'm right here, fuckface," she said. "Talk to me."

She was at least six inches shorter. She had to tip her head back to glare up at him.

The dealer stepped forward, thrusting his pelvis into her. Pushing her until she was against the brick wall of the alley. Then he ground himself against her.

He was twenty-five at most but looked ancient. Like something dug up at some primitive burial site. They all did. A mass grave, under micrograms of fentanyl, on the streets of Montréal.

His breath on her face smelled of rotten eggs. Of sulfur. Of hellfire.

"You know why I'm here," she snarled, not bothering to push him away. "You know what I want. What I can't get in Vancouver."

He thrust his body against her.

"You came for this, did you?" Grinding his pelvis into her. "I remember you, little girl. Amelia."

He said her name in a drawl, dragging it through the mud.

"You have one thing I want." She reached between his legs. "And it isn't this."

She squeezed. Though what she felt was soft. Like a mitten in his pants.

"That's it, little girl. Squeeze harder."

She brought her hand up from his crotch to his throat and gripped it in exactly the way the martial-arts instructor at the academy had taught her.

Then she squeezed.

"Like this?" she asked.

His eyes widened. And she tightened her grip on his throat.

His eyes bulged. And still she squeezed.

"Amelia," said Marc. "Stop. You'll kill him."

"Nothing to lose," she snarled. And squeezed until she felt his larynx begin to collapse. "I want the new stuff. I came all the way back for it. And if I can't get it, I'll take something else. Just." She squeezed. "For." Tighter. "Fun." Still.

And saw terror in his eyes.

Everyone stepped away, including Marc, while the dealer made a gurgling noise.

"I beg your pardon. What did you say?" she asked. And went through his pockets with her free hand as his eyes began rolling to the back of his head.

She found packets of pills. Packets of powder.

None of it was what she was looking for. She put the packets in her pocket.

Then released him.

He coughed and sputtered, then lunged at her. Amelia stepped aside, pushing him face-first into the wall and pinning him there.

"I'm not a little girl, shithead. I'm a fucking bitch," she hissed into his filthy ear. "But you know what else I am, you pathetic piece of *merde*?"

She twisted his head so that he could see her.

139

"I'm the one-eyed man. Tell that to your supplier. Tell him to watch out."

She gave him one last shove, turned around, and left. Marc scurrying behind her.

"What was that supposed to mean?" he asked. "What did you just do? They'll kill you."

"Maybe. Maybe not. I don't actually care." She handed him most of the packets. "One for you. Sell the rest."

"What about you?" He slipped through the snowy street, trying to catch up with her. His arms wrapped around his chest, his coat too thin to keep him warm on this bitter night.

"I have better things to find," she said.

The next morning she woke up in Marc's room, in Marc's bed. With Marc staring at her.

"Jesus, girl, what did you get up to last night? When I left you, you were looking for the new shit. Did you find it?"

She shook her head. "How'd I get here?"

"I carried you. Found you in an alley. I thought for sure you were dead. But you were just passed out. What did you take?"

She rubbed her hand over her face, feeling the grit of dried sleep, or tears, down her cheeks.

"I don't know."

Amelia had been stoned before. Lots of times. But never like this. Her head felt like it was splitting open, and she struggled for breath.

She tried to remember what had happened the night before. But all she saw were flashes that twisted and tilted in her memory. Turning her stomach until she thought she'd puke.

There was one that kept repeating.

A little girl. She was six or seven years old. Bright red Canadiens tuque on her head. She was wearing moose mittens and holding out a baggie of dope.

The child was swaying on her feet. Staring ahead of her.

But Amelia knew it wasn't so much a memory as a hallucination. Brought on by the shitface dealer calling her a little girl.

"You made quite an impression," Marc said, getting into bed beside her and pulling up the covers. "Everyone wants to know who you are."

"What did you tell them?"

Putting his arm around her, Marc hugged her to his bony chest. Speaking into her dirty hair, his voice muffled, he said, "I told them, Sweet Pea, that you're the one-eyed man."

CHAPTER 17

Armand strained to reach the hand. And the body attached to it.

"What is it?" shouted Myrna.

Pinned behind him, she couldn't see what he was doing, or why. But she could feel his almost frantic movements.

She tried to open her eyes, but the filth in the air kept forcing them closed. Billy, facing her, also had his eyes screwed shut. And his hands tightly clasped hers.

But Armand kept his eyes open, focused on the hand. Hoping, hoping to see movement as he stretched his arm out toward it.

He leaned as far forward as he could. But couldn't. Quite. Reach.

"What?" asked Benedict. "What's happening?"

"There's someone buried with us. I see a hand."

Benedict started to cough, and Armand eased up. Realizing he was pressing himself too hard against Benedict. Hurting the living to get to someone who was almost certainly dead.

They heard shouting and digging above them.

Still Armand reached out. In an unconscious imitation of *The Creation of Adam*. Two fingers, almost touching. But where Michelangelo had depicted the beginning of life, Armand knew this was the end. For someone.

"Who is it?" Armand asked.

Jean-Guy closed the door behind him and sat on the bench of the ambulance.

143

Armand was the last, by his choice, to be looked at by the medics. Benedict had been taken to the hospital for scans, given the injury to his head. After being checked out, Myrna and Billy were told it would be best to also go to the BMP Hospital, but both refused.

"All I want is to go home," said Myrna. "Have a bath. See my friends."

Jean-Guy sat across from Armand, who, despite having his eyes rinsed out several times by the paramedics, blinked against the irritation of the tiny bits of grit still in them.

His face was smeared with grime and sweat and water from the rinsing. But no blood.

Jean-Guy barely dared believe it. Not only was Gamache alive. They all were. Saved by a sturdy doorway.

"And Benedict," said Armand, coughing a little and using a Kleenex to wipe the filthy saliva from his mouth. "He pulled us into that doorway. And then protected me."

He could still feel the rubble hitting his arms, his legs. Crushing into him, into them, from all sides. His chest constricting, his breathing difficult.

What he could also feel, though not see, was Benedict. Using his own body to protect Armand.

And he could hear sobbing that died to whimpering.

The boy was terrified. Knowing he was about to die. And yet he'd chosen, as what might have been his last act, to try to save a near stranger, almost certainly at the cost of his own life.

Jean-Guy was nodding, agreeing.

He'd been just about the first one to them. Breaking free of the hands holding him back, he'd scrambled up the pile, slipping and stumbling on the snow and loose debris.

And then he heard them. Calling, crying out for help. Billy, Myrna, Benedict. But the one voice he was frantic to hear was silent. Panic had set in, and he began to dig with his hands. Throwing aside rubble he normally would never be able to shift.

Until the leather of his gloves was ripped away. Until he'd found them.

First Billy, then Myrna, then Benedict. And finally another face turned to him, squinting in the sunlight.

And the voice, rasping. "Jean-Guy, there's someone else."

While a rescue team, with dogs, dug out the body, Jean-Guy had helped free the others.

Myrna had some bruising on her legs, and Billy had a sprained ankle. Benedict had the blow to his head, and possibly other injuries from the original collapse and his night in the cold.

And Armand came away virtually unscathed.

Their heavy boots and heavy coats, thick tuques and mitts had, for the most part, protected them. Along with the doorway. And Benedict.

Armand blinked again, trying to bring Jean-Guy, sitting a couple feet from him in the ambulance, into focus. It felt like someone had smeared pebble-infused Vaseline into his eyes. Everything was opaque. The grit near blinding.

Like the others, he refused the offer of the hospital and, like the others, only wanted to go home.

But while Billy and Myrna had been driven back to Three Pines, Armand stayed. Needing to hear about the other one.

"They've just uncovered the body," said Jean-Guy.

He held out a wallet.

Armand opened it and saw the driver's license but couldn't read it. He shut his eyes tight to clear his sight, but still the words, the face, were blurred.

He handed it back to Jean-Guy. "Can you read it for me?"

Myrna slipped deeper into the tub, until the hot water was at her chin and the suds were piled so high she couldn't see over them.

"Oh God," she whispered as the chill and terror subsided.

What the warm bath couldn't do, the scent of lavender, the dark chocolate brownie, and the huge glass of red wine did.

Outside her bathroom door, she heard Bach. Concerto for Two Violins. And below that, unintelligible but recognizable, the murmured voice of Clara and very, very softly another sound.

"Fuck, fuck, fuck."

She closed her eyes.

Billy Williams rarely had baths and had never, ever had a bubble bath.

It wasn't that he considered them unmanly, he just never considered them.

But Madame Gamache had invited him in, to get clean and warm. And to stay for a meal. He was cold and hungry and about to decline when he smelled the scent of roses and followed her down the hall, limping, to the bedroom and the large bathroom attached. The tub was full, and high with foam from bubbles that smelled like his grandmother's rose garden.

It was too inviting to decline.

"I'll leave you to it," she said. "I'm going over to see how Myrna is doing."

"Say—" began Billy, then stopped. Considering. "Say hi from me."

"I will. There're clean clothes on the bed and stew warming in the oven."

When Madame Gamache had gone, he stepped into the bath, then sat. Sliding deep into the hot water. Feeling his taut muscles loosen as the water, and suds, rose over his aching body.

On a table beside the bath, he found a beer, his favorite kind. And a huge slice of pie. His favorite kind.

Lemon meringue.

Billy closed his eyes and sighed.

Amelia Choquet stood in the shower. Weak still. Bleary.

She'd wanted to take a bath. Long and hot. But Marc's bathroom was so disgusting, with a ring of dirt around the tub, stains in the toilet. Hair, both long and stringy and short and curly, clogging the drains. She wanted to spend as little time in there as possible.

She closed her eyes and felt the warm water cascade over her throbbing head. With the cracked, cheap soap, she washed her body and her hair. And for a moment felt almost human. She imagined that when she opened her eyes, she'd be in the clean, bright shower rooms of the academy.

Amelia held on to the fantasy as long as she could. Then opened her eyes and started scrubbing. And scrubbing.

It was then she noticed something written on her left forearm. A new tattoo, among all the others.

She took a closer look. No. It wasn't a tattoo. It was done in Magic Marker.

David.

That's all it said. Just, David. And a number: 14.

It wasn't her writing. Someone else had put it there.

She scrubbed harder. Until her arm was almost raw.

But the name wouldn't go away.

David. 14.

CHAPTER 18

Jean-Guy Beauvoir hung up the phone in the kitchen, then asked his father-in-law if he could use the one in the study.

"Of course."

Armand watched him go, then turned back to the others in the room. Reine-Marie. Billy. Annie.

Benedict.

Armand and Jean-Guy had gone straight to the hospital and found him in triage. Bruised. Ravenous. With a bandage on his head, at his hairline.

"He's one lucky fellow," said the doctor. "No fractures or internal bleeding, not even a concussion. Your son?" the doctor asked. Jean-Guy. Who gave the young doctor a filthy look.

"No, he's not my son," he snapped, and saw Armand smile. "He's his grandson."

"That's not completely true," said Armand, but he did not completely deny it either.

The doctor looked at the two men, disheveled, dirty. Then at Benedict. Dirty. Disheveled. And didn't see the need to argue. "Well, he's all yours."

They'd taken Benedict home then. To the Gamache home.

Now, all showered and in warm clothes, they'd joined the others in a meal of beef stew and warm apple crisp with thick cream. Comfort foods that rarely failed in their one great task.

It was now midafternoon, and they sat warming themselves by the woodstove in the kitchen.

They'd asked, of course, about the body. The dead man. Wanting to know who he was. But Jean-Guy had explained that he couldn't tell them until the family had been notified.

That had been the call.

When Jean-Guy returned a few minutes later, he took a chair beside Annie, and after a brief glance at Armand he said, "The dead man is Anthony Baumgartner."

"What?" said Benedict. "But we just saw him yesterday."

"Baumgartner?" said Reine-Marie. "A relative of the Baroness?"

"Her son," said Armand.

"Poor man," said Annie. "Did he have a family?"

"*Oui*," said Jean-Guy. "His ex-wife's been told, and she's going to tell their children. They're in their late teens."

"What was he doing there?" asked Reine-Marie.

"That's the question," said Jean-Guy. Though there were other questions arising from the call he'd just received. And made.

"You're sure you didn't see or hear him when you arrived last night?" Jean-Guy asked Benedict, who shook his head. "And you saw no one else?"

Again Benedict shook his head while Armand looked at his son-in-law with interest.

"I saw the car," said Benedict. "But only when Billy and I got my truck started. It was in the headlights. I knew it'd take a while for the truck to warm up, so I went into the house, to get out of the cold."

"And I left you there," said Billy. "I'm sorry."

"That's okay. Not your fault. I was just stupid. Should never have gone in."

"The house was unlocked?" asked Armand.

"Yes."

Armand wiped tears from his cheeks as his irritated eyes again overflowed, and then he tossed the sodden tissue into the woodstove.

The medic had told him not to rub his eyes. That the grit could scratch the corneas and cause permanent damage.

But his eyes were crying out to be rubbed, and it was near impossible not to do just that.

Seeing this, Reine-Marie reached out and held his one hand while he sat on the other.

"Mind if we join you?" came a voice from the living room, and in walked Myrna and Clara. "I'd heard you were sprung from the hospital." Myrna hugged Benedict. "You okay?"

Billy had jumped up and offered Myrna his seat, blocking Clara from taking it. Reine-Marie's eyes lit up, and she grinned at Armand.

"Just a bump," said Benedict.

"A bimp," said Clara. "You minkey."

Benedict stared at her, in much the same way Armand stared at Billy when he spoke.

"I don't think you've met," said Myrna. "This's Clara Morrow, a neighbor."

"Hello," said Benedict, enunciating clearly and speaking loudly.

"You've never seen *A Shot in the Dark*?" asked Clara. She turned to Myrna. "Another movie we need to see again."

"Good idea."

"Clouseau?" Clara asked Benedict, who continued to stare, tilting his head slightly as though that might help decode this unkempt person.

"'My hands are lethal weapons.'" Clara lifted her hands in a karate chop, trying another movie quote, but now Benedict just looked alarmed, and, taking a step back, he bimped into Armand.

"It's all right," said Armand with a smile. "She only uses them to paint."

"Finger painting?" asked Benedict. "I had an aunt who did that. Therapy. Not quite right in the head."

"Speaking of which, your head's okay?" asked Myrna, returning to the original question.

"They did a scan, and apparently I have a thick skull."

He said it with such earnestness that they couldn't help but laugh.

Benedict, not quite getting it at first, looked confused. Then smirked.

"But a big heart," said Reine-Marie, patting the blanket at his knee. "You saved their lives."

"They saved mine."

"It must've been cold in that house," said Armand. "No heat."

"It was."

"Good thing you were able to light that fire to keep warm," he said.

"But it scared the crap out of us," said Myrna. "We could smell it and thought the place was on fire. Like just collapsing wasn't bad enough."

"Can you tell us now?" asked Clara, accepting Armand's chair as he pulled another over from the kitchen table. "Do we know the name of the person who was buried?"

"I just told them," said Jean-Guy. "The dead man is Anthony Baumgartner."

Myrna's face opened in shock. "The Baroness's son? We just saw him yesterday afternoon. At his house."

Benedict had said the same thing. Most people did, Armand knew. It was as though seeing someone recently should be protection against sudden death.

He turned to Benedict. "You were telling us that when you went into the home, it was unlocked. But you didn't see any evidence of Monsieur Baumgartner?"

"No, none. I called hello, thinking someone must be there, with the car and all, but there was no answer. I started looking around, using the flashlight on my iPhone. Just wandering, really, waiting for my truck to heat up. But then I got to thinking about maybe trying to save the place, so I went in further, to take a closer look. That's when it happened."

The young man went quiet.

Armand and Jean-Guy, both with personal experience of trauma, recognized the signs.

"What happened?" asked Armand softly.

His therapists had taught him something he tried to pass along to all agents in the Sûreté. The need to talk about what had happened. The physical, but also the emotional wounds.

And now he coaxed it out of young Benedict. He of the thick skull and big heart.

Henri, lying between Armand and Benedict, rolled onto his back. His huge ears flopping flat on the floor like two small area rugs.

Benedict bent down and rubbed Henri's tummy. Not meeting anyone's eyes.

"I could hear the cracking," he told Henri, who was listening closely. "I thought it was the frost getting into the wood. It happens with old places. I wasn't afraid. At first. I thought I knew what it was. But then there was another, huger noise. I was in the kitchen. I could hear something, like a train coming, and the place started to shake."

His voice was rising, and Myrna reached over and held his hand. Not to stop him but to reassure him.

Benedict looked at Myrna, then over at Armand.

Though his own eyes were bleary, Armand could clearly see the boy's terror.

"I began to run for the door," Benedict continued. "But a beam fell, right in front of me. I just managed to stop in time. And then—" He faltered.

"Go on," said Armand gently.

"And then it just felt like explosions everywhere. I got confused and froze."

He looked around, his eyes wide, and settled on Jean-Guy, who was looking at the young man not with pity, or sympathy. Not even with understanding, though Jean-Guy understood.

His expression held one thing. Reassurance. That what Benedict felt then, now, how he reacted, what he did or did not do, was natural and normal.

Freeze. Run. Cry. Scream.

Jean-Guy had done all those things himself. And he was trained. This boy was a carpenter. A builder.

"I know," said Myrna. "I froze too. When the place started to fall down. It was—"

"I was alone."

Myrna's mouth, open with the next words prepared, remained open. And silent.

"I was alone," Benedict repeated, in a whisper now.

And there was the difference. The gulf. Between their horror and his. They'd also faced death, but together.

He'd been alone.

Benedict's lower lip trembled, his chin puckering with the effort to hold it in.

"I was so afraid," he whispered. "When I finally did move, I saw the doorway and prayed it was under a support beam. I jumped in and got down. And waited. Everything fell around me." As he spoke, he hunched his shoulders. "And then the crashing stopped, but I was trapped. I shouted and shouted, but there was nothing. And then it got really, really cold. And dark. I'd dropped my iPhone, so I couldn't call or text. I didn't have any light. And then it got real quiet."

He was hugging himself and staring into the fire.

"But you had matches," said Armand.

Benedict nodded. "I'd forgotten about them. I made a little pile of wood. It was so old and dry that it burned easily. Every once in a while, there'd be more shifting, but I kinda got used to it, and once I had the fire, I felt better. I talked to myself. Telling myself how well I was doing. How great everything was. How smart I was. How lucky I was. And that someone would come find me." He looked at Billy. At Myrna. At Armand. "And you did."

"You never heard another sound?" asked Jean-Guy. "A human sound?"

"No. Not until you came."

They nodded, thinking. Imagining. Remembering.

And in at least one case, wondering.

"Why were you there?" Armand asked Benedict.

"To get my truck."

"Yes. But you promised not to drive it without snow tires. You gave me your word. So why did you?"

Benedict dropped his eyes from Armand. "I'm sorry." He heaved a sigh. "It sounds so stupid now, but after a couple of beers it seemed such a good idea. It's pathetic, I know, but there're two things I really care about. My girlfriend and my truck. I miss her. And I was worried about it. When Billy here offered me a lift, I took it."

He raised his eyes to Armand.

"I was going to call you in the morning. Tell you where I was. I'm sorry. I really am."

It was exactly the kind of reckless behavior a cop, and the father of a son, recognized. Armand nodded but kept his eyes on Benedict. Armand did not find it difficult to believe that this young man might have lapses in judgment. Witness the hair and sweater, the business card. Nor that he could be reckless. Witness trying to navigate a brutal Québec winter without snow tires.

But he found it difficult to believe that Benedict broke promises. And especially one he knew was being taken seriously.

And yet he had.

Which, Armand knew, meant he'd been wrong about the young man. In that. But in other things too?

The sun was setting, and Annie quietly got up to turn on some lights.

"Could anyone else use a drink?" she asked.

"Yes, please," said Myrna, getting up.

"I'll help," said Clara.

"Can we talk?" Jean-Guy asked Armand. "In your study?"

Once there, Jean-Guy closed the door.

"There's more, *patron*. Something I can't tell the others yet," he said. "The medical examiner doesn't think Anthony Baumgartner died in the collapse of the house."

"Then how?"

"His skull was crushed. There was concrete and plaster dust on the wound, but none actually embedded there."

"Internal bleeding?"

"None."

"Lungs?"

"Clear."

Gamache gave a curt nod and waved Beauvoir to a chair, sitting down himself.

"He was dead before the place collapsed," said Gamache, grasping the implication immediately. "Could it have been a heart attack or a stroke?"

"Dr. Harris considered both and doesn't think so," said Beauvoir. "She's ready to say the cause of death was the wound on the head, before the house came down."

"That's the phone call you made."

"*Oui*. I've classified it as a homicide and assigned Inspector Dufresne to the case. I'll be leading the investigation."

"Good," said Gamache.

"What can you tell me about your meeting with Baumgartner yesterday?"

Gamache thought. He'd already told Jean-Guy about it, and the will, but not in any detail. It had just been an odd event. He'd not seen it as a precursor to murder.

But now he reconsidered.

He described the gathering, the home, the others present. Their reactions to the will.

"So he questioned why you were a liquidator?" said Beauvoir.

"Yes. He'd thought he and his brother and sister were. They'd been led to believe that by their mother."

"Something must've happened, then, something must've changed, for her to take them off."

"But she still left everything to them," said Gamache. "If there'd been a falling-out, you'd think she wouldn't just take them off as liquidators but remove them completely."

Beauvoir was nodding. Thinking.

"Anything else strike you as strange, *patron*?"

Had it? Not at the time, but now? In retrospect?

He could appreciate how easy it was, how tempting, for people to overinterpret things.

Glances. Tones. Flare-ups. At the time they'd been guests and didn't realize that they were also witnesses.

He tried now to be accurate. Had something been said or done that had led, just hours later, to the death of Anthony Baumgartner?

It was the question he'd always asked himself when kneeling beside a body.

Why is this person dead?

And he asked himself that now. Why was Anthony Baumgartner dead? What had happened?

"It does seem too much of a coincidence," he admitted. "That the will is read and a few hours later one of them is murdered. But for the life of me, I can't remember anything happening at that meeting that could've sparked it. When we left, though, Hugo and the notary were still there with Anthony. Something might've happened after I left."

"What do you make of the will, *patron*?"

"I think from our perspective it was unexpected and even unhinged, but I have to say, her children, including Anthony, didn't seem at all surprised by it. They'd have been more surprised if she hadn't left all that money and property."

"Right," said Beauvoir, getting up. "It begins. We'll find out all we can about the Baumgartners."

"Including the Baroness," said Gamache. "I can't help but think if she were still alive, her son would be too."

He rose and went to the door but returned to his desk when the phone rang.

"*Oui, allô.*"

Gamache waved Beauvoir to a chair but remained standing himself.

Jean-Guy saw Gamache's expression change.

"No, you did the right thing. She's still in there?" He listened, sitting slowly back down. "Tell me again what happened. . . . I see. And you're sure that's what she said?"

There was a pause during which Beauvoir could see Gamache's lips thin and whiten.

"Keep on it. . . . No, no. Do nothing. . . . Of course I know it's illegal," he snapped, then reined himself in. Taking a deep breath. When he spoke again, his voice was even. "Use your judgment, but understand that you're there simply as observers. Do not interfere."

When he hung up, Jean-Guy asked, "That was about Cadet Choquet?"

Gamache had told him what had happened the day before at the academy, and he knew the Chief was having Choquet followed.

"Former cadet," said Gamache, but he nodded. "*Oui.*"

"She's on the streets?"

"*Oui.*"

The Chief Superintendent seemed reluctant to speak. Not because he didn't want Beauvoir to know what was happening but because he himself seemed unsure.

"Her friend found her passed out in an alley and took her back to his place."

"*Merde,*" said Beauvoir, shaking his head. "Stupid, stupid girl." Then he looked more closely at Gamache. "But really, you can't be surprised, *patron.*"

He stopped just short of saying, *I told you so.*

Beauvoir had been warning Gamache about the young cadet since she'd been admitted to the academy by Gamache himself.

This was the one great divide between them. This was the Chief's weak spot. His soft spot.

Gamache believed people could change. For the worse, yes. But also for the better.

But Jean-Guy Beauvoir knew better. People did not, in his experience, fundamentally change. All that changed was their ability to better hide their worst thoughts. To put on the civilized face. But behind the smiles and polite conversation, unseen in the gloom, the rot grew and grew, and when the time was right, when the conditions were right, those terrible thoughts turned into horrific actions.

"What're you going to do?" asked Beauvoir. When Gamache didn't answer, Jean-Guy studied his boss and mentor. And got it.

"You're following her. Not to protect her but to see if she finds the opioids."

"*Oui.*"

Not so soft after all, Beauvoir thought, and tried not to let his shock show.

"The Montréal police have assigned two undercover agents to monitor her and report to me," said Gamache.

"You'd sacrifice her?"

"I'd sacrifice myself if I could," said Gamache. "But I'm not the one, the only one, who can lead us to the shipment."

Jean-Guy tried to keep his civilized face in place, but still, he suspected his feelings showed through.

Chief Superintendent Gamache had asked great sacrifices of his people before. Had placed himself in danger, many times.

But it had always been with knowledge and consent. They knew what they were in for.

This was different. Very different. The man in front of Beauvoir was using a troubled young cadet, without her consent. Placing her in danger. Without her consent.

It showed Beauvoir two things.

Just how desperate the Chief was to stop those drugs from hitting the streets.

And just how far he was willing to go to do it. But Jean-Guy could see something else.

The toll it was taking on this decent man.

Beauvoir wondered if he himself would be able to do something so horrific.

"David?" said the junkie. "No, no David."

Amelia pressed on. She didn't even know if this David was French or English. Was she looking for Day-vid. Or Dah-veed?

It seemed a small point, but in the underbelly of this world small points mattered. Like the tiny tear of the skin a needle made. Yes, this was a universe of small points. And big pricks.

She was pretty sure this David had tagged her because she was asking questions about the new shit. It was a warning. That he could get that close.

But Amelia wasn't going to be scared off.

In fact, just the opposite. She knew he'd made a mistake. Shown himself. And she now had a focus for the search.

Find David. Find the drug. And then her worries would be over. Then she'd show Gamache exactly what she was capable of.

Her feet, in running shoes, were wet through and caked in slush. Why hadn't she brought her boots when she left the academy? All she'd grabbed were her books.

She hadn't been back to the rooming house since leaving the day before, but she'd have to go back later that night. Marc needed his room. For business.

And she had her own business to do.

"I'm looking for David," she said to a prostitute.

"Unless you're looking for pussy, I can't help you, little man."

Amelia bristled, then realized that in her coat and tuque and jeans she did look a bit like a little man.

She trudged along rue Ste.-Catherine, a street named for the patron saint of illness. Peering into the dark alleyways, she saw the dregs, the detritus, the sick, the addicted, the whores, the near-dead and dying.

All kids. Most younger than herself. What had happened in the two years she'd been gone?

But she knew the answer. Opioids had happened. Fentanyl had happened. And worse was coming.

Amelia stared down a dark alley and thought she saw a child. In a bright red tuque. But it was just a hallucination, she was sure. An echo from the drugs she'd taken the night before.

Armand turned off all the lights in the house but didn't go to bed, though he was longing, after that horrible day, to crawl under the warm duvet and hold Reine-Marie close. In the curve of his body.

Instead he settled into an armchair in the living room, with a pillow and blankets.

Just down the dark hallway were the bedrooms where Billy and Benedict slept. Peacefully, he hoped.

But if one should wake up with night terrors, Armand needed to be there.

Clara turned off the lights in the loft above the bookstore. She'd made sure that Myrna was fast asleep and was about to leave when she paused at the top of the stairs and looked back.

And thought of all the times Myrna had stayed with her. After Peter. To be there when the nightmares began.

Clara put on the kettle, made herself a strong cup of Red Rose tea. And settled into the large armchair by the fireplace.

Armand sat up with a start. Some sound had awoken him, but as he listened, the house was silent.

And then it came again. A cry.

He threw off the blanket and walked swiftly down the hallway.

"Benedict?" he whispered, knocking on the young man's door and listening. There was the sound again. More like a whimper now.

Armand went in, and, pulling a chair up to the bed, he found Benedict's hand. And held it. Repeating, softly, over and over, that he was safe. And when that didn't work, he began to quietly sing. The first song that came to mind.

"'Edelweiss, Edelweiss . . .'" Until the boy stopped crying and his breathing relaxed. And he fell asleep.

In the next room, Billy Williams lay awake staring at the ceiling. In the darkness it seemed to be dropping, plunging toward him. He gripped the sides of the bed and repeated to himself it was just a hallucination.

I'm safe. I'm safe.

But he could barely breathe for the debris on his chest, and still the ceiling kept collapsing.

He heard a cry and felt his adrenaline spike. It was that very same sound he'd heard in the shrieking house. Inhuman.

And then he heard whispering. Murmuring. And then something else. Unintelligible but familiar.

His grip loosened, and his lids closed, and he fell asleep to someone softly singing.

Amelia pounded on the door to the landlady's room. It opened just enough for the ferret eyes to see who was there.

"What the fuck do you want?" the old woman demanded.

Her stained bathrobe was open, revealing more than Amelia wanted to see.

"I want my room. Someone else's in it."

"Yeah, someone who pays." The landlady's anger was replaced by satisfaction. "You had that room in exchange for cleaning. But you didn't, did you? You kicked over the bucket. I had to clean it up."

It was a lie, Amelia knew. She'd found the overturned bucket and mop still lying in the hallway outside her room.

The tiny eyes looked at Amelia through the crack in the door.

"Get out, before I call the cops," she said, and went to close the door, but Amelia's body stopped her.

"My things, give me my things, you filthy old slut."

"Don't have them."

161

"Where are they?"

"You feel that heat?" The old woman paused. Then smiled. "That's your stuff."

Amelia relaxed her pressure on the door as the landlady's words, and what they meant, hit her. In that moment the door banged shut and the dead bolt was pushed into place.

"You bitch," she screamed, and threw herself against the door. Over and over, until her voice was raw and her shoulder was so bruised she had to stop. Until she slid to the floor, exhausted.

She felt the carpet, crusty beneath her. She smelled the stale tobacco, and shit, and sweat, and piss. And she felt the warmth.

Her head dropped into her hands. And Amelia wept. For her life in ruins and her books in flames.

And then, the warmth too painful, she got up and walked back into the cold. In search of a drug so new, so powerful, it could take her away, far away, from there. Forever.

Reine-Marie found Armand nodding by the fire.

On seeing her, he roused and told her about Benedict. "I need to stay here."

"*Oui*," she said, and, after adjusting the pillow and blankets, she pulled up a chair and sat beside him. Holding his hand and talking softly about Honoré. About their granddaughters in Paris. About Gracie and Henri.

Until he fell into a deep and peaceful sleep.

CHAPTER 19

The sun was streaming through the mullioned windows of the bistro, hitting the wide-plank floors, the comfortable chairs, the pine tables. The patrons.

But it didn't quite reach into the far corner, beside the large open fireplace, where Myrna, Benedict, and Armand sat with Lucien.

Armand had called the notary and asked him to meet them there and to bring some documents with him.

The notary listened, his face getting more and more slack as Myrna and Benedict related what had happened the day before.

"The house I was just in?" he asked when they'd finished. "Fell down?"

"Yes, we're feeling much better," said Myrna, responding to a question unasked. "Some bruising, but the bath last night helped. Thank you."

Lucien looked at her, puzzled.

They sat in wing chairs, their breakfasts and cafés au lait in front of them. Beside them the fire roared, fed by large maple logs.

"A body was found when the farmhouse fell," said Armand. "It was Anthony Baumgartner."

The notary's eyes widened. "Monsieur Baumgartner? He's dead?"

"*Oui.*"

"But we were just with him."

"He must've gone to the house after we left," said Myrna.

"But why?" asked Lucien.

"We don't know."

Gamache had decided not to tell them, yet, that Beauvoir was investigating it as a homicide. The longer that could be kept quiet, the fewer people who knew, the less guarded that people would be.

It would come out soon enough.

"Did Monsieur Baumgartner say anything to you after we left, about going to the house?" asked Gamache.

Lucien shook his head. "No, nothing. We just made small talk while I organized the papers. I didn't stay long, but it all seemed normal."

Both Myrna and Armand knew that Lucien might not be the best judge of what was normal human interaction. But even he would've noticed a fight breaking out.

"Do you know why they were replaced as liquidators in their mother's will?" Gamache asked.

"Not a clue," said Lucien. "And we don't really know that they were ever liquidators. They thought they were, but who knows?"

"Your father would've known," said Myrna. "And there must be an old will around."

"If there is, I don't know about it."

"Did you bring his papers with you?" Armand asked.

When he'd called the notary, Gamache had asked him to go through his father's files and bring anything relating to the Baumgartners. Now Lucien placed a neat pile of papers on the table.

"Your father wasn't the notary for Anthony Baumgartner, was he?" asked Gamache, putting on his reading glasses.

"No. Just for the mother."

"Have you read what's in there?" Gamache asked, pointing to the stack.

He blinked a few times and squinted a little, trying to get his still-blurry eyes to clear.

When he woke up that morning, he found that while his body was stiff and sore from the events in the collapsing house, his eyes were less irritated. But still the words in front of him refused to come into sharp focus, and he struggled to read.

"No," said Lucien. "I didn't have to. I've found what we're looking for."

"An old will?" asked Myrna.

"A very old will," said Lucien. "But not one belonging to Madame

Baumgartner. This's one I found when I did my own search. I believe I know why Bertha Baumgartner called herself 'Baroness.'"

Myrna turned in her chair to fully face him. Armand removed his reading glasses. And Benedict, after taking a huge bite of toasted buttered brioche, leaned forward.

Lucien paused, enjoying the moment.

"Oh for God's sake, just tell us," snapped Myrna.

The moment, it seemed, had passed.

"Fine. After our meeting with the family yesterday, and the extraordinary provisions of the will, I decided to try something. I did a will search under 'Kinderoth.' It took me a while, but I finally came on this."

He picked up a sheet of paper from the top of the pile and handed it to Myrna.

It was a printout of an old document, written in longhand with official-looking stamps all over it.

"This's in German," she said.

"Yes. I read a little," said Lucien. "It seems to be a case contesting the will of one Shlomo Kinderoth. The Baron Kinderoth."

Myrna's eyes widened, and she gave Armand a meaningful look, then handed him the paper.

He put his reading glasses back on and studied it, trying to focus, then handed it to Benedict. "Does the date at the top of that say 1885?"

"It does. This"—Lucien grabbed it from Benedict and held it up—"is a printout of the original filing in a court in Vienna in 1885. Seems Shlomo Kinderoth left everything to his two sons."

"Yes," said Myrna.

"Equally."

"*Oui*," said Armand.

"I'm not putting this well," said Lucien, and no one contradicted him. "He left everything to his twin sons. Both men inherited the title as well as his wealth, which was, according to the filing, vast. Estates in Switzerland. Homes in Vienna and Paris—"

"Wait," said Myrna, holding up her hand. "Are you saying he left the same thing to both?"

"Exactly."

"But how can he?"

"He can't. That's the thing," said Lucien, enjoying himself now.

"That's how all this started. I guess they didn't get along. They sued each other."

"And?" asked Benedict.

"And nothing. It was never resolved."

"What does that mean?" asked Benedict.

"You're not saying the will is still being contested," said Myrna. "That's a hundred and twenty years ago."

"One hundred and thirty-two," said Lucien. "And no, of course I'm not saying that. The Austrians are almost as efficient as the Germans. No, this would've been decided long ago. I just haven't found the judgment yet."

"But we can assume it wasn't in favor of Madame Baumgartner's side of the family," said Armand.

"Then why would she believe she was entitled to it?" asked Myrna.

But even as she asked that, and saw Armand's grim face, she knew the idiocy of her question.

Bertha Baumgartner clung to that belief because she wanted to. It served her purposes.

The Baroness lived in a fantasy world, where the fork in the road favored her. A world where she was both victim and heiress. A baroness cleaning woman. A walking Victorian melodrama.

How many clients had Myrna sat across from as they complained about having been "done wrong"? Whose grip on grievances was so tight it strangled reason. They'd give up sanity before giving up these injustices.

In some cases, in some people, it went on for years and years. The thorn planted firmly in their side. And while Dr. Landers had listened, guided, made suggestions on how to try to let their pain go, still they'd let it fester, until she'd finally realized some clients didn't want freedom from their resentments, they wanted validation.

Entitlement was, she knew, a terrible thing. It chained the person to their victimhood. It gobbled up all the air around it. Until the person lived in a vacuum, where nothing good could flourish.

And the tragedy was almost always compounded, Myrna knew. These people invariably passed it on from generation to generation. Magnified each time.

The sore point became their family legend, their myth, their legacy. What they lost became their most prized possession. Their inheritance.

Of course, if they lost, then someone else had won. And they had a focus for their wrath. It became a blood feud for the bloodline.

Myrna looked at Armand, who had taken back the document from Lucien and written something on it.

"So she thought her side of the family got screwed," said Benedict.

Myrna compressed her lips. All her psychology classes, her Ph.D., her years of study and work, and this young man put it more succinctly than she could.

Bertha thought her family had been screwed. For generations.

"What do you think, Armand?" Myrna asked.

"The sins I was told were mine from birth," he remembered Ruth's obscure poem, *"and the Guilt of an old inheritance."*

"There's a reason Anthony Baumgartner went into that farmhouse," he said.

"Maybe he just missed his mother," said Benedict.

Maybe, thought Gamache.

There was, after all, something precious in the house. The one thing that couldn't be stripped away.

The place was filled with memories.

He saw again the growth chart. And the photograph in Anthony's home, of the three children in the garden of flowers, beautiful and treacherous.

Armand Gamache knew that memories weren't just precious, they were powerful. Charged with emotions both beautiful and treacherous.

Who knew what lived on in that rotten old home?

Gamache studied the printout again. It was written in German, so he couldn't understand much. And he could barely read the writing anyway.

Is this what started it all? A crazy will written one hundred and thirty years ago. And another, equally crazy one, read two days ago?

"Where was Madame Baumgartner when she died?"

"In a seniors' home. The Maison Saint-Rémy," said the notary. "Why?"

"Cause of death?" Armand asked.

"Heart failure," said Lucien. "It's on her death certificate in your dossier. Why?" he asked again.

"But there was no autopsy?"

"Of course not. She was an elderly woman who died of natural causes."

"Armand?" asked Myrna, but he just gave her a quick smile.

"Do you mind if I take this?" He picked up the printout.

"I do," said Lucien. "I need it for my files."

"*Désolé*, but I shouldn't have put it in the form of a question," said Gamache, folding it up and putting it into his breast pocket. "I'm sure you can print out another copy."

He got up and turned to Myrna. "Is your bookstore open?"

"It's unlocked," she said. "Comes to the same thing. Help yourself."

Armand spent the next few minutes browsing the shelves of Myrna's New and Used Bookstore before he found what he wanted. Leaving money next to the till, he put the book into his coat pocket.

When he returned to the bistro, he saw Billy Williams heading to his truck.

"He shouldn't be driving," said Myrna, going to the door. "With his bad ankle."

She called to him, and, as Gamache watched, Billy turned, saw Myrna, and smiled.

"He's a nice man," said Armand. "A good man."

"A handy person to have around," she said. "That's for sure."

They watched as Billy approached the bistro. And while Armand couldn't understand a word Billy Williams said, he did understand the look on his face.

And he wondered if Myrna saw what he did.

CHAPTER 20

Jean-Guy Beauvoir stared down at the body of Anthony Baumgartner as the coroner went over the autopsy results.

Unlike Gamache, Beauvoir had not seen him in life, but still he could tell that Baumgartner had been a handsome, distinguished-looking man. There was about him, even now, an air of authority. Which was unusual in a corpse.

"An otherwise healthy fifty-two-year-old man," said Dr. Harris. "You can see the wound to the skull."

Both Gamache and Beauvoir leaned in, though it was perfectly obvious even from a distance.

"Any idea what did it?" asked Gamache, stepping back.

"I'd say, by the shape of it, a piece of wood. Something similar to a two-by-four, with a sharp edge, but bigger, heavier. It would've been swung like a bat." She mimicked a swing. "Hitting him on the side of the head, with enough force to do that sort of damage. Not as easy as you might think, to cave in a skull. What is it?"

Gamache was frowning.

"Are you sure it was done before the building collapsed?"

It was, of course, a vital question. One was accident. One was murder.

"Yes. I'm sure."

His eyes, still bloodshot and watery, watched her closely.

Dr. Harris sighed, and, stripping off her surgical gloves, she tossed them into the garbage can.

She knew Chief Superintendent Gamache and Inspector Beauvoir well. Well enough to call them Armand and Jean-Guy. Over drinks.

169

But over a body they were Chief Superintendent, Chief Inspector, and Doctor.

She didn't take offense at being pushed on this point. The Chief was a careful man, and nowhere was that care more necessary than in tracking down a killer.

And while she knew that Gamache was still on suspension, she'd continued to consider him head of the Sûreté, until someone forced her not to.

"Anthony Baumgartner had been dead at least half an hour before the place came down. I can tell by the condition of his organs and the lack of internal bleeding. Besides, he was hit on the side of the head. A building doesn't normally collapse sideways."

"I'm going to make a call," said Chief Inspector Beauvoir, pulling out his cell phone and stepping away.

"There were two collapses, is that right?" Dr. Harris asked Gamache.

"Yes. A partial one sometime in the night and then the final one yesterday afternoon."

"The one you were caught in," she said. "That revealed the body."

"*Oui.*"

He explained, briefly.

"Sit down," said Dr. Harris, indicating a stool.

"Why?"

"So I can flush your eyes out."

"I'm fine, they're getting better."

"Do you want to go blind?"

"Good God, no. Is that a possibility?"

She could see he was genuinely shocked.

"Remote, but who knows what material was in that building? The sooner you can get all the grit out, the better. It's possible it's scratching the cornea. Or worse, getting behind the eyeball."

He sat, and she leaned into his face, first taking a close look at his eyes, and then she brought the water up and squirted. He winced away as the water hit.

"Sorry, should have warned you it would sting."

When she'd finished, he grimaced, widening, then blinking his eyes.

"Don't rub," she warned, and took a good look in both eyes, finally clicking off the light on the instrument. "Better. Much better."

They didn't feel better. Now he could barely see, and his eyes were both irritated and painful. He sat on his hands.

"What did you say to him?" asked Beauvoir, returning from a call. "You've made him cry."

Dr. Harris laughed. "I told him the bistro had run out of croissants."

"Are you trying to kill the man?" asked Jean-Guy.

"Enough. I can still hear, you know," said Gamache. His sight was coming back and the irritation subsiding. "What did Inspector Dufresne say?"

"They're going over the wreckage, looking for the weapon," said Beauvoir. "And trying to work out where he was when he was killed."

"What do they think?" asked Gamache.

"Dufresne thinks probably in a second-floor bedroom. When the roof finally collapsed, it brought his body with it. That's what it looks like now."

Dr. Harris walked to the sink while Armand returned to the metal autopsy table. Clasping his hands behind his back, he stared down at Anthony Baumgartner.

So unlike his mother, who looked like an elderly British character actress playing a monarch in a comedy.

This man appeared to be the real thing. Even in death there was something almost noble about Anthony Baumgartner. Gamache wondered, in passing, who the title went to now. Caroline or Hugo?

Did primogeniture apply to fictional titles?

He picked up the white sheet and replaced it over Anthony Baumgartner's face.

And still the Chief Superintendent considered the sheet, and what was under it, for a long moment before he spoke.

"Do you think this was meant to look like an accident?"

"That seems pretty obvious," said Beauvoir. "Yes. We're supposed to think he was killed when the house fell down. And we might have, if Benedict hadn't been there and said there was no one else in there. No one living, anyway."

"True. But for it to look like an accident, the farmhouse had to fall down."

"Well, yes," said Dr. Harris, glancing over her shoulder from the sink.

But Beauvoir returned to the table, looking first at the Chief, then down at the white sheet.

"That's true," he said. Understanding what it was that Gamache meant.

It wasn't just a simple statement of fact. It was a vital element of the investigation.

Then Dr. Harris, drying her hands, turned around, and Jean-Guy could see that she also understood what Gamache was saying.

"How did the killer know the house would collapse?" asked the coroner.

"There's only one way," said Beauvoir.

"He had to make it fall," said Gamache.

"And there's only one person in the picture right now who might be able to do that," said Beauvoir.

Gamache stepped away from the body and put in a call.

After listening to Chief Superintendent Gamache, Isabelle Lacoste considered for a moment.

She'd agreed immediately to his request but now had to figure out just how this could be done.

Then she'd called a taxi. It had dropped her off, into a pile of snow and slush.

Lacoste walked carefully across the icy sidewalk. Her cane in hand. And stood at the entrance to the apartment building.

It was a low-rise, with windows that were so frosted up it would be, from the inside, impossible to see outside.

She tried the front door. It was unlocked.

Limping into the entrance, she had to make her way around a large pile of circulars on the floor. Clearly if there was a caretaker, he or she was taking the day off. Or the year.

Isabelle Lacoste checked again the information Chief Superintendent Gamache had texted her.

Benedict Pouliot. Apartment 3G.

After looking around for an elevator and realizing there was none, she stood in front of the stairs, took a deep breath, and began climbing.

After their meeting with the coroner, Jean-Guy dropped Gamache at a café on rue Ste.-Catherine.

"Bit scuzzy," he said, looking around. "You sure you want to wait here?"

"I used to come here as a young agent." Gamache looked around. "All I could afford. Even brought Reine-Marie here."

"On a date? Are you mad?" Beauvoir looked at the dregs slumped in booths. But the place itself seemed clean enough. The sort of diner where Mom and Dad and drug-dealer son could share a poutine together.

"I guess Reine-Marie likes the bad boys," said Armand, and Jean-Guy laughed.

"Yeah, they don't get much more brutal than you, *patron*. Now, you have everything you need?"

"I need you to leave," said Gamache.

And now Jean-Guy stood in front of the closed door in Sûreté head-quarters. A room he was fast becoming familiar with. And growing to hate.

He lifted his hand, but it opened before he could knock.

"Chief Inspector," said Marie Janvier.

"Inspector," he said.

"Thank you for coming." She stepped aside to let him in.

"Thank you for having me."

If she was going to pretend this was a social event, so could he.

"We have just a few more questions for you." She indicated the same chair he'd sat in last time.

The same people were at the same table, but now there was also an older man in a comfortable chair off to the side.

Beauvoir was prepared this time. He knew, despite the pleasant smiles, what it was they wanted from him.

Instead of taking his seat, he walked past the investigator, directly up to the quiet man in the corner.

"And who are you?" he asked.

The man stood up. He was not in uniform, but he held himself like an officer. Police or military. Senior.

173

He was slightly shorter than Beauvoir, middle-aged, with a trim body. There was an ease about him, and an alertness. The sort of attitude that came from years of being in charge, in difficult situations.

And this, it seemed, was a difficult situation.

"Francis Cournoyer. I'm with the Ministère de la Justice."

Beauvoir was surprised, even shaken. But tried not to show it. "Why're you here?"

"I think you know why, Chief Inspector."

"This has become political."

"This was always political. I expect your Chief Superintendent knows that. Knew that, even when he made the decision to let the drugs pass. But you don't need to look at me like that. I'm not the enemy. We all want the same thing."

"And what's that?"

"Justice."

"For whom?"

Francis Cournoyer laughed. "Now that's a good question. I serve the people of Québec."

"As do I."

"And the Chief Superintendent?"

Beauvoir couldn't contain his outrage. "After all he's done, you'd question that?"

"But his service needs to be seen in its totality. Yes, he's done a lot of good, but can you really say he's served the population well when he let loose what amounts to a plague?"

"To stop something worse."

"But how do we know it would've been worse?" asked Cournoyer. "All we do know is if that drug hits the streets, tens of thousands, maybe hundreds of thousands, will die. Either by the drug itself or the violence that comes with it. Is that justice?"

Even Beauvoir, not a political animal, could see that Francis Cournoyer was trying out the line that would be used on journalists. In talk shows and interviews.

To justify this assassination.

However apparently well-meaning the head of the Sûreté had been, he'd made a terrible blunder. And had to pay.

"What do you want from me?"

"You have a chance to limit the blowback, Chief Inspector. You were his second-in-command. This can mar the entire Sûreté, just when it's beginning to win back some credibility."

"You want me to say it was all his decision? All his doing?"

"You have a choice. Gamache is going to be blamed. There's no way around that. His ruin was inevitable, from the moment he made that decision. He knew it. And did it anyway. There's nothing you can do to stop that. You can't save him. That bullet has left the barrel. What you can do is stop the collateral damage to others."

"Including myself?"

Francis Cournoyer just shrugged.

"Including the Premier?"

Cournoyer's face grew grim.

"We've drawn up a statement, Chief Inspector. Take it with you if you like. Read it. Put it in your own words. But sign it. Do the right thing. Don't be blinded by your loyalty."

"You're kidding, right? You'd say that to me?" Beauvoir was trying to keep his voice down and his tone civil, but his anger was clawing its way out. "Releasing those drugs allowed us to break the largest drug rings working in North America. It was a Sûreté action that almost cost a senior Sûreté officer her life, and instead of thanking us, you treat me and the Chief like criminals?" Now he dropped his voice. "And I'm the blind one?"

"You have no idea what I see."

"Oh, I think I have an idea. We're a detail in your big picture, right?"

And he had the satisfaction of seeing, fleetingly, a moment of hesitation in Cournoyer's eyes. Of very slight surprise.

"It's nice you think we have a big picture," said Cournoyer, recovering. "But believe me, we're just bumbling along, responding to events and trying to do the right thing by our citizens."

Beauvoir didn't say anything, but he did know one thing. This Mr. Cournoyer did not bumble.

Gamache sat at the melamine table in the booth, sipping water and looking out the window.

Then he got a text.

"I'll be back," he said to the server, handing her a twenty. "Please hold the table for me."

"Oui, monsieur."

Pulling his tuque down over his ears and putting his gloves on, Gamache squinted into the bright, cold day. His feet crunching on the sidewalk, pedestrians hurried past him, in a rush to get where they were going.

But he was in no hurry. Up ahead and across the road, two people were also walking slowly. One tall, thin, gaunt even in the winter coat. The other shorter, fuller, more stable on her feet.

Amelia.

Gamache matched their pace for two blocks, and when they paused, he stepped into an alleyway. There, hunched into his parka, he watched, leaning against the cold bricks of the abandoned building.

He saw the dealers and addicts and prostitutes, going about their business in broad daylight. Knowing no cop would stop them.

This part of rue Ste.-Catherine wasn't so much an artery as an intestine.

He could see two scruffy men, in filthy clothing, going through garbage cans. Occasionally shoving each other. Fighting over cans and stale crusts.

Gamache watched, impressed.

The young officers were doing well. Taking this seriously. As they should. There would be few things in their careers more important than what they were doing at that moment. Though they didn't yet know it.

He'd had a text, a brief update, from one of them. Advising him where Amelia was. But they had no idea where he was. No idea that the head of the Sûreté had joined them and was also watching the former cadet.

Gamache stepped back further into the shadows, as Amelia and her friend approached a dealer. Both men looked frail, especially compared to Amelia.

The one-eyed man, thought Gamache.

Then Amelia did something odd. She shoved the sleeve of her left arm up to her elbow and held it out to the dealer, who shook his head.

Amelia said something, appearing to argue, before turning her back on the dealer and walking away. Her friend hurrying to catch up.

"Twenty bucks for a blow job." Gamache heard the male voice behind him.

Ignoring it, he continued to watch until he felt a poke in his back.

"I'm speaking to you, Grandpa. You want a blow job or not?"

Gamache turned and saw a man younger than his own son. Tattoos over his ravaged face. He must have been handsome once, thought Gamache. He must've been young, once.

"No thank you," he said, and turned to watch the exchange across the street.

"Then fuck off."

Gamache felt two fists hit his back with such force he was propelled out of the alley and across the icy sidewalk. Putting out both hands just in time, he thudded against a parked car, narrowly missing skidding onto the street. And into oncoming traffic.

A driver leaned on his horn and gave him the finger as he passed.

"You okay?"

Gamache felt a thin hand, like a skeleton's, on his arm and turned to look into a cavernous face. The cheeks were so sunken the thin skin barely stretched across the bones. And the eyes, with dark circles, were dilated. But kind.

Gamache looked across the road. His eyes sweeping over and past the couple a block away now.

Amelia had glanced back at the sound of the horn, but Gamache had already turned away and was looking at the person who held his arm.

"Do you need help?" asked the soft voice.

"*Non, non.* I'm fine. *Merci.*"

She looked behind her, shouting into the alley. "You fucking asshole. You might've killed him."

"Fucking tranny" came the reply out of the dark. "Get off my block."

The woman turned back to Gamache. They were about the same height, and it was clear she had once been robust but was withered, whittled down. She wore a short leather skirt and a pink, frilly coat. Her makeup was carefully, skillfully, applied, but couldn't hide the sores on her face.

"You sure you're okay?" she asked. "It isn't safe here, you know."

"You're very kind, thank you," he said, reaching into his pocket.

"Don't." She laid the same skeleton hand on his arm.

Gamache brought out a notebook and pen and wrote down his personal number.

"If you ever need help." He handed it to her, along with his gloves. "My name's Armand."

"Anita Facial," she said, shaking his hand and taking what he offered.

Amelia continued walking with Marc. She'd slept in the hallway outside his tiny apartment the night before and tried not to hear what was going on inside.

And now they were off again. He to find another score. She to find David.

A car horn had blasted just behind them, and she'd turned in time to see a prostitute holding the arm of a man who'd almost wandered into traffic.

She watched for a moment as the man gave the prostitute what must have been money for services. Some things never changed.

Amelia continued trudging down rue Ste.-Catherine. She bent her head into the wind and narrowed her eyes and repeated, as she had the night before, the familiar poems and favorite phrases seared into her memory. She went through them, her personal rosary. Over and over. Round and around. Until the bitter day faded. Until the addicts and whores and trannies faded and she was left with the warmth of the words from books now ash.

Gamache walked back to the café.

He knew it was probably unwise to have come here, but he wanted to make sure Amelia was indeed on the streets and was doing what he expected.

Looking for the carfentanil.

He was under no illusion about what would happen if she failed. If he failed.

Fentanyl, he knew, was a hundred times stronger than heroin. And carfentanil was a hundred times stronger than any fentanyl.

It would be like taking a flamethrower to every kid on the streets.

As he walked slowly back, he thought about what Beauvoir had said. That no one was more brutal than him. It was said in jest, but it was also, Gamache knew, true.

Armand felt a slight pain in his back where the young male prostitute had hit him from behind. There were two spots, side by side, that throbbed. If he were sprouting wings, that's where they'd be.

But Armand Gamache knew with certainty that he was no angel. Though he did wonder if there was ever another war in heaven, on which side he'd be placed.

After sliding back into the booth and ordering coffee and a sandwich, Armand put on his reading glasses and opened the book he'd bought that morning at Myrna's bookshop.

Erasmus's *Adagia*. His collection of proverbs and sayings.

The print was small, and Armand's eyes were still blurry, but he knew the book well and now read the familiar entries.

> *One swallow doesn't make a summer.*
> *A necessary evil.*
> *Between a rock and a hard place.*
> *A rare bird.*

And then he found the one he'd been looking for.

In the kingdom of the blind, Amelia recited to herself as she trudged along—

—*the one-eyed man is king*, Gamache read.

"Chief Inspector?"

Beauvoir turned and saw Francis Cournoyer walking down the corridor after him.

"A word, please."

Jean-Guy had been interrogated for an hour and finally been allowed to leave. But he hadn't made it very far down the hallway before Cournoyer caught up with him.

The Ministère de la Justice man looked around, then pulled Beauvoir into the washroom and locked the door.

"You forgot this." He held out a manila file folder.

Beauvoir looked at it. It contained the statement.

"I didn't forget it. I'm not signing. Ever."

"It doesn't say anything we don't already know," said Cournoyer.

"But signing it would say a lot about me, wouldn't it?" said Beauvoir. "Drop it. Drop this whole thing. Do what's right."

Cournoyer smiled. "Is it so clear to you, always? What's right? It isn't to me. And it isn't to Gamache."

"That's a lie. He did what was right."

"Then why do so many decent people think it was wrong? Not just them"—he jerked his head toward the interview room—"but others. Good people, yourself included, disagreed with his decision."

He looked closely at Beauvoir.

"You're surprised I know that? By the Chief Superintendent's own testimony, you pleaded with him to stop the shipment of opioids. Every one of the agents in the inner circle begged him to stop it. He admits that. But it didn't stop him. He let it onto the streets, to potentially kill thousands."

"It hasn't hit the streets yet, and he's gotten most of it back."

"But not all. And it will hit the streets, any day now. Any minute now. Every young death will be laid at his feet."

"You think he doesn't know that? Isn't that bad enough for him? You have to make it a public lynching? It's disgusting. You're disgusting. I won't have anything to do with it."

"You'll change your mind. Before this's over, you'll sign."

"I won't. What's your endgame in all of this? It can't be just protecting politicians."

Cournoyer unlocked the bathroom door, and then, looking back at Beauvoir, he seemed to make up his mind.

"Ask Gamache."

"What?"

"Ask him. He knows far more than he's telling you."

Cournoyer tossed the file, with the statement, onto the floor and left.

Jean-Guy stared at it. Then picked it up.

CHAPTER 21

"Your Benedict . . . Pouliot does not live in 3G, as it turns out," said Isabelle Lacoste, picking up the burger with both hands and taking an almighty bite.

"But he does live in the building?" asked Gamache. "With his girl-friend?"

He had to wait while Isabelle chewed and chewed.

Beauvoir, who'd just joined them in the diner on rue Ste.-Catherine, waved at the server. "I'll have one of those too, please, and a hot choco-late."

It was difficult for a grown man to order a hot chocolate with authority, but he tried.

Armand smiled. But his amusement faded on catching the look Beau-voir gave him.

And Armand felt a slight chill, as though a locked door had opened, just a little.

"*Oui,*" said Lacoste, finally swallowing. It had been a while since she'd been this hungry. "Well, sort of. They used to live in . . . 3G, but she moved out a month or so ago, and he moved into a smaller apartment. Same building. Did you know he's the . . . caretaker?"

She went to take another bite, but Gamache put his hand on her arm to stop her.

"I didn't know that. So he has no girlfriend?"

"Not anymore. Not that the neighbors know. I spoke to half a dozen of them. They all said pretty much the same thing. They'd lived to-gether for a couple of years. The parting seemed . . . amicable."

She took another bite. The place might look like a dive, but the burger was freshly made, perfectly charbroiled, and delicious.

She did not mention that she'd hauled herself all the way up three flights of stairs, pausing at every second step to catch her breath. Only to discover that someone else now lived in 3G and the apartment she was looking for was actually just off the lobby.

"Fuck. Fuck. Fuck," she'd mumbled with each careful step down.

"What do they think of Benedict?" Beauvoir asked.

"They said he's polite. Nice. Trustworthy. There're a lot of older people in the building, and they seem to have adopted Benedict."

"He has that effect on people," said Gamache. "He's a good handyman?"

"Yes," said Lacoste. "According to the other tenants, he seems to know . . . what he's doing. But he hasn't been around for a couple of days."

This description of Benedict was far from conclusive. A handyman could fix a leaking faucet. He could not, necessarily, make a building collapse. At will.

Although a carpenter might. A builder. And that was Benedict's other job.

"But if Benedict killed Anthony Baumgartner," said Beauvoir, "he messed up. His plan couldn't possibly have been to get trapped himself."

"Probably not," said Gamache.

"What do you mean 'probably'?" snapped Beauvoir. "It's obvious."

Both Lacoste and Gamache stared at him in surprise.

"Is something bothering you, Jean-Guy?"

Beauvoir took a deep breath. "I'm sorry. I'm just hungry and tired."

His sponsor in AA had warned him about H.A.L.T. Hungry, angry, lonely, and tired were triggers.

He'd readily admit to hungry and tired. And the meeting had angered him. But it was the lonely that was surprising and upsetting Beauvoir. Cournoyer's final comment had left him feeling very alone.

Ask Gamache.

"It wasn't too much for you, Isabelle?" Gamache asked. "Going to the apartment building?"

"Are you kidding, *patron*? The best . . . therapy I've had in months."

She didn't tell them that she'd slipped and fallen into a snowbank and had struggled to get back onto her feet. Then it had taken another ten minutes to flag down a taxi.

She'd arrived at the restaurant frozen through and bushed.

But it was the most fun she'd had in months. Since the shooting.

She'd been afraid she'd be sidelined forever. Treated by well-meaning colleagues as a charity case. Someone to be patronized, coddled, pitied. And finally ignored.

But Gamache had done none of those things. Instead he'd trusted her with this task, and she'd proven to herself and him that she could do it.

"I've arranged to meet Baumgartner's brother, sister, and ex-wife at his home." Beauvoir looked at his watch. "At three o'clock. I'd like you there if possible, *patron*."

"*Oui. Absolument*," said Gamache. "They know he's dead, of course. But do they know he was murdered?"

"Not yet."

Though it was possible one of them knew perfectly well.

After Gamache headed to the archives to look up some documents, Lacoste was left alone with Beauvoir.

"Okay, spill," she said. "What's wrong?"

"Nothing."

"Oh for Christ's sake, don't make me drag it out of you. You're angry at the Chief about something. What is it?"

He told her about the conversation with the man from the Ministère de la Justice.

As he described what had happened, it all sounded ludicrous. And it would seem silly if he hadn't seen the look on Francis Cournoyer's face.

What's your endgame? Beauvoir had asked, the scent of disinfectant heavy in the air.

Ask Gamache.

With those two words, Cournoyer had thrown a bomb into Beauvoir's world. Though it had been, really, more of a crumble than an explosion. As he'd stood there in the men's toilet. Trying to grasp what was being said.

Cournoyer had more or less said that the person at the center of it all wasn't some vindictive politician. Wasn't some shadowy government operative.

It was Gamache. He wasn't the target, he was the sharpshooter. He wasn't the victim, he was the perpetrator. And he knew perfectly well what was happening. Why. And where it was leading.

And he was keeping Beauvoir in the dark.

And all of this—the investigation, the sneaking around, the threats—were meant to confuse, to dazzle. To misdirect. While something else was happening.

That's what Francis Cournoyer had said. With those two words.

Ask Gamache.

Jean-Guy could feel a headache coming on. The distant throbbing at the base of his skull. Like heartbeats at the birth of dark thoughts.

"But it doesn't mean that the Chief knows anything," said Lacoste. "This Cournoyer man might've been messing with you. Probably not his first mindfuck in a public washroom."

And despite himself Beauvoir snorted. Then heaved a heavy sigh.

He wanted to agree with her. But she hadn't been there. Hadn't seen Cournoyer's triumph as he'd said it.

"Gamache knows way more than he's saying," said Jean-Guy.

"Isn't that a good thing?" asked Isabelle. "You're just pissed off that he didn't tell you."

"Just?" demanded Beauvoir. "Just? I'm being grilled. My career possibly ruined. And he knows why all this is happening, and he's not telling me?" Jean-Guy's voice rose as he wound himself up. "Yes, I'm fucking angry."

There was silence for a long moment.

"You do know," she said, leaning across the table toward him, her voice so quiet he had to also lean in, "that he's the head of the entire Sûreté? Of course he knows more than you. Or me. Or anyone else in the force. He'd better. He's in charge. He's had to navigate these waters for years. So yes he knows more, sees more, than you, or me. And thank God he does."

"He's keeping secrets."

"And that surprises you, Jean-Guy?"

"He's playing me."

186

"Or maybe he's protecting you. Have you thought of that? Can't you see it?"

"Of course I can't see it," snapped Beauvoir. "He's keeping me in the dark. Letting me just waltz into these interrogations like an idiot. I'm tired, Isabelle. Just . . . tired."

And now he looked it. With an index finger, he pushed a fry around on his plate. Then looked up at her. And sighed. "You know?"

She nodded.

"I'm tired of playing catch-up," Jean-Guy said. "Of wondering what monster is around the next corner. Not the murderers. Them I can handle. It's the other stuff. The political games that aren't games at all." He shook his head, then looked down and spoke quietly. "I'm not good at it."

"You don't have to be. He is." She smiled then. "And you're far better at it than you let on. I know that. He knows that."

"But he's better."

"Monsieur Gamache is twenty years older than you. He's been at it a lot longer, at a much higher level. But you're up there now. He trusts you. And, more than that, he cares very deeply about you. For you. If you don't know that by now, you never will."

She flagged down the server again.

"I think we need some tea, don't you?"

She smiled at Beauvoir, who couldn't help but smile back.

Tea.

The Anglos in Three Pines were always pressing tea on each other in times of stress. Even Ruth. Though her "tea," while looking like it, was actually scotch.

He'd thought it vile at first. The tea. But then, somewhere along the line, he found he looked for it. Hoped they'd offer it. And drank it with pleasure, though he didn't show it.

He found now that just the aroma of Red Rose calmed him. He didn't even have to drink it.

The waitress returned, and the scent of the tea enveloped him. Strong. Fragrant. Calming. And yet Jean-Guy could still feel the throbbing radiating from the base of his skull, until it covered his head like a membrane that kept tightening.

He had to think. To be clear. To try to see what was really happening and not what others wanted him to see.

But all that kept coming to mind was Matthew 10:36.

His first day on the job, Chief Inspector Gamache had called him into his office.

The two men were alone, for the first time. And Agent Beauvoir took in two things immediately.

The sense of calm that came from the man behind the desk. It was unusual. Most senior officers Beauvoir knew gave off a "fuck you" energy. Something Agent Beauvoir had learned to copy.

The other thing he noticed was the look in the Chief Inspector's eyes.

Smart, bright. Thoughtful. None of that was particularly unusual in a senior Sûreté officer. But it was something else, in those eyes, that had taken Agent Beauvoir by surprise.

Kindness. Clear enough for a rattled young man to see.

"Have a seat," the Chief had said. And had proceeded to outline, quickly, clearly, what would be expected of Jean-Guy Beauvoir. It amounted to a code of conduct. It started with the four statements that lead to wisdom: I don't know. I need help. I was wrong. I'm sorry. And ended with him saying, simply, "Matthew 10:36."

"You can take all of what I've said to heart," the Chief had said, leading the young agent to the door. "Or none. It's your choice. As are the consequences, of course."

Jean-Guy Beauvoir was used to being told what to do. Ordered around. By his father. His teachers. His superiors.

The concept of choice was new. And more than a little baffling. As was the Chief's habit of tossing what appeared to be random quotes into conversations.

It wasn't until a few years later, and many experiences with the Chief in horrific investigations, that Agent Beauvoir had looked it up.

Matthew 10:36.

Jean-Guy had expected some inspirational biblical saying. From St. Francis, perhaps. Or something from one of those long letters to those poor, and almost certainly illiterate, Corinthians.

Instead what he read struck dread into his heart.

And a man's foes shall be they of his own household.

Far from inspirational, it was a harsh warning in a gentle voice. A whisper out of the darkness.

Be careful.

"I'm tired, Isabelle. Tired of all this." He waved his hand, to indicate not the dingy diner but a world that couldn't be seen. The world of suspicions. Of constant questioning. Of ground shifting.

He just wanted to rest. No, he wanted more than that. He wanted to curl up on his own sofa, in front of the fireplace. With Annie and Honoré in his arms.

And he wanted it all to go away.

He drove her home. At the door she hugged him and whispered, "Be careful."

It was so close to what he'd been privately thinking a few minutes earlier that he felt the hairs go up on the back of his neck.

"I've got Cournoyer's number now," he said. "Not to worry."

"Not of Cournoyer."

"Gamache," said Beauvoir.

"No. You."

As he drove back through Montréal, to pick up Gamache, he could smell a familiar, very, very faint scent. Of rose water and sandalwood.

And he could see, again, those kind eyes. Intelligent. Thoughtful. Trying to communicate something to a hardheaded young agent who was radiating "fuck you."

He watched as pedestrians leaped away from the wall of slush splashed up by cars. As elderly men and women clung to each other to keep from falling. As people, neutered by the bitter cold, scuttled from shops.

And Jean-Guy imagined walking along the Seine with his family. Taking them to the galleries and cathedrals and parks of Paris. Weekend trips to Provence. To the Riviera. Where sun gleamed off the Mediterranean and not off snow.

CHAPTER 22

—

"Ruth, what're you doing?" asked Myrna.

Clara and Gabri stopped tapping on their computers and looked up from their screens.

All four had driven in to Cowansville and now sat in the computer room of the local library, each at a laptop around the large conference table.

They'd come in not for the computers but for the high-speed connection.

Ruth had joined them when she found out where they were going.

Now the elderly poet sat at her laptop, fingers moving swiftly and noisily over the keys as she pounded rather than tapped. A look of satisfaction on her face that would have frightened Genghis Khan.

"Nothing," said Ruth.

Far from being computer-illiterate, Ruth in her early eighties had embraced the Internet.

"As a way," Gabri had guessed, "of spreading her empire."

If there really was a darknet, Ruth Zardo would find it. Conquer it. Become its empress.

"Queen of the Trolls," Gabri had said, and Ruth had not contradicted him.

Though they knew for whom she trolled. Not schoolchildren. Not people who were scorned for being different.

She trolled people who trolled them.

She attacked the attackers.

"Madame Zardo," the librarian had said, practically bowing when Ruth limped in. Elderly, unsteady. Stooped.

But when she sat at the table, behind "her" laptop, she was nimble. Strong. Unyielding. Relentless. No bully could hide. Ruth's hat was so black it was white.

The library was in the process of renaming this room: A F.I.N.E. Place.

"What's she doing?" Clara whispered to Gabri.

"I have no idea," he said.

"Anything?" Myrna asked, and Clara turned her laptop around.

Both Gabri and Myrna took a look.

Clara was in the Austrian registry of births, deaths, and marriages. With a worldwide interest in ancestry, these records were being made available online.

She was following the Baumgartner family, root and branch. Back in time.

To where it grafted onto the Kinderoths.

And then she followed them. To see where, and if, they became the Rothschilds.

"It's interesting, but I'm getting a bit lost. Who's related to whom, and then names change not just with marriage but to avoid discrimination. Obviously Jewish names become Christian. In fact, not only do the names change, but lots of them actually converted. But you see here?"

She pointed to one old document. A name changed from Rosenstein to Rose. But a Star of David remained above Rose. And followed it, through the generations.

And then it stopped. And there was just blank space. Except for the notation "10.11.38."

"What does that mean?" asked Gabri.

Myrna sat silent. Staring. She knew but couldn't say it. She was looking at the names. The ages.

Helga, Hans, Ingrid, Horst Rose. All born in the 1920s. With stars beside their names.

And then the simple notation. 10.11.38.

And then nothing.

"It's a date," Myrna finally said.

Ruth leaned over and looked. Then returned to her computer.

"Kristallnacht," she said, tapping even harder. "November tenth, 1938. When good, decent people revealed themselves for who they really were and turned on their neighbors. The Jews."

"Kristallnacht," said Myrna. "Because of all the broken glass."

"More than glass was broken that night," said Ruth. "It was particularly brutal in Austria."

She spoke as though she'd been there, and while her face was blank and her voice flat, her fingers pounded the keys even harder. In pursuit.

"The Baumgartners?" asked Myrna. "The Baroness's family?"

"Looks like they got out before the Holocaust," said Clara. "I'm trying to track them. Interesting thing is, they aren't called Baron and Baroness."

"So maybe they lost the case?" said Myrna.

"Seems obvious they must have," said Gabri.

"Shlomo Kinderoth left his fortune to both his sons," said Myrna. "You've found the part of the family that became the Baumgartners. How about the other branch?"

Clara spent some moments clicking through. "It's going to take time, but so far I can't find any more references to Baron or Baroness Kinderoth."

"You don't think—" Gabri began.

10.11.38.

"I don't know," said Clara.

"Any luck with the will?" Myrna asked Gabri.

"I have no idea," he said. "I got into the archives, but they're in German. I can't read them."

"I hadn't thought of that," said Myrna.

Armand Gamache sat in the quiet back room of the National Archives. The records he was looking for weren't Canadian. Or Québécois.

He'd used his pass code to get into Interpol. Then over to the Austrian records. The ones he had access to were more detailed than those available to the public.

But he quickly ran up against the same problem Gabri was having.

He could read the names. Baumgartner. Kinderoth. But he couldn't understand the court judgments.

What he did understand was that there were judgments. Plural. Lots of them. From 1887. Then 1892. Then another. And another. All involving Baumgartners and Kinderoths.

Against each other.

They stopped for a few years. And then started up again. Like trench warfare, only pausing to retrench. And then the combatants went at it again. More fiercely each time, he guessed. Such was human nature.

While he could understand the larger issues, the fact this was a case that was tried over and over again, he couldn't get the details. And it was the details that interested him. Though it was far from clear that they'd lead him to whoever had killed Anthony Baumgartner, 132 years after the death of Shlomo, the Baron Kinderoth.

Gamache knew he needed help. He did another search, and then, after finding what he was looking for, he got up and paced.

He was alone in the room, so no one saw him muttering. Gesturing. Finally, after a few minutes, he pulled out his phone and placed a call.

"*Guten Tag,*" he said, and asked for the Kontrollinspektor.

"*Am pursuing powerful informations about a resolve.*"

The voice at the other end of the line was deep, calm, apparently intelligent. And yet Kontrollinspektor Gund couldn't help feeling he was dealing with a lunatic.

"And you are who again?" he asked.

The call had been put through to him by his subordinates. Who enjoyed playing jokes like this in the middle of a long shift, in the middle of the night. It was far from clear this was even a real call and not one of his own agents seeing how far they could push him.

"*I be Armand Gamache, Head Chief of that Sûreté du Québec.*"

"In Canada?"

"*That is the direction*" came the voice, sounding relieved. "Canada."

194

Gamache rolled his eyes. He knew he was making a balls-up of this.

He'd asked, at least he thought he'd asked, for a senior officer who spoke French. Or English. And had been put through to someone who clearly spoke neither.

It might've been the receptionist's idea of a joke, though the Austrians, renowned for many things, were not famous for their hilarity.

Before calling he'd practiced, dragging up from the mists of time whatever German his grandmother had taught him.

He'd sit at the kitchen table, and she'd chat away, in French. And then in German. With a smattering of Yiddish. Of course, as a child, Armand hadn't made the distinction.

As he paced the small room in the National Archives, he mumbled to himself. Repeating the words and phrases as they surfaced. Trying to cobble together an intelligible sentence or two. As he paced, and muttered, the scent of fresh baking became more and more pronounced. Wafting to the surface along with the words. And images.

He could smell, more and more clearly, the madeleines his grandmother had made every Friday.

She'd give him one fresh from the oven, but not before dribbling a spoonful of cod liver oil over the top and letting it soak in. So that when Armand took a bite, it was both delicious and vile. Comforting and gagging. It was like being hugged and shoved at the same time.

"*Sehr gut, meyn tayer.*"

"Very good, my darling," she'd say in Yiddish, and hug him to her so that his eyes came within inches of the tattoo on her left forearm.

"I'm investigating a murder, and a will is part of it," said Gamache into the phone. Or at least thought he was saying. "I need to find out how an estate was settled. It's an old case."

"*Me inspecting a dead murder body, and a resolve is . . .*"

There was a pause as Gund's subordinate at the other end pretended to search for a word. One that, Gund was sure, would be ridiculous.

"*. . . measure.* No, that's not right. *Is a . . .*"

Gund almost hung up. Enough was enough. And yet he was curious. And not completely convinced anymore that this was a bored agent playing a joke.

As the man on the other end struggled with what he was trying to say—

"... *amount*. No. *Quantity?* ..."

Gund turned to his computer and put in "Sûreté du Québec. Gamache."

"... *part*. That's it. *A resolve be part of it*. But resolve might be quite not right. *Oy gevalt*. What's the word?"

Gund read, raising his brows, then looked at the phone and tried to reconcile what he was reading with what he was hearing. Now the deep voice was saying, "*Force. Nein*. I almost have it. Will. That's it. *Gott im Himmel. Danke*." There was a sigh. "*Will. A will be part of it*."

"Chief Superintendent Gamache," said Gund. "If I understand correctly, you would like me to look into a decision about a will?"

He spoke slowly. Clearly.

"*Ja, ja. That is correctly. It is an elderly event*."

Gamache winced, as much from the scent of cod-infused cakes now surrounding him as the stream of near nonsense coming out of his mouth.

"An old case," said Kontrollinspektor Gund.

"*Ja*."

"Can you give me the name of the deceased and the date of the will?"

Gamache did, reading from the printout in front of him.

He also gave Gund his personal email address.

"I'll get back to you as soon as I have the information. It's a murder case, you say?"

"*Ja. Danke schön*."

"*Bitte schön*."

As Gamache hung up he felt that conversation had gone both well and badly. Was comforting and nauseating. Successful and humiliating. And almost certainly not German.

"Such a *tuches*."

CHAPTER 23

—⌣—

Inspector Dufresne had already arrived with the homicide team. Their vehicles were parked discreetly along the road, waiting for Chief Inspector Beauvoir's signal to join him.

At Beauvoir's knock the door to Anthony Baumgartner's home opened and Anthony's sister, Caroline, stood there.

Tall. Elegant. The only evidence of grief were the circles under her eyes.

"Madame," said Beauvoir, introducing himself, though leaving out the department he headed. "I believe you know Monsieur Gamache."

Caroline had shaken Beauvoir's hand, but on seeing Gamache she stepped forward.

And hugged him.

It was quick and might have surprised her more than him.

When he'd been head of homicide, Gamache learned that people reacted to sudden death differently. The emotional could become restrained. Holding themselves back, for fear of what would happen if they cracked.

The restrained became emotional, not skilled at managing feelings.

The strong collapsed. The weak strengthened.

In grief people were themselves and not themselves.

Caroline hugged him.

Then led them both into the living room.

The place, Gamache knew, would soon be searched by those homicide agents waiting outside. Anthony Baumgartner's life would be laid as bare as his body now was.

Inspected. Dissected.

Pulled apart. As they, like the coroner, searched for the cause of death.

Dr. Harris's job was done. Anthony had died from a blow to the head. But theirs was just beginning.

Once they were in the living room, Hugo Baumgartner stepped forward and offered a hand but otherwise stood like a gnome in a garden. Concrete, mute, ugly. And yet, somehow, the dumpy little man dominated the elegant room.

"This is my sister-in-law, Adrienne Fournier," said Caroline. "Adrienne, this is Chief Inspector Beauvoir and Chief Superintendent Gamache."

They offered their condolences.

"*Merci*. It's terrible. I'm afraid I'm still struggling with it. I expect to see Tony come down the hall in his slippers." Then she smiled. "I can see you're a bit confused. Tony and I have been divorced for a few years but managed to remain friends. Probably should've just been friends all along."

"Probably?" asked Caroline.

Adrienne shot her a look but ignored the aside. "Though we have made great children."

She was of average height and well dressed. Over fifty, with hair dyed a rich brown, judicious makeup, and a trim figure. Her clothing was stylish without being showy.

"Before we begin," Beauvoir said after taking the chair Caroline had indicated, "I have some news for you. It's not good."

There was a snort from Hugo, who turned to Caroline when she gave him a look.

"What?" he said. "Like any news at this point could be good. It's all shit." He turned to Adrienne. "Sorry."

His former sister-in-law was regarding him with something close to amusement. Certainly affection.

"You're right, Hug. This is shit."

Caroline turned away. Distancing herself from them. Gamache couldn't help but see an iceberg breaking off from the mainland.

And drifting away.

Though he suspected that had actually happened long ago. Caroline might drift close but would always be separate. And vulnerable to currents and undertows. To the ebb and flow of opinions and judgments.

Probably since childhood.

Behind them he could see the photographs on the bookcase. And while it was too far away and his eyes still too blurry, he could make out the small silver frame and the vague suggestion of three grinning kids. Wet, sagging bathing suits. Tanned arms slung easily over one another's shoulders.

Caroline in the middle, bookended by her brothers.

Had she been happy then? Happy once?

Or had the cracks already begun to form? The cooling, the hardening. The distancing.

Was it in her nature, or had something happened?

And always, always, in the background of Gamache's thoughts, the main question.

Why was one of them dead?

"Your brother," Beauvoir said, looking first at Caroline, then to Hugo. Before moving his gaze to Adrienne. "Your former husband." She gave him a slight acknowledgment. "Wasn't killed in an accident. His death was deliberate."

He paused for a moment, then went on.

"He was murdered."

It was a short, sharp statement.

Both Beauvoir and Gamache knew that people's minds couldn't easily grasp the fact of murder. It was too big, too foreign. Too monstrous. Most just stared, as they stared at him now. As the word and its meaning sank in. Then sank further, from their heads to their hearts.

And there it would live forever.

Murder.

Caroline stiffened, and Hugo, after a pause in which his pudgy face opened in shock, reached out. And took his sister's hand.

In, it seemed to Gamache, an automatic, unscripted, instinctive act of mutual support.

Adrienne, sitting alone in a wing chair, closed her fingers over the arms of the chair. And pressed until her knuckles were as white as her face. She looked, Gamache thought, as though she might pass out.

Beauvoir got up and went to the kitchen, returning with glasses of water. But not before going to the front door and signaling Inspector Dufresne.

Gamache could hear the murmurs of voices in the front hall and the rustling as the Sûreté homicide team entered the house.

The postmortem had begun.

Hugo had abandoned his glass and gone to the bar.

"Screw water," he said, pouring three scotches. His hands trembled as he gave them to Caroline and Adrienne.

Adrienne took a great swig of the scotch, color returning to her face. Hugo downed his in a single shot. But Caroline simply took the glass and held it, as though she'd forgotten how to do everyday things. Like drink. And breathe.

"How?" she asked.

"Why?" asked Hugo.

"Are you sure?" Adrienne asked.

This last was the most natural of questions. Even though she knew the answer. Of course Chief Inspector Beauvoir was sure. He wouldn't have said it otherwise. But still, she had to ask.

And yet the other two had not.

They'd asked other natural questions. How? Why? But what the other two hadn't done was question the statement that someone had murdered their brother.

"We're sure," said Beauvoir. "Do you know of anyone who might want him dead?"

At that moment, on another continent, Kontrollinspektor Gund sat back in his chair.

It was getting on for midnight. A quiet evening in his precinct, and he'd had time to noodle around for the senior Québec cop.

He'd thought it would be a routine search into albeit a very old will.

An elderly event. He smiled as he remembered the epic struggle that poor man had had with the language.

But his smile faded as he read his screen. Then scrolled down.

Further. Further.

It was then he'd sat back and marveled.

"No life is blameless," Caroline began, her voice prim. "But I can't think that Anthony hurt anyone so badly they'd want him dead."

"It's not necessarily that he's hurt someone," Chief Inspector Beauvoir explained. "Motives can be"—he searched for the word—"complex. Your brother might have had something someone else wanted, badly. He might have stood in someone's way at work, for instance. Or have found something out."

Gamache sat quietly on the periphery of the circle and listened. And observed. Searching for some insight. Some reaction.

But all three were shaking their heads.

"Monsieur Baumgartner worked for Taylor and Ogilvy Investments," said Beauvoir. "As an investment adviser, I believe."

"That's correct," said Caroline.

"He invested people's money."

"He acted as a sort of money manager," Hugo clarified. "He'd design a portfolio, get the client's approval, and then others would do the actual trades."

"I see."

An agent, off to the side, was taking notes.

"We'll follow up, of course," said Beauvoir, "but was there anything at his work that was unusual? An unhappy client? A bad investment? Any suggestion of impropriety?"

"None," said Caroline.

"Was he good at his job?"

"Very," said Adrienne.

"I'm sorry to interrupt, but do you mind if I ask a question?" said Gamache.

"Please," said Beauvoir.

"Did any of you invest with him?"

They looked at each other, then shook their heads.

"Why not?"

"I did. A long time ago. But then it didn't seem a good idea to mix business with family," said Caroline.

Hugo was being uncharacteristically quiet, and Adrienne was sitting bolt upright.

"Madame?" Gamache turned to her.

"When we divorced, I moved my money over to another firm, of course."

"Even though you remained friends?"

"Well, that took a while."

"I see. And your children?"

"What about them?"

"I'm wondering if they have any investments, any money in trust or a college fund. That sort of thing."

"Yes, they each have an account."

"With their father?"

"No."

"That too was moved?"

"*Oui.*"

Beauvoir noticed that Madame Fournier's answers were getting more and more clipped. And there was not much more to be clipped before she'd lapse into silence altogether.

And, indeed, silence fell.

Where other investigators pressed and pushed during interrogations, especially when finding a weak spot, Gamache had taught his agents the power of silence.

It could be, often was, far more threatening than shouting. Though that too had its place. But not here. Not now.

Now silence filled the room.

Hugo fidgeted. Adrienne reddened.

And Caroline? She smiled.

Slight. Fleeting. But unmistakable.

Satisfaction.

Hugo made a noise, but Caroline shut him up with a small sound of her own. A quiet cross between clearing her throat and a hum.

It was as though brother and sister understood each other at a primal level, where grunts were enough.

Again the silence encroached. Enveloping them, so that even the young agent off in the corner fidgeted.

"What do you want from me?" Adrienne finally said.

"We want to know what you know," said Gamache. "That's all."

"Just tell them, Adrienne," said Hugo. "It was years ago, and they'll find out anyway. There's no shame."

"For you, maybe." Again there was silence as everyone stared at Anthony Baumgartner's ex-wife.

"My husband was having an affair with an assistant," she finally said. "I found out about it, and it ended our marriage. That's why I took not only my money but our children's money away from the company. From him."

"How long ago was this?" asked Beauvoir.

"Three years."

"Are they still together?"

"No. That ended."

"And the assistant's name?" asked Beauvoir.

"Does it matter?"

"It might. People hold grudges. Her name, please."

And again the slight smile from Caroline. Fleeting. Smug. Cruel.

"His name was Bernard."

Beauvoir raised his brows. "I see."

"Do you?" asked Adrienne. "I wonder what you see? The humiliation? The lies. The little ones and then that great shitty one that was our marriage? I loved a man who didn't, couldn't love me. Not in the same way. Never had, he admitted. Never would. We stood over there." She pointed to the fireplace. "That's where our marriage ended. Right there. When I confronted him and he admitted it. Didn't even try to soften the blow. He just seemed relieved. The bottom had fallen out of my life, and all he felt was relief. Nothing for me. Or the children. He just wanted out, he said. Out."

"Well, he didn't get all that far out, did he?" said Hugo.

"He never came out?" Beauvoir asked.

"No."

"And why not?"

Adrienne was on the verge of answering when she paused. Her shoulders, which had crept up to near her ears, slowly lowered.

She looked at Hugo, who gave her a small nod of support. Her eyes traveled past Caroline, not pausing, then stopped at Beauvoir.

"I don't really know. I never asked. I think, if I'm honest, I was just relieved he was being discreet. For the children's sake. Maybe," she added, "for myself too. I never stopped loving him, you know. I'd have remained with him, had he wanted. I never admitted that to anyone. I loved him, not because he was a straight man but because he was Tony."

She looked around. "I hate this room."

Gamache wondered if it was just the room she hated.

CHAPTER 24

———

"Excuse me," said Chief Inspector Beauvoir, ceding his place to Inspector Dufresne. "I'll leave you with the Inspector and Chief Superintendent Gamache."

He got up, and after nodding to his inspector he caught Gamache's eye.

Gamache, of course, knew exactly what Beauvoir was about to do. The same thing he'd done when he was head of homicide.

Beauvoir had listened to the family. Now it was time to meet the dead man. Or as close as he could come.

Beauvoir walked from room to room, looking in. Sometimes going in.

Agents were photographing. Taking samples. Opening drawers and closets.

They acknowledged him.

"Chief."

Beauvoir nodded back but was, for the most part, silent. Watching. Taking it in. Not monitoring their activity but absorbing the surroundings.

It was always an odd feeling, walking around a person's home uninvited. Seeing it as they'd left it in the morning. Not realizing they'd never return. Not realizing it was the day of their death.

There was something solid, comfortable, restful about this place. It was a home, not a trophy.

The colors were muted. A soft blue-gray for the walls. But there were touches that seemed almost playful.

A lime-green geometric print on the curtains in the master bedroom. Vintage Expo 67 posters were on the walls of the hallway.

Some clothes were tossed casually on a chair in the bedroom. There were balled-up tissues in the wastepaper basket. Some loose change sat on the chest of drawers, along with a framed photo of Baumgartner with his children. A boy and a girl.

On the bedside table, there was a nonfiction book about American politics and a copy of *L'actualité* newsmagazine.

Taking out a pen, Beauvoir pulled open the drawer. More magazines. Pens. Cough drops.

He closed the drawer and looked around for evidence of someone else living there. Or visiting. Overnight.

No one else's clothes, or toothbrush, seemed to be there.

If Baumgartner had a partner or a lover, there was no evidence.

Beauvoir walked down the hall and turned the corner into the room Baumgartner used as a study. And stopped dead.

He didn't know much about art. Did not recognize any artist. With one exception. And that exception was on the wall, over the fireplace in the study.

It was a Clara Morrow. And not just any "Clara," it was a copy of her painting of Ruth. But not just Ruth.

Clara had painted the demented old poet as the aging Virgin Mary. Forgotten.

Embittered.

A clawlike hand gripped a ragged blue shawl at her neck. Her face was filled with loathing. Rage. There was none of the tender young virgin about this grizzled old thing.

Ruth.

But. But. There. In her eyes. Was a glint, a gleam.

With all the brushstrokes. All the detail. All the color, the painting, finally came down to one tiny dot.

Ruth as the Virgin Mary saw something in the distance. Barely visible. Hardly there. More a suggestion.

In a bitter old woman's near-blind eyes, Clara Morrow had painted hope.

Beauvoir knew that most people who looked at the painting saw the

206

despair. It was hard to miss. But what they did miss was the whole point of the painting. That one dot.

The few who got it, though, never forgot it. Dealers and collectors then went back and discovered more treasures in Clara's odd, sometimes fantastical, sometimes deceptively conventional portraits.

But it was Ruth who'd made her reputation and career. Ruth and a dot of light.

Beauvoir nodded to the portrait and heard the old poet snarl, "Numbnuts."

"You old hag," he murmured.

The agents, working in the study, looked at him, but he just gave them a curt nod to continue. Chief Inspector Beauvoir walked around the room, trying not to get in anyone's way. He paused at the mantel, to look at the photographs.

Baumgartner with friends. With politicians. At business banquets. More photos of his children. One of Baumgartner and his now ex-wife. They looked good together. A confident and attractive couple. Then Jean-Guy picked up a small picture in a silver frame. It was black and white. This must have been his parents.

The father was slender, handsome, unsmiling. Severe. A tough man to please, Beauvoir guessed.

And his son took after him, at least in looks. In personality too? It didn't seem so, from the pictures. He was almost always smiling in them.

But then Anthony Baumgartner was good at hiding what he was really feeling. That much had been proven.

Beauvoir's attention shifted to the other person in the photograph. The Baroness.

She was, by just about any measure, ugly. No way around that. With a round body and sagging spaniel eyes and a complexion that even in the old photo looked blotched.

But she was smiling and had a look of near-permanent amusement about her. There was a gleam in her eyes too. And Beauvoir found himself smiling back.

The Baroness, despite all appearances, was far more attractive than her husband.

Though there was also a slight haughtiness, a suggestion of cunning, in that face.

Hugo Baumgartner obviously took after her.

And Caroline Baumgartner? More the father than the mother, though the Baroness's haughtiness was there. But what passed for cunning in the mother came out as cruelty in the daughter.

The photographs were interesting—revealing, even, in some ways—but what he was really interested in was on the desk. Baumgartner's laptop.

"Finished?" he asked the agent who'd been sitting at the desk, going over the papers.

"Oui, patron."

He got up and relinquished the chair to the boss.

Beauvoir sat in front of the blank screen.

There were papers to the left of the computer. With numbers. And a few letters.

They weren't to Baumgartner but from him. Signed by him. Ready to be mailed out, presumably.

Beauvoir read one. It seemed a fairly standard explanation of investments and the state of the market.

The other papers looked like financial statements.

He opened the desk drawers. More paper. Stuffed in there.

"You've been over these?"

"Oui."

Beauvoir pulled the papers out and began going through them. The mess in the drawers was in contrast to the neat desktop. Many people's lives were like that. The neat room and the messy closet. The well-ordered counters and the chaos in the cabinets.

But he also knew that, as homicide detectives, what they were looking for often lived in that gap, between the public and the private.

As they went through Baumgartner's life, that cavern, between public and private, would begin to narrow. Squeezing out whatever lived inside.

Now Beauvoir scanned each piece of paper, smoothing out the wrinkled ones and placing them to the right of the laptop.

He was looking for one specific thing.

When he'd finished, he turned to the laptop and considered it.

Baumgartner, like most people, almost certainly protected his devices with a security code. His iPhone had been found that afternoon in the wreckage of his mother's home. Smashed. But there were hopes some information could still be retrieved.

Beauvoir knew that almost everyone did four things, when faced with modern technology. First they created passwords. Then they forgot them.

Then, on being forced to create new ones, they simplified and went with only one, which opened everything. And then they wrote it down. And hid that paper somewhere.

That way they only had to remember the place, not the password.

Beauvoir grunted as he got onto his knees, then lay on the carpet, staring at the underside of the desk. Nothing. Rolling over, he got to his feet.

"Did you find anything that might be a code for the laptop?" he asked the team.

"Nothing," the lead agent said.

"Well," said another, "there was one thing. There's a piece of paper behind the painting of the crazy old lady."

Beauvoir felt his heart speed up as he walked over to take a look. Sure enough, there was a piece of paper Scotch-taped back there. With a number. And the words "Virgin Mary."

"*Merde*," he whispered.

Beauvoir had learned enough about paintings, and the art world, to know this was a numbered print of the Virgin Mary. And that was the number.

Sitting back down at the desk, his eyes settled once again on the papers Baumgartner had left beside his laptop.

Getting up, he walked down the hall to the master bedroom.

"Agent Cloutier? Would you join me, please?"

"*D'accord, patron.*"

The woman, in her late forties, looked both relieved and worried to be called away by Chief Inspector Beauvoir.

"Hugo?" said Gamache.

"Yes?"

"You're being very quiet."

"I have nothing to add. My sister's doing a good job, as is Adrienne. I can't think of anyone who'd want to hurt Tony."

"What do you do for a living, monsieur?" Inspector Dufresne asked.

They'd already established that Caroline was a real-estate agent. Successful, she said. In the top five percent.

They'd later learn that was true. After a fashion. Top five percent in her company, in her area. Who specialized in condos. For young families.

Which put her in the bottom five percent of agents in Québec.

"I'm an investment dealer," said Hugo.

"The same as your brother?" Dufresne asked.

"Yes."

But Gamache had noticed the very slight hesitation and tucked it away.

"You worked together?"

"No. Different firms. I work for Horowitz Investments."

Gamache's expression didn't change, but he took this in.

This was the same firm he and Reine-Marie used for their investments. While Montréal based and founded by Monsieur Horowitz decades ago, it was now global, with offices in New York and Paris.

"And what do you do there, sir?" asked Dufresne.

"I'm a senior vice president. I have a portfolio of clients whose wealth I manage."

Hugo smiled, which, perversely, made him look even uglier. Like a jack-o'-lantern.

Without consciously realizing it, Gamache had put Hugo Baumgartner down as a bit of a rustic. If he worked at Horowitz Investments, it was in some support role, doing it affably, if somewhat lackadaisically.

Without ambition. Though perhaps not without resentment against a brother who'd fallen into a bucket of good luck at birth. While Oog had fallen into something else.

Gamache now smiled to himself. Humbled, yet again, by a mistake. How often had he warned agents against making assumptions? Leaping to conclusions.

And here he was, having done exactly that.

It never occurred to Gamache that this rough-hewn man might be a wealth manager, looking after tens of millions, perhaps hundreds of millions of dollars.

A phone call would have to be made.

But that was far down the list of things that occurred to the Chief Superintendent at that moment. Another question was forming, just as Beauvoir appeared down the hallway and caught his eye.

"A word?" Beauvoir mouthed.

Gamache was torn. He wanted, needed, to ask the question, but he also knew that Beauvoir would never interrupt unless it was important.

"*Excusez-moi*," said the Chief. He got up and nodded to Dufresne to continue.

"Find something?" Gamache asked as he accompanied Beauvoir down the hallway.

"I'll let Agent Cloutier explain."

Beauvoir's voice, while low, was excited.

Gamache turned the corner into the study and came face-to-face with maniacal Ruth. His brows rose, and then his gaze continued on, to the woman sitting at the desk.

She turned and immediately got up upon seeing Gamache.

"*Patron.*"

"Agent Cloutier." Gamache nodded. "Tell me what you have."

She was a fairly recent transfer from the financial division of the Sûreté. A bookkeeper. A bureaucrat. Not a field agent. Indeed, her accounting wasn't even forensic. She worked on the Sûreté's own budget.

But Chief Superintendent Gamache had been impressed with her, and after discussions with Chief Inspector Lacoste he'd arranged a temporary transfer to homicide. To see if it was a fit.

There was a whole division for financial crimes, but money, hidden or otherwise, was so often the motive for murder that Gamache felt it would help to have someone with financial expertise specifically assigned to homicide. And Lacoste had agreed.

Isabelle had been happy with Cloutier. Cloutier, though, had a very different reaction. Being called to a murder scene, or even being assigned to search a victim's home, was not simply foreign to her. She felt, at the age of forty-eight, as though she were experiencing an alien abduction.

She was not happy.

And even less so at this moment, as she faced the big boss. The head alien. Though he didn't look alien at all. But then, her whirring mind said, they so rarely did.

She had been grief-stricken, horrified by the raid that had so badly wounded her boss, Chief Inspector Lacoste.

She'd also been terrified at the thought that these things happened. That she herself could have been on that raid. Not realizing they'd have ordered the headquarters cat to arm up before they got to her.

But still. It was brought into stark relief that the Sûreté wasn't figures on a ledger. A matter of funding, or cutting, this department or that.

Lives were at stake. Lives were lost.

And she wanted nothing to do with taking or, worse still, giving a life.

She'd never met Chief Superintendent Gamache and had no idea he'd been behind her transfer and had been watching her progress, or lack thereof.

Gamache himself had had to admit that the transfer had not been a great success. It was clear she was unhappy, and a discontented agent never did her best work. Cloutier had been on the verge of being transferred back to the accounts department when the raid happened. And everything changed while, at the same time, staying the same.

The great Sûreté du Québec was in stasis until the leadership issue was resolved. For the moment Agent Cloutier was stuck. And Acting Chief Inspector Beauvoir was stuck with an agent who'd gnaw off her own arm if it would get her out of homicide and back into accounts.

But for now she was theirs. And there. In Baumgartner's home. Staring at the Chief Superintendent. Almost mute. But, sadly for her, not quite. A slight babbling was escaping her, an excruciatingly slow leak of lunacy.

Chief Superintendent Gamache saw this and tried to help, by guiding her.

"What did you find, Agent Cloutier? Was it in those papers?"

He pointed to the pile on the desk.

"Those and these." She pointed to the same stack of papers, confusing Gamache and herself. "Well, these are those, of course. Ha. Yes, well. Definitely something, but not definitive."

Inspector Beauvoir, watching this, sighed.

What he didn't know was that not that long ago Gamache himself had sounded almost exactly like Agent Cloutier, while on the phone to Vienna.

He might've sounded like an idiot, but Gamache knew he wasn't one. Just as he knew that Agent Cloutier wasn't.

"Is it to do with Anthony Baumgartner's personal finances?" Gamache threw her a lifeline.

He could see that the papers contained a lot of figures.

"Yes. No. I don't really know."

Now they all stared at one another, and Beauvoir thought maybe he should take away her gun. Not that she was likely to shoot anyone. Not on purpose. Really. Maybe.

Gamache smiled. "Let's sit."

He waved her to the comfortable chair behind the desk and dragged up two others for himself and Beauvoir.

"Now, Agent Cloutier, tell us what first caught your eye?"

"This." She picked up one of the papers before the laptop. "These look like financial statements, from Taylor and Ogilvy." Her voice was growing more confident. "I take it he worked for them?"

"*Oui.*"

"It's unusual, even unethical, for a money manager to bring home private and confidential papers," she said. "It's one thing to have them on a computer, which is protected by codes, but a printout? That anyone could read? I'm presuming Monsieur Baumgartner was senior enough to know that."

"Then why would he?" asked Gamache.

"I don't know for sure, of course," she said. "But there're two possible reasons. He was behind in his work and figured no one would notice or care. Or he was up to something."

"That something being . . . ?"

"Before I go into that, there's something else odd," she said. "About the papers."

She paused, letting her two *patrons* think about it.

"They're papers," said Beauvoir, getting there first. Getting it. "Wouldn't he be working directly on the laptop? On an electronic file?"

"You'd think so, yes. Assembling statements. Writing cover letters. Not working on hard copies."

"But I get my statements by mail," said Gamache. "Not emailed."

"Yes, for security most are still mailed out," she said. "Email can be hacked. But the mailing's the last step, normally done by an assistant. There's no reason for Monsieur Baumgartner to have the actual print-outs. And certainly not at home. They're of no use to him."

"No legitimate use," said Beauvoir.

"Exactly."

"So what's the illegitimate use?" Gamache asked.

"He'd have these statements here at home"—she looked toward the tidy pile on the desk beside the laptop—"because he didn't want any-one else to see them. And certainly not his assistant, who'd know immediately that something was up."

"And what was 'up'?" Beauvoir asked.

"Until I can get into his computer, I won't know for sure. But it's easy enough to see that they're addressed to different people and show portfolios in the millions. Transactions were done. Stocks bought and sold. These look like legitimate statements."

"But aren't?" said Gamache.

"They might be," she said. "But I'm not sure."

Chief Superintendent Gamache nodded. Financial crimes came under the Sûreté jurisdiction. Every year they uncovered a number of offenses. Some petty and downright stupid. Some close, but not quite crossing a line. A line Gamache had privately told the Premier should be changed.

Others, though, didn't so much cross the line as tunnel under it. Deep. Dark. Long-standing.

And when they were found, personal savings crumbled. Retirement funds disappeared. People were ruined. Often elderly people who could never recoup.

It was tragic and intentional. A fraud, a theft, committed not just over years but over lunches, dinners, weddings, bar mitzvahs, and chris-tenings. As the adviser. The accountant. The manager. Got closer and closer to the family. All the while stealing from them.

After all, who else could cheat you of everything except someone you never questioned?

Gamache stared at the papers, then at the blank screen. Then looked around the comfortable study.

Finally he got up.

"Call Taylor and Ogilvy," said Beauvoir, also getting to his feet, as did Agent Cloutier. "Find out what you can about Anthony Baumgartner. But be discreet."

"Yessir."

"And find out everything you can about Baumgartner's own finances. His accounts, hidden or otherwise."

"*Oui, patron.*" Her voice was crisp, efficient. Excited.

This she could do. And do well.

Gamache followed Beauvoir back to the living room.

When he'd been called away, Gamache had had one question he needed to ask. Now there were many.

CHAPTER 25

━━━

They stared at Chief Inspector Beauvoir as though he'd lost his mind.

As though, like Gamache earlier in the day, he'd lapsed into a language that did not actually exist.

"Tony?" said Adrienne. "Steal from clients?" She almost laughed. "Of course not."

She looked at Caroline and Hugo, who were also shaking their heads.

"You didn't know my brother," said Caroline. "He could never do such a thing. He volunteered at a hospice, for heaven's sake."

It was a non sequitur, though not altogether nonsense. Gamache knew the point she was trying to make.

Only a terrible person would steal from clients. Her brother did a beautiful thing by volunteering in a hospice. Hence he was not a terrible person.

It, of course, did not track. A shocking number of criminals were, in other areas of their lives, model citizens.

"Monsieur?" Beauvoir turned to Hugo Baumgartner.

Gamache was listening and watching. Paying close attention.

"I could believe it of myself before I could believe it of Tony," he said. "There's absolutely no way he'd do anything unethical, never mind criminal."

"Out of interest's sake." Beauvoir turned back to Caroline. "Before he came out, did you know he was gay?"

She shook her head, baffled by the change of topic.

Beauvoir looked at Adrienne and Hugo, who also shook their heads.

"Is it possible, then," he said quietly, "you don't know your brother as well as you thought?"

Caroline's cheeks reddened immediately, and Hugo looked, for the first time, angry.

"It's not the same thing," said Hugo. "One is nature and has no effect on character. The other is choice. People choose to break the law. They don't choose to be gay. Just because my brother was gay doesn't make him a criminal."

"I wasn't saying that, sir, and I suspect you know it," said Beauvoir, keeping his voice steady, though with a slight inflection of annoyance. "The point I was making is that your brother was very good at keeping secrets. He led two private lives, why not two professional ones? And would you even know?"

"Then why did you ask?" asked Adrienne.

But Gamache knew the answer to that. Beauvoir asked because he knew that the answer would tell them more about the family than about the victim.

Hugo glanced down the corridor. Then back at Beauvoir.

"You found something in his study, didn't you? Let me see. I can straighten you out. Explain anything that might look odd or incriminating."

Chief Inspector Beauvoir considered for a moment, then said, "Come with me."

They all did. Caroline leading the pack.

"A moment, madame." Beauvoir stopped her from entering the study.

Going in first, he had a word with Agent Cloutier, who was on the phone. She nodded, then left the room.

Caroline and Hugo entered with Beauvoir, but Adrienne stopped at the doorway, not realizing, perhaps, that Gamache stood behind her.

This was Anthony Baumgartner's private space. His sanctuary. The well-worn leather chair in front of the fireplace had taken on his form. There was the laptop on his desk. The books on the shelves. The photos of private family moments and of business triumphs.

This room even looked like him. Elegant. Masculine. Comfortable. Slightly playful, with the orange shag rug.

Watching her sag, Gamache was struck by how much this woman

really did love this man. It was, he thought, the sort of intense love that could curve back on itself and turn to hate.

"Is this all you have?" asked Hugo, pointing to the papers beside the laptop.

"It is," said Beauvoir, not cowed by the tone.

"He was working on his clients' accounts," said Hugo. "That's all."

"At home?" asked Beauvoir.

"Well, it's unusual," admitted Hugo. "But you could just as easily conclude that he was hyper-responsible. Doing things for his clients in his own time. This isn't evidence of any crime. Just the opposite."

"Why paper?"

"Pardon?"

"If he was working on a client's statement, wouldn't he do it on the computer?"

"Some people prefer a printout," said Hugo. "Especially those of us who are older. I often have spreadsheets printed out. Easier to study them."

"Spreadsheets, yes," said Beauvoir. "But not a statement. Is that fair?"

Hugo shrugged. "We all have our systems. How you can look at these few pages and decide my brother was stealing, is . . . well, I have to say, unfair. He's the victim. Not the criminal."

"*Merci, monsieur,*" said Beauvoir. "Now the laptop. Do you know his password?"

The Baumgartners looked at each other and shook their heads.

"The children's names?" suggested Adrienne.

"The house number?" said Caroline.

Without realizing it, Beauvoir suspected they'd just given away their own codes.

Once again Hugo was silent. But his eyes kept returning to the pile of statements.

"I have a question," said Gamache from the doorway, and he saw Adrienne startle at the sound of his voice behind her.

"Your accounts." He looked at Caroline. "Who has them now?"

It was the question he'd wanted to ask for a while, and now he watched her closely.

There was a long pause.

"They're with me, Chief Superintendent," said Hugo.

"Why did you really take your money from Anthony?" Gamache continued to look at Caroline. "You said it was because you didn't want to mix family and business. That obviously wasn't true."

"Hugo and I have always been closer," she said. "It felt natural."

"And that would make sense if you'd started with Hugo, but you didn't. Your money was first with Anthony, but something made you take it away from him. What was it?"

His voice was reasonable. Not betraying the fact he'd just cornered her.

"Anthony and I had a falling-out," she said.

"About what?"

"Does it matter?" asked Hugo.

"Do you know why she moved her money from your brother to you?" Gamache asked, turning his considerable attention to Hugo, who immediately regretted saying anything.

"It was her decision. I had nothing to do with it. And I certainly didn't poach her."

"That wasn't my question," said Gamache. Though it was an interesting answer.

"Sir?"

Agent Cloutier had returned. She was holding her phone to her palm, muffling any sound.

"Not now," said Beauvoir. "Wait for us in the living room."

"Yessir."

She left, holding the phone in front of her as though it might explode in her hands.

"Now." Beauvoir turned back to the Baumgartners. "Chief Superintendent Gamache asked you a question."

"I don't know why the account was transferred to me," said Hugo.

"You didn't ask?" asked Gamache. Then he turned to Caroline. "You didn't tell him?" He stared at her. "Of course you did. We're going to find out. Probably best we hear it from you."

"You tell him," Caroline said to Hugo. "You can explain it."

"Fine." Hugo took a deep breath. "It wasn't a falling-out. That's just what we told anyone who asked. Three years ago my brother had his license to trade suspended."

"Why?" asked Beauvoir.

"The man he'd been having the affair with was the assistant to a senior partner. That assistant stole money from some clients. Tony caught it and told the firm. The money was put back, the assistant fired, and Tony was kept on, but they suspended his license."

"Why? If he'd done nothing wrong?"

Beauvoir glanced at Gamache, who was quietly listening.

"Exactly, Inspector," said Adrienne. "Exactly what we thought. He'd done everything right, but still they came down on him."

"Why?" asked Beauvoir again.

Hugo was shaking his head and shrugged. He was slouched over and looked less like a garden gnome and more like a gargoyle.

"As with most things, it was political. Internal politics in his company. The partner didn't want to be accused of using bad judgment in hiring the assistant, so they shifted the blame to Tony. Said it was gross negligence. That he'd given the assistant information on clients that he shouldn't have."

"By having printouts at home?" suggested Beauvoir.

"I don't know. All I know is that they made an example of him."

"So he was punished?" asked Beauvoir.

"Yes. After that his career was pretty much over, at least internally. He'd never be promoted to partner. Tony stayed on the accounts, but the trades were done by someone else in the firm. He'd done nothing wrong, but still they suspended and humiliated him."

Again Beauvoir glanced quickly at Gamache, to see his reaction to this. Then away.

"And that's why you moved your accounts?" Beauvoir asked Caroline.

"I didn't want to, but Anthony insisted. He thought they were better with Hugo, who could both advise and trade."

"And were they?" Gamache asked. Seeing the blank look on Caroline's face, he clarified. "Better?"

"I think so," she said, glancing at Hugo.

"My brother knew the market well, Chief Superintendent. The truth is, while I'm good, Tony was better. It was shitty that his license to trade was pulled."

"Did he see it that way?" asked Beauvoir. "Did he hold a grudge?"

"No," said Hugo. "He was grateful to the partners for being discreet.

They could've made a public announcement. They could've fired him. I thought they were shits, but Tony was loyal."

"*Merci*," said Beauvoir. "Was your brother in a relationship right now?"

"Not that I know of," said Caroline.

"Do you know this Bernard's last name?"

They shook their heads.

"The less I knew about him the better," said Adrienne when Beauvoir turned to her.

"Is there anything we should know? Anyone you can think of who might've wanted Monsieur Baumgartner gone?"

They thought about that and again shook their heads.

"You stayed behind with your brother after the reading of the will," Gamache said to Hugo. "Is that right?"

"Yes. We often had dinner together. Two bachelors. I brought the wine and Tony cooked."

He lowered his eyes, perhaps, Gamache thought, the reality of his brother's death and all that had changed being brought home to him.

"What did you talk about?"

Hugo threw his mind back. In time it wasn't all that long ago, but measured in events, it was an eternity.

"We talked about Mom. About the Baroness. She was a one-off." Hugo gave his pumpkin grin. "We talked about how much we miss her."

"I do too," said Caroline.

But her voice spoke more about herself than of any affection for her mother. About a need to be included and, perhaps more crucial, a fear of being left out. Left behind.

"What time did you leave?" asked Beauvoir.

"It was an early dinner. I was home by eight," said Hugo.

"Did he mention wanting to go to your mother's house?"

"No, though we talked about whether it should be saved or not. You think that's why he went there?"

"Could be," said Beauvoir.

He handed them one of his cards with the standard request that they call should they think of anything.

Then he asked for their keys to the house.

They looked surprised. Then not surprised. And handed them over.

After the Baumgartners left, Beauvoir and Gamache joined Agent Cloutier in the living room.

"She hung up," said Cloutier. "But said I could call back when you were ready."

She made the call and handed the phone to Beauvoir.

"*Bonjour?* Madame Ogilvy? This is Chief Inspector Beauvoir. I'm the head of homicide for the Sûreté du Québec. Yes, it is about Anthony Baumgartner."

He explained briefly what she would soon see in the news anyway. Then asked the question.

"He had papers at home?" asked Madame Ogilvy. "Statements? Hard copies?"

"Yes. Can you think why?"

She paused before answering, "No."

"I think you can, madame. I'll let you consider the question a little longer. Can we meet tomorrow? I'll bring the statements and letters with me."

Before he hung up, Gamache touched his arm and whispered something.

"One more question," said Beauvoir. "Do you have any clients named Kinderoth?"

"We have thousands of clients, Chief Inspector."

"Can you look it up?"

"Our clients' names are confidential."

"We can get a court order."

"I don't mean to be difficult, but I'm afraid you're going to have to."

Beauvoir rolled his eyes but could tell there was no arguing. If and when it became known that she'd given out confidential information, Madame Ogilvy would have to prove it was forced from her.

Everyone covers their asses, Beauvoir knew.

"Seems there's a lot of that going around," said Beauvoir once they were back in the car.

"What's that?" asked his father-in-law.

"Suspending people who've done nothing wrong. Shifting blame."

There was a slight grunt of amusement beside him.

This was Jean-Guy's form of apology. For being abrupt with Gamache. For allowing the man from the Ministère de la Justice, Francis Cournoyer, to get into his head.

He now suspected that had been the whole purpose of the meeting. Everyone else, everything else, were all just props. Extras.

The quiet man in the corner was the lead. And Beauvoir was the audience.

He felt ashamed of himself for letting it happen. For even once believing that when Cournoyer had said, "Ask Gamache," it was anything other than, as Isabelle had put it, a mindfuck in a public toilet.

Gamache turned to him and smiled. "You do know that all the things I'm accused of doing, I did. I admitted it. Freely. But, unlike Monsieur Baumgartner, I'm not likely to keep my job."

Now it was Beauvoir's breath that hung in the air. Hung in the silence.

"What do you mean?"

"When this suspension is lifted, I won't be returning as Chief Superintendent."

"You can't know that."

"I do. There can't possibly be a head of the Sûreté who's broken the law."

Beauvoir stared straight ahead and let that sink in. The heater, on full blast, had melted the frost off the windshield, and although he put the car in gear, his foot remained on the brake.

"The fact Anthony Baumgartner kept his job," said Gamache, "doesn't mean he didn't do it. It's possible that young assistant took the fall for him. Not the other way around. Who are the partners more likely to protect? A young man barely starting out or a vice president of the company?"

"And you?"

"Me?"

"Is there more happening than you're telling me?" Beauvoir asked.

Ask Gamache. Despite himself, Beauvoir had just done as Cournoyer suggested.

"Where did that come from?" Gamache asked. "Is that what's been bothering you? Has someone said something?"

"Is there?"

"If there is, I'm as much in the dark as you. This is political. We both know that. But how high up it goes and what the purpose is, I don't know. What I do know is that it doesn't matter."

"Doesn't it?"

"No. All that matters is getting the drugs back. That's it. My punishment for releasing them goes far beyond anything a disciplinary committee can possibly do."

Jean-Guy could see that was true, and already happening. He could see the punishing weight of responsibility. Of guilt. Of fear.

He could sense the anxiety growing to near panic as the Chief struggled to find the last of the drugs.

It was evident in the lines at the mouth. Between the brows. The hands that even in casual conversation were clenched, as though in pain.

That bullet's left the barrel, Cournoyer had said. And now Beauvoir could see it had reached its target.

"We'll find it, *patron*."

"We have to."

It was said with cold determination, and Jean-Guy wondered at the lengths Gamache would go to to get the drugs back. But then he remembered their conversation. About Amelia Choquet. And he stopped wondering.

"Home?" Beauvoir asked, pointing the car in the direction of Three Pines.

"A home, for sure," said Gamache. "But not ours quite yet."

Half an hour later, they were at the Maison Saint-Rémy.

The head nurse greeted them and invited the Sûreté officers into her office.

"What can I help you with? You say you're with the police?"

She spoke English, and the two officers quickly switched languages. As they'd waited for her at the front desk, Beauvoir had picked up a brochure and noted that this was an English seniors' home. One of the few where services were primarily English.

Even those who were bilingual preferred, at the end of their lives, to live it out in the tongue they'd learned from their mothers.

"*Oui*," said Beauvoir. "We'd like to know about the death of Bertha Baumgartner."

"The Duchess?"

"The Baroness," said Gamache.

"Why? Is something wrong?"

"We just need a few questions answered," said Beauvoir. "What did she die of?"

The head nurse turned to her computer and, after a moment, replied, "Heart failure." She took off her glasses and turned back to them. "Vague, I realize. It's almost always heart failure. Unless the family asks for an autopsy, that's what the doctor writes. The people here are elderly and frail. Their hearts just stop."

"Was it expected?" Beauvoir asked.

"Well, it's almost always expected, and yet a surprise. She wasn't sick. She just went to bed and didn't wake up. It's the way most of us hope to go."

"Did she have many visitors?"

"Her sons and daughter would come, but they work and it's difficult." Beauvoir heard what was unsaid. They did not visit often.

"They called her often, though," said the head nurse. "Unlike some here, Madame Baumgartner clearly had a family who cared. They just couldn't visit as often as they might have liked."

"And the day she died?"

"I'd have to look it up."

"Please do," said Gamache, and they followed her to the reception desk, where there was a sign-in book.

Flipping back, she came to the date. It was empty.

"Joseph?" she called to a middle-aged man, who went over. "These men are with the Sûreté. They're asking about Madame Baumgartner."

"The Countess?"

"The Baroness," said Beauvoir, barely believing he was defending the title. "You're at the front desk?"

"*Oui*."

"Did she have many visitors?"

"*Non*. Her family every now and then. Mostly on weekends. And the young woman, of course. She always made it a point to see her."

"Young woman?" asked Beauvoir. "Do you have her name?"

226

"Yes, of course," said the nurse, walking back to her office. "She's the one we called when the Empress—"

"Baroness," said Gamache.

"—died. Yes, here it is." She was at her computer once again. "Katie Burke."

"Can you spell that, please?" asked Beauvoir, pulling out his notebook.

He couldn't see how the natural death of an elderly woman in what appeared to be a well-run and caring seniors' home could possibly have anything to do with her son's murder a month or more later. Still, he took down the information she gave him.

"Why did you call her when Madame Baumgartner died?" asked Gamache. "Is it that you couldn't reach the family?"

"We didn't try."

"Why not?"

"Because Mademoiselle Burke's name was at the top of the contact list. Ahead of her children."

CHAPTER 26

—⁓—

"So, numbnuts, where's your boss?"

"He's at home, babysitting Ray-Ray," said Jean-Guy, passing the salad bowl to Olivier, who was sitting next to him at Clara's long kitchen table.

The fact he'd actually begun answering to "numbnuts" was a little worrisome to Beauvoir, though he'd been called worse. By murderers. Psychopaths. Ruth.

"Babysitting? Just the job for a fourteen-year-old girl," said Ruth. "He's reached his level of competence, I see."

When Clara's invitation for dinner came, Beauvoir at first thought to beg off. He was tired, and it was dark and cold.

He'd assigned an inspector to find this Katie Burke, then settled down to read the reports that were coming in. He'd head back to Montréal and the office first thing in the morning. But for now all he wanted was to put his feet up and nod off by the fire.

But then Annie had whispered the magic words.

Coq au vin.

There was a wild rumor, racing through the Gamache home, that Olivier had made his famous casserole and was taking it to Clara's.

"Don't toy with me, madame."

"And for dessert? Salted," she whispered again, her breath fresh and warm, "caramel—"

"Nooo," he moaned.

"—and burnt-fig ice cream."

"Okay, I'm in," he said, getting up. "You coming?" he called into the study as he made his way to the front door.

When there was no answer, he backed up.

"Patron?"

Armand was peering at the computer, a book open beside it on the desk.

"What're you doing?"

"Trying to translate something, isn't that right, *mein Liebling*?"

He held Honoré on his knee as he read, consulted, blinked to clear his bleary eyes, and wrote longhand in a notebook.

"Coq au vin," said Reine-Marie, joining Jean-Guy at the door.

"Ahh, so the rumor is true," said Armand. "But we already have dinner plans, don't we?" He looked at his grandson. "Sweet potatoes. Yum. Maybe some avocado. Yum-yum. Some gray stuff that they say is meat." He looked up then. "You all head off, we'll be fine. Eh, *meyn tayer.*"

"There you are," said Annie. Her coat already on, she came over and kissed her son. "Don't let him get into any mischief, now."

"You're talking to Honoré, aren't you?" said her father.

"I am."

"You sure you don't want to bring him to Clara's?" asked Reine-Marie.

"Non, merci," said Armand. "We have a full evening planned. Dinner. A bath. A movie. A book. Some all-star wrestling—"

"Were you planning on putting him to bed at any stage?" asked Jean-Guy.

"Eventually. Maybe."

"Dad," said Annie.

"Okay, but we will read a book, right?" he asked the boy. "And I'll recite 'The Wreck of the Hesperus': 'It was the schooner Hesperus, / That sailed the wintry sea—'"

"Dear God," said Jean-Guy. "Flee. *Sauve qui peut.*"

"What about Honoré?" asked Annie in mock terror.

"We can make more. Run, woman, run."

Armand rolled his eyes as Reine-Marie laughed and wondered what would happen if anyone ever called Armand's bluff and realized that all he knew of the dreadful poem were the opening lines.

"Work?" She nodded toward the computer.

"A bit."

"Want me to stay?" Jean-Guy asked.

"And miss coq au vin?"

"Ruth will be there. Sorta evens out."

"Myrna's made her whipped potatoes," said Reine-Marie.

"You're on your own," Jean-Guy said to Armand just as a rush of cold air hit them.

Annie, Reine-Marie, and Jean-Guy turned and shouted, "Close the door."

It was a chorus more familiar than the national anthem.

"Man, it's cold out there," they heard, along with foot stomping. "And this one," Armand could hear Benedict saying, "takes her sweet time doing her business."

Armand smiled. Benedict couldn't bring himself to say "poop" or even "pee." He knew the young man was referring to Gracie, and he sympathized. He'd spent many a cold night begging the little creature to do something, other than chase Henri.

Benedict had taken it upon himself, in exchange for room and board while he waited for his truck to return, to walk the dogs.

Armand felt this left them owing Benedict.

"I'll bring you back something," said Reine-Marie, kissing the top of Honoré's head before putting her hands on the side of Armand's face and kissing him on the lips and whispering, *"Meyn tayer."*

He smiled.

"Is that German?" she asked, glancing at the screen.

"It is. Taking me a while to read it."

"Your eyes still sore?" she asked, looking into them and seeing the bloodshot.

"My German is a little rusty," he said.

"Rusty. Is that German for 'nonexistent'?"

He laughed. "Just about."

She looked at the screen again. "It's long. Who's it from?"

"A police officer in Vienna."

She tied the scarf at her neck. "See you soon."

"Have fun."

He returned to his computer, leaning over Ray-Ray and smelling his fragrance as he read about a family ripping itself apart.

Jean-Guy looked at the tender pieces of chicken along with mushrooms and rich, fragrant gravy, next to the mountain of potatoes.

Whipped, Myrna insisted. Not just mashed.

He was so hungry he thought he might weep.

"So it's true, then," said Ruth. "The Baroness's son was murdered."

Jean-Guy had told Clara and Myrna as soon as they'd arrived for dinner, taking them aside quietly. And word had spread, of course, as others arrived at Clara's home.

"I thought you were lying," said Ruth to Myrna.

"Why would I lie about that?"

"Why do you say your library is a bookstore?" asked Ruth. "Lying is just natural to you."

"It is a bookstore," said Myrna, exasperated. "Don't think I don't see you taking books out under your coat."

"Oh, there's a lot you don't see," said Ruth.

"Like what?"

"Like Billy Williams."

"I see him. He shovels my walk and brushes off my car."

"Doesn't brush off my car," mumbled Clara, and catching Olivier's eye, they both grinned.

"What's that supposed to mean?" asked Myrna. "He's a nice man, that's all."

"Then why isn't he here?" asked Ruth.

"Here?" said Myrna, looking around. "Why would he be here? Does something need fixing?" she asked Clara.

"I'd have to say yes," said Ruth, and Rosa beside her nodded.

"Let's change the subject," said Reine-Marie.

"Well, if murder's out," said Ruth, "and the librarian here being prejudiced is something we're not allowed to talk about—"

"Prejudiced? I'm not—"

"I saw one of your paintings today," Jean-Guy leaped in, spouting the first thing that came into his head.

"You are prejudiced, you know," said Ruth. "You only see the surface and then pass judgment. Billy Williams is just a handyman."

"One of my paintings? Really?" asked Clara. "Where?"

"A print, actually," said Jean-Guy. "One of the numbered prints."

"And who's calling the kettle black?" demanded Myrna. "Did you see the Baroness as anything other than a cleaning woman? Did you even know her name?"

"Isn't it about time you proposed to Gabri?" Annie asked Olivier, jumping onto the conversational pile. "We're all waiting."

"You're waiting?" said Gabri. "If he waits much longer, I won't be able to fit into my going-away outfit."

"And there's your answer," said Olivier.

"You don't have to know someone's name to care about them," said Ruth.

"And you cared?" said Myrna. "Did you even know she'd died?"

"I saw your painting at Anthony Baumgartner's place," said Jean-Guy, raising his voice.

"The dead man?" asked Clara.

"Hey, I thought we weren't allowed to talk about murder," said Ruth. "That's not fair."

"We're not talking about murder," said Jean-Guy. "I'm talking about art."

"You?" Annie, Gabri, Olivier, Clara, Myrna, Ruth, and even Reine-Marie said. As one.

Rosa looked startled. But then ducks often did. And often for good reason.

"What?" said Jean-Guy. "I'm cultured."

"With a capital K," said Annie, patting his hand.

"That's right," he said. "*Merci.*"

They laughed, then Myrna turned to Ruth.

"I'm sorry I snapped at you about the Baroness. But that's a terrible thing to say about someone. That they're prejudiced."

"Not 'they,'" said Ruth. "You. Just because you're a pot, that doesn't mean you can't—"

"I'm a what?"

"Which painting did he have?" asked Reine-Marie.

"The one of—" Jean-Guy jerked his head toward Ruth. "Not the original, of course."

"No, we have the good fortune of having the original here," said Reine-Marie.

"I meant not the original painting," said Jean-Guy.

"Did you?" said Reine-Marie, and she smiled.

"Oh that's right," said Clara. "I gave that print to the Baroness. I'd forgotten."

"Annie's not wrong, you know," said Gabri to Olivier. "You'd better pop the question soon if you want a dewy husband. I'm not going to be thirty-seven forever."

"Well, you have been thirty-seven for quite a while now," said Olivier.

"I guess she gave it to her son," said Clara. "It's just tragic. Do you have any idea who killed him? Oh, sorry, not dinner-table conversation."

Though it wouldn't be the first time a murder had been discussed around that table, by those people, in the flickering candlelight.

"Well, Ray-Ray," Armand murmured as he took his reading glasses off and wiped his hand over his weary eyes. "What do you make of that?"

They'd had dinner and a bath, and now they were on the sofa in the living room in front of the fireplace. Armand reading his rough translation of the Kontrollinspektor's email. Honoré, in his favorite bear pajamas, was lying in the crook of his grandfather's arm, with Henri on the sofa on one side and Gracie on the other.

Honoré knew exactly what to make of that. While not understanding the words that were spoken, he understood the deep, warm resonance coming from his grandfather's body. Each word radiating into him.

So that they were in tune.

And it was a nice tune.

He gripped the large hand holding him securely and felt a soft pat. And a kiss planted on his head.

And he smelled the familiar scent. Of Papa.

While Papa read about a reason for murder.

And then Armand put down his notebook and carried Honoré upstairs to bed, where he picked up *Winnie-the-Pooh*. And Honoré fell asleep listening to the adventures of Tigger and Roo and Piglet and Pooh. And Christopher Robin. In the Hundred Acre Wood.

"It still gives me goose bumps," said Reine-Marie, looking at the original oil painting in Clara's studio.

"Almost gave me a heart attack," said Jean-Guy. "When I saw Ruth in Baumgartner's home. Hovering above his fireplace."

"There must be a lot of these out there," said Reine-Marie. "It was your big success. Your breakout work."

"Nah, the gallery hardly sold any," said Clara, contemplating her masterwork. "Though they did print lots. People love looking at it. And then they like leaving. Really, who wants that"—she jerked her spoon, with ice cream on it, toward the easel—"in their home?"

"Apparently Anthony Baumgartner," said Jean-Guy.

All three looked at the rancid old woman in the painting, then leaned back and looked out the doorway of Clara's studio, into the kitchen, at the rancid old woman at the table.

Ruth was still arguing with Myrna. This time, it seemed, about how choux pastry should be made.

"And that's why they call them loafers," they heard the old woman say.

"Like a loaf of bread? Really?" said Benedict.

"No, not really," said Myrna. "It's c-h-o-u-x. Not shoe. Or loafer."

"Well, that doesn't make any sense."

They returned to the painting leaning against the wall of the studio.

"I wonder what it says about the dead man," said Reine-Marie. "That he was drawn to this particular painting."

"Besides that he had great taste in art?" asked Clara.

"But he wasn't drawn to it," said Jean-Guy. "His mother was. You said that she's the one who wanted it. Then she gave it to him."

"But he hung it," said Reine-Marie. "He didn't just put it away in the basement."

"True." Jean-Guy continued to stare at Ruth on canvas. "Do you think the Baroness understood what the painting's about? Not bitterness but hope."

They looked at him in undisguised—and fairly insulting, he felt—surprise. Annie came over and put her arm around his slightly thickening waist.

"We'll make an art aficionado of you yet," she said.

"Aficionado," he said. "That's a type of Italian ice cream, isn't it? I think what you meant to say is an art gelato."

"And I think you're in the wrong conversation," said Annie. "I believe the one you want is over there."

She pointed to the trio of Myrna, Ruth, and Benedict. Who were now discussing the difference between semaphore and petit four.

"No thank you," said Jean-Guy. "Besides, I already know all I need to about art. Chiaroscuro." He said the word triumphantly, as though opening the Olympic Games or launching a ship. "That's it. My one word of artspeak, but it impresses the pants off people."

"What was that word again?" asked Gabri from the freezer, where he was getting more ice cream.

"Please don't tell him," said Olivier.

"Are there any leftovers? I'd like to take some home to Armand," asked Reine-Marie, walking over to the kitchen.

Olivier pointed to a container on the island, filled with coq au vin and whipped potatoes. "All ready for you."

"*Merci, mon beau.*"

"So," Ruth was saying to Benedict, "if anyone offers you a semaphore, don't eat it."

"But a petit four?"

"You give that to me."

Benedict was nodding, and both Myrna and Rosa were staring, glassy-eyed, at them.

Jean-Guy tapped Benedict on the shoulder. "Come and help me do the dishes."

While Jean-Guy washed, Benedict dried.

"Why did you lie?" Beauvoir asked quietly.

"About what?" asked Benedict, taking a warm, wet glass.

"About your girlfriend."

"Oh. That."

"Tell me the truth," said Jean-Guy.

"Does it matter?" asked Benedict.

"This is a murder investigation. Everything matters. Especially lies."

"But the man who died has nothing to do with me."

"Do you really believe that?" asked Beauvoir. "You're a liquidator on a will in which he was a major heir. It was read just hours before he was murdered. His body was found in an abandoned home where you were also found. You were there when he was there."

He let those words sink in.

"But I didn't know that," said Benedict.

"And how do I know you're not lying now? Again?" He watched the young man's face. "And now you see why lies matter. The actual fib might not matter, but what it shows us is that what you say can't always be trusted. You can't always be trusted."

"But I can," he said, his cheeks a fluorescent red now. "I don't lie. Not normally. But I . . . I hate saying it out loud."

"What?"

"That she left me. That we broke up. It's too soon."

"It's been a couple of months."

"How do you know that?"

"I'm the acting head of homicide for the Sûreté du Québec," said Jean-Guy, handing a soapy plate to Benedict. "Do you really think we wouldn't ask questions about you?"

"Then you've gotta know my relationship has nothing to do with what happened."

"Doesn't it? You lied again to Monsieur Gamache when he asked why you went to the farmhouse last night. You said you missed your girlfriend and wanted to go home. But that wasn't true, was it?"

Benedict concentrated on the glass he was drying.

"It is true, sorta. You wouldn't know what it's like, to have your heart broken and then to be around people who're happy."

He looked at Jean-Guy.

"You. Your wife. Ray-Ray. Monsieur and Madame Gamache. You have what I want, what I wanted. And lost. I couldn't take it anymore. It hurt too much. I had to leave."

Benedict's eyes were wide. Pleading.

For what? Jean-Guy wondered. *Understanding? Forgiveness?*

No, he thought. *He wants what I wanted, when I was heartbroken. He wants me to stop poking the wound.*

"I understand," he said. "No more lies, right?"

"I promise."

Beauvoir turned to face the young man and stared him squarely in the eyes.

"Why do you think Madame Baumgartner put you on as a liquidator of her will?"

"I don't know."

"You must've thought about it. Come on, Benedict. Why would she do that? You must've known her."

"I didn't. I swear. I never met the woman. The Baroness. You can give me a lie detector. Do they still do lie detectors? I should ask Ruth."

Beauvoir sighed. "She's a lie manufacturer. She knows nothing about detecting them."

"But if you make something, wouldn't you normally recognize them?" asked Benedict.

It was, Jean-Guy had to admit, insightful. And true. Ruth was an expert in lies. It was the truth that sometimes eluded her. And, perhaps, eluded this pleasant young man.

Across the room, Clara was watching the conversation between Jean-Guy and Benedict.

"What're you thinking?" Reine-Marie asked her.

"That I'd like to paint that young man."

"Why?"

"There's something about him. He's both transparent and . . . what's the word?"

"Dense?" ventured Reine-Marie.

Clara laughed. "Well, yes. And yet . . ."

And yet, thought Reine-Marie, watching her houseguest. *And yet not.*

As they left, Ruth handed Jean-Guy a gift.

"A poetry book," she said. "One you might appreciate. But don't read it to my godson."

"Why not?" he asked, his eyes narrowing.

"You'll see."

"One of yours?" Annie asked, looking at the gift, wrapped in old newspaper.

"No."

"One of mine?" asked Myrna.

"None of your business," said Ruth.

"I bet it is my business," muttered Myrna as she put her boots on.

At the door the two women embraced and Myrna offered to walk Ruth home.

"We'll see her home," said Olivier.

Out of the darkness, just as she closed the door against the biting cold, Clara heard Gabri say, "Oh look. An ice floe. Come on, Ruth. It has your name on it."

"Fag."

"Hag."

And a sleepy, soft "Fuck, fuck, fuck" as the door closed.

Armand greeted them at the door.

"Have fun?"

"Ruth was there," said Jean-Guy.

Armand smiled. Understanding.

"You've probably already eaten," said Reine-Marie. "But in case you're still hungry."

She offered him the container.

"Oh you savior. I'm starving." Armand kissed his wife and took the container into the kitchen.

"Did you manage to translate the email?" Jean-Guy asked.

"Yes, I think so. At least the gist of it."

"Which was?"

Armand was about to tell him but could see that Annie was waiting for her husband to join her.

"I'll tell you in the morning. Do you mind if I drive into Montréal with you?"

It was meant to be a rhetorical question, but, to his surprise, Jean-Guy hesitated.

"I don't have to," said Armand. "I'm sure someone else—"

"*Non, non,* of course I'll drive you. It's just that I'm not coming back out, and I have an early meeting. We'll have to leave here early."

"I can drive you in, sir," said Benedict. He'd had his head in the fridge and now came out with pie. "If you don't mind my using your car. I really need fresh clothes and should check on the apartment building. Then I can drive you back out. My truck might be ready by then."

"That would be perfect," said Armand. "*Merci.*"

"Why're you going in?" asked Reine-Marie.

"I'm having lunch with Stephen Horowitz." He turned to Jean-Guy. "Horowitz Investments."

Jean-Guy nodded. Hugo Baumgartner's firm.

Annie and Jean-Guy said their good-nights, and Benedict took a huge slice of pie and a glass of milk to his room.

"Anthony Baumgartner must've been an interesting man," said Reine-Marie as the leftover coq au vin warmed up.

"Why do you say that?"

"Well, because Jean-Guy told us that he had Clara's painting in his study."

"Yes. Quite unexpected."

Armand thought about the email he'd spent the evening translating.

Like the painting, it was infused with bitterness. But there was also hope. Though a different kind from the one in Clara's painting.

This was hope of revenge. Of retribution. It reeked of greed. And delusion. And profound optimism that something horrible would happen to someone else.

And it had.

Hope itself wasn't necessarily kind. Or a good thing.

Armand wondered what Baumgartner saw when he stood in front of the painting and looked into the eyes of the Virgin.

Did he see redemption or permission to be bitter?

Maybe, in that face, he saw his own mother. Glaring down at him.

In all her madness and delusion, disappointment and entitlement.

Maybe he saw what happens when false hope is spread over generations.

Maybe that's why he liked it.

Maybe he saw himself.

240

"You go to bed," he said to Reine-Marie. "I'll be along soon. Still have a little work to do."

"So late?"

"Well, Honoré wanted to watch the second *Terminator* movie, and then we visited the casino, so there wasn't much time to work."

"You're a silly, silly man," she said, kissing him. Her thumb traced the deep furrow of scar at his temple. "Don't be late."

She took her tea with her but left behind the delicate scent of chamomile and old garden roses, mingled with the rich, earthy aroma of coq au vin. Armand stood in the kitchen and closed his eyes. Then, opening them again, he headed to his study.

Henri and Gracie followed and curled up under the desk. Armand put in his password and saw that the photos and video he'd opened had finally downloaded.

Amelia and Marc had parted ways early.

It was dark now. The time when hungry people slipped out of tenements and rooming houses. On the hunt.

She'd gone from alley to back street, to parking lot, to abandoned building. Saying the same thing. Over and over.

"I'm looking for David."

A few times she thought she saw a flicker of interest, of recognition, but when pressed—"Where is he? How can I find him?"—the person turned away.

She'd attracted, though, a group of mostly young women. Some prostitutes. Some transsexuals. Most hard-core junkies. Who'd steal, suck, tug anything for a hit.

They came to her because she didn't ask anything of them. And she could fight. Had fought. And won.

They didn't know it was possible. To fight back.

But now they did.

Armand looked at the photos of Amelia taken just a few hours earlier.

They were shot from a distance.

He could see that in one of them she was making a gesture. Grabbing her forearm in what he assumed was a fairly common curse. He could imagine what was also coming out of her mouth.

He looked closer.

She was grubby. Hair unwashed. Clothes dirty. The lower part of her jeans was soaked in slush.

He tried but couldn't see her eyes. Her pupils.

Then he clicked on the video.

"You know, don't you, you shithead," she snarled. "Where's David?"

"Why do you want him?"

"None of your fucking business. Tell me or I'll break your arm."

The dealer turned away.

A semicircle of young women stood behind Amelia. They were barely more than girls.

"Don't you turn your goddamned back on me."

Amelia moved swiftly. Much quicker than the stoned dealer could react. She pushed him into the wall. Then, grabbing his arm, she twisted it behind his back. Jerking it up in a quick, practiced movement.

He let out a shriek that scattered those around. The onlookers scampering away.

The man, barely more than a boy, slid to the ground, weeping. His arm hung at a terrible angle. Useless.

"Next it's your leg. Then your neck," said Amelia.

She squatted beside him and slid the sleeve of her jacket up, exposing her forearm.

"David. Where's David?"

Armand moved this way and that, as though changing his vantage point would let him see better.

But her body was blocking it, and despite the fact there was sound in the recording, her back was to him and he couldn't hear very well.

He did see her get up, and with her foot she pushed the man over.

He heard him cry out. Then Amelia, and her gang, left the picture. The young men who'd stood with the dealer now turned away. And followed Amelia.

Armand narrowed his eyes and scowled. Then went back to the beginning of the video and watched again and again. Until something caught his attention.

He froze the frame. Then enlarged it. As he did, the image grew less and less defined. But still he zoomed in. Closer and closer.

And brought his face closer and closer to his screen, until his nose was almost touching it.

She wasn't just making a gesture with her forearm. That arm, he saw on closer inspection, was uncovered.

In minus twenty degrees, Amelia had shoved her jacket and sweater up so that her skin was exposed.

There were two reasons he could think of that someone might do that.

To shoot heroin, though she hadn't.

Or to show someone something.

And there was something there. Her tattoos. He'd seen them licking out from the cuffs of her uniform but had never seen the actual images. Now he could.

The needle work seemed fine, refined. No pictures. Just words, intertwined. All up and down her arm. Though he couldn't read what was written, he could see that some words, phrases, were in Latin. Some in Greek. In French and English.

Her body, it seemed, was a Rosetta stone. A way to unlock, decode, Amelia.

He wished he could read what was actually written there.

But one thing did stand out. Something scrawled boldly on her skin. More like graffiti than the fine etchings of the other words.

He looked closer. Then sat back hoping that, as with paintings, distance would give him perspective. It didn't.

He zoomed closer. Cursing his bleary vision.

D he could make out. At both ends. And then, with his finger, he traced the lines. Slowly. Having to back up when he realized he'd taken a wrong turn and was now deep into Latin or Greek.

V.

A.

DAVD.

"David," he whispered.

And beside the name some numbers. "One. Four," he mumbled.

He unfroze the image, and the now-familiar video rolled on. He watched as she once again used the move they'd taught her at the Sûreté Academy and dislocated the dealer's shoulder.

Then Amelia and her followers left the frame. Along with his friends. Her entourage was getting larger and larger and now included young men.

Her influence was growing.

It hadn't taken long. And he probably should have seen this coming, and maybe he had and just didn't want to admit it.

He'd not only released a deadly narcotic onto the streets of Québec. He'd released Amelia.

And she was doing what Amelia always did. She was taking over.

"What are you up to?" he whispered. "And who's David?"

The video continued to roll, but all that was left was the heap on the ground, like garbage.

And the whimpering.

Armand was about to turn it off when he noticed movement. A little girl in a bright red tuque. She walked out of the darkness and paused on the sidewalk. Alone. All alone. Then the girl turned and walked out of the frame. After Amelia.

He stared, his face pale. His mouth slightly open. Sickened to see a child alone on the streets.

He was so absorbed by what had just left the frame that he almost missed seeing what remained.

There was someone else, he now noticed. A man. On the very edge of the screen. He was leaning, almost casually, against the wall of the alley. His arms folded, he stared after Amelia. And appeared to be thinking. Then he made up his mind. Pushing off from the wall, he moved. But he didn't follow the others. Instead he stepped over the writhing dealer and walked in the opposite direction.

Armand wondered if he'd just met David.

CHAPTER 27

By midmorning, when Armand and Benedict left for Montréal, Jean-Guy was long gone.

And because Armand wasn't with him, he didn't see Jean-Guy stop in back of the building and look around before being buzzed inside.

The large conference room was empty when he arrived.

Jean-Guy sat but soon got up. Restless, he paced back and forth in front of the windows. Then around the table. Pausing to look at a familiar painting. A copy of a classic Jean Paul Lemieux.

Then he paced again, looking out the window at Montréal, slightly obscured by ice fog. Like a veil of gauze.

He gripped his hands behind his back and puffed out his cheeks before exhaling.

I have a family now, he told himself, *and need to put them first*.

Yes. That was why he was there. Not for himself. Not because he was a chickenshit. Or just a chicken. Or just a shit.

The door opened, and he turned around to see the now-familiar men and women who'd interviewed him. Who'd made the offer just a few days earlier.

He'd declined to accept. Which did not make them at all happy. Apparently not many said no.

He'd explained that he was loyal to the Chief Superintendent. And they'd explained the advantages, and distinct disadvantages, of refusing their offer.

He was being worn down. Acting Chief Inspector Beauvoir recognized the technique, even as he recognized it was working.

But sitting in bed the night before, Annie asleep beside him, he'd gone back over the papers. Reading. Rereading. Would it really be so bad if he signed? Could anyone really blame him?

Ironically, it was the sort of thing he'd normally discuss with the Chief. But could not. Not this time. Not this deal.

He had, of course, discussed it at length with Annie. The options. The consequences.

And now here he was. About to do something he'd never have thought possible.

After shaking hands, they all sat. In the awkward silence, while an assistant brought coffee, Jean-Guy pointed to the Lemieux.

"I like it."

"I'm glad," the woman said.

"A numbered print?" he asked.

"The original."

"Ah," he said. "Chiaroscuro."

A man next to her smiled. "I see you know your art. Yes. Not many realize that it's the play of light and dark, of subtleties and extremes—"

Beauvoir nodded and smiled. But all he could think of, for some reason, was ice cream.

When the coffee arrived, rich and strong, he took a long, restorative gulp. He was ready for them.

And they for him, it seemed.

The woman in charge pushed a small stack of papers across the table, with a pen lying on top of them.

"We're so glad you've changed your mind."

He picked up the pen and signed quickly. He couldn't afford to hesitate now. It was one of the early lessons in homicide from then–Chief Inspector Gamache.

Once an action has been entered, you cannot hesitate. Once committed, you cannot second-guess. Never look back.

This action, Beauvoir realized as he put the cap on the pen, had been entered months ago. When he and Gamache had been suspended. And the investigation had begun. When their own people had questioned not just their actions but their integrity, their commitment.

It had all led here. To this moment. In this room.

He pushed the document back across the table.

"Keep it," said the woman, when Beauvoir went to hand the pen back. "I'm glad you've decided to join us."

She was smiling, they were all smiling. She put out her hand, and after a brief hesitation he shook it.

It was the schooner Hesperus, the deep voice came to him. *That sailed the wintry sea.*

That's as far as it ever went, and Jean-Guy always laughed at the running joke. But now, as he looked out the window at the falling snow and felt the pen heavy in his breast pocket, he remembered the title.

And he wondered if, in his effort to get to safety, he wasn't fleeing from a wreck but causing it.

Benedict proved a careful, though tense, driver.

He gripped the wheel at the ten and two positions and sat bolt up-right, his eyes never wandering from the snowy road.

Car after car passed them on the autoroute. But Armand was in no hurry and preferred safety to recklessness. He also knew that it was his presence that was making the boy extra cautious. Tense, even.

He'll relax soon enough, thought Gamache.

They talked about mundane things, like home ownership and Benedict's job as caretaker and what could go wrong with buildings. Large and small.

Armand told him about renovations they were considering to their home.

"I hope you don't mind my picking your brain," said Armand. "There're quite a few bedrooms, but when our son, Daniel, and his wife and two daughters come, along with Annie and Jean-Guy and their family . . . well, there won't be enough room."

"So you'd like an addition?"

They discussed possibilities. Benedict suggested going up instead of out and renovating the attic. And how to do it without making the whole place fall down.

"One collapsed house is more than enough," said Armand, and Benedict agreed.

Gamache tucked the information away. Not about renovations he had no plans to undertake but that Benedict did indeed know how to prevent a house from falling. And would therefore, presumably, also know how to bring one down.

Benedict dropped Armand off in downtown Montréal, at the quite splendid offices of Horowitz Investments, and promised to pick him up later.

It was snowing lightly. Prettily. Covering the grime of the city. At least for a little while.

Gamache watched Benedict drive around a corner, then hailed a cab and gave an address on rue Ste.-Catherine.

"Are you sure?" the driver asked, looking Armand up and down.

His fare was nicely dressed, in a good parka, with a white shirt and a tie just visible below the scarf.

"I'm sure. *Merci.*"

He leaned back in the seat, and as he did, his face settled into a grim expression.

"Wait for me, please," he said when they reached their destination.

"I won't wait long," the driver warned. Though he hadn't yet been paid, he was willing to leave rather than be carjacked, or beaten and robbed by junkies.

This was, every cabbie knew, a no-go area. Or, if you had to go, it was a place you didn't linger.

He locked the doors and kept the car in gear.

Still, he was curious and watched as his fare walked with more confidence than he should have had, then turned in to what the driver knew was an alley. Clogged with garbage cans and whores.

He waited a minute. Two. Then crept up until he was idling at the mouth of the alley.

The cabbie watched as his fare shook the hand of another tall person. But this one was emaciated. A prostitute. A transsexual.

He passed her money in a thick envelope. Oddly, the woman appeared to try to give it back, but his fare insisted. Then he turned and, on seeing the taxi, nodded.

The man walked back to the car with ease, with authority. And while the driver was tempted to leave him there, after whatever disgusting thing had just happened in the alley, he didn't.

Armand thanked the driver, then sat back in the seat and exhaled as he looked out the window. Scanning the icy streets for a little girl. A child. In a red hat.

But he felt confident his new friend, Anita Facial, would find her. And call him. And he'd go and get her.

He knew in coming here today he'd risked blowing the whole thing. Risked being seen. But there were lines, there were limits. And Armand Gamache was tired of crossing them. Of exceeding them. He was tired of the tyranny of the greater good.

He'd found a line, in the fleeting image of a little girl, that he would not cross.

"'It was the schooner Hesperus,'" he whispered, his breath creating a small circle of vapor on the window, "'That sailed the wintry sea.'"

He realized everyone suspected he only knew the opening lines of the epic poem. That was part of the joke. But the truth was, he knew it all. Every word. Every line. Including, of course, how it ended.

"'Christ save us all from a death like this,'" he quoted under his breath as he looked out the window.

Beauvoir grabbed a quick sandwich in his office as he read over reports of the Baumgartner murder. Updates on interviews. Background checks. Preliminary scene-of-crime evidence. Photographs.

He chaired the morning briefing with lead inspectors about other homicides they were investigating.

He then called Agent Cloutier into his office to get a report on her findings.

She balanced the papers on her knee, then knocked them off. Then her glasses fell off as she stooped to pick up the papers. Beauvoir went around the desk to help her.

"Let's sit over there," he said, taking a pile of papers to the table by the window. One he'd sat at hundreds of times, going over cases with Gamache.

"Tell me what you know," he said to her.

And she did.

"These"—she laid her hand on the statements found in Anthony Baumgartner's study—"are not legitimate. The numbers don't add up.

The transactions look good until you cross-check and realize the buy and sell figures are off."

"So what are they?"

"A play."

"A what?"

"They're like a theater production. An illusion. Something made to look real, but isn't. Monsieur Baumgartner must've known that these clients wouldn't look too closely. Most don't. And the fact is, you'd have to be an expert to figure it out, and even then it takes time."

"Was he stealing from them?"

The clarity, the simplicity of the question seemed to surprise her. She thought about it, then nodded. "Absolutely."

"Have you found the funds?"

"That'll take longer, sir. And a court order."

Beauvoir went to his desk and brought over a paper. It was the court order, allowing them full access to Baumgartner's finances. Another one granted access to the Taylor and Ogilvy client list.

He'd put that in his satchel, along with the copy of the statements Cloutier had given him.

"It would also help if we could get into his computer," he said.

"I'm working on it, *patron*."

The taxi let Armand off where it had picked him up. Outside the offices of Horowitz Investments. They were just down rue Sherbrooke from the Musée des Beaux-Arts and Holt Renfrew. On Montréal's Golden Mile, where glass towers were fronted by old Greystone mansions.

A cab ride, and a lifetime, away from where he'd just been. What separated them, Gamache knew, wasn't hard work but good fortune and blind luck. That picked some and not others. That introduced some to opioids and not others. Five years ago, two years, even a year ago, the futures of the ghastly figures on the street looked very different. And then someone introduced them to a painkiller. An opioid. And all the promise, all the good fortune of birth and affluence—of a loving family, of education—were no match for what came next.

Loved. Beaten. Cared for. Neglected. University graduate or drop-out. All ended up in the gutter. Thanks to the great leveler that was fentanyl.

What was on the streets now was not, Gamache knew, his doing. They were opioids. Killers. Hollowing out a generation. And so far the carfentanil he'd let through hadn't yet gone into circulation.

But it would, he knew. Soon. And if it was bad now, it was about to get incalculably worse.

He'd read a report recently that said an American state with the death penalty was considering using the drug to execute prisoners. It was swift and lethal and guaranteed to do the job.

He'd stared at that report, feeling the blood drain from his face. It wasn't telling him anything he didn't already know. But it did put a word to what he'd done. What he was.

The executioner.

"Armand."

Stephen Horowitz came out of his office, hand extended. His voice still lightly accented from his European upbringing.

All of ninety-three now, he was as vibrant as ever. And as rich as Croesus.

"You're looking well," said Armand, taking the firm hand and shaking it.

"As are you."

The sharp eyes traveled over Gamache before coming to rest on his face.

"Have you been crying?"

Armand laughed. "Seeing you always makes me emotional. You know that. But *non*. Just some irritation."

"That sounds more likely. Most people find me irritating."

Armand did not disagree.

"I've made reservations at the Ritz. Too pretentious, but I like seeing which of my clients are there and think they can afford it."

They walked the two blocks to the Ritz, with Horowitz taking Armand's arm every now and then, far beyond being bashful about any frailty.

He'd been Armand's parents' financial adviser. In fact, Armand's father had helped set Horowitz up in business when he'd been a young refugee after the war. One of the displaced people who never forgot how that felt. Nor, seventy years later, had Stephen Horowitz forgotten that act of kindness.

There was now a shockingly generous account, in Annie's and Daniel's names, with Horowitz Investments. One Gamache himself didn't even know about.

Horowitz had left instructions in his will, and only then would the Gamaches find out.

"I hear you're still suspended," said Stephen, allowing a liveried waiter to flap open the linen napkin before laying it on his lap. *"Merci."*

"I am," he said in response to Stephen's question.

Sparkling water with lime was on the table waiting for them, along with two scotches and two plates of oysters.

"Merci," said Armand as the napkin was laid on his lap.

"Stupid of them." The elderly man shook his head. "Would you like me to make a call?"

"To whom?" asked Armand. "Or do I want to know?"

"Probably not."

"You've already made one call, I know. Thank you for that."

"You're my godson," said Stephen. "I do what I can."

Armand watched him prepare his oysters. With precision. Knowing exactly how he liked them.

Stephen Horowitz was as close as Armand came to having a father. The investment dealer had been disappointed when the young man had chosen the law over finance, though Stephen had his own three children to leave the business to.

Armand's relationship with Stephen was divorced, as far as Armand knew, from money. It was about other forms of support.

"See that man over there?" Stephen was now engaged in his favorite thing. Passing judgment. "Runs a steel company. A complete dickhead. My people have just discovered that he's planning on giving himself a hundred-million-dollar bonus this fiscal year. Excuse me."

To Armand's alarm, though no real surprise, Stephen got up and walked over to the man, said something that made the man turn purple, then returned to the table, grinning all the way.

"What did you say to him?" Armand asked.

"I told him that I was dumping all the shares Horowitz Investments holds in his company. I gave the order just before we left. Look."

And as Armand watched, the man pulled out his iPhone, punched some numbers, and stared. Pale now. As he saw his shares tumble.

"When the stock reaches a low, I've told my people to buy it. All," said Stephen.

"You've bought the company?" asked Armand.

"Controlling interest. He'll see that in a few minutes too."

"You'll be his boss."

"Not for long."

Stephen raised his hand, and the maître d' hurried over, bent down, nodded, then left. Armand raised his brows and waited for an explanation.

"I told Pierre that I'd pay for that table. The man won't be able to afford it after this, and I don't want the restaurant stuck with a bad debt."

"You're very thoughtful," said Armand, and he watched as Stephen smiled broadly. "Did you know he'd be here when you booked?"

"It's Wednesday. He's always here Wednesday."

"So that's a yes."

"Yes."

Wheels within wheels, thought Armand as their lunch arrived. And most of the wheels were running over some poor sod who got in Stephen's way. Or did something he didn't approve of.

"Have you ever heard of Ruth Zardo?" Armand asked, cutting into his sea bass on a bed of pureed cauliflower with braised lentils and garnished with grilled asparagus and grapefruit wedges.

"The poet? Yes, of course." He lowered his knife and fork and looked into the distance, recalling the words: "'Who hurt you once so far beyond repair / That you would greet each overture with curling lip.'"

"That's the one."

"Why do you ask?"

"I just thought you two might get along."

Stephen went back to his food. "Are you hurt, Armand?" He spoke into his Dover sole.

253

"Not beyond repair, no."

Stephen looked up then. His eyes clear and searching. "I don't mean physically. Those wounds heal. I mean by the Sûreté investigation. By this suspension that seems to be going on a long time."

"There're things you don't know, Stephen."

"True. But I know you. It would be a terrible shame to lose you as head of the Sûreté."

"*Merci.*"

"Are you sure I can't put in a call?"

"Don't you dare," said Armand, pointing his knife at the elderly man in mock threat.

Stephen laughed and nodded. "Fine. Now, why did you want to see me?"

"It's delicate."

"Let me guess. It's about Hugo Baumgartner."

"Well, so much for delicate."

"His brother was just killed, so it wasn't hard to guess. Murdered, according to the news. But you can't be involved in the investigation. You are, as we've established—"

"Suspended. *Oui.* But I'm a liquidator on his mother's will and came at it in a roundabout way."

He explained about the will, and Horowitz listened carefully before thinking it over and finally saying, "That's some weird shit."

Armand laughed. "Your considered opinion. Well, you're not wrong. But I want to ask you about Hugo Baumgartner. He's one of your senior vice presidents."

"He is. Ugly as original sin. Vile to look at. Really quite disgusting. But, like many ugly people, who look like villains, he has to make up for it by being obviously decent. If I didn't have three children capable of taking over the company, I'd consider him."

"He's that good?"

"He is. He's as good as his dead brother was bad."

"So you know about that."

"I do. Hugo didn't tell me. He's protective of his brother. But word on the street—"

"Does everyone know?"

"If they don't, they're dumber than I thought. Why else would a senior VP at Taylor and Ogilvy have his license suspended? That's a serious move. Not done lightly."

"Hugo says his brother was railroaded, made an example of. That it was the assistant who actually stole the money."

"Yeah, yeah," said Stephen, gesturing with his knife and fork. "Blah, blah. What else's he going to say?" The elderly man leaned toward Armand. "Who's more likely to know how to steal money from a client's account and be able to cover it up for months? The VP or the assistant? Who's more likely to have access? And who's more likely to be fired? I'll give you a hint—the answer to the last question is different from the first two."

Armand nodded. He'd gotten that far himself. "What can you tell me about Taylor and Ogilvy?"

"They're a relatively new firm. Been around for about thirty years, though they like to give the impression they were created by royal charter in the 1800s."

"Victoria banked with them?" asked Armand.

"Something like that. Magnificent offices, clearly meant to impress."

"And yet?"

"I'm always suspicious of anyone who feels they need to impress with surroundings rather than track record."

"You're suspicious of everyone," Armand pointed out. "Hardly telling."

"True," admitted Horowitz with a smile.

"You think they're hiding something?" Armand asked. "Are they legitimate?"

"Oh yes. Just sail a little close to the edge."

"You do know that the earth is round."

"The earth might be, but human nature isn't. It has caverns and abysses and all sorts of traps."

"Taylor and Ogilvy exists on the edge of one such trap?"

"If they employ humans, then yes."

"You employ humans," Armand pointed out.

"But I watch over them," said Stephen. "And I'm immortal."

"And infallible."

"Now you're getting it."

"Hugo Baumgartner," said Armand. "He's about as human as they come. Can he be trusted?"

"As far as I know. But you're not asking me to transfer your account to him, are you?" He watched his godson. "No. You're not sure about him, are you, Armand?"

"Dessert?" asked Armand when the waiter took their plates.

Stephen smiled and accepted the dessert menu. After they'd ordered warm apple tarts, tea ice cream, and coffee, Stephen spoke again.

"It's the will that interests me. I've known families torn apart by them. Expectations. Those're corrosive. Combined with greed or desperation, it can get pretty nasty. Go on for years."

"Generations," said Armand.

"Do they really believe that a title and all those possessions belong to them?"

"They say not, but—"

"What's bred in the bone," said Stephen. "Sometimes we think we haven't bought into someone else's craziness until it's tested. They're Jewish, aren't they?"

"Yes. Does it matter?"

"It might. From Austria? Vienna?"

"*Oui*."

Stephen was nodding.

"You have an idea?"

"Nothing as good as an idea. More like a vague thought. I just wonder if the old woman—the Baroness, you call her?—if she might've been right after all, without realizing it. Let me do some research." He waved for the bill. "That's what you wanted, wasn't it? For me to do some digging."

"I wanted your company," said Armand. "And a delicious meal."

"You got a nice meal, and I just got fed bullshit." He shoved the silver salver across the linen tablecloth. "Here. You can pay."

Armand smiled and shook his head. It had always been his intention to pay. He always did. And now, it seemed, he was also, thanks to Stephen, paying for the meals of four people he didn't even know.

"Let's hope my suspension is over soon," said Armand, laying down his credit card.

"Why? So you can pay for this? Don't worry, you can afford it."

"No." He nodded toward the steel magnate, who, ruined over his meal of veal sweetbreads, glared at Stephen as he left. "So I can solve your murder."

The old man laughed.

CHAPTER 28

⌒

Jean-Guy looked around the waiting room of Taylor and Ogilvy.

He was on the forty-fifth floor, but you'd never know it. There was oak paneling, and oil paintings, and even a bookcase with leather volumes, as though to say if your investment adviser could read, he was sure not to screw you.

Jean-Guy expected, when he looked out the window, to see the magnificent garden of an estate, and not Montréal from the air.

Illusion.

What was it Agent Cloutier had said?

A play. A set. Something that looked like one thing but was actually another. This place was made up to look like a solid, conservative, trustworthy firm. But was it something else?

He peered at the paintings, then got up to look at one in particular. A numbered print.

Not exactly a fake, but not the real thing either.

"Do you like it?" a woman's voice behind him asked.

He turned around, expecting it was the receptionist who'd spoken, only to find a very elegant and surprisingly young woman standing at the open door.

"I do," said Beauvoir. "I'm here to see Madame Ogilvy."

"Bernice, please." She extended her hand. "Have I heard correctly? Tony was murdered?"

"I'm afraid it looks that way."

Her eyes narrowed in a wince, absorbing the words. "Jesus. I'll do whatever I can to help."

"*Merci.*"

She turned, and he followed her down the hushed corridor. Taking in the offices on either side, where brokers, mostly men, sat speaking on telephones or tapping on laptops.

The hallway was paneled in wood and art.

"Nice paintings," he said.

"Thank you. Most are prints, but we do have some originals," she assured him. "Some awful things my grandfather bought, thinking they were good investments. They were not. We hide those in the offices of the partners, as a reminder."

"Of what?"

"Of what happens when we think we know about something when we do not." She stopped then and smiled at him. "You must run into the same danger in your profession, Chief Inspector. Only your mistakes can cost lives."

"As can yours."

Her smile faded. "I'm aware of that."

She turned and continued her chat about the art. It was, he could tell, rehearsed. A patter she repeated for everyone. To put them at their ease.

"We specialize in Canadian art. Québec, wherever possible."

"But not always originals."

"No. The originals are often not available, so we buy numbered prints. But only the low numbers."

He laughed, then realized she was serious. "Why's that?"

"Well, because they're more valuable. Everything's an investment, Chief Inspector."

"Everything?"

"Everything. And I don't just mean in business. As humans, we invest not just money. We spend time. We spend effort. There's a reason it's put like that. Life's short, and time is precious and limited. We need to pick and choose where we put it."

"For maximum return?"

"Exactly. I know it sounds calculating, but think about your own life. You don't want to waste your time with people you don't like or doing something you don't find fulfilling."

Beauvoir felt there should be some clever response, but all that came to mind was to say, *That's bullshit.*

A few years ago, he might've. But then a few years ago he wasn't the Chief Inspector.

"What're you thinking?" she asked.

"I'm thinking that's bullshit."

Oh well, if life really is short, might as well be himself.

She stopped and looked at him. "Why do you say that?"

He looked around before his attention returned to her. "It's the sort of thing someone who works here would say. I'm not saying you don't believe it. I'm saying most people don't have the luxury to pick and choose. They're just trying to make it through the day. Taking whatever shitty job they can. Trying to hold the family together. Maybe in a shitty marriage with kids who're out of control. You live in a world of choice, Madame Ogilvy. Most don't have investments. They have lives. And they're just trying to get by."

"A zero-sum game?" she asked. "That's bullshit. And patronizing. People might not be able to choose to work here, or live in a mansion, but they still have choices. And investments of time if not money."

They stared at each other, the strain obvious. Beauvoir didn't care. He preferred it like this. Pushing people. Seeing what they're really like underneath.

He found it interesting that when he'd become crass, she'd changed. Used exactly the same language. The difference was, it was natural to him. Not to her.

Here was a chameleon. Who adapted to situations, and people.

It was a useful skill. Both a defense and an offense. It was designed to lower people's guards. *I'm just like you*, she was saying. *And you're "one of us."*

It was a subtle and powerful message. One that put people at ease and let her into their confidence.

Elegant and refined when called for. Foulmouthed when called for.

Demure. Scrappy. Crass. Classy.

All things. And nothing. Except calculating.

One of the many things he loved about Annie was that, while adaptable, she was always herself. Genuine.

This woman was not.

Still, this was going to be, if he was smart, a good investment of his time.

"Do you have any Clara Morrows?" he asked as they turned a corner.

"No. I tried to buy one of her Three Graces, but there were no prints left. Only the one of that old woman. Scared the *merde* out of me."

"You should see the original," said Beauvoir. "Better than an enema."

She laughed and showed him into her office.

It was like walking from the past into the future or, at least, a very glossy present day. It was a corner office, of floor-to-ceiling glass. There, before him, spread Montréal. Magnificent. In one direction he could see the Jacques Cartier Bridge across the St. Lawrence River. In the other, Mount Royal, with its massive cross. And in between, office towers. Bold, gleaming, audacious. Montréal. Set for the future with roots deep in history. It never failed to thrill him. And the ice fog only made it more otherworldly.

Her desk was wood. But sleek and simple. An age-old material with a modern design. There was a sofa, some chairs, and the art, like everything else, was contemporary.

"No one you'd know," she said as he scanned the walls. "Students mostly. We fund a scholarship for young artists to study at the Musée d'art contemporain. What I ask in return is one of their works."

"In the hopes one day it'll be worth something?" he asked.

"There's always that, Chief Inspector. But mostly I hope they do what they love."

"And do you?" he asked, sitting down.

"As a matter of fact, I do. Born to it, I suppose. Investing, finance, the market. Both my parents are in investing."

"Your father's the CEO and your mother's the chair of the board."

"You've done your homework."

He felt himself getting prickly. It was such a condescending thing to say.

"Not difficult. A simple Google search. Is that how you got your job?"

Two can be insulting.

"Well, it's not a coincidence my name is Ogilvy. But I earned this office. Believe me. Investing not only comes naturally, it fascinates me."

"How so?"

"The chance to make a real difference in people's lives. To secure their retirement. Their children's educations. Their first home. What could be better?"

The truth, thought Beauvoir. That could be better. This was, like the patter down the hallway, a practiced speech. More oak paneling. More fake originals.

"And you?" she asked.

"Me?"

"Do you love what you do?"

"Of course."

But the question surprised him. He'd never really thought about it. Did he love it?

He certainly hadn't stood over corpses, hunted killers all these years for the money or glamour. Then why had he? Was it possible he did love it?

Beauvoir brought the warrant from his satchel and placed it on the desk.

Madame Ogilvy didn't bother to look at it. "I also did some research. In answer to your question yesterday, we don't have any clients named Kinderoth. Now. But we did. Both have died. One five years ago and one last year. They were elderly and in ill health."

"Did Anthony Baumgartner look after their finances?"

"No. They were with another adviser, and, frankly, it was such a small account that when it was divided among the heirs there was hardly anything left. Though I understand the will was a little strange."

Beauvoir felt that frisson that came with an unexpected find.

"How so?" his voice betrayed none of his excitement.

"I can't remember the exact details, but it seems they left far more than they actually had. We talked to the adviser, of course, about why they thought they had what amounted to a fortune, but he was as baffled as anyone. We did our own investigation, and there was absolutely nothing wrong with our accounts."

"Do you know if there was an aristocratic title involved?" He asked this as though it were a perfectly natural question. And braced for ridicule.

But she wasn't laughing. She was looking at him with genuine surprise.

"How did you know that? As a matter of fact, there was. We think they must've been suffering from dementia, or some sort of collective delusion. Monsieur Kinderoth was a taxi driver and Madame Kinderoth had raised the children. They had a very modest house in East End Montréal and a small retirement income. And yet in their will they left millions, and a title."

"Baron?"

"And Baroness, yes. Apparently that's what they called themselves."

Beauvoir could feel his heart speeding up and his senses sharpening, as they always did when he was closing in on something. Or, really, had fallen face-first into it.

But his voice remained neutral. His own oak paneling. His veneer in place.

"Do you have the address of their children?"

"I thought you might ask. They had two daughters, both living in Toronto. Both married. What does this have to do with Tony Baumgartner's death? As I said, they weren't his clients."

Her hand rested on a slim manila folder.

"I'm afraid I can't tell you that."

He saw a flash of annoyance, quickly there and rapidly hidden. Here was someone not used to hearing no. And someone who clearly thrived on information. No surprise there. You didn't land in this office by being ignorant.

And you weren't the acting head of homicide for the Sûreté by handing out information.

He extended his hand, and she gave him the folder.

"*Merci*. No relatives living in Québec?"

"Not that I know of."

He nodded. They'd done searches from the government databases for Baumgartners and Kinderoths. Both, fortunately, unusual names.

While there were a few Baumgartners scattered around, perhaps distant cousins or not related at all—agents were checking—there were no more Kinderoths in Québec.

Jean-Guy's mind was working quickly, to absorb this news of another strange will. One, he suspected, that left exactly what the Baroness Baumgartner had left. He'd have agents check. The Kinderoth will would be in the public domain by now.

"Thank you." He held up the file before tucking it into his satchel. "Now, the main reason I came here is to ask you about Anthony Baumgartner."

"Exactly," she said, and leaned forward in her chair. "How can I help?"

"What was he like?"

"He was a brilliant analyst. He understood—"

"We'll get to that in a moment. I'd like to hear what he was like as a person."

Beauvoir's technique was very different from Gamache's. The Chief wanted to remain quiet. To listen. To put people at their ease. Draw them out and have them almost forget this was an interrogation. He used silence. And calm. Reassuring smiles.

While Beauvoir could see the benefits and the results of that, his own approach was to get in their faces. Keep them off balance so that they'd erupt.

He asked a lot of questions. Interrupted answers. Let them know who was in charge. And kept turning up the pressure.

"As a person?" Bernice Ogilvy asked.

"You know. A human being. Not an investment."

He saw her color. "I understand. He was nice—"

"You can do better than that. Did you like him?"

"Like him?"

"It's a feeling," he said. "How did you feel about Anthony Baumgartner?"

"He was nice—"

"Puppies are nice. What was he? How did you feel about him?"

"I liked him," she snapped. "A lot."

"A lot?"

"Not like that."

"Then how?"

"He was nice—"

"Come on. What was he to you?"

265

"An employee."

"More than that?"

"Of course not."

"Did you know he was gay?"

"Only when he told me."

"Is that true?"

"Yes. It didn't matter. He was—"

"Nice?"

"More. He was like a father."

It came out almost as a shout. Defiantly. Challenging Beauvoir to challenge her.

He did not. He had what he wanted.

"To you?"

"To everyone. All of us. Even the older men, they looked up to him."

She regarded him, expecting another interruption. But Beauvoir had learned from Gamache when to keep his mouth shut. And listen.

"He never forgot a birthday or an important anniversary," she said. "And not just of the partners but everyone. Assistants, cleaners. He was that sort of man."

A good man, thought Beauvoir. Or just good at appearances.

"When I came into the firm, I used my mother's maiden name. I didn't want anyone to know who I was. I started as Tony's assistant. He was patient and kind. Taught me more about the market in six months than I'd learned in four years at university. How to read trends. What to look for. To not just study the annual reports but to get to know the leadership of companies. He was brilliant."

"And what happened when he found out who you really were?"

She raised her brows and compressed her lips.

"He wasn't happy. He took me out for drinks, and I thought he'd be pleased. He'd mentored someone who'd one day have—" She raised her hands to indicate the corner office.

"But he wasn't," she said. "He told me that this was a business built on relationships and trust. Not on tricks. Not on games. He wished I'd been honest with him. And that it didn't speak highly of him, or of me, that I felt I needed to pretend. That I didn't trust him. He didn't say it, but I could see I'd disappointed him. It was awful."

And I bet you've spent the last few years trying to make it up to him,

266

thought Beauvoir. Was Baumgartner that clever? To play her like that. To talk about trust when he himself was violating it?

Beauvoir reached into his satchel and placed the statements on her desk.

"I've had an agent working on these. I suspect you'll come to the same conclusion."

Madame Ogilvy put on glasses and picked up the statements, without comment. A minute. Two. Five went by. Jean-Guy got up and wandered the office, examining the walls and the art. Glancing at her every now and then.

His iPhone buzzed, and he looked at the text. It was from Gamache, asking if he could meet him over at Isabelle Lacoste's place in an hour.

He sent back a quick reply. Absolutely.

Finally Madame Ogilvy put down the statements. Her face was bland. Almost blank. Though he saw her fingers tremble, just before she closed them into fists.

"You were right to be concerned, Chief Inspector." Her voice now held none of the emotion of before. It was clipped. Controlled. "I'm glad you brought these to me."

"Are you?" he asked, sitting back down.

Her smile was thin. Her eyes cold. This was not a young woman. This was the senior partner in a multibillion-dollar investment firm. Who didn't get the job because she was the CEO's daughter but because she could do just this.

Absorb information quickly. Break it down. See the implications and options. And not hide from reality, no matter how unpleasant. They were skills that would have served her well in any business. Including his.

"I am," she said. "It would come out eventually. Better we have a chance to manage the situation."

At least she was being honest about that, thought Beauvoir. But he wasn't fooled by her sangfroid. Agent Cloutier had made it clear that embezzlement on this scale, for what appeared to be a long time, would probably need the collusion of someone very senior.

They were far from sure Anthony Baumgartner had been in it alone.

In fact, Beauvoir had begun to formulate a theory.

That Baumgartner was corrupt, that much seemed obvious, but he was also a tool. He'd set up the shell, directed the play, to use Cloutier's analogy. But someone else wrote the script.

Who better than the CEO's daughter? Baumgartner's former protégée?

Had the story she'd just told him been more bullshit? Beauvoir wondered. About disappointing Baumgartner? About him not knowing who she was? About his decency?

Had he in fact taught her things she didn't learn in business school? Like how to steal from clients?

Who, after all, was in a better position to hide what was happening? And to protect him if caught. As he had been.

Instead of firing his ass, they'd fired the assistant.

And then there was the question of where the money went.

Anthony Baumgartner's lifestyle showed none of the fruits of this labor. He lived in the same home he'd been in for years. Drove a nice, though midrange, vehicle. Had not gone on any luxury vacations.

It was a rare person who was greedy enough to steal clients' money and then disciplined enough not to spend it.

Unless the lion's share was going somewhere else. To someone else.

"And how do you manage this situation?" he asked.

"Well, the first thing I do," she said, reaching for the phone, "is call the regulatory commission and report this."

"We've already done that."

"I see. I'll call as well, later." She put down the phone, slightly miffed. "We will, of course, replace any money taken from clients."

"Stolen."

"Yes."

"Bit awkward, isn't it?" he said. "This isn't the first time Anthony Baumgartner embezzled from clients."

"You're talking about what happened a few years ago," she said. "That wasn't him. Not directly. It was the assistant of one of the senior partners."

"You?"

"No."

"They were having an affair, I believe," said Beauvoir.

"That's true. The assistant apparently used Tony to get at his access codes and was siphoning money from various accounts. He was bound to be caught. Not very smart, really. But he did get away with quite a bit before it was discovered."

"Who caught him?"

"Tony. He came to us immediately, and we acted."

"By firing the assistant."

"Yes."

"And not Monsieur Baumgartner."

"He'd been foolish, trusted someone he shouldn't have. But his actions weren't criminal."

"And yet you suspended his license."

"There had to be a consequence. Other brokers had to see that if you're tainted in any way, there will be a punishment."

"And his clients?"

"What about them?"

"Were they told?"

"No. We decided not to. The money was replaced, and it was decided Tony would work with another broker, who'd put in the tickets and do the actual transactions. But Tony would continue to manage the portfolios. Make the decisions. It wasn't necessary for this to be spread on the street."

"The street?"

"Our language. It means the financial community."

The street.

Beauvoir was beginning to appreciate that the only thing that separated this "street" from rue Ste.-Catherine was a thin veneer of gentility. But once that was peeled away, what was revealed was just as brutal, just as dirty, just as dangerous.

"Baumgartner was fine with the new arrangement?"

"He understood. Look, he didn't have to come to us. He probably could've figured out how to cover it up. But instead he sat right where you're sitting and told me everything. About the affair. About finding out Bernard had stolen his access codes for the accounts. He offered to quit."

"But you didn't take him up on it?"

"No."

"Why not?"

"I've already told you."

269

"You know as well as I do that you could've fired him. And given what's happened, perhaps even should have." He looked at the statements. "I want the truth."

She took a deep breath and continued to hold his eyes.

"He was the best financial adviser we had. Brilliant. I am, after all is said and done, my father's daughter, Chief Inspector. I know talent, and I want to keep it. Tony Baumgartner was that. And so we chose a middle ground. Suspending his license to trade but allowing him to continue managing portfolios."

"So if he could no longer trade, how did he manage to steal all that money?" Beauvoir pointed to the papers on her desk.

"No, no, these are all fake. There were never any trades. That's the whole thing. He made it look like there were, but it's all gobbledygook. If a client actually bothered to read this"—she put her splayed hand on the paper—"what they'd see are numbers that are both impressive and mind-numbingly boring. No one, other than another financial wonk, would bother to study these."

"So where did the money go?"

She shook her head and took a deep breath. "I don't know. But it looks like millions. Tens of millions."

"More," said Beauvoir, and, after a small hesitation, she also nodded.

"Depending on how long this's been going on, yes. It'll take us a while to work it all out."

"But wouldn't people, his clients, realize? When there was no actual money in the account?"

"How?"

"When they asked for it."

"But people don't," she said. "They give it to their investment dealer, and at best they cash in the dividends or take the profits. But the capital remains in the account. Weren't you ever told by your parents never to touch the capital?"

"No. I was told not to touch my brother's bike."

She smiled. "Point taken. But a truism in investing is that people take the profits, the dividends, but leave the capital."

"Is this a Ponzi scheme, then?" he asked.

"Not quite, but similar. This's even harder to find, since he's made it look like these clients were investing through Taylor and Ogilvy, but

270

they weren't. He's used our letterhead, our statement format. Our address. Everything. Except our accounts. The money just went into Tony's personal account."

"Where?"

"I have no idea."

"So you wouldn't know it was happening?"

"Not at all. Our auditors would never catch it, because it's not there to catch."

Beauvoir was beginning to see the genius of this. The simplicity.

"So he had two sets of clients? There were the ones whose accounts he was legitimately working on, and then there were those he kept at home. The ones he was stealing from."

"That's what it looks like."

"We'll need to know if any of these clients also have legitimate accounts with Taylor and Ogilvy."

"Of course. May I keep these?" She looked down at the offending statements.

"Yes."

"You'll be questioning them?"

"Yes," he said again.

She nodded. Like mad Ruth in Clara's painting, Bernice Ogilvy could see just the hint of something on the horizon. Far off, but approaching. And gathering speed. Something that had been there a very long time. Waiting. Inevitable.

But where Ruth saw the end of despair, Madame Ogilvy saw the beginning of it.

Once this got out, and it would, no one would trust Taylor and Ogilvy again. It might be unfair, but such was life, when everything depended on something as fragile as trust. And human nature. And a thin oak veneer.

"Is this why Tony was killed?" Madame Ogilvy asked.

"Possibly. We'll need to interview everyone. Are you really so surprised that Monsieur Baumgartner was stealing?"

"I don't know anymore." She'd been so sure of herself, so in control of the room and her emotions. But now a crack appeared.

"Is it possible he was behind the original embezzlement, and not the assistant?"

She nodded, slowly. Thinking. "It's possible."

"It might've been a test run," said Beauvoir. "And he learned from it."

Now she was shaking her head. "I can't believe it."

"That he did it?"

"That, yes. But also that I didn't see it. When I looked at Tony all I saw was a good, decent man."

"That's why it's called a 'confidence game,'" said Beauvoir. "It depends on confidence."

"Suppose it isn't true?" she asked.

"It's true."

"But just suppose, for a moment, that it isn't. That Tony was telling the truth about the assistant and that he didn't do this." She laid her hand on the statements.

Beauvoir was silent. Not wanting to feed this delusion.

It was one of the many tragedies of a murder. That there was an inquiry, into the life of the dead person. And it often revealed things people wished they'd never known. Often things unrelated to the murder. But exposed nonetheless.

And when this happened, friends and family refused to believe it. The affair. The theft. The unsavory acquaintances. The pornography on the computer. The questionable emails.

It got messy. Emotional. Sometimes even violent, as they defended the honor of the dead. And their own delusions.

"Thank you for your time," he said, getting up and walking to the door. "An agent Cloutier will be in touch, probably later today."

She colored. Not used to having her statements ignored. "You asked for Bernard's name and address? My assistant will give it to you as you leave."

"*Merci*. You'll cooperate?"

"Of course, Chief Inspector."

She might as well cooperate, he thought. The damage was done. The deed was done. No amount of hiding, of wishful thinking, of lying, would stop, or even slow down, what was hurtling over the horizon.

Driving through Montréal, on his way to Lacoste's home, he thought about Madame Ogilvy's final question.

Suppose Anthony Baumgartner wasn't stealing clients' money.

That would mean someone else was.

Anthony Baumgartner's name was on the statements. His signature was on the cover letters.

Beauvoir edged forward, through the snow-clogged, car-clogged streets.

It would have to be someone close to Baumgartner. Who knew the system. Who knew his clients. Who had access to his files and the letterhead. Who knew the man well.

Someone in Taylor and Ogilvy.

Now Beauvoir was seriously considering the question.

Suppose Anthony Baumgartner hadn't done anything wrong. Hadn't been stealing. Suppose those statements were in his study, overseen by mad Ruth, because he'd found out that someone else was. And he was poring over them, to figure out who at the company was stealing millions of dollars from clients.

Suppose, Jean-Guy thought as he turned in to Lacoste's narrow street and looked for a parking spot amid the piles of snow still waiting to be cleared, suppose Anthony Baumgartner was exactly what Madame Ogilvy had described.

A good, decent man. An honorable man. Who'd offered to resign when someone else had done wrong. Who understood the value, and fragility, of trust.

What would a man like that do if he discovered corruption on that scale, or any?

He'd confront the person. Demand an explanation. Threaten exposure.

And what would that person do?

"Kill Anthony Baumgartner," mumbled Beauvoir, backing carefully into a spot.

CHAPTER 29

"And what do you want from me?" asked Lucien as he looked at the two women in his office.

"I'd like to know why you said you'd never met the Baroness," said Myrna, "when you had."

She laid his father's agenda on the desk.

Beside her, Clara tried not to fidget. All around them were towers of boxes. Each the same height. Six feet. Placed, it seemed, consciously, strategically, around the office. Like an obstacle course, she thought.

Though there was something else vaguely familiar about them. Were they meant to resemble those ancient rock formations? Like Stonehenge. Or the mysterious heads on Easter Island.

The boxes—files, she saw—were stacked one on top of the other and seemed far from secure. Why not just pile them along a wall, like any sensible person would?

But she could tell that Lucien Mercier was far from sensible. Rational, yes. In the extreme. But "sensible" demanded the person also be sensitive. In order to make good, sensible decisions.

This man was not.

Clara was all for creativity. But the precarious files looming around them were not works of art. They were, she felt, projections of something innate to Lucien. Something intimate, private. Unhappy.

It sounded almost silly to put it that way. Too simplistic. But how razor-sharp was that simple word? Unhappy.

"In fact," Myrna went on, "you'd been at her house, with your father. You were there when the will was discussed. It's in his notes."

Lucien remained unmoving, except for his eyes. Which moved freely, from woman to woman. They flickered to a stack of boxes behind them. Then back.

He was like, Clara thought, a child who thinks that if his body is immobile, no one will notice his eyes moving. Or if he closes his eyes and sees no one, then he himself becomes invisible.

It was, she knew, a highly egocentric state. One most children grew out of.

Clara was watching him closely. Openly.

She was there at Myrna's request. Her friend wanted a witness. Not because she was afraid of this reedy little man but because, after reading his father's papers, Myrna realized the son could not be trusted. That he could say one thing to her, then change his story later.

"But you have to pay attention," Myrna had warned Clara in the car driving over. "Promise me you will."

"What did you say?"

"Come on, I'm serious. I know you. You look like you're following a conversation, nodding and smiling, but in fact you're trying to work out some issue with your latest painting."

Myrna was, of course, right. As they drove over to the notary's office, Clara had been letting her mind wander. Freeing it up. To see what her subconscious might do with Benedict. He of the silly haircut and goofy grin. And happy eyes.

She wondered if she might paint him as a sort of cartoon character. All bright colors and pastel outlines in bold strokes.

But now that she was in this office, all thought of the shiny young man was banished as she sat in the shadows of the boxes and watched Lucien.

And considered how she might paint him.

"I didn't lie," said Lucien. "I just hadn't remembered. I meet a lot of people."

"Why did you go there with your father? Why did he take you there?"

"He was a cautious man. He always wanted a witness when meeting with elderly clients. A second opinion."

"About what?"

"If the person was competent."

"And was the Baroness?"

"Of course. Otherwise he'd never have allowed her to do that will."

Charcoal, thought Clara. That's what she'd use.

Bright crayons for Benedict and the charred remains of something once living for this man.

"Why can't I find David?" asked Amelia.

Marc shrugged.

He'd given it absolutely no thought. What was left of his mind was taken up with only one thing, the search for more dope. He was like a Neanderthal, completely driven by survival.

Though he recognized that while he was focused on one hit, the next hit, Amelia was looking at the mother lode. At having more shit than they knew what to do with, except use and sell. To get high and get rich.

But still, he couldn't get past worrying. About the next hit.

Amelia was standing in his kitchenette, making peanut-butter sandwiches with the loaf they'd stolen from the convenience store. It was stale and beginning to mold. The fresh loaves had been lifted by others, earlier in the day.

She'd have to remember that.

"Here."

She handed one to Marc, who looked at it with disgust. It was all he'd eaten for months. Peanut fucking butter. The very smell turned his stomach.

Taking a bite, he grimaced. It tasted like despair.

"He's out there somewhere," she said, walking to the window. "But if he has the new shit, why isn't he selling it? What's he waiting for?"

Marc joined her at the window. The sandwich hanging loose in his thin hand.

For just a moment, he allowed himself the aroma of pancakes and bacon on a Saturday morning.

Then he locked it away again. In the private room he was saving. He'd crawl into it, and curl into a tiny ball, and close his eyes. And sit at his mother's table. Eating pancakes, and bacon, and maple syrup. Forever.

He stared down at the junkies and trannies and whores gathered out there. Waiting for Amelia. To do what?

They only wanted one thing. He only wanted one thing. For the pain to stop.

"This David doesn't want to be found," said Amelia.

And for good reason, she knew. If they were looking for the carfentanil, others would be too. And he wouldn't have it in his pocket. He'd have to have a whole operation.

"Like a factory," she said out loud, though she knew she was still just talking to herself. "Right? 'Cause he'd have to cut it. Package it. Prepare it for the streets. Thousands and thousands of hits. He'd need space. And time. He'd know that once it hit the streets, all hell was going to break loose. Between the cops, the mob, the bikers. Every piece of shit within thousands of miles will come to Montréal, looking for it. Looking for him. Right?"

Marc's sandwich hit the floor with a soft thud. But he remained standing. Swaying slightly. Like a cow asleep on its feet. Not aware it was in the abattoir.

"So he'd have to sell as much as he could, as fast as he could, then get the hell gone," said Amelia. "That's why it's not out yet. David doesn't want to sell it until he can sell it all. It must be in some basement. Some drug factory."

This David had marked her. To warn her off. Thinking she was just some newcomer junkie, making inquiries.

She might not know who David was, but he clearly had no idea who she was. And what she was capable of.

CHAPTER 30

—

Chief Superintendent Gamache was already there when Jean-Guy arrived at Isabelle Lacoste's home.

He joined them at the kitchen table.

They looked at each other, and then, in unison, all three said, "Tell me what you know."

"You first, Jean-Guy," said Gamache, smiling at his son-in-law and naturally taking charge.

Beauvoir told them quickly, succinctly, about his meeting with Bernice Ogilvy. And his thoughts as he drove over to meet them.

"Do you think it's . . . possible Baumgartner knew nothing about it?" asked Lacoste. "That someone else was stealing the client's . . . money and using his name?"

"And Baumgartner was killed because he found out?" said Beauvoir. "Follow the money. One of the first rules of homicide."

He looked at the Chief Superintendent. They'd spent much of their apprenticeship as agents watching Gamache break not the law but the so-called rules of homicide investigation. Which was why, as Beauvoir and Lacoste knew, his department had a near-perfect record of finding killers.

"Murderers haven't read the rule book," he'd told them. "And while money's important, there are other forms of currency. And poverty. A moral and emotional bankruptcy. Just as a rape isn't about sex, a murder is rarely about money, even when money's involved. It's about power. And fear. It's about revenge. And rage. It's about feelings, not a bank balance. Follow the money, certainly. But I can guarantee when you find it, it'll stink of some emotion gone putrid."

"Go on," Gamache now said to Beauvoir.

"It would sure be a good reason to kill Baumgartner," said Beauvoir. "Whoever was stealing from the clients was facing not just ruin but prison if Baumgartner exposed him."

"In killing Baumgartner he kept his wealth and freedom," said Lacoste. "Pretty good motive, I agree."

"And now," said Gamache, "pick it apart. What's wrong with that theory?"

Far from being annoyed at this challenge, Beauvoir found it one of his favorite things to do. He was very good at finding fault, even with his own theories. And this was far from a theory he owned or, as Madame Ogilvy would say, was invested in. It simply interested him.

"Okay," said Beauvoir. "If he wasn't stealing from his clients, then what were the statements doing in Baumgartner's study?"

"He'd just discovered what was happening," said Lacoste, taking on the devil's-advocate role, to Beauvoir's delight. "He was shocked and angry and needed to study them to make absolutely sure before accusing anyone."

"But how would he know, just from those papers, who was doing it? They only have his name on them."

"He's a smart man," said Lacoste. "He knows Taylor and Ogilvy and who was likely to be able to do it."

It was a weak argument, they recognized. One the devil would probably lose in court. But possible.

"And who would that be?" Gamache asked. It was unusual for him to interrupt this part of the process. He preferred to listen and absorb.

This showed he thought they just might be onto something.

"The broker doing the trades for him," suggested Beauvoir. "I'm having him brought in for questioning."

"And?"

"The obvious," said Jean-Guy. "Bernice Ogilvy."

"What did you make of her?" Gamache asked.

"She's young, bright. Got there because of her family, of course, but she has the skills and temperament to keep the job. She's smart. Ambitious. Adaptable."

"Greedy?" asked Gamache.

Beauvoir thought about that. "Entitled, maybe. I think she'd do just about anything to protect what's hers."

"Would she steal from clients and blame her former mentor?" asked Gamache.

Jean-Guy Beauvoir found himself coloring slightly at the mention of betraying a former mentor. And he wondered, fleetingly, whether Gamache could possibly know about the meeting that morning. And the paper he'd signed.

"She understood very quickly how it could be done," said Beauvoir. "Maybe too quickly. And she strikes me as the sort who thinks she's smarter than those around her."

"Probably . . . because she is," said Lacoste. "Besides, who really believes they're going to get caught? Madame Ogilvy knows the . . . business and knows how to get around any scrutiny."

"Just set up fake accounts," said Gamache. "It's so simple. No one at Taylor and Ogilvy would see them. And the clients would have no idea. They'd continue to get what looked like real statements, with real transactions. They'd have dividends and profits deposited in their accounts. All would look perfectly normal."

"Except she'd be putting the capital, their initial investment, into her own account," said Beauvoir. "And paying out generous so-called dividends to keep clients from asking any questions."

"Could they have been in it together?" Lacoste asked. "Ogilvy and Baumgartner?"

"Agent Cloutier suspects there'd have been two of them," said Beauvoir. "And don't forget, Baumgartner himself wasn't exactly splashing money around. He lived in the same house. Drove a decent but sensible car. Why would he steal and not spend the money?"

"Retirement," said Lacoste. "Squirreling it away in some offshore account. Then one day he disappears."

As Gamache listened, a series of photos in Baumgartner's home came to mind. Of Baumgartner and his children. Happy. Radiant, in fact. Was this the face of a man willing to turn his back and never see them again? Disappear to some Caribbean refuge? For what? A power boat and marble bathrooms?

"*Désolé*," said Gamache. "I've taken you off course. Back to the

281

arguments. You were making the case for Anthony Baumgartner's finding out about the embezzlement and confronting whoever was doing it."

"Right," said Beauvoir, refocusing. "So he stumbles on what's happening. Maybe one of the so-called clients calls him or he runs into them at a party, and they ask about their account. An account he knows nothing about. Baumgartner does some digging, finds the fake statements, and brings the evidence home. He pores over them, then arranges to meet the person he suspects was—"

"Why?" Lacoste interrupted.

"Why what?"

"Why not just go to his manager?"

"Maybe the manager's the one who's doing it?" said Beauvoir.

"Then why not go to the industry regulator?" asked Lacoste.

"Because he's not sure," said Beauvoir, feeling his way along more slowly now. "Or he is sure and doesn't want to believe it. He wants to give this person a chance to explain or clear themselves. Or maybe he doesn't realize he's talking to the guilty party."

Gamache shifted in his chair and tilted his head.

This was interesting.

"Maybe he asked to meet someone he thinks will be an ally," said Beauvoir, gaining more confidence in this unexpected theory. "To show them the evidence and ask what they think."

"And the person kills him?" asked Lacoste. "Bit of an . . . overreaction. Can't the person just muddy the waters or send B- . . . Baumgartner off in the wrong direction? They must know that if they kill Baumgartner then the cops, aka us, will definitely be involved, and asking questions."

"Why?" asked Beauvoir, turning the tables on her.

"Why ask questions? It's kinda how we . . . solve murders, isn't it?" asked Lacoste.

Armand Gamache was watching this. Two smart young investigators, hashing out the most vile of crimes. His investigators. His protégés. Now more than capable of running whole departments on their own.

He missed this. Not simply sitting around kitchen tables trying to solve a murder. But doing it with these two. With Jean-Guy and Isabelle. Going at it like siblings.

"I know you prefer to just arrest the first person you meet in an . . . investigation," said Isabelle. "But the rest of us actually investigate."

"*Merci,*" said Beauvoir, smiling thinly and recognizing the patronizing tone as a ruse, an attempt by Isabelle to get under his skin. It worked more often than he was willing to show.

"But I meant why would we ask about an embezzlement?"

"Because"—now she sounded patient in the extreme—"the investigation would uncover it."

"But would it? I hope so, but it's far from a given, especially if Baumgartner had nothing to do with it," said Beauvoir. "Look, suppose Baumgartner was inadvertently meeting with the person who was actually responsible for the embezzlement—wouldn't he take along his evidence? Even if he was meeting with someone he suspected, he'd take it along. As proof."

"Right," said Lacoste, her voice guarded. Trying to see where this was going. "So?"

But Gamache could see and was smiling slightly.

"So that person would know two things," said Jean-Guy. "That there was nothing linking Baumgartner to the thefts. On his computer or files or anywhere. So any investigation into his death would reveal exactly nothing. And the killer would reasonably expect that whatever papers Baumgartner had with him were probably his only copies. Might even have asked, to make sure they were."

"So he'd kill Baumgartner and destroy the evidence," said Lacoste, forgetting to argue.

"Exactly."

Gamache waited to see if either of them would spot the flaw in that argument. He waited.

And waited.

"If those were his only proof," said Jean-Guy, "why were the statements found in his study?"

And there it was, thought Gamache. The problem.

If Baumgartner was meeting someone to either confide suspicions or confront them about the embezzlement, he'd take proof. And the person, after killing Baumgartner, would take that proof and burn it.

So why were there copies of the incriminating statements next to his computer?

And there was another problem with this theory.

"Why the farmhouse?" asked Lacoste.

Yes, thought Gamache. Why meet at the farmhouse?

"Familiar ground," suggested Beauvoir. "Maybe he was going to be there anyway, a final look around before it was torn down. Maybe the reading of the will brought up childhood memories and he wanted to visit. Convenience, coupled with the need to be in what he, even unconsciously, considered a safe place."

"At night? Without electricity or heat?" asked Lacoste.

Beauvoir nodded. Hugo had said they'd had dinner together. He'd left early, but still, it would have been dark.

"And why was he upstairs?" asked Lacoste.

"Looking around," said Beauvoir. "In his childhood bedroom."

It was credible, though hanging on to believability by a thread.

"Don't forget," said Beauvoir, "Baumgartner didn't expect to be killed. Either he thought he was meeting a friend, someone who'd help him, or he thought he'd be confronting someone. That it would be a shitty conversation. But he clearly didn't see this person as any physical threat. Or he'd never have agreed to meet him—"

"Or her," said Lacoste.

"—there."

"There's another problem," said Lacoste. "The convenience of the building falling down."

"But was it convenient?" asked Beauvoir. "It meant Baumgartner's body was found, maybe sooner than the killer expected. If it hadn't fallen, it's possible his body wouldn't have been found for a long time."

"I guess it's also possible Baumgartner didn't arrange to meet this person at the farmhouse," said Lacoste. "Maybe he was followed there and killed."

"What do you mean?" asked Beauvoir.

"Suppose Baumgartner got in touch with the person he suspected and arranged to . . . meet them the next day, at the office. The person, knowing they were in trouble, drives over to Anthony Baumgartner's . . . home, maybe to kill him there, but then sees him leaving. He follows him to the abandoned house and kills him there."

"Bit convenient for the killer, *non?*" asked Beauvoir.

"But it fits, and it explains the timing, with the will," said Lacoste, warming to her just-discovered theory. She turned to Gamache. "You and Myrna and Benedict read them their mother's will. While . . . ridiculous, it was very much the Baroness. It stirs feelings of childhood, and Anthony decides to drive out and see the old . . . place before it's torn down or sold."

Beauvoir snorted, but Gamache tilted his head. He drove, every now and then, past the house he grew up in. And after Reine-Marie's mother died and before they sold the family home, she'd wanted one last walk around.

What Lacoste was describing was emotionally valid. Though Beauvoir was also right. It did seem a bit too convenient for the murderer. That Baumgartner would just happen to be in a remote farmhouse, designed for quiet murder.

"*Bon*," he said. "Let's move on to the more likely theory. That Anthony Baumgartner not only knew about the money being stolen but was responsible. Who killed him then?"

"One of his targets," said Beauvoir. "Someone who found out."

"But why kill him? Why not just tell someone at his company or, better still, go to the police?" asked Lacoste.

"Because the company had been told once and nothing happened to him," said Beauvoir. "A slap on the wrist. Why trust Taylor and Ogilvy to do something this time, when they did nothing last time?"

"Okay, but my question stands," said Lacoste. "Why not go to the police or a lawyer? Why not sue his . . . ass? Why confront Baumgartner?"

"Because they weren't sure," said Beauvoir. "Most people can't believe someone they trust is stealing. They'd ask first, and if they didn't like the answer, then they'd take the next step."

"Right," said Lacoste. "A lawyer or the police. Plan B surely isn't to kill the guy. But you're saying that's what . . . happened. What would that achieve?"

"It was a bang on the head," said Beauvoir. "Has the makings of a sudden rage, not something planned out. As much as Baumgartner didn't expect to be killed, I'm betting whoever did this didn't expect to kill."

Gamache was listening. But there remained one big problem with that theory. A familiar one.

"Why the farmhouse?" Lacoste asked. "Would Baumgartner really agree to meet a client, someone he was stealing from, there? Even if he didn't know . . . what it was about, that's a long way to go. Out in the middle of nowhere. And a pretty personal space. I just don't buy it."

Gamache was listening to this and thinking that it wasn't so easy to find a place to kill someone. Even in rural Québec. A forest would make sense, but how do you lure a client, who's already suspicious, into the woods?

"Come on," said Lacoste, following the same line of thought. "Would the client really agree to meet in an isolated, abandoned home? I wouldn't."

"Why not?" Beauvoir turned to Gamache. "You did. When you got the letter from the notary."

Gamache gave a short laugh. "True, but I wasn't going there to confront someone. And I didn't realize it was abandoned until I got there."

"And there you have it," said Beauvoir. "The client who's being screwed wouldn't know either. He'd gone that far, and I'm sure Baumgartner explained it was his mother's house. It sounded okay. Safe."

It was possible, thought Gamache. But far from probable. Though it did explain why those statements were still in Baumgartner's study. He was doing the stealing. And the killing. And he expected to be home.

"So," said Lacoste. "We have two theories. That Anthony Baumgartner was doing the stealing and that he wasn't."

"Doesn't feel like progress to me," admitted Beauvoir.

"Let's move from theories to facts," said Gamache.

"*D'accord,*" said Beauvoir, putting a slip of paper on the kitchen table. "I have information on the assistant who was fired. His name's Bernard Shaeffer. Taylor and Ogilvy had his address from when he worked for them, but nothing since."

"Bernard Shaeffer," repeated Lacoste. She took the paper and entered his name in her laptop. "His address is the same," she said, reading from the government files. "Looks like he's now working for the . . . Caisse Populaire du Québec."

She looked over the screen of her laptop at her colleagues. Her brows rose.

"A bank?" asked Jean-Guy. "The Caisse hired him after what he did at Taylor and Ogilvy?"

"Let me make a quick call," said Gamache, picking up his iPhone.

He dialed, waited, then gave his name and asked for Jeanne Halstrom. The president of the Caisse Populaire. After inquiring about her family, he asked a few other questions, listened, thanked her, then hung up.

"Bernard Shaeffer was hired as a financial adviser eighteen months ago. He had Anthony Baumgartner down as a reference. According to the personnel file, Monsieur Baumgartner vouched for him and said he'd been an outstanding employee. They'll start an investigation into Shaeffer's activities, including if he's set up any unusually large accounts in his or Baumgartner's name. We'll need a warrant, but she'll get things started."

"We might've just found out where the client's money went," said Beauvoir. "Looks like Baumgartner didn't break off contact with Bernard. Just the opposite."

"He wouldn't be so stupid as to have the accounts in his own name, would he?" asked Isabelle.

"We'll find out," said Gamache. "Even if it's offshore, the Caisse can probably track Shaeffer's activity."

"And I'll go visit young Monsieur Shaeffer right after this." Beauvoir thought for a moment. "Better still, I'll have Agent Cloutier bring him in for questioning."

He made a call, then hung up. "She's on her way."

"Good," said Isabelle. "She's found her . . . footing?"

"Yes. Finally. But she's frustrated about not being able to get into Baumgartner's laptop and get at his personal files. We all are. We're still trying, of course. Put in the names of his children, and his mother. And father. All the obvious ones."

"Maybe it's not a name," said Gamache, "but a number."

"We've tried the children's birth dates. His birthday. But you asked for facts, *patron*. There is something else I found out from Bernice Ogilvy," said Beauvoir. "Not about Baumgartner this time. It's about

287

Kinderoth. An elderly couple by that name had an account at Taylor and Ogilvy."

There was a beat while they took that in.

"With Baumgartner?" asked Lacoste.

"*Non.*"

She deflated a bit. It was probably too much to ask.

But Gamache was leaning forward. He knew Jean-Guy well. Very well. And he could see this wasn't some aside. This was, perhaps, the main course.

"Go on," he said.

And Beauvoir told them what Madame Ogilvy had said about the Kinderoths. And their will.

Beauvoir watched for their reaction and wasn't disappointed. Gamache smiled, and Lacoste was almost throbbing with excitement.

The three sat around the kitchen table, as they'd sat around so many tables, across Québec, across the years. Sipping strong teas and coffees and discussing terrible crimes.

So much had changed over time, but the core remained the same.

Beauvoir thought about the question Bernice Ogilvy had asked. Did he love his job? The answer, he knew for certain, was yes. And it wasn't just his job he loved.

Chief Superintendent Gamache sat back, a look of extreme concentration on his face. Then he brought a notebook out of his breast pocket.

"This came in last night," he said. "From Kontrollinspektor Gund in Vienna. I'd asked him to look up that original will."

"The one going back a hundred years," said Isabelle.

"A hundred and thirty. Baron Kinderoth, Shlomo, had two sons, twins," Gamache reminded them. "He left them each the entirety of his estate. We'll probably never know why he did it, but we can see the effect it had. It clearly caused hurt and confusion. Who inherited? I asked the Kontrollinspektor if he could do some searching through their records. This's what he sent back."

He put on his glasses while Beauvoir and Lacoste leaned closer.

"I won't read it verbatim," said Gamache. "My translation is pretty bad, but I think I got the gist of it. I've sent it on to an acquaintance who does speak German, but in the meantime this'll have to do. Both sons took it to court, of course, and after a few years it was decided in favor of one son, the one deemed the firstborn of the twins. By then both men had themselves died, and the heirs of the other son contested the decision. Because of the complexity and confusion over who was really firstborn, the case lingered. It took another few years to be heard and another few years for a decision. This time it was in favor of the supposed younger son. He worked in the family firm, and the first seems to have been, in the words of the court, a rotter."

"How long out from Shlomo Kinderoth's death did this happen?" asked Lacoste.

"That decision for the younger son, and now his heirs, was thirty years after Shlomo's death. Again the family of the older son contested the decision."

"And the money?" asked Beauvoir.

"It remained in trust," said Gamache. "Growing, but not dispersed."

Lacoste did a quick calculation. "Thirty years. That would put that decision around 1915."

"Exactly," said Gamache. "World War One. According to records the Kontrollinspektor found, much of the family was killed, at least the young men. Austria was in turmoil. It wasn't until the 1930s that the family took another run at it. By then the descendants of one of the sons had become Baumgartners, through marriage. And had since moved to Canada. Montréal. The Kinderoths stayed in Austria."

"Oh dear," said Lacoste.

"*Oui*," said Gamache. "All I have are the court records. That's all I asked for, and I'm not sure if more detailed accounts are possible, but it does seem that at least one Kinderoth survived the Nazis and came to Montréal after the war. There might be others still in Europe somewhere. Kontrollinspektor Gund is looking."

"Why Canada?" asked Beauvoir.

"Not just Canada," Lacoste pointed out, "but Montréal."

"Where the Baumgartners had settled," said Gamache. "It cannot be a coincidence."

"Were they looking for family?" asked Lacoste. "After what happened, maybe distant and even unpleasant family was better than none. It might be instinctive."

"It's possible," said Gamache. "But I think by then their instincts had warped and something else motivated them. Shortly after the war ended, another petition was filed in the Austrian courts. For the Kinderoth fortune."

"My God," said Lacoste. "Don't they ever give up?"

"Was there even a fortune left?" asked Beauvoir.

"I doubt it," said Gamache, "but they wouldn't know that. I think they were still going on family lore."

"Or maybe they knew something the authorities didn't," said Lacoste. "Some Jewish families managed to convert their money into art, or jewelry, or gold, didn't they? And then hid it or smuggled it out of the country."

"Yes," said Gamache. "But neither the Kinderoths nor the Baumgartners could get at the money. It was held in trust. And the Nazi regime would've confiscated it. Stolen it."

"So they've been fighting over nothing?" asked Beauvoir. "All these years?"

"Nothing tangible anyway," said Gamache. "But who knows? It was there once, so I suppose there's a possibility—"

He left it hanging.

"And now?" asked Lacoste, looking down at the notebook and the careful writing there.

"And now, according to Kontrollinspektor Gund, a final decision is about to come down in the Austrian courts."

"When?" asked Beauvoir.

"Anytime now. According to Gund, it's been expected for a year or so, but there's a backlog, of course, of lawsuits dating from the war. They're getting through them slowly."

"This slowly?" asked Beauvoir. "Most of the people who brought them would be long dead."

"Their descendants would benefit," said Gamache. "And the Austrians want to be very careful. To be as fair as possible, especially about anything to do with the Jewish population and what was stolen. They can't, of course, undo the Holocaust, but they can try to make reparations."

"Why don't the Kinderoths and Baumgartners just decide to divide it equally?" asked Lacoste. "This would've been settled generations ago."

"Maybe you want to suggest it to them," said Jean-Guy, and he got a glare from Isabelle.

"Up until now it's been unpleasant but civil," said Isabelle. "Do we really think Anthony Baumgartner's death—"

"And maybe his mother's," said Beauvoir. "She died suddenly and then was cremated."

"*Oui,*" said Lacoste. "Okay. Maybe the Baroness too. But do we really think they were murdered because of a century-old will?"

"One that was about to be settled," said Gamache.

"And contested again," said Beauvoir.

"*Non.* The courts have said they won't tolerate another appeal. They have too many old cases to go through to keep retrying the same one."

"So whoever wins could inherit a fortune," said Lacoste.

"Real or imagined," said Gamache. And this seemed, he thought, a family rich in imagination. Clinging on to the myth of aristocracy and power and wealth, even as they drove cabs and cleaned toilets.

Beauvoir shook his head.

Why kill Anthony Baumgartner now? Did they think Caroline and Hugo had murdered their brother for a larger stake in a fictional inheritance?

He'd met these people. They seemed intelligent. And no intelligent person would believe in the fairy tale of an old fortune that had somehow survived wars and pogroms and the Holocaust to come to them now.

And suppose the other arm of the family won? The Kinderoths? What then? A fratricide for nothing?

The three of them stared into space. Thinking. Trying to see through the tangle of time and motives.

Gamache looked at his watch. He was meeting Benedict in downtown Montréal in twenty minutes. He'd have to be leaving soon to make the rendezvous.

"And there's still the issue of the liquidators of Madame Baumgartner's will," he said.

"Very suspicious lot," Beauvoir said to Lacoste, who nodded agreement.

Gamache smiled patiently. "We don't know why Myrna and I were on it, but we at least have some connection through Three Pines, where the Baroness worked. But are we any closer to knowing why Benedict was a liquidator?"

"Not at all," said Lacoste, who'd been charged with finding out. "There seems absolutely no connection. He never worked in the area. He never met her. How Madame Baumgartner even knew he existed, never mind trusted him enough to put him on the will, is a mystery."

"Dead end?" asked Beauvoir, needling her.

"Never," said Lacoste. "There's a reason, and I'll find it. I plan on speaking with his ex. This Katie might know something or remember something he'd forgotten. I've never met him, but by your description Benedict does seem pretty scatterbrained."

Once again Armand felt the body of the young man on his back. As Benedict protected him from falling debris.

And then, when the worst was over and he could straighten up, Armand had looked, through grit-clogged eyes, at the young man in the silly hat. With blood streaming down his face. From a chunk of concrete that would almost certainly, Armand knew, have struck him.

It was an act of extreme selflessness. And instinct. It spoke of Benedict's good heart, though it was no use denying that his brain was perhaps not the sharpest.

Gamache got up. "I've got to go meet him. He's giving me a lift back to Three Pines. I'm probably late already."

"Can I drive you over?" Jean-Guy asked as they walked to the front door.

"If you don't mind."

Beauvoir went down the outside stairs to start the car.

Gamache thanked Isabelle. And she thanked him.

"What for?" he asked.

"For this. For not leaving me behind."

"Never." He kissed her on both cheeks, then walked carefully down the flight of icy steps. But at the bottom he stopped. Dead.

Then, as Beauvoir watched from the warming car, Armand turned and raced back up the stairs, taking them two at a time. Shouting to Isabelle.

Beauvoir got out of the car and was halfway up the stairs himself when Gamache emerged from Isabelle's home.

"What is it? What's happened?" Jean-Guy asked.

"What was the name," Gamache asked, his voice brusque, "of the young woman who was at the top of the contact list for Madame Baumgartner?"

As he spoke, he came down the stairs quickly, faster than he probably should have.

"In the seniors' home?" asked Beauvoir. "I can't remember."

"Can you find it?"

"I can find my notes."

"Great," said Gamache as he got into the passenger seat. "Give them to me, please."

Beauvoir handed them over, then drove as Gamache turned on the reading light and scanned, not even bothering to put on his glasses. After a couple minutes, he lowered the notes, wiped his eyes, and stared out the windshield.

"Katie Burke," he said.

"Yes, that's it," said Beauvoir. He glanced over at Gamache. "What is it?"

Something had happened.

"I asked Isabelle for the full name of Benedict's girlfriend—"

"Katie Burke," guessed Beauvoir, and he saw Gamache nod. "Holy shit," exhaled Beauvoir. "Benedict's girlfriend not only knew the Baroness but was her first contact?"

He was elated, but as he shot a look at Gamache, he could see that far from being triumphant at finding this unexpected connection, Gamache was subdued.

There was silence as they drove through the now-dark streets of the city, and both men considered what this might mean.

When he pulled over to drop Gamache off, Beauvoir said, "Benedict lied."

"Yes."

"Do you want me there when you speak with him, *patron*?"

"No, that's not necessary. You have a lot to do. Isabelle said she'd find out all she can about Katie Burke and report back to you."

"Well, at least we now know how Benedict got onto Madame Baumgartner's will," said Beauvoir. "But we don't know why."

"We will," said Gamache, his voice clipped.

It was going to be, Beauvoir thought, a very long drive back to Three Pines, for both Gamache and the young man.

It was never a good idea to lie to the Chief.

Jean-Guy headed off for his interview with Bernard Shaeffer, who even now was waiting in an interview room at Sûreté headquarters.

Gamache stood on the sidewalk, scanning for Benedict. The warmth of the drive over slid off him as the biting cold seeped up the cuffs of his sleeves and down his collar and settled against the exposed skin of his face.

But he felt none of that. He was staring ahead. Thinking. Trying to bridge the chasm between what he knew and what he felt.

"Chief Superintendent" came a familiar voice, and Gamache turned to see Hugo Baumgartner approaching. "You look deep in thought," said the ugly little man.

A thick winter coat, a tuque, and cheeks ruddy with cold did nothing to improve Baumgartner's appearance.

But his eyes were bright and his deep voice warm.

"I was."

"Can I help you with anything?"

"No, I'm just waiting for my lift, *merci*."

"Would you like to wait inside?" Hugo waved behind him, toward the office building he'd just come from. The head office of Horowitz Investments.

"No, I'm fine. Thank you."

But Hugo didn't leave. He stood beside Gamache, shifting from cold foot to cold foot. And thumping his gloved hands together. He looked like a lug, a pug, a failed boxer who made a living being beaten up by his betters in practice rounds.

Gamache turned to him. Clearly Hugo had something to say.

"I hear you had lunch with Mr. Horowitz."

"I did," said Gamache. "How'd you know about that?"

"Ahh, the street. Everyone knows everything. For instance, I know that during lunch Stephen approached that moron Filatreau and told him he was dumping his stock."

"True. Do you know what Monsieur Filatreau had for lunch?"

It was meant as a joke, but Hugo answered, "Sweetbreads. And you had sea bass."

Gamache's smile faded, and he nodded. The street, it seemed, was well informed.

"What else do you know, Monsieur Baumgartner?"

"I know you asked about my brother and that Stephen said he was a crook. Mr. Horowitz is a financial genius and a good judge of character. But he isn't always right. He likes to imagine the worst in people. His worldview is that everyone's a crook. Or about to be."

"He spoke highly of you."

"Well, maybe I have him fooled," said Hugo. "My brother was a good man. He wouldn't steal. Word's spreading that that's why he was killed. You have to find out who did this, please. It's bad enough what happened. Anthony's reputation can't be ruined too."

"What do you know about the will?"

"My mother's? Just what you do. That she believed the hokum about some long-lost family fortune that was really ours. It was amusing to us as kids but grew tiresome."

"And yet when we were reading the will, and your brother and sister seemed embarrassed by it, you defended your mother."

"Her, yes, but not the will."

"As I remember, you did defend it, saying you thought maybe she was right."

Hugo looked around and again shifted from foot to foot. "I loved my mother and hated when anyone mocked her. Even Tony and Caroline."

"You're a loyal man."

"Is that such a bad thing?"

"Not at all. I admire it. But loyalty can blind us to the truth about people. Though, as it turns out, your mother might've actually been right."

"What do you mean?"

Hugo had stopped shifting and stared at Gamache.

"I think you know exactly what I mean, monsieur. Think about it, and call me when you decide you do know."

He gave Hugo a card.

Just then Gamache saw Benedict draw up in his Volvo. It was rush hour and dark, and it didn't take long for other cars to start honking at Benedict, who was gesturing at Gamache to hurry.

"There's one more thing," said Gamache. "Who's Katie Burke?"

"Who?"

"It's cold, and my ride is about to be murdered by other drivers, so just tell me. You know I know."

"Then why ask?"

"To see just how truthful you decide to be. So far you're not doing well."

"I've told you the truth about my brother."

"Did you?"

There was a pause, and all they could hear were more horns joining in, a veritable shriek of rage from rue Sherbrooke. Directed at Benedict.

"Who is Katie Burke, Monsieur Baumgartner?"

"She used to visit the Baroness in the nursing home."

"Why?"

"I don't know. But Mom liked her, and it sort of relieved us of some responsibility, I'm ashamed to say."

"She was at the top of your mother's contact list."

"Was she?"

"You didn't know?"

By now Benedict had lowered the window of the Volvo and was pleading with Armand to get in.

Hugo shook his head. "Does it matter?"

"Would I ask if it didn't?" Armand gestured toward the card in Hugo's gloved hand. "Your mother's will, Monsieur Baumgartner. Give me a call when you decide to tell the whole story. Don't wait too long."

He walked to the car and waved at the line of cars behind Benedict. More than one driver raised a finger in return.

"Thank God," said Benedict, exhaling and pulling into traffic. "Who was that? Looked like you were speaking with something from *Lord of the Rings*."

"Hugo Baumgartner."

"Oh right. I didn't recognize him."

Armand buckled up, and as they headed over the Champlain Bridge, he found himself humming under his breath.

"'Edelweiss, Edelweiss . . .'"

CHAPTER 31

Bernard Shaeffer sat in the spartan interview room at Sûreté headquarters. Looking around. Crossing and recrossing his legs. Trying to get comfortable on a metal chair that would never allow it.

Chief Inspector Beauvoir looked through the two-way mirror.

"Did he say anything on the ride over?"

"*Non, patron*," said Cloutier. "Only asked if this was anything to do with the death of Anthony Baumgartner."

"And what did you say?"

"Nothing. Here's his iPhone."

She handed Beauvoir the device. It was now the first thing they did with suspects. Relieve them of their devices, so they couldn't contact anyone or delete anything.

Monsieur Shaeffer was not what Beauvoir expected. He'd been prepared for a young buck. Someone sharp. Attractive.

Not this average-looking, nervous young guy wearing a good but not exceptional suit.

Though, Beauvoir dropped his eyes and noticed Shaeffer's shoes. Pointy and on point. Completely of the moment.

Fashionable and expensive.

Jean-Guy knew. He too tried to be fashionable but could not afford this level of expense.

While suggestive, it was far from definitive. Some people bought expensive cars. Some spent their money on vacations. And some single young men spent their money on clothes.

It did not mean Shaeffer was living beyond his means. Or was a thief.

"Right," said Beauvoir. "Come with me."

Cloutier followed him into the interview room, where Beauvoir introduced himself.

"My name's Jean-Guy Beauvoir. I'm the acting head of homicide. You've met Agent Cloutier."

This was said for both Shaeffer and the recording.

They took seats, Beauvoir across from the young man.

"Thank you for coming in. We just have a few questions for you."

"About Tony?"

"Mostly, yes." Beauvoir's tone was friendly. "Tell us about your relationship with him."

"We worked in the same office. Taylor and Ogilvy. This was a few years ago. I was an assistant, and Monsieur Baumgartner was a senior vice president."

Shaeffer was watching Beauvoir closely and seemed to come to a decision.

"We had an affair. And then I was fired."

"Why?"

He'd made it sound as though it was because of the affair.

"You might as well tell us, Bernard." Beauvoir smiled encouragingly. "You must know we've already visited Taylor and Ogilvy."

"I was accused of stealing from clients' accounts. But I didn't do it."

"Then why would they fire you?"

"They had to blame someone, didn't they?"

"If you weren't doing it, who was?"

Shaeffer hesitated.

"Come on, Bernard. The truth. It's all right. Just tell us."

"Monsieur Baumgartner."

"Anthony Baumgartner?"

"Yes."

"But if he was stealing, why would he go to Madame Ogilvy and tell her about it?"

"He thought they were going to find out, so he went and blamed me."

"His lover."

Shaeffer nodded.

"What did you do?"

"What could I do?"

300

"I don't know. Tell the truth?"

Shaeffer laughed. "Right. Me against a senior vice president. Let's guess who they'd believe."

"So you just left?" asked Beauvoir, and when Shaeffer nodded, Jean-Guy stared at him for a long moment. "Then why did you put Anthony Baumgartner down as a reference at the Caisse Pop?"

Shaeffer reddened. Clearly they knew far more than he realized.

"Tony told me if I kept quiet, he'd find me a job at the Caisse and vouch for me."

"So you accepted?"

"What choice did I have? If I refused, I'd be thrown out on my ass anyway. I was pretty well screwed."

An agent walked into the interview room and whispered in Beauvoir's ear, then left.

"So," said Beauvoir, "you're saying Anthony Baumgartner was stealing and you were completely innocent?"

Shaeffer straightened up. "Well, okay, I knew what he was doing. But I wasn't involved."

"He told you?"

"He'd had too much to drink. He was relaxed, and he talked too much. He knew I wouldn't tell anyone."

"Why wouldn't you?"

"Because I cared for him. A lot."

"And?" said Beauvoir.

There was silence again as Shaeffer fidgeted. "And he said if I told anyone, he'd say it was me, not him."

"Which he did anyway."

"Yes."

Beauvoir studied the unremarkable young man.

"Were you ever in his home?"

"Once. He wanted help putting up a picture his mother had given him. I think it might've been of her. She looked kinda crazy. Anyway, we hung it above the fireplace in his study and then had a few drinks. He asked for help setting up his new laptop, so we had a few more drinks, then fiddled with the computer for a while and got sorta giddy—"

"Did you get the laptop working?" said Beauvoir.

"Yes."

"And did he put in a security code?"

"Yes. I remember because it took him a while to come up with one. He said he was running out of ideas for new codes."

"And do you remember the code?"

The question was asked casually, but the room crackled with the tension between the Sûreté officers.

"No idea. He didn't tell me."

"Did he hint? Say anything?" prodded Beauvoir.

Shaeffer thought. "If he did, I can't remember."

"Did you sneak a peek? Look over his shoulder when he entered it?"

"Of course not."

"'Of course'? Come on, Bernard. We all do it. Just out of curiosity. Did you watch while he put it in?"

"No."

"Then what did you do?"

"Huh?"

"In the study, while Monsieur Baumgartner put in his password, what did you do?"

"I stared at the picture. I don't know why anyone in their right mind would have that thing in their home."

Beauvoir considered. It could be true. That painting of Ruth was as riveting as it was revolting. As Clara herself said, it was hard to look away.

But this was a sharp young man, and given a choice between finding out the password to a laptop and looking at the picture of a mad old woman, Beauvoir was pretty sure he knew which one Bernard Shaeffer would choose.

"What happened next?" Beauvoir asked.

"We got drunk and had sex."

"For the first time?"

"Yes. We'd been sorta feeling each other out, but I wasn't sure he was gay. But he kept sending these signals, and then—"

"What was he like?" asked Beauvoir.

"As a lover?"

"As a man."

Shaeffer considered the question. "Kind. Smart. Decent. I thought."

"Until he blamed you for stealing and got you fired."

"Yes."

"When he got you the job at the bank, did he ask for any favors?"

"Like what?"

Beauvoir stared at him for a moment, then stood up.

"I'll let you think about that. Excuse me."

Beauvoir nodded to Agent Cloutier, and they went out, leaving Shaeffer to stare at the slowly closing door. Then at the blank wall across from him.

The ice fog that looked pretty when stuck like crystals to branches was a lot less attractive when it settled onto the roads. And then was covered by the soft snow falling.

Benedict and Gamache made small talk, as Benedict drove carefully back to Three Pines, watching for black ice on the highway.

They talked about their day. About the weather.

Benedict asked about Gamache's eyes.

"Better, thank you. I'm seeing much more clearly."

They'd lapsed into what appeared to be companionable silence.

But appearances deceived.

Once again Chief Inspector Beauvoir introduced himself and Agent Cloutier, then sat down in the interview room.

"You are Louis Lamontagne?"

"I am."

"And you work for Taylor and Ogilvy as a broker?"

"I do."

He was forty-five, maybe slightly older, thought Beauvoir. Plump but not heavy. Just a little soft. "Comfortable" was the word that came to mind. His hair was trimmed and graying.

He looked upright. Intelligent. Conservative in every way. If "trustworthy" had a poster child, it would be the man across the table, thought Beauvoir.

And he wondered if he was looking at another numbered print. Close, but not the real thing.

"You did Anthony Baumgartner's trades for him, I understand."

"Yes."

"How does that work?"

"Well, Tony was a wealth manager, so he created portfolios for his clients. Given their age, their needs, their tolerance for risk, he'd decide which vehicles to put them into. Then he'd ask me to do the actual buying and selling."

"And that was fine with you?"

"Absolutely. More than fine. He was a brilliant investment adviser. To be honest, if he bought a stock, I'd often put my own clients into it. He had a knack for seeing how apparently unconnected elements came together and could affect the market. It's a terrible loss. A really sad thing to happen to a fine man. Do you have any ideas who did it?"

"We're hoping you can help."

"Anything."

Beauvoir slid the statements across the table and watched as Monsieur Lamontagne picked them up.

After a minute or so, Beauvoir saw his brows rise, then draw together in concentration and consternation. His blue eyes blinked behind his glasses, and his head leaned to one side. Just a little. Perplexed.

"None of these people are on Tony's client list. I didn't do any of these trades." He looked at Beauvoir over the papers. "I don't understand."

"I think you do."

Lamontagne went back to the statements, going from one to another and rereading the cover letter.

"I can guess," he said, finally putting them back down on the table. "But I can't explain."

"Try."

Louis Lamontagne held Beauvoir's eyes, in a look that was smart, assessing.

"I think you already know," the broker said.

Beauvoir held the gaze but said nothing and saw Lamontagne's eyes open in surprise.

"You think I had something to do with this."

"What is 'this,' monsieur?" asked Beauvoir.

Watching closely, Agent Cloutier took mental notes. On what the

Chief Inspector was saying and not saying. How to imply. How intimating became intimidating. It was subtle, and all the more powerful for it.

In her previous assignment, in the accounting department, she never ended up in interview rooms.

This she found fascinating.

It took nerves, she saw. And intense concentration, while appearing to be completely relaxed. Her instinct was to come out with things. To show how much she knew. Now she could see the value of saying very little. And letting the other person come to their own conclusions about how much was known. Let their fears take hold and take control.

"'This,'" said the broker, "is a scam. Someone set up a shell and made it appear to be Taylor and Ogilvy business."

"Someone?"

"I know you want me to say it was Tony, but it could've been anyone."

"Including yourself?" It was said casually, with a touch of humor.

Lamontagne smiled, but his color betrayed him. "I supposed I could have, but I didn't."

Beauvoir waited.

"All right, I admit, it looks like it was Tony. His name's on the statement and the cover letter."

"With Taylor and Ogilvy letterhead," said Beauvoir. "The clients would think their money was being managed through the company, but in fact he was stealing it and paying out generous dividends to keep them from asking questions."

Lamontagne nodded, staring at Beauvoir. "Yes. Exactly." He picked up the paper again. "Tony must've chosen people he knew weren't plugged into the market. Who almost certainly never read the business pages or the statements."

"Does this surprise you?" asked Beauvoir.

Lamontagne shifted in his chair.

"I'd have to say it does."

"But you've heard the rumors about Monsieur Baumgartner."

"I know his license to trade was pulled. That's why I was asked to do his trading for him. That's a serious penalty. I'd heard it's because he was involved in something with clients' money. But not directly. Apparently it was an assistant who did it, and Tony was the one who blew the whistle. And took some of the blame. The street loves a rumor, and a scandal, and especially loves a fall from a great height, even if it's unfair. Especially if it's unfair."

"You make the street sound like it's a machine," said Beauvoir. "And not brokers like yourself."

"I wasn't involved in those rumors."

"But did you do anything to stop them?"

"I didn't feed them."

It wasn't the same as stopping them. As defending Tony Baumgartner.

"Did you think there was truth to the rumors?" asked Beauvoir.

"I saw no reason to believe them," said Lamontagne.

"Did you see any reason not to believe them?"

"This business is made up of more than its fair share of wide boys." When Beauvoir looked puzzled, he explained. "Mostly young men desperate to make a killing. Make a mark. They throw money around, they talk loud. They have all sorts of theories about investing that sound good but are bullshit. They genuinely think they're brilliant. And their confidence convinces clients to invest with them. They're snake-oil salesmen, and most don't even realize they have no idea what they're doing."

"And Anthony Baumgartner was one of them?"

"No, that's what I'm saying. He wasn't. And from what I saw, he didn't tolerate it. That's why he turned that young fellow in. He must've known there'd be blowback and some of the shit would land on him. And it did. More than he probably realized."

"So how do you explain this?"

Beauvoir placed his index finger on the statement.

Lamontagne stared at it and sighed. "He was in his mid-fifties. He'd been screwed over by the company. A company he'd helped build. By a woman he'd mentored. He'd been made an example of. Humiliated. It's possible he saw a bleak future and decided to hell with it. If that's what came of decency, maybe it was time to be indecent."

Beauvoir saw another set of documents, pushed toward him. Across a sleek boardroom table. And he saw himself signing. Was he so very different from Anthony Baumgartner? Disillusioned. And now indecent.

"But if that was the case," Lamontagne went on, "I never saw it. In all the trades I did for him, he was smart and fair. Often brilliant and prescient. He made his clients a lot of money."

"You're of course talking about the clients he wasn't stealing from," said Beauvoir.

The broker hesitated, then nodded. "Yes. I honestly thought he was one of the good guys." He smiled. It was more wistful than amused. "There's a book we're all told to read when we first get into the business. Tony gave me his copy as a thank-you gift when I agreed to use my license to do his trades. It's called *Extraordinary Popular Delusions and The Madness of Crowds*. I guess we're all deluded at times."

"Could Monsieur Baumgartner have set that up"—Beauvoir pointed to the statements—"by himself, or would he need help?"

"No, he could do it himself. It would take organization, but I suspect he started small, then grew it. All he'd need is a hidden account and to choose his targets wisely."

"People who wouldn't see," said Beauvoir.

"People who wouldn't question, Chief Inspector. And there are a lot of those."

Lamontagne looked at the statement on the table. A few slender sheets of paper, but, like Madame Ogilvy that afternoon, the broker could see what they meant.

Ruin.

This scandal would kill Taylor and Ogilvy. And throw them all out of work. And maybe Anthony Baumgartner would, in death, have his revenge.

Beauvoir thanked Monsieur Lamontagne and made his way back along the corridor to the interview room where Bernard Shaeffer waited.

Delusion and madness, he thought as he reentered the room. There was a lot of both in this case.

It was close. Amelia could feel it.

Even those around her, the junkies, the whores, the trannies who'd been drawn to her, could feel it. They couldn't feel their fingers and toes. Their faces were numb and ravaged.

They'd lost all compassion. All good sense. Even their anger and despair were gone. They'd lost their families, and they'd lost their minds.

But this they could feel.

Something big was coming.

It didn't yet even have a street name. Whoever controlled it would get naming rights. For now it was just "it." Or "the new shit." And that seemed to only add to the excitement, the mystique.

Amelia knew what "it" was.

Carfentanil.

She also knew that whoever had it, whoever controlled the carfentanil, would win. And Amelia was determined to win.

But time was short. Once it hit the street, it was out of her hands.

Amelia stood at the window, but the view was obscured by thick frost and grime, so that all she saw were blurry streetlights.

Though she couldn't see them, she knew they were out there. Waiting for her.

The junkies and whores and trannies. Who'd turned to her for protection. Because she had muscle on her bones and a brain not completely fried. And she could see around corners. What was hiding. What was waiting. What was coming.

They slept in the corridor outside Marc's room, armed with guns and knives, and some had clubs, and waited for her to come out. And lead them.

Their eyes glowed in ways their mothers would never recognize.

They had nothing to lose and one thing to find. It.

Out there somewhere, in the hollowed-out core of Montréal, there was a factory cutting and recutting the drug. And this David knew where it was.

If she wanted to find it, she'd have to first find him.

"So, Sweet Pea," said Marc as they prepared to leave. "What're you going to call it?"

"What?"

They'd stepped out of his room, and Amelia saw, up and down the dingy hallway, skeletons struggling to stand on pin legs. On feet clad in boots stolen from corpses of friends who'd OD'd.

Bodies. Pale. Frozen. Picked up by dark vans and taken to lie on autopsy tables, then in drawers. Unnamed. Unclaimed. By mothers and fathers, sisters and brothers, who'd spend the rest of their lives wondering whatever became of their bright-eyed child.

"It. The shit," said Marc. "Ha. It rhymes. It the shit."

Amelia had to smile. She thought her favorite poet, Ruth Zardo, would like that little morsel. It the shit.

"When you find it, you'll have naming rights," said Marc. His eyes were unfocused and his words indistinct. Mumbled. His lips and tongue no longer able to work properly. He shuffled and muttered like an old man after a stroke. He put his arm around her shoulders. "Dragon. Wicked. Suicide. Something terrifying. Kids like that."

She felt, even through his winter coat, his bones.

There was hardly anything to him anymore. He was being eaten alive. Consumed from the inside out. They all were.

Except Amelia. At least not so that it was visible. But still she wondered if her mother would recognize her anymore. Or claim her as her own.

Beauvoir took his seat across from Bernard Shaeffer and smiled.

"Tell me."

"What?"

"No more games," said Beauvoir, his tone cold but calm. "Baumgartner set you up at the Caisse Populaire, a bank, for a reason. Now I want that reason."

"I don't—"

"Tell me."

"There's—"

"Tell me," Beauvoir snapped. "Where do you think I was just now?"

Shaeffer looked from Beauvoir to Agent Cloutier, his eyes wide. He clearly hadn't given it any thought. Now he did.

"I don't know—"

"I was next door, in another interview room." Beauvoir glared at him. "Asking questions and getting answers. Now I'm giving you a chance. Answer the question. What did Baumgartner want from you?"

There was silence.

"Now," shouted Beauvoir, bringing his open hand down on the table with such force that Shaeffer nearly jumped out of his skin. As did Agent Cloutier, who dropped her pen on the floor and had to quickly bend to scoop it up.

"An account," said Shaeffer. "Okay? He wanted me to set up an off-shore account. And put the money he sent into it."

"For both of you?"

"No. Just under the name Anthony Baumgartner."

"He used his own name?"

The question seemed to surprise Shaeffer. "Of course. Why not?"

"Easy to trace."

"He didn't expect to be caught."

"How much is in it?"

"I'd have to check, but I think it's somewhere around eight million," said Shaeffer.

"And how much did you take for yourself?"

"Nothing."

"Oh for Christ's sake," said Beauvoir. "How stupid are you? You know we'll find out." He turned to Agent Cloutier. "She's in charge of forensic accounting for the entire Sûreté. Nothing gets past her. She's brought down business leaders, politicians, mob heads. She'll bring you down too. Before breakfast. So save us the trouble."

Shaeffer looked at Cloutier, who now wished she hadn't stuck the pen in her mouth and chewed it.

"Okay," he said. "Maybe a little. But don't tell him."

"That I can promise," said Beauvoir.

Shaeffer shook his head. "Sorry. I forgot he's dead."

Beauvoir hadn't missed the tone of Shaeffer's voice when he'd, just for a moment, forgotten that Baumgartner was dead.

He was afraid of him, thought Beauvoir. Genuinely afraid. In fact, Jean-Guy thought as he got to his feet, that might've been the most genuine moment in this whole interview.

"Give Agent Cloutier the information on the account, please."

"I can go?"

"We'll see."

They were getting closer, thought Beauvoir as he walked toward his office. Closer to embezzlement, if not murder. But he knew Gamache was right. When they found the money, it would be infused with delu-

310

sion. With madness. With the stink of emotions rotten enough to lead to murder.

Amelia could hear the footsteps of the junkies and whores and trannies following them as she and Marc walked down the concrete stairs. Marc gripping Amelia's hand for support.

The air got colder and colder the closer they got to the front door.

Amelia braced for the frigid blast as soon as the door opened, but still it took her breath away and made her eyes water.

"Oh, fuck," she heard Marc say, coughing and choking on the air.

Through watery eyes Amelia saw a little girl in a red hat with the Montréal Canadiens logo. She stood alone, at the mouth of an alley.

Amelia could just see, poking out of the darkness, a pair of legs. On the ground. In ripped fishnets. The rest of the body was in darkness. But Amelia had no doubt. It was a body.

She caught the eyes of the girl, who looked to be five or six years old.

Amelia took a step toward the girl but was stopped by a single word. "David."

A skinny black kid had come up to her. No more than fifteen, she thought. He was staring at her with eyes far too big for his head.

"What about him?" she said, and felt, more than saw, the junkies and whores and trannies form a semicircle behind her.

"I'd heard you want him. I know where he is. For a tab I'll tell you."

"Yeah, right. Get outta my way, shithead," she said, and shoved past him, heading across the street. To the girl, who was still standing there. Staring.

"David," he repeated, and pushed the sleeve of his thin coat up. To expose his forearm. "Look."

And there, written in Magic Marker, was the same word she'd found on her own arm. The word that was still there. Indelible.

David.

Like a calling card.

And beside the name there was a number: 13. No. It was 1/3.

She pushed up the sleeve of her jacket and took a closer look at her forearm. "David," it said. And the number. Not 14 but 1/4.

Amelia stared at it and felt her heart beating in her throat. "Where is he?"

"I have to show you. Now. Before he leaves." He put out his hand.

"Give him one," said Amelia, and Marc handed over a single pill. "You'll get another when we get to meet David."

The kid pocketed the currency and without another word turned and walked down the dark street.

Amelia looked behind her. To the mouth of the alley. But the little girl was gone.

"Almost there," Marc whispered as they followed. "Come up with a name yet?"

"Sweet Pea," she said. "You started calling me that when I was five years old."

"That's what you're going to name the shit? Sweet Pea?"

"No. I'm going to call it Gamache."

"After the head of the Sûreté? The guy who got you into the academy?"

"The guy who got me kicked out. The genius who gave us the shit. He deserves to have it named after him. To know that the last thing tens of thousands of kids will say will be his name. It'll become synonymous with death. Gamache."

"You hate him that much?"

"He ruined me," said Amelia. "Now it's his turn."

CHAPTER 32

"Oh look," said Benedict. "I think my truck's back."

They'd crested the hill leading down into Three Pines. There were lights at the windows of the homes, and in the bistro they could see figures moving about.

The headlights of Gamache's car caught the swirl of snow as it fell, and where the beams hit the surrounding forest, the trees were alternately dark and bright as snow rested on the branches.

Armand knew there'd be fires lit in each of the homes, including his own. But before he could join Reine-Marie in front of it, there was something that had to be done.

Benedict pulled up behind his truck, and, getting out, he went to inspect the tires.

"They're very good," he said. "The best. Are you sure I can't pay for them?"

"I'm sure," said Armand.

Benedict tossed the tail of his tuque around his neck and over his shoulder and looked about him. "I'm going to miss it here. What is it?"

Armand was regarding him in a way that made Benedict uncomfortable.

Isabelle stared at her laptop.

Her husband had returned, and the kids had come in from playing, and all around was pandemonium.

But she was sitting at the kitchen table in her own little bubble.

313

Where all was deadly quiet. There were just the two of them. Isabelle Lacoste and Katie Burke.

"So that's who you are," whispered Lacoste. And reached for the phone. While the kids chased each other and the dog barked and her husband called to them to wash up for dinner.

Jean-Guy Beauvoir had his feet crossed on the desk. A file on his lap. The information Madame Ogilvy had had her assistant give him on the Kinderoths, and Bernard Shaeffer, and Anthony Baumgartner.

He slowly lowered the file and stared at his own reflection in the window. Then, dropping his legs off the desk with a thud, he muttered, "Gotcha," as he reached for the phone.

Benedict picked up the keys to his truck from Madame Gamache and thanked her profusely and sincerely for their hospitality.

"I don't know what I'd have done," he said. "Without you."

"You're welcome back anytime, right, Armand?"

"Let me walk you to your truck," said Gamache.

As the door closed, he could hear the phone ringing.

"I don't know how I can ever thank you, sir."

"You promised me a driving lesson." Gamache looked around. There was a good four inches of snow on the road. Billy Williams would be by soon to clear it, but right now it was accumulating. "You can thank me by giving me that lesson."

"Now?"

"Is there a better time?"

"Well, it's dark, and you must be tired."

"It's six thirty. I'm not quite that old."

"I . . . I didn't mean that," stammered Benedict.

"Get in," said Gamache, walking around to the passenger side and climbing up. "Let's drive a few kilometers out of the village. I have a spot in mind."

He was quiet as they drove, and then Gamache asked, "Who's Katie Burke?"

"Who?"

Gamache was silent, staring at the snow swirling in the headlights. "She's my girlfriend."

The truck was speeding up, exceeding the limit now.

"My ex."

They were gathering speed.

"Your ex? Are you sure?"

"Yes."

"How long ago did you break up?"

"Two months."

"About the time Bertha Baumgartner died?"

The engine growled as Benedict pressed harder on the gas.

"I guess. I don't know."

"Did she know Madame Baumgartner?"

"Of course not."

"Are you sure? Be more careful with your answers."

"Maybe you should be more careful with your questions. Leave Katie out of this. You wanted a lesson? Here goes."

He put his foot to the floor just as they crested a hill.

"Benedict—" Gamache began, but got no further.

Benedict hit the brakes, and the truck spun, veering out of control.

Gamache was thrown against the door, hitting his head on the window. He heard Benedict grunt as he was tossed sideways.

"Let go of the brake," Gamache shouted.

But Benedict's foot was jammed onto the pedal as he yanked the steering wheel first one way, then the other. Fighting for control. The snowbank approached, then the truck caught and fishtailed in the other direction. Toward the other bank. And the drop-off.

Gamache released his seat belt and forced himself forward. Grabbing the wheel, he tried to steer into the spin, but Benedict's grip was too tight, and it was now almost impossible to tell which way was forward. And which would send them into the trees.

Benedict was bucking against Gamache's body, which was pinning him to the seat. Partly to try to force his foot from the brake and partly to help protect the young man against what now seemed the inevitable crash.

Gamache grabbed Benedict's pant leg, pulling it as hard as he could. Trying to yank his foot off the brake.

It finally lifted, and Gamache could feel the truck catch and slow, but he knew it was too late. In the headlights he saw the snowbank approaching and, beyond it, the trees.

He closed his eyes and braced himself.

The truck shuddered and then slowed.

Gamache opened his eyes and turned to look out the windshield. And saw not the woods but the road.

He shoved the gear into neutral, and the truck glided to a stop, pointing straight ahead.

Both men stared straight ahead, gathering themselves.

Gamache took a deep breath and exhaled while, beside him, Benedict was hyperventilating. His breaths coming out in short puffs.

"Katie Burke," said Gamache. "Tell—"

"Leave her out of this."

"Are you really prepared to kill us both? To protect her?"

"Leave her alone," said Benedict.

"Was it her idea or yours?"

"Enough."

"Or what? You'll run us off a cliff? More death? Does it get easier, Benedict, the more you do? I'm giving you a chance to tell me yourself."

Benedict was staring at him, wild-eyed, desperate.

"No?" said Gamache. "Then I'll tell you. Katie knew Madame Baumgartner. She was her first contact in the nursing home. That's how you got onto the will, isn't it?"

Benedict continued to glare at Gamache, but now with more surprise than hostility.

"Murder, Benedict. Is that what you wanted? Was it planned?"

But Benedict seemed too stunned to answer.

"Tell me. The truth now."

As soon as they walked back into the house, Reine-Marie said, "Both Jean-Guy and Isabelle have been calling. They'd like a callback."

It sounded to Armand that they would more than just "like" a call.

"You're back," said Reine-Marie to Benedict. "Everything okay? You look pale."

"He's just going to rest for a bit," said Armand, making for the study. "We've been testing the tires. We gave each other little lessons on driving in dangerous conditions."

Benedict collapsed into an armchair facing the fire.

"What did you do to him, Armand?" Reine-Marie whispered at the door to the study.

"Taught him a lesson," said her husband. "If he tries to leave, let me know. But I don't think he will."

Armand held up the keys to the truck.

Then, picking up the phone to return the calls, he noticed there was a message. A soft, now-familiar voice told him that she'd found the girl. And Armand could come get her anytime. She'd be safe.

Now it was Armand's turn to sit, almost collapse, into a chair. He closed his eyes briefly, and exhaled, whispering, *"Merci."*

Then he called Jean-Guy, who was in his car. "On my way down, *patron*. I'll be there in a few minutes."

"Great, but why?"

He explained. Then Gamache called Isabelle.

When he left the study, he found Benedict still in the armchair, a mug of hot chocolate, untouched, on the table beside him.

He was staring blankly into the cheerful fire. Reine-Marie had just put a fresh log on, and Henri was lying in front of it, while Gracie slept on the sofa. It was, to all appearances, a tranquil domestic scene.

But, as he'd just heard from Isabelle and Jean-Guy, there was delusion at work. And a certain madness.

After he'd hung up, he called Myrna and asked her to come over. She had to hear this.

"Would you like me to leave, Armand?" Reine-Marie asked. She recognized his manner and knew this was no longer a social occasion.

"Non, stay if you'd like."

Just then Myrna arrived, shaking snow from her tuque and kicking off her boots. "This'd better be good. I left a bowl of soup and a glass of wine to come here."

But, taking a seat by the fire, Myrna could see that whatever was happening, it wasn't good. It was bad.

"What is it?" she asked, looking at Benedict, who seemed almost comatose. "What's happened?"

"In a moment," said Armand as he went to the window. He'd seen headlights flash by.

A minute later Jean-Guy walked in.

"This," said Beauvoir as he stepped aside, "is Katie Burke."

"Katie?" said Benedict, getting up.

CHAPTER 33

⌒

"Are you fucking with me?" Amelia shouted after the boy, who stopped and turned.

They'd been wandering the back alleys for an hour. Marc was beginning to tremble, not from the cold, or fear, but from withdrawal. His mumbles had become a plaintive whine.

"I need something. Anything."

He'd already taken a tab of acid, but he was used to stronger. Needed stronger. And was getting weaker and weaker.

They all were.

The junkies and trannies and whores who straggled along after Amelia as she followed the boy from alley to tenement to empty lot. Some had broken off, desperate now for a hit. Preferring to go it alone.

Those who had stayed, the junkies and trannies and whores, were too far gone to make a decision. They just trudged after her, afraid of being left behind. Again.

"No, no, he was here an hour ago," said the kid, looking around. "He told me to come find you. It's ready."

"What is?"

"Dinner. He's made dinner for you. What the fuck do you think I mean? The shit's ready."

"Then why does he need me?" asked Amelia, feeling a surge of adrenaline.

"How should I know?"

Amelia looked over at Marc. Wanting to ask him, to ask anyone, for advice. She was tingling and wasn't sure if it was excitement or a warning. This wasn't right. Every instinct told her she was being set up. That she should stop. Turn around. Go back. Go home.

But she had no home. There was no "back" back there. Only forward.

The stud in her tongue knocked against her teeth as she considered her options.

The kid was on the move again, slipping and sliding through the slush in his running shoes.

"He must've left," he was muttering, looking this way and that. But it was night, and hardly any light from the street penetrated down these back lanes. David could've been standing feet away and they wouldn't see him.

Making up her mind, Amelia grabbed Marc's hand and dragged him, staggering, forward.

Click. Click. Click.

The sound of her stud joined the chattering of his teeth.

Katie and Benedict sat side by side on the sofa in front of the fireplace.

A platter of roast beef, chicken, and peanut-butter-and-honey sandwiches had been put out on the coffee table, along with drinks.

Katie wore a long boiled-wool skirt over bright pink jeans and a sweater made up of what looked like meatballs but were actually brown pom-poms. They hoped.

Henri was looking at her in a way that demanded monitoring.

She had the same haircut as Benedict. Almost shaved on top, and from just above the ears down it was long.

They held hands and looked very young as Katie stared at the adults surrounding them and Benedict stared at the sandwiches. And Armand stared at Henri. In warning.

Once again Armand noticed a resemblance between the shepherd and the carpenter.

"I hope you know," he began, lifting his eyes to the young couple, "that it's far too late for lies. And there've been far too many already."

While his words were firm, his voice was gentle. Encouraging. Like coaxing fawns from the forest.

Katie nodded, and Benedict's eyes met Armand's.

"How did this begin?" Gamache asked. There was no doubt that the question was aimed at Katie.

"Well, I guess it started before I was born—"

"Maybe the more recent events," said Armand. "How did Benedict get onto Madame Baumgartner's will?"

"She knows?" asked Myrna.

"And she knows why you're on too," said Beauvoir. "Don't you?"

Katie nodded again. She might look like a lunatic, but her eyes were sharp and bright and glowed with intelligence.

She was, Gamache suspected, a remarkable young woman. Certainly a one-off.

"I met Madame Baumgartner in the seniors' home," said Katie Burke. "I don't know if you know, but there aren't all that many Anglo homes around."

"Why would it matter?" asked Jean-Guy.

Katie looked at him with a weary patience, as though she were the adult and he was very, very young.

"What language would you choose to die in? It matters. We were lucky to get my grandfather into this one. I was visiting him and noticed that this one old woman hardly ever had visitors. Her family came when they could, and they seemed to care, but the days are long when you're sitting all alone. She always smiled at me and had the nicest face. A little eccentric, you know?"

The adults, as one, nodded. They could see that this young woman would be drawn to the eccentric.

"So one day I took her a tin of homemade cookies."

"Those cookies with a hole on the top filled with jam," said Benedict. "Except Katie's holes are different shapes—"

Katie patted his hand, and he stopped talking.

"Thank you," she said.

Far from being a way to shut him up, it was said with great kindness.

Affection, thought Armand. He was not only listening closely, he was watching them closely as well. Studying the dynamic. Often what seemed obvious was not a fact, or even the truth.

"We got to talking," Katie continued the story, "and she asked me to call her 'Baroness.' Well, I thought that was strange."

"Who wouldn't?" said Myrna.

"No, I mean I found it strange because I called my grandfather 'Baron.'"

"Why?" asked Myrna, her voice wary.

"It was just what he liked to be called. He was Baron, and my grandmother was Baroness. I didn't think anyone else did that. Madame Baumgartner reminded me of my grandmother, who I adored, so I'd sit with her in the home and we'd talk. Then one day I suggested they should meet. The Baron and this new Baroness. My grandmother had died the year before, and I know he was lonely."

"Did you know who she was?" asked Armand.

"By then, yes."

"And, knowing who she was, you still suggested they meet?"

Armand was leaning forward. His voice was friendly, as though this were a pleasant gathering of friends and murder wasn't hovering in the background.

"Yes."

"Did he know?" he asked.

Katie smiled for the first time. It was, they both knew, the vital question.

"He did. The Baroness Baumgartner."

Armand sat back on the sofa, not bothering to hide his amazement. "Did she know who he was?"

"No. I was afraid she'd refuse to see him. It wasn't until I introduced him that she found out."

"Who was he?" asked Myrna.

"The Baron Kinderoth," said Jean-Guy. "Katie here is a Kinderoth."

He'd discovered that when he'd been going over the file on the Kinderoths from Taylor and Ogilvy. In it were notes on the estate and who got the small amount of money in the investment account. The Kinderoths had two daughters. One had married a Burke and moved to Ontario. And had a daughter named Katherine. Katie Burke.

While Jean-Guy had started with the Kinderoths and ended up with Katie, Isabelle Lacoste had started with Katie and ended up with the Kinderoths.

She too had called Gamache and told him her findings, confirming what Beauvoir had just told him.

Different roads, but the same destination. Here. Now.

Myrna stared at Jean-Guy, taking this in. Then turned to Katie. "You're a Kinderoth?"

The young woman nodded.

"And you knew the history between the Kinderoths and the Baumgartners?" asked Myrna.

"Yes. I was raised on the story. That my great-great-grandfather was the eldest son. And the money, the title, the estates were ours. But the Baumgartners—filthy, greedy, cheating, and lying Baumgartners—had been trying to steal it for more than a hundred years."

"A hundred and thirty-two," said Benedict.

"What happened when they met?" asked Myrna.

"I introduced my grandfather. The Baron Kinderoth. He was in a wheelchair but managed to get up. He offered her the flowers he'd asked me to buy for him. Edelweiss. Then he bowed and called her Baroness."

The only sound in the room now was the muttering and crackling of logs in the fireplace. Shadows from the fire threw macabre, distorted shadows against the walls.

"And Madame Baumgartner?" asked Armand.

"She stared for a long time. It seemed forever," said Katie.

"A hundred and thirty-two years," said Benedict.

"Then she got up too. I went to help, but she refused. She stood straight, staring at the Baron. I thought she was going to say, or do, something awful. Then she reached out and took the flowers. '*Danke schön*,' she said." Katie smiled. "'Baron Kinderoth.'"

They sat in silence. Imagining the moment.

Then, very softly, as though from far away, Myrna heard humming. *Edelweiss. Edelweiss.*

She looked at Benedict. *Edelweiss*, he hummed.

"What happened then?" Myrna asked.

"I wish I could say all was forgiven on both sides, but it wasn't," said Katie. "Each time I visited, I'd take my grandfather into the solarium to have tea with the Baroness. They'd sit in silence. Then, one week, they were already there. Talking quietly together. I just left the cookies in their rooms and went home."

"They became friends?" asked Reine-Marie.

"It took a while," said Katie. "But yes."

"So how'd they get over all that history?" asked Myrna.

She'd known clients of hers when she was a practicing psychologist who never got over much less deep-seated resentments.

"Loneliness," said Katie. "They needed each other. They understood each other in ways no one else could."

"Ahhh," said Myrna. There was nothing like the pain of the present to cure the pain of the past.

"After a month or so, they were almost inseparable. Eating every meal together. She got him out into the garden, and he got her playing cribbage."

"Did they tell their families?" Armand asked.

If they had, the Baumgartner siblings had chosen not to mention it.

"They were planning to," said Katie. "But they were worried that too much damage had been done. They knew the judgment in Vienna was coming soon, and both worried that when it was announced, which- ever family won wouldn't want to share. And the family that lost would have their bitterness cemented in place. But they had a solution."

"They'd get married," said Benedict. And, not for the first time, he saw a group of people staring at him as though he were mad.

"Married?" asked Myrna. "Because of the money?"

"Because they loved each other," said Katie. "I think he loved her even more than he loved my grandmother. She made him laugh. He'd had a hard life, and it'd hardened him. But with her he could just be himself. A taxi-driver baron."

"And she could be a cleaning-woman baroness," said Reine-Marie.

"Yes. They thought if they made that sort of commitment to each other, not just in words but in action, the rest of the family would have to accept it and drop the feud."

"And share the fortune?" said Myrna. "No matter who won?"

"Yes. The plan was to leave everything to each other, with the pro- viso it be split equally among both families, when the last one died. But of course they wanted their children to not just accept grudgingly but wholeheartedly. As they had."

"But—" said Myrna.

"But my grandfather died before they could get married."

"Oh," said Reine-Marie as though she'd suffered a physical blow. "It must've been awful for the Baroness."

"It was. She hadn't told her children, and by then it was too late.

His death sent her into a tailspin. Partly physical, but mostly mental. She became confused. She called the notary in, with the intention of changing her will, as she and the Baron had discussed. Leaving everything, in the event she won the case in Vienna, split equally between the families."

"But the notary wouldn't do it," said Benedict.

"He saw the state she was in," said Katie, "and said he couldn't in all conscience allow her to change her will. He thought her mind wasn't sound. He knew the family history, the court challenges, and felt she must've been coerced somehow. He believed that the Baroness, who'd been so embittered about it all her life, would never willingly share with a Kinderoth."

"Just what the Baron and Baroness had feared from their families," said Reine-Marie.

"Yes," said Katie. "It confirmed her fears. If the notary thought she was nuts, her family sure would. But he did allow her to change one thing."

"The liquidators?" asked Myrna. "Is that when she put us on the will?"

"Yes."

"But why?" asked Armand.

"So that you could execute not just the will but her real desires. She knew that her children never would. There was too much history there. But with new liquidators there'd be none of that. The notary was right, of course. She was confused. But one thing was clear to her. The plan she had with the Baron to share the fortune had to be followed through. It became an idée fixe. A kind of obsession. It wasn't about the money, it was about letting go of all the bitterness. They could see the damage they'd done in passing it along to their children. Freeing them of it would be their real inheritance."

"But if it was that important to her," asked Reine-Marie, "why not just write her own will and sign it? Isn't that legal?"

"A holographic will," said Armand. "As long as it's written in longhand and signed by witnesses, yes, it's legal in Québec. But the notary had already seen her and decided she wasn't of sound mind."

"Exactly," said Katie. When she nodded, as now, her entire meatball sweater bobbed up and down.

It was amusing, disconcerting, and slightly nauseating. A cross between performance art and dinner.

Henri sat up and started drooling.

Armand motioned with his hand for the shepherd to lie back down, which he did, reluctantly.

"So," said Myrna, "the only thing the Baroness could do was change the liquidators."

"Yes. She took her three children off and put you on."

"But again," said Myrna. "Why us? We didn't even know her."

"Exactly. That's why. We needed someone who had no idea of the history."

"We?" asked Armand.

"I meant she."

"Of course," said Armand. "So that's why she changed liquidators, but why us specifically? Madame Landers and me?"

"The Baroness had heard that the head of the Sûreté had moved into the nearby village. She was enough of a snob to like the idea that someone so prominent would be executing her will. She also figured you'd keep her family in line. To be honest, her next choices were the queen, followed by the pope. But when she heard about you"—Katie turned to Myrna—"she immediately agreed you'd be perfect."

"A senior police officer and a respected psychologist," said Myrna, nodding. "Makes sense."

"You're a psychologist?" said Katie. "No, apparently Madame Zardo told the Baroness you were a cleaning woman. That's why she wanted you. Someone who'd understand."

Myrna's eyes narrowed in a glare, daring anyone to laugh.

The only one not smiling was Armand.

"How did the Baroness know to ask about changing the liquidators?" he asked.

"Like I said, the notary wouldn't let her change the actual will—"

"Yes, I heard. But does anyone else here know that it might be possible to change the liquidators?"

He looked around, and they all, to a person, shook their heads. Including Benedict. Who, after a sharp squeeze of his hand, stopped.

"So let me ask again," said Armand. "How did an elderly and admittedly confused person know to even ask about the liquidators?"

326

There was a pause before Katie answered. "It was my idea. I looked it up and suggested it to her. The Baroness agreed it was worth a try."

"And the choice of liquidators?" asked Armand.

"Was hers."

That sat there, taking in the odor of a lie. Armand let the pause stretch on. And the stench sink in. Before he finally spoke again.

"Including Benedict?"

Reine-Marie was watching this closely. Not Katie but Armand. Watching him take away, with a civility that was almost frightening, the props for her story. Until it collapsed.

"That was my idea," Katie admitted. "The Baroness actually wanted me as the third, but I said that wouldn't work. If they found out my mother's maiden name was Kinderoth, her family would accuse me of influencing her."

Jean-Guy raised his brows but chose not to say what everyone else in the room was also thinking.

"So it was agreed that my boyfriend, Benedict, would be a liquidator in my place," said Katie. "I could vouch for him. That he's honest and kind and will do what's right."

Do what she tells him, thought Jean-Guy.

"But you broke up," said Reine-Marie. "Benedict told us."

"That was planned," she said. "There couldn't be any connection. Not even the notary knew."

"So you didn't actually break up," Jean-Guy said to Benedict. "You appeared to but didn't. That was another lie."

Layer upon layer. Lie upon lie. Covering up some rotting truth. That they still hadn't reached.

"Didn't you think we'd find out?" asked Armand.

"I didn't think anyone would really ask," said Katie.

"We didn't think we were doing anything wrong," said Benedict.

Armand turned to him. "As a good rule of thumb, if you have to lie, you might be doing something wrong."

"You told me you liked my hat, sir," said Benedict, staring at Gamache. "Was that a lie?"

The question, and unmistakable challenge, sat there while Gamache stared back. Assessing and reassessing the young man.

"That was opinion," said Gamache. "Not fact. If you're lying about the facts, there's something wrong. And the two of you have been doing a lot of lying. Can you really be so surprised when we doubt you?"

"That was a great deal of effort to help an elderly woman," said Myrna.

Gamache, still watching Benedict, agreed. Though the word that came to his mind wasn't "effort" but "premeditation."

"I wasn't just helping her," said Katie. "I'd seen what this whole feud had done to my mother, my aunt, my grandparents. Myself. Spending our whole lives believing our lives could be, should be, better? Thinking we'd been screwed by the Baumgartners. Waiting for some judgment a continent away? To make us happy. It was awful." She placed a hand over her stomach, as though feeling ill. Benedict put his hand on her knee. "I agreed with the Baron and Baroness," she said. "It had to end."

"And, conveniently, make sure that whatever the judgment in Vienna was, you'd inherit?" asked Armand.

There was, Reine-Marie noticed, considerably less civility in that question. But this was not, after all, a party. The idea was not to be friendly but to get to the heart of a murder.

"We both know, monsieur, that there's nothing to inherit," said Katie. "Not after all this time. The cost of the lawsuits alone would be ruinous, never mind what the Nazis did to any Jewish property. All I'd inherit would be outrage. I don't want that. For me or my family."

Armand looked at this young woman and wondered if she really was that immune to the family plague. The creeping disease of hatred. The bindweed in the garden.

Benedict caressed Katie's hand in a way that was supportive and intimate.

"But still," said Armand, "it doesn't explain everything. As liquidators we're charged with honoring the provisions of the will. Not doing what we think is fair."

"That's why she wrote the letter," said Katie.

"What letter?" asked Armand.

"The Baroness wrote a letter, to be given to her eldest son, after the reading of the will. In it she explains everything."

"Why give it to him and not us?" asked Myrna.

"She didn't want her children to hear it from strangers," said Katie. "And she thought he'd understand."

"Understand about sharing the fortune?" asked Jean-Guy.

"About ending the fight."

"Why would she think Anthony would understand, more than the others?" asked Myrna.

"Something to do with a painting," said Katie. "Of a crazy old woman who wasn't really crazy, or something like that. Apparently the others hated it, but he wanted it. I didn't really understand what she was saying. She was rambling by then. I think she was getting confused between the painting and herself. But for some reason the painting was important to her. And to him, I guess. Anyway, she decided her eldest son was the one to get the letter."

"Did he?" Myrna asked.

Armand and Jean-Guy exchanged glances.

"We didn't find anything like that among his papers," said Jean-Guy.

Armand got up. "Will you come with me, please?" he asked Jean-Guy and Myrna.

They went to his study, and, closing the door, he made a call.

CHAPTER 34

"Do you know what time it is?" came Lucien's voice.

Gamache looked at his watch.

"Ten past eight," he said.

"At night."

"*Oui.* I'm sorry for calling after hours. Myrna Landers is with me, as well as Chief Inspector Beauvoir. We have you on speaker. We have some questions."

"Can't it wait?"

"If it could, do you think we'd be calling?" asked Jean-Guy.

"Did Madame Baumgartner leave a letter to be given to her son Anthony?" Gamache asked.

The television in the background was put on mute.

"Yes, she did. I found it in my father's file attached to the will."

"Why didn't you tell us about it?" asked Myrna.

"Why should I? Your job is to liquidate the will. This wasn't part of that."

"But still," said Myrna, "you could've mentioned it."

"And after Baumgartner was killed?" asked Beauvoir. "When it was clear it was murder? Didn't you think to mention it then?"

"A house fell on him," said Lucien. "The letter didn't kill him."

"How do you know?" asked Gamache. "Did you read it?"

"No."

"The truth, Maître Mercier," said Gamache.

"I did not. Why would I care what was in the letter?"

That at least had the ring of truth to it.

Unless the letter was about himself, which clearly it was not, Lucien Mercier would not be interested.

"When did you give it to him?" Beauvoir asked.

"Right after the reading of the will. After the rest of you left."

"It was just the two of you?"

"No, I think Caroline and Hugo Baumgartner were still there."

"Actually, Caroline left with us," said Myrna.

"Did he read the letter while you were there?" asked Armand.

"No. I just handed it to him and left. I have no idea when, or even if, he read it. Why does it matter?"

"It matters," said Beauvoir, "because her son has been murdered. And you gave him a letter just hours before it happened. A letter that might've led him to contact someone. Meet someone. That might explain why he went to the farmhouse and who he met there. Do you have any idea why he might've gone there that night?"

"No, none."

"Do you know what was in the letter, Maître Mercier?" Gamache asked. Again.

"No."

The three in the study exchanged glances. Not at all sure whether to believe him.

Though they could not think why he would lie.

"Lucien Mercier, the notary, confirmed that when the reading of the will was over and we'd left, he gave Anthony Baumgartner a letter from his mother," said Armand when they'd returned to the living room.

"Does he know what was in it?" Reine-Marie asked.

"He says he doesn't," said Jean-Guy, sitting back down.

"So no one knows what was in the letter?" asked Reine-Marie.

"I think one of us does."

Armand turned to Katie.

She looked at Benedict, who nodded.

"You're right," she said. "I was there when she wrote it. In the letter she explained about meeting the Baron. About hearing his side of it. About seeing he wasn't a greedy monster at all, just an old man carrying on an even older fight. She said something about a horizon. I don't know what that was about. But she did say in the letter that if Anthony loved her, as she knew he did, he'd do one last thing for her. If they won the court case, he'd share the inheritance with the Kinderoths."

"A beautiful letter," said Reine-Marie.

"And very clear," said Armand, who continued to watch Katie.

"I wonder if he read it," said Myrna. "And how he felt about it."

"And if he told his siblings," said Jean-Guy. "Pretty good motive. Without Anthony and the letter, the money was theirs. With him, they'd have to share. People are killed for twenty bucks. We're talking millions."

"That don't exist," Myrna pointed out.

"But how do we know?" asked Jean-Guy. "How do they know? We don't and they don't. Not until the court case is decided. And it doesn't really matter if it exists, just that they believe it does, or hope it does."

Myrna nodded. People were capable of believing almost anything. And hope was even more sweeping and powerful.

Reine-Marie was listening to this but watching Armand as he got up and threw another log on the fire, poking it and sending embers up the chimney. Then he turned around, the poker still in his hand.

"Who wrote the letter?" he asked.

"The Baroness," said Katie. "I told you."

But the meatballs on her sweater were trembling.

Her heart, Gamache knew. Beating so ferociously it was setting them off. Still, she was looking at him apparently calmly. Apparently coolly.

She has courage, Gamache thought. But he also thought it was a shame she needed it. So much courage demanded to look him in the eye and tell him such a lie.

"An elderly woman, declining mentally and physically, picked up a pen and wrote a letter?" he asked. "Setting it all out so clearly?"

Instead of being harsh, accusing, his voice was reasonable. Soft. Inviting her, once again, to come out of the woods.

"Yes. I watched."

Benedict took her hand and held it. "Katie," he said, and nothing else. Just the one word.

Katie.

She dropped her eyes to the rug. To the dog staring at her and drooling.

"She dictated it, but I wrote it for her."

"*Merci*," said Armand, replacing the poker and sitting back down. "You know what that means, of course."

"It means even if you find the letter, it's in my handwriting. There's no proof they were her words."

"*Oui*," said Armand.

What he didn't say, but that was clear to him and, he suspected, to Beauvoir, was that there was no proof of any of this. This could all be lies.

The reconciliation. The desire to marry. Wanting to share the inheritance.

It could all be a lie.

Anyone who could confirm the story was dead. The Baron. The Baroness. And now Anthony Baumgartner.

The other thing that was clear was that Benedict wasn't the passive boy toy he appeared to be. Dressed, styled, molded, and manipulated by Katie Burke.

He had, with one word, gotten her to speak the truth. Not, Gamache suspected, because Benedict believed in telling the truth. But because he could see that lying was no longer working.

"There was one more thing in the letter," said Katie.

"Let me tell them," said Benedict.

He looked at Gamache. "The Baroness wanted the farmhouse torn down."

"Why?"

"Because she wanted them to make a clean break. Start their own lives, fresh. She knew they'd never move on as long as that house was standing. It was where she'd brought them up. Where she'd told them all those stories about the inheritance. She wanted it gone."

"Is that why you went there?" asked Armand.

"Yes," said Benedict. "I wanted to go at night, when I knew the Baumgartners wouldn't be there. I needed to see how hard it would be to take it down. I know you said you'd have it condemned, sir, but suppose that took a while, or what if it wasn't? I felt it was up to me to make sure it was done."

"I asked him to do it," said Katie.

"I found the support beam in the kitchen and gave it a couple of good whacks with a sledgehammer. Just to test it."

"It failed the test?" asked Myrna.

"Well, yes. The place fell down. That wasn't planned."

Katie held his hand tightly as he looked across at Myrna, Jean-Guy, Armand.

"You came and found me," said Benedict. "Thank you."

"Thank you," said Katie.

Reine-Marie saw a young man.

Jean-Guy saw the cloud of concrete and plaster and snow. And heard the roar.

And the shouting. Screaming. His own. As he fought to free himself from those who held him back.

Myrna saw the huge beams and slabs coming down all around. She felt the rubble crushing in around her and the overwhelming terror, and disbelief, as she realized she was about to die. And she felt Billy Williams holding her hand.

Armand looked at Benedict in front of the cheerful fire and felt the young body on top of his, trying to shield him, as the house of Baumgartner fell and the world came to an end.

And then he saw Benedict's dust-covered face, with the blood. And beyond it the hand, thrust up through the rubble.

Anthony Baumgartner.

Amelia was beginning to shiver almost uncontrollably.

They'd been at it for hours now. Amelia recognized what this was. They were being deliberately worn down. Led by the nose through the freezing streets until they had no will, no fight left.

Her feet were soaked through, and beside her, Marc was weeping. Begging. She didn't know what for. He was just begging.

Probably for this to stop. For them to stop.

But Amelia couldn't afford to. Even as she recognized the manipulation, she had to see it through.

Up ahead the boy turned and gestured.

"I found him."

CHAPTER 35

⌒

Murder was essentially simple, Beauvoir was thinking as he walked with his father-in-law into the kitchen.

The motives, even the method, might look complicated, until you figured it out. And they were figuring this one out.

Armand closed the door into the kitchen.

"What do you think?"

"I think it's all bullshit. I think there was no friendship between the Baron and the Baroness, never mind love. Katie Burke's story's almost laughable. It sounds like a fairy tale."

"Most fairy tales are pretty dark," said Armand, taking the tarte Tatin out of the fridge and handing it to Jean-Guy. "Have you read any to Honoré? Rumpelstiltskin? It starts with a lie and ends with a death."

"I'll keep my eyes peeled for an elf," said Jean-Guy.

"An imp," said Armand. He plugged the kettle in and turned to watch Jean-Guy cutting the caramelized apple tart.

They were there, ostensibly, to get dessert, but when Reine-Marie came in to help them, she saw the look on her husband's face and went back out.

"I think she's pregnant," said Armand. "Katie, I mean."

"What makes you say that? Did the elf tell you?"

"Imp, and no. It was the way she put her hand over her abdomen when she talked about ending the family legacy of hate. And then he touched her in a way that was very tender. The way I saw you reach out for Annie when she was pregnant with Honoré. He loves her."

"They love each other," said Jean-Guy, licking his fingers and thinking. "If she is pregnant, it could be even more of a motive."

"But for what?" asked Armand. "To end the feud or to keep it going? One keeps them happy but in poverty, the other comes with a fortune but at a price. What do they want for their child? Money or peace?"

"Money," said Jean-Guy. "Always money. Peace is for people with a bank account. Look at them. He's a so-called carpenter but really a janitor, and she's a . . . what? Wannabe designer? She's never gonna make money, unless it's designing clown suits. And neither is he. And now they're looking at a baby coming? No, their only hope, their last hope, is the judgment in Vienna."

"She said she didn't believe there was any money."

"What's she gonna say? Sure, maybe her more sane self tells her there isn't a fortune left. But she's been raised on a pretty dark fairy tale. Of huge wealth coming their way. Who doesn't dream of that? No, you can't tell me that Katie Burke doesn't believe, deep down, that there's a fortune. And it belongs to them."

Delusion and madness, thought Jean-Guy. Like most fairy tales.

"Trust me," he said. "Those two are in it up to their necks."

Armand told him about what had happened in the truck.

"Do you think he was trying to crash?" asked Jean-Guy, shocked by what he heard.

"No, I think he felt cornered and was overcome with anger when I questioned him about Katie."

Though they both knew that at the root of anger was fear. And fear was what propelled most murders.

"You think they killed Anthony Baumgartner?" Armand asked.

"I do. I think there was something in that letter that sent Baumgartner to the farmhouse. Benedict met him there and killed him."

"Why kill him?" asked Armand. "If the letter is telling Baumgartner to share the fortune, why would they need to kill him?"

"Because the letter didn't say that. Katie was lying. We have no idea what was in the letter. The Baroness might've dictated one thing, like Anthony should share, but Katie wrote down something else. Like Anthony should go to the old farmhouse alone the night the will was read. Which he did. Thinking it was his mother's wish."

"We don't know that."

"No, that's my point. We have no idea what was in that letter. Katie might even be telling the truth."

Though Beauvoir clearly did not believe that.

"All we know is that Baumgartner read it, then went to the farmhouse."

"You make it sound like cause and effect," said Gamache. "Something else might've happened to send him there."

"That's true."

"It's interesting that Katie knew about the painting of Ruth. The only way she could know about it was if the Baroness told her."

"But that doesn't mean it was in the letter."

"No, no it doesn't," said Gamache. "So, to recap, we have two theories. One, that Katie wrote down exactly what the Baroness dictated. Two, that she did not."

Beauvoir was nodding. "We don't seem to be much closer."

Though that was often the odd thing about a murder investigation. They could appear to be getting further from the truth, lost in the dust thrown up by all sorts of contradictory statements. Evidence. Lies.

But then something was said, or seen, and everything that had seemed contradictory fell into place.

"That damned painting keeps coming up," said Jean-Guy. "Bernard Shaeffer even mentioned it today when I spoke with him."

He told Gamache about that interview.

"So he was there when Baumgartner hung it in his study," said Gamache. "Then he helped get the laptop up and running."

"That was supposedly why he was there," said Beauvoir. "But then it turned into something else."

"Shaeffer told you that Baumgartner was trying to think of a new password? Did he find one?"

"If he did, he was smart enough not to tell Shaeffer."

"According to Shaeffer," said Gamache.

"True. We're still trying to crack it. We've searched the home, of course. I even looked behind that damned painting, but all I saw there was the print number."

Gamache nodded, and then his brows drew together. "What did you see there?"

"It's a numbered print. They write the number on it, so buyers know what—"

"Yes, yes," said Gamache. "I know. We have some here, including one of Clara's."

He walked over to the wall by the long pine table. Beauvoir had seen the picture many times, including the original in Clara's studio, when she'd first painted it.

Now he and his father-in-law stood in front of it.

Clara called it *The Three Graces*. But instead of showing three beautiful young women, naked and intertwined in a more than slightly erotic way, she'd painted three fully clothed elderly women from the village. Including the woman, Emilie, who used to own the Gamaches' home.

They were wrinkled, sagging, frail. They held on to each other. Not because they were afraid or feeble. Just the opposite. These women were roaring with laughter. The work radiated joy. Friendship. Companionship. Power.

"The number of the print," he said, reaching out to take the large painting off the wall, "is written on the back."

"Actually—" Armand began, but it was too late. Jean-Guy had it off and had turned it around.

Something was indeed written there. But it was in Gamache's familiar hand.

"For Reine-Marie, my Grace. With love forever, Armand."

Jean-Guy colored, and, after quickly putting it back on the wall, he turned to look at Armand, who was watching him and smiling.

"Not exactly a secret," said Armand. "Or a code. What I wanted to show you is that."

Gamache pointed to the front of the painting. On the lower right corner were Clara's signature and the numbers 7/12.

"I've seen that," said Jean-Guy. "But I always thought that was the date it was finished."

"No. It's the number of the print. Seven of twelve."

"She only printed twelve?"

"It was before she became successful," said Armand. "She didn't think she could even sell twelve."

"So this must be worth—"

But he stopped and stared at *The Three Graces*. At the number. And grunted. "Huh. So what's with the number on the back of Baumgartner's painting?"

Gamache raised his brows, as did Jean-Guy. Who then walked quickly over to the phone in the kitchen and placed a call.

"Cloutier? The painting in Baumgartner's study. Yes, the crazy old woman. There's a number on the back. Did you make a note of it? Can you go over to the house and see? Better yet, bring the painting in. No, I'm not kidding. No, I don't want it in my office. Keep it by your desk. Okay then, turn it to face the wall. I don't care. Just get that number and try it on his laptop. I'll be there in an hour."

Beauvoir hung up and turned to Gamache.

"We'll know soon. I don't know what we'll find on that computer, but I'm still betting those two out there"—he jerked his head toward the living room—"are in it over their ridiculous haircuts. I think Anthony Baumgartner was greedy. Scheming. Criminal. I don't think he had any intention of sharing the wealth."

"And you think that's why he was killed?"

"I do. Don't you?"

Gamache glanced toward the closed door, and Jean-Guy, who knew him well, could guess his thoughts.

"Look, *patron*, I know you don't want Benedict to be the one. You like him. I like him. He saved your life. But—"

"You think that's why I don't believe it was Benedict?" asked Armand. "Because he did a nice thing?"

"It was a pretty nice thing," said Beauvoir.

"True, but we've arrested too many nice killers to be fooled. I just don't see any proof. That they've lied, yes, but if everyone who lied to us was a killer, there'd be slaughter in the streets. I just don't believe it."

"You don't want to believe it."

"Show me the proof and I will."

"You talked about separating facts from all the lies in this case. Well, here's a fact for you. Benedict was in the farmhouse when Baumgartner was there. He had opportunity and motive. I'm betting under all that rubble we'll find the sledgehammer, or whatever weapon he used. And then their story will collapse, like the building. With them in it."

The two men were used to arguing over cases. Challenging each other. Challenging theories, questioning evidence. This was nothing new. Though there was a slight edge to it, and Armand knew why.

Was he refusing to see what was so clear to Beauvoir? What would be so clear to him if he didn't keep feeling the trembling body on top of him and hearing the crying. Of a young man terrified of dying but instinctively protecting another. A veritable stranger.

Could such a man, just hours earlier, have taken a life?

But Armand knew the answer to that. Yes. One was instinctive. The other well thought out. Premeditated. And maybe also, at a profound level, instinctive.

A parent would do a lot to provide for his child. And if that meant killing a—what had Katie called him?—filthy, greedy, cheating, and lying Baumgartner, then so be it.

Yes, Armand had to admit. It could have been Benedict.

They returned to the living room, and Jean-Guy said his goodbyes, explaining that he had to get back to Montréal.

Myrna got up. "I'll be leaving too. Those brownies won't eat themselves."

"I thought you said it was soup you left behind," said Reine-Marie, walking her to the door.

"You must've misheard," said Myrna.

"What about us?" asked Katie.

"You're free to go," said Beauvoir.

"Me too?" asked Benedict.

Beauvoir hesitated for a moment, then nodded.

They thanked the Gamaches for their hospitality.

"And the tires," said Benedict, with a smile that a day earlier Gamache might have found disarming but now struck him as possibly calculated. "I won't forget."

"And neither will I," said Armand, shaking the young man's hand. Then he turned to Katie. "I really do like the hat, you know."

Beauvoir watched them leave, then said to Gamache, "Next time I see them, it'll be with an arrest warrant."

Gamache put on his boots and coat and hat.

"Taking the dogs for a walk?" asked Beauvoir, pulling on his mittens.

"*Non.* I'm going in to Montréal too."

"Good," said Beauvoir. "I'll drive you. You can stay over with us, if you like."

"*Non, merci.* I'll drive myself. I'll be coming back out."

"Your eyes okay?"

"They're just fine."

Beauvoir paused, studying his father-in-law. "Are you sure?"

"You're not accusing me of being blind again, are you?"

"Only to evidence so obvious your infant grandson could see it," said Beauvoir. "But I think you're okay to drive."

Gamache laughed and said good night to his son-in-law, then went and explained to Reine-Marie that he had to go into the city but would be back later.

"Would you like me to come?" she asked.

"*Non, mon coeur—*"

Just then the phone rang.

"I'll get it," he said, and went into his study.

When he reached for the phone, he paused. The number lit up on the handset was one he recognized.

He glanced out into the living room, then, with his foot, swung the door closed.

"*Oui, allô,*" he said.

His voice sounded strange in his own ears. Oddly calm, while his heart pounded.

"Monsieur Gamache?" asked the man at the other end. "Arnold Gamache?"

"Armand. *Oui.*"

"My name is Dr. Harper. I'm one of the coroners in Montréal. I'm afraid I have some bad news for you."

Gamache felt light-headed. Physically sick.

Annie? He thought. Honoré? Had there been an accident?

He stood straight but put out his hand to steady himself against the desk. Preparing for the blow.

"Go on."

"We found your name and phone number on a body that was just brought in. There was no other identification."

"Go on," said Armand. He felt his extremities going cold and tingling. He wondered if he might pass out.

"Male. Over six feet. Slender. Emaciated, really. Dressed in women's clothing."

Armand sat down and closed his eyes, lifting a trembling hand to his forehead. He exhaled.

Not Annie. Not Honoré.

"Seems to be a pre-op transsexual," the coroner was saying. "He had your name on a piece of paper in his pocket."

"She," said Gamache, sighing.

"Sorry?"

"She. Does she have on a pink coat? Frilly?"

"Not anymore. No coat. No boots, no gloves. He—"

"She."

"She was almost stripped. Do you know her?"

"Was she the only one?" asked Gamache, realizing what this might mean. "Was there anyone else with her when she was found?"

"Another body, you mean?"

"A little girl. About six years old."

"I don't know, I was only given this body."

"Well, check," said Gamache, fighting to keep from snapping at the coroner. "Please."

Normally the coroner, new to the job, wouldn't have taken orders from a stranger on the phone, but this man spoke with such authority he found himself saying, "Just a moment."

And going to check.

Gamache was put on hold. He got to his feet and paced as he waited. And waited. Finally Dr. Harper came back on.

"No. No little girl. Not in the morgue at least. Are you that Gamache? Head of the Sûreté?"

"I am."

"Do you know who this body is?"

"I think I do, but I'd have to see her. What did she die of?"

"Looks like an overdose. We're running tests."

"I'll be there in an hour."

"Yessir."

Armand headed for the door but changed his mind, and, returning to his study, he grabbed some syringes from the locked drawer in his desk.

Then he left.

Gamache stood beside the metal autopsy table, looking over at the clothing, tagged and piled on a side table. Bright purple nylon blouse, bought because it resembled silk, he suspected. Faux-leather miniskirt. Torn fishnet stockings.

Then he turned his attention to the thin body and saw the care she'd taken, for people who wouldn't care. Her bouffant blond wig was askew. The thick makeup, now smeared, had, that morning, been skillfully applied. Though nothing could cover the scabs and sores on her face.

In that wretched place, she'd made a stab at beauty.

He looked down at the body and felt overwhelming sadness.

The coroner and the technician, on hearing the head of the Sûreté muttering what sounded like the last rites, stepped away.

More from embarrassment than respect for privacy.

Gamache crossed himself and turned to them.

"Her name's Anita Facial," he said. When there was the beginning of a guffaw from the technician, he stifled it with a stern look. "Not, of course, her birth name. I don't know what that is. If you need help finding her next of kin, let me know. I'll do what I can."

Gamache noticed the mottled skin, the blue veins. The terror in the eyes, red from burst blood vessels. This was not a blissful death. Anita hadn't drifted away on a cloud of ecstasy. She had been torn from this life.

"It's carfentanil," he said.

"What?" asked the coroner.

"It's an analogue of fentanyl. An opioid."

"He's right, sir," said the technician, who'd gone to the computer. "We just got the blood work back. He has—"

"She," said the coroner.

"She has carfentanil in her system. Though not much."

"Doesn't take much," said Gamache.

"Never heard of it," said Dr. Harper. "You know it? A new opioid?"

"Newish," said Gamache. "New to the streets."

The coroner gave a deep sigh and muttered, "Goddamned drugs."

"May I?" Gamache reached out, then asked permission before touching Anita's arm.

Her body was marked with what looked like homemade tattoos. Hearts. Butterflies. On the back of one hand was *Esprit*.

Spirit.

And on the other, *Espoir*.

Hope.

Esprit. Espoir.

But it was her left forearm that interested him. More writing, in a different, though familiar, hand.

Not a tattoo, it was written in Magic Marker.

David.

And after the name there was a number: 2.

Dr. Harper went over to the computer and said something to the technician, who tapped on a few keys.

"Holy shit," he said, and turned to the coroner, who studied the screen, then turned to Gamache.

"There've been six deaths here in Montréal in the last three days. Four since this morning. All homeless. All junkies. All the same drug. What is this stuff?"

But Gamache didn't answer. It was rhetorical anyway. The coroner knew exactly what it was. A nightmare.

Gamache felt his chest tighten.

He was too late. It was being released. Six deaths already. He looked over at Anita. Seven.

But still, he hadn't heard from the undercover cops. Amelia hadn't found any. So maybe this was the forerunner, a sort of foretaste.

The main body of the drug would be on the streets soon. Perhaps within hours. But not quite yet.

"Can you bring up the autopsy pictures?" Gamache asked, stepping over to the terminal.

They did.

"Zoom in on the left forearms."

First one, then another. Then another.

"Shit," said the technician. "We missed that."

Gamache didn't respond. He was staring at the images on the screen. They had several things in common.

All junkies. All dead by carfentanil.

All with David written carefully on each left forearm. Though the numbers were, for the most part, different.

"What does it mean?" asked the coroner.

"I have no idea what this means," said Gamache, still studying the screen.

"So if a kid overdoses on this carfentanil," the coroner asked, "is there an antagonist? A rescue medication?"

"Naltrexone," said Gamache. "The Sûreté and local forces are being given it. But—"

But if all the carfentanil was released onto the streets, there wouldn't be nearly enough rescue drug out there. And not enough time to administer it. Carfentanil killed too fast for much hope of rescue, unless you got there immediately.

Gamache returned to the body of Anita Facial. And heard her soft voice on the message she'd left for him that afternoon.

She'd found the little girl. She'd keep her safe until he came to get her. But he hadn't. And she hadn't. And now the girl was still out there. Alone.

In the midnight and the snow!

"'Christ save us all from a death like this,'" he muttered under his breath as he left the mortuary and returned to his car.

But he knew Christ wasn't responsible. He was. And prayer, no matter how fervent, wouldn't stop it.

Once in the privacy of his car, he placed a call.

"What the fuck is it?" came the gravelly voice.

"It's Gamache."

"Oh, shit, sorry sir," the young man whispered. "I shouldn't be talking."

"Have you seen any sign of the carfentanil? Any sign at all that it's hit the streets?"

"No, none. But there's lots of anticipation."

"There's a little girl," Gamache said. "Red tuque. Five, six years old. I want you to find her."

"I can't."

347

"This isn't a request, it's an order."

"But, sir, Choquet's on the move. I think this's it. I think she's found him."

"David?"

"Yes. I can't talk. If anyone sees . . ."

Gamache knew it was a terrible risk, calling. No homeless man should be shuffling along and talking on a phone. But now he faced a choice.

The girl or the drug.

But there really was no choice to be made.

"Stay with her," he said. "We'll be tracking you. You have the naltrexone?"

"*Oui.*"

"Good luck," said Gamache.

He called his counterpart at the Montréal police and alerted him.

"We have the cell signal," said the assault-team commander. "We're ready to move as soon as we get the word."

"You'll need masks."

"Got them. You're there now?"

"Close."

"God, let's hope this's it."

The commander hung up, and Gamache drove toward the rotten core of the city he loved.

Agent Cloutier was still at her desk past midnight when Beauvoir arrived at Sûreté headquarters.

Ruth, leaning against the wall and clutching the thin, torn blue material at her throat, glared at him as he walked into the homicide department.

"Sorry," he said to Ruth, and turned her around.

"I have it here," said Cloutier, of the number he saw written there. "But waited for you to come before putting it in."

"Thanks for waiting," said Beauvoir as he pulled up a chair and nodded to her.

"Where is he?" asked Amelia, looking around.

This was an alley off an alley off a back lane. Impossible to find, except by those who were lost. She was pretty sure it wouldn't be on any map.

But once found it was never forgotten. And probably never left.

All her senses were alert, her eyes sharp, her hearing acute.

"Who?"

The voice was deep. Calm. Amused.

Not the kid anymore but someone else, speaking from a doorway.

Amelia turned and saw a figure. Arms crossed. Legs apart. Watching her.

He was young, she could tell. There was about him something that was missing from everyone else in the alley.

Except her.

Meat on his bones. And life in his voice. This man was fully alive. And, like her, fully alert.

"David," she said.

"Yes, I'd heard you were looking for him."

"Are you David?"

He laughed and stepped from the doorway. But the alley was dark, and she couldn't see him clearly. He tossed a small packet at the kid, who grabbed it and melted away.

"No," he said. "I'm not David. You already know him. Quite well."

Amelia's mind was racing. What had she missed?

"Show her," he said, and the junkies and dealers, who'd been leaning against the wall of urine frozen to the bricks, pushed up their sleeves.

All had "David" written on their forearms.

Then the man shoved up his sleeve. Even from a number of feet away, Amelia could see the tattoos. But not the name.

What did it mean? Her mind flickered this way and that, looking for the answer. It meant something.

Everyone else had "David" written on their arms. Including herself. Everyone except him.

He must have lied. He must be David. He wouldn't need to write his own name on his own forearm. Would he?

But she knew, quickly, instinctively, that he hadn't lied. He didn't need to. He was in control.

If he said she'd met this David before, then she had. But who? When? When he'd written his name on her arm, of course. But she couldn't remember anything about that. It was a complete blank. She'd passed out, far too stoned to remember anything.

She'd woken up hours later with the indelible ink on her arm.

David. Then the numbers 1 4. But actually it was 1/4.

Why was this man going around writing his name on junkies?

"Oh Christ," she whispered.

David wasn't a man. David wasn't even human.

David was the drug.

CHAPTER 36

"Damn," said Beauvoir.

He sat back in the chair and stared at the screen.

It hadn't worked. The number on the back of Clara's painting wasn't the code.

He'd been so sure of it. Had had Agent Cloutier reenter it. Two more times.

Nothing.

"Sorry, *patron*. It was a good idea," she said, and Beauvoir couldn't help but think that things were pretty desperate when Cloutier was patronizing him.

"We'll get it eventually," she said, not making him feel better. "But I do have some news. Bernard Shaeffer's handed over the information and access to the offshore money. It's a numbered account in Lebanon. Let me show you."

She brought it up, and there, very clearly, was the name Anthony Baumgartner and the amount. Just over seven million.

Beauvoir raised his brows. "A lot, but not actually as much as I expected."

"Me too," she said. "The numbers don't tally. According to the statements, the clients, all told, gave Baumgartner several hundred million. So where's the rest?"

"In another account," said Beauvoir, thinking. "With another person."

"Shaeffer?" asked Agent Cloutier.

Chief Inspector Beauvoir was nodding. Thinking.

Another reason for murder. Suppose Baumgartner realized his former lover wasn't quite as stupid, not quite as intimidated as he thought? Suppose he found out Shaeffer was stealing from him?

He'd confront Shaeffer. And Shaeffer would have killed him. Would have to, if he wanted to be free of Baumgartner and keep the fortune.

Beauvoir looked at the painting, then turned it back around so that Ruth was again scowling at him.

"A code can be symbols as well as numbers and letters, right?"

"Yes. It's even better, more secure, if some symbols are used. Why?"

"There's a symbol for you. And numbers."

He pointed to the lower right corner.

Gamache drove slowly down rue Ste.-Catherine, scanning the street.

Then, finding a parking spot, he pulled in and got out. His cell phone was connected to the agents tracking Amelia as she closed in on the back-street factory.

But right now Gamache had someone else he had to find.

"A little girl," he said to a prostitute. "She's five or six. Red Canadiens hat."

"You don't want a little girl," she said. "You want a big girl."

She grabbed her breasts.

"I don't mean for that," he said, his voice so stern the woman lowered her hands and stopped the act.

"You her father?" asked the prostitute. "Grandfather?"

"I'm a friend. Have you seen her?"

"Yeah, with Anita this afternoon."

"Anita's dead."

"Oh, not Anita too." She looked up and down the street. "I can't help you. I'm just trying to stay alive."

"You want to stay alive?" he said, handing her a fifty. "Get off the streets."

"And go where, honey? Your place? You and your nice wife gonna help me? Get out of the way and let me do my job."

"I'm serious," he said. "There's a new drug that's killing people. It killed Anita. Stay away from it."

"You look like a nice man. Let me give you some advice. Stay away from here."

But, of course, he couldn't leave. As the prostitute watched, he walked up one side of the street, then down the other.

His face grew numb in the bitter cold. He had to turn his back now and then against the wind, to catch his breath. But he kept on.

Talking to near-frozen junkies and trannies and whores.

But while most knew who he was talking about, none knew where the little girl was.

And then he saw. A bit of red. Down an alley. Disappearing into a doorway.

He followed, quickly. Once at the door, he yanked it open and saw a man holding the girl by the hand. Leading her down the corridor and into a room.

Gamache shouted, and the man, looking back and seeing him, shoved the girl into the room and slammed the door.

Breaking into a run, Gamache got to the door. It was locked. He pounded on it.

"Open up."

When there was no response, he threw himself against it. Again. And again.

Finally he broke through and stumbled into the room.

A man stood there. Middle-aged, or at least aged. Disheveled. Eyes sunken and red.

He held the girl in front of him, his large hand around her small throat.

"Give her to me," said Gamache, advancing into the room.

"I found her." His hand tightened around her throat. "She's mine."

"You need to let her go."

"I won't."

Gamache knelt down and looked into the little girl's eyes. But they were unfocused. Staring blankly ahead. Her mouth was open, and she was breathing rapidly. The Canadiens tuque had fallen off, and Gamache could see her hair, blond, filthy, matted.

"Can you close your eyes?" he asked her gently. She just continued to stare. "It's going to be all right. No one will hurt you."

But he suspected she'd heard that before. Just before she'd been hurt. Maybe beyond repair.

"I'm here to help," he said. "I know you might not believe it, but I am."

Then he stood back up.

"I won't hurt her," he said to the man. "But I will hurt you unless you let her go, right now."

"Fuck o—" was as far as he got.

Gamache took a long, rapid stride forward and hit the man so hard in the face that his nose broke. He dropped to the floor, bleeding, as Gamache grabbed the girl and lifted her into his arms.

"It's all right," he whispered, holding her tight and averting her fixed gaze from the broken man on the floor. "It's all right. You're safe."

Behind him he heard the man screaming. But the sound got fainter and fainter as Gamache and the girl went down the corridor and out into the cold night.

He got her buckled into his car and gave her a chocolate bar from his glove compartment. Jean-Guy thought he didn't know about the stash, but he did.

The girl just held it in front of her. Like a celebrant holding the cross.

"My name's Armand," he said, swinging the car back onto Ste.-Catherine. His voice was calm. Intentionally authoritative. "I'm with the police. You're safe now. I promise. I have a granddaughter your age. She lives in Paris. Her name's Florence. We call her Florie. She has a younger sister named Zora. What's your name?"

But she remained mute. Frozen in place. Barely even blinking.

Just then the cell phone burst into life.

"We've got it," said the agent. "The factory's in an abandoned building down a side street just off St.-André, north of Ste.-Catherine. She's gone inside. Should we go in?"

Gamache pulled over and hit his phone, about to say no, but the Montréal commander got there first.

"No" came the crisp voice. "Wait for us. We're five minutes away. Chief Superintendent, I have you even closer."

Gamache knew exactly the area the agents were talking about. And he was close.

He looked at the little girl. He couldn't leave her alone in the car. But neither could he take her with him.

He scanned the street and saw the answer.

"Chief Superintendent Gamache?" came the voice of the Montréal tactical commander.

"I'll be there in two minutes," he said, and then, stopping the car in the middle of the street, he bundled the girl in his arms, whispering calmly, gently, "Everything's fine. You're safe."

But he wondered, even as he spoke, if that was the biggest lie so far.

Pushing open the door into the diner, he looked around, then walked up to the waitress who'd served him two days earlier.

"My name's Gamache, I'm with the Sûreté. I have to go. Please look after her until either I return or someone from the Sûreté comes to get her."

"Are you kidding me?"

"You must." He placed the girl in one of the booths and turned to the worn waitress. "Please."

She held his eyes for a moment, then gave a curt nod.

"*Merci.*" Gamache brought out his wallet and gave her all he had. Then he knelt down and held the girl's dirty face between his large hands. Bringing out his handkerchief, he wiped her face and said quietly, "It'll be all right. This nice woman will bring you a hot chocolate and something to eat. No one will hurt you."

He stood up and looked at the waitress. "That's right, isn't it?"

She frowned and looked unhappy about all this. But he could see it was an act.

The girl would be safe.

He left, running across the street, dodging traffic, then up St.-André. He'd pulled out his phone and called Jean-Guy.

It rang and rang as he ran.

"*Patron—*"

"They've found the factory. It's off St.-André, north of Ste.-Catherine. You can track using my signal. And, Jean-Guy, there's a little girl in that diner we were in, on Ste.-Catherine. Have Lacoste come and get her. Hurry."

Without waiting for a reply, he clicked back to the map and the pulsing blue dot. And the white dot. On the horizon. Getting closer.

Beauvoir stood up and instinctively put his hand to his hip. And felt his gun there.

"I need to go."

"But we just broke the code. We're in."

By then Cloutier was talking only to Ruth, who continued to scowl. Though she did seem to be seeing something, very far away.

"What do you mean, you're going out?" demanded Lacoste's husband.

"And so are you. You need to . . . drive me."

While their neighbor looked after the kids, they drove into downtown Montréal.

"I'm not sure this's safe," said Isabelle's husband, glancing around.

"It could be worse," said Isabelle, staring out the window and wondering about the others.

Amelia was warm. Finally.

The cold that had gotten into her core and gripped her bones was letting go. Thawing.

She felt the heat slowly spreading, radiating out along her arteries and veins.

And she felt her muscles relax. Go limp. It felt . . . wonderful.

She'd bucked and fought, but they'd pinned her down. Here. In the factory she'd worked so hard to find.

She'd followed the man into the basement of the building and found something she'd only ever seen in class, at the academy. In training footage of raids on labs.

Hundreds of people were working at long tables. They wore protective gear. Masks. Rubber gloves. Smocks. In front of each was a scale, sensitive enough to show micrograms.

"Better stay back," the man said. "Did you know that the Russians used carfentanil in that hostage taking a few years ago? They pumped it into the air supply, to knock everyone out. But they had no idea what they were dealing with," he said with a laugh. "Killed most of the hostage takers and hundreds of hostages."

"All I know is that it's an elephant tranquilizer," said Amelia, standing as far back as she could from the long tables and the mounds of white powder.

"It was, but this"—he gestured toward the tables—"is another generation. Evolution. It's a wonderful thing but can also be a bit confusing. For instance, when this shit fell into our hands a few months ago, we knew what we had but didn't know how much to put in each hit."

He spoke matter-of-factly, as though talking about a soup recipe.

"So we experimented. As the release got closer, we began giving it to different people to see what happened."

Amelia looked down at her arm. Then at him.

"That's what this means. You wrote it on everyone you experimented on."

"Yes. The name of the drug, David, and the dosage. You got a quarter gram. Others weren't so lucky. But now we know the best hit. We don't want to kill too many of our customers. Of course, if they're stupid enough to take more than one dose at a time . . . well. Too dumb to live, I guess. Evolution."

"You fucker. You gave it to me?"

"You brought it on. Showing up out of nowhere. Asking questions. Beating up my dealers. You didn't think you could just arrive on the streets and take over? You really thought I'd allow it?" He laughed again, then grew serious. "I know who you really are. Not the one-eyed man. You're as blind and stupid as the rest of them, Amelia Choquet. Cadet in the Sûreté Academy."

"Former. I was kicked out."

"Mmm, yes. Trafficking. And yet instead of arresting you, they just threw you out? Now, why was that?"

"Why do you think? Oh, wait a minute. You think this's a setup? Yes, that makes sense, you dumb turd. That way I could get kicked out, move into a shithole with a junkie, and freeze my ass off. I'm living the dream. You think you're so clever. But we both know that this"—she nodded toward the long tables—"fell into your lap. And you're going to need help keeping it. Once this hits the streets, every dirty cop, every mob boss, every gang member, every wannabe cartel chief will be after you. You're right. I'm not the one-eyed man. I have two good eyes, and what I see is you gutted in some alley. You need me."

He was nodding. And then he looked past her and raised his brows.

Hands gripped her shoulders, and she was dragged backward onto the floor.

She fought, at one point thinking she'd broken free, but then a blow knocked her down and almost out. Dazed, she was turned onto her back, so that she was staring into his eyes.

"I don't think so," the man whispered, kneeling over her. "You're too dangerous. You betray everyone and everything, and eventually you'd betray me."

He stood up and nodded to someone. "Do it. Then toss her out."

Amelia bucked and fought and shouted. And felt the needle go in.

Then felt the warmth. Then it got hotter and hotter. Until it began to burn. Until her blood felt like it had turned to lava.

She opened her mouth to scream, but her eyes just rolled to the back of her head. Then turned red.

Gamache found the agents, their weapons drawn.

They gestured toward a door where two well-armed guards stood.

Then the agents pointed up. More guards stood on a fire escape and on the roofs of surrounding buildings.

Gamache gave a curt nod, then carefully backed down the alley. He turned, only to find the tactical commander and his assault team.

"Two out front," Gamache whispered. "Two on the fire escape opposite and three on the roofs."

He gestured, and the commander nodded.

"Got it." He handed Gamache a mask. "Do you have a weapon?"

"No," said Gamache.

"I might get shit for doing this, but—"

He pressed an automatic into Gamache's hand.

"*Merci.*"

"Let us go in first."

"Of course."

The commander signaled behind him. Weapons were raised, and with a few rapid silenced shots the guards dropped.

Gamache was about to move forward, right behind the commander, when he felt a hand on his shoulder.

It was Beauvoir, his own gun drawn.

"*Patron*," Jean-Guy whispered.

"Lacoste?"

"On her way to the girl."

As he spoke, his sharp eyes were on the door, with the tactical team pouring through.

He started to move forward, but Gamache stopped him. "Amelia Choquet's in there."

"So she did lead you to the stuff," said Beauvoir. "Fucking junkie. What did I—"

"She's with us. She's following my orders. We have to find her. Here." He handed Jean-Guy the mask. "Put this on."

The fight was brutal.

The tactical team arrived in force and didn't hesitate to use that force, firing on the armed guards with precision.

They moved swiftly through the lab, the first wave targeting those with weapons, the next wave of armed officers shoving workers away from the tables. Pushing them against the wall. Frisking those who complied. Subduing those who did not.

Beauvoir, gas mask on, went through ahead of Gamache and almost fell over the body.

He gestured to Gamache to back out, and, grabbing the collar of Amelia's coat, he dragged her back through the door. Away from any drug that might be floating in the air. Kicked up by the attack.

Once out the door, Beauvoir ripped off his mask and knelt by Gamache, who was on his knees beside Amelia.

Beauvoir kept his gun trained on the open door as automatic fire burst out. Ignoring it, Gamache wasted no time feeling for a pulse. He pulled the syringe from his pocket and plunged it into Amelia.

Her eyes were open. Glassy. Red. As though possessed.

Only then did he feel for a pulse as Beauvoir, still focused on the open door, called for medics.

"How is she?"

"No pulse."

Gamache tore open her coat as bullets hit the bricks above them. Beauvoir ducked, instinctively, but Gamache kept on with the compressions. Counting. Under his breath, his face fixed, his focus complete. Ignoring the gunshots all around.

"Three. Four. Five."

Beauvoir sensed movement through the door into the lab at the same moment he heard a click. Turning quickly, he saw the gun rising. Pointing at them.

A young guy held the weapon like an expert.

But Beauvoir was more expert. He fired. Three quick shots. Boom, boom, boom. And the man dropped.

When the ringing from the shots stopped bouncing off the walls, he heard Gamache beside him, still counting. Not losing a beat.

"Twenty-nine. Thirty."

The medics arrived.

Gamache bent lower and gave Amelia two breaths.

"Carfentanil," he said, continuing the compressions while Beauvoir watched the door into the lab and counted for him.

"Seven. Eight. Nine."

"I gave her the antagonist," said Gamache as he rocked back and forth, keeping the rhythm of the compressions.

"Which one?" asked the medic, kneeling beside him and preparing the defibrillator.

"Naltrexone. Less than a minute ago."

"Okay," said the medic. "Step aside."

Gamache did, watching as the medics worked on Amelia. And other medics moved forward into the factory. To care for the wounded. Even as the shots continued. And more wounded were made.

Gamache looked over at Jean-Guy, who was now kneeling beside the young man he'd shot. And killed.

CHAPTER 37

"You look awful," said Isabelle's husband with a sympathetic smile. "Here."

He handed Gamache a scotch and offered Beauvoir a coffee.

"*Merci*," said Armand, accepting the drink but putting it down. "Where is she?"

It was well past midnight, and he felt like he'd been hit by a truck, but the evening wasn't over yet.

"In our daughter's room," said Isabelle. "Would you like to see?"

"Please. Do you know her name?"

"No. She hasn't spoken."

"Social services?"

"I thought I'd wait 'til morning."

"Good."

Gamache and Jean-Guy followed Isabelle down the hall.

Her husband stayed behind in the living room, watching the three of them go. Recognizing that while he and the children would always be the most important parts of Isabelle's life, these three also formed a family.

The door was open, and a night-light was on. In one bed lay Sophia, Isabelle's daughter. Fast asleep.

In the other was the little girl. On her side, curled into a tight ball under the comforter. Eyes staring. Her hands clutching the pillow at her head.

Armand walked in quietly and knelt down.

When last he'd seen the girl, her hair was matted and caked with filth. Now it was clean and brushed. She'd had a bath and smelled very faintly of lavender.

"It's Armand," he spoke softly. "We met earlier. I'm the police officer."

She cringed away, her eyes widening.

"It's all right. I won't hurt you. No one will. You're safe." He was careful not to approach further. Not to touch her. "You can go to sleep now."

He smiled in a way that, he hoped and prayed, didn't betray how his heart ached for her.

But she continued to stare at him, in terror.

"May I?" he asked, turning to Isabelle and indicating a book on the bedside table.

Isabelle nodded.

Armand brought over a chair and opened the book.

"'. . . in which we are introduced to Winnie-the-Pooh and some bees,'" he read, his voice deep and soft and tranquil. He looked up then, into her wide eyes. "'And the stories begin.'"

"Amelia?" Isabelle asked Jean-Guy.

They'd left the Chief Superintendent reading to the girl and had returned to the living room.

"We just came from the hospital," said Jean-Guy, dropping into an armchair. "They got her heart going, and she's breathing on her own."

"Brain damage?" asked Isabelle.

"They're doing tests, but we won't know until she wakes up. We're going back there right after we leave here."

She nodded. "If there's anything I can do."

"There may be. Thank you. I'll let you know."

"So she was working with the Chief all along? Did . . . anyone know?"

"No."

"Not even you?"

"No. I knew he'd expelled Amelia in hopes she'd lead him to the carfentanil, but I had no idea she was in on it."

Isabelle looked at Jean-Guy closely. "Are you okay with that? With not being told?"

He lifted his fingers off the arms of the chair, then dropped them. What could he say? What could he do? It was, he knew, the nature of the job.

Secrecy. Secrets.

Lacoste had them. All senior officers had things they kept close to the chest.

God knows, he himself had his secrets. One in particular.

He knew he'd have to tell his father-in-law soon. And this one hit closer to home and was far more personal than the secret Gamache had kept from him.

"The carfentanil?" asked Isabelle.

"Looks like we got it all, except for what was used in the experiments."

"What experiments?" Isabelle's husband asked.

"This particular opioid's so new that no one really knows the safe dose. And, of course, that also depends on weight, body type. Health. So many addicts have weak hearts, and very little will push them over the edge. This guy—"

Boom, boom, boom. Beauvoir saw, in a flash, the man drop. Dead.

Something he would never unsee. Another ghost for his long-house.

"—experimented on junkies. Giving out different doses and writing on their arms the amount. A milligram. Two. To see who survived and who died."

Isabelle shook her head, and then her brow furrowed. "Why did he call it David?"

"It's his father's name."

Isabelle took that in. Not sure what it meant. Was it meant as a tribute or an attack, an accusation? Was it meant to thank or to hurt?

She suspected the latter.

"You okay?" she asked Jean-Guy. She could guess what he was thinking.

That he'd just killed a young man. Troubled. Criminal. A killer. It was self-defense. But he was still dead. And one day soon, Jean-Guy would have to face the boy's father. David.

"I'm tired," said Jean-Guy, and she could see that it would take much more than a shower and a good night's sleep for him to recover.

"The sound of maple logs in an open fire," she said quietly. "A hot dog at a Canadiens game. Honoré's hand . . . holding yours."

"These things I've loved," Jean-Guy whispered. *"Merci."*

She glanced down the hall to where the children were sleeping. A delicate, almost reedy sound was coming from there.

Jean-Guy and Isabelle went quietly down and looked in.

Armand had closed the book and was leaning toward the child, his elbows on the torn and filthy knees of his slacks.

He was humming. While, in the bed, the little girl's eyes were closed.

Edelweiss. Edelweiss.

Hours later Amelia Choquet opened her eyes, squinting into the bright light.

She felt a hand on her shoulder and startled.

"It's all right, you're in the hospital. My name's Dr. Boudreau. I'll be looking after you."

He spoke slowly. Clearly.

"Can you tell me your name?"

There was a pause.

"Amelia . . . Choquet."

"That's right. And do you know who this is?"

Dr. Boudreau looked at the man standing beside him.

"Shit. Head," she mumbled.

"Wha—" the doctor began, but Gamache gave a gruff laugh.

"She got that right too," he said, and looked across the bed to Jean-Guy, who was smiling with relief.

"I'm sorry, Amelia," said Gamache. "For this."

"Did you—"

"Yes, we got it all."

She closed her eyes, and Gamache thought she'd drifted off. But she spoke again, her eyes still closed.

"Girl."

"We have her. She's safe," said Jean-Guy. "Your friend Marc is here in the hospital too. They're looking after him."

Amelia nodded, then went silent.

Gamache took the doctor aside. "Will she be all right?"

"I think so. She's healthy, and you got the rescue med to her in time. She's lucky."

"Yeah, well," said Jean-Guy, "I can hardly wait to hear her version of that when she's fully awake."

Before he left, Armand took the worn little book from his pocket and pressed it into her hands.

"Erasmus," he whispered, though he wasn't sure she could hear him. "For company."

They left the hospital, but there was one more stop they had to make before the day, or night, was over.

Agent Cloutier was asleep in her chair but awoke quickly and stood up at her desk when she saw the Chief Superintendent come in with Chief Inspector Beauvoir.

Both men looked exhausted. Unshaved and disheveled.

She'd heard what had happened and had begun toward them when she stopped. And smiled. Broadly. On seeing who walked slowly in behind them.

"Chief Inspector," said Cloutier, going over to Lacoste and hugging her.

"Is that how we greeted each other, *patron*, when you were head of homicide?" asked Jean-Guy.

"Only in private."

Beauvoir laughed and pulled over two chairs to join the two already in front of the laptop on Cloutier's desk.

Isabelle sat and took a moment to look at Ruth glaring back at her.

"Amazing," she said. "I keep expecting her to say 'numbnuts.'"

"Why would the Virgin Mary say that?" asked Cloutier.

"Not important," said Beauvoir. "Show us what you have."

As Agent Cloutier walked them through the files they'd found on Anthony Baumgartner's computer, a pattern emerged.

The three of them stared at the screen. Then at each other. Then at Agent Cloutier.

Beauvoir had known some of this when he'd been called away. But most of it Cloutier had uncovered on her own.

"It's genius," Cloutier said in admiration. "Almost too simple to believe, and that made it hard to find." She shook her head. "Incredible."

The other three were leaning forward. Examining the details.

"It's suggestive," said Gamache.

"It's more than that, sir," she said. "It says it all."

"No. It says one thing, but there's no proof this is what actually happened," said Gamache.

"We need proof, Agent Cloutier," said Jean-Guy. "But this at least tells us where to look."

"I have proof," she said. "Follow the money."

She smiled and started tapping rapidly on the keys. Different pages popped up and disappeared from the screen.

"This is," she said as she typed, "the same route Anthony Baumgartner took. Circuitous, but then it would have to be."

There, finally, on the screen was the home page of a corporation in the British Virgin Islands.

"Is that where Baumgartner hid the rest of the money?" asked Beauvoir.

"With Shaeffer's help. But it's a launch point, not the final stop," said Cloutier. "People who want to hide money set up a corporation in a tax haven like BVI, then funnel it to a numbered account. Switzerland used to be the country of choice. But then came the crackdown. This"—she hit another page—"took over."

A bank in Singapore came up.

"How do you know this's where Baumgartner hid his money?" asked Beauvoir.

"Because I found the account."

"How?" he asked.

Agent Cloutier glanced over at Ruth. "A little help from the crazy lady."

Lacoste and Gamache looked puzzled, but Beauvoir's brows cleared.

"The number on the back of the painting," said Beauvoir.

"Yes. It wasn't his password, it was the account number. He wrote it there so he wouldn't forget it."

She put in the numbers, and up popped the account. Under the name Baumgartner.

"Three hundred and seventy-seven million dollars," Lacoste read off the screen.

"A motive for murder," said Beauvoir. He stood up and placed a call. Ordering agents to arrest Bernard Shaeffer.

The sun was up and flooding into the offices of Horowitz Investments when Beauvoir arrived. He'd had time to shower and change and had asked Hugo and Caroline Baumgartner to meet him in Hugo's office.

The office was as impressive as Hugo Baumgartner was unimpressive. Floor-to-ceiling windows looked out over the city. It spoke of success but didn't drip wealth. It was restrained, while saying all it needed to say.

Jean-Guy took note. Wondering if he could make over his office like this.

The siblings sat side by side, like a princess and a toad. Caroline self-contained and elegant. Hugo squat and disheveled. No tailor could ever make him look tailored. But his bulging eyes were warm and encouraging, and he rested his hand on his sister's.

"You have news, you said?"

"We do," said Beauvoir.

He'd brought Agent Cloutier with him. He'd invited Gamache as well, but having also showered and changed, he had another meeting to go to. With the Premier Ministre du Québec.

The review board had come down with its recommendations.

Just before entering the meeting with the Baumgartners, Beauvoir had received a call from Gamache.

"I've had a message from Kontrollinspektor Gund in Vienna. There's been a decision on the will."

Beauvoir listened, and then, after wishing Gamache good luck, he hung up and entered his own meeting.

"You know who killed Anthony?" asked Caroline.

"Yes. Early this morning we arrested Bernard Shaeffer."

She closed her eyes and exhaled. "Oh, poor Anthony."

"But why would Shaeffer kill him?" asked Hugo. "Revenge for being fired? That was a couple of years ago."

"You'd be surprised how long people can hold on to things."

"Were they still seeing each other?" Caroline asked.

"Not that we can tell," said Beauvoir. "Not as lovers anyway. But there's evidence that your brother got him a job after he was fired. He's working at the Caisse Populaire."

"At a bank?" asked Hugo. "Why would Tony do that? It doesn't make sense."

"It does if you need to set up false accounts and hide money."

Hugo opened his mouth to speak, then shut it and stared at the Chief Inspector.

"You have proof?"

Beauvoir nodded. "Shaeffer admitted he'd set up a shell company and a numbered account in Lebanon in your brother's name, in exchange for the job and his silence. We found millions."

Caroline looked at Hugo. "What does this mean? Anthony really was stealing?"

"It looks like it. Are you sure it was him, Chief Inspector? Maybe Shaeffer set up an account in Tony's name but used the money himself. Tony found out, confronted him, and Shaeffer killed him."

"We considered that possibility," said Beauvoir. "That your brother actually knew nothing about it. There was also the strange issue of the amount in the account. Slightly over seven million."

"Sounds like a lot to me," said Caroline.

But Hugo understood. He was watching Beauvoir, his ugly face expressive. "According to the statements you showed me, he'd taken hundreds of millions. So where's the rest?"

"Exactly."

Beauvoir nodded to Agent Cloutier, who put Anthony Baumgartner's laptop on the table and set it up.

"It took us a while, but we finally got into your brother's computer." Beauvoir looked at them. "I hope this won't upset you."

They looked at each other, and Caroline gave a curt nod. "Best we know. I expect it'll all be made public soon enough."

"The interesting thing about your brother," said Beauvoir as Cloutier brought up the files, "is that almost without exception he was described as decent, brilliant. A great mentor and a man of integrity, who when he discovered wrongdoing, turned the person in, knowing he'd get some of the blame."

"That was the Tony we knew," said Hugo.

"But his actions told a different story. A man who was brilliant, yes, but deceitful. Embezzling not just tens of millions but hundreds of millions. Who betrayed a young co-conspirator and turned him in when it looked like they'd be caught. It's a familiar story for those of us in homicide. People lead double lives. They appear to be one thing while actually being not just something else but something totally opposite to what people think."

"How else do they get away with it?" said Hugo.

Beauvoir was nodding. "Except most don't. Let me show you what we found on his laptop."

The Premier stood at his desk, and Gamache rose also.

He'd been in the Premier's Montréal office less than ten minutes.

These things didn't take long.

"I'm sorry, Armand," said the Premier, looking down at the unopened envelope on his desk. "If there was any other course possible, I'd have taken it."

"I appreciate your telling me yourself, and in person. I knew what would probably happen when I made those decisions. It could've been worse. You could be arresting me."

"You've made some enemies, Armand, but you have a lot more friends. I hope you know I'm one of them."

"I do."

"And you got the drugs back, that's what matters. I've been reading the preliminary report on what happened. You do know that if you hadn't already been suspended, you'd have been suspended for what you just did." He looked at Gamache closely. "And no one else knew you'd had a cadet thrown out of the academy and that she was working with you?"

"No one."

"Not even Beauvoir?"

"Not even him. Just Cadet Choquet and me."

The Premier nodded slowly. But decided not to question it further. The less he knew . . . He walked forward, to show Gamache the door.

"How is she?"

"Recovering. She'll be running the Sûreté one day."

"Yeah, well, the job's open. Apparently you have to be half crazed to accept it, so that bodes well for her. I just hope I'm long retired by the time there's a Chief Superintendent Choquet."

Gamache smiled, then paused at the threshold. "There is something you can help me with."

"Name it."

"There's a little girl. . . ."

Gamache called Reine-Marie and told her what happened, then drove across town to the low-rise apartment building and pressed the button for the caretaker's apartment.

Benedict let him in, and a few minutes later Gamache was sitting on a worn sofa in the tiny basement apartment. Katie and Benedict were across from him, sitting on boxes.

"Have you figured out who killed Monsieur Baumgartner?" Benedict asked. "You know, I thought for a minute yesterday, at your place, that you suspected us."

"More than a minute," said Katie.

"No, I haven't come about that. Chief Inspector Beauvoir will be by later this morning to talk with you."

They exchanged glances, then Katie asked, "Why have you come?"

"There's a decision in the court case in Vienna. It came down this morning."

Benedict took Katie's hand, and they waited.

"They ruled in favor of the Baumgartners."

The couple sat still for a moment, then Benedict put his arm around Katie and she nodded.

"It's what we expected," said Katie. "And without that letter the Baron and Baroness's wishes won't be followed. They'll keep it for themselves."

"It's theirs to keep," Benedict said. "You did your best. We'll be fine."

He hugged her closer.

"The sins I was told were mine from birth / And the Guilt of an old inheritance," thought Gamache as he left them and headed over the Champlain Bridge toward Reine-Marie and home.

Maybe it stops now, with their child.

Hugo Baumgartner was staring at the laptop, his lower lip thrust out in concentration.

"Are you following?" asked Agent Cloutier.

"Yes, thank you," he said with a patient smile. And returned to the screen. After a few minutes, he sighed. "So Tony and Shaeffer were working together after all. I was wrong. I'm sorry. I really didn't think Tony had it in him."

"I'm afraid that's what it looks like," said Beauvoir. He scrolled down as he spoke.

Hugo was studying the screen, nodding. "They've taken the usual routes to hide money."

"You know a lot about it?" asked Beauvoir.

"More than some," he admitted. "But less than most. Mr. Horowitz asked me to head a committee investigating offshore accounts."

"To set them up?" asked Beauvoir.

Hugo gave him an amused look. "To make sure we weren't inadvertently helping clients hide money. Partly moral, but also practical. Mr. Horowitz is wealthy enough, he doesn't need that money, and he sure doesn't need the trouble if the regulators and the media find out."

"Did you find any?" asked Beauvoir.

"More than we expected, Chief Inspector. The wealthy have a way of justifying things. They live in distorted reality. If everyone at the club's doing it, it must be okay."

"'They'?" asked Beauvoir. "You don't consider yourself one of them?"

"Wealthy? No," he laughed. "I'm very well off, rich by most standards, but these people have hundreds of millions. I'm not in that club, nor do I wish to be. I'm happy where I am."

Hugo returned to the screen. "One thing I do know is that we'll need to find the number of the account in Singapore. Has Shaeffer given it to you?"

371

"He says he doesn't have it. In fact, he seemed surprised about this second account."

"He must be lying," said Hugo. "Unfortunately, the bank in Singapore won't tell you, and they can't be compelled to give out the information. But Tony must've written it down somewhere."

"Well," said Beauvoir. "You're right about that. It was written down."

"You found it?" asked Hugo.

"Behind the painting," said Agent Cloutier.

"Which painting?" asked Caroline.

"The one in his study," said Beauvoir. "Above the fireplace."

"Of the crazy old lady?" said Caroline. "That's where Anthony hid it?" She thought for a moment, then said, "Smart, actually. It'd be pretty safe there. I can tell you that no one goes near it. God knows what the Baroness saw in that thing. Miserable piece of so-called art. You thought the same thing, didn't you?"

Hugo nodded.

"Poor Anthony ended up with it," she said. "Told her he liked it. Something about a white dot in the distance. He was just being polite, and look where it got him. She gave it to him, and he had to hang it up. No matter what you say he did, there was a lot of kindness in him."

"I haven't said he did anything," said Beauvoir. "At least not anything illegal."

"What do you mean?" She pointed to the laptop. "Isn't that the proof?"

Beauvoir nodded to Cloutier, who started putting the numbers in.

"After all our high-tech hunting, it was writing on the back of a painting that finally gave us the proof we needed."

Cloutier hit enter, and up came the account.

Caroline's eyes widened.

"Three hundred and seventy-seven million," she whispered.

Then her expression changed, to confusion.

"But I don't understand. That says Hugo Baumgartner." She turned to her brother. "Was Anthony trying to make it look like it was you?" And then she understood.

Jean-Guy Beauvoir stood, and Agent Cloutier experienced another first.

Her first arrest for murder.

CHAPTER 38

"So." Ruth's voice, querulous, stalked in from the living room to the kitchen, where Armand and Reine-Marie were preparing warm hors d'oeuvres. "The idea is to run around the village green at minus twenty, in our bathing suits, wearing snowshoes?"

"Yes," said Gabri. "It was Myrna's idea."

"Was not."

"Was too."

"I think it's brilliant," said Ruth. "Count me in."

"We're doing this at night, right?" Clara whispered to Gabri.

"Now we are."

"Have you heard from Justin Trudeau yet?" Myrna asked. "Is he coming?"

"Oddly, the Baroness Bertha Baumgartner here has not yet heard back from the Prime Minister's office," said Olivier.

"You used her name?" asked Ruth.

"It was Myrna's idea," said Gabri.

"Was not."

"Was too."

"That's . . . that's . . ." Ruth struggled to find the right word. "Brilliant too. She'd have liked that. But I can't believe Justin Trudeau isn't keen to strip down and race around a tiny village. He's taken his shirt off for less. He once did it for a bag of Cheetos. I think."

"We still have time," said Gabri. "He'll reply. The winter carnival isn't until the weekend."

"If there was a ribbon for faint hope, he'd win," said Olivier with pride.

"Okay, here's a question," said Ruth. "One that philosophers have been asking for centuries. Which would you rather have? A numb skull or a numb nut?"

"Dear God," whispered Reine-Marie, peering around the corner of the kitchen at their assembled guests. "What've we done?"

"Ahh, the age-old question," said Stephen Horowitz, sitting beside Ruth on the sofa. "I believe Socrates asked his students the same thing."

"It was Plato," said Ruth.

"Was not."

"Was too."

"I think," Armand said to Reine-Marie, "we should keep an eye out for two more Horsemen."

"Well, he's your godfather," she said. "And it was your idea to invite him down to meet Ruth."

"I kind of thought they might cancel each other out."

"More like Godzilla meets Mothra," said Gabri, walking into the kitchen and taking a grilled parmesan on baguette off the tray they were preparing. "Tokyo is not safe. We, by the way, are Tokyo."

"There you are, Armand," said Stephen when they returned to the living room. "I have some questions for you."

"Numb skull," said Armand.

"No, not that. Though that is the right answer." The elderly man looked at the hors d'oeuvre platter and asked, "Caviar?"

"They're provincial," said Ruth. "Come over to my place later. I have a little jar and a chilled bottle of Dom Perignon."

"Taken from us on New Year's Eve," muttered Olivier, still fuming.

"The jar of caviar was open," said Clara. "By now it'll probably kill her."

"That's the one you took," said Myrna. "We ate it the next day, with chopped egg on toast."

"Oh right. Never mind."

Stephen held out his glass, and Armand refreshed it. "You know what I'm going to ask."

"I'll let Jean-Guy explain," said Armand, correctly guessing what was on Stephen Horowitz's mind. "He's the head of homicide. He figured it out."

Jean-Guy looked uncomfortable, and not just because Rosa was sitting on his lap. Beside him, in the crook of his arm, Honoré was staring at Rosa, transfixed by the duck, who was muttering, "Fuck, fuck, fuck."

Then Jean-Guy heard another voice repeating the same word.

His eyes widened, and he looked at Annie, who was staring at their son.

His first word.

Not "Mama." Not "Papa."

"Shhh," said Jean-Guy, but by now others had noticed the odd echo coming from the armchair.

"I think," said Annie, going over and scooping up their son, "it's time for a bath."

And that's when Honoré let loose. One great, long "Fuuuuck!"

Even Rosa looked startled, but then ducks often did.

"Ahh," said Reine-Marie and looked at the fire, while Armand raised his eyes to the ceiling, suddenly finding the plaster fascinating.

Ruth hooted with delight, and Stephen said, "Attaboy, Ray-Ray. You tell 'em."

Armand dropped his eyes and looked at his godfather. "Nice. *Merci*."

"Only you, my dear boy, could have a grandson whose greatest influence is a mallard."

"Is she a mallard?" Clara asked Ruth, who shrugged and took a long swig of Stephen's drink.

"Okay, off we go," said Annie while Honoré, in her arms and noticing the reaction his first word got, wailed it all the way down the hall.

"Good God," sighed Reine-Marie.

"Good lungs," said Stephen.

Beauvoir tried not to notice the tightly pressed lips of Clara, Myrna, Gabri, and Olivier. Even Armand and Reine-Marie looked amused.

"You have some questions, sir?" Jean-Guy asked Stephen.

It had been a day since the arrests of Bernard Shaeffer and Hugo Baumgartner. One for embezzlement, one for murder.

"Hugo. What happened? I can follow the scheme," said Stephen. "But I don't know the details. He wasn't just my employee. A senior vice president. I trusted him. I must be getting old."

"You're already there," said Ruth.

"I can tell you most of what happened," said Jean-Guy.

Everyone leaned forward.

Even Myrna, who already knew. Armand had told her. And she, in confidence, had told Clara. Who had told Gabri in confidence, who immediately told Olivier, swearing him to secrecy. Who then spilled it to Ruth in exchange for the crystal water jug she'd also lifted on New Year's Eve.

"Yes," said Clara. "Please, tell us."

"The idea started when Anthony turned Shaeffer in. Shaeffer was fired, and Anthony Baumgartner had his license to trade taken away," said Jean-Guy.

"The original embezzlement," said Stephen.

"Yes. Hugo knew Anthony wasn't to blame, but he also knew his reputation had been damaged. The street, as you call it, believed Anthony Baumgartner was also in on it and that only his senior position in the firm had saved him. They believed he was as dirty as Shaeffer. Hugo saw his opportunity. He approached Bernard Shaeffer, who was clearly a crook, and offered to get him a job in the Caisse Populaire, in exchange for certain favors."

"Hugo was the one who wrote the letter of recommendation to the Caisse," said Myrna. "Not his brother."

"And what were the favors?" asked Olivier. They knew the broad outlines of the crime, but not the details.

"Shaeffer would use the facilities and connections of the bank to set up an account in Anthony's name."

"Don't you mean Hugo's name?" asked Clara.

"No, that was the brilliance of what Hugo did. He was setting Anthony up. If anyone clued in to what was happening, they'd only find Anthony's name, on a numbered account in Lebanon."

"They put seven million into it," said Stephen. He was listening closely. So far this wasn't anything he didn't already know.

"*Merde*," said Olivier. "Wish he'd incriminated me."

"That was nothing," said Beauvoir. "The real money was going into a numbered account in Singapore. Not even Shaeffer knew about that. He had no idea of the scope of the embezzlement."

He looked at Gamache, inviting him to join in. Armand leaned forward, his glass of scotch between his hands.

"It worked well for a few years," said Armand. "As with most things, it started small. A little money from one or two. But when Hugo realized they weren't questioning, as long as they got their dividend checks, he increased the amounts and the number of clients."

"He got greedy," said Clara.

"Greed, yes. But I've seen this sort of thing before," said Stephen. "It becomes a game. A thrill. A sort of addiction. They have to keep increasing the hit. No one needs three hundred million. He could've stopped at fifty and been safe and comfortable for the rest of his life. No, there was something else at work. And I didn't see it."

He looked not just upset but drained.

Despite her kidding, Reine-Marie knew perfectly well why Armand had invited his godfather out for a few days. And introduced him to Ruth.

It was so he wouldn't be alone with his thoughts. With his wounds.

Things were pretty dire when Ruth was the healing agent.

"So what went wrong?" asked Gabri.

"Anthony ran into one of the so-called clients on the street last summer," said Beauvoir. "The man thanked Anthony for the great job he was doing. Baumgartner didn't think much of it until he started going through his client list and realized this fellow wasn't on it. He contacted the man and asked for the financial statement."

"So he knew someone was stealing, and using his name," said Stephen. "I got that. But how did he figure out it was his brother?"

Ruth, sitting between Gabri and Stephen, had fallen asleep and was snoring softly. Her head lolling on Stephen's shoulder. A bit of spittle landing on his cashmere sweater.

But he didn't push her away.

"He didn't. Not at first," said Beauvoir. "When we got into his laptop and uncovered his search history, we found that he seemed to be searching for something. At first we assumed he was looking around for places to put the money, but then we checked the timelines and realized it wasn't that."

"He was trying to retrace someone's steps," said Armand. "To figure out who was responsible."

"He started with his own company," said Jean-Guy. "With Madame Ogilvy, in fact. Then spread it out. When all else failed, he began looking further afield."

"Or closer to home, really," said Armand. And not, he thought, in a field but in a garden. Apparently healthy but actually choked with bindweed.

He tried to imagine Anthony Baumgartner's shock when he realized who was stealing. And setting him up.

Matthew 10:36.

Armand sometimes wished he'd never paused on that piece of Scripture. And he certainly wished he didn't know the truth it contained.

"What I don't understand is how Anthony Baumgartner even found that trail," said Stephen. "Hugo would've hidden it well."

"Let me ask you this," said Armand. "If you were going to embezzle, would you use your own computer?"

Stephen's face opened, and he gave a small grunt. "No. I'd use someone else's and take the opportunity to implicate them while I'm at it, in case it's ever caught. Smart Hugo."

"Smart Hugo," said Beauvoir. "He and Anthony got together once a week for meals. While Tony cooked, Hugo used his brother's laptop, supposedly to get caught up on the markets."

"But actually to transfer money," said Stephen.

"But wouldn't it be obvious?" asked Olivier. "I do our accounting online, and it's all right there."

"Not hard to bury it," said Beauvoir. "Especially if you want to. And Hugo wanted to. But not too deep. He also wanted people to be able to find it, if need be. And we eventually did. And yes, it made it look like Anthony was the one doing it. Why wouldn't it? Without the password for the numbered account in Singapore, there'd be no proof it was anyone other than Anthony."

"But Anthony found it?" said Clara.

"*Oui,*" Beauvoir continued. "We found Anthony's searches. He'd made no attempt to hide those. They were more and more frantic, it seems. And then, in September of last year, they stopped."

"He had what he was looking for," said Armand.

"He knew then, months ago, that Hugo was stealing?" said Stephen. "Why didn't he stop it then? Why wait until now to say something? Denial?"

"Maybe," said Armand. "But I think it might've been something else."

"His mother," said Clara. "He waited until his mother died."

"Yes," said Armand.

"I can see why Hugo would need someone else to blame, but why not use Shaeffer for that too?" asked Olivier. "Why drag his own brother into it?"

"Hard to tell," said Jean-Guy. "There was the convenience of the laptop and the fact Anthony was already tarred by the street. Hugo isn't admitting anything."

"I think there was something else," said Myrna. "Jealousy. And can you blame him?"

"For killing his brother?" asked Clara. "I think I can."

"No, I mean for being jealous. Resentful. One tall, handsome, respected, decent. Married with children. The other squat, physically unattractive, even slightly repulsive. Imagine growing up together?"

"But lots do," said Gabri. "I have a younger brother who's not nearly as attractive as me. It hasn't led to murder."

"Early days," said Olivier.

"But there was more," said Myrna. "Who was the Baroness's favorite? Who understood Clara's painting? Hugo might've looked like his mother, but Anthony was more like her in every way that mattered. That's why Hugo dragged Anthony's name into it."

"'The sins I was told were mine from birth,'" said Stephen, looking down at the woman drooling on his sweater, "'and the Guilt of an old inheritance.'"

Ruth woke up with a snort. "Guilt? Sin?"

"You were singing her song," said Gabri.

"Wait a minute," said Stephen. "I know about these numbered accounts. You got the number for the one in Lebanon from that Shaeffer fellow, but what about the other?"

"We found it behind Clara's painting," said Beauvoir.

"Yes, yes, but how did Anthony Baumgartner find it and put it there? These codes are closely guarded. The bank only sends them out over secure, encrypted emails. There's no way Anthony could've just stumbled on it and then written it behind that painting. By the way," he said to Clara. "I'd like to see the original. Is it for sale?"

"Ten bucks and she's yours," said Gabri, pointing to Ruth.

"We can talk," said Clara.

"You're right," said Jean-Guy. "Anthony could never find the code.

It's the one thing that Hugo knew would incriminate him. The only place where he needed his real name. On the account in Singapore that had three hundred seventy-seven million in it."

Olivier groaned.

"So how did Anthony find it and get into the account?" asked Stephen.

"He didn't."

They stared at Jean-Guy.

Armand crossed his legs and sat back. Marveling at Jean-Guy. His protégé, who now no longer needed any protection. He was soaring on his own.

"Anthony Baumgartner didn't write the access code there," said Jean-Guy. "Hugo did."

"And Anthony found it?" asked Myrna.

"No. He didn't. When he confronted Hugo that night at their old farmhouse, he didn't have the final proof. I think he must've begged Hugo to explain, but when Hugo couldn't, Anthony told him he'd have to turn him in."

"And that's why Hugo killed him," said Ruth.

"*Oui.*"

"Do you think Hugo meant to kill him?" asked Gabri.

"How should I know?" asked Ruth.

"I was asking the head of homicide," said Gabri. "Not the demented poet."

"Oh," she said. "Well, go on, numbnuts."

"Hard to tell," said Jean-Guy. "He was a man who planned. He must've had some sort of exit strategy, in case the embezzlement was found out. But I doubt his plan was to kill his brother."

"He was cornered," said Armand. "And when Anthony refused to turn a blind eye, he lashed out."

"You see what comes of integrity, Armand?" said Stephen. "Of decency?"

"Some godfather," said Myrna.

"Decency didn't kill him," said Armand. "Indecency did. Jealousy. Greed. Resentment."

"We were looking at one feud when it was another that did the damage," said Myrna.

They were quiet for a moment, until Gabri broke the silence.

"Is it rude to say I'm hungry?"

"So'm I," said Stephen. "What's for dinner? Lobster?"

"Stew," said Olivier.

"Eh," said Stephen. "Let's call it boeuf bourguignon."

"I see you're reading the book I gave you," Ruth said to Jean-Guy as they got up. She pointed to the coffee table.

"You gave him *The Gashlycrumb Tinies*?" asked Stephen. "By Edward Gorey? Oh, I think I really do love you," he said to Ruth.

While Stephen read the book out loud, Jean-Guy took Myrna aside.

"We found the letter," he said.

"In the wreck of the farmhouse?"

"Yes. Torn and dirty. It was exactly what Katie Burke described. Written in her hand, though the envelope looked like it was written by the Baroness. In it she asked Anthony to share the fortune should it come their way. Which it did."

"Thank you for telling me," said Myrna.

Annie caught her husband's eye. Jean-Guy took a deep breath, and then, excusing himself from Myrna, he approached his father-in-law.

"I'm going to say good night to Honoré. Want to come? Gets us out of preparing dinner."

"After dinner to avoid the dishes would be better," said Armand, but he followed Jean-Guy to their room.

As he left, he noticed Annie taking Reine-Marie into the study and closing the door.

"Why didn't you accept the job you were offered?" asked Jean-Guy, once in the bedroom with the door closed.

After calling Reine-Marie the day before, about his meeting with the Premier and the decision of the disciplinary committee, he'd called Jean-Guy. And told him he'd been asked to resign as Chief Superintendent.

Which he'd done. He'd had the letter prepared and in his breast pocket.

"You told me about resigning," said Jean-Guy in a whisper so as not to wake up his son. "But you didn't tell me you were offered your old job back. As head of homicide."

"True," said Gamache. "It was academic. I was never going to accept."

"Because of Lacoste?"

"*Non*. I made it a condition of my resignation that Isabelle was offered the post of Superintendent in charge of Serious Crimes. It'll be held for her until she's ready. Did you know they've started the paperwork to foster the little girl?"

"No, I hadn't heard. That's terrific."

Beauvoir sat on the side of the bed and looked at the crib where Honoré was sound asleep. He gave a deep sigh.

"I hope she accepts," said Armand, joining him. "The Sûreté needs her."

"It needs you, *patron*. So if not because of Isabelle, then why turn down Chief Inspector of Homicide? Ego?"

Gamache laughed and tapped Beauvoir's knee. "You know me better than that, old son."

"Then why?"

"You know why. It's your job. Your department. You're more than ready. You're Chief Inspector Beauvoir, the head of Homicide for the Sûreté. And I couldn't be more pleased." His smile faded, and he looked serious. "Or proud."

"Take the job."

"Why?" asked Armand, his eyes narrowing slightly as he studied Jean-Guy.

"Because I'm leaving."

He saw his signature, scribbled quickly before he could change his mind, on the papers that had been pushed across the polished desk.

"I've accepted a position with GHS Engineering. As their Head of Strategic Planning."

There was a long silence finally broken by "I see."

"I'm sorry. I wanted to tell you sooner but couldn't find the right time."

"No, no. I understand. I really do, Jean-Guy. You have a family, and it comes first."

"It's more than that. These last few years have been brutal, *patron*. And then to be suspended and investigated by our own people? It was just too much. I love my job, but I'm tired. I'm tired of death. Of killing."

They sat quietly, looking at the sleeping child. Hearing his soft breathing. Inhaling the scent of Honoré.

"Time to live," said Armand. "You've done more than anyone could ever ask. More than I could ever ask or expect. You're doing the right thing. Look at me."

Jean-Guy dragged his eyes from the crib to look at Armand. And he saw a smile that started at his mouth and coursed along the laugh lines. Up to the deep brown eyes.

"I'm happy for you. This is wonderful news."

And Jean-Guy could see there was genuine happiness there. "One more thing," he said.

"*Oui?*"

"The job's in Paris."

"Ahhh," said Armand.

"So that's the famous picture," said Stephen, taking a seat beside Ruth and gesturing toward Clara's painting.

"No, that's of the Three Graces," said Ruth. "The one the Baroness had is of me."

"The Virgin Mary," said Clara.

"The Virgin Mary as me," said Ruth.

"Other way around," said Clara.

"There you are," said Gabri as Jean-Guy returned. "Our little boy learned any new words? '*Merde*'? '*Tabernac*'?"

"No, he's sleeping. Papa's just tucking him in," said Jean-Guy, serving a portion of stew and creamy mashed potatoes and handing it to Annie.

"And Mama's gone to help," said Annie, taking it and catching his eye.

"You okay?" Armand asked Reine-Marie.

She'd closed the door behind her and put a hand on Armand's back as he held the sleeping infant.

It was a good thing, thought Armand, putting his face close to the child's head and inhaling, that the scent was uniquely Honoré. If he ever came across it unexpectedly—on a walk, in a restaurant, from a passing infant—he'd be overwhelmed with the grief he felt now.

And yet there was happiness there too.

It was wonderful and terrible. Joyous and devastating.

And there was relief.

Jean-Guy was out. He was safe. And so were Annie and Honoré. Safe and far away.

He handed Honoré to his grandmother, then put his arms around them both, smelling again the scent of the child mixing with the subtle perfume of old garden roses. He closed his eyes and thought, *Croissants. The first log fire in autumn. The scent of fresh-cut grass. Croissants.*

But it would take a very long list of things he loved to overcome this.

Reine-Marie held her grandson and breathed in the scent of Honoré and sandalwood. And felt Armand's embrace and the very slight tremble of his right hand.

She never thought Paris would break their hearts.

After dinner Stephen took Armand aside.

"I have some news for you."

"But first I want to thank you. Jean-Guy's accepted the job," said Armand. "And he'll be good at it. Strategic planning's what he's been doing for years at the Sûreté."

"Only now no one will be shooting at him," said Stephen.

"Exactly. But he must never know it came from you or me."

"I'm a cipher."

"You didn't tell me the job was in Paris."

"Would it have mattered?"

Armand considered for a moment before answering. "*Non.* It just would've been nice to have had warning."

"*Désolé.* I should have told you."

"What's your news?"

"Remember I told you that I had an idea and would do some digging around about that will thing?"

"I do remember, but you don't need to anymore. It's been decided in favor of the Baumgartners."

"Yes, I heard. I asked colleagues in Vienna to look into it. That

384

Shlomo Kinderoth was a piece of work. He must've known the trouble it would cause, leaving the estate to both sons."

"Maybe he just couldn't decide," said Armand.

"Or maybe he was a numbskull. A hundred and thirty years of acrimony. My people tell me there's no money left. What didn't go in legal fees was stolen by the Nazis."

Armand shook his head. "Not a surprise, but tragic."

"Yes, well, there's more. Besides the money, the Baroness left a large building in the center of Vienna."

"Yes."

"But, unlike the money, that building is real. It's still there and actually did once belong to the family. She wasn't totally delusional. It's now the head office of an international bank."

Armand nodded, but Stephen kept looking at him. Waiting for more.

"What is it?" Armand asked.

"The Nazis. There's reparation, Armand. The Austrian government is paying billions to families who can prove that the Nazis took their property. There's clear title."

"What're you saying?"

"That building's worth tens of millions. Maybe more. If the Baumgartners and Kinderoths can get together and file a joint claim, the money will be theirs."

"My God," said Armand. He was silent for a moment, thinking of the young couple in the basement apartment. "My God."

After dinner Ruth invited Stephen back to her place.

"To look at her prints," said Stephen with a gleam in his eye and a duck under his arm.

"Don't be late," said Armand. "I'll be waiting up."

"Don't," said Ruth.

Myrna had left with Clara.

"Nightcap?" asked Clara at the door to the bistro.

"No, I can't."

Clara was about to ask why not when she saw why not.

Billy Williams, all scrubbed and shaved and in nice clothes, was sitting by the fire. Two glasses of red wine and a pink tulip on the table in front of him.

"I see," said Clara. After giving her friend a hug, she walked back to her home. Smiling and humming.

Pausing at the door, Myrna tilted her head back and looked up into the night sky. At all the dots of light shining down on her.

Then Myrna stepped forward.

ACKNOWLEDGEMENTS

A funny thing happened on my way to not writing this book.

I started writing.

The truth is, I've known since I began writing *Still Life* that if Michael died, I couldn't continue with the series. Not simply because he was the inspiration for Gamache, and it would be too painful, but because he's imbued every aspect of the books. The writing, the promotion, the conferences, the travel, the tours. He was the first to read a new book, and the last to criticize. Always telling me it was great, even when the first draft was quite clearly *merde*.

We were truly partners.

How could I go on when half of me was missing? I could barely get out of bed.

I told my agent and publishers that I was taking a year off. That might have been a lie. In my heart I knew I could never write Gamache again. (And, sadly, would have to give back the next advance.)

But then, a few months later, I found myself sitting at the long pine dining table, where I always wrote. Laptop open.

And I wrote two words: Armand Gamache

Then the next day I wrote: slowed his car to a crawl

And the next day: then stopped on the snow-covered secondary road.

Kingdom of the Blind was begun. Not with sadness. Not because I had to, but with joy. Because I wanted to.

My heart was light. Even as I wrote about some very dark themes, it was with gladness. With relief. That I get to keep doing this.

Far from leaving Michael behind, he became even more infused in the books. All the things we had together came together, in Three Pines. Love, companionship, friendship. His integrity. His courage. Laughter.

I realized, too, that the books are far more than Michael. Far more than Gamache. They're the common yearning for community. For belonging. They're about kindness, acceptance. Gratitude. They're not so much about death, as life. And the consequences of the choices we make.

Now, the publishers, wonderful people, had no idea I was writing. It wasn't until six months later that I told them. But even then, I warned them the book might not be ready in time.

My wonderful agent, Teresa Chris, and Andy Martin, my U.S. publisher with Minotaur Books, were magnificent. Telling me not to worry. To take whatever time I needed. Stop writing, if I needed.

And that was all I needed, to keep going.

And so *Kingdom of the Blind* was born. It is the child that was never going to be. But happened. My love child.

I want to thank a number of people for their patience and kindness.

My assistant, Lise, my great friend, who held my heart when it was too heavy for me.

Andy Martin, the head of Minotaur Books in the U.S. My editor, Hope Dellon, to whom this book is dedicated. Paul Hochman and Sarah Melnyk. Sally Richardson and Don Weisberg. All so much more than colleagues.

Thank you to Kelley Ragland, for leaping in where needed.

To Teresa Chris, my long-suffering and passionate agent and friend.

To Ed Wood, Kirsteen Astor, David Shelley, and all the team at Little, Brown UK.

Thank you to Louise Loiselle at Flammarion Québec, for placing the books in the hands of so many French Canadians.

Thank you, Linda Lyall in Scotland, for the great social media design, and for answering so many of the emails.

I want to thank Kirk Lawrence and Walter Marinelli, for their unwavering friendship and support. And Danny and Lucy at Brome Lake Books.

Thank you to Rocky and Steve Gottlieb for their courage in allowing me to use a story from their own lives.

Thank you to Stephen Jarislowsky, a great character himself, for being, with good humor, the inspiration for a new character.

To Troy McEachren, who helped me with a legal plot point. Where there's a will . . .

And my family. Rob and Audi. Doug and Mary. My nieces and nephews. For enveloping me in their lives. I promise not to make too much of a mess.

As I sit here, at the long pine table, writing to you, I see forests and hear birds. I see a bench inscribed with *Surprised by Joy*. Just down that path through the trees is a café, and the bookstore.

I choose to live in the beautiful little Québec village of Knowlton. For the simple reason that this is home.

I want to thank my neighbors, for their patience and kindness. For saving a place at the table for both Michael and me.

And I want to thank you. For your company.

We are very fortunate, aren't we? To have found each other in Three Pines.

EXCLUSIVE CONTENT
FOR LOUISE PENNY'S

~

KINGDOM
OF
THE BLIND

The World of Three Pines

Rivière Bella Bella

Du Moulin

Old Sta

Du Moulin

When I started writing about Three Pines, and creating the characters that would populate my Armand Gamache novels, I often turned to the world around me here in the Eastern Townships of Québec. It quickly became clear to me that the setting was also a character. Three Pines came alive, not just because of the villagers but because of the places where Armand, Clara, Olivier, Gabri, Ruth, and foulmouthed Rosa and company could be found. I wish I could say I invented those places, but the truth is, they were inspired by where I live. By where I shop. Two of them, La Rumeur Affamée in the village of Sutton and Brome Lake Books in Knowlton, became the inspiration for specific shops in Three Pines—Sarah's Boulangerie and Myrna's New and Used Bookstore. One provides food for the body, the other for the mind. Both vital. Just as we love introducing friends to each other, so I want to introduce you to these places that mean so much to me. I asked their owners to tell us about them, and this is what they wrote. I hope this visit to the boulangerie and the bookshop gives you a glimpse into the world that has inspired the Gamache books.

–LOUISE PENNY, NOVEMBER 2018

LA RUMEUR AFFAMÉE

"More people go to Sarah's Boulangerie than ever show up at
church," snapped Ruth. "They buy pastry with an instrument
of torture on it. I know you think I'm crazy, but maybe I'm the
only sane one here."

—*from* The Cruelest Month, *chapter one*

Nestled in the picturesque Eastern Townships of Québec lies the enchanting hamlet of Sutton and its acclaimed ski hill, "Mont Sutton."
La Rumeur Affamée General Store is located in the center of the village and is the meeting place for local residents, including Louise, and
tourists alike.

Entering La Rumeur Affamée is a sensory experience. After taking
in the eye-appealing décor, our well-trained professional team members welcome you with friendly *"Bonjours"* and smiles from behind the
bread and cheese counters, but the truly exceptional greeting is from

the enticing smell of freshly baked breads, croissants, brownies, and our signature *Tarte au Sirop d'érable* (maple syrup pie).

You are immediately drawn to the original handcrafted, all-wood counters and display cases, well-used hardwood floors, and high ceilings from the 1860s that instantly make you feel like you have entered an era of times gone by.

Sutton was settled by Loyalists following the American Revolution. The Town Hall was built in 1859, and in 1861, George Henry Boright, a settler from New Hampshire, built the brick building that housed his general store, post office, and stage coach depot which La Rumeur has now occupied since 1999. It is truly the heart of the community.

In the early days, the main economy of Sutton was driven by farming, and in 1960, the Mont Sutton ski resort opened and the village has since become reliant on tourism. The town has become a popular year-round destination for its vineyards, art galleries, mountain biking, road biking, hiking, and, of course, skiing, snowboarding, and cross-country skiing.

Sutton is populated by the highest proportion of artists in Canada, hosting annual festivals such as Le Tour des Arts, the International Sculpture Symposium, and many art galleries. Sutton has historically been an English enclave in a predominantly French province. The ratio now sits at approximately 40 percent English to 60 percent French.

La Rumeur Affamée roughly translates to "The Famished Rumor." Kelly Shanahan, co-owner of La Rumeur Affamée, certainly knows how to quash that rumor by providing a vast selection of irresistible baked goods, local and international cheeses, charcuteries, sausages, locally raised duck products, delectable ready-made meals, tantalizing sandwiches, aromatic coffees, extra virgin olive oils, vinegars, mouthwatering chocolates and desserts, Québec craft beer, wine, and non-gluten and certified organic products.

Kelly has an impressive background as a foodie, having owned and operated L'Aperitif—a fine food shop in the neighboring town of Knowlton—managed a massive cheese department at Central Market in Dallas, Texas, and worked at David Woods Fine Foods' signature store in Toronto, as well as having offered cooking classes and working many years in the restaurant world.

Being a former executive in the chain restaurant business, I recognized the value of supporting my wife of thirty years in her culinary endeavors in a small-town environment. A native of Québec City, I worked in the fast-paced cities of Toronto, Vancouver, Montréal, and Dallas before accepting Kelly's challenge of a simpler life.

The Great Wall of Bread at La Rumeur awaits you with freshly baked baguettes and artisanal loaves of spelt, kamut, quinoa, flax, rye, nut, olive, and cheese. Our nongluten and nonlactose breads include quinoa, rye, raisin, and nut bread. Our chocolate orange muffins are to die for as is the selection of croissants, chocolatines, and *vienoiseries*.

Kelly says, "Although it's hard to beat the mind-boggling aroma of fresh bread, our signature maple syrup pies are the hands-down winner with our regular patrons." Fresh daily fruit pies, cookies, squares, cakes, and *sucre à la crème* round out the alluring selection of baked goods.

The fact that the town has a population of less than 4,000 defies the general store's ability to maintain a massive selection of almost 200 cheeses from around the world, including over half from Québec.

"Our 1608 cheese was crafted in 2008 in the Charlevoix region to celebrate the 400th anniversary of Québec City, the oldest city in Canada. Using raw milk from Ancien Canadien cows, of which there are less than 1,000 head left in the world, this semi-firm award-winning cheese is a huge seller," says Kelly.

Seeing the wide-eyed reaction of first-time customers as they take in the old-world charm and enticing odors of our 1860s-style general store is reward enough for the lovingly hard work we put in daily.

It is easy to see why Louise Penny drew inspiration from this jewel in the Eastern Townships for the local boulangerie in her best-selling novels. The joie de vivre is alive and well at La Rumeur and chances are you might spot L'inspecteur Gamache sampling one of our many Québec craft beers, remarking *c'est si bon* the next time you drop in.

—WAYNE SHANAHAN, CO-OWNER, LA RUMEUR AFFAMÉE

Sutton is located six miles north of Vermont, one hour southeast of Montréal, four hours northwest of Boston, and six hours north of New York City. La Rumeur Affamée, 15 Principal North, contact: 450-538-5516 or find us on Facebook.

BROME LAKE BOOKS

"You feel you're letting down a friend," said Reine-Marie.
"Partly, but I run a bookstore," said Myrna, looking at the
row upon row of books, lining the walls and creating corridors in
the open space.

—*from* The Nature of the Beast, *chapter four*

So often, a visit to a bookshop has cheered me, and reminded me
that there are good things in the world.

—Vincent van Gogh

Founded in 1998, Brome Lake Books is a little village bookstore with
a lovingly curated collection of new titles and old favorites for the discerning booklover. Local authors and books on the area are featured

in their own sections. Wooden shelves made by a local craftsman line the walls. Lower units in the middle of the room are fitted with casters for smooth movement along the wide plank pine floors (you do have to be prepared for those impromptu dance parties). The high tin ceiling and a large wall of Victorian windows overlook the park and the mill pond in the heart of the Loyalist village of Knowlton.

Originally a farming area, the natural beauty of the townships soon attracted wealthy families escaping the city heat who came to build lavish summer homes along the shores of Lac Brome. More recently the area has become a hub for visual artists who have set up home studios and art circuits. Wineries and local breweries have sprung up and the bookstore reflects this diverse and eclectic community. Classic story books for the grandchildren visiting for the summer, *New York Times* bestsellers for the young professionals, edgy crime thrillers for the brooding artists, and lots of beautiful photographic books to spark the imagination of them all.

A reading area is dedicated to Louise Penny with a little woodstove and three pine tree–shaped shelves to display Louise's books, Three Pines café-au-lait mugs, F.I.N.E. T-shirts, and a decanter of licorice pipes. On the wall is a framed copy of the Three Pines inspirational map. A braided rug made by a friend's mother along with two cozy armchairs and a little coffee table complete the area. Lining the top of the bookshelves are samples of Louise Penny's books in various languages.

On most days my wife, Lucy Hoblyn, and I may be found puttering around the store. We walk in to work early with our Portuguese sheepdog, Watson, or the "big hairy carpet," as he is often called. Watson is the official greeter at Brome Lake Books and he has many friends that stop by for a friendly wag. Our three boys, Angus, Adam, and Benjamin, have all grown up with the bookstore and have inherited a love of reading—the very best gift a parent can give.

In May of this year, Brome Lake Books moved into a building across the street and we were overwhelmed by all the generous help that we received. Thirty-five friends, neighbors, and customers turned up to carry boxes and boxes of books and heavy shelves. A local book club prepared a sumptuous picnic lunch for all of us to share. One of

the happy helpers was none other than Louise Penny herself. Everyone was smiling and jovial and then someone starting singing their A-B-C's as it helped put the books in alphabetical order. It was a very Three Pines day.

One of the great pleasures at Brome Lake Books is having the chance to meet and correspond with the many fans of Louise Penny. Whether it be Arleen from Texas, Diana from Nova Scotia, or Andrea from Australia, Louise always has the best fans. Louise inspires us to be kind, caring, and thoughtful people. Her books are more about love and community than murder, more about art, poetry, and food than crime. More about living than dying. *Vive Gamache, vive Louise!*

–DANNY MCAULEY, CO-OWNER, BROME LAKE BOOKS

GIANTS

The Dwarfs of Auschwitz

The Extraordinary Story of the
Lilliput Troupe

Yehuda Koren & Eilat Negev
With a foreword by Warwick Davis

The Robson Press

Revised edition first published in Great Britain in 2013 by
The Robson Press (an imprint of Biteback Publishing Ltd)
Westminster Tower
3 Albert Embankment
London SE1 7SP

First published in Germany by Econ Verlag in 2003.

948.5318S   ISBN 978-1-84954-464-1

10 9 8 7 6 5 4 3 2 1
948-631503

A CIP catalogue record for this book is available from the British Library.

Set in Sabon

Printed and bound in Great Britain by
CPI Group (UK) Ltd, Croydon CR0 4YY

CONTENTS

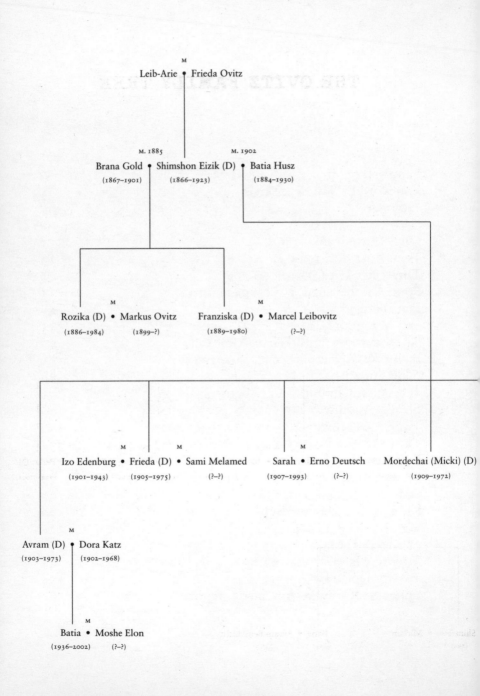

M
Leib-Arie • Frieda Ovitz

M. 1885   M. 1902
Brana Gold • Shimshon Eizik (D) • Batia Husz
(1867–1901)   (1866–1923)   (1884–1930)

M   M
Rozika (D) • Markus Ovitz   Franziska (D) • Marcel Leibovitz
(1886–1984)   (1899–?)   (1889–1980)   (?–?)

M   M   M
Izo Edenburg • Frieda (D) • Sami Melamed   Sarah • Erno Deutsch   Mordechai (Micki) (D)
(1901–1943)   (1905–1975)   (?–?)   (1907–1993)   (?–?)   (1909–1972)

M
Avram (D) • Dora Katz
(1903–1973)   (1902–1968)

M
Batia • Moshe Elon
(1936–2002)   (?–?)

THE OVITZ FAMILY TREE

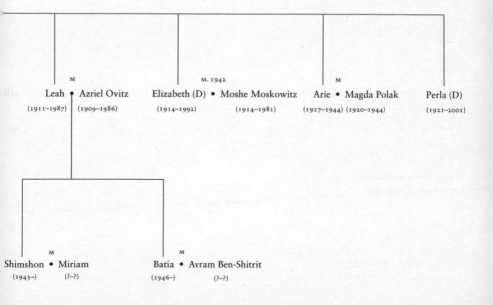

M	M. 1942	M	
Leah • Azriel Ovitz	Elizabeth (D) • Moshe Moskowitz	Arie • Magda Polak	Perla (D)
(1911–1987) (1909–1986)	(1914–1992) (1914–1981)	(1917–1944) (1920–1944)	(1921–2001)

M	M
Shimshon • Miriam	Batia • Avram Ben-Shitrit
(1943–) (?–?)	(1946–) (?–?)

FOREWORD BY WARWICK DAVIS

Several years ago, I was researching the subject of short people in entertainment for a potential film or documentary idea. My doing this was also borne out of a personal curiosity about such performers, and why they did what they did. Among tales of medieval court jesters, Tom Thumb and the dwarf town in Coney Island, I found the inspirational story of the Ovitz family. My research was not thorough or in-depth at that point, but what I did discover about the family left a lasting impression.

In the spring of 2012, I was approached by a television producer who wanted me to tell the story of the Ovitz family for a documentary. This was one of those offers that needed no consideration and I agreed to it immediately. I remembered what I'd read about the family of seven dwarfs all those years ago and how amazing I thought their story was.

Before production started, I wanted to research more thoroughly the family, their lives and their ordeal at the hands of Nazi doctor Josef Mengele, but I was stopped. The director of the documentary wanted this to be a journey of discovery for me, as well as for the viewer, so I closed the textbooks and opened my mind.

In October 2012, I set off to Romania and to the village of Rozavlea, where the Ovitz family were from. I spoke to people who knew them and visited the house where they all lived together.

One of the most pleasing things I discovered about the 'Lilliput Troupe', as they were known, was that they were professional performers through and through. These were not seven dwarfs who went up onstage as some sort of novelty act – these were proper entertainers who just happened to be short. This really resonated with me. I started my acting career at the age of eleven, getting a part in *Star Wars: Return of the Jedi* because I was three feet six inches tall. It wasn't because I was a great actor; it was simply because I was the right height for the job. However, even at that early age, I realised that to sustain this as a career I would have to focus on my performance and that being short should not be my selling point.

Not only are the Ovitzes inspiring as performers, but as people too. They survived Auschwitz, the notorious Nazi death camp, by sticking together, supporting each other and never giving up hope.

On a cold, bleak day in late November 2012, I went to Auschwitz II (Birkenau) to film the final sequence for the documentary. Actually being there had a really profound effect on me. I was able to stand where the Ovitzes stood, see the things they saw, in particular the view of the chimneys from the crematorium that Perla Ovitz had described seeing after disembarking from the train onto 'the ramp'. I also went to the accommodation block where the Ovitzes had spent much of their time in Auschwitz. I took two handmade tiaras that belonged to Perla and Elizabeth, part of their stage costume that had been loaned to me by the authors of this book. I laid the tiaras there for a few minutes as a mark of respect for the family, and a symbol of their triumphant survival. It was a very poignant moment.

My only wish is that I could have met Micki, Elizabeth, Perla, Rozika, Franziska, Avram and Frieda. I would like to have been able to get to know them, relate to them and find out where they found the strength and courage to survive their time in Auschwitz. However, Yehuda Koren and Eilat Negev have allowed me the next best thing by writing this book.

It manages to convey all the vibrancy, passion and hope that these seven wonderful souls gave to the world. They should never be forgotten.

It leaves me both inspired and humbled. Thank you.

Warwick Davis
December 2012

PROLOGUE

There's a long pause after the chime echoes inside. No ray of light sneaks from under the door. No movement. No muffled noises disturb the quiet afternoon.

Two peepholes, one above the other, catch the eye. The lower is just thirty inches above the ground. Until not long ago, Perla Ovitz would drag herself and peek out, trying to guess by the look of the trousers or dress hem if it was a friend or foe. Nowadays, confined to her bedroom, she's too weak to make the journey. Her vigorous voice erupts from a loudspeaker in the hallway; it demands identification. Only then is there a buzz, and you can push the heavy brown door open. You blink in the dusky corridor. You are not sure how to continue, for fear of slipping or bumping into concealed furniture, or worse, trampling over the hostess. She's less than three feet tall, and you might squash her unintentionally.

Her voice is your compass, guiding you forward. You grope blindly towards a diminutive silhouette that clings to the doorway of the dimly lit room. She waits at the threshold in a full-length majestic crimson dress, and allows her visitor to tiptoe past. You step carefully inside. Only then, she waddles in.

It is her bedroom. The legs of the double bed have been sawn off and, although it is almost lying on the floor, a small stool stands next to it, to enable her climb into sleep. Beyond a kindergarten table and chairs is a child-high washbasin. From your towering angle, there's not much difference in her height if she's standing up or sitting on the edge of the bed. Your first impulse is to shrink down, so as not to dwarf her with your presence. She nods towards the normal-sized sofa beside her bed. You take care to keep your feet on the ground, as crossing your legs will push your shoes straight into her face.

The raven-black hair of the ageless doll-like lady is carefully combed back, and held in place by a velvet bow, in old-fashioned Hollywood style. She's theatrically made up at all hours, her cheeks are rouged, her nails are lacquered shiny red. A pair of earrings, a necklace and rings ornament her. 'As long as you breathe, you should look your best. I don't want people to pity me' is a recurrent motto of hers.

She enchants with her dazzling smile and her bubbly talk is studded with unexpected aphorisms: 'a beaten dog dreads even the kindest people' is how she excuses her cautiousness. She spends most of her time sitting on her petite chair or reclining, dressed, on her covered bed, as these days she can stand no more than a minute or two unaided.

She's on her own most of the day, and needs everything to be easily accessible – a packet of chocolate cookies and a plastic box of sliced apples lie on the bed should she get hungry. A thermos with water waits within reach.

She can't move without her cane, which serves as an extended hand, to pull, press, push. Tiny stools scattered through the house allow her a brief rest in her movements around the flat. All the light switches have been lowered to her height. The kitchen has a knee-high stove and a special mechanism allows her to open the refrigerator door with a push of her cane. All the food is stored on the bottom shelf.

Vases that stand tall as her hold abundant bouquets of silk

and plastic flowers, in her favourite colours: sharp violets, soft pinks. A heavy red curtain at the wide entrance to the living room is pulled to both sides and gathered in thick cords, as if a show were about to begin. Forty-five years have passed since Perla Ovitz took her last bow, but the stage stays with her still. Once, when all her family was still around, she loved the lights: she even flooded herself with them off stage, at home. Now, trapped alone in this big empty apartment, she seeks the economy and safety of dimmed lamps and half shadows.

Perla's memories, though, remain vivid in their glories and their horrors. Hers is a true story of seven dwarfs, with no benevolent Snow White but a beast. While reading like a fairy tale, it moves into some of the darkest corners of hell human beings have ever experienced.

ONE

TRANSYLVANIA, 1866

The tale begins with giants.

In long gone days, it is said, in hilly northern Transylvania, the Dolhai Valley was strewn with tribes of giants. For ages upon ages since the creation, they lived and prospered and roamed the earth. And then came the deluge, and they all fled up to the sleek peaks of the mountains. There, one by one they perished, and when the waters receded, the sole survivors emerged: a giant and his daughter, Roza Rozalina. Her eyes black as coal, her hair red as flame and as long as the sadness of the fir trees. Sorrowfully she wandered through the valley.

'Father,' she sighed, 'I'm withering with loneliness, will I ever find a mate?' She headed towards the Iza River and, daydreaming, strolled along the bank. All of a sudden, she spotted tiny creatures slipping between the grass blades. Roza Rozalina was astonished: never had she seen creatures so similar to her, and yet so small. She picked up a handful and nestled them in her apron. These moving toy-like creatures would rescue her from boredom, she thought. She examined them closely; one in particular caught her eye. He was handsome as the moon and appeared to be less frightened than the others. Her cheeks blushed as she felt the pangs of love.

When she showed her catch to her father, he was alarmed: 'Alas, my daughter, our time is up! These tiny creatures will inherit the earth. Return them immediately to their place!' But Roza Rozalina was incapable of obeying. Soaked in tears, she begged the Almighty to tie her fate to that of the small, handsome brave one. And the Almighty shrunk her a little and stretched him a lot, until they became in size like twins. Eventually their descendants filled the land. They named the place Rozavlea after their giant, ancestral mother.

In that sleepy little Romanian village, the ancient legend has been passed on from one generation to the next. Every August, the roughly 7,000 peasants who live there celebrate the festival of Roza Rozalina, with the schoolchildren staging the story. And in the same village, so proud of its legendary giantess matriarch, a real dwarf was born in 1866.

It was the third pregnancy for Frieda Ovitz and, having already given birth to a healthy daughter and son, she was distressed to discover that her baby had stopped moving inside her. In that remote part of the world, she could only take recourse to prayer or an amulet, or the hope of a miracle. Being an Orthodox Jewish woman, she sought the advice of her rabbi.

'Your child will live,' he assured her, safely glancing at her belly from behind the table that separated them, 'but he won't grow tall.' Heartbroken, Frieda and her husband Leib decided to try halting destiny by naming their newborn son 'Shimshon Eizik', after Samson, the biblical giant. The first years passed without apparent complications and the parents began to believe they had been spared. But when the child reached the age of seven, even they had to admit that he had long since stopped growing. They probed each other's memory and they asked their elders. As far back as anyone could remember, in all their family history, there had never been anyone who had not grown tall. Little Shimshon Eizik was shuttled between doctors, healers and sages; he was prescribed medications and charms, spells and potions. But to no avail – they added not a millimetre to his stature. Frieda gave birth to two more boys; she was relieved when they passed the fateful age and continued growing normally.

Like the rest of Transylvania, Rozavlea was part of the Austro-Hungarian Empire. The peasants of that rural area were wretchedly poor, with whatever limited opportunities there were certainly out of reach for a three-foot-tall youth like Shimshon Eizik. He could never hope to lift an axe, or cut a tree, or push a plough, and every farm animal was an immense and menacing monster. When Frieda and Leib Ovitz realised their son would never be able to support himself by physical labour, they invested in his schooling instead. Furnished with tutors, he excelled in his studies, gilding his path through life with brightness and good nature.

As a teenager, he tried to come to terms with his lot. The sages of the Halacha, the ancient Jewish code of law, were aware that the sight of human malformations could evoke scorn and derision. Shimshon Eizik thus found solace in the Halachic imperative that if one sees a black man, a red man or an albino, a giant, a crooked-faced man or a dwarf, one should say, 'Blessed be God, who alters man'. In this way, the negative response to disfigurement was channelled instead into admiration for God's diverse powers of creation. Traditionally, the blessing was recited only on one's first encounter with the deformed person, as it was meant to overcome the initial repulsion and treat the 'altered' as an equal.

But when Shimshon Eizik read further into the holy texts, he was upset to learn that they defined a dwarf as a cripple, and thus disqualified him from certain functions only normal-bodied men were allowed to perform. Even if born to a line of holy priests, a dwarf was, for instance, never allowed to serve in the temple. So a forlorn Shimshon Eizik realised that in spite of an apparent tolerance for anomalies, Judaism tended to exalt those blessed with a perfect body.

Furthermore, Jewish folk tales often portrayed dwarfism as a punishment for some wrongdoing or sin. Sometimes it could also represent the lesser of two evils. In one old tale, a childless couple frequents the cemetery to beseech God for offspring. One day, in the midst of their weeping and pleas, an angel descends to them from heaven. 'God has heard your prayer, and granted your wish,' the angel tells them, 'but you must choose: you can have either a son who will grow no larger than a pea or a tall, healthy daughter who will leave you and convert to Christianity at the age of thirteen.' The couple does not hesitate: 'Let him be as small as a pea.'

Dwarfs, however, could also serve as symbols of distinction and merit, as in the case of Rabbi Gadiel, who has been immortalised by author S. Y. Agnon. A kind of Jewish *Agnus Dei*, Gadiel the Dwarf heroically sacrificed himself to save his community from blood libel – the accusation that his congregation had murdered a Christian child to acquire blood for the baking of unleavened Passover bread. And yet, before the advent of modern genetics, the third-century Talmud sternly warned that 'Giants should not marry each other, as they will give birth to a flagpole, and midgets should not couple, as they will produce a thumb.'

Tiny in stature – no taller than a boy of five – but at the same time a lively and self-confident nineteen-year-old, Shimshon Eizik Ovitz was searching for an average-sized bride. In a deeply religious society which valued learning, Shimshon's excellence in rabbinical studies and his piety compensated for his physical deficiency. He could offer his bride the prospect of a better livelihood, along with the community respect he enjoyed as an educated person. Nevertheless, the choice of eligible spouses was meagre, as only about 200 Jews lived in Rozavlea and no more than a few thousand in the neighbouring villages, the Jews then totalling just 20 per cent of the population. After much searching, the local matchmaker suggested eighteen-year-old Brana Gold, from the nearby village of Moisei. As usual in a prearranged marriage, Brana did not have much say in the matter.

For one or another reason, Shimshon Eizik decided to discontinue his studies. By then, not only had he succeeded in overcoming any feelings of shame and unease for his own body, which created a stir wherever he went, but he had also learned to manipulate public curiosity and transform mockery into adoration. His audience would soon forget his size and shape, captivated instead by his quick tongue and charisma.

The Jewish communities of the region preserved an older, traditional way of life, resisting modern, liberal trends. There was no official job that the community could offer him, not even as a schoolteacher, since he would be the mock of the class. But he harnessed his eloquence and the attraction generated by his odd appearance and slipped easily into the cultural role of *badchan* or merrymaker – a colourful, virtually indispensable figure at wedding festivals, occasions which provided a harsh life its most joyful moments. Life, in fact, stood still when the community celebrated nuptials, which were often as lavish as carnivals, and which gave a rare chance for people to let their hair down in an acceptable way.

During the wedding feast, the *badchan* would entertain the guests with drollery, riddles and anecdotes. Only a learned person, with a deep knowledge of the wedding protocol and a knack for organisation, could orchestrate such a complex enterprise involving hundreds of guests. All in all, the creation of a new family was an event that called for perfection: opulent food served with the choicest tableware, eaten while wearing ravishing clothes and listening to the finest orchestra. Though it was a conservative, superstitious community, fearful of the 'evil eye' which could damage the health of expected offspring, Shimshon Eizik Ovitz's deformity did not deter potential clients from hiring him: his skills had made him famous throughout the region, and beyond.

Months before the wedding, the fathers would book him for the week. They would negotiate his fee, cover his travel expenses and arrange his lodgings. In the weeks leading up to the wedding, Ovitz prepared for the occasion by gathering information about the newlyweds, their parents and the community dignitaries. He would then write songs and ditties based on family histories, assorted facts and anecdotes, rumours and gossip, all aiming at a good laugh. At the occasion itself, Ovitz appeared in the decorated courtyard dressed smartly in a black suit and hat and carrying a small cane. Before the guests arrived, his assistant, who always travelled with him, lifted him onto a chair standing on a table which served as his podium. From there, as a master of ceremonies, he would make his audience shed tears one moment, roar with laughter the next. With his ditties, he encouraged both bride and her all-female entourage to weep, for his verse offered them a cathartic antidote to the fears and apprehensions of an uncertain future:

> Cry out your eyes, O graceful bride,
> Your diamond tears enhance your charm.
> Now is the time to wail out loud,
> As soon you'll become a wife.

Ovitz thus expressed his sympathy for both the young bride and groom, each having to depart a familiar, secure childhood home to live with a person practically unknown to them. In his sermon, he would remind them of their respective conjugal roles and responsibilities. But the tension was broken immediately after the taking of vows and declaration of man and wife. Now Ovitz would put on his funny face and work hard to create a jovial mood, encouraging the guests to dance until they dropped. From time to time he announced a special guest and offered a witty verse about him and praised the gift he had brought. As a jester, Ovitz was allowed to toss little barbs of irony at the community's hypocrites and misers.

Shimshon Eizik Ovitz was an earnest jester. He amused his audience with puns and limericks based on familiar quotes from Talmudic thought. He gauged the mood of the wedding guests and told the orchestra which tunes to play. He showered witticisms upon the grandmothers of the brides as they whirled in their customary dance, after which it was the men's turn, the revelry going non-stop until the early hours of the morning. When he could, he would grab moments of rest and slump into his chair, for Ovitz's small feet and short legs provided only meagre support.

●

The morally strict Jewish society in Eastern Europe at the end of the nineteenth century allowed entertainment only on certain holidays and festivals; the theatre was banned as indecent. The wandering *badchans* were, in essence, the pioneering actors of the Jewish world, the founders of Yiddish theatre. They enjoyed great popularity because they ministered to a basic human need: release. Years later, when Jewish orthodoxy had lost its grip, Ovitz's children would follow in his footsteps by establishing their own vaudeville troupe, which would take the entertainment first offered in religious ceremonies onto the stages of theatre halls, all for the sake of pure fun.

On 2 November 1886, Shimshon Eizik Ovitz was lost in prayer when he heard the first cry from the bedroom. Peszele Fogel, the midwife, emerged and announced that he had a daughter. They named her Rozika. When the toddler began walking, she swayed from side to side like a duck. Shimshon Eizik Ovitz recognised the dreaded signs all too well. On 27 January 1889, Franziska was born, and she too proved to be a dwarf like her father and sister. If Shimshon and Brana feared the mark of heredity would strike their progeny again and again, they had to suppress it and obey the biblical command to procreate. A daughter, Mancie, and a son, Judah, soon followed, but they both died in their first year and took the secret of their future growth to their tomb.

As a merrymaker, Ovitz would impress his audience so much with his Talmudic wisdom that before and after the wedding people would approach him with various religious and personal dilemmas. Many of the region's Jewish communities were so small they could not afford a rabbi, and the scholarly Ovitz filled the gap. He moulded himself into the rabbinic role, dressing and behaving like a sage. In fairy tales dwarfs grow long beards, but in real life most of them decline to do so, as it makes them look even shorter. But Ovitz groomed his beard to look respectable.

Gradually he stopped performing as a wedding jester, moving into his new role as an esteemed, wandering rabbi in Maramureş County. He would settle in a small village for a week or two, conduct prayers and preach. For its part, the community provided him with lodgings and furnished a consulting room.

He frequently had to deal with questions regarding the dietary laws (*kashruth*) and, in particular, the separation of meat and milk: for which housewife did not agonise over the dictum that she must pour away a bucket of precious milk if she suspects that a speck of meat accidentally fell inside?

While giants were traditionally deemed to be stupid, all body and no brains, dwarfs – whatever the mixed biblical and rabbinic opinions – were popularly believed to have been born with great wisdom and magical powers as godly compensation for what they had been deprived of in inches. Shimshon Eizik Ovitz benefited from this folk belief. He rapidly became famous for his spiritual powers and people flocked to see him wherever he went.

Surrounded by people who believed in miracles, the charismatic Ovitz added amulets, spells and charms to his repertoire. He would lay hands on the head of a sick child and recite a prayer. For an infertile woman, he would inscribe a blessing in ancient Hebrew letters on a piece of parchment to be worn at all times. Often he provided the services of a lay psychologist by listening to the laments of wives with matrimonial problems and advising them how to restore peace – and stray husbands – to the household.

Ovitz was paid handsomely for his opinions and advice, especially by certain businessmen who consulted him regularly before signing new deals. He himself had a good head for business, investing his earnings in property and land. Official Maramureş County documents attest to Shimshon Eizik Ovitz's popularity, prosperity and social mobility: at first, he was registered as a 'cantor'; in later years as a 'wizard'; and he finally gained the status of 'landlord'.

●

Great healer though Ovitz was, he was powerless when his own wife Brana fell ill and died of tuberculosis in the winter of 1901 at the age of thirty-three. Since he spent most of his time travelling to make a living, he could not take proper care of his two teenage daughters – nor could he simply leave them to their own devices. Furthermore, for the sake of distance from improper thoughts, the community expected this well-known religious authority to find a new wife.

Barely had the usual thirty days of mourning passed when the matchmakers began knocking at the door. Ovitz refused to consider widows and divorcees, as they were burdened with their own children. But he did find Batia Bertha Husz, a girl from a distant village only two years older than his daughter Rozika, much to his liking.

What might have persuaded a pair of loving parents to give their pretty, healthy, eighteen-year-old daughter to a crippled widower not only twice her age, but also with two dwarf daughters? Shimshon Eizik Ovitz's reputation as a prosperous healer and spiritual superman must have worked for him. To head off the anticipated gossip about Ovitz's preference for a young virgin, everyone was told that the bride was already an old maid of twenty-four. In any event, Shimshon hoped that with this fresh chapter in his life, his hereditary luck might also change. It didn't. On 26 September 1903, Avram was born, a dwarf. In June 1905, a baby girl was born, named Frieda after Shimshon's mother. She proved to be a dwarf as well.

When the third child was born in August 1907, the Ovitzes had reason to believe the spell had finally lifted, since Sarah was the first child to grow healthy and tall. But in July 1909 came Micki, a dwarf. Two years later, the pendulum once more swung in the opposite direction, Leah being average-sized, with child number eight, Elizabeth, arriving in April 1914 – again a dwarf. Three years later came average-sized Arie, and the youngest of them all was born on 10 January 1921.

Choking, suffocating, she emerged with the umbilical cord tied around her neck. The despairing midwife took her away from the exhausted mother and placed her quietly aside, waiting for her to die. At first, Batia Ovitz didn't understand. She asked to see the baby and when the midwife ignored her, she became alarmed. 'Let her rest in peace,' advised the midwife, hinting consolingly at the baby's critical condition. 'This child must live! Bring her to me!' ordered Batia, forcing herself upright. The midwife obeyed. Batia hugged her baby and noticed that its jaws were locked. She bent its head back and, inserting her index finger into the tiny mouth, she almost tore it open. The baby responded with a deep cough.

Later Piroska Ovitz – her Yiddish name 'Perla' reflected her pearl-like size and beauty – liked to blame her mother for her big mouth. In Perla's infancy, it was hard to tell whether or not she would join her three normally growing siblings. Every symptom was analysed both ways, and the signs seemed to indicate that she would escape the six dwarfs' fate. She didn't. Shimshon Eizik's genetic trait had once more asserted its dominance, as it had in seven out of his ten children: the largest recorded dwarf family in the world.

Ovitz built a new home for his large clan. He rented the old shed in the back yard to the new village doctor, so they now had a physician at hand. Although their house stood next to the synagogue, Ovitz and his seven dwarf children found it difficult to cross the muddy earth in the long, cold winters to attend daily prayers. When they did manage, unavoidably they created a great deal of fuss, for in order to see the cantor and the Holy Ark, they all had to be raised onto small stools placed on the bench.

To make things easier on them all, Ovitz converted one of his rooms into an everyday prayer room. As one of the community philanthropists, he eventually donated part of his land and money to help renovate the community synagogue, which he attended mainly on the high holidays. He continued his travels, leaving Batia at home to take care of the ten children. Since she treated her husband's two daughters from his first wife as her own, Perla grew up without knowing that Rozika and Franziska had a different mother: 'As they were miniatures, I didn't realise they were almost mother's age. They helped her a lot to raise us.'

In September 1923, Shimshon Eizik Ovitz attended a wedding in a faraway village. Immediately after the meal, his body temperature soared, and he began sweating and vomiting. His assistant and coachman, Simon Slomowitz, rushed him home. Ovitz was wracked with pain. The fish he had eaten was poisonous. He died after a week of agony, at four in the afternoon on Sunday 16 September. He was fifty-seven years old.

Only a few tombstones from the extinct Jewish community of Rozavlea have survived in the abandoned cemetery. Miraculously, one of them marks the grave of Shimshon Eizik Ovitz. The fading Hebrew inscription reads:

Here lies an honest, virtuous, learned man, a charitable benefactor of the poor, all of whose deeds were for the honour of God.

TWO

ROZAVLEA, 1923

For a widower with ten children, the matchmaker could still find a spouse. But there was no chance that at thirty-nine the newly widowed Batia Ovitz would find a man willing to take on the burden of providing for her and her children, five of them under fourteen, seven of them dwarfs.

The family struggled to rearrange itself. Having just turned twenty, Avram stepped into his father's shoes – he had already accompanied Shimshon Eizik on his travels as his apprentice, observing him perform the roles of rabbi and *badchan*. With the same small frame as his father, he would occasionally mount the table and join him in rousing the crowd. The double-bill dwarf act had been a success.

As both the new provider and the head of the family, Avram Ovitz strove to maintain his father's contacts in the villages scattered throughout the region, with the aid of the ever loyal Simon Slomowitz, his father's coachman and travelling assistant. Gradually he gained confidence, composed his own witty lines and developed his own style of performance.

Perla, who was eighteen months old when her father died, had no memory of him. As a child, the only man she called 'Papa' was her brother Avram. No one at home corrected her; perhaps out of pity, her siblings wished to postpone the bitter truth of her being fatherless as long as possible. Avram took

13

charge of her education, testing her in her studies. When she wanted sweets, she turned to Avram for money. By the time she reached the age of six she was about his height, but this did not strike her as odd.

One day, while Perla was helping a girlfriend who lived across the street with her homework, she began bragging about the generosity of her father. The girl's mother overheard Perla's boasts, and felt obliged to correct her.

'You really can't call him father – he's your brother!' she said to Perla.

'He is *too* my father – he gives me all my things. Everybody's got a father, and so do I!' Perla contended. But the neighbour wouldn't let it drop. 'Actually, you don't have any father! He's dead!'

Perla rushed home. Sobbing, she told her sisters what the neighbour had said. 'She's lying!' she cried. 'Come and tell her she's wrong!' As Perla's sisters hugged her and tried to console her, it started to dawn on her that the neighbour might have been speaking the truth. Then, for the first time, her sisters told her the story of her real father, Shimshon Eizik. For years to come, Perla had to bite her tongue to keep the word 'Papa' from slipping out when addressing her brother Avram.

The Ovitz clan buzzed with bee-like cheerfulness. Each member played a specific part in the household and mother Batia orchestrated them all. The average-height teenagers Sarah and Leah took care of day-to-day physical tasks like washing and cooking, or carrying the basketfuls of laundry to the Iza River to be scrubbed on a wooden plank. For years they also did the sewing, until Elizabeth and Perla were old enough and skilled enough to make clothes for all their sisters. The dwarfs refused to wear children's clothes: 'They looked ridiculous on us. People tend to view dwarfs as children anyway, and we wished to look respectable.' The age span between the oldest and youngest sister was thirty-five years, but since they were almost the same height and size they could all wear identical clothes. In their all-blue or all-pink dresses, they were often mistakenly thought to be twins or triplets. The five female dwarfs also combed each other's hair and painted shiny varnish on each other's nails. They never wore high-heeled shoes, since these were unstable to stand on and could make no real difference to their height. 'Shoes had to be custom-made for us anyway, because of our unusually broad soles.'

The interior of their wooden home, which was painted white, resembled a doll's house. Decorated with a great deal of hand-made lace and tapestry, it was furnished with low washbasins, beds with sawn-off legs, tiny chairs and many stools. The four average-height members had to adjust, although there was also furniture suitable for them and for the occasional guests. The dwarfs had to be careful using the toilet hut in the back yard, which was a simple hole dug in the ground. A smaller wooden tier made just for them narrowed the hole so they wouldn't fall through.

The Ovitzes had everything they needed in their small paradise. The front garden was full of flowers and the back yard was an orchard: apples, plums, peaches, pears, grapes, hazelnuts. They raised chicken and geese and kept a few cows in the shed. While they had to rely on hired help to pick the fruit, milk the cows and pump water from the large stone well in front of the house, they were able to bake their own bread, smoke their own geese, churn their own butter and make jam.

The Ovitz house stood on Rozavlea's main street. Relatives of Shimshon Eizik Ovitz – his three brothers and one sister – lived nearby with their families. The two younger brothers,

Israel Meir and Lazar, were also artistically inclined and Uncle Lazar, together with five of his ten sons, formed a *klezmer* troupe that played at weddings. Influenced by local Gypsy bands, the now-famous *klezmers* – the Hebrew–Yiddish word actually means 'musicians' – had been playing folk tunes, dance tunes and Hasidic melodies, all over Europe, for centuries. They were popular not only in the Jewish communities, but also among the non-Jewish town dignitaries and the bourgeoisie, who preferred the Jewish *klezmers* to their Gypsy counterparts, since the Gypsy music was considered coarse.

'The heart is like a violin: you harp on the strings and melancholy tunes pour out,' goes a Yiddish proverb. The fiddler – in a well-known painting Chagall has depicted him gliding with his fiddle over the village rooftops – was the *klezmer* band's leader. Next in importance was the clarinet player, whose music could at once make eyes water and feet tap, while the bassist provided rhythmic and harmonic underpinnings. As the band's primary purpose was to crowd the floor with dancers, the beat of the percussions was firm and steady. Instead of piano, larger bands also had an accordion, as well as a cimbalom.

Like all *klezmers*, Lazar Ovitz and sons were natural musicians with no formal musical education and could not read notes. Spontaneous, skilled improvisers, they mastered their instruments through instinct and emotion, playing with ecstasy. There were around 5,000 *klezmers* in Eastern Europe at the time. Competition was so intense that sometimes a band would pay parents to perform at a wedding, and then hope to make some small profit from the tips they would get for playing favourite tunes. Despite the meagre earnings, *klezmers* stuck to their trade for it was also a passion, even when it had to be financed through manual labour – for instance, Lazar Ovitz and sons were horse traders. While both the *badchan* and the *klezmer* made their living from weddings, they enjoyed different levels of esteem, Jewish society valuing the word more than the tune. The *badchan* earned more respect for his learning and verbal facility than the low-class *klezmer*, whose joie de vivre was aligned with fickleness.

The musicians in most *klezmer* bands did not come together by chance but were carrying on a family trade, with talent and melodies they had inherited from parents and older relatives. This is how Rozika and Franziska came to play the violin: they picked up the music and mastery from their uncle and neighbour Lazar. In pious families, however, it was unheard of for young women to travel alone, so the two sister violinists accompanied their brother Avram on his trips to weddings. The three Ovitz dwarfs soon became a major attraction, Rozika and Franziska exciting audiences with their child-sized violins and winning applause when they sang in their high-pitched voices. Thus began a family pattern. Each child would learn to play an instrument and at sixteen would join the musical troupe of the Ovitzes.

•

Being surrounded by six brothers and sisters her own height made it easier for Perla to come to terms with her dwarfism.

Like every child, I expected to add a few centimetres every year and grow like a flower. But when I saw the others, I realised I'd never grow tall. It saved me from feeling inferior and helped me accept myself as I am. In my dreams, my legs and arms don't lengthen, and I've never fantasised about a good fairy coming to double my height. Being a dwarf is no punishment. The difference in height does not diminish my pleasures. Our life is as worthwhile as anyone else's.

On 1 December 1918 – two years before Perla's birth – Romania annexed Transylvania from Hungary as part of the Great War's peace agreements. The major change was felt at school, with the official language becoming Romanian and Hungarian culture publicly eradicated. But like most Transylvanian Jews, the Ovitzes prided themselves on their historical and cultural connections with Hungary, and maintained them at home. Perla picked up the language and old songs by listening to her sisters. She had a musical ear and a good singing voice: 'From infancy, I imitated my sisters and sang from morning to night, causing everyone a headache. Our tenant doctor continually bribed me with chocolates to shut me up.'

She was a bright child and began reading even before she started to attend the local primary school, which was just a few houses down the road. Although she could manage the short distance well enough, she often found herself in the arms of teachers and classmates hoping not so much to spare her legs but – more so – to have fun leaping around with a living doll. No one bothered to ask her permission and she did not protest, afraid of losing their company. She especially liked to play hide-and-seek with the neighbouring boy Arie Tessler. Whenever he caught her, he would spontaneously swing her in victory around the room. 'I have always believed she was my age and only recently learned to my surprise that she is in fact six years older than me. Her tiny build fooled me,' recalls Arie.

In school plays she was often cast as a baby in a cradle – a role she did not seem to mind at all. She certainly didn't miss the daily humiliation of blackboard arithmetic exercises, since she could not reach the board. She was also exempt from gymnastics and avoided the schoolyard during playtimes, for fear of being knocked down by the full-size children. Instead, she used the time to do her homework, thus becoming popular among her classmates as she willingly let them copy her notebooks. 'They all needed me for their studies, so they never mocked me, and treated me with respect.' In return for her help, they escorted her home, carrying her books and guarding her from the dogs, which all seemed to her huge and threatening. A dog, no matter how friendly, could tip her over just by brushing against her or trying to lick her face.

One day between classes, Perla was standing alone in the empty schoolroom staring at a large map of Romania. In her hand, she held the teacher's pointer, which was longer than she was tall. She was unaware that a supervisor had stepped inside, until he thundered, 'What are you doing here, little girl?' For a moment she was dumbfounded, but she soon composed herself. 'I'm studying. I know the map by heart and can point wherever you want, even with my back to the wall,' she boasted. He challenged her to find Cluj, then watched in disbelief as she turned around and, magician-like, lifted the pointer over her shoulder and hit the town on its dot. Amazed, he asked for more towns and then mountains. Each time, the tip of her pointer landed on the exact spot. The act made her famous in school, and she repeated it again and again. Not once did she reveal even a flicker of stage fright.

There were happy times for the family when one after the other, three of the female dwarfs got married. The first was Rozika, the oldest, and already an old maid of forty when, on 2 May 1927, she married her 28-year-old cousin Marcus Ovitz. The twelve-year gap in their ages didn't show since like most dwarfs, she looked much younger than her years. Next to wed was Franziska, who married Marcel Leibovitz, followed by Frieda, who exchanged vows with Ignaz (Izo) Edenburg, an electrician from the nearby town of Sighet. The village gossips, who couldn't get over the fact that all three grooms were healthy men of average height, concluded that they must have been drawn to the family fortune.

Because the three newlywed wives refused to leave their kin, their husbands had no choice but to move in. Each couple had a room of its own and the new spouses were expected to earn their keep by helping the family dwarfs with daily chores. This arrangement would apply to all future weddings as well. Some spouses would adjust. Others would find it a strain and divorce. 'My uncles and aunts, the seven dwarfs, were so attached to each other they were like a mythological creature, one body and seven heads,' explains Perla's nephew Shimshon Ovitz, who was named for his grandfather.

Summer departs early in Transylvania, and September is often a capricious month. The sunshine is deceptive and the chilly air behind its beams can be dangerous. One such September day in 1927, a neighbour of Batia Ovitz implored her to share a swim in the river, the last chance before winter. It was Friday and although Batia had nearly finished preparing the Sabbath meal, she did not feel inclined to join in the adventure. But her friend insisted until Batia gave in. The two women headed towards the Iza, whose banks were serene, the water glimmering with temptation. Batia Ovitz was almost glad that she had overcome her misgivings, as she braved the river's grey-green water. She barely noticed the chill in the light September wind. Then, suddenly, she felt a stab in her chest and let out a scream. Leaning on her frightened friend, she struggled her way home. The doctor was called in; he diagnosed tuberculosis.

For almost three years, Batia Ovitz lay bedridden. Every day, when Perla returned from school, she would rush to her mother's bed and, to make her happy, recited her lessons. 'But I was not allowed to cuddle with her, like I was used to. Let mother rest, I was always told, and sent from the room.' Once the door was shut, her mother would cough out blood.

On 8 February 1930, Saturday evening, the Ovitz house was filled with gloomy-faced people.

I asked my sisters why they were all dressed in black and what all the strangers were doing. I was told they came to take Mummy to the doctor. I was puzzled as to why they needed so many people to accompany her. My sisters didn't answer. I thought they were crying because of her illness.

Nine-year-old Perla was not taken to her mother's funeral. For weeks, the entire family evaded her questions. She refused to eat in her mother's inexplicable absence and rapidly lost weight. Her sisters finally had to lock her like a goose between their knees and force food down her throat. Eavesdropping one day, Perla heard anxious whispers from the next room: 'If she goes on with her hunger strike, very soon she'll join mother.' Perla could not contain her happiness. She pushed the door open and pleaded: 'Please let me join Mummy.' The whispers resumed and then her sister Sarah turned her way: 'Promise not to cry.' Perla nodded. 'Mother has gone,' said Sarah.

'So let's go where she is,' urged Perla.

The sad truth began to sink in only when her sisters couldn't stop sobbing.

THREE

ROZAVLEA, 1930

His name was Hershel Weisel, but he was known in the region as *Hershel der Langer* (Hershel the Tall One), for he was a giant. In his boat-like shoes he stood seven feet, two inches tall, and with wild-grown beard, protruding teeth and thundering voice, he might have been feared as a monster. Instead, he was a laughing stock. Unable to find a job because of his massive size, he was reduced to begging. To earn some money, he toured the villages with his average-height wife, and Long and Short, as they were called, leaped around like dancing bears, to the applause and ridicule of all.

Batia Ovitz had feared that a lone dwarf would be twice as helpless as such a giant: her children's only strength, she believed, lay in numbers. On her deathbed, she imparted to them a rule to guide them through life, a rule that in fact would eventually save them: 'Through thick and thin, never separate. Stick together, guard each other, and live for one another.' She exhorted them to cultivate a common skill, so that they could earn their living together with no need to rely on the kindness of strangers – to find a profession in which they would be neither isolated nor ostracised, but rather welcomed, a profession in which they would flourish.

The stage seemed to be the perfect choice, for there would they not be applauded, courted, honoured? Three of the dwarfs had already been in the wedding show business, and they could continue to try their luck with a *klezmer* band. But that option would leave out the remaining four, so it was rejected. On the other hand, establishing their own wedding band also presented problems: some *klezmer* bands featured one woman or maybe two, but a group of five female and two male musicians would have been too much for the more conservative revellers to allow. And in any event, prospective clients might well be reluctant to book an all-deformed band for their children's great day. Furthermore, the small, weak lungs of the Ovitzes did not permit them to play any wind instrument – an essential for weddings. All in all, they had to admit that playing energetic dance music for endless hours on their crooked feet would be an intolerable strain. Lastly, the socio-economic status of *klezmers* was already low and the Ovitzes suspected that as dwarfs they would be doubly discriminated against.

Because they deviate from the norm, dwarfs have always had a problem earning a living. Yet, historically, they have fared better than sufferers from other major deformities. The public has, of course, always been interested in the diversity of creation and in oddities of nature: an elephant man arouses aversion and pity; a giant evokes astonishment; a girl with three legs prompts apprehension. But dwarfs make people smile. Unlike 'freaks' – historically labelled *mirabilia monstrorum*, or 'monstrous wonders' – dwarfs are *mirabilia hominum*, 'human wonders', maybe because every adult was once a child, and so finds it easy to identify with the plight of a small person in a world dominated by tall people and big objects. Then too, the diminutive stature of dwarfs can seem cute and kindle a parental instinct. Indeed, dwarfs have often been treated like children, picked up like babies and spoken to in patronising tones. Perhaps, in the disturbing disproportion between a dwarf's normal-sized head and short limbs, is perceived the symbol of an eternal child.

●

Dwarfs had their golden era in ancient Egypt. There, dwarfs were honoured and venerated like gods and, in fact, one of them was a god, whom the Egyptians named Bes. His realm was midwifery and he also looked after misfits neglected by the other gods.

Pharaoh Pepi I (2332–2283 BC) enjoyed the company of Danga, his dwarf jester, who sharpened his perception of the relativity of size and supremacy. 'I am the gods' Danga,' Pharaoh Pepi observed, 'for they must find me as ridiculous as I find my Danga.' Augustus Caesar, too, was deeply attached to his dwarf Lucius, so much so that upon Lucius's death, Augustus had his statue sculpted and inserted with precious stones for eyes. Court dwarfs played their handicap to their advantage: they survived by making others laugh, often through pranks and foolery, and frequently with astonishing wit. Only they could speak critically and frankly to the pharaoh, king or tsar, without having their heads severed from their bodies. Only Bahalul, the dwarf of Caliph Harun al-Rashid, could have insulted his master so obnoxiously, with practical jokes and verbal forays, all while pretending to be an idiot.

No palace has been complete without dwarfs. Those at the Viennese court were described by the writer Lady Mary Wortley Montagu (1689–1762) as 'devils bedaubed with diamonds'. Royal families exchanged dwarfs as presents: King Charles IX of France, for example, happily received four from the King of Poland, Sigismund Augustus, and three from Maximilian II of Germany. Notably, thirty-four dwarfs served in Rome as waiters, and objects of curiosity, in a banquet given by Cardinal Vitelli in 1566. The Duke of Buckingham presented the eighteen-inch-high Jeffrey Hudson to Henrietta Maria at her marriage feast to Charles I. Hudson was brought to the table hidden in a cold pie 'from which he sprang forth at a given signal, to the great amusement of the Queen and her guests'. With ever greater fanfare, Valakoff, the favourite dwarf of Peter the Great, was mated with the female dwarf of Princess Prescovie Theodorovna in 1710. The Russian Tsar invited seventy-two dwarfs to the special party, and then allowed the newlyweds to spend their wedding night in his royal bedchamber. On a more practical level, the endearing quality of adult intelligence locked inside a child's body made male dwarfs safe companions for little princes, while female dwarfs escorted the princesses. In regal court paintings, dwarfs are often found standing next to dogs or monkeys, stressing their similar role as royal pets. In the first third of the twentieth century, the court-dwarf tradition had not fully expired: once when Perla Ovitz performed in Bucharest, she and her family were invited to the palace of King Carol II:

> We gave a special performance, the king sitting on his throne surrounded by his entourage. They all applauded fervently, and we bowed to the floor. The king beckoned us to approach, and we gathered around him. He fondled us, as if deciding if we were real people or mechanical dolls.

Still, by the end of the nineteenth century, the court-dwarf fashion had fizzled. Life in the service of nobility had nonetheless left its mark in dwarfs' stage names, which included a Princess Martha, Princess Elizabeth and Princess Pauline. At a bit less than two feet tall, Princess Pauline is the shortest woman listed in the *Guinness Book of Records*. For their part, male dwarfs honoured themselves with military ranks, like the great American showman General Mite, as well as his famous colleague and the star of the Ringling Bros. and Barnum & Bailey Circus, General Tom Thumb, who entertained Queen Victoria at Buckingham Palace.

Unlike giants or other people with physical deformities, performing dwarfs borrowed not only the titles of the nobility but also their style of dress: dashingly elegant gowns, spectacular hats, an abundance of fake jewellery. Their regal appearance and imperial manners were so convincing that they sometimes confused the public, especially as certain kings and generals were also strikingly short: Attila the Hun, Charles III of Sicily and Naples, Władysław I of Poland. Napoleon himself was no giant. As royalty tended to marry within the family, they had a higher than normal rate of bodily deformations – a phenomenon made eloquently clear in Velásquez's paintings.

Vittorio Emanuele III, King of Italy, was so embarrassed by his height of five feet that he was never seen without his high heels. To compensate for his heredity, he married the giant Princess Elena of Montenegro, who stood nearly two feet taller than him. Wherever Perla and the other dwarfs travelled, people inquired whether they were Vittorio Emanuele's relatives: 'Vittorio Emanuele was the most famous European dwarf of the time, and we were a very famous troupe, so everyone thought there had to be a family connection.'

Of course, dwarfs' lives were not usually gilded. More often than not, dwarfs were abused and mistreated, as in the salons of aristocratic Roman ladies who commanded them to run about naked. They appeared naked, as well, at Roman festivals, where they were tossed into the arena either to fight one another or as prey for wild beasts. Queensland, Australia, has provided its own modern manifestation of such cruelty, with a sadistic game called 'dwarf bowling', in which the human bowling balls are lifted in one arm and thrown against the pins. This practice has not yet been banished and, in January 2012, a thousand people gathered in Windsor, Canada, for a dwarf-tossing competition.

At the end of the nineteenth century, the Darwinian concept of evolution sparked excitement not only among scientists, but also among the public at large, and staring at freaks or evolutional anomalies was regarded as 'an educational experience'. From 1840 to 1940, in fairground tents all over Europe, the 'freak show' flourished. Spectators rushed in droves to see disfigured and malformed people doing mundane tasks that should have challenged them: an armless lady making tea, a legless man riding a bicycle – or a dwarf mastering a musical instrument.

Already the objects of public curiosity, dwarfs felt that they might as well make a living from it. From the beginning, they were part of these freak shows, along with fire-eaters, bearded women and legless men. Dwarfs with some artistic talent sang and danced; others entertained by juggling or performing impressive physical feats that might have overpowered even an average-sized man. Those suffering from severe abnormalities and distorted, helpless bodies were often displayed in closed tents or cages, simply to provoke revulsion.

When a dwarf wished to be appreciated for his real talent and true artistry as a performer (as opposed to his dwarfism), it generally proved impossible. Frank Delfino, who started his showbiz career in the Midget Village at Chicago's 1933 World's Fair, hoped to gain recognition as a virtuoso violinist. He insisted no mention be made of his deformity in publicising his concerts, but to no avail; his impresarios billed him as 'the world's smallest violinist'. Although he would appear in films like *Planet of the Apes* and *The Incredible Shrinking Woman*, he became better known for his role in McDonald's hamburger commercials, which he played until the age of eighty.

Traditionally, many dwarfs have performed in circuses as clowns and acrobats, often mounted on ponies or elephants. Nearly every circus used to employ a troupe of dwarfs – in Russia today, there are still some all-dwarf circuses. The most famous Jewish circus dwarf was Zoltan Hirsch, half of the duo Gérard and Zoli. Born in Hungary in 1885, Zoli was the only short person in his family, his condition being due to rickets. A wandering circus that had settled in his town caught his imagination and he spent his days among the performers. He found wearing a top hat, smoking jacket, oversized silk tie and shiny black shoes far more appealing than being a blacksmith – his destined profession. In a career that took him from Russia to England, South Africa and Latin America, he enjoyed celebrity status everywhere. He also appeared in films, and published an autobiography, appropriately titled *The Great Life of a Small Man*.

Dwarfs found their stage not only in tents or fairgrounds. At the end of the nineteenth century, Berlin was entranced by Fatmah and Smaum, sibling dwarfs from Ceylon. They appeared daily between two and ten o'clock in Hagenbeck's Ceylon Teahouse. When Fatmah died at sixteen, her brother switched to sports and performed at the Berlin Wintergarten and Zirkus Busch. In 1904, Samuel W. Gumpertz founded a midget city in Coney Island's 'Dreamland'. He gathered 300 dwarfs from various fairs and circuses around the world, and offered them both a steady salary and residency in his 'Lilliputia', named after Lilliput, the land of the little people in Jonathan Swift's *Gulliver's Travels*. Lilliputia was built as a replica of fifteenth-century Nuremberg; every building was in proportional scale to the height of the four-foot (and shorter) inhabitants. They had their own parliament, theatre, shops, cafés, restaurants, post office, a barber shop, as well as diminutive horses and chickens. Reflecting Gumpertz's fine eye for details, the laundry man was a Chinese dwarf. They had their own beach, with a miniature lifeguard tower. The midget city's fire department responded hourly to false alarms, with midget firemen rushing through the narrow streets with their hoses. Visitors could walk around the miniature town and, peep-show-like, watch the dwarfs go about their daily routine. When the park was closed at night, the dwarfs were free to follow their own pursuits.

Gumpertz's idea caught on quickly. In 1913, Leo Singer established his own version, Lilliputstadt, in Vienna's famous Prater amusement park. Similar dwarfs' towns were subsequently built in Berlin, Paris, Budapest, Chicago and San Francisco. Carl Schaefer's Märchenstadt Lilliput toured several German cities. The format was revived decades later and, in July 2009, an amusement park, The Empire of the Little People, was opened near Kunming, China, housing 100 dwarfs from all over the country. At the outbreak of the Great War, Singer sailed with fifty of his dwarfs on a world tour that passed through Asia, Australia and South America before landing in the United States. The dwarfs performed from coast to coast and were President Harding's guests at the White House. A few decades later, in 1939, Singer would supply Hollywood with 124 dwarfs for the filming of *The Wizard of Oz*.

Since they had economic value, dwarf actors were relatively well cared for by their impresarios. They counted themselves lucky to be holding a safe, decently paid job, and to be living among peers who could be supportive of them in their many moments of frustration. It is estimated that in pre-Second World War Europe alone, at least 1,500 dwarfs made a living out of show business. Seventy-one different impresarios represented them, Leo Singer himself employing twenty-five agents who scoured remote European villages for dwarfs, and sometimes purchased even a tiny ten- or eleven-year-old from their parents.

•

Somehow, Singer's agents never reached Rozavlea, but if they had knocked on the Ovitz door, it would have been slammed in their faces.

> Circus was not for us, as we didn't have the physical strength or inclination. We abhorred the idea of being animals in a human zoo, of people crowding us for hours, pointing their fingers and saying, 'Look, she's cleaning the windows.' We never wanted to make a living out of exhibiting our deformity. We always wanted to be taken seriously as professional actors.

The Ovitzes conducted their lives communally; every step they took was discussed and every decision they made was debated in a family council. After much discussion, they determined that the only acceptable career for them lay in an improvement upon the *klezmer* idea, but not simply as an all-dwarf band. At the time, there were other all-dwarf bands in Europe, but they were invariably just one act in a whole vaudeville show. The Ovitzes wanted a show of their own.

With the experience he had gained writing gags as a merry-maker, Avram Ovitz began scripting them for his sisters and brother. Instead of dance music, they put together a programme of love songs and local hits. 'Onstage it was all romance, because we knew that is what people crave in real life.' And the audience went mellow when Perla, rocking from side to side, sang,

Nobody loves you
as much as I love you.
Nobody hugs you
the way I do.
The flowers are blooming just for you
and it's all because I love you.

She always preferred the tragic love ballads and, sixty years on, her voice still carries the emotion with which she sang

Since you left me and went away,
I've been waiting in vain
Although you'll never return.

Not everything being either roses or thorns, the Ovitzes tailored their two-hour programme to fit all moods and tastes. Between the songs – which they performed in five languages – they kept their audience roaring with laughter with broad jokes and hilarious stand-up scenes. From the Hasidic branch of their family, they had inherited both the dictum 'serve the Lord with joy' and the notion that music, song and dance were superior to words of prayer as expressions of faith. For the Hasidim, to live in joy was a virtue and to yield to melancholy was anathema. To kindle the spirit, and rise to a state of joyous ecstasy, the Hasidim shook their torsos and clapped their hands with fervour during prayer. With similar enthusiasm, the Ovitzes could be at peace with God, the community and themselves when making money out of laughter.

Still, as Orthodox Jews, they had to weigh the propriety of singing frivolous hits like 'I left my heart in Hawaii'. They found justification in the cabbala for performing current pop tunes; the *nizozoth,* or divine sparks, says the cabbala, fell down from the Spheres of Holiness and were scattered throughout the entire universe – even into non-Jewish music. Through singing, the sparks are released, to be lifted up and purified.

The Ovitzes set out to buy musical instruments and they chose mainly those in children's size. The two oldest sisters, Rozika and Franziska, already had their quarter-size violins and for the raven-haired, dramatic Frieda, a local craftsman made a cimbalom with shortened legs. Micki played both a half-size cello and a small accordion, while the energetic Elizabeth took on the drums, the only regular-size instrument they had in their band. And Perla got a tiny, four-string pink guitar that looked like a toy. Perla, however, would not immediately join her family on its performance-tour, as she was barely ten; she would first have to finish four more years of schooling. Of the seven, only Avram – singer, actor, and the master of ceremonies – performed without a musical instrument.

Costumes were of the utmost importance. Mistresses of the sewing machines, the sisters stitched together glamorous dresses: fluffy, silky evening gowns, in bright, cheerful colours, all of them identical in cut and design, with bows and lace to accent them, and with sequins, little pearls and spangles to make them shimmer in light. The men wore white jackets and bow ties. Hair presented a problem, for in Orthodox Judaism, hair is considered seductive. Every married Jewish woman in Rozavlea shaved her head completely and then covered it with a shawl to demonstrate her modesty. Since childhood, the Ovitz girls had witnessed the monthly visits of a rough, bony woman with whom their mother would lock herself in the bedroom. Shyly, Batia would then lift part of her scarf to reveal new growth of hair, and the woman would shave it away. After covering the freshly shorn area again with her scarf, their mother would bare another patch of hair to her visitor's razor.

But such a custom would not serve Batia's five performing daughters. They needed their beautiful, voluminous hair to enhance their presence onstage. Likewise, during performances, Avram and Micki exempted themselves from the prescript that Jewish men cover their heads at all times with a hat or a skull-cap. Fortunately, the dwarfs' diminutive size placed them beyond the strict Orthodox Jewish code of dress and appearance, as did their profession. Because their livelihood depended on their dress and looks, the Jewish community accepted their aberrant immodesty.

The 'Lilliput Troupe' seemed an obvious choice as both name and trademark. Since it was a family business, they decided not to hire a professional manager. Avram, already the head of the family, took responsibility for marketing and contracts. While the dwarf siblings were the stage stars, the average-height family members worked behind the curtains. Sarah assumed the duties of the wardrobe mistress: she laid out the costumes for each scene, and helped her dwarf sisters undress and change when they rushed from the stage between scenes. Izo Edenburg, Frieda's husband, worked as stage hand and arranged for transportation. Leah stayed behind at the family farmhouse in Rozavlea, where she attended to the animals and crops, and kept the house ready for the troupe on its return from long, exhausting tours. With her good business sense, she also ably dealt with the accounting and bookkeeping for the family enterprise.

The only sibling who did not participate in the family

business was Arie. He had a good singing voice, but chose to lead a life of his own. A tall, handsome man, with a talent for handicrafts, he became a first-rate tailor and moved to the town of Satu Mare. Leaving the family would turn out to be his doom.

FOUR

ON THE ROAD, 1931-1940

On Sunday mornings, Simon Slomowitz would stop, horse and carriage, at the Ovitzes' door. Then, he and Izo Edenburg would pile the cimbalom, the set of drums and the cello, all of them sealed in their crates, onto the carriage and tie them securely with a rope. After that, they would add to the load a large box of props, two suitcases packed with neatly folded costumes and a box filled with food for the journey: smoked goose thigh, fruit and vegetables from their garden, a jug of cider made from their own apples, dry cake and round loaves of bread. Then the seven Lilliput Troupers would step out from their one-storey house and gather around the carriage. One by one, they'd wait to be lifted up onto the carriage by the strong arms of Slomowitz and Edenburg. Wrapped in bulky overcoats, the dwarfs would huddle together on the benches, the women guarding their elaborate coiffures against the damp and dusty wind in colourful scarves.

In the absence of buses and paved roads, Slomowitz supplied the only shuttle service between the village of Rozavlea and Sighet, which was twenty-two miles away. Because few villagers had business in the town, Slomowitz found himself generally underemployed, so he was able to work regularly at the Ovitz home as a handyman. When the troupe began travelling, he became their loyal, reliable coachman as well. Already as a young man, Slomowitz had spent much of his time with the Ovitzes, since he had assisted their father, Rabbi Shimshon Eizik. 'They made him feel needed and important, and he stayed well beyond his working hours. More than feeling pity for their helplessness, he enjoyed their cheerfulness, the music and the cultivated atmosphere,' recalls his son Mordechai Slomowitz. It didn't hurt that, for years, Simon had been – and was still – in love with the beautiful, coquettish Frieda, despite the fact that she was married to Izo and that he himself had a wife, Chaya, and seven children. Chaya Slomowitz deeply resented her husband's absence from home for days on end, but she refrained from rocking the boat as her family's livelihood depended so completely on the Ovitzes.

The first performances of the Lilliput Troupe were local, in Maramureş County. Handwritten posters announced their arrival in the isolated villages and money changed hands at the door just before the show started. Not many artists bothered to tour this wretched, godforsaken region, so the local stars from Rozavlea quenched the deep thirst of the villagers for amusement. The troupe's success was in fact instantaneous, although they soon realised they would not be able to make a steady living off a population of 175,000, many of them peasants too poor to afford the price of a ticket.

Not many villagers ventured out of the Iza Valley, but the Lilliput Troupe was thinking big – as their father had. The tales of Shimshon Eizik's far-flung travels, of the fame they had brought him and the fortune he had gained, had become legend to his children; in the legend, they found a model: like a small army, they set out to conquer the nearby districts one by one with their entertainment. Starting with appearances in shabby village halls, they moved on to town theatres and cinemas. Success followed upon success. The troupe's confidence grew, and so did their reputation and appetite for more. With the news of their spectacular show travelling fast, they soon found themselves performing all over Romania, Hungary and Czechoslovakia.

They travelled mostly by train. Since there was no railway station in Rozavlea, first they had to endure the bumpy three-and-a-half-hour ride by carriage to the depot in Sighet. They could easily have afforded a move to Sighet, but they preferred the safety and intimacy of their pastoral village. Each concert tour lasted several weeks. The troupe would stop in one town for a few days, where they'd present two or three performances each day, usually to loud applause and full houses, and then move on to another stop. Life on the road is difficult for any actor, but for them it was ferociously exhausting. Outside the security of their home, its every detail tailored to their small-ness, they struggled in alien territory that was fraught with continually surprising obstacles.

Indeed, they could not make a move without the help of their entourage: they had to be lifted like babies from the plat-form into the train wagon and then raised up to the seat; in restaurants they needed a hand to climb onto a chair; perfor-mance halls and hotels confronted them with endless stairs. Furthermore, they had to carry their small wooden stools with them on their travels, in order to reach hotel beds and wash-basins or simply take a moment's rest.

The troupe's tour schedule was coordinated with local festivals, market days and annual fairs; their programme was adjusted to the audience, the country and the event. They were fluent in several languages – Hungarian, Romanian, German, Yiddish – and could sing in a few more. They could perform on an improvised platform under the sky as easily as on a proscenium in a hall lit by crystal chandeliers. The only

exception was weddings – not a disgrace, but not for professional artists. 'An artist should keep his standards – the moment
you lower them you'll never get them back' was one of their
mantras. But when invited as guests to family weddings, they
would, of course, often be asked to entertain the crowd; with
considerable reluctance they would agree.

Orthodox Jews were in fact not permitted to enjoy show
business in any form. Still, when Isaac Peri – an Israeli historian
of Romanian Jewry – was seven, he could not resist. Everyone
in Târgu Mures was talking excitedly about the Lilliputs – 'the
dwarfs are coming, the dwarfs are coming' – except Isaac's
father. A very religious man, the leader of his town's congregation, he would not allow his son, even should Isaac dare
to ask, to attend such a circus. Desperate to see the amazing
dwarfs, Isaac snuck into the open-air theatre. A man in the
audience placed him on his knees, so that little Isaac could see.
His father never learned his secret.

At another performance, Arie Tessler, Perla's childhood play-
mate, was astonished to see the girl he used to swing around
the room in jest now standing majestically onstage, and singing grandly in the company of her family. He recalled:

> They swept everyone off their feet with their jokes and songs.
> One scene has stuck with me. I was standing by the postal
> manager, one of the more educated and respected people in
> our village – throughout the show he was very enthusiastic.
> Suddenly he shouted the name of a Russian song, something
> having to do with heartache, and when Perla sang it, he cried
> like a baby until the end.

Every song was greeted with a storm of applause and master
of ceremonies Avram would have to beg for quiet. At the end

of the show, they were hailed with flowers and often money was thrown onto the stage. Once, when Perla, beaming, turned about to make her bow to the audience, she was struck in the chest by something sharp and heavy. It nearly knocked her down but, fortunately, it had not hit her face. When she recovered her breath, she picked up the object from the floor: it was a banknote, tied around a heavy coin so that it would fly across the hall and land on the stage. From then on, Avram warned audiences to be cautious when expressing enthusiasm and advised them to place their gifts on the apron of the stage – not to hurl them and place the Lilliputs in peril. At evening's end, the troupe would collect bouquets, coins, notes, chocolates and even small bottles of perfume. 'We were very friendly towards our audience. An actor should be warm, not conceited, though not everyone can restrain his arrogance.' As a promotional gift, they had cards printed with a picture of all seven dwarfs, and autographed 'Souvenir from the Lilliput Troupe'. Decades later, the cards, carefully preserved in photo albums kept by devoted fans, would emerge from oblivion.

In every town they performed in, the Lilliput Troupe would be invited into the homes of the affluent Jews, just as their peers in past generations had been fitted in castles of kings and nobles. Tables loaded with kosher delicacies would overwhelm the dwarfs, for their frugal upbringing and orthodoxy had accustomed them neither to lavish banquets nor to bohemian life. They refrained from hanging out with their fans and from drinking in taverns, and from dining in fancy restaurants after a show. When the stage lights darkened, they quickly returned to their hotel, where seven dwarfs and their three-man entourage would squeeze themselves into three plain rooms. Nor would they indulge in extravagant shopping sprees, not even when touring the big cities. In any case, they wouldn't find clothes or shoes in their size on the shelves. The Ovitz sisters had a lifelong passion for cosmetics, however, and they also loved to visit fabric shops, where they bought endless yards of silk and satin for their dresses.

•

The Lilliput Troupe embarked on its career in the early 1930s; the timing was good. Dwarfism had by then reached the height of its popularity and an all-dwarf family band performing with miniature musical instruments was an irresistible novelty, with great commercial value. Importantly, too, by the 1930s dwarfs had become objects of curiosity not just onstage, but also in respectable academic circles, where the border between the freak show and the lecture hall commonly got blurred. The topic of dwarfism gained popularity among physicians as much for its clinical interest as for its quaint appeal.

Doctors working side by side with freak-show impresarios broke all professional taboos by issuing medical certificates that described in detail the patient's aberration. These certificates, read aloud at the freak shows, were offered as proof of authenticity, to enhance the commercial value of the miserable human exhibit. Dwarfs were also hunted down by doctors at fairgrounds and amusement parks, then taken away to medical schools for research. Many dwarfs simply hired themselves out for academic research, which for the most part involved endless measurements of every inch of their body. Head size commanded particular interest among advocates of the pseudo-science of phrenology. The findings of such research were often presented to full houses in medical and anthropological societies around Europe, sometimes with the human guinea pig onstage.

It was not only living dwarfs that intrigued the doctors; their skeletons did too, and they were mounted for the public in permanent museum displays. In his performances, the legendary Owen Farrel – a dwarf strong enough to lift four grown men, two sitting astride each arm – would lie down on the ground and allow a cart to be driven over his chest. He sold his body in advance to a surgeon for a weekly pension, to be paid to him until his death. Especially terrible is the case of Caroline Crachami, allegedly born in Sicily, but raised in Dublin. She weighed 450 grams at birth and her health was frail. At an early age she suffered from a persistent cough and a certain Dr Gilligan persuaded her parents to allow him to take her to London, supposedly for the benefit of a better climate. He then exhibited the one-foot-seven-inch-tall girl not only in London, but also in Liverpool, Birmingham and Oxford, everywhere advertising her as 'the smallest person on earth'. This 'Sicilian Fairy' had an 'unearthly voice', which enchanted royalty and the aristocracy. And for an extra shilling, gentlemen visitors could line up to touch and fondle her. In 1824, after one such evening in which she met more than 200 guests, Caroline collapsed. She was not quite nine years old at her death. Her grieving father rushed to the doctor's clinic in London to take his daughter back to Ireland for a family burial. He was a week too late. Gilligan had already sold the child's body to the Royal Academy of Surgeons for skeletonisation. For the 500 shillings that they paid him for the body, he threw in her miniature, two-inch-long shoes, her pair of socks, a tiny ruby ring and her thimble.

Caroline Crachami is exhibit 227 at London's Hunterian Museum. The room next to her exhibits the skeleton of Charles Byrne, also from Ireland. A giant, well over seven feet tall,

Byrne left his impoverished land to appear in the exhibition halls of affluent London. There, in 1783, he met the surgeon John Hunter, who convinced the city's new 22-year-old sensation that giants have short lives anyway; since his body had scientific value, he should sign documents permitting the doctor to dissect him after death. After signing the contract, Byrne had second thoughts; tormented by the idea of his flesh being boiled from his bones, he paid an undertaker to ensure that upon his death his corpse would be sunk in the Thames with leaden weights. He died soon after of excessive drinking. The press reported his death and anatomists' fight to obtain the body. John Hunter placed the highest bid, rumoured to be over £500. He hurriedly chopped the body into pieces and boiled it down into the bones, assembling it again for presentation. This skeletonisation technique and the general quest for skeletons would be repeated often in the pathological laboratories of Nazi doctors during the Second World War.

●

In Arie Tessler's memory – he saw the Ovitzes perform on several occasions – although the dwarfish stature of the Lilliput Troupe was their primary attraction, 'Still, people don't dress up, spend money on a ticket and sit for a couple of hours just because the performers are dwarfs. If they had been lousy musicians, everyone would have booed them off the stage after five minutes. Their long career speaks for itself.' Indeed, even as the Ovitz family accumulated fame and fortune, they did not slow down. Because they could not predict how long good health and success would last, they worked tirelessly, and conducted their finances cautiously. They invested heavily in gold and jewellery, which they took care to stash away. They fascinated the neighbours with their stories of distant wonders and there was an aura of magic about them. Although they performed only in adjacent countries, the Rozavleans, to this day, boast that the Ovitzes renowned tours took them 'all over the world'.

The Ovitzes were quick to appreciate the potential of a new invention – radio. Izo Edenburg used his electrical training to install an antenna on the roof, so that they could listen to distant stations and keep up to date with the latest developments in popular music – and thus expand their repertoire. Since the dwarfs could not read notes, they had to learn their music by ear. They would gather around the big, brown Telefunken, first humming, then adding their voices and finally accompanying the radio on their musical instruments.

In the mid-1930s, the whole village was astounded by a previously unseen arrival: a big, dark car stopped in front of the Ovitz house. Edenburg looked dashing driving the Italian model, which was spacious enough to accommodate easily the whole troupe, as well as their costumes, props and musical instruments. To have a car then meant more than it does to own a private jet today. The Rozavleans would crowd around the new acquisition and fight for permission to wash and polish it. An ex-Rozavlean, Benjamin Samuelson, recalled that 'being able to be even close to a car was so rare, it was like a privilege'. He was seven years old at the time, and was always puzzled by how they all fitted in the car. One day he was sitting with his friends on the bank of the Iza River

when we had a stroke of luck. They allowed us to wash their car. This was an unbelievable experience, an honour we didn't expect but took full advantage of. We were being asked, even encouraged, to touch the car. This state of grace lasted for a few years. Whenever they came back home, the car would be taken to the river, where my friends and I would wash it for them.

The automobile made such an impression on the villagers, that even now, more than six decades later, merely mentioning the name Ovitz elicits an instant smile from the few old peasants, along with a comment, 'Ah, they had the first and only car in the whole region. Up to then, we never had a carriage without horses.' They can still describe the auto in minutest detail and they still wonder how, of all people, it was the weakest of the weak who had come to own such a marvel, while never in their life could they afford one.

FIVE

HUNGARY, 1940

L ya Graf had travelled far to pursue success. Full of hope, the exquisite twenty-year-old dwarf had taken the boat to New York and was immediately snatched up by the Ringling Bros. and Barnum & Bailey Circus.

The circus's publicity man thought hard to come up with a gimmick that would garner public attention for the new discovery. He took Lya to Washington and on 1 June 1933, he tiptoed with her up the stairs of the Senate building. They were heading for the Senate Banking and Currency Committee room, where J. P. Morgan, the leading American financier of his time, was due to testify.

Spotting his prey, the publicity man quickly plopped Lya onto Morgan's lap. He snapped his fingers and the press photographer, who was in on the stunt, snapped a picture. When the blazing flash dissolved, the whole room fell silent. The 66-year-old Morgan was famous both for his lack of humour and for his aversion to physical contact. That morning he was especially out of sorts because of the inquisitive Senate hearing. Yet, after a moment's bewilderment, and to the considerable surprise of all, his face widened into a big smile. The following day, all the major American newspapers carried the photograph of the enchanting, wavy-haired, blonde dwarf and the powerful, bald multi-millionaire. The *American Heritage Magazine* would later comment.

Morgan, and even Wall Street as a whole, profited adventurously from the encounter. From that day forward until his death a decade later, he was in the public mind no longer a grasping devil, whose greed and ruthlessness had helped bring the nation to near ruin, but, rather, a benign old dodderer.

The shy and sensitive Lya Graf, however, gained little she valued from the 'adventurous encounter'; the exposure and attention that the photo brought her proved to be too much for her to handle. Unable to bear the prospect of becoming a celebrity freak, a dwarf on exhibition instead of a recognised artist, she returned to her native Germany two years later. In 1937, she was arrested by the Gestapo. Not only did her dwarfism get her categorised as 'useless for society', but she was also half Jewish. In 1941, she was transported to Auschwitz, where she soon died.

The Ovitzes were not aware that the earth was trembling under the feet of Jews throughout Europe. They were oblivious to Hitler's rise to power, the Nuremberg Laws, Kristallnacht, concentration camps. Not even the outbreak of a world war and the subsequent cancellation of their performances in Nazi-occupied Czechoslovakia awakened them to the disturbing new reality. Like many other Jews in Transylvania, they simply did not feel personally connected to the events unfolding in distant Germany: they continued to do what they had to do to make a living. They performed. Their admirers, after all, were waiting for them and they could not let them down.

But it did not take long for events to catch up with them. During the twenty-two years of Romanian rule over

Transylvania, Hungary had never abandoned its hopes of retrieving its former province. The right moment arrived in June 1940, when the Soviets issued Romania an ultimatum demanding the return of Bessarabia. Hungary, for its part, called for the restitution of Transylvania. As Hitler was secretly planning to invade Russia in 'Operation Barbarossa' and thus needed both Hungary and Romania as allies, he could not risk the possibility of military confrontation between the two countries. On 30 August 1940, German foreign minister Joachim von Ribbentrop and his Italian counterpart Count Galeazzo Ciano dictated their arbitration terms: Hungary was to receive northern Transylvania which had a population of 2.5 million.

The months prior to this agreement had seen the collapse of law and order in Romania and with it the rise of a new wave of anti-Semitism. The Romanian government had long been antipathetic to the Jews, so the Ovitzes, like all Jews in the region, welcomed what they perceived as a return of the golden era of Austro-Hungarian rule. However, what they failed to realise was that the current Hungarian regime was itself anti-Semitic.

On 13 September 1940, the transfer of government was completed, but within a few days, the flowers of hope proved to have sharp thorns. Hungary quickly implemented anti-Jewish measures. All Jewish newspapers were shut down, along with social and sport clubs. Jews were expelled from secondary schools and universities. Civil servants, doctors, lawyers, teachers and other white-collar professionals lost their jobs. Jewish businesses were confiscated, with only a lucky few able to hand over their keys to non-Jewish partners and thus maintain at least a partial livelihood.

Performances by Jewish artists were restricted to Jewish audiences. But most Jews, financially impoverished and emotionally ravished, had neither the inclination nor the money for song and dance. Their careers in crisis, the Ovitzes travelled to Budapest, now their capital, knowing that the audition lying before them – to get the newly required Hungarian identity cards – was a mission that dared not fail. They stormed the government office in full feather, radiating the natural charm and theatrical self-confidence they'd gained through years of celebrity. The seven contagiously cheerful dwarfs so dazzled the officials with their fairy-tale presence, publicity photos and bubbly chitchat, that they were never asked the one essential question. The word 'Jew' did not appear on their freshly issued official identity cards.

So the dwarfs could go back on the road – but not, to be sure, as if the world was waging no war: for nearly four years they lived in racial disguise and constantly ran the risk of arrest for breaking Hungarian laws that forbade them as Jews to perform for non-Jewish audiences. They stopped speaking Yiddish in public; they pricked up their ears for gossip. Rumours, whispers, hints of apprehension could quickly cut short a commitment in any town or village. If they were booked for a Friday evening or a Saturday matinée – the Jewish Sabbath – one or another of the troupe would then play ill, a doctor would be summoned to the hotel to fill out a certificate. A large apology notice would be posted on the doors of the performance hall and the disappointed audience would be promised an extra performance on Sunday.

They could still feel relatively safe in their own village. Their home remained a popular venue for the celebration of the Jewish festivals and villagers who had not been invited would glue themselves enviously to the windows. On hot summer days, if they were not on tour, the Ovitz women, as always, would take their small wooden stools out into the shade of the garden's fruit trees, and in the cool afternoon hours they would move to the pavement where they could see and be seen by the neighbours. All would stop to greet the sisters and to share gossip.

According to one of the neighbours, Rosa Stauber, in this period

> people in the village would wear rustic clothes, sheep-skin jackets, makeshift boots, and the children ran in the mud barefoot. And there they were in the latest fashion – city clothes, delicate flowery dresses, black lacquered shoes. They were the only women in the village with manicured nails, red lipstick, powdered cheeks and eyelashes painted black. It was an attraction – a free show. They were so beautiful and aesthetic and sweet smelling, like elegant dolls.

The village children would sneak up on the Ovitz men, quickly measure themselves against them, and shout 'I'm taller! I'm taller!' to their friends – a practice that Avram and Micki tolerated as an innocent game. On Saturdays after the prayer service, they would stroll down the peaceful main street of Rozavlea, a sight remembered by all who survived the pending horrors: a procession of seven strolling dwarfs followed by the taller members of the family. The seven celebrities would exchange benevolent smiles and waves of the hand with the village people. If they detected any mockery, the Ovitzes tried not to show it.

According to world statistics for this period, the marriage rate among the general population was approximately 75 per cent; however, wedding bells rang for only 30 per cent of people with restricted growth. The Ovitz family managed much better: five of the seven dwarfs ended up married, all of them to average-height spouses who moved into and became part of the Lilliput household. Perla Ovitz had a whole set of suitors, and was confident of eventually marrying.

> But I never went hunting. I didn't need to – they were all after
> me. Men were attracted to us because we had pretty faces and
> good manners. The fact that I was small didn't bother them.
> Some men prefer dolls. Height and body size are no sign of
> health or fertility; some rings have huge worthless stones,
> others have tiny precious ones. Just as diamonds can be small,
> so were we.

She met some of her suitors after performances. They would buy tickets to successive shows, never once taking their eyes off her, and sometimes dare to make the next move by squatting at the artists' entrance. Feeling too young to make a romantic commitment, and not ready to leave her family or to desert the stage, Perla consistently responded to her suitors with rejections. Her brother Micki, a bachelor in his thirties, never reconciled himself to being single, maybe because it is generally more difficult for women than men to accept miniature partners. Time and again, Micki or members of his family would try to persuade a girl to marry him. They all declined with a diplomacy that veiled deep offence.

Dwarfs, of course, can have children; statistics show the chance of passing on dwarfism to be 50 per cent. One British dwarf couple, Robert and Judith Skinner, a little less than two feet, three inches tall each, managed to have fourteen average-sized children. None of the female Ovitz dwarfs, however, ever conceived. Their doctors had in fact advised them not to, as their pelvises were too narrow for safe delivery. Married to the tall and full-bodied Dora Katz, Avram Ovitz was the only family dwarf to father a child, Batia, born in 1936. She developed normally.

In the summer of 1941, the Hungarian authorities rounded up 35,000 Jews who had settled in Transylvania after 1919 and could not prove their Hungarian origins. They were deported to the Hungarian-occupied parts of Galicia, where they were led to believe they would be resettled on deserted farms. Soon after, on 27 and 28 August, 23,600 of them were massacred. A man from Sighet did survive: he was hit by a bullet, fell into the freshly dug mass grave and was covered by corpses. He managed eventually to crawl out from under the dead bodies and, at great peril, returned to Sighet. Trembling, he described the atrocities he had witnessed to the Jewish community leaders. Few believed him; most branded him insane. Still, his awesome testimony passed from mouth to ear – but even those who responded to it more with serious concern than instinctive scepticism took solace in the fact that they were true Hungarians and had lived in the region for generations. The government would not visit such horrors upon them.

The massacre at Kamianets-Podilskyi was the first large-scale murder in what would emerge as the Nazi project of genocide known as the Final Solution. On 20 January 1942, the systematic implementation of the programme in all countries under German rule would be discussed at the notorious Wannsee Conference in Berlin. Soon after began the herding of millions of Jews into the cattle cars of trains that would deliver them to death camps or to their execution in the slaughter pits. But the Hungarian government was, in fact, delaying the deportation of its Jews.

The Lilliput Troupe's routine was not hindered and they entertained their audiences all over Hungary. At home, they enjoyed happy moments: Moshe Moskowitz, the manager of a Jewish theatre in Cluj, became a frequent visitor. He had seen the Lilliputs perform numerous times and knew their repertoire by heart. He was so enthusiastic that he suggested a merger with his own group. The Ovitzes declined, out of concern that they'd lose their independence, and fear that they'd see their income cut in half. But Moskowitz, who had come to take them over, found the tables turned – he had fallen in love with Elizabeth and, as a result, became the Lilliputs' new manager.

In her memoirs, Elizabeth Ovitz claims she was a romantic seventeen-year-old when the tall, mature Moskowitz proposed to her. But her recently discovered birth certificate shows, however, that she was actually twenty-eight at the time, the same age as her prospective husband – her miniature size and childlike looks had made it possible for her to subtract eleven years from her age without suspicion. They married on 6 November 1942. Throughout their career, the dedicated, industrious Lilliput Troupe had hardly ever turned down a job offer; on occasions, to fulfil several conflicting requests, they would split into performing duos, trios or solos. So it was that Elizabeth, on her first weekend as a married woman, set out to honour a solo-star engagement at the physicians' ball in Sighet. Her husband stayed at home and she was chaperoned by her sister Leah. It was almost morning when she returned to find him awake and furious. But the newlyweds had no time to fully develop their first matrimonial quarrel, since a week later they were forced to part.

From 1941, all Jewish males between the ages of eighteen and forty-eight were conscripted into Hungarian army labour-units and driven to the Ukrainian front. They disarmed land mines, paved roads, constructed bridges, built fortifications and dug in copper mines. Under deliberately harsh conditions, many of the men died from exhaustion, starvation and torture. The aim of the general conscription was not only to gain manpower but to weaken the communities into near starvation by keeping the bread-winners away. With the able Jewish men far away, the possibility of resistance to future brutal measures was forestalled.

Within a short time, the Ovitz family lost four men to the conscription: brother Arie, who left behind his young pregnant wife Magda; Azriel, who had just recently married Leah, and would not witness the birth of his first son; Izo, torn away from his beloved Frieda; and Moshe, separated from Elizabeth, his wife of only ten days. The Ovitz dwarfs had two new worries: the fate of their loved ones and the management of their daily life without essential help. They could no longer use their indispensable car, since Izo Edenburg had been the only one who could drive.

The Transylvanian Jews had lost control of their daily lives and were suffering from collective anxiety-based paralysis. Although hundreds of Polish-Jewish refugees, who had witnessed firsthand Nazi murders and massacres, had fled to the region with terrifying tales, very few of the Ovitzes' neighbours responded by fleeing as fast as they could into deepest Romania. In any event, given their physical helplessness, this was an option the Ovitzes could not even contemplate.

By the start of 1944, more than 4 million Jews had already been murdered; hundreds of thousands more were still penned up in ghettos and concentration camps. Nevertheless, despite their new hardships, the Ovitzes managed to maintain their careers. Remarkably, they continued to book even extended tours that would take them hundreds of miles away from their village. Like many others, they imagined the war would soon be over – that the flames would die out before they themselves would be burned.

On Sunday night, 19 March 1944, they were back in their hotel rooms in Szolnok, Hungary, after a well-applauded show at the National Theatre. They had just started a new concert tour with three more weeks of performances before their return to Rozavlea for Passover. They were exhausted and all but Micki soon fell asleep. Lying awake in bed, he was listening to the soft night sounds when suddenly they were interrupted by loud music blaring through the hotel walls. At first he was drawn to the persistent rhythm, its heavy beat, and he couldn't help drumming out its tempo on the blanket with his fingers. But when it showed no sign of stopping, he became irritated. Banging on the wall was not his style, so he grumpily got dressed and went down to the lobby to complain.

SIX

MARAMUREŞ, EASTER 1944

T he same sounds were spilling triumphantly into the dimly lit lobby. Micki Ovitz was puzzled. 'There's no news on the radio, but rumours say the German army has invaded,' explained the receptionist. Micki realised the game was up. He clambered back up the stairs and banged on his sisters' doors. It took some time before they opened. Micki's news stopped their grumbling at the early hour. Some of the hotel guests had already gathered for breakfast in the dining room when the seven Lilliputs, their sister Sarah, and their stage hand assembled in the lobby with their luggage. They fought hard to conceal their panic while Avram Ovitz paid the bill and apologised for their untimely checkout. News of a sudden illness back home, he said, as he slipped the cashier a few folded notes.

Two taxis got them to the railway station where a crowd full of equally anxious passengers blocked the aisles with stacks of baggage. Hordes of gendarmes and armed soldiers marched up and down the hall as the drivers helped the Lilliputs settle themselves in a corner. In the past, Avram, head of the troupe and family, had always gone to the booth to purchase their tickets. But it occurred to them that times had suddenly changed. It was not going to be an ordinary ticket purchase: a ticket agent could arbitrarily determine their fate. They decided that the coquettish, assertive Elizabeth would get the best results. Tall sister Sarah paved her way.

'Papers!' grumped the man behind the barred window.

Elizabeth stepped out of the line, while Sarah hurried back to the group to collect the identity cards. The cashier was too busy to notice there was no face in the window, only a tiny hand with short, puffy fingers capped by shiny crimson nails laid the pile of documents on the counter.

With some suspicion he flipped through the pages, then mumbled that only one train was going in their direction and already demand for tickets was close to exceeding availability, even for eligible passengers. Elizabeth suspected that 'eligible' meant 'non-Jews' and had to remind herself that the Ovitzes' cards did not indicate their Jewish origins. She stretched out on her tiptoes. 'Our husbands are at the front, fighting for the fatherland,' she told the agent. Looking for a hero's wife, the agent had to bend forward and even then he could glimpse only the top of her shiny black hair. 'And do you have enough money for nine tickets?' he asked in a tone reserved for children. Swallowing her pride, Elizabeth handed him the pile of notes she had taken from Avram's wallet.

Her smile of relief was signal enough for the Lilliputs to pick up their baggage and prepare to move. As they all headed towards the train platform, they tried to avoid bumping into the stiff-faced gendarmes. To their horror, a patrol spotted them and strolled over. The Lilliputs froze; the gendarmes gathered around them. It took a minute before the Lilliputs realised the soldiers were not after their papers but were looking for a laugh. Promptly, the Lilliputs complied, with an account of the previous night's performance and standing ovation. Avram provided a juicy joke and proffered the gendarmes an open invitation: 'Whenever you see our posters, tell the cashier you're our guests – he'll let you in free.' Once again, they had won over their audience and the gendarmes, like VIP escorts, cleared the Lilliputs' path to the platform, lifted them up onto the train and passed them onto their car. Throughout the journey, they trembled at every stop, careful not to utter a word that might give them away. Twelve hours later, they were home.

By this time, the Russian front had tightened and Hitler had stopped trusting his Hungarian allies, who were seeking a way to break from the Nazi embrace. The invasion of Hungary – named 'Operation Margarethe I' – ended four-and-a-half years of relative safety for the Hungarian Jews. Until then, the Hungarian government had rejected Germany's directive that all Jews be deported to the death camps. Following the invasion, the new Fascist government was eager to make Hungary *Judenrein* – free of Jews.

For the first time in their lives, the Ovitzes felt overpowered by circumstances. They cancelled all their scheduled shows, and did not venture out to perform even in the vicinity of Rozavlea. Shutting themselves inside their house in anxiety, they waited for the fog of persecution to clear. Anti-Jewish decrees were issued daily. By national order, every Jew aged six and up had to wear the yellow Star of David. Elizabeth and Perla used their couture skills to fashion dozens of yellow stars and meticulously stitch them to coats and jackets. Perla would nurse her pain long afterwards: 'We felt like walking dart boards, available for stabbing or a shot in the heart.' Jews were not allowed to leave their towns and villages. All their valuables – gold, silver, jewellery, carpets, furs – had to be surrendered to the local authorities. Affluent Jews were summoned to the police station, where every last gem was interrogated, beaten and tortured out of them. Christians were threatened with severe punishment for hiding valuables for Jewish neighbours.

Nevertheless, many Jews attempted to find hiding places for their possessions. Some of the Ovitzes' friends crept in the dead of night to the isolated cemetery on the far bank of the river and there dug a pit for their valuables in the heavy soil. For the Ovitzes – all their husbands away in the labour camps – this was not an option. Fortunately, though known to be rich they were somehow escaping police scrutiny. Certain that in the inevitable house search their wooden floors would be torn up, the walls hammered open and the upholstery slashed, they searched the courtyard for other alternatives, but nothing seemed safe enough. Then their eyes fell on the family car, which had been standing idle for two years. They carefully wrapped their gold and jewellery in cloth before cramming it into a tin box. In the dark of night, their small size now an advantage, Avram and Micki crawled beneath the car, scooped out a hole in the ground and stashed away the box.

Special Hungarian police squads and local clerks called at every Jewish household to record the names and ages of all the tenants and to obtain a full description of the house with a list of its facilities and contents. As it was a time of emergency, and as the officials left carbon copies of their documents with the residents, the Ovitzes found it reasonable to assume the survey was being done for their benefit. In fact, the documents provided the authorities with a ready means to track down anyone trying to run away or hide. They also proved very useful in the efficient seizure of Jewish property and its distribution to the neighbours.

To foster isolation from the outside world, Jews were ordered to surrender their radios. The Ovitzes dared to hang on to their big brown wood-panelled Telefunken; they listened to it furtively, they prayed for news of a German defeat. Since no one else in the village owned a set, they were quickly informed on. They counted themselves lucky, however, for though the radio was confiscated they were not punished for the offence. On Friday evening, 7 April 1944, the Ovitzes sat down for their Passover Seder. More emotionally than ever before, they recited the Haggadah. Profoundly moved by its account of the Hebrew enslavement in Egypt, they prayed that God would repeat their ancestors' miraculous exodus, when the waters of the Red Sea parted to provide a path to freedom and then converged to drown the enemy that pursued them.

They tried to take solace, too, in the possibility that Maramureş, a remote Hungarian province far from the central government in Budapest, might be spared. They did not know that just a few hours earlier, the interior minister had signed a decree ordering the ghettoisation of all Hungarian Jews. The implementation started with Maramureş, since it was the closest county to the Russian front. They celebrated the seven days of Passover in ignorant bliss. Then on Saturday 15 April, before they had a chance to store the special festive plates and cutlery for the next year's Seder, they heard the chilling announcement in the street. 'We were ordered to pack our suitcases and move to the synagogue,' remembers their cousin Regina Ovitz.

> We were in shock; we couldn't decide what to do first. We thought that since the Red Army was approaching, we were being taken away from the border for a temporary stay in a safer part of Hungary. The pessimists among us concluded we were being sent to labour camps. No one thought about dying.

The Jews of Rozavlea rolled pots and pans in blankets, as they could not be sure of kosher conditions in their new place of residence. They selected their best clothes, gathered necessary supplies and packed the food left over from Passover. Expecting to continue their professions, the men bundled up their tools: an awl, an axe, a hammer, a saw. Reasoning that in the new place, and especially there, people would welcome the pleasure of entertainment and find in it a source of unity as well as remembrance of bygone days, the Ovitzes packed the instruments they could most easily carry: Rozika and Franziska's violins, Perla's guitar, Elizabeth's small drum. They locked away their bulky cello, cimbalom and big drum. They selected their favourite stage costumes and make-up kits. After hastily watering their garden and scattering food for their chickens and cows, they asked their long-time neighbour to keep an eye on the place. At the entrance to every pious Jewish home, a small holy scroll with a metal shell, known as a *mezuzah*, is nailed to the right doorpost, above one's head, so that it can be touched for its blessing upon entering and leaving. In general, the Ovitzes had fitted everything down to their scale, but they had exempted the *mezuzah*, as they didn't wish to debase it. Now, on the brink of a lengthy journey, they lingered on the ritual. One by one, they lifted their right hands up towards the *mezuzah* and kissed their fingers in prayer. As they were about to lock the door, a gendarme supervising their departure stretched out his hand. 'Don't bother,' he said. 'I'll keep the keys.'

The synagogue could hardly contain the village's 650 Jews with their baggage. The Ovitzes tried to make themselves safe in a corner by erecting a fence with their luggage so as not to be crushed. The doors of the synagogue had been sealed and Hungarian militia surrounded the building so that no one could flee. As the hours passed, the heat and stench became suffocating. Rozika and Franziska, the older Ovitz sisters, fainted, and the village doctor was brought in. 'It's too crowded for the dwarfs here; it may put their lives in danger,' he told the officer in charge. The black rooster feather in his helmet bobbing, the officer consulted his superior and returned with a positive reply. The Ovitzes gathered up their belongings. As their house stood next to the synagogue, there was not much walking to do.

That night, there was a bang on their door. With great apprehension they answered it – and discovered a rowdy group of tipsy gendarmes standing before them with guns, bayonets and bottles. The frightened dwarfs stood aside to let them in. The men in uniform slumped onto the red velvet sofa: 'Let's have some fun!' they demanded. Bewildered, the Lilliput Troupe took out their instruments, arranged them-selves in a corner, and hesitatingly started to sing and play. The drunken gendarmes joined in, clapping ecstatically, command-ing the dwarfs to play their favourite songs again and again. Occasionally one of the gendarmes would pull himself up and, swaying heavily, lift a female dwarf away from her instrument and try to dance.

Not long before they had been a paying audience; now they had us for free. They wanted us to drink with them, but we explained we'd be too sick to play. They were away from home, longing for a woman, so again and again they demanded love serenades. I was in no mood for romance, all I wanted was to cry, but we had no choice. When they left at dawn, we were shattered, humiliated. We couldn't stop thinking, what does our whole miserable community, suffocating in the next-door synagogue, think of the merry sounds coming from our home?

And on every night of the following week, the scene was repeated. The Lilliputs felt vulnerable without the barrier of the proscenium arch, the stage lights, the curtains. But they realised that once again their deformity was playing to their advantage. A week later, a new order was issued – they were all to march the seven-and-a-half miles to the village of Dragomireşti, to be locked in the ghetto together with Jews from thirteen other villages.

The militia allowed only small children, the elderly and invalids to use carts instead of walking. A villager who had worked on the Ovitz farm offered the Lilliputs his carriage. On arrival in Dragomireşti, they were herded into a closed section of the village, cramped with a total of 3,500 Jews. The more fortunate arrivals were quartered with twenty other ghetto-dwellers all squashed into one flat. The less fortunate made sheds, barns and stables their makeshift dwellings, or else they simply slept outdoors. The Ovitzes managed to squeeze themselves into the flat of a family friend. The curfew was lifted an hour a day for purchasing essentials. Time was too short for the dwarfs, and Leah, Sarah and sister-in-law Dora served as the legs for all, rushing around frantically each day to meet the needs of their survival.

In an effort to avoid any resistance, the Hungarian militia – guided by German officers – segregated the leaders of the communities and detained them in separate quarters. To break the general spirit, the militia issued degrading decrees. Most humiliating was the forced shaving of the men's beards and the cutting of their ear-locks, which had been religiously groomed since early manhood and were an integral aspect of their appearance. The Ovitz men were spared the disgrace, since on professional grounds they had never grown beards.

Most of the non-Jewish villagers in Maramureş turned their backs on their Jewish acquaintances, who had often employed them to do farm work. Indeed, some of them welcomed the plight of the dispossessed and immediately began plundering their property. A small minority, with altruism and empathy, took the time and trouble to visit their former employers or neighbours, and on occasion to bring them food. According to Haim Pearl,

> they sometimes travelled for hours carrying vegetables, fruits, eggs, oil and flour from the deserted Jewish farms. My uncle was seventy-six, a rich landowner, and his peasants kept coming to the ghetto to consult him about sowing and cultivating the land for the coming season. When they saw their dignified master, pale, exhausted and beardless, crouched with his bundle on the floor like a pauper, they burst into tears, and drew us into weeping along with them.

Still, with every day spent in the ghetto, more of its inmates became convinced that they would survive to see the next – in part because the Hungarian militia nurtured the notion by disseminating false information.

In the evening of Sunday 14 May, all men between the ages of eleven and sixty were ordered to assemble in the school-yard, which had been turned into a horse stable and was full of excrement. Only a handful of German officers walked around, but the operation was executed wholly by Hungarian gendarmes. Dozens of them stood on the bridge leading into the compound, to create a wall of bludgeons, with which they battered their captives as, terrified, they were forced to cross the bridge. Some tried to escape and fell into the water, to roars of laughter and cheers from the local villagers. When dawn broke, the militiamen herded the women and children over to the schoolyard.

As Perla Ovitz remembers it, the dwarfs were wearing three layers of clothing, one on top of the other – they wanted to carry as much with them as they could, yet not to be too heavy to move. A reporter and a photographer arrived to cover the local exodus, and as always, the dwarfs stole the show. To get a most catching photo, the creative photographer put a soldier next to them, for size comparison. The photos that appeared in the next day's newspaper showed the Ovitzes dragging themselves along on their walking sticks and preparing to mount a horse cart. Although it was a hot day in May, the dwarfs are wrapped in overcoats and scarves as if it were the dead of winter. They look calm enough, Rozika and Franziska have even managed a smile when they spotted the media. Unheeding to the tragedy of it all, the obtuse news editor titled the story 'Jewish Dwarfs at the Ghetto'. The caption reads: 'The family arrives at the compound with its baggage. The soldier next to them seems like a giant, but actually he is of medium height.'

As the photos indicate, the Ovitz dwarfs were put on a cart, as were Dora, Leah and their children. Sarah had been ordered by the gendarme to dismount and walk. She was immediately swallowed up in the crowd. Frantic and tearful, her sisters spotted one of the officers who had spent several nights at their home. Pleading their helplessness without the aid of their full-size sister, they begged him to restore her to the cart. Thanks to her grass-green coat, they could see her from afar and Sarah was retrieved just in time before being totally lost in the crowd. The human colonnade was wriggling up the hill towards the train station at Vişeu de Jos. Propelled forward by blows from the gendarmes, they were not allowed a moment's rest during the fifteen-mile march. The climb was steep and the sun was scorching. They were deathly thirsty. They stumbled; some fell. The villagers, running alongside the doomed convoy, waited for their chance to dash forward and snatch a fallen blanket, a rolling kettle, a sack of potatoes.

They had walked nine hours and it was already twilight

when they reached the station. They beheld in silhouette a never-ending line of freight wagons, their doors wide open, waiting to swallow them up. In a frenzy now, the soldiers used the butts of their rifles and waved their bayonets to get the exhausted Jews into the wagons. The air resonated with alarm. Mothers were screaming and children yelling as families were torn apart in the commotion.

Swept up into the chaos, gripped by panic and misery, dozens of the Ovitzes' friends and relatives, including Uncle Lazar, the *klezmer*, and his sons and grandchildren, were desperately trying to find each other. The cart carrying the Ovitzes halted at a distance from the train, and the coachman helped them down. They were left on their own. The swarm soon pulled them forward to the freight train. They lifted their eyes. The floor of the wagon was higher than their heads; they could not possibly mount it. Clinging to their belongings, they tried to shield themselves as people stepped, tripped or climbed over them to get into the train. It was Simon Slomowitz, their handyman, who suddenly noticed their distress. He pushed aside the crowd and made his way towards them, his wife and children chasing after. One by one he lifted the dwarfs into the wagon before tending to his own family. They all huddled together in a corner of the wagon. A German officer counted them all and wrote the total number in chalk on the doors, which were then slammed shut. The inside of the wagons went dark. The train, around forty wagons, crawled out of the station.

The wagons were intended for transporting cattle, so there was no light. The single small hatch in the ceiling let in hardly any air – and certainly not enough for the eighty frightened people packed into each wagon with their suitcases, boxes and bundles. Space was so tight that they had to stand for endless hours and could sit only in turns. To spare their weak legs, though, the Lilliputs were the only adults allowed to crouch together on a small island on the floor. But pressed on every side by scores of people who towered and swayed above them, they were robbed of the scant air that came through the hatch and fainted regularly throughout the journey.

As no one had any idea how long the journey would last, each family rationed the meagre food they had brought with them. In the boiling hot wagon, teenager Mordechai Slomowitz, together with his five younger siblings, began crying for water. 'Father added some vinegar to the bottle to keep us from drinking too much and wasting the precious fluid,' he remembers. Some people were yelling, some were praying; others were simply too numb to react. The unbearable stench of urine and excrement filled the wagon. A single bucket in the corner served as the toilet for the entire car. It was too wide for the Ovitzes to sit on; compassion prompted someone to offer the use of his child's chamber pot.

When they left the station, they thought they were heading east. But the train stopped so often, and so frequently reversed or altered its route after waiting for hours on a side track, that they soon lost their sense of both time and direction. Each day at a brief stop in an empty field, with no road signs or local residents to disclose their location, they were allowed to breathe, stretch and attend to their bowels – but always at gunpoint.

Before they were granted permission to climb down from the train, they were warned that if any of them ran away, the entire wagonload of people would be shot. The Ovitzes did not dare leave the train. They travelled for three days and nights, famished and dehydrated, sweating and suffocating. At last, the train came to a final halt.

The door slid noisily open. The cool night air caressed their faces, revived their souls. For a moment.

SEVEN

AUSCHWITZ-BIRKENAU, MAY 1944

A second deep breath filled them with a sickening stench – a mixture of scorch and smoke. Before they could define the foul odours, they were deafened by shrieks and roars, and a loud barking of dogs. Beams of light from powerful projectors made them blink as they stood paralysed at the wagon doors. The ramp beneath them teemed with vicious dogs and helmeted soldiers. Men in odd striped jackets leaped onto the wagon and began pushing them downward. 'Leave your luggage on the wagon, you'll get it later!' they were ordered in Yiddish. Simon Slomowitz was the first to jump down; then, cradling the dwarfs in his arms one by one, he lowered them to the ground. Their layers of clothing made them bulky and awkward to hold.

A soldier passing along the ramp was shouting '*Zwillinge heraus*! *Zwillinge heraustreten!*', which sounded bizarre: 'Twins step out!' Other soldiers were hollering, 'Men to the left, women and children to the right!' as they split the crowd in two. 'Five in a row' was the next command. Simon Slomowitz and nineteen-year-old Mordechai helplessly watched mother Chaya and the five younger children drift away – the human tide was tearing families apart. Everything was happening too quickly for the Ovitzes to follow. Shoved aside, they clung desperately to each other in a tight ring: the seven dwarfs, their two tall sisters, sister-in-law Dora and the two children. The strange, immobile coil of twelve attracted the attention of the SS men. Once again, the Lilliputs had become a magnet.

Turning back to look for her husband and son, Chaya Slomowitz saw that the Ovitzes had been enveloped by soldiers' helmets. For a few seconds, Chaya stood stock-still. Then, despite the grudge she harboured against the Lilliputs – and quite contrary to her own nature – she gathered her children behind her and, in one of those inexplicable fatal decisions, fought her way back through the crowd to the Ovitzes.

Oddly enough in that infernal site, the Lilliputs were calm and composed, no doubt because the soldiers were not harassing them the way they were the others. 'And who are you?' barked the officer. 'We're all one family, from the same village,' said Mrs Slomowitz firmly, although they were not related, and her only connection to the Ovitzes was through her husband, their coachman and handyman.

The Lilliputs kept silent. They had no idea where they were or where the future would take them, but if Mrs Slomowitz wished to link her destiny to theirs, so be it. The officer allowed Mrs Slomowitz to join the Lilliput circle; encouraged, she played her trump again. 'My husband and son are over there, with the men. Can they join us, too?' Surprisingly, the officer complied. A soldier was sent to fetch Simon and Mordechai. Now they were twenty.

No longer effaced in a human mush, the Lilliputs quickly regained their confidence – so much so that they began to behave like stage stars besieged by ardent fans. Micki Ovitz felt enough at ease to draw from an inner pocket in his coat a pack of autographed fan cards, which he handed around to the SS men. Two other neighbours from Rozavlea, Gitel Leah Fischman and her daughter, stopped to peer at the surreal scene. 'Don't tell me you're another of their relatives!' sneered the amused officer. Before the Fischmans could come up with an answer, Micki Ovitz jumped to the rescue. Pointing out the exquisite twenty-year-old Bassie, he announced, 'Not yet, but she'll soon be. She's my fiancée!' The officer did not pursue the point. 'Never mind. Step aside and don't move until *Hauptsturmführer* Dr Mengele arrives!' He instructed some soldiers to guard the group of now twenty-two detainees: 'No one is allowed to take them away until Dr Mengele sorts things out!' Another soldier jumped on his bicycle and rode away. It was past midnight, the morning of Friday 19 May 1944.

They were standing at the edge of the ramp, watching the backs of their uncles and aunts, cousins and friends, all the neighbours from Rozavlea, disappearing in their march towards a building with two chimneys that ceaselessly poured out flames and smoke. 'What's that fire all about?' asked Perla Ovitz. A man in a striped jacket looked at her with revulsion: 'Don't you know where you are? This is no bakery – this is Auschwitz, *Kever Yisroel*, the Grave of Israel, and you'll soon end up in the ovens, too!' He spoke not out of malice but from furious despair. Reduced to a mere shadow of a man, he was a Polish Jew who had been in hell for too long and was indignant at the new arrivals' ignorance of what their brethren had been through for the last few years.

Suddenly, each flame looked like a human being, flying up and dissolving in the air. We went numb, then started thinking about the unknown man we were waiting for – if this was a graveyard, what was a doctor doing here?

•

Josef Mengele was known in his Bavarian hometown – Günzburg – for his musical and dramatic talents. In his teens he wrote a play based on fairy tales; its success earned profits that were donated to local orphanages. In high school, he was considered more ambitious than brilliant. The eldest son of a well-off engineer and industrialist, he was expected to take over the prosperous family agricultural equipment factory. According to his school friend Julius Diesbach, Mengele did not want simply to succeed but to 'stand out from the crowd', and he once told Julius he would one day find his name in encyclopaedias. It appears that throughout his life, Mengele instinctively bowed to authority figures; a charismatic science teacher shifted his interest from the arts to the natural sciences.

In 1930, Mengele enrolled as an anthropology and medical student at the University of Munich. With the life of a medical practitioner seeming too mundane, he became intrigued by the wider, burgeoning field of heredity and eugenics. Mengele's doctoral advisor was Professor Theodor Mollison, who liked to boast that he could tell a Jew just by looking at his photograph. In 1935, Mengele received a PhD in anthropology, attempting to demonstrate that one could differentiate racial groups according to jaw shape. A year later, 25-year-old Mengele got his licence to practise medicine.

Mollison's enthusiastic letter of recommendation won Mengele a highly coveted position as a research assistant at the Institute for Hereditary Biology and Racial Purity at the University of Frankfurt. In the words of Mengele's biographers, Gerald Posner and John Ware, 'Mengele was now at the epicentre of Nazi philosophical and scientific thinking, which held that it was possible to select, engineer, refine and ultimately purify the race.' He became the favourite student of Professor Freiherr Otmar von Verschuer, a renowned geneticist and ardent admirer of Hitler. Mengele assisted his mentor by writing expert opinions on legal paternity issues. (In a court case that accused a young man of violating the Nuremberg Laws by having an affair with a German woman, Mengele argued that the man was a Jew and, therefore, guilty. The court, however, chose to believe the neighbours' account that the man's natural father was German. Upset by the decision, von Verschuer complained to the Minister of Justice that the court preferred domestic gossip to serious scientific research.)

Mengele was particularly fascinated by the genetics of dominant abnormalities. A man blessed with good looks, he began his quest by close scrutiny of himself in the mirror. His structural dental problems aligned with his academic writing on palates and jaws. Having a dimple on his chin and a flat round disk on his ear cartilage, which he was embarrassed about, inspired a paper on the 'Hereditary Transmission of Fistulae Auris' – a condition that is characterised by an abnormal opening in the ear cartilage – and its coincidence with chin dimples.

In 1937, Mengele joined the Nazi Party and a year later the SS. He was also awarded a second doctorate for his work on 'Genealogical Studies in the Cases of Cleft Lip-Jaw-Palate', in which he claimed that these dental irregularities were hereditary and tended to appear with other hereditary abnormalities, like idiocy and dwarfism. Robert Lifton sees this work as a prefiguration of Mengele's genetic research in Auschwitz.

This work, along with similar research on harelip, was listed in the 1938 edition of the prestigious *Index Medicus*. Von Verschuer now enjoined Mengele to participate in his research on twins. Mengele's academic career was flourishing but it was interrupted in June 1940 when he was drafted into the army and applied for membership in the Waffen-SS.

His two years of service, mostly on the Russian front, earned him four decorations, including the Iron Cross First and Second Class, and a wound that withdrew him from the battlefield. Reassigned to the *Reichsarzt SS und Polizei* at the Berlin headquarters of the Race and Settlement Office, which was responsible for concentration camp medical experiments, Mengele was able to resume his close relationship with his patron: von Verschuer had himself recently moved to Berlin to take up his new post as the director of the Kaiser Wilhelm Institute of Anthropology, Human Heredity, and Eugenics.

Professor von Verschuer's monumental research on twins had suffered a setback because of the war: he had no supply of new case studies. He therefore suggested that Mengele apply for a position at Auschwitz, where they would have continual access to an unlimited supply of human specimens. On 30 May 1943, now thirty-two years old, Mengele arrived in Birkenau, about two miles from Auschwitz. Birkenau had begun operating in February 1942; Auschwitz was no longer large enough to deal with the mass of racially undesirable peoples.

Appointed chief physician of the Gypsy family camp, Mengele was responsible for camp hygiene and, in rotation with other doctors, for selecting which of the new Birkenau arrivals on the ramp should be sent to their immediate death and which should be assigned to slave labour. His enthusiasm, ambition, charisma and cruelty set him apart from the other death-camp doctors. His first task after his arrival at Birkenau was to crush a typhus epidemic that had contaminated a third of the inmates of the women's camp. When two SS guards also caught the disease, the camp command took extreme measures. In her book *Prisoners of Fear*, Ella Lingens-Reiner, a former inmate-doctor from Vienna who worked with Mengele, reports that Mengele's method of decontamination was to send an entire barrack of 498 women – mostly Jewish women from Greece – to the gas chambers. Then, the emptied barrack was disinfected. In the next step, the women in the adjacent barrack were disinfected and then transferred to the first disinfected barrack – this process of 'musical barracks' being continued until all the women had been disinfected.

In the service of Professor von Verschuer, Mengele was collecting twins, but he was also using his long, diligent shifts on the ramp to select unusual and striking human mutations. Like a demonic impresario casting the ultimate freak show, he plucked out from the masses hunchbacks, pinheads, hermaphrodites, giants, dwarfs, extraordinarily obese men, grotesquely corpulent women and anyone else suffering from a growth disorder. Sara Nomberg-Przytyk, an inmate in the Birkenau infirmary, recalls that:

> Mengele loved to single out those who had not been created in God's image. He once brought a woman to our area who had two noses; another time a girl of about ten who had sheep's wool on her head instead of hair; on another occasion, he brought a woman who had donkey ears.

•

Contrary to most testimonies by Auschwitz-Birkenau survivors, that Mengele was the one who personally selected them, it is clear that he could not have been on the ramp day and night, week after week. On the night the Lilliputs arrived at Birkenau, Mengele was fast asleep in his room at the nearby SS headquarters. All the troopers on duty at the ramp, however, well knew his passion, his collector's mentality. To gain favour with the freak-hunter, they were always on the lookout for new specimens to enrich his 'human circus'. While a lone dwarf did not provide reason enough to knock on Mengele's door in the middle of the night, seven dwarfs, along with their tall, normal-sized siblings, seemed to be a good cause for disturbance.

His mentor Professor von Verschuer had always emphasised that heredity could best be researched on complete families, so when Mengele was told that a large family with dwarf traits had just arrived he did not waste a moment. He hurried out to see the new acquisition. Crowding around him, the Ovitzes did not waste their chance to dazzle him. They answered his questions eagerly, in chorus. They told him about Rabbi Shimshon Eizik and his two tall wives, Brana and Batia; they told him about the birth of ten children, seven of them dwarfs, and about their marriages, their in-laws, fiancées and cousins. And Mengele was indeed dazzled: 'I now have work for twenty years,' he said joyfully.

Unable to suppress her feelings, Perla involuntarily slapped her cheek and muttered: 'Oh, my God.'

Mengele turned to her: 'Yes? Anything wrong?' he inquired. With the eyes of her family piercing her like bullets, she didn't dare utter another word. 'He was polite and curious, but as he was only interested in dwarfism and our family tree, I thought to myself, I won't survive him, not in this place, and definitely not twenty years.' Anxious not to lose his precious find in the death-mill named Auschwitz, Mengele turned and whispered some orders to the officer in charge, then disappeared to find suitable accommodation for the group.

He was a choosy collector. After a brief look, he had often rejected as 'uninteresting' specimens of twins and dwarfs, and without a second thought sent them on to their deaths. Had the Ovitzes arrived separately, scattered in various transports, most of them – and surely average-sized Leah, Sarah and the children – almost certainly would have been killed. Their desirability lay in their number and in their anomaly as an entire family. Batia Ovitz's admonition that her children stay together was once again proving to be wise.

They all slumped onto the ground but, though exhausted, were too afraid to doze off. The ramp was now empty. Groups of men in striped jackets were throwing the piles of ownerless luggage into trucks. Only three hours had passed since their arrival, and all the noisy confusion, all the anguish and hysteria, had yielded to a heavy, dull silence. Nearly all those who had come with the Lilliputs were now dead, and already their bodies had been dragged from the gas chambers and fed to the crematorium. Of the Dragomireşti transport of 3,500 people, fewer than 400 would survive the night. These lucky ones had been selected for forced labour and were going through various stages of admittance: having all their body hair shorn, taking a brutally cold shower, quickly donning striped prison clothing; followed by a hastened march to the barracks. It was nearly dawn when their train rolled back outside the camp, to clear the rails for the next train in line.

A black army truck pulled up to the hushed group of the Ovitzes. Simon Slomowitz and his son helped everyone get up onto the bed of the truck. They were all sitting on the metal floor, so they couldn't see where they were being taken. The truck stopped. Their bones cracking, they dismounted, and an officer led them into a building. A pungent odour assaulted them. Hooks with numbers were attached to the walls; there were wooden benches to sit on. They were the only ones inside, all twenty-two of them. 'Take off your clothes!' the officer bellowed. Then, in the anxious silence, everyone looked to the seven Lilliputs for guidance. 'We are Orthodox Jews and can't undress together, men and women, brothers in front of sisters,' pleaded Avram Ovitz. The officer was impatient. From the tone of his voice, they knew they had better not argue. Averting their eyes from each other, they shed layer after layer of their clothes. Judah Slomowitz was eleven at the time: 'I had never seen a naked woman before and I was bewildered and intrigued with so many of them around me: my mother, my sisters, the dwarf ladies. It excited me to embarrassment. I couldn't help myself and burst out laughing.'

A heavy door opened and the wave of stuffy heat assailed their faces. They'd barely crossed the threshold, groping their way inside, when the door slammed behind them.

It was almost dark and we stood in what looked like a large washing room, waiting for something to happen. We looked up to the ceiling to see why the water was not coming. Suddenly we smelt gas. We gasped heavily, some of us fainting on the floor. With our last breath we cried out. Minutes passed, or maybe just seconds, then we heard an angry voice from outside – 'Where is my dwarf family?' The door opened, and we saw Dr Mengele standing there. He ordered us carried out and had cold water poured on us to revive us.

The event indelibly etched the imminence of death on their memory: they were beginning to be gassed – and everyone would have died if Mengele had not suddenly reappeared.

Nevertheless, the story's verification with specialists and relevant documentary evidence suggests it is unlikely any gassing was scheduled for the Ovitz group that day. The gas chambers were designed to kill between 500 and 2,000 people at once, depending on the size of the hall. Zyklon B was effective only in a room temperature of 27° Celsius, which was achieved by cramming a mass of people together. Gas chambers were simply not operated for merely twenty-two people; small groups were shot. Furthermore, according to the camp's rigid safety orders, the SS personnel had to wear gas masks when operating Zyklon B. Although the victims died within fifteen minutes, the SS men routinely waited half an hour before turning on the powerful fans that dispersed the gas from inside the chamber. Only then were the doors opened. The operators themselves did not enter; instead, Jewish inmates from the *Sonderkommando* were sent in to drag out the bodies for cremation.

Consequently, if the Ovitz group had been consigned to a gas chamber, once the extermination process had begun, it could not have been halted, as by then it would have been impossible to open the doors. What seems more likely is that the Lilliputs had been taken to the camp sauna for disinfection, where the water poured over heated stones would have produced much steam and fumes, as well as temperatures intense enough to open wounds and cause someone to faint. The sauna would have had a particularly traumatic effect on both small children and fragile dwarfs – an effect that might easily have created the impression of being gassed.

In any case, the twenty-two members of the Ovitz group returned to the dressing room where they lay on the benches until they regained their senses. They were exempted from the sauna's second phase, in which they would have been forcibly shoved into the next hall to shower in ice-cold water and then to towel-dry with ten people to one flimsy towel. They were also spared the invasive search of all bodily orifices for gold or jewellery. Contrary to standard procedure, they were given their own clothes back, after they'd been disinfected. It was a practical move on the part of Mengele, a seasoned laboratory scientist, who cared for his human subjects the way he did his lab rats, according to their particular needs. And Mengele realised they needed their own specially sewn clothing. To dress them in clothes that had been stockpiled in storerooms after being stripped from some of the hundreds of thousands of children murdered in Auschwitz-Birkenau simply would not do: though Lilliputian in height, the Ovitzes had the bodies of adults, with breasts and curves and wide bottoms. Finally, the long night ending, a truck drove them to the *Familienlager* – the 'Family Camp'. Situated not far from Auschwitz-Birkenau's main gate, the family camp had been opened in September 1943 for Czech Jews who were transported from the Theresienstadt ghetto in their homeland. Its purpose was similar to that of Theresienstadt: Czech families were kept there as evidence that would refute reports of mass extermination in Auschwitz-Birkenau in the event of a Red Cross inspection.

The residents in the 'Family Camp' were not gender segregated, unlike the 100,000-plus inmates of Auschwitz-Birkenau. There, the fundamental rule was separation between the sexes, so strictly enforced that even a pair of three-year-old mixed-sex twins being kept alive for experimental purposes was separated and held in different camps according to their gender. Although the 'Family Camp' did not fall under Mengele's medical supervision, he managed to find a room there for the dwarfs, who, to their profound relief, were thus able to stay together. Mengele's attention, however, did not spare the dwarfs Auschwitz-Birkenau's institutional tattoo. Though painful, tattooing was welcomed by inmates, as it indicated that they had, for the time being at least, escaped execution. The administration at Auschwitz-Birkenau, the only Nazi concentration camp that tattooed its prisoners, kept extremely meticulous inventory lists, and each day recorded any change in the number of prisoners. Death among inmates due to torture, disease, exposure and generally harsh conditions could total as many as several hundred in a single day, and the only way to identify a corpse, and thus strike it from the list, was by the number tattooed on the left forearm.

On that same fateful Friday, the males were tattooed. The first to stretch out his arm was Simon Slomowitz – in blue ink the needle etched the number A-1438 into his skin. He was followed by his sons Mordechai, Joseph and Judah. Next came the turn of the Ovitzes: first, forty-year-old Avram; next, 35-year-old Micki. The small arm of fourteen-month-old Shimshon, sister Leah's baby, was almost totally covered by the number A-1444. The names and numbers were recorded, and a copy of the list was sent to the head office of the Auschwitz-Birkenau camp: inventory item 148855 notes that seven Jews from Hungary, among them twin brothers, were admitted to the camp after selection and given numbers A-1438 to A-1444. The bureaucratic error by which the dwarfs were classified as twins probably originated in their connection to Mengele, who had selected them for his experiments, most of which involved twins.

Three days later, the women and girls of the group were tattooed, though not in any particular order. Perla, the youngest dwarf, stood first in line and received the number A-5087. Next came her eldest sister, Rozika, and then, in succession, Frieda, Franziska, Elizabeth, Sarah and Leah. Avram's wife, Dora, hugged her eight-year-old Batia while the child bore the pain that came with A-5094. The mother extended her own arm next, followed by Gitel Leah Fischman and her daughter Bassie. Seventeen-year-old Fanny Slomowitz became A-5098. Her mother Chaya and two sisters, Helene and Serene, were the last in line. 'Some of us fainted during the ordeal, and our arms were so swollen that they ached the rest of the week.'

On that same day, Monday 22 May 1944, a train from Satu Mare stopped at the ramp. Among the passengers were Magda, the 24-year-old wife of Arie Ovitz, along with her parents and her four-month-old baby. When anti-Jewish decrees were issued in March 1944, the Lilliputs had cabled Magda and begged her to join the rest of the family in Rozavlea, as Arie had been inducted into a Hungarian army labour camp. Nor had the Ovitzes yet seen the baby, named Batia after their mother. Magda had cabled back that she could not leave her parents. The Ovitzes had invited all to come over, but Magda's parents did not want to leave their home. Now, on their own on the ramp, without the Lilliputs, the four of them stood no chance. Perla never ceased to lament them. 'Not a day has passed since without the tormenting thought that if we had all come together to Birkenau, they would have survived.'

EIGHT

AUSCHWITZ-BIRKENAU, JUNE 1944

June saw the height of the carnage.

Since April 1944, the camp headquarters had been fervently preparing for the arrival of Hungarian Jewry. The crematoria had been thoroughly renovated and the chimneys reinforced with iron hoops. An improved platform enabled the trains to disembark closer to the gas chambers. The Ovitz transport in mid-May was among the first to arrive. From then on, several times a day, a new train hauling forty wagons, each one crammed with eighty people, unloaded its human cargo.

The thirty-six furnaces in the four crematoria couldn't burn them all and many corpses had to be incinerated in open pits. According to the official records of the Auschwitz State Museum, over 400,000 Hungarian Jews were murdered in the course of sixty days. Their belongings – clothes, shoes, kitchen utensils, toiletry, spectacles, toys – piled up in huge mountains outside the storage blocks, waiting to be shipped to Germany to ease the lot of the populace. Of every ten people who stepped down onto the ramp, nine were sent directly to the gas chambers. The SS didn't bother to register their names or tattoo their arms.

The Ovitzes sensed they were enjoying special treatment, but couldn't determine precisely why. The shortage of manpower in German industry and the high expenses incurred by the war had delayed the programme for the total extermination of the Jews. Most of the new arrivals at the camp – the 10 per cent spared the gas chambers – now provided slave labour in branches of well-known German factories that had been built near Auschwitz. Others quarried rocks or farmed the nearby fields, or helped to maintain the camp by cleaning sewage or pushing carts loaded with corpses. The work, of course, was not so much a liberation as a brief, tortured interval before certain death. It was in any case obvious to the dwarfs that they were not being kept alive for work. But perhaps they might be expected to entertain the exhausted labourers, so as to raise their morale. They could only wonder and speculate as they waited, idle, in the barrack.

All the inmates were quartered in barracks originally designed as stables for the German army. Each stable, planned to shelter fifty-two horses, had been modified to house more than 500 prisoners under inhuman conditions. Each prisoner was allotted a bunk – or wooden plank – less than sixteen inches wide, in three tiers, one above the other. Only a line of narrow hatches admitted scarce rays of light. The roof always leaked and the floor – or rather, the dank swampy ground – swarmed with rats.

Two small rooms that flanked the entrance to each barrack had been designed for the exclusive use of the 'block elder' – a veteran prisoner in charge of enforcing the daily routine. Concerned that his dwarfs might end up trampled by the mass of full-size inmates, Mengele appointed one of those small rooms for the Ovitzes and their entourage. Whereas Birkenau inmates slept two or three to a ragged blanket in their single set of clothes on thin, louse-infected mattresses stuffed with sawdust, the Lilliputs enjoyed individual wool blankets, sheets and even pillows. 'The dwarfs slept on the lower berth and even this was too high for them to mount,' remembers Joseph Slomowitz, who was thirteen at the time. 'We had to help them up and down. Our parents and the tall Ovitzes slept on the middle berth, and we children climbed up to the top one.'

Every morning in Birkenau began with a nightmare: the *Appell*, a roll-call. It forced all inmates to rush outside at four o'clock and stand at attention for endless hours in rows of ten, while they were counted over and over again. Motionless, clad in their rags, they stood exposed to heat, cold, rain, snow: their torture knew no season. At the end of the day, after eleven hours of hard labour, they went through the same process again – and, on occasion, at midnight or whenever the SS chose. Those who collapsed were dispatched to the gas chamber. It was obvious that none of the seven dwarfs could survive a single *Appell* and Mengele not only exempted the dwarfs from the ordeal, but also extended the privilege to the entire 'family'. All of them were counted in their room, to help them maintain their physical and mental condition. Mengele had plans for them.

The inmates' thin striped uniforms offered no protection against the harsh weather at Birkenau, and they were always dirty, torn and ridden with lice. Their ill-fitting wooden clogs caused painful abscesses. But those in the Lilliput group had been allowed to keep their own clothing. Perla could wrap herself warmly in the brown sheepskin coat she had brought from Rozavlea. On it, she stitched the required identification sign – a red triangle topped with a yellow stripe. The dwarfs took meticulous care of their clothes, washing them frequently since they knew it would be difficult to replace them. Elizabeth especially cherished her antelope shoes, which she kept on repairing, sewing them by hand when the seams ripped open. When they became tattered past hope, she was taken to *Kanada* – the Auschwitz storerooms, named for a dreamland of wealth and comfort – where she was allowed to select a suitable pair of children's shoes. The dwarfs enjoyed another privilege, too – not because some shred of altruism on Mengele's part prompted it but because his research required it: they were not forced to shear their hair.

Nor were they subjected to corporal punishment. Flogging inmates until their torn flesh bled or hanging them by their hands was common practice in Auschwitz. Likewise, the arbitrary selection of prisoners for the gas chambers and the random shooting of inmates were daily routines. In a world of shaven heads and ragged striped uniforms, the Lilliputs' hair and clothes were a shield of protection, for every SS soldier instantly recognised the dwarfs as Mengele's pets, hence not to be damaged. But there was no special protection from the death camp's food: in the morning, a barrel of darkish, cold, unsweetened and diluted coffee substitute was brought to the barrack. Sometimes it was a mixture of water and herbs that was supposed to pass for tea. Lunch was either a watery soup made of potato and a few leaves of cabbage, or else roots, the sort normally fed to cattle, that had been boiled in a huge vat of water. The quantities were meagre, and Perla found the taste nauseating, rancid with the smell of rotten vegetables and more suspicious substances – some sort of poison, she feared. 'Once when they poured us soup, I saw worms crawling in the bowl.' There were bits of glass, buttons, things looking like teeth and little fingers of children. Dinner offered no more than a piece of stale bread and water. The contaminated water caused severe diarrhoea, so even in the summer heat the dwarfs refused to drink it and were constantly thirsty.

The barracks had no sanitation facilities. Instead, the roughly 10,000 inmates of the 'Family Camp' had to manage with the

270 faucets and 174 toilet holes in the sanitation barrack. They were allowed to use the facilities twice a day, the time allotted being extremely short so they were always fighting for places. On the rare occasions that they were allowed to shower, the inmates had to undress in the barrack and then rush naked to the cold-water showers, come rain or snow. Many inmates caught pneumonia, which worked as effectively as – if less efficiently than – a bullet or gas in their extermination. The dwarfs, however, benefited from Mengele's well-known obsession with hygiene.

He was manicured, immaculately clean, and always wore white cotton gloves. He demanded that we wash every day. He knew we would be crushed and frozen in the latrines, and ordered that a colourful curtain be hung in a corner of our room. There was a warehouse full of little chamber pots that parents had taken for their babies on the long train journey. The babies were all killed, and Dr Mengele furnished us with one of the pots, as well as an aluminium bowl to wash in. Simon Slomowitz would bring a bucket of water from the washrooms and we would wash each other with the help of Sarah and Leah. Sometimes we used the undrinkable tea to shampoo our hair. It was important to be clean, to keep the lice away from our hair and body. Dr Mengele ordered us to stay away from people, so as not to become contaminated. Obedience was the first lesson we learned in the camp. You had to know how to behave in that place: not to be a spoilt child and desire something you could not have.

Every day the Lilliputs groomed themselves, scrubbing and brushing each other for hours in preparation for their summons to Mengele's cabinet. They dressed up in their finery, powdered their faces and rouged their cheeks. Make-up had always been essential to them and they'd had the forethought to ferret some away in their pockets when they boarded the train to Auschwitz. They could stroke in a black line along the lids of their eyes, and they could pout their lips and colour them red.

•

The first time that the Lilliputs were summoned to the *revier* – the clinic – and the doctors in white gowns examined them, they thought it was a routine admission procedure. But when the examinations were repeated day after day, it soon dawned on them that they had been selected for some medical purpose. Josef Mengele was only one of dozens of doctors who performed criminal experiments on the inmates of Auschwitz-Birkenau. Whereas German law protected laboratory animals, there were no limitations whatsoever on what could be done to human guinea pigs in the death camps. Dr Hans Münch, whose laboratory for the Waffen-SS's Institute of Hygiene was located in Auschwitz's notorious block 10, had free rein with the prisoners:

> The working conditions were ideal. The laboratories were excellently equipped, and the cream of academia was present – people with an international reputation. I could carry out experiments on human beings usually only possible on rabbits.

Mengele felt no compunction about experiments conducted upon the Jews. He argued that since they were all doomed to die anyway he caused them no worse harm through his research and it would be a waste for science not to use them. He was proud of his work and told his son Rolf that his experiments had saved thousands of people from certain death. Some of the experiments were commissioned by the army: inmates would be injected with poisonous substances in order to discover what methods and means soldiers might be using to get themselves disqualified from service on the eastern front. German pharmaceutical companies and medical specialists took advantage of the unlimited pool of subjects to test any new substance or procedure that captured their eugenic interest, such as efficient, cheap methods of implementing mass sterilisation and eliminating the mentally, genetically or racially unfit. So it was that thousands of young prisoners suffered radiation, repeated injections with various chemical substances, operations without anaesthetics, castrations. Those who did not die in the name of German science often ended up gruesomely maimed.

Grants that Professor von Verschuer's Kaiser Wilhelm Institute received from Germany's main research foundation, the *Deutsche Forschungsgemeinschaft,* financed Mengele's research at Auschwitz, initially on specific proteins and eye colour. Such funding likewise furnished Mengele's laboratory with the latest and most sophisticated medical technological equipment. Acting on the instructions and under the supervision of von Verschuer, Mengele dispatched to the Kaiser Wilhelm Institute blood samples, limbs, and eyeballs in different colours. He had whole families of Gypsies killed specifically for their eyeballs.

According to Professor Benno Müller-Hill from the Institute of Genetics, University of Cologne, 'The goals of the research project of Mengele and von Verschuer were to decipher genetic differences of Jews, Gypsies and others in resistance to various infectious diseases, and to assemble as much material as possible from genetically affected twins or families.' Dr Jan Cespiva, a former Auschwitz inmate, testifying against Mengele in 1963 before the public prosecutor in Frankfurt, stated:

I was able to see with my own eyes how he infected twins with typhus in the sick room of the Gypsy camp, in order to observe whether the twins reacted in the same way or differently. A short time after being infected, they were sent to the gas chambers.

To Professor Berthold Epstein, a distinguished Jewish paediatrician imprisoned at the camp, Mengele confided that his only goal in the war was to stay alive and use his work at Birkenau as a springboard towards a professorship. In order to escape being sent back to the front, he was looking for an insurance policy in the shape of a scientific treatise that would confirm his professional stature and the indispensability of his research at Auschwitz-Birkenau. 'We are enemies – you will not get out of here,' Mengele bluntly told Epstein. 'If you perform scientific work for me and I publish it in my name, you will prolong your own life.' As a result, Epstein extensively researched a deadly gangrene of the face and mouth, conducting tests on Gypsy children and adolescents.

The ambitious Mengele was not long content with his position at Birkenau as von Verschuer's assistant. He wanted a research niche of his own. In the spring of 1944, with Birkenau preparing for the massive influx of Jews soon due from Hungary, he saw his chance. Previously, during his first year in the camp, he had mainly experimented on a few dozen cases, most of them sets of twins, that he had discovered among the Gypsies and Czech Jews in Birkenau's separate sub-camps. But now, with the imminent arrival of hundreds of thousands of Jews, research vistas of unlimited scope and variety were about to open up for him.

According to research assembled by Danuta Czech for the Auschwitz State Museum, the category 'twins selected and admitted to the camp' is first recorded in registry documents on 17 May 1944 – just two days before the Lilliput Troupe's arrival. Importantly, the term 'twin' in the records does not simply signify multiple births; rather, it refers to any child or adult selected by Mengele for his experiments. On his first day of hunting, he found thirty-nine promising human specimens. In a fortnight, he had enriched himself with 192 new subjects, and by the end of July he had already collected 300: 177 females and 123 males, mostly twins, with ages ranging from infancy to old age. The day he discovered the Lilliput Troupe, 19 May, 'he was beside himself with joy', remembered Olga Lengyel, one of the Jewish doctors whom he forced to assist him.

●

Eighty-five years earlier, an Austrian monk named Gregor Mendel was experimenting with peas that he grew in a greenhouse in the Augustine Abbey of St Thomas in Brünn (now Brno, the Czech Republic). In 1865, Mendel, who was also interested in various human deformations, published an article in an obscure scientific journal summing up his experiments. While, as is well known, he was the first to suggest the existence of genes and the principle of genetic heredity, his findings were essentially ignored for three decades. Nevertheless, in the period after 1900 (a good fifteen years after Mendel's death) his botanical research would emerge, transformed, as the monster of eugenics. Fused with social Darwinist ideology and its version of 'survival of the fittest', the fixation on genes would culminate both in Mengele's selections for the gas chambers and for the experimentation blocks – as it happens, a mere 120 miles from Mendel's solitary room.

Working within a particular utilitarian tradition, eugenic scientists claimed that heredity accounted for most physical and social ailments. Distinguishing between 'good' and 'bad' genes, they set out to root out the bad ones – through sterilisation. By 1920, twenty-five American states had legalised sterilisation for the criminally insane, the mentally ill or handicapped and others considered genetically inferior. But all told, the American laws were applied to a relatively modest degree. While modelling its own programme of compulsory sterilisation on both American and Scandinavian precedents, Nazi Germany pioneered the zealous implementation of such a programme. In June 1933, the Law for the Protection of Hereditary Health established the criteria for compulsory sterilisation. Among those to be sterilised: the mentally retarded, manic depressives, schizophrenics, epileptics, the hereditarily blind and deaf, and alcoholics, along with people suffering from grave bodily malformations or arrested growth. Once the law was implemented, a total of roughly 400,000 German citizens would fall victim to it.

All doctors, nurses and midwives had to report any patient and every newborn child who evinced deformations of head or spine. More aggressively, under a policy initiated in 1938, the state authorised the killing of all children suffering from severe physical or mental problems; in October 1939, this euthanasia policy was extended to include adults. This T-4 euthanasia programme was executed in six killing centres equipped with gas chambers in Germany and Austria. It is estimated that more than 200,000 German citizens whose lives were considered 'unworthy of living' were killed. Deformed people with homes and families were relatively safe; those institutionalised were at the mercy of caretakers and doctors. For instance, Dr Hans Grebe, Mengele's colleague at the Kaiser Wilhelm Institute, told Professor Benno Müller-Hill that his research on dwarfism in 1942–3 became impossible and had to be abandoned, because so many of his subjects in governmental institutions had disappeared.

So it was that all the diversities of creation and wonders of nature that had drawn crowds of parents and children to Sunday fairs, to Lilliput cities, the Vienna Prater, the Berlin zoo and elsewhere – had become outcasts. Once showered with flowers and besieged for autographs, these entertainers and performers were now declared a social burden, a genetic error that the state set out systematically to erase.

•

Mengele had at least three clinics in Birkenau – in the men's camp, the women's camp and the Gypsy camp. Several laboratories supplied him with medical services. Before fleeing the camp in January 1945, he hastily packed into a trunk what research data, documents and specimens he could. The rest he set on fire. It's a small victory of history that in a place so dedicated to destruction, in the registry book of the X-ray clinic and in laboratory report-forms on samples of blood, saliva, urine and faeces, several thousand lab results were found intact, after the liberation of the camp. Of these results, seventy-five pertained to the Lilliput group.

The earliest surviving Lilliput lab records are dated 28 June 1944 – a very busy day, evidently, as all twenty-two of the group were taken to Mengele's clinic, in block 32 of the Gypsy camp. To Joseph Slomowitz, it looked like any ordinary clinic – the staff in white gowns, stethoscopes dangling on doctors' chests, files containing each subject's personal data and test results. The Slomowitz family, all average height, had no blood connections to the Ovitzes, but they had conned Mengele into believing they were kin. Thus they were always taken along with the Ovitzes to the clinics and on their medical forms all the Slomowitzes are categorised as dwarfs. That they were all so tall puzzled Mengele. Fearful that Mengele would discover the truth and send the family to the gas chambers, the Slomowitzes drew his attention to their youngest, Serene. She was seven, but they told Mengele that she was thirteen and had long stopped growing. Since they had no identity papers there was no way he could verify the information and on the premise that Serene was indeed a dwarf, he extracted bone marrow from the spines of the entire family in an attempt to ascertain why all but Serene had grown tall. The pain they endured was terrible.

On each visit to the clinic, they all waited on a bench in the corridor as one by one they were called in. Even the youngest children had to face the doctor's syringe alone. The examinations lasted for hours, and no one could return to their barrack until the last one was through. Perla noticed that Mengele had everything worked out. At the end of each day he would prepare the schedule for the next; then, every evening, the block elder would come to their room and call out from a list the numbers of those in the group who were summoned for the next day's test. If it was to be done in the nearby barrack, they would walk there, but otherwise an ambulance would fetch them.

Every few days the doctors drew blood. The night before, we had to fast. It was a big syringe, the amount they took was enormous and, being feeble from hunger, we often fainted. That didn't stop Mengele. He had us lie down, and when we came to our senses they resumed siphoning our blood. The nurses and doctors were prisoners too, but they didn't try to make it easier on us. They punctured us carelessly and blood spurted.

We often felt nauseous and vomited a lot. When we returned to our barrack, we would slump on the wooden tier, but before we had time to recover, we would be summoned for a new cycle.

In the 1940s, medicine was obsessed with blood and its constituents. It was generally believed that blood plasma retained all traces of illness and contained all genetic traits. German scientists considered blood as a key to the differentiation between superior and inferior races. This premise accounts for the particular ordeal of Shimshon Ovitz. Born prematurely, Shimshon was still markedly smaller than normal at a year old. Both his parents were of average height, but his mother had had a dwarf father and had seven dwarf siblings; thus, Mengele was extremely eager to learn Shimshon's genetic destiny. The baby intrigued Mengele more than any other member of the group, and he showed the infant no mercy. Because the veins in his arms were too narrow for extractions, Mengele had blood drawn from Shimshon's fingers and from behind his ears. The stabs of the needles left his soft skin black and blue. To extract enough blood to fill a single tube seemed to take an eternity. The baby often fainted; his aunt Perla would give him her own precious sugar cube, which she received to revive her after the blood taking. Once, his aunts later told him, the test tube fell to the floor and, smashing, splattered blood all over the examination room. The staff doctor was terrified, as he knew that Mengele was impatient for results and that the extraction of another tubeful of blood was impossible. The only possible cover-up seemed to be to extract blood from his mother, Leah, instead, and present it as Shimshon's own. Although she had already supplied her quota, Leah again had a rubber band squeezed tight around her arm; she fainted as the blood flowed.

Frequent extraction of blood often proved to be fatal to weakened, hungry and exhausted victims. Hani Schick came from the neighbouring town of Sighet, ten days after the Ovitzes. She arrived with her husband and three children, five-year-old Otto and twins Joseph and Hedi, who had just turned one. Her husband was selected for death and Hani would have met the same fate had it not been for Mengele, who noticed the twin babies clutched in her arms. The twins and Hani were examined and weighed. Large quantities of blood were drawn from the two babies, under Mengele's supervision. On 4 July a staff doctor drew 200 ml of blood from each of them and the next day Joseph died in his mother's arms. The body of one-year-old inmate number A-12087 was laid outside the barrack, to be added to the death-cart and taken in the morning to the crematorium. Eleven days later, inmate number A-7044 joined her twin brother. For eight months, Hani Schick managed to hide her son Otto in the sick women's barrack. Two weeks after the liberation, the child died of a liver infection.

Jewish gynaecologist Dr Gisella Perl, also from Sighet, was forced to work on Mengele's team. In her book *I Was a Doctor in Auschwitz*, she recalls that:

the healthy, the talented, the beautiful, were ruthlessly exterminated, but everything abnormal was a source of constant amusement and enjoyment to our jailers, because only when comparing themselves with these freaks could they feel superior. There were days, though, when the midgets served other purposes than entertainment. Often, altogether too often, he took great amounts of blood from their veins, in order to play around with it in the laboratories reserved for German 'scientists'. The poor midgets grew paler and weaker as time

94

went on, although Dr Mengele paid generously for the blood he took, by giving them a double ration of bread on such days. The ordinary bread ration, the same we received, was insufficient even for midgets. I shall never forget the little lady midget who told me one day that the double bread ration made her so happy that she did not even mind the cruel, painful and sickening process which made her earn it.

As an SS officer who enjoyed three-course dinners of, say, thick tomato soup, half a fried chicken and a scoop of vanilla ice cream, Mengele was totally detached from the depravation and hunger that his dwarf specimens daily suffered. Whenever he saw them, he would exclaim, 'Surely you've enough to stuff yourself with!' Hungry as they were, they never dared to complain. Most Auschwitz inmates showed grave symptoms of emaciation and Mengele did try to improve the diet of his specimens. Still, some milk soup, a slice of white bread, a tea-spoon of beet-jam, a slice of cheese and a piece of sausage – indulgences that other inmates could not even dream of – hardly improved it enough for the Ovitz group. They were constantly, severely fatigued from the loss of blood.

He gave us some porridge, baby food, but we had passed the age and hunger drove us crazy. The children were always crying for food. One of the Slomowitz boys said, 'You're small, you don't need to eat much, give me your portion, I have to grow.' He constantly threatened to tell Dr Mengele the secret of us not really being family if we didn't give him our food. One day, I had enough and grabbed his hand, pulled him out of the barrack, and pointed up at the smoking chimney at the end of the camp. 'Go tell Dr Mengele, that's where he'll immediately send you and your family!' That reduced him to silence.

Analysis of the surviving lab reports shows that Mengele divided the Lilliput group into subsections. On different dates, he would summon the males and not the females, the dwarfs and not the average-sized ones, or only mothers and children.

> He made never-ending comparisons. He drew blood from our older dwarf sisters who were born to another mother, comparing it to ours to see if we were really from the same father. He compared our blood to that of our tall sisters to see in what way it was different – he couldn't stop wondering how such a high quota of dwarfs could be produced from two tall mothers and one dwarf father.

No special forms were printed for the experiments, and Mengele had to use the standard medical forms issued by the 'Hygienic Bacteriologic Laboratories of the Waffen-SS' for the soldiers' sick parade. By the entry for 'SS rank and number', he filled in the name of the prisoner and his Birkenau number; by the entry for 'clinical diagnosis', he wrote *Zwerge* (dwarf); and by the entry for 'address of transmitting office', he indicated the sub-camp and barrack where the Lilliput group was sequestered. He personally signed each lab form with his flamboyant signature, followed by his full rank. The forms indicate that the Lilliput blood samples were sent to the laboratory of the SS-Hygiene Institute in block 10 of Auschwitz. Far from recording any effort to break the genetic code for dwarfism, the surviving forms reflect, instead, the routine healthcare procedures of the 1940s: the laboratory checked the blood for 'Takata-Ara' and 'Rest-NaCl' as well as vitamin C, in order to trace kidney problems, liver function and typhus.

'Looking at the remaining medical tests done on the dwarfs, it seems that although Mengele acted according to the practices of his time, he had no idea what he was looking for. Hence the repeated tests and the large amounts of blood he took,' observes Professor Raphael Falk of the Hebrew University's Department of Genetics. More sophisticated tests had to be performed at the Kaiser Wilhelm Institute in Berlin. Elizabeth Ovitz recalled that she once saw in Mengele's clinic a box of big, new syringes that had arrived from Berlin; the inscription on the outside of the box read, 'The Protected Jewish Hungarian Dwarf Inmates'. Her account is confirmed by Professor von Verschuer himself, reporting to the *Deutsche Forschungsgemeinschaft* that 'blood samples are being sent to my laboratory for analysis' by 'my post-doctoral assistant, MD Ph.D. Dr Mengele'. Whenever a lab form returned with the stamp 'Blood Homolyzed Condition not Separable', blood had to be taken again. The medical forms show that because of laboratory failure, Elizabeth Ovitz had to give blood for a Wassermann test three times in ten days. It's hard to comprehend why Mengele insisted several times on looking for syphilis in the children as well, including eleven-year-old Judah, nine-year-old Helene, eight-year-old Batia and even baby Shimshon. They, as well as the adults, all proved negative.

NINE

AUSCHWITZ-BIRKENAU, JULY 1944

From the first frame, the story of *Snow White and the Seven Dwarfs* enchanted Dina Gottlieb. This first-ever full-length animation film became a box office hit at the same historical moment that anti-Semitic laws barred Jews from public places in German-occupied Prague. The fragile, blonde, blue-eyed art student knew the Disney film virtually by heart. She had seen it half a dozen times and each time she had risked her life to do it, for each time she had removed her yellow star to slip into the cinema. In September 1943, Dina and her mother Johanna were sent to Auschwitz-Birkenau, where they were placed in the Czechoslovakian 'Family Camp'. In an effort to mask the horrors of the place from their children, the Czech Jews set up a barrack for playing and studying. Dina volunteered to decorate the walls of this bizarre island of sanity: 'I painted a meadow with some trees, and was about to insert cows or sheep when I noticed that all the children had gathered behind me. I turned and asked what they wanted, and in a chorus they all shouted, "Snow White and the Seven Dwarfs!"' Dina duly painted a graceful Snow White dancing with Dopey, surrounded by clapping dwarfs, one of whom played an accordion. Her large, brightly coloured fresco inspired the children to write and stage their own version of the fairy tale. They named it 'Snow White in Auschwitz'.

The fresco inside block 31 drew the attention of an SS doctor, who reported it to Mengele. Certain she was going to be gassed or shot, Dina Gottlieb was terrified when she was summoned to Mengele's office. As she recalls it, Mengele was leaning behind a tripod and looking through a camera at a group of Gypsies standing in front of him. He beckoned her to approach and take a look – he was not satisfied with the quality of the colour in photographs previously taken. Might she be able to more accurately record the skin tones in paint, he wondered? She said she would try.

She was supplied with paint and brushes, and the gates of the Gypsy camp were opened to her for models. As she walked around, she observed scenes of daily life that seemed almost normal: children chasing each other in a game of tag, old women chatting, a young man playing a guitar. It was the sad beauty of a young French Gypsy woman, however, that captured Dina's artistic eye. She found an interpreter and learned that the young woman's name was Céline, that she was twenty, the same age as Dina herself, and had just lost her two-month-old baby daughter due to the lack of milk. 'Tell her that Dr Mengele asked me to make some portraits. I want to paint her. Can she come tomorrow to his office?'

Every morning at seven, when Dina arrived, her subject was already there waiting.

I worked very slowly, hoping to gain time for Céline to get back on her feet. With her grieving face, I painted her as a Madonna veiled in a blue scarf. My workroom was next to Mengele's office, and occasionally he would drop by to inspect the progress. Once, he pulled up Céline's blue scarf – rare conduct for Mengele since he preferred to avoid touching prisoners. He demanded that the Gypsy's ears be emphasised, as part of his racial research.

Céline was suffering from severe diarrhoea and could not digest the camp's coarse, dry black bread. Coaxing a slice of white bread each day out of Mengele, Dina secretly passed it on to Céline. The two young women became friends, and found ways to overcome the language barrier. They had moments of laughter and Céline taught Dina a French song. After a fortnight, Mengele declared the painting complete. Dina would never see Céline again.

Not happy with Gottlieb's apparent preference for good-looking Gypsies, Mengele himself chose Dina's next set of models: a selection of elderly women and men. She got the impression that the doctor wanted simply to acquire visual documentation to support his racial theory, as Dina's series of eleven Gypsy portraits were intended to illustrate the book that Mengele was hoping to write. When she had completed the final portrait, Mengele seated himself in front of her, folded his hands in his lap and asked her to draw him.

I picked up a pencil and looked into his eyes – they belonged to a dead man. The squeak of the chalk on paper was the only sound in the room. He broke the silence, teasingly asking if I noticed anything special about him, something only his wife would know. I hesitated before I dared to point at the mark on his left ear. It was a flat, round disk on his cartilage. Mengele smiled with approval.

In the workroom next to Dina's, a female Polish prisoner took the hand- and fingerprints of all the inmates selected by Mengele for his experiments. Mengele instructed Dina to sketch their skulls, ears, noses, mouths, hands and feet. She nearly fainted, though, when she was ordered to draw a heart that had been split in two and stored in a jar of formaldehyde; the heart's owner had been shot in an attempt to escape.

Then one day, I saw a column of dwarfs trotting towards me, like a film scene. There were seven; I could not believe my eyes. It was as if all my animated dwarfs – Dopey, Grumpy, Sneezy and all the rest – had descended from the mural in the children's barrack and come to life. But I was no Snow White and they were real. I could not help smiling in response to the dwarfs, and to the magic number of seven – there was something optimistic and encouraging about such fragile beings managing to survive here.

On Saturday 1 July, Perla, Avram and Micki Ovitz were driven to the X-ray clinic in the main camp of Auschwitz. Perla was extremely worried: Why had she been summoned again, after already having had seven X-rays taken just three days earlier, together with her sisters Rozika, Franziska and Elizabeth? Had the X-ray revealed something suspicious? She listened to her body and tried to discern if she was experiencing some unusual aches or discomfort. And if she was ill, would she be treated for the disease or disposed of?

Mengele always insisted on rigorous medical procedures. Hungry as the dwarfs were, they had to fast before most of their blood tests, and before every abdominal X-ray they were given laxatives to purge their withered bowels. All night they'd be running to the chamber pot in the corner of their room. The clinic registry book shows that on 1 July at the end of a busy day, the three Ovitzes were scheduled for extended X-ray sessions that could last for hours. While they sat naked on the black swivel-chair, the giant machine was repeatedly adjusted to their size. While all other inmates listed in the register had a single X-ray – an arm, ribs, a leg, a shoulder – the Ovitzes were subjected to ten different shots each. Starting with the head and proceeding to the chest, pelvis, hands and feet, their entire bodies were X-rayed. A few days later, Mengele laid the X-ray negatives on Dina Gottlieb's desk and gave her transparent tracing paper. She pasted the negatives to the window to get more light and followed the contours with her pencil. She immediately noticed the tiny fingers. At first she thought that they belonged to children but Mengele pointed out to her the different bone structure: the fingers had an extra bone that could be detected only in X-rays. This bone, Mengele explained, protruded at the age of eighteen months in individuals born to dwarfism and thus enabled physicians to make an early diagnosis of the condition. Meanwhile, Perla heard nothing from Mengele and she convinced herself that her new set of X-rays had turned up nothing clinically wrong.

Block 28 of the main camp at Auschwitz was equipped with the most sophisticated gear of the time: a photographic workshop and studio. For the most part, the photos that were processed there depicted political prisoners, although Mengele also took advantage of the studio and workshop to compile a photographic record of his research subjects. One of the photographers was Polish prisoner Wilhelm Brasse. He had started working with Mengele at the end of 1943; at first, he photographed Gypsies with gangrenous faces; twins, triplets and even quadruplets came later. Then one day, in the summer of 1944, the truck from Birkenau brought the dwarfs. They all had to undress, and Brasse took the standard shots: one frontal, one from the side, one from the back. In addition, at Mengele's instructions, he also took close-ups of the dwarfs' hands and feet – of particular interest, as their trunks were nearly normal.

The female dwarfs felt ashamed standing naked in front of Brasse, and it was embarrassing for Brasse as well. He had been ordered not to converse with the petite women with beautiful faces; nonetheless, he tried to make them feel at ease, by moving about gently, speaking softly, apologising that he had no choice in the matter. Later on, the SS brought to Brasse's workshop an extraordinarily obese man and a Ukrainian with a giant penis. After he took both men's photos, they were shot outside the studio.

Mengele's research relied primarily on blood tests, X-rays and anthropometric measurements. He had neither the time nor the inclination to test his hundreds of victims personally but then, he did not need to – not with the abundance of expert professionals among the hundreds of thousands of people passing through the gates of Auschwitz-Birkenau: Countess Dr Martina Puzyna, for one. A member of the Polish resistance movement, she was captured and jailed in March 1943, then sent to Auschwitz five months later. Unlike many of the imprisoned medical doctors who were enlisted as aides by the SS physicians, the 42-year-old Puzyna was assigned to hard physical labour. Soon afterward, she contracted typhus and was hospitalised. In Mengele's rounds at the hospital – he checked on patients with bad prognosis – his brief pause at a bed could mean death. He had a quick look at the critically ill Puzyna, and was about to move on when an accompanying doctor remarked that she was an anthropologist from the University of Lvov. Mengele promptly turned back and asked her about her training. Her voice feeble, her speech faint, she mentioned her assistantship with the famous Professor Czekanowski. Impressed by both her scientific and aristocratic background, Mengele ordered Puzyna to report to his office.

Too weak to walk on her own, Puzyna had to be carried

to Mengele's office by two female prisoners. Mengele greeted her by asking what she had been doing at the camp since her arrival; when she answered that she had been carrying heavy stones, he burst out laughing. They discussed anthropology, his interest in comparative research on twins, and the appropriate techniques for measurement. Mengele ordered additional food for her and he had her billeted as a prisoner-physician. 'He was interested in seeing my work capacity restored as fast as possible. Compared to my former situation, it was heaven on earth.'

Dr Puzyna was assigned a special workroom equipped with all the necessary tools – Swiss-made callipers, protractors, compasses, slide rules – and was furnished with two assistants, a female former anthropology student to help her do the measurements and a young girl to note the findings. While Mengele's specimens sat naked for long hours in the unheated room, Dr Puzyna fastidiously measured the length and width and shape of the eyes and nose as well as the various distances from the tip of the eye to the nose, the ear, the other eye, the jaw. 'Turn left! Right! Bend over! Stretch up! Don't breathe!' The inmates were bombarded with orders. Tediously and repeatedly, she measured finger after finger, joint after joint, and every digit was carefully recorded in its proper place on the chart.

When the Ovitzes came in for measuring, they seemed to her to be consistently cheerful. Mengele never indicated to her the purpose of the Lilliputian measurements, although her impression was that his interest in heredity had prompted him to research the topic more thoroughly through pathology. According to Perla Ovitz, the measurements themselves did not hurt, but the process was exhausting and irritating, not to mention degrading. 'It was as if my body was being dismantled into its smallest components, and I had no idea why they measured the same limbs again and again. We had stopped growing ages ago and certainly hadn't expanded or shrunk since the previous week.' As a doctoral student, Mengele had published an article criticising scientists who lost themselves in details; he had argued that 'it is not useful to take as many measurements as possible: one must restrict oneself to the most significant ones'. However, with the unlimited time, human resources and research possibilities available at Auschwitz-Birkenau, Mengele neglected his own golden rule, as he unleashed himself and his team on his subjects in a relentless quest for detail.

A veteran member of the Polish resistance, Martina Puzyna did not abandon her underground activities. She collected incriminating documents regarding Mengele's medical crimes – a sample of her own measurements, a psychiatric test for twins, an X-ray of a female prisoner's lungs – and smuggled them out of the camp in October 1944. Yet she remained ambivalent in her judgement of Mengele's work and insisted long after the war that its results 'were of immense value to the science of anthropology. I recognised this fact at the time, and tried to secure these results for myself. I prepared copies and concealed them in containers, and buried them near my office barrack.'

When the war ended, she hurried to her barrack to retrieve the documents, but she was unable to locate the exact spot where she had hidden them; they had disappeared forever. Documents she had smuggled out earlier have survived, including the anthropometric measurements of 296 Jewish girls and women from Hungary, 111 of them twins, on sheets of fading paper partly damaged by weather and time. Long columns in dense handwriting are filled with each prisoner's number, age and Dr Puzyna's twenty-four different measurements for each person. But even if the buried documents had been found intact, Puzyna would have found them difficult to use, because the monstrosity of the medical–anthropological activities at Auschwitz, which quickly became evident after the war, made Mengele's name notorious.

Dr Miklos Nyiszli, a Jewish pathologist who was forced to work side by side with Mengele, himself witnessed to his daily horror how the inmates were 'exposed to every medical examination that could be performed on human beings. Blood tests, lumbar punctures, exchanges of blood between twin brothers, numerous other examinations, all fatiguing and depressing.'

Kalman Braun was just over thirteen when he arrived at Auschwitz with his twin sister, Judith, and their mother, from whom the children were immediately separated, never to see her again. When he entered his assigned barrack, Kalman felt completely lost. He stood at the entrance, frozen, when suddenly a bespectacled child came forward and said, 'Come, come, boy, you can be with me.' After a second or third glance, Kalman noticed that the hands which greeted him, like the smiling face, were wrinkled. This was no child. 'Where are you from?' asked the man. And as they exchanged names of towns and people they knew, they were surprised to discover a close family connection. For it turned out that the small, kind, bespectacled man was Ludovit Feld, forty years old and a prominent painter in Košice, Czechoslovakia. Feld's older brother was married to Braun's maternal aunt. 'How come I've never heard of you?' asked Kalman. 'Because I converted,' answered Feld. His family first rejected him because of his deformity; once he converted, they ostracised him completely. Nor did Feld's conversion save him from Auschwitz. When the Nazis came, he was sent there with his parents, his three sisters and their children. All fifteen average-sized members of the family had been exterminated; only the three-foot, seven-inch-tall Ludovit was left alive.

'A Jew cannot cut himself from his roots, just as a dwarf cannot alter his size,' says Kalman Bar-On, formerly Braun.

From that day onwards, I shared the same bench and blanket with my Christian relative, sleeping cuddled together like spoons. He was a source of advice, wisdom and comfort, and thanks to him, I had someone in the world. In return, I offered him the experience of parental feelings for the child he never had. In matters of daily survival, Ludovit was the child, and I the adult, since he was afraid of being crushed while queuing for food. With the heat of my body I kept him warm at night.

Feld endured the same cycle of medical tests that the Ovitz family did. Although they shared the same handicap and fate, the Ovitzes resented Feld because of his conversion, and refused to exchange a word with him when all of them sat together in the clinic. Once Dr Puzyna had completed the initial round of anthropometric measurements, Feld was examined by a team of specialists: an internist, a neurologist, a psychiatrist, an ophthalmologist, a dermatologist, a surgeon, a urologist, and an ear, nose and throat man – all of them prisoners, of different nationalities. While Mengele reviewed all the results, he himself conducted none of the actual examinations. According to Feld, Mengele behaved properly and politely during his visits; he even offered the dwarfs cigarettes.

The team of prisoner specialists thus evaluated the dwarfs' entire anatomy by comparing the physical features and psychological characteristics to those of average-sized humans in search of irregularities that would account for their arrested growth. Feld and the other dwarfs supplied samples of urine, stool and saliva that were analysed in the biological, pathological, bacteriological, chemical and serological laboratories of Auschwitz's Hygiene Institute. The laboratories had been fitted with the latest scientific equipment and financed by German academic institutions. When it came to the relation between nurture and nature, Mengele's position was clear: he was looking for signs of heredity everywhere – in the hair, skin and teeth; in the hormones in the blood; in the pigments and blood vessels in the retina of the eye. According to Perla Ovitz, the doctors poured first boiling then freezing water into the dwarf's ears, an experiment that was not only excruciatingly painful but nearly drove them crazy as well; the doctors placed glass eyeballs next to those of the dwarfs, for purposes of colour-identification; drops in the dwarfs' eyes blinded them for hours. 'Healthy teeth were extracted, hairs and eyelashes were plucked out – all to see if there was a difference between us small ones and the tall ones.' The married female dwarf sisters were strapped to a table and subjected to such close gynaecological scrutiny that it left them deathly pale and so shaken that they refused to tell Perla what they had endured. She feared they would do the same to her, but the doctors said, we'll wait with this one, she's too young for it.

All the medical victims in Auschwitz had their own, ever-growing medical files, with diagrams, charts, photographs, X-rays and test results. As Mengele had no access to their medical records in Rozavlea, and since the dwarfs had brought no documents with them, he grilled them endlessly with questions regarding their origins and family history. Again and again, they had to repeat the story of their father and his two wives, to name every aunt, uncle and cousin, and specify their former occupations and places of residence. Mengele filled his notebooks with scores of names, as each household had ten to twelve members. He pressed them to recall if there were any other dwarfs in their extended family, no matter how often they told him there were none.

Mengele's psychiatrists employed numerous questionnaires to check the Ovitzes' intelligence. Seasoned world travellers locked into Lilliputian bodies, they had Mengele marvelling at their wit and incredulous at their knowledge and insight. At one point, he expressed his intention of exhibiting them at a prestigious research institute in Berlin. The eight members of the Slomowitz family underwent exactly the same thorough examinations as the twelve Ovitzes. Only the Fischmans, mother and daughter, were exempted, as Bassie had been falsely presented as Micki Ovitz's fiancée. Mengele had other plans for the beautiful twenty-year-old.

Being less than content with visual representations of his specimens in X-rays, Dina Gottlieb's illustrations and Wilhelm Brasse's photographs, Mengele also ordered Ludovit Feld to draw his dwarfs and twins. One of the latter was Peter Grünfeld, aged four and separated from his mother and twin sister, who were placed in the women's camp. '*Lajos Baci* ("Uncle Lajos") – that's what we called Ludovit Feld – would place me before a window to catch the light,' Grünfeld remembered.

> He would sit on a small stool with a big sketchbook, slowly drawing me in charcoal. Very quickly, I would lose my patience, fidget around and Feld would rebuke me: 'Sit still on your butt, I can't work when you're moving.' Almost sixty years later, his words still echo inside me.

Feld had to deliver all his paintings to Mengele because any form of creative self-expression by inmates – writing, painting

– was forbidden and punishable by death. But Feld, however, furtively tore small pieces of paper from Mengele's allotment and sketched scenes of camp life that he then hid under the mattress. Under Mengele's instruction, Feld also drew the doctor's own portrait – 'He loved so much to be painted, and forced me to constantly draw him.'

On 23 June 1944, an International Red Cross delegation had visited the ghetto of Theresienstadt, Czechoslovakia, to investigate reports that the Jews there were being transported for extermination. The delegation was scheduled to proceed next to Poland in order to inspect the Czechoslovakian 'Family Camp' at Birkenau. The Red Cross delegates had been highly impressed by the showcase Jewish habitat of Theresienstadt, especially when they were shown postcards written by former residents of Theresienstadt affirming that everyone was alive and well in Auschwitz-Birkenau. What the delegates didn't know was that the postcards had been written under duress just a few hours before their authors were gassed. Also, the cards were all dated two weeks after the gassing. The International Red Cross decided that with everything being so satisfactory, a trip to Poland was an unnecessary investment of time and energy. The Germans no longer had to fear an inspection of Auschwitz-Birkenau. Further camouflage became unnecessary and the liquidation of the 10,000 inmates of the 'Family Camp' could begin.

It was to be Dina Gottlieb's second selection, scheduled for 2 July 1944. The Seven Dwarfs of the fairy tale had saved her from her first selection, on 8 March. She and her mother had been among the twenty-seven people selected for life; 3,800 others were sent to the gas chambers.

Dina's parents had divorced when she was a baby and her father had remarried. For years, Dina and her father had not been in contact; then one day in the 'Family Camp', she saw him, with his new wife and two children. She became very fond of her half-brother, Peter, who was eleven. He was constantly hungry and she smuggled bread to him whenever she could. But she could not save him or anyone else in the family, that awful July.

> We all had to march half-naked before the inspecting eyes of Dr Mengele and his team. I knew them well from my work, and I was friends with one of them, Dr Koenig, Mengele's assistant. Much to my relief, when my turn arrived, he was looking straight into my eyes and not at my naked body.

Gottlieb and her mother, among the handful selected for life, were moved on to the women's camp. Three thousand other young, relatively healthy men and women were selected for slave labour in Germany. The rest, 7,000 Czech Jews, now faced extinction. Perhaps more than any other inmates they were well aware of the camp's real purpose, for they had lived for months right under the crematorium chimneys, eyewitnesses to the hundreds of thousands of new arrivals instantly swallowed by the gas chambers. On 10 July 1944, a curfew was imposed on the 'Family Camp'. Three thousand Jewish Czechs were taken out to be killed. The day after, it was the turn of the remaining 4,000.

With the 'Family Camp' in the process of liquidation, Mengele could no longer house his dwarfs there, as they might mistakenly be gassed with the others. He had to find them new accommodation. For the first time in their lives, the Ovitzes were forced to separate. The women and girls, along with little Shimshon, were taken to the infirmary of the women's camp, while their brothers Avram and Micki, as well as Simon

Slomowitz and his three sons, were sent to the men's infirmary. Their barracks were too far apart to make mutual sustenance possible any longer. They all worried about the uncertain length of their separation and the strong possibility that they would never see each other again.

TEN

AUSCHWITZ-BIRKENAU,
AUGUST 1944

I t was only midday, but Regina Ovitz was so feeble she felt
herself slipping into sleep. She picked up a broken brick
and arranged it under her head. She dozed off immediately on
her makeshift pillow, indifferent to the rough earth beneath
her and to the shrieks of the guards.

From afar, like voices in a dream, she heard fervent shouts:
'Look, Lilliputians! Lilliputians!' The joy in the voices
evaporated inside her as her reverie continued. Suddenly, a
downpour of rain hit her.

Instinctively she coiled herself up to protect her body from
the heavy drops. Only when she became soaked to the bone
did she manage to rouse herself. Shuddering, sleep-drugged,
she looked blearily at the barrack, the wet earth, the broken
brick. The cry 'Lilliputians! Lilliputians!' still echoed inside her
head; it prompted her to circle the barrack and enter a forbidden zone. Then she saw them, on the path across from her: five
little figures.

Twenty-four-year-old Regina was a relative of the dwarfs.
Her grandfather, Israel Meir Ovitz, was the brother of
Shimshon Eizik, the Lilliputs' father. The two families came
from the same village and had travelled on the same train, but

in different cattle cars. All forty members of Regina's family had been killed, while she had been assigned into slave labour to harvest grain in the fields near the camp. Bending her back for hours on end had begun to cripple her. Her head shaven, her arms and legs bare, she'd been sunburned all over in the scorching heat. Abscesses covered her limbs and she could hardly walk. Wracked by pain, she had stopped going to work. She'd have lain listlessly all day on her bunk had it not been for the block elder.

'If they find you in the barrack, you'll be taken to the clinic,' she had warned Regina, out of pity and concern. 'It's a short stop from there to the gas chambers. Go out! Find somewhere to hide and stay there!'

Regina had responded with an apathetic shrug and had not moved. The block elder got her to her feet and pushed her out the door. She told Regina to wait until the others came back from work and only then return to the barrack. That's when Regina hid behind the barrack and fell asleep.

When the rain awakened her, and she saw the dwarfs, Regina recognised them immediately. For the other prisoners the dwarfs' parade was just a curious scene, but for her it was an unbelievable family reunion. She had come to Auschwitz with her grandfather, mother, aunts, uncles and nieces, and she had lost them all at once upon their arrival; but suddenly there they were – her five cousins, Rozika, Franziska, Elizabeth, Frieda and Perla.

They were elegantly dressed, as if for their Sabbath stroll in Rozavlea. I couldn't get near them, so I did all I could to attract their attention, jumping up and down, waving my aching arms and frantically calling out their names. I was afraid that, being escorted by an SS man, they wouldn't dare respond.

But the parade slowed, then halted. They turned their heads and Regina saw their puzzled look.

'Who are you?' asked Elizabeth Ovitz suspiciously. 'I'm Bella, Bellush from Rozavlea,' Regina pleaded, calling out her Yiddish nickname. As one, the five women hid their faces in shock. Without her hair, her body clad in a thin, soaking wet dress, her limbs covered with sores that crumbling paper bandages could not protect, their cousin was unrecognisable. The SS man stepped towards Regina and with the butt of his gun he struck her on the head for interrupting the march. In the excitement of her discovery she didn't immediately feel the pain, but the blow was heavy enough to knock her backward. She stumbled and then, as she leaped away, the soldier shouted, 'Halt or I'll shoot!' He had mounted his gun; Regina froze. She could see the five Lilliputians saying something to the soldier. She could not hear their words, but he lowered his gun. Then they all withdrew, and continued on their way.

Regina stumbled over to the block elder and begged her to find out where the Lilliputians had been taken, for, incredibly, she had found her family. The block elder agreed and took advantage of the relative freedom of movement that block elders enjoyed in the camp. She returned for Regina a half-hour later.

The Ovitz sisters were about to enter the washroom when the two women approached. Their first words to Regina were, 'Where's your mother?' and they all burst into tears when she replied, 'You know pretty well where she is.'

When they met with Mengele two days later, Elizabeth told him that they had discovered a cousin of theirs in the work camp. 'How many more relatives are you going to find here?' Mengele teased her. 'There's just this one,' Elizabeth quickly assured him. Because Mengele wanted to enlarge his research pool, he was ready to be persuaded, and Elizabeth was sent with her block elder to fetch their ailing cousin. For the next sixty years, come any sudden downpour of rain, Regina has shuddered with gratitude for that summer shower in Poland. 'If it wasn't for the rain, I would not have woken up to see the Lilliputians, and with my open blisters I wouldn't have lasted the week.'

Now they were twenty-three. The sixteen women and little Shimshon had a room of their own at the women's camp. The six men were kept with Mengele's male twins and misfits, sharing three wooden bunks in block 14 – the experimentation block in the men's infirmary. Avram and Micki Ovitz needed help for everything, so Simon Slomowitz dressed and undressed them, washed them and helped them clean up at the toilet. Whenever they had no transportation, and had to walk a long way to the clinic, his son Mordechai helped him carry them.

Efraim Reichenberg, who was sixteen when, mistaken for a twin, he was imprisoned with his brother in the experimentation block, remembers Avram and Micki:

Alongside the surprise of encountering dwarfs in the real world and not just in fairy tales, came the astonishment of viewing them with treasure, in the form of prayer shawls and phylacteries. I don't know how they managed to have them but they were the only ones in the whole block and we envied them for that. To be able to meditate in prayer and cry to God, retaining such a significant element of your identity, supplied some remedy to the soul in the hell of Auschwitz.

The camp authorities strictly prohibited religious practice and anyone caught engaging in Jewish ritual was severely beaten for subversion. So when either Micki or Avram stood in prayer, the other dwarf stood guard outside to warn his brother. For their part, the female dwarfs placed themselves in similar peril each week when they plucked threads from their sheets and twisted them into a wick, which, with a small piece of wax, made a Sabbath candle.

The men's infirmary bordered the huge *Kanada* warehouse, which overflowed with personal belongings seized from the masses sent to the gas chambers. The prisoners who worked there illegally traded in food supplies so essential for survival. The Ovitz men managed to find among them messengers to smuggle whatever scraps they could get their hands on to their sisters in the women's camp. Naturally, everyone seized any opportunity to come by an extra morsel of food; the kitchen had a magnetic pull and grovelling before the staff had its rewards. But to the dwarfs, who stood knee-height to the kitchen workers, the boiling pots and sharp carving knives were menacing. On one occasion, the German kitchen supervisor beckoned Elizabeth Ovitz to follow her into her private cubicle. They walked slowly, in silence. When the door slammed behind them, the woman slumped onto her bed. Elizabeth, fearful, stood and waited, and could only wonder what was in store for her. 'Sing me something sad,' said the German woman. Elizabeth breathed a sigh of relief and her mind raced through her repertoire to find one of the songs that had always brought the audience into tears.

'O, yellow rose, if only you could speak, you'd know that life is not worth living,' Elizabeth began hesitatingly, but as the melancholy song flowed forth and tears streamed down the cheeks of her solitary listener, her voice regained its old confidence. Wiping her eyes, the supervisor asked for an encore. 'Wherever you are, forget me not. When you left me, you took my soul with you,' sang Elizabeth, squeezing from every word the utmost of its melodrama. In the end, both women had been deeply moved by the heartbreaking, forlorn melodies; they took care to dry their faces before returning to the kitchen. Elizabeth was secretly rewarded with nigh-incredible bounty: a potato, a piece of bread, an onion, a bulb of garlic. She would repeat her private concerts and her grateful audience of one, sobbing on her bed, would always pay handsomely – so much that Elizabeth could feed her brothers, too.

Regina Ovitz was promptly enrolled in the same cycle of medical examinations and subjected to the same painful tests as her Lilliput cousins. Still, her improved situation quickly revived her – her abscesses healed, her hair grew. Perla taught her how to manage sewing with an improvised needle and thread, and when Regina did some mending for the block elder, she was given a sugar cube.

One of the X-ray technicians was a Czech inmate. He ordered me to take my clothes off, and measured my bust, waist, thighs and the inside of my legs, each of my limbs. When it was over, he asked me if I was hungry. I confessed I was and he gave me a sandwich the likes of which I hadn't seen for ages – made with white bread, a piece of cheese inside, a pepper and a tomato, a heavenly flavour. Before leaving, he put four cigarettes in my pocket. In my village it was unheard of for a Jewish girl to smoke, so after returning to the barrack, I traded them for a piece of pork fat. But since on religious grounds I couldn't use that either, I tried for another exchange. The only thing I managed to get was a small onion. Everyone told me I had been cheated.

●

By August, the mass extermination of Hungarian Jewry was over. The camp authorities now turned to the Gypsies. The Nazi regime had been undecided in its policies towards them: should they be exterminated as an inferior race, or should they be locked away and sterilised as anti-social elements? By 16 May 1944, the die had been cast. The SS surrounded the Gypsy camp in Birkenau in an attempt to lead all 6,000 inmates to the gas chambers. The troopers, however, met with fierce opposition – men and women armed with knives, iron pipes and any metal object, dull or sharp, that they could find – and were forced to retreat. As a result, the camp administration changed its plan. Able-bodied Gypsy women were sent to slave labour camps, and Gypsy men from Germany were sent to the Wehrmacht to serve as live mine detectors.

Karl Stojka, a fourteen-year-old Gypsy, was transferred to Buchenwald, but he was found unfit for work and was to be sent back to Auschwitz – and certain death. Stojka's brother and uncle appealed to the SS, falsely saying that he was not a skinny child but a tough adult dwarf, fit for any work. In normal times, dwarfs were treated for the most part as outcasts who were generally denied employment; in these extreme times, though, deformity could prove to be a lifeline. So Karl Stojka, a average-sized boy, exploited the stereotype of dwarfs famous for extraordinary strength. He was allowed to stay in Buchenwald, survived the war and became a painter.

The liquidation of the Gypsy camp was scheduled for 2 August. After the evening *Appell*, a general arrest was ordered for the whole of Birkenau. All the prisoners curled onto their bunks and listened to the roar of the trucks. They could hear the dogs barking savagely and tried to guess to which part of the camp the SS was heading, and whose turn it was now. Mengele had opposed the annihilation of the Gypsies from the outset, and had tried to sway his superiors against it – not out of sympathy for the *Mischling* (half-breed) Aryans or, as some have speculated, because of his own dark, 'non-Aryan' appearance. Rather, he was simply reluctant to lose a group of his specimens. The Gypsies had served him as a steady pool for blood samples, he had plucked their eyes and extracted their skeletons, which were carefully wrapped in large sacks of strong paper – all to be forwarded to the Kaiser Wilhelm Institute in Berlin, marked 'Urgent! War Materials!' He had always managed to find ways to move his Gypsies through one selection after another and thus preserve them for the sake of his research. Annihilation of the Gypsies totally disregarded his needs and, once it had been initiated, Mengele was not allowed to keep his subjects alive in another part of the camp. For the first time in his Auschwitz career, he faced the limits of his influence – and his human research subjects faced the loss of privilege and protection.

Throughout his year as chief physician for the Gypsy camp, Mengele had developed cordial relationships with its inmates. He had displayed fondness for the twin children and often smiled when they called him 'Uncle Mengele'. But when he received the final order to liquidate the remaining 2,897 Gypsies, most of them women and children, he carried it out obediently and diligently. Wholeheartedly embracing the manhunt for his former favourites, he now made use of their blind trust by enticing boys and girls out of their hiding places with the same candies he had offered them after painful experiments. As he led them to their death, he ignored their frantic pleas.

Listening to the shrieks of the Gypsy women and children that sounded through the night, Dina Gottlieb moaned over the fate that awaited all her painting models. When the Gypsy camp was nearly empty, two more children were discovered hiding. Mengele offered them a ride in his car, as had sometimes been his custom. Only this time the trip ended at the gas chambers.

Even at the scene of the gassing, though, Mengele lost no opportunity to advance his research. A large group of children had already stripped naked and was about to enter the gas chambers when Mengele suddenly pulled aside twelve sets of his twins. The children gathered eagerly around him, for they believed he had come to their rescue. With his special blue chalk, he drew the capital letters 'ZS' on their bare chests. Their faulty German led them to assume they were being singled out as *Zwillings*, twins, but they were actually being marked for dissection – *Zur Sektion*. He then sent them back to the hall. The doors slammed shut. As the granules of Zyklon B were released, Mengele turned to the *Sonderkommando* and ordered them to take great care not to burn the ones he had marked with blue letters but to bring them, instead, straight to the pathology laboratory in the same building.

'In this collection of bodies, there were twins of all ages, ranging from newborn infants to sixteen-year-olds,' remembered inmate-pathologist Dr Miklós Nyiszli.

For the moment the twelve pairs of corpses were stretched out on the concrete floor of the 'morgue'. Bodies of black-haired, dark-skinned children. The job of classifying them by pairs was a tiring one. I was careful not to mix them up, for I knew that if I should render these rare and precious specimens unusable for his research, Dr Mengele would make me pay for it with my life.

Dr Nyiszli conducted his pathological studies on the Gypsy

twins for several days running, and with the greatest possible care. He meticulously prepared every dissection report, which was to stand as the concluding document in each child's personal file. One long afternoon, he and Mengele became immersed in discussion over a group of unresolved pathological questions. Nyiszli did not hesitate to contradict Mengele – 'as if this was a medical conference of which I was a fully fledged member'. It appeared that Mengele was willing to tolerate the inmate's firm assertion to the contrary: when it was time to leave, he gave Nyiszli a cigarette.

A week later, Irene Mengele decided to pay her husband a visit. He had not been home for many months – had not even found time to visit after the birth of his first son, Rolf, in March 1944. She left the baby with Mengele's parents and took the train to Auschwitz. It was a double celebration: her twenty-seventh birthday and their fifth wedding anniversary. In her diaries, which were never published but were made available to biographers Gerald Posner and John Ware, she described happy days in the SS barracks. They swam together in the nearby Soła River and picked blackberries, from which she made jam in his kitchenette. Their delight in their 'second honeymoon' was further enhanced by a most favourable official report on Mengele by his garrison commander, *SS-Standortzarzt* Dr Eduard Wirths:

During his employment as camp physician at the Auschwitz concentration camp, he has put his knowledge to practical and theoretical use, while fighting serious epidemics. With prudence, perseverance and energy, he has carried out all tasks given him, often under very difficult conditions, to the complete satisfaction of his superiors, and has shown himself able to cope with every situation. Furthermore, as an anthropologist he has most zealously used his little off-time duty to educate himself further; utilising the scientific material at his disposal due to his official position, he has made a valuable contribution in his work to the anthropological science.

In addition, Wirths praised Mengele for his 'tact and reserve', while also noting his 'popularity' among his subordinates and the 'respect' they accorded him. Following the report, Mengele was awarded the War Cross of Merit, Second Class with Swords. After the annihilation of the Gypsy camp, he was appointed First Physician of the Auschwitz-Birkenau camp and moved his office to the men's infirmary. He continued to orchestrate the myriad medical tests on his 350 Jewish victims, 250 of them twins and dwarfs, and even intensified them.

The Ovitzes were never told which tests were going to be performed on them on any particular day, but they learned to guess quite accurately by what route the ambulance would take. They would find themselves lying naked and face down on the examination tables, and the bustle of medical activity around them only intensified their anxiety as they wondered where precisely their bodies would be pierced or jabbed or poked, and to what violent and devastating effect.

To be forcibly subjected to a long series of medical tests and trials that one knew were designed to bring about some remedy would be difficult enough, but the Ovitzes felt they were consistently being violated for apparently needless and endless samplings, puncturings and probings. They saw their medical files grow steadily thicker, document by document, yet they could see no medically constructive or beneficial purpose whatsoever behind it all. And it seemed that the tests would never end. Still, after their separation, the clinic afforded the family's men and women their only opportunity to meet. The pain and apprehension caused by the medical tests were thus tempered by the hope of seeing their kin from the other camp. On those rare occasions, the guard would turn away and allow them to exchange news, gossip or a word of comfort.

Solomon Malik was thirteen-and-a-half when he arrived in Birkenau with his parents and five siblings. His father and two of the children were immediately gassed; but it was Mengele's passion for twins that saved Solomon and his twin sister as well as two younger, three-year-old twin brothers. Their mother was kept alive to take care of the toddlers. They had lived in Moisei, a village next to Rozavlea, so Solomon had occasionally snuck into the Lilliputs' performances. Now he was in a barrack with them and they were often taken to the clinic together. As their numbers were called, they would silently mount the ambulance that would drive them to the medical block:

We waited outside the door like strangers and although we went through the same tests, we didn't share or compare our experiences when we returned to the barrack. In Auschwitz, no one moaned about his hardships, as we were all suffering to the same degree. Each minded his own business. You were only interested in your bunk-neighbour if he had a slice of bread you could steal from him. I felt like a slaughtered rooster that keeps on running for a few seconds, oblivious of his slit throat, until he drops dead. We knew we would all end up in the chimney, so there was no point in making friends for the short time we still had.

The last two weeks of August were particularly terrible. The surviving medical records at the Auschwitz State Museum archive show that starting in the middle of the month the

Lilliput group had to endure an increasing number of tests. On 16 August, Simon Slomowitz and his three sons were taken to the clinic with Avram and Micki Ovitz. Blood was drawn for a variety of tests, including syphilis. Two days later, the five dwarf sisters underwent the same tests. On 21 August, eight-year-old Batia Ovitz was driven alone to the X-ray lab in Auschwitz. The next day, a syphilis test was administered on two Slomowitz girls, their mother, and Leah and Dora – all of them average height. Two days later, it was the turn of baby Shimshon and Batia, as well as Elizabeth and Sarah. On 29 August, the four female dwarfs, excluding Perla, were summoned again.

With so many tests, they feared they were entering a new, far more brutal and agonising phase in the research. Or worse, that Mengele was terminating his project and that they would soon be killed. One day, at the end of August, Mengele brought Dina Gottlieb a huge roll of paper. It was so long that she could not spread it open inside the clinic. She took it outside and stretched it out on the ground, holding the corners down with stones. Then, crawling along it, she enlarged various charts, and mapped out an extremely complex family tree. She filled the square frames with names, years and gender, as well as symbols – some large, some small – next to each name. She had no idea what it was all about, but Mengele seemed to her to be very tense those days.

ELEVEN

AUSCHWITZ-BIRKENAU,
SEPTEMBER 1944

It was almost twilight when Mengele entered the Lilliput room at the women's camp. He was holding a small parcel under his arm. 'Good evening, *Herr Hauptsturmführer*,' they chorused, jumping to their feet at the unexpected visit. He signalled them to sit down and rested his boot on a chair. Then, clasping his waist, he announced that tomorrow he would be taking them on a special journey to a beautiful place they had never seen. They had to get ready, he said.

Their faces grew pale. Mengele flashed a grin, in an attempt, it seemed, to put them at ease. He said that they were to wear their finest clothes and that their hair should be perfectly coiffed and their faces made up – for they were going to be appearing onstage in front of some very important people. Before he left, he laid his gift on the low wooden table. For a long time, the Ovitz sisters stared at the parcel, too terrified to move and touch it. Finally, warily, they unwrapped it and discovered to their delight a face-powder compact, crimson rouge, and brilliant turquoise and green eye shadow. Shiny red lipstick was tied together with a matching jar of nail varnish. And there was an extra treat – a bottle of eau de cologne.

Thrilled with Mengele's gift, the sisters fiddled with the make-up. They sniffed the scent and rubbed it joyfully on their skin. They already had their own mirror and a small make-up kit – unheard of in Auschwitz – but the items in Mengele's parcel, they had to admit, were of much higher quality. They went through their few dresses. Each sister selected her most presentable one; then they tried to match each other's colours. Sitting on the low bunk, they reinforced the seams, and with the flats of their hands, smoothed away the wrinkles in the fabric. As they discussed what to sing the next day, they wondered how they would manage without their two brothers with solely feminine voices. In the past, they had sometimes split the troupe and performed in duos or trios, so they decided to trust their fifteen years of artistic experience and just improvise. They did not sleep a wink that night. They lay awake hoping that tomorrow's performance would transform their destiny.

At dawn, Friday 1 September 1944, Sarah and Leah rushed out to get a bucket of water so they could help their sisters wash. They dressed each other and combed each other's thick, black hair. In turns, they held up the small mirror for one or another to powder her face. To their lips, eyes and cheeks they applied a heavy, theatrical layer of make-up. Their glamour restored, they felt jubilant.

Mengele had ordered that the Lilliput Troupe's five female members be accompanied by another contingent, which included their two average-size sisters, Sarah and Leah; baby Shimshon; sister-in-law Dora and her daughter Batia; and Chaya Slomowitz along with her three daughters. Regina Ovitz, Bassie Fischman and her mother Gitel Leah were the only three who had been excluded. With a mixture of envy and worry, they watched the preparations and could not help but wonder what this separation would mean for them.

A truck stopped near their barrack and Perla was struck silent with joy: her brothers, dressed in their best clothes, were sitting inside, as were Slomowitz and his sons.

Indifferent to the convoys' exultation, the prisoners in the yard simply nodded at the spectacle. In the code of Auschwitz-Birkenau, any special gesture – the promise of a journey, a hearty meal – was a deadly omen.

The truck passed through Birkenau's gate, but instead of driving to the main gate of Auschwitz it entered a nearby camp they had always bypassed before. It was the SS residential camp and administrative centre. Well-guarded and off limits, here there were no shabby barracks; no hairless, emaciated inmates who could barely drag themselves around. Instead, spotless brick buildings faced lush green lawns brightened by colourful beds of flowers.

The group of twenty Jewish women and men was escorted to a corner in the shadow of a large, new building. Cars stopped at the entrance and unloaded scores of uniformed SS officers.

They were astounded when china plates and silver cutlery were laid out on the lawn in front of them. For the first time since they had left home five months previously, they were having a proper meal. They balanced their plates, heaped with food, on their laps and strove not to spill anything on their clothes. Delight and indignation accompanied every morsel. The officers entering the building glanced incredulously at the dwarfs' picnic and chuckled.

After a while a sergeant came to fetch them. They walked in a column, the seven Lilliputs in front followed by their family, the Slomowitzes ending the procession.

We tiptoed into the building, hearing muffled sounds amplified by loudspeakers. It sounded like a speech or something. We were heading backstage, when suddenly two men carrying a stretcher with a body shrouded in black passed us by. We were numb. Where was Dr Mengele? We hadn't seen him all day. Where had he brought us? Was this going to be our end too?

Nevertheless, eager to be back in the limelight, they managed to stifle their apprehension. They did wonder, though, why their tall sisters, the Slomowitzes and the children, none of whom had any theatrical experience, were being led to the stage with them.

'Off you go,' the sergeant whispered. Marching forward in a long line, they mounted the stage. To their relief they saw Mengele at the front of the stage. A solemn master of ceremonies, he waited for them to take their places in a line that stretched from one end of the stage to the other.

The auditorium was packed; they had never seen so many medals and decorations. There was a murmur in the hall. The audience stared at the assortment of men, women and children onstage. The Lilliputs smiled in confusion, for they did not know how to begin. They looked to Mengele for a cue.

He turned to them and snapped, 'Undress!'

Aghast, their hands trembling, they fumbled with their buttons. The Lilliputs tried to shrink into themselves and wished they could disappear altogether. They bent their shoulders forward, in an attempt to cover their genitals with their hands. 'Straighten up!' barked Mengele. Standing to attention like soldiers on parade, they fixed their eyes at imaginary points at the end of the hall to avoid seeing their naked relatives next to them.

It was not the first time Mengele, like some freak-show impresario, had exhibited the Lilliputs and their group. 'This zeal had earned him great praise,' recalls Auschwitz survivor

Ella Lingens-Reiner. But in the past the show had always taken place in the privacy of their room or in his clinic.

We always had to be prepared for Dr Mengele and wear make-up, since he had told us, 'You're something special, not like the rest of them, and I want my fellow officers and professors to see you.' He would bring them to our room and we would stand to attention until he allowed us to sit down. He used to boast to his visitors, 'I have a whole family; they are like dolls, only real.' Sometimes we remained dressed, sometimes we were naked. The guests would touch our bodies and measure us and repeatedly inquire about our parents. Once Dr Mengele asked us to sing – we sang something in German, and they all clapped their hands. Dr Mengele was so pleased that he then shook hands with each of us.

Since 1938, Mengele had been engaged in a race against Dr Hans Grebe. Three years his junior, Grebe was also an assistant to Professor von Verschuer and specialised in dwarfism. The rivalry between the two men became increasingly more heated and, by 1944, Grebe had already published two papers on dwarfism, in part because he was able to spend his time doing research in Berlin. He was about to become the youngest professor in Germany. In Auschwitz-Birkenau, Mengele was conducting himself as if he had established his own research institute, a modest rival to the Kaiser Wilhelm Institute. To pursue his project, Mengele had recruited several distinguished inmate-doctors and put them to work in his well-equipped laboratories. He occasionally organised colloquiums at his Birkenau facilities, and chaired discussions of case studies.

But 1 September 1944 was a very special occasion: it was the inauguration of the new *Lazarett* (hospital) in the SS camp.

Many high-ranking guests from Berlin were in attendance and Mengele was the main speaker. After Mengele's years in uniform, away from the podium, the Auschwitz conference was his chance to retrieve his place in the academic limelight. His wife, Irene, sitting proudly in the audience, noted the title of his lecture in her diary: 'Examples of the Work in Anthropological and Hereditary Biology in the Concentration Camp.' Mengele was, in fact, going public with his work for the first time. Until then, afraid of competition and sabotage, he had been very secretive. After the war, his close assistant, the prisoner-anthropologist Dr Martina Puzyna, testified before the Frankfurt general prosecutor that, even to her, he did not reveal 'what he was aiming for in the final analysis and evaluation of the measurements we conducted for him'. Mengele kept everything locked in his cabinets. Dr Lingens-Reiner would not forget her surprise when one day he proudly invited her to glance at some of his files. She leafed through the papers, which were full of charts and measurements of heads and bodies of twins and dwarfs. 'Isn't it interesting? What a pity all this will fall into the hands of the Bolsheviks,' he said. Lingens-Reiner would continue to be struck by this startling moment of indiscretion.

In the *SS-Lazarett*, Mengele stepped behind his trembling human display. He stood near the large map of the dwarfs' family tree that Dina had drawn. Perla remembered the scene in great detail:

> Dr Mengele started lecturing, and I couldn't stop thinking about the long billiard cane he was holding. He was very knowledgeable about our history, including our father's two wives. Whenever he mentioned the name of one of us, he pointed at the map and then touched us with his cane. 'This is Rozika, daughter of the first wife; this is her sister; this is Avram, the first son of the second

wife; these are his wife and daughter, who are normal-sized.'
He then moved to the podium and from his notes described the
tests he did on each of us. From time to time he turned to us
and touched various of our body organs with his billiard cane.
It lasted for ages – we nearly dropped from fatigue. It was hot
and we were dripping sweat and shame, but no one offered us a
glass of water.

•

Since the start of the twentieth century, genetics had been at the
forefront of science, perceived as holding the potential for the
promulgation of positive traits and the eradication of negative
ones. Some geneticists had tried to develop blood tests by which
they could establish the physiological basis for dwarfism. There
was also a popular theory that the condition might be rooted
in hormonal deficiencies. Thus, the thyroid gland came under
close scrutiny, as some types of dwarfism were known to result
from the lack of a specific hormone. Other speculation centred
on accidents at birth and lack of vitamins. For their part, the
leading German geneticists constructed complex family trees
as a means of tracing the progress of the malformation. While
still a university student, Mengele studied *Human Heredity*
by the renowned German scientists Baur, Fischer and Lenz.
The work described various kinds of restricted growth and, to
classify the Ovitz dwarfism, Mengele embraced the authors'
definition of a condition known as 'achondroplasia', in which
'the limbs are dwarfed, whereas the head and the trunk are of
approximately normal size'.

Recessive inheritance of dwarfism is much more common
than dominant inheritance, and the Ovitz family offered an
excellent example in which a negative trait was inherited

through a dominant gene, not in one instance but in seven, and in seven instances out of ten – a rarity indeed. According to inmate-pathologist Nyiszli, however, Mengele was aiming not only 'to discover the biological and pathological causes of the birth of dwarfs and giants' but also to demonstrate that 'in the course of its long history, the Jewish race had degenerated into a people of dwarfs and cripples'.

Within many cultures and many ideologies, the term 'dwarf' has in fact had a pejorative or even degrading connotation. One of the favourite images of Jews in Nazi propaganda was of a bald, fat and hunchbacked dwarf. A caricature published on the front page of *Der Stürmer* in July 1939, for example, shows such a dwarf Jew struggling with a blond, athletic, half-naked Aryan. The Aryan is drawing a sword and the caption reads: 'He who subordinates himself to the Jews is only a dwarf, never a hero.' But despite his deeply held convictions concerning the Jews' racial degeneracy, after three-and-a-half months with the Lilliputs, Mengele actually had very few findings to report. He knew that the greatest impact he could make upon his peers that September day was simply the sheer presence of the Ovitz dwarfs onstage. He bombarded his audience with figures and details about the complex family, going so far as to include the eight Slomowitzes – who of course were no kin to the Lilliputs.

Perla Ovitz recalled that an officer in the front row was filming them with his movie camera. Fifty years later, Hannelore Witkofski, a historian and advocate in Germany for the rights of short people, and Shahar Rozen, an Israeli film director, searched on Perla's behalf through various archives in Germany and Poland, but could not find the film.

It annoys me to this day that our naked humiliation was preserved for all to see. Maybe Dr Mengele took the film with him when he fled to South America and it's hidden somewhere. Maybe his wife or son have it. I won't feel easy about this until it's found and destroyed.

The search has been documented in a film titled *Liebe Perla*.

•

Colleagues, prisoner-doctors and historians have expressed varying opinions of Mengele's professional demeanour and scientific ability. 'He was the most pleasant companion. I have only the best to say of him,' stated SS Dr Hans Münch, Mengele's colleague at the Waffen-SS's Institute of Hygiene in Auschwitz. Münch also described both Mengele's elegance and intelligence as outstanding in the 'intellectual desert' that was Auschwitz. On the other hand, some of the inmate-doctors have characterised Mengele in less flattering terms, pointing to his plodding diligence, pedantry and his fanatical, enthusiastic devotion to his concept of genetics. According to anthropologist Martina Puzyna, 'It cannot be said that research on twins was a Nazi idea alone. It has always played an important role in anthropology.' Mengele's research on heredity in twins and dwarfs, then, was in line with accepted anthropological methods of his time; in Puzyna's view, what gave him a singular scientific advantage was the unlimited human pool at his disposal in Auschwitz. Thus, he could conduct his research 'on a big scale, to gain results by statistical methods, with acceptable values', she testified. Although 'Mengele was clearly capable of killing people to obtain certain research results', he was 'at times genuinely interested in serious, factual scientific work. Having myself worked as a scientific assistant, I deemed him capable of doing serious work.'

But others who worked with Mengele have been far less generous in their assessment: 'How we hated this charlatan! He profaned the very word "science"!' writes Olga Lengyel, who was part of Mengele's medical team. 'His experiments lacked scientific value – they were no more than foolish playing.' And while pathologist Dr Nyiszli concurs with Dr Puzyna that medical research was 'the most important thing on Mengele's agenda', he also dismisses that research as 'nothing more than a pseudo-science. Just as false was his theory regarding the degeneracy of dwarfs and cripples, sent to the butchers in order to demonstrate the inferiority of the Jewish race.' Finally, with the sobriety that comes from historical distance, Robert Lifton observes in *The Nazi Doctors* that 'Mengele's method was a product of his scientific training and early experience, his Nazi ideology and the peculiarities of the Auschwitz settings.'

•

When Mengele finished his lecture, the audience rose to applaud. Some SS officers left for lunch, but many others darted forward onto the stage. The swarm of uniformed men soon engulfed the Lilliput group. They stood motionless, naked, waiting for permission to dress. Shimshon Ovitz, only eighteen months old at the time, has no memory of the Lilliputs' humiliation, but he notes that throughout the years his aunts and uncles would constantly allude to or recall 'the performance'.

The SS officers wanted to see us from close range. They stared at the doll-like figures and peppered us with invasive questions. One of them came close to my mother – she was holding me in her arms – and touched her naked breast. I flung out my hand, so I'm told, and pulled at his swastika with all my might. It fell to the floor, and my mother panicked and started crying, sure he would draw his pistol and shoot us on the spot. She then stooped to pick up the swastika but the officer calmed her down, '*keine Angst, keine Angst* – never mind, he's just a baby, he doesn't know what he's doing'. He picked it up himself, but we only relaxed when he left the hall.

Once Mengele's presentation was over, the Lilliput group was offered some refreshments but they were too devastated to touch a thing. The truck took them back to the camp and the families separated again. Entering their barrack in silence, the women and girls were greeted with amazement, as if they had returned from the dead. Back in the SS compound, the Mengeles looked forward to another week of vacation before the cheerful, easygoing Irene had to return home. But on the eve of her departure, she contracted diphtheria, which quickly developed into an inflamed heart muscle. She was hospitalised with a high fever, her devoted husband then visiting her three times a day.

In truth, the small empire Mengele was running in Auschwitz was a thorn in the flesh of his fellow SS doctors. They envied his stardom; they resented him for stealing the show at the *Lazarett* inauguration event; they coveted the acclaim he had won for his research. The latter had earned him not only a medal but also a recommendation for promotion outside Auschwitz. Some of his SS colleagues tried to emulate him by concocting research topics and employing inmate-doctors to labour on their behalf. Others, like SS Dr Heinz Thilo, actually tried to sabotage Mengele's research. Thilo – who owes part of his notoriety to his epithet for Auschwitz: *Anus Mundi* (anus of the world) – was known to whistle opera arias while performing his selections, just like Mengele. Thilo had been in the camp longer and they were the same age, yet already Mengele was a *Hauptsturmführer*, while Thilo was only an *Obersturmführer*. Thilo was waiting for the right moment, which soon came his way.

To take some joy in the last days of summer, a football game was organised at the men's infirmary one afternoon. Two teams of twin boys were kicking the ball, to the cheers of the crowd. Judah and Joseph Slomowitz were among the players, and their father and brother encouraged them from the touchline. Avram and Micki Ovitz watched the game from their small stools. Suddenly, the tall frame of Thilo shadowed the yard. 'Why are you all idling about?!' he demanded, and called for an immediate *Appell*. They all stood in line. Then they had to march in front of Thilo.

'Your number!' he barked at those he chose, and the *kapo* (an inmate assigned to supervise the other inmates) noted it down. A curfew was set, the barrack was sealed and the doors were boarded. As Mordechai Slomowitz told us,

Dr Thilo selected dozens of twin children, as well as Avram and Micki Ovitz and my two young brothers, who were eleven and thirteen. They were all put aside in the barrack. The double portion of food brought in that evening was a sign they were doomed. The Nazis wanted you to gain weight so you could burn more quickly. My father and I decided that when the truck to the crematorium arrived, we would mount it as well. The SS wouldn't mind killing another two.

'Let's pray,' said Avram Ovitz, and they all wept and supplicated.

Zvi Spiegel was a 29-year-old twin whom Mengele had placed in charge of the twin children; he became known as the *Zwillingsvater* of Auschwitz. Spiegel, himself a victim of Mengele's experiments, acted not only as father to all the twins, comforting and encouraging them, but also as Mengele's eyes and ears in the barrack.

> Mengele warned me frequently that if anything happened to the twins, I would be hanged. Somehow I managed to open the bolted door of the barrack. I've no idea how I dared, but I ran towards Mengele's office. It was dangerous, because the SS on the watchtowers shot anyone who ran in the camp, but I knew time was of the essence. The SS guards in Mengele's clinic knew me. I told them, 'I need to speak to Dr Mengele!' Imagine a Jew wanting to speak to Mengele. This was a bit like saying you wanted to speak with God. Only it was easier to have a hearing with God. To this day I don't know why they didn't shoot me for making the request.

The guard picked up the phone and dialled. 'The *Zwillingsvater* is here, he says Dr Thilo was in the infirmary this afternoon and selected some of your twins and dwarfs!' If Thilo had counted on Frau Mengele's illness to provide him the opportunity to damage his rival's human collection, he had got it wrong. Mengele's reaction was swift – not only did he cancel the selection, but he also dispatched one of his subordinates to ensure that no harm befell his research subjects.

Irene Mengele had suffered further complications from the diphtheria and she badly needed her husband's attention, but he nonetheless continued to fulfil all his duties, including his selections on the ramp. On 29 September, he welcomed 2,499 Jews from the Theresienstadt ghetto. He sent 1,900 of them to their deaths. The rest he admitted to the camp. Among them were three pairs of teenage twin boys.

September, season of the Jewish high holidays, was favoured by the Nazis for especially extensive killings. In the arrest warrant and indictment issued in Frankfurt am Main in January 1981 by the twenty-second criminal division of the Frankfurt *Landgericht*, Mengele was charged in absentia with having sent 328 children to the gas chambers on Rosh Hashanah – the Jewish New Year's festival – in 1944. In addition, the charge read, during the fast of Yom Kippur a week later, 'he hung a batten between the goal posts of a football pitch' and 'approximately 1,000 children under the required height' were sent on to their deaths.

TWELVE

AUSCHWITZ-BIRKENAU, OCTOBER 1944

For some time now, the Lilliput Troupe had been living not only in a house of horror, but also in an environment appallingly unsuited to their size where every object presented a monstrous obstacle. Even short distances seemed vast and arduous to their undersized, bowed legs and tired feet. Their situation was made slightly more bearable by Mengele; he had small wooden stools built for them in the camp carpentry shop, which was located on the first floor of crematorium II. Wherever they went, they carried their stools like artificial limbs so they could rest in the course of a journey that was bound to quickly exhaust them. The Lilliputs had always disliked being lifted like babies, partly out of fear that they'd be dropped, or placed in chairs too high for them to get out of. The stools thus became their makeshift ladders to independence.

When the weather was nice and they were not in the medical clinics, the Ovitz ladies would go outside to the square in front of their barrack, set up their stools, and watch the world go by, just as they had done in Rozavlea. Remarkably, in spite of the horrific events transpiring daily in the camp – or maybe because of them – the magnetic Lilliput Troupe continued to attract public attraction. The camp was always abuzz with rumours;

the tale of dwarfs basking in the sun or strolling about on parade soon spread. Even inmates from distant barracks would find ways to pass by and gaze. Some of the Lilliputs' former fans were surprised to discover them behind barbed wire, as they had not known the dwarfs were Jewish. Others were amazed and delighted that these star performers had not been changed drastically by the camp, for there they were, still in all their finery – as if the world had not really been turned upside down.

Auschwitz was a Babel of tongues and nationalities, from Italian and French to Greek and Polish. Having lost their families, inmates naturally gravitated to any surviving fellow townspeople, and to anyone who spoke their language. So it was that even strangers from Maramureş County came to chat with the Lilliputs – to enquire who had died, who had survived. Ibby Mann, whose theatre-loving father had invited the Lilliput Troupe to dinner in his home after one of their performances in the happy days before the deportation, recalls:

> Mother knew they were expert dress makers and at the end of the evening she presented them with a colourful fabric to make outfits for their show. Only my twin sister Sarah and I had survived the selection, so when I heard that the Lilliputs were in the camp I rushed over to see them. They not only remembered their visit but had been looking for us in the camp. One of them went back into their barrack returning with a dress made from the fabric mother had furnished. I caressed the doll-sized dress and cried. A matching shawl accompanied the dress and they let me have it – the only memento I had left from my mummy.

The Lilliputs clearly enjoyed the other inmates' pilgrimages – they had always loved being the centre of attention, and they welcomed this relief from the bleak anonymity of Auschwitz.

They also appreciated their relative luck, so they were always cheerful and patient with their less-fortunate visitors. The Lilliputs also made an impression on inmates who had previously never heard of them. When testifying about Mengele's atrocities before the public prosecutor in Frankfurt twenty-five years later, a number of survivors recalled seeing dwarfs in the camp. Nurse Regina Teresa Krzyzanowska remembered the 'Lilliputians who were in block 23 and came to the camp from Hungary. They were whole families. They were circus artists and tried to stage a few shows.' In her memoir *Sursis pour l'Orchestre*, Fania Fénelon, a singer in the Auschwitz women's orchestra, speaks of '[dwarfs] jumping, doing acrobatics, shrieking at the top of their voices; there was a banal scene of clowns, their chubby little hands slapping ridiculously: what a pathetic sight'. The recurrent mistaken notion that the Ovitzes were circus performers may have arisen from the tradition that stereotypes dwarf artists as clowns and jesters. The Lilliput Troupe's style of performance was, by necessity as well as choice, far removed from clowning – their bowed legs and short, weak arms prevented them from doing any acrobatics whatsoever.

With brightly coloured dresses, painted faces and coiffeured hair, the dwarfs were a surreal, mirage-like presence in Auschwitz-Birkenau. Witness Elzbieth Piekut, for instance, recalls 'seeing a sort of Lilliputian family camp through the barbed wire, the men strolling about in tall hats and frock coats, the women in crinoline dresses'. And Fania Fenélon similarly describes a scene of Lilliput men wearing frock coats and bow ties and women in gala dresses made from magnificent fabrics.

They were all sinking under the burden of jewellery, necklaces hanging down to their bellies, double bracelets on their wrists, their earrings lightly touching their shoulders, framing their painted faces, diamonds shining in their well-coiffeured hair. The genuine mixing with the fake, immense wealth, incredible!

Growing up with fairy tales about dwarfs, children, too, were attracted to the Lilliputs' barrack. Starved for amusement, they frequently visited the Lilliput yard. Leah Nishri notes that

someone who was not imprisoned in Auschwitz-Birkenau will find it impossible to understand what it was like seeing dwarfs there. The selection on the ramp was so severe that only the strongest and fittest could pass it, and even then many would not survive the harsh conditions. As an orphaned, desolate girl of fourteen-and-a-half, I gained heart from these small handicapped people surviving intact against all the odds.

The teenager savoured the presence of the dwarfs for a few hours and was astonished when a tall, robust woman from the group grasped her daughter's hand and said, 'Let's go meet Daddy.' It was Dora Ovitz and her eight-year-old daughter Batia.

Those totally ordinary words hit her like lightning. As if hypnotised, Leah followed Dora and Batia to the electrified barbed wire fence, where Avram Ovitz was waiting on the other side, along with Mordechai Slomowitz, who carried the stool for him.

I watched the reunion from a distance with aching, not believing this glimpse of normality. There were no families in the camp and if a woman had a young child both would be automatically sentenced to death. In my curiosity, I followed them back to their barrack, where they had a room for themselves, private and very spacious. Another dwarf lady appeared – decades later

I recognised her on TV and learned that her name was Perla Ovitz. She was wearing a reddish-brown leather coat, padded with fur. A tall woman was walking behind her, carrying a bucket filled with potatoes. One potato was an unattainable dream to us, but a full bucket? In the camp I had never seen such a quantity. Perla was walking proudly, like an elegant lady returning with her servant from shopping. No other Jew in the camp walked with so much self-assurance. It seemed these people could get whatever they wished.

Mengele's painter, Dina Gottlieb, gained a similar impression:

They did not look trapped like we did. They seemed hopeful and cheerful unlike the rest of us, who were frightened and pessimistic. It seemed they did not believe they'd be killed. They had a very good life before the war as VIPs, and continued to see themselves as special and privileged.

Living in the same barrack as the dwarfs, Sara Nomberg-Przytyk was less than admiring. In her memoir *Auschwitz: True Tales from a Grotesque Land*, she derides them for their endless prattle about Mengele:

'How beautiful he is, how kind,' they repeated it every minute. 'How fortunate that he became our protector. How good of him to ask if we have everything.' They almost melted in adoration. They were accustomed to exposing themselves in public, and this was like another show for them.

One afternoon, continues Nomberg-Przytyk, Mengele entered the barrack, and

ABOVE 'Through thick and thin, never separate' was Batia Ovitz's dictum to her children. *Top row, l to r*: Leah, Simon Slomowitz (their coachman and handyman), Sarah, an unidentified cousin; *middle row*: Arie, Frieda, Batia Ovitz, Avram, Micki; *bottom row*: Perla, Elizabeth. Rozavlea, 1927.

LEFT They excited audiences, winning applause when they sang in their unique high-pitched voices. *Top*: Rozika and Franziska; *bottom*: Elizabeth and Frieda. Rozavlea, 1930s.

Micki, in a cabaret-style publicity photo, 1930s.

Elizabeth impersonating Charlie Chaplin.

SUVENIR DE TRUPA LILIPUT

'Souvenir from the Lilliput Troupe', a fan card of the kind Micki handed out to the SS upon arrival at Auschwitz-Birkenau.

ABOVE The Ovitz family leaving the ghetto, May 1944.

RIGHT Medical document, signed by the 'Angel of Death', Dr Mengele, instructing that blood will be taken from Perla Ovitz.

An order to take blood for a syphilis test from Simon Slomowitz, his sons and the two male dwarfs.

The Slomowitz family: father Simon, sons Judah and Joseph, daughters
Helene and Serene, and mother Chaya. Sighet, 1946.

Avram with his wife Dora and ten-year-old daughter Batia. Sighet, 1946.

P
R
O
G
R
A
M
M
E

P
R
O
G
R
A
M
M
E

I.

1). Marsch
2). Hoffmans erzeilung
3). Hamavdil
4). Hitz
5). Je suis seul ce soir
6). Cu dona soapte dulci
7). Dus pintele Jid
8). Fiarin Fiarel
9). Nö
10). Hikovtzi
11). Di veiber

II.

Komedie in 1 act
DI FALSE LIEBE

Anteil nemmer :

Ovici Dolfy
in rol van git bazitzer Kalman Klaps
Ovici Greta
in rol van di almune Madam Flamenzip
Ovici Elisabet
in rol van di gardi dame Lora
Ovici Paula
in rol van di dinst mojd Fania
Ovici Markús
in rol van kutscher Don

Bine bearbeiting in Regie von Jakob Cyterman

ABOVE In Antwerp, Belgium, the Ovitzes resumed their career. Here, a programme from their musical and comedy review.

RIGHT A favourite part of the Lilliputs's act was to bring tall men on stage to offer a comic contrast.

ABOVE Though they were successful artists, for six years the Ovitzes lived in a wooden barrack in an immigrants' camp in Haifa. (*L to r*): Elizabeth, Perla, Rozika, Frieda, Franziska and Avram.

LEFT Frieda and Micki, backstage in Israel, early 1950s.

RIGHT The Israeli
audience responded more
enthusiastically to tragic-
comic material than they
did to songs. Perla (*right*)
and Elizabeth.

BELOW To avoid rivalry,
the Lilliput Troupe split the
leading roles equally. (*L to r*):
Avram, Micki and Perla.

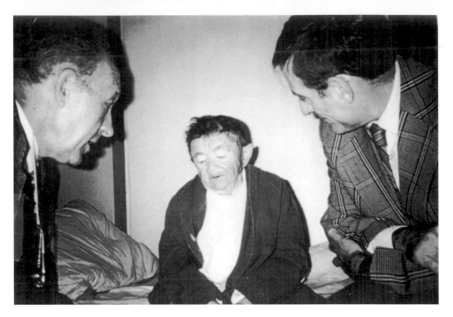

Ludovit Feld with Kalman Bar-On (*left*) and Peter Grünfeld, who shared the experimental block with him. Slovakia, 1989.

The entire Ovitz family. *Back row, l to r*: Sarah, Azriel and his wife Leah and daughter Batia, Moshe Moskowitz (Elizabeth's husband), an unidentified woman, Avram's daughter Batia and wife Dora. *Front row, l to r*: Micki, Franziska, Perla, Elizabeth, Rosika, Frieda, Avram, and Azriel and Leah's son Shimshon. 1949.

we all stood at attention, including the midgets. Next to them, we looked like giants. He looked at them very closely. Then one of them stepped out of the row and fell at his boots. She was just about as tall as his boots. She hugged it with feeling and started to kiss it. 'You are so kind, so gorgeous. God should reward you,' she whispered, enraptured. He did not move for a minute, then he simply shook her off his boots. She fell. She lay there, tiny, spread out on the floor.

Perla Ovitz firmly denies that such an incident ever occurred.

Dr Mengele never yelled or swore at us and, God forbid, never hit us. We all knew he was ruthless and capable of the worst forms of sadistic behaviour – that when he was angry he would become hysterical and literally shake from rage. But even if he were in a bad mood to begin with, the moment he stepped into our room he would immediately calm down, becoming a well-behaved boy. When he was in a good mood people would say, 'he probably visited the little ones'.

And prisoner-doctor Katarzyna Łaniewska seems to confirm this: 'Mengele would often come to barrack 23 where the dwarfs were living, to chat with them and even crack jokes.'

Sara Nomberg-Przytyk's view of the Ovitzes – their boot-high size and their theatrical gestures – may have been distorted by both her envy and her perspective. From her own towering angle, every curtsy or nod of a dwarf could be easily interpreted as servility – even as boot-licking. Of course, there may have been other cause for envy besides the Ovitzes being the treasured subjects of Mengele's research. In fact, they had many things going for them. For one, unlike most inmates, they were fluent in German and could communicate with Mengele and the SS officers. For another, they had remained intact as a family. For a third, as a group, they had managed to maintain some of the glamour attached to their showbiz identity. Wearing their artistic persona enabled them to be detached from the daily misery of the camp and to put up a façade. In their pretty faces and perfumed finery lay much of their appeal for Mengele. He himself was immaculately groomed. His hands were well manicured; his riding crop was polished; his uniform perfectly fit his body, upright and militarily borne; his neatly pressed trousers were inserted into glistening black boots. He found his exquisite dwarfs, with their cheerful nature and theatrical manners, unusually pleasant company. And Perla was aware of the Devil's charm:

> Dr Mengele was like a movie star, only more good looking – he could have got prizes for his good looks. Anyone could easily fall in love with him. Nobody who saw him could imagine that behind his beautiful face a beast was hiding. He was a beautiful beast. Among ourselves we always asked how a man like that could become a Nazi.

In return, Mengele praised the Lilliputs for their appearance. Perla recalls the sorts of compliments he would offer Frieda – the prettiest of them all – and her replies:

> 'How beautiful you look today!' Mengele would say.
> 'I knew that *Herr Hauptsturmführer* was coming, so I took great care to make myself up in his honour.'
> 'If it was indeed for me, do continue to do so. But tell me, before arriving in Birkenau, did you also put on make-up every day?'
> 'Of course I did, I'm an actress!'

If Dr Mengele was not satisfied with Frieda's make-up, he would inquire, 'Are you in a bad mood today? Why didn't you apply your beautiful red lipstick?' Once he said to my sister Elizabeth, 'You've lost weight. That's not good!' When I heard this I panicked and started to cry, knowing that when he said 'it's not good', it had only one meaning: 'To the ovens!' 'Why are you crying?' he asked me. I said, 'Because *Herr Hauptsturmführer* said "it's not good".' Dr Mengele lifted his hand. 'Don't worry.'

Despite the apparently intimate nature of the dialogue, they always took care to address him by his full SS rank and medical title, then to grace it all with 'Your Excellency'. 'We approached him the way one addresses a king, because he was King of Birkenau.'

While the main purpose of Auschwitz-Birkenau was to eradicate its inmates' identity, some professions – mainly music and medicine – did offer better survival prospects. Doctors were employed in the camp clinics and laboratories; musicians played in one of the three camp orchestras – all of them applauded by Mengele, the music lover who whistled arias from Verdi and Wagner while carrying out the selections. For the Lilliputs, he composed a special couplet that he often sang to them:

Auf den sieben Bergen
Habe ich sieben Zwergen.

Behind seven hills
I have seven dwarfs.

In the world of fairy tales, dwarfs always lived behind *sieben Bergen* – seven mountains – but Mengele was also punning here on the proper noun *Siebenbürgen*, the German name for

Transylvania, the region the Ovitzes came from. Because the dwarfs tried hard to please him, he composed another couplet for them:

Die ungarischen jüdischen Zwerge
geschützte Häftlinge.

The Hungarian-Jewish dwarfs
are excellent prisoners.

When he asked them to sing for him, they were reluctant, as they were afraid of what the other inmates might think. 'We don't have our full orchestra with us,' they protested. 'If I can sing *a capella*, so can you,' Mengele answered, and to prove it he hummed a line from a Hungarian Gypsy song that had been making the rounds of the restaurants in central Europe: 'There's only one girl in the world for me.' His joviality somehow injecting confidence into them, for a moment they felt safe in his hands and, as a token, they sang him one of their favourites: 'Come make me happy.'

One day while chatting with the dwarfs, Mengele let slip that ever since childhood he had loved the Grimm Brothers' *Snow White and the Seven Dwarfs*. Never, though, had he imagined such a real-life encounter. The similarity between life and fiction intrigued him: in both instances, the symbolic number of seven; the group of diligent happy dwarfs all living and working together, never separating. Disney's *Snow White* had been a huge success in Hitler's Germany, as well as the rest of Europe. In Disney's animated film, the dwarfs had their own band and they played instruments similar to those of the Ovitzes: guitar and accordion, bass and drums. Audiences loved the tale's moral, in which the legendary dwarfs, living apart from society in the thick of the forest, have each – along with Snow White – discovered the benefits of mutual help. Disney's dwarfs protected their princess and secured her future, while she attended to their daily needs.

Historically, in their traditional role as court jesters, dwarfs were the only subjects who dared speak their minds to the king without paying with their lives. Likewise, the Ovitzes played jesters to Mengele's king, and dared to voice their complaints.

'Forgive me for asking, Your Excellency, but when will this all be over so we can go home?' asked Frieda, with all the charm she could conjure up.

'What do you mean, *meine Liebe*? Don't I have a family that I want to see? I can't go home myself!' Mengele raised his voice. 'I'm not working here for pleasure but under orders. You've got nothing to complain about! As long as you're here with me you're better off!'

Weakened by hunger and suffering the stress of countless tests, the small and skinny eighteen-month-old Shimshon Ovitz preferred crawling to walking. Mengele could not decide whether the child was a late developer or was displaying the early signs of dwarfism. The blond, long-haired boy never cried and he had yet to start speaking. Still, emulating his mother and aunts, Shimshon tried to stand to attention whenever Mengele entered the Lilliputs' room. He had never known his father, Azriel, who had been taken away for slave labour before he was born:

My mother told me that whenever I heard the name 'Dr Mengele' I would say '*tatti*', and that word was the only one I knew. When he came over to see us, I would toddle towards him mumbling '*tatti, tatti*'. Mother apologised to Dr Mengele: 'He thinks the *Herr Hauptsturmführer* is his father.' But he was actually very pleased, and smiled: 'No I'm not your father, just

Uncle Mengele.' He showed affection for me, playing with me and giving me candies and toys that had belonged to children he killed: 'Look what Uncle Mengele has brought you.' I took my first steps on the cursed soil of Auschwitz, and Dr Mengele was the man I would run to as 'Daddy'. This has spoiled my life.

The members of Mengele's human zoo were not officially recognised by the camp administration and received no special status and privileges. Only the young twins and their mothers were exempt from work; all the other experimental subjects were assigned to hard labour. Nevertheless, because of their deformity, the seven dwarfs had been allowed to remain in their barrack and, furthermore, so had their entourage. Then, one day in October, they were hit with a new decree: all average-sized adults in their group were to begin slave labour.

Deeply upset and fearing for the lives of their loved ones, the five female dwarfs decided to appeal. This time it was Elizabeth whom they sent to try to soften Mengele's heart. At first he dismissed her: 'In times like this, everyone has to take part in the war effort. I work, my wife works and so will your family!' But Elizabeth persisted:

> I appeal to Your Excellency like a child in need, pleading to his benevolent father. We depend on Sarah, Leah and the others for our existence – to mount our beds or get some water. We're lost without them; we won't be able to survive a day. If *Herr Hauptsturmführer* sends them away to work, he'd better send us too.

She was frantic, crying; the words streaming out of her mouth were drowned in sobs. She failed to notice Mengele's smile. 'Come to Mengele, Elizabeth. All right, I'll let them stay with you.'

A few weeks later, however, the dwarfs' efforts to shield the able-bodied members proved to be futile. The fierce onset of the winter had killed many people in the camp and with the crematoria no longer working – one of them blown up by rebelling inmates and the others shut down – extra hands were needed to burn the dead in open pits. Sarah Ovitz was among the women forced to load emaciated female corpses into the death carts and empty them into the gaping pit. Simon Slomowitz and his sons, including eleven-year-old Judah and thirteen-year-old Joseph, had the same task in the men's camp.

•

Survivors of the death camp had the impression that the Lilliput Troupe had no fear of Mengele, but Perla tells a different story:

> In his presence, we shielded ourselves with smiles, but inside we were trembling like fish out of water. We were never fooled by his amiability. When Dr Mengele said that as long as we were with him, we were not 'over there', it didn't make us feel any safer, but rather the contrary. He often said, 'I've enough work on you for twenty years', but that was no relief either – it was no guarantee he'd keep us alive all those years. He could finish the tests in a short time, toss us in the flames and work on the findings for as long as he wished.

THIRTEEN

AUSCHWITZ-BIRKENAU, NOVEMBER 1944

Irene Mengele's recovery was proceeding very slowly. After five weeks at the camp hospital, she was finally able to move to her husband's new flat in the doctors' barracks. In another fortnight, she was well enough to travel with her husband to Freiburg, where, for the first time, Mengele met his eight-month-old son, Rolf. Mengele's absence afforded the Ovitzes momentary relief from the endless tests, but it also caused them considerable anxiety. 'We were used to seeing Dr Mengele nearly every day. As much as we dreaded him, we were twice as petrified when he was away. Our hearts stood still then. We were utterly dependent upon him, and were well aware anyone could kill us in our saviour's absence.' A week later, he was back in his office. 'Guess where I've been,' he teased Dina Gottlieb as, tanned and smiling, he stepped into her workroom by his office. He didn't wait for her answer. 'In Argentina,' he said. 'I had no idea why he picked Argentina,' remarks Dina Gottlieb. 'He handed me a bag of cookies and two packs of choice English cigarettes. He said, "I'm having a late celebration of the birth of my son."'

Two orchestras were operating in Birkenau, one at the men's

camp and one at the women's camp. Their melodies could be heard twice daily, keeping pace and order as the inmates marched to their labour at dawn and as they returned from their labour in the afternoon. Music also provided an artistic interlude during the camp commander's speeches; it was featured at official ceremonies – and at the open-air hangings. On summer Sundays there were outdoor classical music concerts for the camp staff but the aloof Mengele, although a music lover, did not attend. The tunes travelled to the neighbouring barracks; prisoners ventured to the nearest electrified fence to catch a sound from another world.

The living quarters of the orchestra members were a centre of attraction, and the SS officers and prisoner-functionaries went there at night for entertainment. The musicians, of course, had no choice but to comply with their whims and wishes. Smaller ensembles were often called upon to play at private staff parties and birthdays. In his book *People and Ashes*, Professor Israel Gutman, an Auschwitz survivor and prominent historian, recalls that:

> Feasts and saturnalias were celebrated at *kapos*' and block elders' quarters. The artistic programme consisted of obscenities and dirty jokes. Sometimes a prisoner with a sweet voice would sing pre-war hits in various languages. The *kapos* especially favoured melancholy tunes. The 'singers' were mostly Jews, who supplied their service for a ration of bread. The famous stars were very popular among the *kapos* and enjoyed a special income, thanks to their art.

Birkenau inmates tried to improve their condition with whatever talents they had. A barber would hope to shave a *kapo* for a piece of bread or two cigarettes; a seamstress might mend the block elder's clothing. SS guards often had Dina Gottlieb draw poster-size portraits from photos of their wives, fiancées and girlfriends, which they hung by their beds. Once, she was handed a postcard of a naked red-haired nymph sitting by a waterfall and was ordered to paint a life-size copy of it by the following morning. She worked frantically the whole night. 'A day later, the SS man brought it back for repairs – there were holes torn into the strategic body parts,' she recalls.

When Mengele heard that a champion chess player was among the inmates, he arranged a game for himself. Late one evening, he came to the *Schreibstube*, the clerk's office, where the chess player was already waiting. Mengele removed his hat and placed it on a stool. Finger by finger he peeled off his white gloves, placing them inside his hat. Then he laid his cane across the upturned hat. The first round lasted a few hours, but the tournament continued over the following weeks. The prisoner was nicknamed 'The Rabbit' – a proper name for one of Mengele's pets. He was clearly kept alive solely to entertain the Nazi doctor. 'The Rabbit' found himself in a tight spot: if he played well and defeated Mengele, he could pay for the victory with his life. On the other hand, if he played badly and allowed Mengele to win, he might be killed for the deceit. 'The Rabbit' played in constant fear.

Eighteen-year-old Abraham Cykiert was among the few permitted to watch the games. Something of a *wunderkind* in his home town of Łódź, he had been accepted into the local Yiddish Writers' Association at the age of fourteen, after publishing only three poems. In the ghetto, he had sold his poetry to the ghetto functionaries in order to support his parents and seven siblings. A poem could get him a few potatoes, a pair of shoes or a shirt. 'Writing poems in Auschwitz was different,' Cykiert recalls.

It wasn't for an additional slice of bread as much as being vital for existence. To continue doing something so essential to me helped me keep my sanity and preserve my identity. I spread the word that I was a Yiddish poet – not a very practical profession in a death camp. But in Birkenau one never knew.

He waited one day outside the *Schreibstube* and ambushed one of the clerks: 'I'm a poet, can you lend me a pencil and paper?' Startled by the youth's innocent recklessness, the clerk furtively and surprisingly obliged. That night, words rushed from Cykiert's mind onto paper and in the morning he searched out his benefactor. The clerk's face was mask-like as he read the poem; Cykiert could not tell if he understood a word. 'Can you also write left-handed poetry?' asked the clerk, to the young man's incomprehension. He then pulled out a sheet of paper filled with jottings and scribbles, and handed it to Cykiert. The young poet blushed as he read gutter-rhymes, obscenities and abominations. 'Try it,' said the clerk.

The next day, Cykiert showed him his latest creation. The clerk was so pleased that he paid the teenager with a hot bowl of soup. 'Can you recite as well as you write?' he asked. Cykiert nodded.

The following night, he took me to the weekly binge of all the inmate-VIPs in the camp: veteran prisoners who assisted the SS in running the place. They were sitting around a table laden with delicacies: cheese, sardines, sausage, fruit. The alcohol flowed freely. There were other inmate-performers with me: singers, actors, musicians. We performed from the back of the room as they devoured the food. We were not allowed to touch anything, but when the party was over we could share the leftovers. I read my pornographic lines and they rolled with laughter. I was consequently accepted as the group's permanent jester. Every week, each of us had to come with new material – to this day I'm ashamed of the poems I was forced into writing. Decades passed before I could start to write again.

Perla Ovitz insists that she and her family never took part in the 'night life' of the death camp: they never performed in these drunken revelries; they never sang in public; they never privately entertained parties of *kapos* and SS men. Yet nearly all witnesses – former fans, acquaintances and neighbours from Rozavlea who were in the camp with them, as well as inmates who shared their barrack – vividly recall the dwarfs performing for the SS. One such witness was Eta Tessler:

> I knew the Ovitzes from Maramureș, as I was from Viseu, a nearby village. In Auschwitz I was part of the *Scheisskommando*. We had to collect the daily excrement of 32,000 women from the latrines, sift it into barrels and carry it outside the camp. All day long we were criss-crossing the camp, filthy and smelling, pushing the heavy cart with overloaded shit barrels. One day I came across two of the dwarf ladies. It was extremely cold, and I envied them for being able to have coats and warm pockets. I asked them where they were going and they answered 'singing'. I would run into them a few more times, walking in the same direction, but I couldn't tell if it was always the same duo or if they took turns.

•

Sunday 30 July was the fast of Tisha B'av, commemorating the destruction of the Holy Temple in Jerusalem. On this day, Jews would cease working and gather in synagogues to lament the catastrophe, which led to a bitter exile. Being familiar with the Jewish calendar, Mengele perversely ordered the leader of the women's orchestra to prepare a special concert. He selected the programme himself: military marches, circus music, waltzes, the foxtrot. The forthcoming concert caused much excitement. The orchestra arranged extra rehearsals, not just to master the exceptional programme but to master it brilliantly enough to please the unusual guest of honour. Rows of wooden benches stretched out over the infirmary yard. Opposite the orchestra stage, a special platform was erected to hold the SS staff and their inmate-assistants, doctors, nurses and camp functionaries. In the centre of the dignitary box sat Mengele himself, the arena's emperor.

As the orchestra struck its first notes, Fania Fenélon, one of the musicians, noticed a group of dwarfs crossing the stage in a straight line. 'It's a very famous dwarf circus from Hungary,' whispered one of her colleagues. Fenélon described the proceedings in her book:

> We start with a foxtrot, Mengele waving his hand, the dwarfs filling the stage, some couples dancing, other participants only managing a kind of grotesque, depressing twist. The men bow with a touch of servility; the women follow. Their jewellery, silk, ornaments, glitter in the sun, igniting thousands of sparkles, dancing, swinging, intermingling. These creatures emit joyful sounds, trying to sing along with Clara, Lotte and me. They have high, shrieking voices. The orchestra plays a march, and they accompany with clapping and stamping. There is something unreal and awful about the fifty tiny hands covered with rings, the bracelets clicking on their little arms, the little legs stamping... The circus is at the foot of our stage, a circle with distorted creatures moving about, clapping like children,

some of them fifty years old. The SS men burst out laughing. The young girls present at the scene start to tremble with fright at the uproar, the music, the dwarfs, the masquerade.

Although Fenélon is wrong about their number – they were seven, not twenty-five – and despite the negative tone, she appears to offer a fairly realistic account. For her part, Perla Ovitz recalls an entirely different musical programme: romantic, melancholy German songs that moved her and her sisters to tears. She maintains adamantly that she and her family did not appear or perform onstage, that day or any other day, and insists that they watched the performance from their tiny stools in the audience.

Against the bleak backdrop of Auschwitz-Birkenau, the evening was so vivid that it became deeply etched in the memory of many survivors. Isaac Taub was present that evening. He was part of the group of twin boys enlisted to carry chairs and benches and arrange them in rows. The children were allowed to stand at the back during the performance; afterwards, they dismantled the seats and carried them back to the depot.

> There were about 200 spectators and it was a full, professional show, with stage lights and music. I remember that the female and male dwarfs stood onstage. If I'm not mistaken, this concert was repeated once more. We all knew that the dwarfs were performing for the Nazis, but it was nothing to be ashamed of.

After two hours, Mengele lifted his hand and declared the concert over. Fania Fenélon recalls that 'Mengele stood in the midst of the smartly dressed dwarfs, in their grotesque outfits and jewellery. He turned to us and said, in his ironic manner, "*Sie haben ein gutes Publikum*" (You have a good audience).'

All the way to Auschwitz-Birkenau, the Lilliputs safeguarded their musical instruments. Everyone in the ghetto had been told that the deportation would be the start of a new life; thus, the craftsmen and professionals had taken their tools with them. But in the havoc on the ramp they were all ordered to leave their belongings on the trains. The Ovitzes were no exception. 'You'll get them later,' they had been promised. 'They were always grumbling about their little musical instruments, which had been taken from them,' recalls Dina Gottlieb. 'They asked me if I could help get them back, as they were entertainers and needed their tools.'

Many survivors recount a surrealistic scene in which a dwarf is playing the violin in a yard between the barracks. Gitta Drettler, who had lived next door to the Ovitz family on the main street of Rozavlea, remembers being:

happy to see them once again in the camp. The Nazis forced them to play in the SS barracks and I could hear the music from outside. They had their tiny musical instruments, and when I met them after the war in Romania and went to hear them playing, they said, 'These are the instruments we had in Auschwitz.'

Likewise, Maria Halina Zombirt, who had worked in the infirmary as a clerk, testified to the Frankfurt general prosecutor that she had heard the family of ten Hungarian dwarfs 'playing on musical instruments – a very peculiar piece'. Kalman Bar-On, who lived in the same barrack as Avram and Micki Ovitz, recalls that

I would call them 'the two Toulouse-Lautrecs'. They always boasted, 'We are an artistic troupe!' They told us they arrived with all their equipment, stressing that it had been important for them to bring their musical instruments, even at the expense of clothes and household utensils, since their whole future depended on it.

And Regina Teresa Krzyzanowska, who worked as nurse at Auschwitz, testified that the 'Lilliputians tried to please Mengele' by putting on 'a few shows' – which naturally would have been impossible without musical instruments.

Since so many survivors have commented on the Lilliput ladies' tiny, glamorous stage dresses, it would appear that at least part of their luggage was located and delivered to them. It is not clear whether the instruments were eventually restored to them as well; it would have been easy enough to replace their equipment with child-size violins and guitars. The *Kanada* warehouse held the plunder from hundreds of thousands of murdered children, many of them musically gifted.

From the moment the Lilliput Troupe set foot on the ramp back in May, and Micki Ovitz began handing out fan cards to anyone who would take them, the dwarfs had not stopped promoting their artistic talents. The news was enthusiastically received by the German criminals who had been transferred from jails in Germany to serve in Auschwitz as heads of barracks or supervisors of labour groups. Having been locked away for years and hungry for amusement, they seized every opportunity to exploit inmates with talent to entertain. The Lilliputs had no choice once they'd been ordered to perform.

Still, though, Perla Ovitz insisted throughout her life that neither she nor her sisters and brothers ever performed in the death camp.

We only sang among ourselves in our room, to remind ourselves of the good old days, have a good cry, and try and forget for a moment where we were. Everyone in the camp knew that we were artists and we could not escape from it completely. So there were occasions when one of us, from fear of being killed or from no choice, succumbed to the demand of a kitchen supervisor or SS officer and sang for a candy or a bit of margarine. But we never put on a performance, and in any case did not have our musical instruments.

Why, despite considerable eyewitness testimony to the contrary, such stubborn and persistent denial? The Ovitzes had always had a strong sense of their own artistic standards. Before the war, they carefully weighed each invitation to perform and accepted only those they considered appropriate showcases for their talent. As pious, God-fearing Jews, they would have deemed public performance in Auschwitz to be an abomination, like partaking of festivities in a graveyard. Nor would performance under coercion have lessened their shame – not with a painful awareness that while they were entertaining Nazis at the camp's notorious SS parties, the chimneys outside never stopped smoking.

All told, it would be no wonder if the Ovitzes strove to erase their experience from the records. And from their minds.

FOURTEEN

AUSCHWITZ-BIRKENAU, DECEMBER 1944

In the middle of December, without warning, the trucks stopped taking the Lilliput group to the clinics. Energetic as ever, Mengele was still running busily about but he seemed to have lost interest in his family of dwarfs, and they were afraid to approach him. The camp was covered in deep snow and they shut themselves in their barrack. Terrified, again and again they discussed the sudden change in Mengele's behaviour towards them, but they could find no reason why he no longer seemed to need them. However much they dreaded new applications of his evil instruments, however much they trembled at the screech of a truck slowing down outside their barrack or at the snap from a piece of paper handed to the *kapo*, Mengele's absence from them was the greater terror.

'Is he going to try and stretch us?' Perla broke their tense silence one afternoon. That was not the worst scenario that haunted them; there were other horrors they imagined but did not speak of. 'Dirty whores' is how Mengele referred to Jewish women, according to Dr Gisella Perl, a Jewish gynaecologist forced to work with him. In her book *Five Chimneys*, Olga Lengyel, another prisoner-physician, recounts how Mengele never missed a chance to ask the women indiscreet and improper questions. He made no secret of his amusement when he learned that one of the pregnant deportees had not seen her soldier husband for many months; another time, he hunted out a fifteen-year-old girl whose pregnancy was clearly dated from her arrival in the camp. He questioned her at length and insisted on the most intimate details. When his curiosity was fully satisfied, he sent her off with the next herd of selectionees. The camp was no maternity ward, it was only the antechamber to hell.

'Now tell me, how did you live with your midget?' In her memoir of Auschwitz, Sara Nomberg-Przytyk recalls Mengele posing this question to Dora, the tall, full-bodied wife of Avram Ovitz. Mengele was pressing on the common stereotype of the male dwarf as a sub-human characterised by an unusually potent sex drive and wild, unnatural desires. Dora Ovitz blushed, dumbfounded, her blood pounding in her ears. 'Speak!' screamed Mengele, and then proceeded to interrogate her, vulgarly, in front of her young daughter, her sisters-in-law and the entire barrack. Had she conceived her child with her dwarf husband, he demanded, or was the father someone else? As Dora responded by praising her husband's intelligence and industry, writes Nomberg-Przytyk,

we all stood there like blocks of stones.
'Don't tell me about that, only about how you slept with him.'
Mengele was salivating. The sweat poured down her face in big drops, on her clothes. She spoke and he asked questions. I cannot repeat the conversation. It was grotesque, inhuman torture.

At times, Mengele's sexual curiosity took him beyond such interrogations. Two pairs of identical teenage twins testified for the Frankfurt prosecution that he forced them to have sex with other twins in order to determine if the girls would bear twins in turn. The Lilliput group feared the same fate. 'We were three young women in the group,' recounts Regina Ovitz:

> Fanny Slomowitz, who was seventeen, Bassie Fischman, who was twenty, and myself, twenty-four years old. We had all been brought up in strictly Orthodox homes and had never been out alone with a man. Since childhood we had known that our marriages would be arranged by our parents and that our husbands would be the only men in our lives. We all knew that Mengele had bizarre ideas – we were terrified he intended to couple us with dwarfs for the sake of the outcome. We were sure this was his next move, the only reason he was keeping us alive.

Whenever Mengele visited their room, the girls wished they were invisible, but they could only stand in the corner, shrink into their bodies and avoid his gaze. Raised in a community that ordered girls to remain virgins until their wedding night, the young women faced an abyss. They feared that their wombs would become laboratories and that they'd be forced to produce offspring which, full-size or otherwise, would themselves be doomed to serve as human guinea pigs; the nightmare would repeat itself again and again at Mengele's discretion. They had long since abandoned any hope of leaving Auschwitz alive, but the wretched prospect that they now faced – insemination by a pair of older dwarfs, one forty-one years old and married, the other a bachelor of thirty-five – deepened the hopelessness into utter despair.

'Among us in the experimental barrack for male twins and dwarfs was a misshapen, hunchbacked gnome, a little less than four feet tall,' recalls Efraim Reichenberg.

> He was forty years old, had a fissure in his skull and could only walk with the aid of two crutches. He had been a watchmaker in Budapest and we came together on the same transport. Each of us was enduring his own private hell, but when he let us know what he was going through, there was still room for pity. Nearly every day he was put in a room and stripped naked. The SS brought him Gypsy women infected with syphilis and forced him to have sexual intercourse with them. The SS doctors stood watching. Every morning when he arrived and at the end of the day before he left, they examined him thoroughly to see if he had already caught the disease. When he first told me I didn't want to believe him, but one day I saw him through a crack in the door. A male nurse was holding him, forcing him down on a woman because he was no longer able. The unfortunate man didn't last long – he died some time later, not of syphilis but of exhaustion.

With the test results piling up over the summer, Mengele's clerks had no respite. Hour after hour, day after day, they filled out forms headed *Klinische Diagnose – Zwerge*, to which they appended lists of names. Ludovit Feld appears on one such list, along with the Ovitz brothers and the Budapest watchmaker – his name will here remain absent. Pointing out the hideous irony of their status in the camp, Feld noted that:

> although our living conditions had been markedly better than those of other inmates, we suffered terribly from an awareness that sooner or later we would be killed, our skeletons displayed

in biological museums. We heard it from the prisoner-doctors and from other prisoners. Word got out that near the crematoria ovens Dr Mengele had a *Sezierraum* [an autopsy room].

Pathologist Miklós Nyiszli has provided a description. The autopsy room

> was located in crematorium II, to the left of the entrance. The walls were painted pale green, the floor red. In the centre of the room, mounted on a concrete base, stood a dissecting table of polished marble, equipped with several drainage channels. At the edge of the table, a basin with nickel taps had been installed.

Like other SS doctors in the camp, Mengele routinely sent his pathologist the bodies of prisoners who had died of disease or hardship – or who had been killed expressly to be autopsied. The autopsy report was the essential conclusion to the research on each subject. Skeletons and organs were regularly exported to the Kaiser Wilhelm Institute in Berlin and to medical schools throughout the Reich. In June 1943, for example, 115 prisoners were transported from Auschwitz to the Natzweiler-Struthof concentration camp near Strasbourg. There they were killed and their bodies, still warm, were sent to *SS-Hauptsturmführer* Professor Dr August Hirt. He was building up a collection of skulls at the Anatomy Institute of the Reich University in Strasbourg, and was looking for 'Jewish-Bolshevik commissar types', as examples of 'a repulsive but typical species of sub-humanity'.

In Leeuwarden, northern Holland, Alexander and Julia Katan had been nicknamed 'The Lilliputians'. 'In a small town, people are straightforward when someone is different,' explains their only son, Alphons. 'Father's pelvis and legs were badly malformed due to a childhood illness, and mother was also very small.' Katan – the Hebrew word means 'small' – was the only dwarf among eight siblings; in 1930, he and Julia rejoiced when Alphons arrived and grew up to be average-sized and healthy.

An extremely energetic and active man, Alexander Katan was an economist and accountant, who spoke seven languages. He was not a practising Jew and in 1940, when Germany occupied Holland, he and his wife refused to stitch the yellow star to their clothes. Katan, who could move outside his home only with the aid of a special cart, was summoned to the head-quarters of the *Sicherheitsdienst,* the security service. 'As father had difficulties climbing the high staircase to their office, I had to accompany him. The Nazis called him in again and again, simply wishing to toy with him and laugh at his deformity.' In July 1942, Alexander was imprisoned in the *Strafgevangenis* (prison for serious crimes) in his hometown. At the beginning of September, he was brought to the concentration camp of Amersfoort and in October was deported to the Austrian concentration camp of Mauthausen. In August, his wife Julia was arrested and on 29 November, she was sent to Auschwitz. Because of her short stature she had no chance of being selected for work; Mengele was not yet stationed at the camp and there was no dwarf research. Julia was killed on arrival.

'I was twelve years old,' recalls Alphons Katan, 'and my aunt managed to convince the German authorities I was not my father's son, but rather the illegitimate child of a Catholic friend of the family. This saved my life. I found shelter with one of my aunt's non-Jewish friends.'

Mauthausen was smaller than Auschwitz – but no less brutal. Block 27 now houses a pathological museum that exhibits 286 specimens of human organs harvested by the camp doctors:

faces, skulls, skeletons, hearts, lungs, kidneys. Prisoners with spectacular tattoos had been put to death and then had their skin stripped from them; an album of tattooed skins displays the most outstanding designs. Physicians from the camp's Race and Hygiene Institute were continually combing the barracks in their search for prisoners with abnormalities whom they could add to their pathological collection. With his distorted limbs, Alexander Katan – Mauthausen prisoner 13992 – caught their eye. For several months, he endured the same sort of tests that the Lilliput group was subjected to at Auschwitz.

Hans Maršálek, then a prisoner working in the camp's administrative department, recalls an occasion when a group of distinguished civilians, led by Commander Franz Ziereis, visited the specimen collection at Mauthausen. One of the tour's high points was the exhibit of The Tall and The Short: the former, the strapping six-foot-two-inch Paul Liese, a delinquent from Hamburg; the latter, Alexander Katan. 'One is a Jew, the other a German, a criminal. Observe the difference between the two,' Commander Ziereis challenged his visitors. Maršálek remembers that 'after this comparison between Jew and Aryan, Liese took Katan in his arms and carried him out of the barrack... They were using Katan as an example of the degeneration of the Jewish race.' The presentation was repeated at every official camp visit.

Joseph Herzler, a prisoner who survived the experiments, was familiar with the pathological unit at Gusen, a sub-camp of Mauthausen:

I particularly remember a Dutch professor. Regrettably, I don't know his name. He was a unique individual. If I were asked to describe his looks, I must say he had a typical midget form. That is, his height was less than one metre. His exterior: a normal head of enlarged form, a full beard and a child-sized body. He was extremely intelligent, had broad knowledge, was a university professor and spoke seven languages fluently. He was kept tied in a corner of the room all day long and was examined by various SS physicians, doctors and visitors from other camps. Of course, he was not spared malicious remarks – 'this is the size of a Jewish existence' and so forth. Once someone said in mock sympathy, 'Well, at least he'll soon be dead since now his fate's been sealed.'

On 27 January 1943, *SS-Sturmbannführer* Dr Karl-Joseph Gross ordered that 43-year-old Katan be given a lethal injection of phenol. It was injected straight into Katan's heart; he died instantly. His body was then skeletonised, with every step of the process documented by a photographer. A special ambulance drove 180 miles to deliver his bones to the SS Medical Academy near the University of Graz. After the war, all that his son knew was that his father had died in Mauthausen. It took Alphons Katan fifty years to muster the courage to go there. What greeted him at the museum in block 27 were four poster-sized photographs of his father; one in which he was wearing the striped prisoner's uniform; two nude photos, front and back, taken just before the deadly injection; the fourth was of Katan's skeleton.

After a long, humiliating battle waged by Alphons Katan and intervention on his behalf by the Dutch government, the Austrian Interior Minister instructed the museum authorities to remove the photographs. Alphons Katan's struggle to restore his father's dignity, however, continues. His father's photographs are still in circulation at various Holocaust museums for all to see and purchase. They are printed in books and displayed at medical conventions; they can be downloaded from the internet. Historians argue that such photographs need to be displayed because they document Nazi atrocities and thus serve as vital tools in the struggle against Holocaust deniers, neo-Nazis and anti-Semites. 'But it's a never-ending humiliation of my father,' pleads Alphons Katan, who argues that the claim of historical truth does not outweigh the dignity of an individual or a family. Katan has demanded, too, that the medical school at the University of Graz return his father's skeleton to him for a proper burial. The university alleges that they are unable to locate the skeleton and cannot provide any information regarding its whereabouts.

The SS doctors were so certain of the scientific necessity of their activities that they did not bother to hide them. With the dirty work being left to the Jewish inmate-doctors, information about the medical atrocities quickly spread among the prisoners. Mordechai Slomowitz recalls that 'we lived under constant fear of our fate being the same as the two male dwarfs who arrived in Auschwitz and were killed, their bodies put in boiling water to be cooked until the flesh separated from their bones'.

This event happened in August 1944. During a selection of Jews transported from the Łódź ghetto, Mengele noticed a hunchbacked man of around fifty. Beside him stood his son, a handsome boy of fifteen with a deformed right foot, for which he wore an apparatus made of metal plates. Mengele waved the two of them aside. When the whole transport had passed into the gas chambers and the ramp was empty, he signalled the father and son to approach. He inspected them briefly, asked a few questions and then took out his notebook and wrote a message to Dr Nyiszli: 'These two men to be examined from a clinical point of view, exact measurements taken and clinical records set up, including all interesting details, and most especially those relative to the causes provoking the bodily deformations.' Mengele tore out the page and folded it. He then handed it to one of the SS guards, with the instruction that he deliver the two men to Dr Nyiszli.

The Hungarian-Jewish pathologist examined the hunchback and his son at some length, chatting with them to ease their tension. He learned that the devoted father, a prosperous wholesale clothing merchant, had taken advantage of business trips to Vienna to visit specialists there and have his son's foot examined and treated. The mother had died in the ghetto. Nyiszli tried to console them – they would probably be sent to a labour camp. As they were famished from the transport, he also saw to it that they were fed.

The father and son had just finished eating when *SS-Oberscharführer* Muhsfeld, accompanied by four members of the *Sonderkommando*, arrived and took them to a nearby room. Muhsfeld ordered them to strip naked. Then, two revolver shots were fired. The bodies were immediately returned to Nyiszli, who was so sickened by the sight that he could not perform the autopsy. He entrusted the dissection to one of the other inmate-doctors. It is not clear why Mengele did not add the short man from Łódź and his crippled son to his living dwarf collection. Perhaps he realised that the father's deformity stemmed from rickets, which was not hereditary and therefore of no interest for his genetic research.

Later that afternoon Mengele arrived at Nyiszli's workroom. He read the pathology report with growing excitement and declared that 'these bodies must not be cremated', as Nyiszli recounts in his memoir, *Auschwitz: a Doctor's Eyewitness Account*. 'They must be prepared, and the skeletons sent to the Anthropological Museum in Berlin. What methods do you know for the preservation of skeletons?' he urgently asked Dr Nyiszli. The two of them discussed the pros and cons of the various methods, and Mengele chose the quickest: cooking.

Bricks were laid in the courtyard, a fire was kindled and 'two casks, containing the bodies, placed upon it. Two *Sonderkommando* men were given the job of gathering wood and keeping the fire hot. After five hours, I tested the bodies and found that the soft parts were now easily separable from the bones.' When the water had cooled, the skeletons were put in a gasoline bath to be cleaned and polished. After they were dry, Nyiszli's assistant rearranged the bones in shape. Mengele, who had come with several other officers, was highly pleased. The group examined the skeletons, and Mengele ordered that they be wrapped and taken by two soldiers to Berlin.

That was the first time Dr Nyiszli was ordered to perform this gruesome task, but it would not be the last. One of the sights that haunted *Zwillingsvater* Zvi Spiegel to his dying day was that of a dwarf being tortured to his death by Mengele. Afterwards, the miserable victim was placed in an acid bath until the flesh was stripped from his bones.

We had reconciled ourselves to the thought that we wouldn't walk out from the camp and would have no grave, just like all the others murdered in Auschwitz. But the notion that our bare skeletons would be exhibited in Berlin, even a hundred years later, people arriving to gawk and stare, was ghastly beyond words. We had never taken part in a freak show or lived in a *Lilliputstadt*, and had not publicly displayed our bodies, considering it degrading. We were professional musicians and that's how the world had regarded us. If there was some relief in the idea of death, there was torment in the idea of being displayed in a museum.

To paraphrase a famous line by the poet Paul Celan, death was indeed a master of Auschwitz. It could strike at any moment, select any inmate as its prey. Its toll each night was piled outside for all to see, like so much garbage waiting to be collected. A space suddenly empty in a bunk did not shake heaven and earth. Those who survived the night walked about, as if wrapped in an invisible shell, praying to live one more day. But the Lilliput Troupe drew the eyes of the inmates beyond their shells, and they cared about their fate and noticed their whereabouts.

'One day, the dwarfs from block 23 were taken away,' recalls Dr Katarzyna Łaniewska. 'I don't know what was done with them.' Her colleague Ella Lingens-Reiner confirms that 'after about three weeks, the family disappeared suddenly. We were convinced they had been gassed.' Another doctor, Sigmond Hirsch, a French-Jewish roentgenologist and a resistance fighter, recalls that the experiments had ended and the dwarfs had been delivered to the gas chambers. Complete strangers to the dwarfs, inmates who saw them only briefly, like Maria Gasiorowska, a block elder at the women's camp, noticed that they had 'disappeared after a relatively short period of time, about two months. Following their disappearance, which attracted attention, there was news around the camp that they had been gassed. The news came from the crematorium workers.'

One of these was *Sonderkommando* Philip Müller: 'The only thing I saw regarding the midgets was how they executed them. He [Mengele] killed most of them, or had them killed, in order to perform autopsies on their bodies.' Maria Halina Zombirt, who had been a clerk in charge of the sick registry, testified for the Frankfurt prosecution that she 'met a group of ten Hungarian dwarfs and was told that they were a family who performed in a restaurant. When one of them died, he was prepared and skeletonised and sent to the museum in Berlin.'

Two survivors have gone so far as to describe the death of the dwarfs in great, appalling detail. Sara Nomberg-Przytyk

GIANTS

remembers Mengele ordering that little Shimshon be brought
to his medical cabinet. When Mengele was finished with
the baby, he locked the door behind him and left. Later, as
Nomberg-Przytyk tells it, Leah Ovitz arrived, and discovered
a terrible scene: she

> grabbed the half-dead child and ran into a mad frenzy of pain.
> Not one drop of blood was left in his little face. 'He will die.
> He has to die,' she said, choked with tears. At night, the little one
> died. He never regained consciousness. In the small room, on the
> little table, lay the little boy. Around him, like pillars of stone,
> stood a large woman, along with the child's mother, slim and
> frail; the three midgets sat in miniature chairs. They did not cry.
> They were all frightened of the torturous death awaiting them.

In the evening, the testimony continues, the dead child was
placed outside the block with the other corpses to be taken
to the crematorium. Nomberg-Przytyk also claims that she
witnessed the awful death of Avram Ovitz: 'The old midget
wanted his wife,' and he tried to slip through the wire; a guard
spotted him and, when Avram got close enough, shot him. 'He
never made it to his wife.'

But little Shimshon did not die on Mengele's operating table
and he survived Birkenau. Likewise, his uncle Avram was
not shot, but lived to see liberation day. What, then, caused
Nomberg-Przytyk to make such basic mistakes? Most likely
she was compressing a number of events, and attributed to the
dwarfs two common occurrences in the daily life of the camp:
the death of a child in his mother's arms and the shooting of
inmates who approached the electrified fence.

In a similar manner, the singer Fania Fenélon maintains that
immediately after the concert, 'the handsome doctor was seen

crossing the camp, followed by his merry, squeaking army of dwarfs'. She describes Mengele as a Pied Piper proudly marching in front, with the dwarfs – joyful, self-assured, apparently unworried – behind him. 'Who could dream of exterminating such tiny creatures, always joyful and happy! Mengele laughs with them, he seems quite amused, he – so enormous, ruling over such small ones.' Fenélon then reports that later Mengele returned alone, his hands in his pockets. She concludes her account with the words ending the opera *Pagliacci* by Leoncavallo: '*La Commedia e Finita!*'

A similar reminiscence was given by Renee Firestone, an Auschwitz-Birkenau survivor: 'The Germans found a community of midgets, transported them to Auschwitz, shot them en masse and then were forced to let them sit in a pile for three days until the crematoria could take them.' A mass killing of dwarfs was not registered only in the memory of camp survivors, however. Documents in the Auschwitz archives have led some researchers to conclude that Mengele killed eleven female dwarfs on 7 December 1944.

In the 'Labour Deployment List' of 5 December 1944, under the heading 'sick and unable to work', a new category appears for the first time: *Zwerge*. It indicates that sixteen female dwarfs were transferred to the women's camp in BIIe. It had previously been the Gypsy camp, but had stood empty since the extermination of all its inhabitants in August. The transfer was part of a rearrangement of Birkenau. The prisoners were being moved into fewer barracks, as the women's camp had been liquidated. Healthy women prisoners were transferred to BIIb, while the ill, as well as female twins and dwarfs, were transferred to BIIe. Three days later, the number of female dwarfs in the roster dropped from sixteen to five; the roster does not indicate the fate of the missing eleven.

Many researchers have tried to decipher the horror behind the figures. 'They probably died the previous day as a result of the experiments conducted on them by SS Dr Mengele,' concludes Danuta Czech, in her extensive Auschwitz research. But although any sort of death was possible in the macabre world of Auschwitz-Birkenau, it is most unlikely that Mengele would have arbitrarily eliminated eleven of his carefully maintained dwarfs at one go, before he had finished his work on them. Furthermore, he considered the autopsy vital to his research and would have been well aware that Dr Nyiszli could not possibly have dealt with eleven corpses in any exacting, productive way.

There were indeed sixteen females in the Lilliput group: the five Ovitz dwarf sisters; their two average-size sisters; Avram's wife and her eight-year-old daughter; cousin Regina; Chaya Slomowitz and her three daughters; Bassie Fischman and her mother. Since Mengele regarded them as an extended family, he moved all sixteen of them to the new accommodations in Birkenau.

But clearly, contrary to the conclusion of the camp historians, the eleven women did not die: all sixteen lived to see the end of the war and then emigrated to Israel or the United States.

It would seem, in fact, that the disappearance of the eleven was simply a bureaucratic error. When the sixteen females of the Lilliput group arrived at their new barrack, they were duly recorded in the camp registry as dwarfs, in accordance with Mengele's note of transfer. But on a recount three days later, the officers in BIIe noticed that only five of the women were in fact dwarfs, and the eleven other average-sized women and young girls were thus excised from the category of *Zwerge*. While they no longer appeared in the same slot on the list, they nonetheless continued to live in the same room as the dwarfs.

This being the case, why is there so much testimony concerning their brutal collective murder? One plausible answer might be that Birkenau survivors, who regarded their own deliverance as miraculous, found the chances slim that someone as helpless as the dwarfs could survive. In addition, the fact that the Lilliputs were transferred several times from one side of the camp to the other caused their fellow inmates to lose touch with them and in Birkenau, when you stopped seeing someone, it could mean only one thing.

•

The new barrack of the group's females was much closer to the men's infirmary, where their loved ones were located.

Though Jewish holidays were set aside for extensive killing, Christmas Eve 1944 in Auschwitz-Birkenau was relatively peaceful – a momentary respite from horror. Elizabeth Ovitz, escorted by her tall sister Sarah, went to wish a merry Christmas to the kitchen staff. On her way back, two SS officers stopped them and took Elizabeth into a back room while Sarah, frantic, waited outside. The officers mounted Elizabeth on a chair and demanded entertainment. Elizabeth's songs won her a shower of cellophane-wrapped candies, a piece of salami and some margarine, all of which she took back to her family. Christmas festivities were taking place in various parts of the camp. Dr Lucie Adelsberger remembers watching a party in the men's infirmary from behind the fence:

> Physicians and nurses were allowed to strike up dance tunes with a jazz group. It was an open-air performance on the grassy area close to the wire. The women crowded around on the other side of the fence, shouting 'Bravo!' and clapping their

hands. The programme was good, nothing was forbidden, no sentry shot into the crowd.

The experience of Solomon Malik, then a fourteen-year-old twin, was even more extravagant:

I went to a Christmas party in a large hall in the *Kanada* camp, near the crematoria. It was open only for camp functionaries but our *kapo*, Frau Schmidt, took me along with her. There was lavish food, drink, music and dance. It was a complete show: someone lifted a table with his teeth, clowns amused the crowd with their tricks. I remember that one of them rode a broomstick and laid eggs, to the cheers of the spectators. The Lilliputs were part of the artistic programme. I don't remember exactly how many of them were there, but they sang and played their tiny instruments.

For the revellers, all of them 'Aryans', the future was bleak. The Russians were closing in; the German Army was engaged in desperate battles. But at the camp, the orchestra played on.

FIFTEEN

AUSCHWITZ-BIRKENAU, JANUARY 1945

By the summer of 1944, the Red Army was already 120 miles from Auschwitz. But the Russians did not become a real threat to the SS at the death camp until four months – and tens of thousands more victims – later. As the thundering of the cannons grew audible, the inmates grew even more uneasy. 'We were always afraid that the Nazis would kill us, the old prisoners, as soon as the eastern front drew close to Birkenau, since we had been witnesses to their crimes,' comments Erich Kulka, a survivor and historian, in his book *The Death Factory*. The steady advance of the Allied forces prompted the Third Reich to begin liquidating the concentration camps and centres of mass extermination. One by one, they were demolished. Auschwitz-Birkenau, the biggest death factory of them all, was the last in line. To cover up unimaginable crimes, the crematoria were blown up. The pits, in which countless corpses had been burned, were filled and covered with earth. Buildings and offices were razed, wooden barracks were dismantled; the construction materials and the furniture were shipped into the heart of Germany.

In January, all the able-bodied members of the Lilliput group were recruited for the task. Sarah Ovitz, who had been hauling the dead to the pits with the *Leichenkommando*, was now assigned to help dismantle the barracks. If her former job had been emotionally straining – she kept visualising her own body swinging lifelessly from the death cart she was pulling – at least, at her new task, she could fantasise about living to see the hell cease. Slomowitz and his three sons had meanwhile been transferred to the *Kanada* warehouse, where they frantically packed shoes, spectacles, clothes, toys and innumerable family treasures to be sent to Germany.

The Nazi war machine was reluctant to lose the enormous force of slave labour it had gathered at Auschwitz. In order to keep exploiting it, the SS implemented a massive evacuation. In a period of five days, 58,000 prisoners were marched on foot in heavy snow about fifteen miles to the train station. From there, they were transported in open wagons to concentration camps in Upper and Lower Silesia.

Twice in the past, Mengele had saved Dina Gottlieb from selections, for he required her skills as an illustrator. With his experiments now coming to an end, he needed her less and left her to her fate. Dina and her mother were among those consigned to what was aptly dubbed 'the death march', for its destination was uncertain and those who could not keep up were simply shot by the SS on the spot. Quenching their thirst by sucking on pieces of snow, mother and daughter made it to Ravensbrück.

Mordechai Slomowitz recalls:

We all stood for *Appell* and an officer shouted, 'All those who can march fifty kilometres, step forward!' Several men and boys did, forming a group. 'Who can march forty? Thirty? Twenty?' One by one, the barrack, including the frail and ailing, was split into groups, which started to walk towards the unknown.

Physically our family could make the journey, but father did not want to desert the dwarfs.

'Can you march five kilometres?' demanded the officer. Simon Slomowitz looked at the two Ovitz dwarfs. The brothers exchanged glances and Avram, the elder, nodded. 'We can make it,' said Slomowitz. It was obvious that the dwarfs could not walk even a hundred metres, especially in the heavy snow; equally obvious was their urgent desire to get away from Birkenau as quickly as possible. Five kilometres was the distance from Birkenau to the main camp of Auschwitz. The men surmised that if the entire Birkenau camp was being liquidated, Auschwitz would be the meeting point with their women.

Simon and his son wandered around, looking for an improvised means of wheeling the dwarfs. Next to the kitchen barrack they found a cart that had been used to distribute bread and to dispose of the dead. They lifted Avram and Micki into the cart and wrapped them in blankets. Then, Slomowitz and his three sons started pulling the cart out of the camp. The roads were buried in snow and in the thick wall of fog they could see no farther than the tips of their fingers. They had only the footprints of the droves of inmates who had ventured out before them, along with some scattered corpses, to mark the way. They had gone no more than a few hundred metres when the heavy wooden cart tipped over. They could go no further. 'There's no point – we'll freeze to death here,' said Simon Slomowitz. 'If we're going to die, let's die in our bunks, not like dogs in the fields.' They wrenched the cart from the snow and retreated. In the prevailing disorder at Birkenau, where the discipline among the SS guards had gone lax, they managed to settle quietly back into their barrack. They wondered where Mengele was and if he could help them. Unlike the other SS doctors, he had continued his research up to the last possible moment, but it had been days since they had last seen him.

Until the evacuation, Martina Puzyna had worked mainly in a special barrack in the former Gypsy camp. 'Written measurement data was kept there. I well remember that Dr Mengele showed up in January 1945, several days before the evacuation, and silently packed his records, preparing them for transport like a wild man.' She had stood aside and watched, since he allowed no one to help him. Flushed from exertion, he stuffed two trunks with instruments, slides and specimens. Leafing frantically through the files in a huge cabinet, he pulled out the essential documents. Then he slammed everything into his car and drove away. It was 17 January 1945.

At midnight, SS officers ordered all the inmate-doctors who had worked with Mengele to collect his remaining medical documents. 'In less than an hour, the documents were gathered in front of the bureau quarters. They were heaped upon the earth and made quite a mound of papers. An SS guard promptly set them on fire,' recalls Olga Lengyel in her memoir. Perla supplements that account:

No one knew that Dr Mengele had left for good – it took several days for us to realise we were not going to see him again. Throughout the months that we'd known him, he had always promised, 'When I move to another place I'll take you with me.' When the camp was torn down, we waited in our room for him to come, but he didn't keep his word. When he ran away, the only thing he took was our papers, which were more important to him than we were.

On 18 January 1945, the SS marched 5,300 women and children out of Auschwitz-Birkenau, among them dozens of twins led by Zvi Spiegel. The Lilliputs, however, stayed behind, along with a few thousand inmates who, too sick to move, remained in the now nearly empty barracks. 'A number of sources indicate that the SS planned to liquidate them, not only as witnesses to their crimes, but also as an unwanted burden,' concludes Polish researcher Andrzej Strzelecki. In essence, the camp had ceased functioning. No food whatsoever was being distributed. The prisoners were now left at the mercy and whim of a small, nervous SS force that spent most of its time looting the warehouses and shooting people for pleasure. Seven hundred inmates were murdered in the camp's final days. More than 200 of them were locked in a barrack and burned alive.

One night in the commotion, Avram and Micki, along with Simon and his three sons, sneaked out of the men's infirmary and stole into the women's camp, where they found their families. Over the following days, whenever one of the remaining SS guards approached the women's barrack, the six men quickly hid themselves. They spent most of their time praying, whispering psalms and imploring God for deliverance. Like other prisoners in the now virtually deserted camp, they raided the kitchen and storerooms, and for the first time in many months they satisfied their hunger with a warm meal cooked by the Lilliput women.

The 'uncanny atmosphere' of Auschwitz's closing days is etched into the memory of Kalman Bar-On.

The busy, densely populated camp became desolate, suspiciously silent. Great fires consumed the remaining goods at the *Kanada* warehouse. Explosions could be heard, as well as collapsing buildings. We were in a no man's land – no SS guards at most of the watchtowers, but the barbed wire of the outer fence was still electrified and we could not get away. From time to time, out of nowhere, soldiers would burst into a barrack, order everyone out and shoot them. One day they called an *Appell*, announcing they would lead us out of the camp the following morning at ten. I sensed a trap that they were going to shoot us the moment we passed the gates. Even if they let us march, it would be very hard to survive. I stood by my uncle Ludovit Feld, knowing that with his tiny legs and weak body he wouldn't be able to make it. I didn't want to leave him and didn't know what to do.

'Son, we're not going anywhere,' said Feld, convincing not only Kalman but also fourteen other teenage twin boys who had remained in the barrack. They covered themselves with blankets and for ten days they lay motionless, on the frozen ground, beneath the lowest wooden bunk. They had nothing to eat but crumbs, and could not go outside to relieve themselves for fear of the SS.

'For the first time in my life, I dared to disobey an SS order,' notes Kalman Bar-On.

It was a strange feeling. I feared their revenge if they found us, but I was happy to be taking my fate into my own hands. Those who walked out of the camp thought they were saving themselves. But for many of them, including my poor mother, the walk meant death. Those of us who followed the advice of a wise and resourceful dwarf who could not move and didn't want to be left alone were saved.

In the last days of January at Auschwitz, Russian cannons were thundering at close range, American aeroplanes were buzzing overhead and the German guards were in panic. But freedom was in the air. Fervently, the Lilliputs prayed that they would not die by friendly or enemy fire at the last moment. At night they slept in their clothes; one of them always stood guard.

On Saturday 27 January around 3 p.m., the first Red Army reconnaissance troops entered Birkenau. The 5,800 remaining prisoners were too exhausted to greet them. According to the Jewish calendar it was Shabbat Shira, the day for the annual reading of the 'Song of the Sea' from the book of Exodus – the eulogy in which Moses and the Children of Israel praise God for drowning Pharaoh and his army in the Red Sea. 'We all felt God's hand was at work, redeeming us on the Saturday commemorating the miracle of our forefathers' deliverance from certain death. But we were not so lucky as to be delivered by the Americans. We got the Russians instead,' Perla commented.

The Lilliput Troupe had performed for Hungarian soldiers and for German soldiers; they now had a new audience, as jubilant Russian soldiers crowded into the barrack to gape at the seven dwarfs. The Russians brought vodka with them and did not have to plead much – the Ovitzes were happy to oblige. For drums, they used some metal pots from the kitchen, on which Micki and Elizabeth hammered out their rhythms with wooden spoons. The party lasted through the night, with the Lilliputs again and again singing the few Russian songs in their repertoire. 'In the midst of the celebrating I was full of fear,' recalls Regina Ovitz.

> The Russian soldiers frequently entered our room, always tipsy, and I didn't like the way they stared at us. Whenever their footsteps grew louder, we three girls hurriedly climbed to the upper bunk. We lay there quiet as mice until they left. I didn't trust them – they made me feel threatened.

All twenty-three members of the Lilliput group were examined by Russian doctors, who found them to be in better health than most of the survivors; none of them required hospitalisation.

'How many dwarfs like you were in the camp?' Ludovit Feld was asked by a Lieutenant Misivrov from the military prosecution office of the Red Army, who was sent to gather evidence. 'In Birkenau where I was, we were ten Lilliputians. Five men, five women.' 'How did the doctors and the SS treat you?' 'The doctors treated us fairly but the SS laughed at us, although they never hit us. Whenever they made selections, we were kept alive.'

This testimony from March 1945 is the earliest evidence on record relating to Mengele's research on dwarfs. It also establishes their precise number: ten. However, this is not a figure on which researchers and survivors agree. Dr Gisella Perl, for example, indicates in her book that, 'One of these barracks housed Dr Mengele's pets, Polish and Hungarian Jewish midgets, about forty of them, some alone, some with their entire family.' Some research places the figure as high as a hundred or more. Nevertheless, there were only seven dwarfs in the Lilliput group and the Ovitzes insist there were only three other dwarfs beside them.

This figure of ten is backed up by the surviving Auschwitz archives: between May 1944 and January 1945, listed under the category *Zwerge* are the names and camp numbers of the seven Ovitzes, Ludovit Feld, Arthur Seligsohn and the Budapest watchmaker.

Arthur Seligsohn, from Breslau, was transported first to Theresienstadt and then, in May 1944, to Auschwitz-Birkenau – he was prisoner number A-1199. Because of his handicap, the 56-year-old dwarf was transferred by Mengele from the Czech family camp to the men's clinic, where he lived with the male dwarfs. He was thus spared the fate that awaited the other Czech Jews when their camp was liquidated. According to the Red Cross, Arthur Seligsohn was alive and well in Grüssau, Poland, in July 1948.

No one knows the number of dwarfs who, like Lya Graf and Julia Katan, arrived at Auschwitz-Birkenau before Mengele's tenure there and were sent instantly to their death. It is likewise difficult to determine how many dwarfs arrived at the camp but failed to gain Mengele's attention and were systematically exterminated.

Close scrutiny of 159 photographs taken by SS men Ernst Hofmann and Bernhard Walter during selections of Hungarian Jews in May and June 1944 – a collection known as the 'Auschwitz Album' – discloses at least three more dwarfs on the ramp: two of them old men, one a teenager. The teenager, evidently too deformed and weak to stand on his feet, reclines in a wicker chair that had been brought from home. These three nameless dwarfs were killed a few hours after being photographed; no doubt Mengele did not find them sufficiently interesting for his research.

When anti-Jewish decrees were imposed on Hungary in 1940, famed 59-year-old dwarf Zoltan Hirsch was expelled from the circus. Soon thereafter he was arrested for wearing a yellow star that did not meet Nazi requirements: it was too small. His defence – that the badge was proportionate to his size – failed to sway the authorities. He was imprisoned and later sent to Auschwitz with the Jews of Budapest. According to Gjorgi Szilagyi, who had run a Lilliputian town in Budapest, the celebrated Zoli was made a doorman in the camp. This remarkable dwarf, who had travelled the world as a favourite of statesmen and kings, was reduced to being a laughing stock for the SS. Day after day, dressed in spectacular uniforms, he stood by the camp gates and saluted the Nazis as they came and went. This service did not save him from the gas chambers. Strangely and poignantly, Zoltan Hirsch has nonetheless been immortalised as a collector's item: the Roli Zoli, a tin wind-up toy of a clown riding a red scooter.

•

Fleeing Birkenau, Mengele travelled to Berlin for a brief meeting with Professor von Verschuer at the Kaiser Wilhelm Institute. Most likely he wanted to discuss the possibility of returning to the institute to continue his work on the material he had collected in Auschwitz. Meanwhile, he had to report to the Gross-Rosen concentration camp in Silesia. He had always wanted fame and was determined to go down in history as a pioneer and innovator. His research on dwarfs was not a marginal item of scientific curiosity.

In his rivalry with Hans Grebe, Mengele lost. By the 1950s, scientists had begun to taxonomise the various types of dwarfism. In 1952, Hans Grebe, now an honoured and distinguished scientist, published his papers on a rare form of short-limb dwarfism, to which he would lend his name: the diagnostic term 'Grebe Syndrome' is used to this day. Grebe identified the syndrome after studying a pair of Brazilian sisters, aged seven and eleven. Mengele had an entire family, seven of them dwarfs, at his disposal. Had he had the time to continue his research he, too, might have identified the Ovitz type of dwarfism that would in honour bear his name. But he did not, and the credit belongs to Maroteaux and Lamy, two French physicians who defined it in 1959. They named it 'pseudoachondroplasia'.

The inmate-doctors who worked under Mengele surmised that he aspired to unlock something resembling a 'genetic code' for dwarfism. But that was an illusion. Decades would pass before science acquired the necessary knowledge for it. What Mengele was looking for, brutally and futilely, in 1944 was achieved in 1995, by a Jewish scientist, Professor Jacqueline Hecht of the University of Texas.

SIXTEEN

ON THE ROAD, 1945

Under the Final Solution, entire Jewish communities, extended families of forty or fifty members, were crammed in cattle cars and transported to Nazi death camps. Almost nine out of ten people who arrived at Auschwitz-Birkenau were sent directly to the gas chambers. Some able-bodied men and women, usually between the ages of fifteen and thirty-five, provided slave labour, a tortured interval before death. It was rare that one person from an entire family survived, let alone two. The Ovitzes and the Slomowitzes were the only families who were deported to Auschwitz and emerged with all members unscathed, the youngest aged just eighteen months, the oldest fifty-eight years old.

The Ovitzes had been doubly doomed by the Nazi racial policy: deemed unworthy of living on account of being Jews and because they were handicapped. But deported to the death camp because they were Jews, their dwarfism saved their lives. In an ideology that praised the survival of the fittest, they proved just the opposite.

The day after liberation, a Russian army film crew arrived at the camp. As the crew had missed the actual historical moment, they decided to stage it. Children always heighten the poignancy of a war story, so when Captain Alexander Vorontsov, a cameraman, chanced upon a group of Mengele's twins leaving the camp, he detained them. Dissatisfied with their randomly improvised clothing, he had them change back into striped prisoners' uniforms.

In his search for a dramatic location, Vorontsov had found a narrow path that ran between two fences of barbed wire. He had another cameraman climb up a watchtower to get a bird's-eye view. Along the path, accompanied by nuns and nurses, the children in striped uniforms were paraded again and again; at the director's cue, they would stop and roll up their sleeves; then they'd point at the numbers tattooed on their arms to the camera. Extracts from the film are screened every half-hour at the Auschwitz State Museum. At first glance, one can hardly discern the bespectacled face and tiny form of forty-year-old Ludovit Feld among the marching children.

Feld's helplessness had left him no choice but to stick with Mengele's twins, with whom he had been imprisoned for the past eight months. 'When the Russians came,' recalls Kalman Bar-On,

> I gave Uncle Ludovit my hand and we walked over to Auschwitz through the deep snow. I left him alone in one of the buildings and began searching for food. There was a huge storeroom with noodles and sugar. I found an empty tin, made a fire and cooked our first meal in freedom.

But the commanders of the 60th Army of the First Ukrainian Front were anticipating a Wehrmacht offensive and they advised those who could get away not to linger. Too weak to undertake a long journey, Feld had to remain in Auschwitz. His nephew Kalman headed for Palestine.

All twenty-three members of the Lilliput group were now reunited. They found strength and safety in their number as they prepared for the journey back to their village. There they hoped to meet up with the husbands of Frieda, Elizabeth and Leah, who had been taken to Hungarian labour camps two years earlier. They would move back into their house, find their hidden money, and resume their career and lives.

Simon and Mordechai Slomowitz rushed back to the camp kitchen; the bread cart still stood where they had left it. The dwarfs and the small children, along with the group's few belongings, were lifted onto the cart. Simon and his son tore blankets into strips, knotted them together, and tied one end to the four-wheeled cart. Slinging the makeshift rope over their backs, holding the other end they slowly pulled the cart out of the camp. Sarah and Leah took turns helping at the front, while the other women pushed the cart from behind. To ease the load, the children struggled alongside in the slippery snow.

'I was sitting between my aunts and uncles, watching my poor mother hitched to the cart like a human horse,' recounts Shimshon Ovitz. After a few kilometres of pushing and pulling, they stopped by the ruin of a bridge. It had been blown up by the Wehrmacht to slow down the Russian offensive. 'There was no way we could slide the cart with the dwarfs across the frozen river,' explains cousin Regina Ovitz.

We unloaded them and Simon Slomowitz picked up Avram, the heaviest of them all. Simon walked warily and we anxiously watched every hesitant step until he succeeded in setting Avram on the opposite bank. He returned for another one. Sarah carried one of her sisters and, since Micki was the lightest, I cradled him in my arms, carrying him like a baby to the other side. I was twenty-four, he a 35-year-old man less than a metre tall, but at the time I didn't feel embarrassed. It was the least I could do to reciprocate for the dwarfs having saved my life.

This incident would take on an ambivalent quality for her months later, when the Ovitzes voiced the hope that she would become Micki's wife.

When everyone was safe on the opposite bank, Slomowitz and his son went back across the river to retrieve the cart. The group then continued the journey. Proceeding at a snail's pace, they struggled both with muddy roads and their own disorientation. They had no idea whether they were still travelling in a zone liberated by the Russians or had in fact wandered back behind German lines. At every crossroad they stopped for a rest and for long, animated debates about where to turn next. Each passing Red Army vehicle presented the threat of robbery or the humiliation of abuse and ridicule – but the human horses pulling the dwarf-laden cart amused the Russians. The drivers would hoot joyfully and the soldiers, springing to their feet, would wave and toss them bread and vodka.

Touched by the refugees' plight, one officer gave them a horse to draw the cart. He also directed them southeast, towards Kraków, the largest town in the area, where they hoped to find a train and start the long journey home to Romania. When the cart began zigzagging erratically, they discovered that one of the gift-horse's eyes was blind. And as they passed through the ruins of demolished Polish villages, they realised that they could not expect their own houses to be intact.

It was dark when they reached the desolate village of Zator. Every shadow seemed menacing. They feared that the peasants, out of sheer hostility towards returning Jews, might decide to kill them; or that they might murder them in their sleep and then rob them of their scant belongings. They decided not to enter the village and spent their first night of freedom in a deserted farm on its outskirts. The next day, they chanced upon a Russian soldier who advised them to head north to the village of Babice and proceed from there to Kraków. It took them a whole day to make the ten kilometres to Babice. Recalls Regina Ovitz:

The Russian soldiers outnumbered the Polish peasants. They invited us to their camp and promised food. Considering what I'd been through in Auschwitz, I was fairly good-looking and they were notorious for their behaviour towards women. I evaded their offer and pleading, and Bassie and Elizabeth went to get the food for all of us. For the first time in my life I ate from a plastic plate.

The news that a company of dwarfs was in the village travelled fast. Soon they were summoned to the local Russian army headquarters. Mountains of food were laid out before them. After months of near starvation, they had to resist devouring the food so as not to overload their shrunken stomachs and risk their lives.

In the morning, they bid farewell to their half-blind horse and clambered onto a military truck. On their arrival at Kraków, the Russians put them up in a hotel near the central square, Rynek Glowny, that previously had been confiscated by the SS. Perla remembers that...

The Russians treated us well, attending to all our needs. They threw a victory ball and we were invited to sing and perform. It was nearly a year since our last concert, but we hadn't lost our touch and they applauded fervently. From then on, throughout our time in Kraków, we performed for them at every birthday or holiday. One of the officers tried to tempt us with an offer for a Russian tour from an impresario-friend in Moscow. We declined politely, as our hearts were longing for home.

Relaxing the rigorous survival instincts which had sustained them in Auschwitz, they surrendered to the joys of Kraków. The city had escaped destruction and retained its splendour. They were enjoying the Russian hospitality and felt flattered to be in demand again. The city restored their spirits and sanity, and so they delayed their departure, unaware that as the weeks were slipping by they were losing their independence and freedom of movement as the Russian army tightened its hold on the region.

And then, stranded at the hotel for days on end with nothing to do, they finally broke down. 'The horrifying suppressed memories began to float out and hit us,' says Mordechai Slomowitz.

> We now talked ceaselessly about the hell that was Auschwitz. While there you got used to seeing people burning and sealed yourself off from your surroundings. We hadn't shared our shock and fear – we had never cried as it would have made us weak. Now in the safety of Kraków, we talked obsessively, not omitting any of the ghastly details. We cried very often and it left us feeling drained.

When the group was finally ready to move on they realised that their considerable number, an advantage in the camp, had now become a burden. Finding transportation for twenty-three people, not to mention food and shelter, complicated every move. The roads were already jammed with refugees, some of them lost and wandering aimlessly, others struggling to find their way home. On top of that, the Ovitzes were given bad advice: to turn west to Katowice, and look for a train to Romania.

It was Easter, April 1945, when Solomon Malik, the fourteen-year-old twin who had lived with the Lilliput men in the experimental barrack, saw the dwarfs again. At liberation he had been ill with typhus and for two more months had remained hospitalised in Auschwitz. Once he'd recovered, he had walked and hitch-hiked the forty kilometres to the refugee camp at Katowice, where he was overjoyed to discover his twin sister and two four-year-old twin brothers. The Ovitzes were with them. Soon, however, the entire camp was on the move: 'The Russians suspected that many German soldiers were getting rid of their uniforms, adopting a Jewish identity and hiding among the refugees,' recalled Malik. 'It was difficult to determine on the spot who was kosher, who a murderer. So they decided to take us all to Russia and do the sorting out there.' The entire camp was taken to the railway station. The Lilliputs were aghast to find cattle cars awaiting them once more. This time, though, the doors were left open and they could look out at the countryside and breathe fresh air during the long voyage. There were frequent stops for food, as well as for relief in the woods.

They were travelling east and as the hours passed, the Ovitzes began to find the landscape more and more familiar. Then the train pulled into the station at Czernowitz, and they could barely contain their joy. Just a few hours' drive by car from their beloved village, Czernowitz had always been one of their favourite stops when they were on tour. They had frequently appeared in the splendid *Fekete Sas* (Black Eagle) concert hall. Only now their destination was the city's secondary school, which was to be their new temporary dwelling. They were allowed to walk around the town as they chose, but under no circumstances could they leave for home. It was the end of the war, 9 May 1945, and they were in an odd situation: in Russian hands, neither captive, nor free.

'We know you're looking for SS soldiers. You don't suspect us of being them, so why don't you let us go?' The dwarfs pleaded with every officer they chanced on. The officers were sympathetic, but shrugged their shoulders. 'The Russians provided us with food and all the necessities,' recalls Mordechai Slomowitz. 'But after all, we were living in town and needed money. Micki and Elizabeth suggested going to the city centre and giving an outdoor performance. I took a small hand cart, mounted them on it and pushed it through the streets like a pram.'

Using the cart as their stage, the two smartly dressed dwarfs immediately attracted an audience. They knew the local people well and remembered the hits they had sung for them just a year or two earlier. Within half an hour, coins had piled up around their legs. Mordechai pulled the cart to another spot and another audience.

After a fortnight, all the refugees were marched to the railway station.

'You're going home,' they were told. Avram Ovitz was sceptical: 'Trust me; I know the place like the palm of my hand. If the train stands on the right platform, we'll see Rozavlea soon. But if it's on the left, we're going to Russia.' The train was on the left platform. Four days later, they were in Slutsk, Belarus.

The camp was much larger than the last one, and was divided by nationalities. According to Solomon Malik,

> there were Jews and non-Jews, Romanians, Hungarians, Poles and people from France. Even an entire Italian football team that had come to entertain the Italian soldiers on the front, and found themselves prisoners of war. I was put in charge of the kitchen storeroom and would steal bottles of spirit, diluting it heavily with water and making a fortune by selling it to the Italians. Our county, Maramureş, had changed hands so often, from Hungary to Romania and back again, that we no longer

knew to whom we belonged. But then Stalin made a goodwill gesture towards King Michael of Romania and allowed all captured Romanian soldiers to return home. We rushed to the camp commander and said, 'We're Romanian too.' He was kind and let us join the soldiers.

As the train approached Sighet, the closest town to their village, the Lilliput group collected its belongings and hurried to the doors. The train came to a halt but no one was allowed to disembark. They all had to continue to the last stop, Arad, 400 kilometres further on, at the far end of Romania. But even there, the Russians, suspecting the presence of SS men among the SS's victims, refused to allow the passengers off the train.

That night, all the suspected were assembled and ordered to raise their left arms; the SS had tattooed the blood group of their troopers into their left armpits. Several men were arrested and sent to Russia. So it was only at the end of August 1945, seven months after being liberated from Auschwitz, that the Lilliput group was finally free.

When all twenty-three of them arrived in Rozavlea, the Slomowitzes returned to their home, as did Bassie Fischman and her mother.

Regina Ovitz, who had lost her entire family in Auschwitz, had nowhere to go: she moved in with her dwarf cousins.

Weeds now covered their flower and vegetable beds, the chicken and geese were no longer running about the yard, and the cows had disappeared from the shed. From the outside, the house, at least, looked to be intact. But the door had been broken open and inside only the childlike furniture, not useful to anyone but the dwarfs, remained. The thick carpets, the flimsy curtains, the hand-embroidered tapestries, all were gone. Other objects had been slashed or shattered. The floor planks had all been torn up, probably in the course of someone's search for gold and other valuables. Avram and Micki rushed outside to the dust-covered car in the yard. Some parts had been damaged and the paint had been scratched by the village children who, it seemed, had used it as a playground. Apparently, though, no one had attempted to move it from its place. They waited anxiously until midnight to investigate the ground beneath it. Avram and Micki crawled under the chassis and groped around until they felt a small hollow. Silently, like moles, they clawed the earth away. The jar was there, just as they had left it, filled to the brim with their jewellery and gold coins.

Bad news soon followed. From Jewish refugees returning from the camps, the Ovitzes learned that their brother Arie, with eight of his friends, had managed to escape the Hungarian labour camp. They had hidden in a deserted farm but a peasant woman had informed on them. All nine were shot on the spot. Devastated, the Ovitzes then learned the terrible fate of his wife Magda, their four-month-old baby girl and her parents, who were all gassed in Auschwitz. More bad news came from a group of men who had been in a slave-labour camp in the Urals: Izo Edenburg, Frieda's husband, had died of hunger. And there was still no news of the husbands of Elizabeth and Leah.

SEVENTEEN

SIGHET-ANTWERP, 1945-1949

Six hundred and fifty Jews had been driven out of Rozavlea in the spring of 1944. A year later, only fifty had survived to return to the village of their birth.

Eyes full of resentment followed the survivors as they retrieved furnishings from the homes of dead family members in order to make their own looted dwellings once more habitable. In their year's absence, some of the houses had been occupied by Romanian squatters and the authorities showed no inclination to evict them in favour of the lawful owners.

Simon Slomowitz nailed their floor planks back down where they belonged; Sarah collected the essential pots and pans; and they agreed that for the time being they could do without curtains. The nights were getting chilly, so they were thankful that at least the fireplace had not been damaged. They lit a bonfire in the back yard and each of them waited with a little pile of the clothes they had worn in Auschwitz. First, Avram threw in his coat, and they all watched as the flames scorched and devoured it. Next it was Rozika's turn and, once her dresses had dissolved completely, Franziska threw hers into the blaze. As if they were participating in an ancient ritual, the Ovitzes stood silently in their circle until every trace – every ruffle, feather, button and patch – had turned to ash.

Soon after arriving back in Rozavlea, Bassie Fischman found

a new love, Abe Glazer, who had himself just returned from Auschwitz. Along with her mother, they applied for immigration visas to America, where Bassie's brother was already living. The Ovitzes, meanwhile, had enlarged their household. They had seen their neighbours' orphaned daughter, Gitta, crying on the stairway of her deserted parents' house and taken her in. 'There were not enough beds, so I shared one, sometimes with Perla, sometimes with Sarah,' recalls Gitta Drettler-Budimsky.

> They did everything they could to cheer me up and taught me some songs. I was a shy, fourteen-year-old Orthodox girl and didn't know any dances. So the dwarf women played some tangos and waltzes, and Micki led me through the living room and taught me the steps. He was such a skilful teacher that I hardly noticed he was half my size. I wanted to do my share of housework, but they wouldn't hear of it.

The Lilliputs viewed their seventeen-month absence from the stage as a forced intermission that could be easily made up for; they intended to resume their lives from the point of the disruption. Rozavlea would once again be home port for their excursions. But Rozavlea had changed. Perla Ovitz:

> When we asked for our belongings, the neighbours refused to return them. They said, 'You suffered in Poland, but we suffered here.' They did not hide their hostility: 'We had it so good without you, why have you returned?' I fired back, 'It was God's will that we survive.' But I was frightened by this homecoming.

Rozavlea had become a graveyard. The stillness of the empty houses, the muted, ruined synagogue, the faces missing from the street – Rozavlea was increasingly unbearable.

They decided to move to the town of Sighet, now a haven for Jewish refugees who had been uprooted from their villages. At 40 Bogdan Voda – on the main street and just a short walk from the only synagogue still standing – the Ovitzes found an apartment: the entire first floor of a grand house that had been the property of a wealthy Jewish family exterminated in Auschwitz. The Slomowitz family followed suit and occupied a flat near the Ovitzes.

Once again, the Lilliputs assembled their orchestra. They replaced the missing instruments and rehearsed their repertoire. On weekends, they converted their spacious living room into a ballroom. The entrance fee was affordable. 'Only the young had come back from the camps. We were on our own, youth with no authority or responsibility, no longer as pious as before the war,' recalls Shoshana Glazer, who lost her parents, grandparents, and six brothers and sisters in Auschwitz. 'Just a year-and-a-half before, Jewish teenagers like myself had not been allowed to mix and never thought of really dancing together. Now, the floor was always packed with dancing couples.'

Nevertheless, their Jewish clientele was limited; the region's bustling community of 154,000 Jews on the eve of the war had been reduced to only a few thousand who were trying desperately to rebuild their lives. Not only were the survivors too poor and too few to provide an audience, but Romanian towns and villages had also been rendered destitute. The Lilliputs soon realised that they could not possibly earn a living in the area, but neither could they leave – Leah and Elizabeth had still heard no word from their husbands.

Just ten days after her wedding in November 1942, Elizabeth had been torn from her husband. In spring 1945, freed from labour-camp slavery, Moshe Moskowitz rushed home to find her. The house was looted and empty, with no sign at all that the Ovitzes had survived. At that time they were still in Russian captivity. Moskowitz lost hope of ever seeing his wife again. As a last memento, he took a photograph he had found in a drawer. In the photo, as elsewhere, Elizabeth is safely embraced by her family.

Taken in 1927, the oval-shaped photo constitutes one of the few remnants of the Ovitz clan's pre-war life. It shows Batia Ovitz surrounded by her children, 24-year-old Avram authoritatively sitting next to her, his legs dangling above the ground; Elizabeth, only thirteen, is lying on the carpet, with her head resting against her six-year-old sister, Perla. All the dwarfs are leaning back, as if they are trying not to strain their weak spines while the photographer takes his time and adjusts his camera. The sons are wearing top hats and bow ties; they have snow-white handkerchiefs folded neatly in the upper pocket of their jackets. Apparently, at that early age, Avram already needed a cane, while Micki, at eighteen, still shy about his handicap, uses an umbrella as a crutch – although it was a warm day. The mother's dark dress has long sleeves and a high neck; a modest scarf hides her hair. Her daughter Frieda, though, is wearing a low *décolletage* and long earrings peep out from her thick black curls. Shortly after that blissful summer, their mother would fall ill and be bedridden until death.

Moskowitz put the photo in his suitcase and headed southward for the Romanian capital, Bucharest, where he hoped to collect some information about the fate of the Ovitz family. He was lucky. At the office of the Jewish community, quite by chance, he ran into his brother-in-law Azriel Ovitz, Leah's cousin and husband, who had also recently visited Rozavlea. Like Moskowitz, he had found no evidence that their dear ones had survived. For days the two men carefully pored over survivor lists, but they found nothing. Then Moskowitz got news that his sister was alive and well in Rome. He travelled to stay with her, while Azriel decided to try his luck again and return to Sighet. The beadle at the synagogue directed him to the Ovitzes' new apartment. There, for the first time, Azriel saw his three-year-old son, Shimshon. A year later, Leah bore a daughter. They named her Batia.

In January 1946, Moskowitz, still in Rome, accidentally bumped into a relative of the Ovitzes who was on his way back to Sighet. On a piece of paper, Moskowitz scribbled some words of love and hope, along with his address, and attached the photograph. He had no idea whether Elizabeth and her family were alive, but he used every opportunity to look for them.

Through the Jewish community in Sighet, the messenger traced the Ovitzes and Elizabeth cabled her husband immediately. Once he arrived at Sighet, the Ovitzes were finally able to leave.

The only country that agreed to provide them with entry visas was Belgium. Although they had never performed there, and had no knowledge of the country's languages, they were encouraged to learn that many of their compatriots had already begun a new life among the diamond merchants in Antwerp's Yiddish-speaking community. In Belgium, too, they thought they would be closer to America.

Cousin Regina, reluctant to join them on their new odyssey, preferred to start a new life of her own in Romania. The Ovitzes allowed her the use of their derelict house in Rozavlea, which she made as liveable as she could. She would always appreciate the parcels of food that they sent her from Antwerp. As for Simon Slomowitz, who had stood by the Lilliputs' side for the past three decades, it was obvious that he would

SIGHET-ANTWERP, 1945-1949

follow the troupe wherever they decided to go. His wife was unhappy with the prospect of Antwerp, especially since their grown children, Mordechai and Fanny, were not joining them: brother and sister had decided to stay in Romania, since they no longer wanted their destiny to be bound with the dwarfs'. Years later, they would emigrate to Israel. Perla Ovitz:

> We took a taxi to see our village for the last time. In the cemetery we bid farewell to our parents. We wept by their tombstones, asking for forgiveness at having to leave them behind for ever. We knew we would never set foot in that country again.

In the spring of 1947, there were a quarter of a million displaced Jews in Europe. Most of them were stranded in tents and barracks at refugee camps, under the administration of relief organisations. The Ovitzes, their family intact, had escaped that bitter fate. In Antwerp, where half of the Jewish community had perished, the Ovitzes easily found a vacant and furnished apartment on Maria Magdalena Street. The Slomowitzes rented a flat just opposite.

The death camps had left the survivors exhausted; all they wished for now was peace and quiet. Placid Belgium afforded the Ovitzes simple pleasures. They enjoyed the life of Antwerp's Jewish community, which had retained remarkable prosperity. Each of the able-bodied men found work – in the diamond market, the furrier workshops or the American Army warehouses – while the seven dwarfs were preparing their comeback. They realised that in their present country of residence, they would need to revamp their performances to suit their new audiences. For the first time in their career, they hired a professional director, Jakob Cyterman. They added French songs to their repertoire ('*Je suis seul ce soir*') and a one-act comedy, *De False Liebe* – False Love. One of the new skits was 'In the tailor's shop'. Perla, Micki and Elizabeth were the tailors, helplessly trying to satisfy the needs of their client, an exceptionally tall man. It was the first time that the Lilliput Troupe was willing to poke fun at their size and the audience roared with laughter.

They were embraced by their next-door neighbours, a childless Catholic couple who owned a fruit and vegetable shop. Perla in particular was the apple of their eye. Whenever she passed by, the greengrocer would lift her up like a doll and plead with her to take whatever she liked: 'You've suffered enough,' he'd say. Perla was twenty-eight at the time but was happy to be babied. The grocer always diverted his eyes from her arm. Begging her to cover her tattooed number, he'd say: 'I can't be reminded of what they did to you.'

•

At this time, Dina Gottlieb and her mother were in Paris. They had survived the death march and the liberation had found them in the Neustadt-Glewe concentration camp. Once freed, mother and daughter headed immediately to their hometown of Brno, where Dina was anxious to rejoin her boyfriend, Karel Klinger. She had not seen him in two years. In Brno, a mutual friend who had been imprisoned with Karel at Dachau handed her a note: 'I declare Dina Gottlib to be my lawful wedded wife.' It was dated a few days before Karel died, on the eve of liberation. He would remain the great love of her life.

With her only reason for staying in Brno gone, they moved to Paris, where Dina had an uncle. She applied for a job as an animator with the Paris office of Warner Bros. The man who interviewed her for the job was Arthur Babbitt, who had been a senior animator on Disney's *Snow White and the Seven Dwarfs*. She was won over. Eventually they married and settled in Hollywood, where Dina became a housewife and raised two daughters. She returned to the art of animation after her divorce, which followed fourteen years of marriage. Despite her long-time fascination with Disney's classic, she could not ever bring herself to paint dwarfs again.

'One day,' Dina recounts,

I met a man who offered to take off my tattooed Birkenau number for fifty dollars. I didn't think much and let him do it. Now whenever I look at the thin white scar on my forearm I regret it. I realise it was my lucky number and I shouldn't run away from my past. When I play the lottery, I use my camp number, 61016, and I've also made it my email address.

In 1973 Dina learned that seven of the Gypsy portraits she had painted for Mengele, including the one of Celine, had miraculously survived and were being exhibited at the Auschwitz State Museum. Since then, she has been battling the museum authorities to retrieve them.

Dina's case embodies a clash between two opposing principles. On the one hand is the American faith in the paramount value of individual rights; on the other, a strong conviction – one solidly grounded in Poland's Communist era – of the paramount value of the collective good. The result is a tangle of conflicting moral and legal rights that King Solomon would have found difficult to solve. The museum claims that everything found and made in the death camp should remain there for ever, as evidence of the Nazis' atrocities and as a memorial to the victims. As the portraits were not undertaken at Dina's initiative but commissioned by Mengele, the museum contends, they are not ordinary works of art; rather, they are medical illustrations that constitute the documentation of a crime.

When she completed her first portrait, Mengele had noticed that she had not signed her work. 'You mean my name or my number?' she asked him. And he said, 'Your name.' And she duly inscribed 'Dina 1944' on all the works she had done for him. 'My paintings saved my life, and thanks to them I lived to raise a family,' she argues. 'They are a part of my soul, and I won't be complete without them. As long as they are there, I'll still be a prisoner in Auschwitz.' Dina died in July 2009, aged eighty-six. Her paintings have remained in the Auschwitz State Museum.

After the liberation, Ludovit Feld, one of the ten dwarfs in Mengele's collection, returned to his Czechoslovakian home-town of Košice. He resumed his artistic career and became one of his country's renowned painters and art teachers. Although his long-standing conversion to Christianity had not prevented his deportation, the experience of Auschwitz did not propel him back to the old faith. When he found no real peace of mind in the church, he turned to various Marxist and Leninist groups, which likewise failed him. Disappointed and disil-lusioned, he gradually re-embraced his native Judaism and began attending synagogue services regularly.

It took Kalman Bar-On and Peter Grünfeld, the young inmates from the experimental block, forty-four years to track down Feld. In the autumn of 1989 they travelled from Israel to meet him. He was eighty-five, had never married and contin-ued to live on his own, almost blind, bedridden. At his bedside, he kept an album of his drawings, entitled *Children are Also Led to Death*.

'Throughout the years, I've been waiting for you,' Feld said to his visitors. 'I can hardly see, but each of the twin's faces I painted in Birkenau is etched deep inside me. I remember the pretty face of one child with special sharpness – Pepicheck, who couldn't sit still when I painted him. What happened to him? Did he survive?' Peter Grünfeld knelt by Feld's bed and let the blind man feel Pepicheck's wet cheeks. Ludovit Feld died in May 1991. A black marble tombstone in the Jewish cemetery of Košice bears his full Hebrew name in Hebrew letters.

•

And now to Josef Mengele and his associates. *SS-Obersturm-führer* Dr Heinz Thilo, Mengele's Auschwitz rival, was transferred to Gross-Rosen concentration camp at the end of 1944. His fate remains unknown; he is thought to have been killed either in Hohenelbe in May 1945 or in Berlin in October 1947. Professor Otmar von Verschuer, Mengele's professional sponsor and head of the genetic and hereditary research programme at the Kaiser Wilhelm Institute, was declared a Nazi sympathiser by a Frankfurt denazification court in 1946; he was fined 600 marks. In 1951, he became professor of human genetics at the University of Munster; three years later, he was promoted to the position of dean of the medical faculty. On his sixtieth birthday, in 1956, he was commended as a 'master and teacher' by the distinguished Italian eugenicist Luigi Gedda in the Italian magazine of eugenics, *Acta Genet.* Similar honours were bestowed on him by the American, Italian, Austrian and Japanese societies for human genetics. He died in 1969; his wicked deeds went ignored to the end.

Mengele's academic rival, Professor Hans Grebe, obtained a teaching position in the department of human genetics at the University of Marburg in 1952; in 1957 he became president of the German Association of Sport Doctors. Grebe, like von

Verschuer, vigorously denied any collaboration with Mengele at Auschwitz. He also destroyed all incriminating documents. The medical records kept by von Verschuer at the Kaiser Wilhelm Institute are not available to researchers: in a bizarre irony, many decades after they were murdered, the Nazi doctors' Jewish victims have been transformed by German officials into esteemed patients whose right to privacy must be steadfastly safeguarded.

In 1948, the Kaiser Wilhelm Institute was renamed 'the Max Planck Institute'; a half-century later, in June 2001, the society's president, Professor Hubert Markl, issued the following statement, admitting that: 'There is scientific evidence proving beyond the shadow of a doubt that directors and employees at the Kaiser Wilhelm Institute were together intellectually responsible for, and sometimes even actively collaborated in, the crimes of the Nazi regime.' This came as no news to Efraim Reichenberg, a survivor of Mengele's experiments. 'Over all these years, I've been aware that Mengele was simply a little cog in the machinery of mass murder. The biggest crime in history was carried out under the direction of leading scientists and distinguished institutions.' Reichenberg and six other victims were flown to Berlin to hear Markl express his formal 'apology and deep regret ... personally and on behalf of the Max Planck Institute ... [that] crimes of this sort were committed, promoted and not prevented within the ranks of German scientists'.

On 17 January 1945, Mengele left Auschwitz, made a short stop at the Kaiser Wilhelm Institute in Berlin, and then travelled to Gross-Rosen, where he shed his SS uniform. Then, dressed in a Wehrmacht uniform, he continued to Saaz in the Sudetenland to work in a field hospital. He carried with him two suitcases filled with his research data. It is highly likely that the data included reports on the Lilliput-group experiments; it is also likely that Mengele viewed the data as a potential noose – as the proof of his crimes – but also as a potential springboard to a new academic career. On the night of 8 May 1945, the date of Germany's unconditional surrender, Mengele deposited the suitcases with a nurse who had worked with him in Saaz. He then fled to Saxony, where he was captured by the Americans in late June 1945. He was registered under his real name in an American POW camp. The United Nations War Crimes Commission had already declared him a major war criminal, but the 'wanted' list never reached the camp, and he was released two months later.

Mengele did not go straight home to his wife and child, nor did he visit his parents. Instead, risking capture by the Russians, he set out on a long journey to the Thuringian town of Gera, where his nurse was keeping the suitcases. With his precious Auschwitz documents, he took shelter on an isolated farm near the Bavarian village of Mangolding. His wife, Irene, afraid that she'd be followed by the American military, hazarded only one visit, in the summer of 1946. Biographers Posner and Ware suggest that around that time their marriage was coming to an end; the fugitive doctor no longer held the promise of a glorious future that Irene had pinned her hopes on.

Mengele must have followed the Nuremberg trial of his former Nazi medical friends and colleagues in December 1946 with some degree of apprehension. Seven of them would be hanged; five would receive life sentences. On the other hand, the apparent social and professional rehabilitation of his superiors – the onset of their embrace by post-war Germany's academic community – must have stirred in him considerable envy. Mengele had decided to stay away from Europe until it tired of pursuing Nazi war criminals. He arrived in Buenos

Aires in late August 1949 and passed through customs with his suitcase of experimental data. A month later, the special German academic commission that had already rehabilitated von Verschuer threw Mengele a lifeline as well, announcing that 'from the available evidence, it is not clear how much Dr Mengele himself knew of the atrocities and killings in Auschwitz during the times in question'. Evidently, Mengele did not consider the lifeline reliable enough and decided to remain in South America.

•

In 1949, the Lilliputs were themselves trying to decide whether to stay on in Europe or leave for good. After two admittedly tranquil years in Belgium, they still felt rootless. 'We were expelled from our parents' house, from a country where we were famous. We managed to survive one Hitler, but who can promise us another miracle?' Perla Ovitz would tell her siblings in their family debates. The memory of Auschwitz clung to all of them and America seemed a safer place. Their career was not taking off and they gladly accepted the occasional invitation to sing at a benefit for the newly established state of Israel. Each Passover, they enunciated the traditional 'next year in Jerusalem' but had never seriously considered turning the prayer into a concrete plan.

Before the war, immigration to Palestine had been controlled by its British rulers, who issued a limited number of entry visas for distribution by the Jewish Agency. The Zionist vision favoured the young and able-bodied. The image of the New Jew – a broad-shouldered, hard-working, sun-tanned pioneer – conflicted rather starkly with the Ovitzes' deformity. In any case, only a handful of their neighbours in Rozavlea had emigrated to Palestine before the war. As Orthodox Jews, the Ovitzes were not eager to follow them, as they were not keen on the new society taking shape there, which turned its back on religion. For the Lilliput Troupe, a new life in a land where Yiddish was frowned upon, where the old culture was scorned and the folk traditions banished, would have been artistic suicide.

Following the war, Palestine had become a desired haven for the refugees who had survived the Final Solution. Still, the obstacles placed in the path to the Promised Land seemed insurmountable to the Lilliputs. The British Mandate authorities were issuing only 1,500 visas a month, so their chances of obtaining even one were virtually nil. Nor were they capable of smuggling themselves illegally, boarding an ancient, over-loaded cargo boat that might land them in Palestine furtively, at nightfall, off one of its deserted beaches. Tens of thousands of Jews had already resorted to just such a strategy, jumping off board into the arms of Jewish underground members who would help them through the water to the shore – and then living in hiding, with a constant fear of being arrested by the British police. Those were the lucky ones; the majority would in fact be caught and sent to internment camps in Cyprus. It was obvious that the Ovitzes were not fit for such an ordeal. And the War of Independence marked the onset of an even worse time for them to emigrate. Israel was thus relegated to last of a list of priorities.

The Lilliputs missed the stage. The offer to perform in Russia was still there and there was a Lilliputian village in Budapest. But they were too independent – some found them superciliously so – for such an enterprise, and they deplored any vulgar exploitation of their handicap. They had reconciled themselves to the idea of a final, if early, retirement from show business when suddenly they received a dream invitation: the impresario Irving Jacobson was offering them a long-term contract to perform in one of New York's Yiddish theatres. He sounded very keen and the financial arrangements were especially tempting. And then, equally out of the blue, they were faced with another option. Israeli immigration emissaries, dispatched throughout Europe, had been channelling Holocaust survivors towards the new Jewish state. When the Belgian branch learned that the Lilliputs were heading for the New World, they knocked on their door. The War of Independence was over, the emissaries told them, and promised financial benefits that matched the American offer.

The Israeli option had now become appealing. While Hebrew had been the dominant language of art and culture in Jewish Palestine, the tens of thousands of European refugees now expanding the population of the new Israeli state meant that Yiddish had gained a new audience. And the Lilliput Troupe had gained a new chance.

When our next-door neighbours in Antwerp heard that we planned to leave, they begged us to stay, promising they would designate us as sole heirs. But while we were divided between America and Israel, we did agree on one thing – not to stay in Europe any longer. In the family discussions I favoured America. I said Israel is like a young chick that has just emerged from its egg, let's go to America, make money and then settle comfortably in Israel with full pockets. Those who preferred going to Israel right away pointed out that our previous fans had been immigrating there by the day, while in America nobody knew us. We were frightened by what people said about America being a competitive, cruel society, about us not being able to live up to its tempo. When we were too weak to perform, we'd be thrown to the dogs.

The head of the family, Avram Ovitz, cast the final vote: 'Enough wandering. It's time we settle down and live among our kin.' So they changed the forwarding labels on their packed crates from 'New York' to 'Haifa'. On 4 May 1949, the *Atzmaut* ('Independence') set sail from the port of Marseille. The Lilliputs and 2,150 other passengers celebrated Israel's first Independence Day in the middle of the Mediterranean.

EIGHTEEN

HAIFA, 1949-1954

On Monday 9 May 1949, Leah Ginzburg-Fried, the correspondent in Haifa for the daily newspaper *Maariv*, took the bus to the port downtown. It was a routine stop on her morning rounds, since thousands of immigrants were disembarking daily and stories were there for the picking. Standing by the gangway, chatting with her colleagues, she threw an occasional glance at the descending passengers. A middle-aged, elegantly clad man walked nonchalantly down a gangplank. The press people instantly recognised the face of Sidney Stanley and besieged him. He had been involved in a British government financial scandal and escaped from London in the middle of his trial. He seemed to feel safe in his new haven, answering questions with considerable arrogance.

Stanley commanded attention, certainly, but out of a corner of her eye, Ginzburg-Fried caught a peculiar sight. Seven dwarfs were carefully negotiating the gangway. They each held the rail with one hand to balance themselves as they stretched out a leg to reach the step below; their strange parade moved slowly forward. Ginzburg-Fried wavered between the two attractions. She hastily scribbled down the fugitive Stanley's statements while keeping an eye on her other newsworthy catch. She lost sight of them for brief moments when the dwarfs got hidden in the general commotion on the dock, but at her first opportunity she dashed over to them.

'The unusual phenomenon of seven dwarfs caused much attention and the passers-by gaped at them,' she later reported in *Maariv*. 'Someone tried to drive the intruders away. Someone else lowered his voice and reproached the onlookers: "They're human beings like us, only small. Of all people, Jews should not be prejudiced and offend handicapped people with an intrusive gaze."' When the crowd began to disperse, Perla Ovitz, in a long black dress and with a red flower tucked into her hair, stepped forward with a buoyant smile. 'We're not intimidated by inquisitive eyes,' she is quoted as saying. 'Millions of people have been watching us throughout our entire lives. Naturally we'd like to be no different than you, but if this is the shape God destined for us, we have no complaints against Him.'

Leah Ginzburg-Fried stooped down. Her pleated skirt touching the ground, her pad resting on her knee, she began to take down the Lilliputs' story, from the limelight of pre-war Romania to the cesspool of Auschwitz. They spared no details and candidly discussed one event in particular – their humiliating presentation at the SS medical convention, when Mengele ordered them to strip naked. In this respect, the dwarfs were unusually frank. At that time, a great many Holocaust survivors, guilt-ridden by their own chance deliverance, had been extremely reluctant to explore their own traumatic memories, let alone to disclose in public the horrors they had been through.

The Lilliput Troupe had planned their grand entrance. The dwarfs refused any assistance, letting no one cradle them down the gangway. They handled the interview skilfully, knowing what to conceal and what to reveal, and what would make a good quote. They showed themselves to be in good shape and in good spirits, for to seek pity or display weakness, they knew, would harm the chances of a comeback. The 63-year-old Rozika Ovitz said she was forty-five; 28-year-old Perla demurely declared she was nineteen. Six-year-old Shimshon, heedless of the shock he was causing, ran around proudly showing off his tattoo. They would ask for no special favours from the state, Ginzburg-Fried jotted down in her notebook. On the contrary, they had a message: 'Our only wish is to bring some laughter and joy to our brethren in our new homeland.'

The photographers now stepped in. Exactly five years earlier, the Hungarian press had documented the dwarfs' expulsion to Auschwitz. On that hot May day in the Dragomireşti ghetto, they had been dressed in layers of winter garments, as they were travelling into an unknown future. Now, for their reception in Haifa they had chosen much lighter fashion – Franziska and Rozika were wearing identical long, flower-printed cotton dresses; Elizabeth wore an elegant two-part summer suit.

This time as well, a uniformed policeman was asked to stand beside one of the lady dwarfs; as before, the contrast between big and small made for an eye-catching image. The United Press International (UPI) photographer set up the seven dwarfs in a semi-circle. For his photo, Micki and Avram have taken off their summer jackets and rolled up their white shirt sleeves; their engraved, silver-handled canes cast aside, they are standing energetically erect. With their neat and fashionable garments, their make-up and styled hair, the dwarfs made everyone around them look shabby. They are smiling at the camera, as if they are about to bow to an applauding crowd. To this day, the UPI photograph is reprinted in a university genetics textbook to illustrate the 'human pseudoachondroplasia phenotype determined by a dominant allele that interferes with bone growth during the development'.

Ginzburg-Fried followed the Lilliput Troupe to the immigrant camp of Bat Galim. In the first year of Israel's independence, the nation of 650,000 had to absorb 200,000 new immigrants. As accommodation for the influx of newcomers was next to non-existent, vacated British army camps, abandoned Arab houses and makeshift tent cities became their temporary homes. The Ovitzes had barely unpacked their suitcases when agents and producers came courting. While the Lilliputs basked in their renewed celebrity, they nonetheless remained cautious and diplomatically postponed a decision. 'First, we want to see the country, then we'll find a place to live. Only after performing for the Israeli soldiers and making them happy, we'll talk about business.'

Starting a new life in Israel would end the Ovitzes' thirty years of friendship with the Slomowitzes. The two families had jointly struggled in a daily battle with the harshest imaginable conditions for human survival. If it had not been for the dwarfs' willingness, at a risk to their own lives, to falsely present to Mengele their neighbours as family, the Slomowitzes would certainly have perished. But with the danger over, the burden of debits and credits no longer served as a bond; rather, it strained the relationship

'Mother demanded that we not see them any more once we set foot in Israel,' recalls Judah Slomowitz.

She was always scolding Father: 'You have a wife and children, whom you neglect all the time to serve those dwarfs hand and foot.' Father was torn: 'They saved our lives! We owe them everything.' But Mother had the last word: 'You're turning us into their slaves and I've had enough of it.' So we sailed on separate boats, and while they settled in Haifa we went south to Ramla.

Their shared fate had bred in the two families a mutual sense of resentment over each other's lack of appreciation. Indebted to the Lilliputs for their lives, the Slomowitzes felt that they could do nothing, ultimately, to sufficiently gratify their saviours. Regina, as well as Bassie Fischman and her mother, felt the same.

'No doubt I owe my life to them, but at the same time they wouldn't have survived Birkenau if we hadn't been there to care for them,' says Bassie Fischman, now Glazer, living in New York. 'We carried them in our arms, stood in line to bring them food, helped them dress and wash up. We were their human horses and without us they couldn't have made the journey back home. We're equal parties – they saved us and we saved them.'

The break was also favoured by the Ovitzes, who felt that they had been exploited by their debtors. But while the rest of the group willingly dropped contact with the Ovitzes, Simon Slomowitz couldn't keep away. To his dying days, in 1977, he would travel discreetly up to Haifa in order to spend some cheerful hours with the dwarfs and provide a helping hand around the house; he would continue, too, as always, to bask in the presence of his Frieda.

All fifteen members of the Ovitz family settled in a long wooden barrack near the sea. Each received an iron bed, a straw mattress, a woollen blanket, two sheets and the maximum settlement allowance of forty dollars. Hanging blankets divided the barrack into small family units and allowed some intimacy. Perla recalls that:

Part of the outer wall was missing, and the blanket we hung in its place did not help much to keep away the wind and chill. There was no escape from the constant noise of the waves, especially at night, and I lay awake for hours. We became bitter: was this the villa they promised when they convinced us not to accept the American contract? Dr Mengele had at least provided us with a room with a toilet; here in our new homeland they didn't want to waste proper accommodations on us because we were dwarfs.

Still, they soon became magnets for the press. One Israeli weekly offered its readers five photos of the Lilliputs engaged in various pursuits: in one, the dwarfs are being interviewed by kneeling journalists; in another, Micki and Avram are wrapped in their prayer shawls; a third shows Rozika and Franziska with their small violins; in the fourth, Frieda is hugging her nephew and niece, little Shimshon and Batia. The fifth – a photo of the elderly sisters powdering their noses – carries the caption 'a woman is a woman, and make-up is essential, regardless of age and size'.

They were approached by Kalman Ginzburg, the Israeli impresario, who persuaded them to join his list of such celebrity clients as Jascha Heifetz, Isaac Stern, Yehudi Menuhin and Leonard Bernstein. He bombarded municipal and governmental offices with letters demanding that the Lilliput Troupe be exempted from the high entertainment taxes. To reinforce the letters, he had all seven dwarfs storm the offices.

The Israeli bureaucracy did not act promptly upon Ginzburg's petitions so, adding more pressure, he organised a press conference at the distinguished Tel Aviv Commercial Club. The invitation promised lunch – one way to ensure a full journalistic presence in a time of austerity; the tables were indeed lavishly laid. Ginzburg opened the occasion by describing the Lilliput Troupe's European career and widespread popularity. He pointed out that the dwarfs had received alluring offers from both Moscow and New York, yet they had chosen to settle instead in Israel, despite the financial sacrifice. He lauded the unique style of their performances, which preserved a Jewish heritage that the past decade had greatly endangered and nearly destroyed.

Then, Avram Ovitz rose and not a single eye missed the tattooed number on his arm. He briefly described the troupe's Auschwitz experiences before taking questions from the floor. To one reporter he explained, 'Our first performances will be in Yiddish, but we are already making an effort to acquire Hebrew as quickly as possible and use it onstage.'

He was vague about their repertoire: 'First of all, we'll show the Israelis what a dwarf family can do.' Soon after the press conference – and before the troupe had publicly performed even one song – the Ministry of Finance had granted their demands. They would receive the same tax-exempt status accorded such celebrated institutions as the Israeli Philharmonic Orchestra and the Habima Theatre. While the ministry did not mention the Lilliputs' dwarfdom, it most certainly influenced the decision; for if the troupe found itself unable to perform and make a living from music, the fifteen Ovitzes would add a far from negligible burden to the state's already sorely overstretched social services.

Some columnists disapproved. 'A short stature is not a guarantee of high standards,' Alexander Tauber wrote in one tabloid. 'The only grounds for judgement is artistic excellence and this even holds true for dwarfs. Let them first perform and if the critics declare that they have raised artistic standards in Israel, then they have grounds to apply for a tax exemption.'

Even before the ministry's decision, the Lilliputs, certain that they would be granted the exemption, had booked the most prestigious halls in Israel for the entire month of August.

Their publicity campaign was intense and expensive. Huge advertisements in ten newspapers and billboards all over the country announced 'The Lilliput Troupe: first performances ever in Israel, in songs and music, folklore, comedy and drama'. Racing against the clock so as not to lose the summer season, they had to hire extra carpenters to work day and night to build the set and props. Assisted by a professional, Egyptian-born seamstress, Elizabeth and Perla made glittering new costumes for the entire cast.

The Lilliput's career was launched anew on 4 August 1949 – exactly five years, by the Jewish calendar, after the performance perversely commanded by Mengele at Auschwitz on the day of the Tisha B'av fast. Observing tradition, the Lilliputs ate nothing the whole day; they prayed and lamented the Temple's destruction. But already one hour after the fast had ended they were onstage in *Armon* (Palace Hall) in their new hometown of Haifa. They had fierce competition for audiences that month. The Israel Opera was staging *La Bohème* and *The Barber of Seville*; mime Marcel Marceau was bringing his show from Paris; the Habima theatre was presenting its big hit *In the Negev Prairies*, a controversial play about the sacrifice of young men in the War of Independence.

But the competition did not diminish the Lilliput Troupe's success. Their show proved to be a tour de force; it ran for more than six weeks and all forty-one performances were sold out. They went onstage twice daily and the matinée was especially designed for children on school vacation. A favourite act was to mount six tall men from the audience onstage, to offer a comic contrast with the stars.

The halls were often packed with immigrants who hadn't seen them perform for years. Yet the show was not merely a trip down memory lane, bathed in nostalgia for a world utterly devastated by war and for loved ones abruptly lost. In the foyer, people who were long thought dead would be suddenly recognised by relatives or neighbours and they would fall into one another's arms. A feeling of triumph charged the place: five years after Auschwitz, the show was going on again. The audience roundly applauded the Lilliputs, of course, but they were also celebrating their own resurrection.

Surviving Rozavleans were admitted to the show for free. One day, the newly married Gitta Drettler-Budimsky spotted a notice of their performance. The last time she had seen the Ovitzes was in the summer of 1945, when they had given her shelter in their house in Rozavlea. A year later, the fifteen-year-old orphan had emigrated with a group of other children and teenagers to Israel, and this advertisement was the first sign of life from her former benefactors.

Throughout the show I was crying and laughing and couldn't wait for the last curtain to fall so I could see them. I rushed backstage then and joined the queue of people who were already waiting. When I entered their dressing room, I was delighted that they immediately recognised me. We hugged and they gave me their souvenir photo, which I cherish to this day.

After the Lilliputs had wrapped up their first season, they prepared their new show, realising that they could not win over the larger Hebrew-speaking public with their old material. In the past, they had always played to homogenous audiences; thus they had specially tailored their shows for each group, be it Romanian, Hungarian or Czechoslovakian. In Israel, with its Babel of languages and numerous cultures, that strategy would no longer suffice. They needed to put together a repertoire with a wider and more general appeal.

A governmental regulation forbade resident artists from performing solely in a foreign language, Yiddish included. The Ovitzes, then, had to add content in Hebrew to their shows. They had noticed that Israelis responded more enthusiastically to tragicomic skits than they did to songs, so Avram sat down to write some. Domestic relationships provided an inexhaustible source of ideas for marital scenes, which had a hidden advantage for the dwarfs: they could sit on a chair or sofa onstage – a welcome relief when doing their second performance of the day.

They made a point of sharing the stardom by evenly splitting the solo parts and leading roles among all members of the troupe. They continued to employ director Jakob Cyterman and incorporated themselves as a company, 'Lilliput Entertainment Ltd'.

After nine months of rehearsals in their flimsy wooden barrack by the sea, they were ready to hit the road again with their new show. The programme was divided into two acts: 'Import–Export' in Hebrew and, after the intermission, 'An Angel Among Men' in Yiddish. In the latter, Perla played the peace-making angel who shot Cupid's arrows at a quarrelsome husband and wife. Throughout her life, she kept her cherished white-winged dress in her bedroom's overflowing wardrobe.

As time went on, the Lilliputs enriched their repertoire:

In one of our most popular plays, *The Double Wedding*, my brother Micki was my fiancé and Elizabeth was Avram's fiancée. We never got to the marriage ceremony, because in the Jewish religion when a man says 'with this ring I thee wed' it's legally binding even if said in jest or onstage. After the show, men would come to my dressing room and timidly enquire, 'Are you really engaged to that man?' I would laugh and reassure them, 'No, I'm only his sister.'

Perla, in fact, had a whole range of new roles. Her school-day experience with the pointer and the geography map inspired her brother to write a skit in which she, as a pupil, impresses the school supervisor with her knowledge. In another piece she played an awkward secretary at a job interview. Although she was the youngest in the troupe, Avram decided that she would be perfect in the role of an old lady. She painted deep wrinkles on her face and, since the Lilliputs never used wigs, she dusted her hair with talcum powder. With a quiver in her voice, she was so convincing that fans who came backstage to compliment the granny were incredulous when Perla's sisters pointed at her. Elizabeth captivated audiences as an unfaithful sweetheart who dances a sensuous tango, until she's discovered by her jealous lover, Micki, who stabs her with his knife. Her melodramatically prolonged dying scene in 'Death Tango' never failed to get a standing ovation.

That summer of 1950 again brought a box office sellout, and they extended the season until winter. Every night, after the applause and the curtain calls, they folded up their extravagant costumes and took a taxi back to the drafty barrack at the immigrant camp. Despite the uncomfortable conditions and lack of privacy, they were reluctant to move. They had not yet found a house that could accommodate all of them, and more than anything they feared separation. Besides, their barrack had become a contact point for people who had known them in their various circumstances.

'After I had brought my jewellery workshop tools to Israel, they kindly agreed to keep them for me, since I was still a soldier and had no home,' recalls Herman Szabo, the next-door neighbours' son from Rozavlea. Zvi Klein – the thirteen-year-old twin who had lived with them in their Auschwitz barrack – recalls that the experience made us kin. I had no one left in the world, so I took to the sea. For fifteen years, whenever I returned to the port of Haifa, I prayed with concern that they were alive and well, and would only breathe a sigh of relief when I saw them in their doll-like prettiness. With each year that passed I viewed their presence as a small victory over the Nazis.

And Arie Tessler remarks that:

they were very cheerful and welcoming and time flew by when we visited. When it was late I would feel uncomfortable and want to leave, but my brother always wanted to stay. He seems to have been fascinated by the contrast between Avram and his huge wife – he was interested in peeping into their makeshift bedroom. Once the partition stirred slightly and he saw Avram lying cuddled up to his wife's legs.

Shimshon Ovitz had turned out to be a late developer, and his parents feared that he was manifesting the Ovitz genetic propensity. Thinking of the future, the family decided to prepare him for joining the Lilliput Troupe. They bought a second-hand piano and hired a music teacher. To help Shimshon overcome stage fright, Avram tailored a small part for him in the show. Over the school vacation, the boy performed onstage with his uncles and aunts, but he could not muster much enthusiasm, and the plan soon faded.

In 1951, the troupe was preparing for its third season and for extending their career abroad. In the midst of preparations for their European comeback, though, they suffered an unexpected blow. Their new impresario, Isidor Gruenberg, had embezzled their earnings. He falsely claimed he had spent the money on hiring performance halls and on visas to Germany. The dwarfs sued him and on 6 May 1953, all seven of them appeared in court. The media came running. While Avram Ovitz was head of the family and manager of Lilliput Entertainment Ltd., Elizabeth Ovitz-Moskowitz was the troupe's ambassador. She assumed the responsibility of presenting the Ovitzes' case. When she entered the courtroom, her lawyers realised that if she spoke from the witness stand she would be hidden from the magistrate. She was thus allowed to testify from the counsel's bench; still, she needed an additional small stool. 'For two hours, she was questioned in Yiddish by the prosecutor, and her confident, self-assured answers proved that she was well-versed in the ways of the world,' reported the influential daily *Haaretz*. 'The dwarfs' appearance in court attracted much attention. Their heads are like those of normal people; only their body and legs are short. They were beautifully dressed, the lady adorned with diamond-studded rings, gold bracelets and other expensive jewellery.' Gruenberg was found guilty and sent to jail.

The Ovitzes' disappointment with Gruenberg was something of a last straw. They had been performing for four years in Israel and felt that they had exhausted the country's small market: the gimmick of seven dwarfs was no longer working. The country was now flooded with Yiddish shows and competition was tough. In any event, life had left its mark on them. They had endured the ordeal of Auschwitz and its aftermath, and they had been performing for more than twenty-five years. Rozika was sixty-eight, Franziska sixty-five, Avram fifty-one. Perla excepted, the others were not far behind. All in all, the demands of theatrical life had become too strenuous for them: leaving the barrack at noon without lunch (so as not to overload their bodies); travelling two hours to the theatre, then performing two hours onstage; a short break after the matinée, then another show, and then the long return journey home; arriving at the barrack well after midnight. The routine was exhausting, and in a family council they discussed their options and decided to change course: they would retire from the stage and search for another occupation, one that would provide a livelihood without forcing them to separate.

They had never given up on the financial promises they had received from the Israeli authorities in Antwerp, and now they presented the bill to be paid. The Jewish Agency responded by offering them leases for a cinema and laundry in the beach resort of Netanya, less than an hour's drive from Haifa. But the Ovitzes did not find the terms adequate. In November 1954, after months of fruitless correspondence, their patience ran out. They travelled to Jerusalem and alerted the press that they would not leave the Jewish Agency's head office until their demands were answered. To avoid bad publicity, the security guards were instructed not to forcibly evict the dwarfs. Instead, the corridor where they were squatting was sealed off from the outside world.

On the third day of the sit-in, Elizabeth felt faint and was taken to the hospital. That afternoon, a spokesman announced that a special committee had been formed to consider the Ovitzes' demands. Only then did they agree to return to their barrack in Haifa.

NINETEEN

HAIFA, 1955-1979

On 30 October 1868, Christoph Hoffmann and Georg David Hardegg of Würtemberg's Temple Society arrived in the Holy Land. Believing in the imminent second coming of the Messiah, they wanted to rebuild the *Tempel Gottes*, (the Temple of God). At the foot of Mount Carmel they laid a cornerstone for their first residential house in Haifa. By the end of the 1930s, 650 Templars had settled in Haifa's flourishing German Colony; an additional thousand were living in six other settlements around the country. The Templars made their living from agriculture, light industry and hostelry. They had their own sports club, a bicycle association, a football team, cafés and restaurants. Of the seven cinemas in Haifa at the time, two were located in the German Colony. One of them, the Stadtgarten – an open-air, 800-seat cinema at the corner of Jaffa Road and Carmel Boulevard – was built on a site owned by Hermann Keller. In time, a second, roofed cinema, the Carmel, was added at the same location.

After the outbreak of the Second World War, all eligible Templar men were called back to Germany to join the Wehrmacht. As the war progressed, any men still living in the Templar settlements were at first detained in camps by the British authorities as enemy residents of Palestine and later deported with their families to Australia. Dozens of women with children, as well as the elderly, were left on their own in Haifa; the Templars' Arab partners and employees, meanwhile, ran the businesses on their behalf. When the war ended, those Templars who had been left behind gradually returned to Germany. The last of them departed when the State of Israel was established, whereupon their houses were confiscated as 'enemy property' for the use of Holocaust survivors. So it was that the Carmel and the Stadtgarten – now named Ganim (Gardens) – were now being offered on lease to the Lilliput Troupe. The vast plot also included a car-repair shop, a locksmith's, a carpentry shop, an upholstery shop and a small waffle bakery; the Ovitzes would collect the rent from these businesses as part of the deal. More attractive to them, though, were the residential apartments in the compound and they did not hesitate to sign the contract.

After six years in the crumbling barrack at the immigrants' camp, the Lilliput Troupe finally moved into proper quarters in the German Colony. Each family had its own space in the cinema compound. Avram and his wife lived on the top floor in one apartment (having married young, their daughter, Batia, was living elsewhere with her husband). Elizabeth and Moshe Moskowitz had a smaller flat for themselves in the building, as did Sarah and her husband, Erno Deutsch. So did Frieda, who had gotten married a second time, to Sami Melamed. Next door Leah lived with Azriel and their two children. In another flat, Rozika and Franziska shared one room, and Perla and Micki shared the other (when she changed clothes, he turned his back). For the first time, each of the Ovitz families now had the chance to run its own affairs; however, they all continued to share Sabbath and holiday meals around a long table.

In 1955, the Lilliput Troupe marked its retirement from the stage with a week of farewell performances that ended with a lavish ball. Thereafter, Lilliput Entertainment Ltd devoted itself not to theatrical presentations, but to promoting films on the silver screen.

It was very convenient to live on the premises, just a few steps from work – I had moved from stage lights to a narrow box office cubicle. It was in no way humiliating since I was still in show business. As a cashier, I needed to know what the film was about, to present the story to the customers in an attractive way. I was always carefully dressed and made up like in the old days when I was the show.

Perla was in fact no ordinary cashier. She was herself an attraction and the cinema's best publicist. Customers enjoyed chatting with her and, to show their appreciation, they often brought her small gifts.

As they always had, the Ovitzes continued to divide the work between them. Avram maintained his role as manager, Elizabeth chose the films and Micki operated the translation roll. Tall sisters Leah and Sarah worked in the cinema buffet and café. When things got hectic, everyone pitched in, except Rozika and Franziska, now nearly in their seventies, and Frieda, who had developed a kidney disease. The porters and ushers were local Arabs.

As in the Lilliputs' theatre days, summer continued to be busy season, as they were operating both the cinemas and offering 1,200 seats for each of the three daily shows. Since they could not afford to rent the expensive Hollywood films, and as their neighbourhood consisted mostly of Arabs and newly arrived Jews from Arab countries, the repertoire for the most part consisted of films in Arabic, Turkish, Greek and Hindu – languages the Ovitzes did not understand. 'I liked the films all the same. They were so sentimental, love stories in different languages. The actors were so handsome and the serenades stirred my heart.'

At the age of thirty-five, Perla was still hoping to find her storybook prince and don the bridal veil. 'There was a butcher who wanted me, quite a handsome guy. But he had a beard and I didn't like it. I always wear make-up so bearded men are not for me.' One day a suitor from her past showed up, although she had already rejected him back in Transylvania, as she had not wished to leave her family. 'He now said, I am single, you are single, we both survived the camps, let's get together. But I didn't want him, because he was a Communist and I would have none of that. I'd suffered enough from the Russians and didn't want one of them in my house.'

Yet another suitor, a waiter named Jonel, did manage to break her wall of resistance. Perla came to terms with her fears, a date was set, invitations were sent, the menu for the celebration was decided upon. But then, just twelve days before the wedding, she learned that the future groom had been boasting that all the Lilliputs' immense property would soon be his. The marriage was called off; the wedding dress was quietly stored away.

Unlike most dwarfs, who depend upon the mercy of others for any sort of livelihood, throughout their lives the Lilliput Troupe had always been able to manage its own destiny. In their theatrical careers, the dwarfs held centre stage, while the other, average-sized family members supported them from the back. The same pattern came into play in their new career. The Ovitz dwarfs were the employers and they bossed the tall relations around. To bystanders the Lilliputs may well have appeared to be the proverbial jolly dwarfs, playing out a utopian fairy tale of mutual assistance and camaraderie in a bustling commune. In reality, they were more domineering and demanding than that.

Working and living under one roof was gradually taking its toll. Individual desires, actions, plans and habits were continually subject to comment and criticism from any – or every – other member of the family. Individual deeds or dreams prompted heated family debates and inevitably split the clan into camps. The Ovitzes functioned rather like a miniature parliament, with coalitions and opposition, pacts and deals. Still, the dwarfs' needs and opinions always held sway, and sibling ties prevailed over the bonds of marriage.

'I didn't grow up in a normal house,' says Shimshon Ovitz.

The place was actually a hellish mixture of hospital, geriatric home and institution for invalids. The tall sisters, Sarah and my mother Leah, sacrificed themselves for the sake of the dwarfs. They were so physically helpless that if you forgot to pour them a glass of water they would dehydrate. Sarah's husband left her because he couldn't cope with it and she gave up on having a family of her own. My parents had no married life whatsoever. When I needed something Mother would say, 'Do it yourself, you have hands and feet, they don't.' So from the age of ten I washed my own clothes, made my own meals. I was never cross with her, because I understood her obligations. In any case, mother couldn't raise me to her liking because all her childless sisters meddled and treated me as their own. I had seven mothers, was flooded with attention, but lacked a single intimate moment with my own mum.

From childhood onward, he had to carry his uncles down the stairs to the waiting wheelchair, which he would then push through the streets. The neighbourhood kids mocked the dwarfs' wobbly gait and short, spade-shaped hands. They harassed Shimshon by shouting 'Midget! Midget!' at him, since he was the shortest in the class. Sometimes he tried to respond in kind: 'As tall as you are, you'll be as short as my uncles, just wait until a car runs over you and cuts off your legs.' That tactic failing, he would get involved in street fights. He soon gained the reputation of a local menace.

Shimshon was so short that throughout his childhood he was himself convinced he was a dwarf. He was relieved when, at the age of thirteen, he started growing again. 'I began to overeat – stuffed myself with food and became a human mountain. If I had remained a dwarf I would have killed myself. It's horrible suffering. With no hands and legs you are totally dependent on others for all your needs.' After his army service, in the mid 1960s, Shimshon became a sailor, in order to escape the family – and himself. He wanted to decorate his body with tattoos like every seaman, but in her letters his mother begged him not to: 'the Nazis have already tattooed us', she wrote. Several times, with drunken resolve, his money paid and the design selected, he sat ready in the tattoo parlour, his shirt off. But then he'd see his mother's face in the shadows on the wall or window, and flee.

When he finally gave up the sea, Shimshon drifted between jobs, got into brawls and had a few run-ins with the law. 'I was the terror of Haifa. These fists sent many people to hospitals,' he asserts with some pride. Still, he was, all in all, an appealing young man, albeit one reluctant to marry, for he feared that genetics would smite his offspring, too. The fact that his cousin Batia, Avram's daughter, had borne healthy children did not ease his mind. He made it a practice to introduce his girlfriends to his dwarf family in order to see their reaction; the visit ended many a relationship. Miriam Shoshani stuck with Shimshon, however, and in 1970 they got married. 'When I was in school I told the children that the tattoo on my arm was my ID number from Germany,' he says. 'Miriam is from Morocco, where the Jews escaped the Holocaust, and she had no idea what the number meant. Once she took some steel wool and tried to scrape it off my skin.'

There were other changes in the Ovitz family. Frieda and Sarah divorced their husbands; Dora, Avram's wife, died; he remarried, divorced, married for the third time – to another Holocaust survivor – and was widowed some years later. The clan celebrated the birth of Shimshon and Miriam's first child, a daughter, Ariella – named after dead uncle Arie. To their great relief, her growth was normal. 'With every pregnancy Miriam and I were terrified,' explains Shimshon Ovitz. 'In two or three cases, when the doctor said, "There's an extra test I want you to have", we quickly arranged an abortion, not wanting to take even the smallest chance.'

•

Pseudoachondroplasia, the Ovitzes' type of dwarfism, is a rare syndrome. Inherited through an autosomal dominant, it occurs approximately once in every 60,000 live births. The head and face are normal in size, as well as the internal organs, but the arms and the legs are short. The total height of an adult with pseudoachondroplasia ranges between two and a half and a little over four feet.

The faulty gene was identified in 1995 by Professor Jacqueline Hecht of the University of Texas's Houston Health Science Centre. She and her group discovered it in the cartilage oligomeric matrix protein (COMP) gene on chromosome 19. The deformation in the protein that produces cartilage restricts the growth of the spine and bones. 'At this time, there is no cure and therapy is mainly symptomatic for the progressive, debilitating joint changes,' write the American physicians and researchers, Muensterer, Berdon, Lachman and Done, in *Paediatric Radiology*, March 2012. Researchers are currently looking for a substance capable of weakening the harmful effects of the flawed gene.

In 80 per cent of cases, the affliction is a result of spontaneous genetic mutation, not heredity. However, a person with pseudoachondroplasia and a average-sized partner have a 50 per cent chance of giving birth to a dwarf. The dwarfism of Shimshon Eizik Ovitz, the family patriarch, was a spontaneous occurrence, as he had been born to average-sized parents. His abnormal gene, however, was dominant and he passed it on to seven of his ten children. Leah, like her two average-sized siblings, had not inherited the abnormal gene. Her son, Shimshon, and daughter, Batia, could thus expect their children and grandchildren to have the same chance for average-sized offspring as the rest of the population.

'Logic and statistics cannot pacify the heart,' says Shimshon Ovitz. 'We have no peace, and fear we will not be spared. Fortunately our three additional children were all healthy, but every pregnancy in the family – and now the grandchildren are coming – is followed by tension. Right now we have five grandchildren and they are developing normally.'

•

In August 1972 the Ovitz clan was shaken when brother Micki died of a heart attack at the age of sixty-three. The obituaries described him as 'an actor and owner of two cinemas'. His body was placed for a formal viewing in front of the Ovitz cinemas so that his many fans and clients could pay their respects. He was buried in a newly purchased family plot in Haifa cemetery. Five months later came another blow, when Avram Ovitz, head of the family, died at sixty-nine. Shortly afterwards, Leah suffered a major stroke that left her speechless and paralysed in a wheelchair for the next fourteen years. Frieda died in 1975. 'It was horrible, agony upon agony, the pain and mourning accumulating and multiplying,' Perla sighs. It became increasingly difficult for the remaining siblings to continue managing the cinemas. In 1979 they sold the entire compound and bought a large flat for the remaining six of them: Rozika and Franziska, Elizabeth and her husband, tall sister Sarah and Perla.

•

When they retired from the stage, the Lilliput Troupe stored away its musical instruments; the dwarfs never touched them again. When they vacated the cinema compound, Shimshon sold the instruments cheaply to a local antique dealer. The collection then disappeared. In late 1997, what were claimed to be the Lilliput Troupe's instruments resurfaced as the property of a dealer who began negotiations for their sale to the Jewish Museum in Berlin. News of the prospective deal reached Yad Vashem, the World Center for Holocaust Research and Commemoration in Jerusalem, which immediately expressed interest in purchasing the collection. Unable to meet the asking price of $80,000, Yad Vashem made an appeal for donors. Ultimately it purchased, at a reduced sum, two child-size violins with missing strings, a bowless cello, a flawed cimbalom and a set of drums. Missing from the collection were both an accordion and a pink guitar of the sort used by Perla. The sale was executed without an expert's appraisal and with no proof of provenance.

Amnon Weinstein, a violin maker and a world-renowned expert on ancient string instruments, has had considerable experience identifying musical instruments that survived the Second World War. He carried out his inspection on the alleged Ovitz collection in our presence, as well as Haviva Peled-Carmeli of Yad Vashem, who is in charge of purchasing articles for the museum's collection.

Weinstein immediately recognises some of the instruments as a collection offered to him in Haifa, in the 1970s. 'The story said to be behind the instruments was very moving,' he recalls, 'but there was something fishy about the whole sale, the instruments and the dealer, so I backed off and never regretted it. In any case I have an excellent memory and some of the instruments now in Yad Vashem are not the ones I saw at the time.'

When sold to Yad Vashem, the delicate string instruments had come stripped of their cases and were not even wrapped in cloth, as professional artists like the Ovitzes would have taken care to do.

Examination of the cello's size and design reveals that it is clearly not the same cello that appears in the Lilliput Troupe's publicity photos. The cello in Yad Vashem, although beautifully carved, is old and badly damaged; Weinstein estimates that a crack in its soundboard dates back at least a century. It could not, therefore, have been used by the Lilliput Troupe before the war or after it, when they resumed their career.

'And on top of that,' adds Weinstein, 'the cello is too big for a dwarf to play.'

Wearing special soft, white, cotton gloves, Weinstein lifts up one of the violins, turns it from side to side, sniffs at it with the care of a detective.

It is a child's quarter-size violin and has the smell and heavy traces of a woman's face powder. Children usually play such an instrument for two or three years, moving on to a larger one as they grow older. The violin is passed on from one child to another so it never becomes worn in the same places. But this worn-down violin was used by the same musician for many years – the chin and fingers repeatedly rubbed it in the same spots.

The violin thus may well have belonged to Rozika or Franziska.

Of much poorer quality is the second violin, which comes from a different manufacturer; it bears no distinctive marks or identifiable traces of make-up and there's nothing to connect it to the Ovitzes. On the other hand, the cimbalom, a folk instrument built by a village craftsman, and the intricate set of drums both probably belonged to the Lilliput Troupe. One of the sticks accompanying the drums, however, is a wooden mallet of the sort used to flatten steaks and schnitzel; it is unlikely it was ever used onstage, although the crack in the mallet attests to a long life in someone's kitchen. The differences in the quality of the various instruments – some finely made, like the drums; others bric-a-brac, like the non-descript violin – makes it doubtful they were used by the same group of musicians.

To determine whether or not the instruments were played in Auschwitz, Weinstein gently inserts a thin, flexible tube into the sound box of the violins and moves it around, while peering through the periscope's eye.

If these are really the instruments that were with them there, there might be traces of human ashes inside, since the black smoke filled the air. But the absence of ash here might only mean that the violins were not played in the open air; they could still have been used indoors.

The general impression is that the original collection was deliberately split up: the particularly valuable instruments may have been sold separately and replaced with items picked up by the dealer in some flea market to complete the ensemble. The fate of the Lilliput collection thus perpetuates the exploitation of Holocaust victims, with objects belonging to them, whether real or forged, being sold to willing buyers at exorbitant prices.

TWENTY

HAIFA, 1980-1992

The intimate encounter with Mengele when he was her 'painting model' had haunted Dina Gottlieb-Babbitt ever since. Years later, in a bus station on Hollywood Boulevard, she panicked at the sight of a man who resembled him. 'I thought, oh my God, he's after me. I was sure he knew I was the only person in the world who could clearly identify him, and he or his messengers would come to silence me.' Throughout her life, she kept her telephone number unlisted and never disclosed her address. Yet her attitude towards the Nazi doctor is unsettlingly ambivalent:

> The entire world was after him, but I decided that if he were ever captured, I would not come forward to testify. Not that I feel any gratitude, he didn't care if I lived or died, and did nothing to save me. But for a fleeting moment he spared me, letting me hang on for a little while and come through.

Early in December 1968, a police officer called at the Carmel-Ganim cinema. Perla had just opened the box office. He introduced himself as Inspector Kolar and had barely mentioned that he was collecting evidence against Josef Mengele when she interrupted him: 'Have you caught him?' she asked.

'We will, we will,' he assured her apologetically. 'But

meanwhile we're helping the German prosecutors to prepare a
dossier against him.'

I was not looking for revenge, but it was clear to all of us that
when an inspector came to investigate Nazi crimes we would
cooperate. Although I must admit I never hated Dr Mengele. I
should have hated him, I know, because he was a murderer, but
he let us live. Not that he liked us, he only used us to further his
ambition of becoming a famous scientist. But thanks to him we
had some human freedom in the camp.

In the family assembly that evening, the Ovitzes decided that
Elizabeth should be the one to tell the story of their ordeal.
The memories came forth readily and Kolar quickly filled four
pages with her testimony.

I don't know what concrete experiments Mengele performed
on me. He was interested in everything; they thus often dripped
a liquid into our eyes that left us nearly blind the entire day.
They gave us shots in our ears and in nearly all our organs. We
often felt sick and miserable and still had to deliver ourselves
into his hands.

It was the first time in twenty years that the Ovitzes had been
asked to tell their story. Upon their arrival in Israel, they had
spoken openly about the torments Mengele had inflicted on
them. Like most survivors, though, they very quickly realised
that their painful accounts fell on deaf ears. So they kept silent.
For the duration of the Second World War, the Jews in
Palestine were cut off from family and friends who had been
trapped in Nazi-occupied Europe. After liberation, successive waves of new immigrants brought with them dreadful

confirmation that parents, brothers, sisters, cousins, uncles and aunts were no longer alive. Horror at the incomprehensible torments of their brethren and guilt over the failure to come to their rescue closed Israeli hearts to the survivors' endless tales of suffering. At the same time, Israel was mourning its own tremendous losses in the War of Independence: a grief so immense and immediate left little emotional space to mourn those killed in a different time and place or to pity the survivors. In a clash of catastrophes, pain at the death of 6 million Jews in Europe came second, at the time, to the loss of 6,000 young soldiers on Israel's battlefields.

'The kids at school echoed the general mood of the country – "Why did you go like sheep to the slaughter? Why didn't you fight back?"' recounts Shimshon Ovitz with some bitterness. 'I was so angry at them. I had only been a year-old toddler then, but even if I could have thrown a rock, what harm could I have done them? We were so weak and hungry; the Nazis, well-armed sadists. Anyone would have responded like we did.' Burdened with agonising and exhausting memories, the survivors withdrew into themselves. Gradually, they learned to put the past aside as they built new lives in a harsh land. But the Ovitzes, who had gone through it all together and survived intact, seemed to be able to live simultaneously in the past and the present.

'Having invaded our veins, Mengele was one of our household names,' says Shimshon Ovitz.

Dr Mengele wanted this, did that. I ate Mengele for breakfast, he was my bedtime story, and I couldn't sleep at night because I was hearing my aunts and uncles scream in their dreams. We breathed Auschwitz the whole day through as if we were still there. Every tiny daily event reminded my family of something in the camp. I grew up on these stories and passed them on to my children. We are all broken vessels who, even if glued together, cannot be whole again. You can't expect people like us to be normal.

Seven decades later, Shimshon Ovitz's refrigerator is always stuffed with food, as if he is expecting a siege or a war. His wife, Miriam, is unable to close the doors of the kitchen cupboards, which are bursting with food in packets, bottles, cans and jars. Obese to the extent that it threatens his life, Shimshon finds his hunger insatiable. He cannot stop eating.

•

After arriving in Argentina in 1949 with forged documents, Mengele had worked for his family's agricultural-equipment firm as its South American agent. In his book, *Mengele: the Angel of Death in South America*, published in 2009, the Argentine historian Jorge Camarasa claims that Mengele continued his genetic experiments with twins. In the early 1960s, he regularly came to Cândido Godói and offered medical treatment to the cattle and to the women of this small Brazilian town. As a result, one in five pregnancies resulted in twins – the usual rate is one in eighty. 'I think Cândido Godói may have been Mengele's laboratory, where he finally managed to fulfil his dreams of creating a master race of blond-haired, blue-eyed Aryans,' said Camarasa.

In March 1954, Mengele divorced his first wife, Irene. Two years later he married his brother's widow, Martha, who had flown with her son from Germany to Argentina to be with him. By 1956 he apparently felt secure enough to officially change his false name, Helmut Gregor, back into his real one at the

West German embassy in Buenos Aires. In 1959, when a court in Freiburg issued the first warrant for his arrest he moved on to Paraguay – a safer place for a war criminal to hide from the American, German and Israeli intelligence services, as well as the scores of journalists and private Nazi hunters who were now trying to track him down. Still, he continued to shuttle between Paraguay and Argentina.

In April 1960, eleven Mossad agents had arrived in Buenos Aires to kidnap *SS-Obersturmbannführer* Adolf Eichmann and bring him to trial in Jerusalem. As one group was spying on Eichmann's movements, another managed to locate Mengele's apartment and learned that he was at home. Eichmann, who implemented Adolf Hitler's Final Solution, was deemed a more important target and the Mossad snatched him first, holding him in a safe house while they waited to take him out of Argentina. Meanwhile, Mengele left his home but the agents believed that it was a temporary absence. Rafi Eitan, who was head of the operation, feared that if they waited for Mengele's return they might risk the exposure of the Eichmann Operation. 'When I have a bird in my hand, I don't start looking for the bird in the bush. I'll take the bird in my hand, put it in a cage and then deal with the one in the bush,' he revealed to *Der Spiegel* in 2008. After nine days in the safe house, Eichmann was smuggled out on an El Al flight. A few weeks later, a Mossad team returned to Buenos Aires but, since the abduction was widely publicised, Mengele had disappeared.

With the opening of Eichmann's trial in Jerusalem on 11 April 1961, the Israeli attitude towards the Holocaust changed dramatically. The public trial, held in the newly inaugurated city theatre, was broadcast live on the radio daily (the country had no TV service yet). People gathered in the streets; riveted by the words coming from the loudspeakers, they followed the proceedings. The testimony of 110 witnesses, each one representing an obliterated community, revealed for the first time to the Israeli public the full scope of the Final Solution. The Holocaust now stood out horrifically on the Israelis' list of national calamities. For the first time, survivors could openly cry their hearts out, and the country cried with them.

Mengele moved to Brazil and, using false identities, hid out on isolated farms and later in a one-bedroom bungalow in a São Paulo slum. Life on the run did not seem to suit Martha Mengele and the couple soon separated. In 1962, the Mossad discovered his whereabouts but the organisation had other 'operational priorities' and he once again escaped justice.

In 1959 in the judicial arena, meanwhile, the public prosecutor Freiherr von Schowingen in Freiburg, anticipating Mengele's arrest, assembled some testimonies of Mengele's victims. In 1964, the Administrative Court of Hesse and the universities of Frankfurt and Munich annulled Mengele's medical and anthropological degrees, because 'of the crimes he had committed as a doctor in the concentration camp of Auschwitz'. Nonetheless, his early research continued to be cited in medical books and articles all over the world well into the 1970s.

In 1969, Mengele's case was transferred to the Frankfurt criminal-judicial system, where the investigating judge, Horst von Glasenapp, had collected 300 more testimonies from around the world. Although he had no authority to look for Mengele, von Glasenapp made several failed attempts to trace him. However, none of the secret services were really making an effort to find the former Dr Mengele.

•

Years, then decades, passed and the survivors of Mengele's experiments grew only more indignant at the lack of any sustained efforts to catch him. Hoping to convey their message beyond Israel to a broader international public, a group called the Children of Auschwitz-Nazi's Deadly Lab Experiments Survivors (CANDLES) organised a trial in absentia in Yad Vashem, Jerusalem. On 5 February 1985, Shimshon Ovitz pushed his aunt Elizabeth's wheelchair out of the pouring rain and into the museum auditorium, while Sarah wheeled her sister Perla.

That day the sky was crying, too. I was sorry that Dr Mengele was absent from his trial. The only reason I wanted him caught was so he could sit days and nights listening to what he did to us. I would have shown him the scars and ailments, tell him about my weak heart and the legs that can no longer support me. I don't believe he would have apologised, but if the judges were to ask me if he should be hanged, I'd tell them to let him go. I was saved by the grace of the Devil – God will give him his due.

Since the dwarf sisters were wearing lookalike hats, raincoats, dresses and handbags, the press mistakenly described them as 59-year-old twins. Elizabeth was in fact seventy-one, Perla sixty-four. To spare them the effort of mounting the podium, Prosecutor Zvi Terlow came down to the first row to conduct the inquiry. As always, Elizabeth spoke out more than her sister but both she and Perla captured the imagination of the world press. *Newsweek*, for example, described how the Lilliputs 'entertained their tormentors. On one hellish night, the entire family was stripped naked and marched on to a stage to perform for SS chief Heinrich

Himmler' – it was not him; he's confused here with a minor Nazi official who strongly resembled him – 'and 2,000 Nazi officers and soldiers. Mengele acted as MC while Himmler sat in the front row and recorded the fun with his movie camera'.

The emotional impact of the 106 witnesses stirred the governments of Israel, the United States and Germany to make fresh efforts in the hunt for Mengele. Besides offering new and increased bounties of a million dollars and a million marks, officials from the three countries met in Frankfurt on 10 May 1985, to coordinate their efforts. They issued a warrant for the search of the Günzburg home of Hans Sedlmeier, a retired executive in the Mengele family firm, who was suspected of flying regularly to South America to deliver money to the fugitive. An address book found in Sedlmeier's flat led the investigators to Brazil.

On 7 June scores of policemen and journalists gathered at Our Lady of the Rosary Cemetery on a hillside in Embu, ten miles from São Paulo. An incredulous Dina Gottlieb-Babbitt watched on television as the São Paulo assistant coroner Dr José Antonio de Mello, standing above an open pit, presented a skull to the cameras' blinding flashes. 'I painted Mengele's portrait and know the shape of his skull,' she says. 'It was not like the one they showed. His face was much wider. My feeling was it was a cover-up by his family and associates to gain him extra time.'

An international team of forensic experts examined the remains. On the basis of the gaps between the skull's teeth – a subject Mengele himself had studied as a young physician – they declared that 'it is ... our opinion that this skeleton is that of Josef Mengele, within a reasonable scientific certainty'.

But many of Mengele's victims, as well as many others, were sceptical and believed he was managing to live on as a free man into a ripe old age. In an attempt to quell such rumours, Mengele's son, Rolf, issued a statement that on 7 February 1979, his father had suffered a stroke while swimming and had drowned. He explained that the family's subsequent six years of silence was a precautionary measure taken to ensure the safety of those who had helped the Auschwitz doctor hide for thirty years.

> I cried all night when I heard that Dr Mengele had died. He always insisted he was just obeying orders and I believed him. The streams of blood he took from us that sometimes spilled onto the floor would pass before my eyes, but still I cried. The heart is the stupidest human organ. Dr Mengele had a heart of stone but mine is human, flesh and blood.

The doubts about Mengele's remains persisted until 1992, when Rolf and his mother Irene provided blood samples and a DNA comparison was made with one of Mengele's bones. The bone-sample matched. Mengele's dossier was closed.

In July 2011, Mengele's diaries were sold by Alexander Autographs, an auction house in Stamford, Connecticut. The thirty-one notebooks contained some 3,000 pages and included stories, poems, reflections and drawings. Unfortunately, they did not include any documents that referred to his experiments on the Lilliput group.

•

For a while, the trial in absentia of Mengele brought the Lilliputs back into the limelight. For months, journalists and photographers courted Perla and Elizabeth, but eventually the fuss abated and they withdrew back into anonymity.

As early as July 1951, the West German government had approved a one-time grant to victims of Nazi medical experiments. Such grants, the government insisted, were not to be interpreted as compensation based on legal claims, but rather as donations to further the victims' recovery. For the most part, money was distributed among residents of Hungary and Poland; none of it reached Mengele's victims in Israel.

In 1985, a group of 'Mengele's twins' sued the West German government on the basis of the 1951 decision. One of the eighty-three claimants was Efraim Reichenberg, who had shared a barrack with the male dwarfs. He had arrived in Auschwitz with his seven siblings, all of whom were killed except for László, who was mistaken for Efraim's twin.

László had a resonant baritone singing voice and frequently entertained the SS, whereas Efraim could barely squeak out a tune. The differences between their vocal cords intrigued Mengele, who repeatedly injected substances into their throats. László began to have breathing difficulties and laryngeal swellings. His lungs were damaged and he died a year after liberation at the age of nineteen.

Efraim himself was not spared. Over the years, his voice dwindled until he lost it completely. Eventually, he couldn't breathe or swallow food. He underwent twenty-two gruelling operations to remove his mangled vocal cords, larynx and part of his oesophagus. He was totally mute until 1984, when a special microphone was implanted in his throat. His speech is slow, it sounds metallic and a pause follows each word emitted from a voice mechanism.

The Germans took my voice away in the camp and gave it back to me forty years later as installed equipment – 'made in Germany'. My case is anything but special, I'm not unique.

Many of us suffer kidney failure, different kinds of cancer and cardiac problems. After Mengele's trial in Jerusalem we demanded our medical files be found so we could know exactly what was done to us and get the right treatment. We appealed to the Americans, the Russians, the Germans and even to the Mengele family, but remain empty-handed, just dying painfully.

To avoid an embarrassing political and juridical debate, West Germany arrived at a compromise agreement with Mengele's Israeli victims, with each of them settling for 20,000 German marks. In the original 1951 offer, the minimum grant had been 25,000 marks and the maximum 40,000 – for cases 'where the victims' whole life has been ruined by the pseudo-medical experiments'. The Ovitz family did not get grouped with the twins nor did it get the belated compensation.

For two minutes, a siren is sounded throughout Israel on each Holocaust Memorial Day; for two minutes the traffic halts and everybody freezes in place. Shimshon Ovitz shivers as the siren carries him back to his childhood in Auschwitz. Then comes anger.

They're whistling in our faces. It makes me furious that billions of German marks Israel got as reparation money have been wasted on extravagant public projects such as buying a fleet of fifty ships, trains and industrial equipment, all made in Germany, while we were stuck in leaking barracks. Israel declares itself the sole heir of the 6 million, demanding that the money once belonging to them be channelled to the state. Nobody cares about the old and ailing survivors. They just need us as a tool to extract more money for projects.

In addition to the money paid to the state of Israel, survivors could apply for personal compensation from Germany. Each member of the Ovitz family had to provide the German bureaucracy with evidence that they really had been interned in Auschwitz, that they had been assigned to the experimentation barrack, that their health had been impaired. 'I'm much sicker than most people my age, all from the eight crucial months of my infancy when I was Mengele's lab rat,' says Shimshon Ovitz. 'Later I supported my family by selling clothes from a street stall, but now I'm too ill to continue. Germany cannot buy itself out with the monthly 800 marks that I get, or even the thousand paid my helpless aunt Perla.'

TWENTY-ONE

HAIFA, 1993–2001

'In Auschwitz I swore that if God let me stay alive I would tell my story again and again until my breath died out so that no one could say it never happened.' Perla is always willing to give interviews, to share her experience with children writing essays about the Holocaust or to lecture about her family history.

On Holocaust Memorial Day, all restaurants, cinemas and theatres in Israel are closed by law. Official ceremonies are held in each town, and schools dedicate the day to remembering the victims and meeting the survivors. When we come to take Perla to meet schoolchildren in May 2000, we find her all dressed up, sitting on the edge of her bed. In her tiny black handbag she has packed her cardiac pills, some cookies and lipstick. She adds a photograph of Mengele. 'I want the children to know his face,' she says.

We cradle her in our arms and take her down the stairs and into the car. She is light as a feather. In a small town thirty minutes' drive from Haifa, we wheel her into the school gym. The children stand up in silence to greet her. Six tall glass candles, a gigantic yellow star and the slogan 'Remember and Never Forget' barely hide the ads for a local beauty parlour and a mechanic's workshop. A ten-year-old boy dressed in the colours of the Israeli flag – white shirt, blue trousers – reaches up to the microphone. His voice is unwavering as he reads the special prayer for murdered children:

> Let the Nation remember her beloved children, innocent and pure, snatched from the laps of their parents by human beasts. Tortured, beheaded, gassed, smothered, burned alive. Babies and infants, smashed against walls, dropped from high roofs, suffocated in sacks, drowned in rivers.

The list of barbaric tortures and perverse methods of killing is repeated again and again by the children in their performances of dramatised readings, songs and dances. The level of horror their programme generates is so intense that it could carry the cinematic warning 'unsuitable for children'. The ceremony ends with scenes of rebellion against shadowy forces, designed to imprint on the children's imagination the necessity of resistance in the event of another Holocaust: 'Never again will we be led like lambs to the slaughter!' the chorus chants. 'The Germans have come! Jews, take up arms! Better die on drawn swords – let's defend ourselves to the last breath! Death to the murderers!'

Perla Ovitz weeps silently; she wipes her tears with a chequered handkerchief. A class of nine-year-olds gathers around her.

'I didn't have a name, just this number.' She rolls up the sleeve of her dress. All eyes are glued to her arm.

'How did they tattoo you?' enquires a boy with a punk haircut. 'Did it hurt?' asks a skinny girl.

'I fainted twice, but that was the easy part.' Perla doesn't spare them the gory details.

'Dr Mengele was my boss, do you want to see him?' Without awaiting a response, she draws his photo from her handbag and passes it around.

The children glance at him with a mixture of amazement and repulsion.

'Did he make you a dwarf?' one of them asks.

'No, Dr Mengele was a very powerful doctor, but even he couldn't make someone a giant or a dwarf.' And she tells them the story of Shimshon Eizik and his two wives.

At the end of the meeting, the children draw out their pocket cameras and photograph themselves with her. Perla flashes the radiant smile of a film star. She signs autographs on pages torn from the children's notebooks. Before they leave, they all pass in line in front of Perla's wheelchair; one by one, they kneel to shake her hand.

A fortnight later, the postman brings her a large brown envelope full of letters. One of them reads:

'Dear Perla, I was so moved by your talk. You are so beautiful and I really love you. If you need anything don't hesitate to phone me and I'll immediately come to help you.' The girl has written her home telephone number on the letter, and decorated it with flowers and two intertwined hearts: they bear her name and Perla's.

•

The fairy tale of the seven dwarfs who stuck together like peas in a pod was drawing to its close. In 1979 five of the surviving siblings and Elizabeth's husband moved into a stone house on the corner of a quiet street at the outskirts of the German Colony. It was just three blocks away from their cinema compound, which would stand deserted and crumbling for almost twenty years – eventually, a glass and marble shopping mall would emerge from its ruins.

Like in their old family home in Rozavlea, they were

once again all living under the same roof. Elizabeth and her husband took the largest bedroom, with a crescent-shaped corner balcony. Rozika and Franziska, inseparable as always, took the second bedroom, while Perla and tall sister Sarah shared the small one between the kitchen and the bathroom. 'At night we tiptoed into our old sisters' room and stood by their beds to check that they were breathing.' Their recently found bliss proved to be short-lived. One by one they were plucked away, and with each death the remaining Lilliputs withdrew further into themselves like snails into their shells. Franziska died in 1980, aged ninety-one. A ycar later, Elizabeth lost her darling Moshe Moskowitz.

The four sisters, in an attempt to fill the void each loss created, moved beds. 'Life was frightening enough as it was, so I joined Elizabeth in her double bed so she wouldn't be so lonely after forty years of marriage,' says Perla. Sarah moved in with the inconsolable Rozika and they closed up the small bedroom.

In 1984 Rozika died; she was ninety-eight. Not many dwarfs reach such a ripe old age. According to the *Guinness World Records*, the record holder is also a Hungarian showbiz personality, Susanna Bokoyni, stage name 'Princess Susanna' – who died that same year in the United States, aged 105.

Since only three of them were now left, Sarah moved a sofa into Elizabeth's and Perla's bedroom, and the door to the second bedroom was closed. Soon thereafter, they were devastated by the untimely death of Ariella, Shimshon's fifteen-year-old daughter, after a year-long battle with cancer. Ariella's heartbroken grandparents, Leah and Azriel, followed. In 1992 Elizabeth died of heart failure and, a year later, Sarah.

Perla, then seventy-two years old, found herself alone. Since the day she was born, she had always been encircled by her family. With her sisters and brothers gone, she felt so utterly abandoned that she joined them in the family plot:

Here lies the last of the family of dwarfs, Miss Perla Ovitz, daughter of Shimshon-Eizik and Batia, who suffered every single day of her life.

The epitaph on Perla's tombstone, which she sees whenever she visits the cemetery, does not strike her as bizarre or macabre; nor does she think that it conflicts with her abandoned joie de vivre. 'The stonecutter suggested it when I told him my story, and I thought it was an appropriate summary of my life. We were happy when we were together and even Dr Mengele couldn't separate us. There in the cemetery we're together for ever.'

In the city of the dead, the Lilliputs dwell as if still around the festive Sabbath table: Perla is on the far right, with Frieda to her left, and she's facing her sister Elizabeth and brother-in-law Moshe.

In the large, mostly empty flat, their presence seems imminent. Family photographs and full-sized, sugary oil paintings of her and Elizabeth, bedecked in clusters of dangling jewellery and long stage dresses, make Perla feel less alone, as if they were still talking to her. On Friday afternoons, at twilight, when she lights her pair of Sabbath candles, Perla lights her dead sisters' candles, too. A special low railing in the stairwell tells of times when she could go out on her own. Nowadays she leaves only rarely, to see her doctor or to visit the bank. A loyal taxi driver lifts her in his arms, carries her down the stairs, places her in the back seat; her folded wheelchair goes in the boot. Her arms have grown too weak to operate the wheelchair, so she must be pushed everywhere. She doesn't visit other people because she is swallowed up by normal-sized furniture.

Perla suffers terrible spine pains due to the abnormal bone and cartilage formation typical of her type of dwarfism; her body weight presses down on her short, knock-kneed and bowed legs. Her chest is narrow, and as a result she suffers from heart and respiratory problems. But in spite of such sufferings, she is usually cheerful and welcoming. 'The heart is crying, but the lips are smiling' is Perla's often declared motto. She has always loved people and since childhood 'whenever I heard a voice in the other room I rushed to see who the guest was. And I've not changed.'

She was never offended when people called her 'dwarf'. 'What else can they call me? I see myself in the mirror and it's a fact.' Still, she avoids using the term; instead she divides the world into 'big people' and 'we the little ones'. She most commonly refers to herself as a girl ('I'm a girl who...'), despite her womanly old age. 'I could marry today if I wanted to!' she exclaims girlishly.

But I don't think that one should marry at any cost and I'm not sorry about never having had a man. I know love; I was in love many times, but not enough to get married. I didn't rush. My brothers and sisters were better than any husband for me. As I grew older, I realised that marriage turns a woman into a man's slave and I didn't want to be one. I didn't need someone bossing me around. When a man is angry he always blames his wife. I would be an excellent wife for any man, but there's nothing a man can give me that I don't have already.

Keeping to a strict schedule, Perla wakes up every morning at six, pours some water from the thermos near her bed and swallows a cardiac pill. She then recites three daily psalms that a local rabbi has recommended and waits in bed. At eight, an aide sent by the social services arrives.

'Look at me. I'm eighty and still have to be washed like a baby,' Perla observes. Her bath done and breakfast on the way, Perla pulls a mirror from the drawer by her bed. She balances it on the stool – 'I sat on this one in Auschwitz' – and, just like an actress about to face an audience, professionally applies her make-up, dabbing on the colours with her fingers. Once a month she dyes her hair raven-black.

Her wardrobe is bursting with rows of identical, vibrantly coloured dresses. 'I instantly sense when the maid hands me one of Elizabeth's by mistake, but I never tell her to put it back since I like being in touch with my sister.' She prides herself on being an accomplished seamstress and she still makes dresses, as well as bed linens and lingerie, with her Singer sewing machine. 'We were like the dwarfs in fairy tales, always diligent and hard-working, better craftsmen than tall people.' Perla watches with hawk eyes as the maid cleans the house, and she is not content until every crochet doily and satin cushion is placed exactly at the right angle. The maid functions as her legs and does the shopping for her. Before she leaves at one o'clock, she serves Perla her lunch and places a napkin-covered supper on the low table by the window.

'I maintain a rigid diet, eating very little, because we tiny people are in danger of being too heavy for our legs and lungs.' She washes the plates herself, at her childlike sink at the corner. In the afternoon she's on her own. She spends most of her time confined to her room, where everything she needs lies within reach: food, water, a telephone, a buzzer to open the front door. Behind a coloured curtain is a low lavatory.

Self-reliant by nature, Perla tries to be as independent as

she can. She would never ask a guest to fetch her something from the kitchen. A guest's first instinct is to sit on a low stool next to her, so as not to overshadow her. But she always insists that guests take a more comfortable seat, one that matches their size. If it's not too hot or too cold, Perla drags herself to the room's adjoining balcony for fresh air and a momentary escape from her prison. She slides the shutter open as if it were a stage curtain, and mounts her tiny armchair.

This is her last podium.

Perla's regal emergence on the first-floor balcony, theatrically dressed and meticulously made-up, attracts attention. Passers-by stop on the pavement; they lift their eyes to greet her and exchange a few friendly words.

'I was an actress!' she declares ostentatiously. She implicitly attributes every aspect of her life to her profession, but memories of the theatre are painful. 'It was the best part of my life, we were all together having fun and it's all gone. When I think of those times I realise how lonely I am now and lose the will to live. Being alone is worse than being in a concentration camp.'

She can no longer go out to the movies or the theatre and, since her last sister's death, she has not been in the mood to watch TV. Her most steadfast companion is an ancient red miniature transistor radio and she sings to its music. When in an especially bad mood, she simply hums to herself. 'Romantic Hungarian tunes are better than cardiac pills,' she advises. She cries when she sings her favourite song:

> I'm going to the graveyard to talk to mother.
> The forest is gloomy and the branches are crying.
> I would have told you, mother, what troubles my heart,
> how bitter is life without you.

Sometimes she falls asleep with the radio on and some nights she awakens with a scream. 'In my dreams I am back in Auschwitz, although I rarely see Dr Mengele. More often I'm in an *Appell*, praying that no one is missing from the count – otherwise we'll all be killed.'

While many Holocaust survivors boycott German products and object to Israeli orchestras playing Wagner, Perla Ovitz works hard at distinguishing the past from the present. Hannelore Witkofski, the historian and advocate for short people's rights, contacted Perla in the 1990s after reading about her, and they soon began corresponding regularly. 'Hannelore is hurt when people look at her as if she were a monster and make clear she should evaporate,' explains Perla indignantly. 'She told me that even today in Germany, many people think that the life of dwarfs and people like her and me with disabilities is worthless and that the Nazi's idea of euthanasia was not bad after all. It's shocking.'

Accompanied by fellow activists, Witkofski has flown to Israel several times to see her. Once she surprised Perla with a new, highly sophisticated wheelchair.

I asked Hannelore how much I owed her. She answered, 'You?! It's us who owe you everything!' She always wears trousers, and was intrigued to try on one of my dresses. It looked so nice on her that I used the same pattern to sew her a red sleeveless summer dress.

●

It's 10 January 2001, Perla's eightieth birthday.

In the stairwell, before pressing the doorbell, we light eighty candles and inflate colourful balloons. Perla is stunned to see us with Hannelore and other friends. Our birthday gifts symbolise the themes of her life: small diamond earrings, a guitar-shaped chocolate cake, a bottle of champagne, French perfume, a CD player, a child-sized walker. Perla is in a good mood and sings from her repertoire to the small audience gathered in her bedroom. She retains the glow of the girl, the *chanteuse*, the darling, the angel, when Romania and Hungary were her stage.

Or perhaps it's the glow of her faith. Perla is steadfast in her religious practice. She keeps kosher, observes the Sabbath and, on holidays, cooks for herself the traditional meals from her childhood, puts on a festive dress and sits by herself to celebrate.

Auschwitz has shaken the faith of many survivors, but not hers.

It's beyond me to understand how he who sees the whole world could watch the flames coming out of the chimneys, devouring his children, and do nothing. There are rabbis who say that the Jews died in the Holocaust because of their sins. Although I'm Orthodox and have the utmost respect for rabbis, I totally abhor this explanation. Our friends and relatives were extremely religious and did nothing to deserve punishment of any kind. We are too small and lowly to comprehend God's intentions. The fire was his will, as it was his will that our whole family would survive.

If I were a healthy Jewish girl, one metre seventy tall, I would have been gassed just like the hundreds of thousands of other Jews in my country. So if I ever wondered why I was born a dwarf, my answer would have to be that my handicap, my deformity, was God's only way to keep me alive.

EPILOGUE

ROZAVLEA–AUSCHWITZ, SEPTEMBER 2000

Our journey into the true story of the seven dwarfs who were liege to no benevolent Snow White but rather to a heartless beast started in 1994, when we came across this brief comment in a history book: 'In 1949, a troupe named "The Seven Dwarfs of Auschwitz" toured the cities of Israel in a song and dance show.' There were no individual or family names, no further identifying details at all. But we were intrigued. We had never before heard of this strange amalgam of death and amusement. That even we seasoned journalists had missed this historical episode was not surprising. After all, half a million Holocaust survivors, each with a separate ghastly and amazing tale, had settled in Israel after the war.

Some sleuthing soon led us to the name 'Ovitz' and the family's hometown of Haifa. We did not expect to find any of them alive after so many years, although we did discover nineteen Ovitzes in the Haifa telephone directory. Each call we made seemed to confirm the futility of our mission. Then we chanced on Perla.

She sounded suspicious over the phone, but then an elderly woman who lived alone in the city had reason to be. She opened up instantly, however, when she heard that we wished to learn more about the Lilliput Troupe and its travails in Auschwitz.

Every fortnight since, we have travelled from Jerusalem to visit Perla. A hearty smile, a kiss on both cheeks: 'Oh, I've soiled you again with lipstick. Never mind, it's a proof of love.' We offer a box of chocolate pralines, occasionally a bottle of red wine: 'Thank you so much, the doctor said it's good for my heart.'

One question is enough to set her sailing on the river of her memories. She describes her village, the main road, the houses she passed on her way to school, the yard where their geese and hens ran free. She leads us through the rooms of her childhood home. Her voice caresses the furniture and curtains, and we get to know not just the house, but the texture of its happiness – as if we, too, had lived there. Her memory is startlingly vivid, as if she had been there just last year, rather than fifty years ago.

She also remembers in gritty detail each of the barracks the Lilliputs inhabited in Auschwitz, and her mimicry of Mengele's speech and gestures brings his unsettling presence into her bedroom. Still, we wanted to see the places with our own eyes; we wanted to find out whether Rozavlea and Auschwitz remembered the Lilliputs. So we flew to Bucharest, then took a one-hour flight north to Baia Mare and from there a two-hour taxi drive to Sighet, the town closest to Rozavlea.

As Perla had stated that the Lilliputs 'always performed in the biggest, most luxurious halls', we wander around the town in a search of the stages on which they had appeared. The largest public hall in town is the 'Teatrul Popular Sighetu Marmathei Sala de Spectacole Studio', across from the Piata Libertatii. The imposing name hangs over a shabby reality. The entrance has evidently fallen into disuse; it is blocked by six heavy, brown iron doors, the type usually installed in warehouses.

On the wall, a tattered poster dated eight months back announces a Laurel and Hardy-type pair of comedians and a

Troupa de Ballet, the Romanian version of a Pigalle nightclub act. The illuminated sign on the second floor reads 'Discoteca No Comment'.

'There's nothing to do here. There are no more theatre shows, only once in a while a travelling troupe comes through,' says twenty-year-old Ramona, a guide in the local ethnic museum; she favours tight blue jeans and speaks MTV English. She leads us to the only other hall in Sighet, a cinema in a state of general deterioration. Its seats are torn and dirty; its programme is mainly trashy American movies. Sixty years on, the town has lost virtually every shred of its former glory. The street names, though, have not changed, and Bogdan Voda is still the principal road. We look for the Ovitz family house, number 40: they lived here for two years after the war. The façade reveals Parisian aspirations, but inside the stairwell it is gloomy and stinking.

Before the war, Sighet had a thriving community of 10,000 Jews. Today only a few dozen remain, most of them old. Half of the town's fourteen synagogues were destroyed by Horthy's Hungarian Fascist regime, the other half by the Communists. Only one is still standing: the grand Sephardi synagogue. The American writer Elie Wiesel is the town's famous son and, because his parents attended this synagogue, it has been lavishly reconstructed recently with generous American donations. Yet, it is not an active place of worship; rather, it is a monument to a dead community. The town converted Elie Wiesel's childhood home into a Jewish museum and a memorial to 'the first man from Sighet to be awarded the Nobel Peace Prize', as the tourist brochure declares. Wiesel is the local guy who made good and attained international celebrity. However, the brochure does not mention the circumstances that led to Wiesel's departure: his transport to Auschwitz as a teenager, along with the rest of the town's Jews.

Sighet, the northernmost town in Romania, lies close to the Ukrainian border. It has 50,000 inhabitants but no car rental agency. And there is still, half a century after the Ovitzes' days here, no train connection to Rozavlea.

We stop by the Jewish community centre. We speak no Romanian and the clerk at the office understands no English. We try Hebrew, but the language of the prayer book provides no bridge either. Luckily for us, a round, short, red-faced man with a raincoat and leather case happens to come in. Everyone calls Josef Tennenbaum 'professor', because he once taught Russian in high school, but in the eleven years since the demise of Ceauşescu and his regime, Russian has been out of style in Romania. So Tennenbaum has much free time on his hands. He agrees to be our translator – with his knack for languages, he's acquired a modest facility in English – and guide.

Tennenbaum doesn't own a car. Not many do in a country where 40 per cent of the population earns as little as a dollar a day and where a pound of meat costs $1.25 and a pack of Marlboros one dollar.

Full of initiative, he rushes outside, returning half an hour later with Berciu Petru, an unemployed technician whose ancient Delta – the Romanian version of a Renault 12 – is in tip-top shape.

The following morning, the four of us ride to Rozavlea, some twenty miles away. 'They owned the first car in the village,' is 76-year-old Ivan Petrovan's first response when we ask him about the dwarf family. He remembers going to school with a dwarf girl. It was Perla.

They had nice clothes, but all the Jews dressed much better than the rest of us. Jews made more money than we did – the best land in the village belonged to the dwarfs. They were especially rich because they also made money from their shows. But now there are no Jews here.

Petrovan seems uncomfortable with the revelation. 'We're not to blame,' he adds hastily.

The Hungarians and Germans forced us to evict the Jews from their homes at gunpoint. I had a horse and a carriage and the militia gave me the name of a Jewish family to drive out of the village. The majority had to walk, and it was a sad sight to see them trailing along with their blankets and pillows over their heads.

When we mention that the Jews claim that their houses were looted, Petrovan grows defensive.

It wasn't us. It was the Gypsies who did that to them. I took nothing, not even a spoon. I do have some Jewish things at home, that's true, but I bought them with good money. A Jew returned from the war and sold me his family property before leaving for Israel. We were on very good terms with the Jews. I had many friends among them and I liked the special cakes they made at Easter.

Visovan Gheorghe, an agricultural engineer who switched to politics, is now serving his second term as *primar* of Rozavlea – he is the village principal. His office is located in a sizeable estate house that once belonged to one of Rozavlea's richest Jewish families; it is the only Jewish house that was not demolished. 'When I was born the Lilliputs had already been gone for many years, but my aunt told me about them. Nothing is left of them now except memories that pass from generation to generation.' The *primar* has a computer, a printer, a fax machine and a mobile telephone. And he has his own private toilet, to which he holds the key. It's a wooden shed in the yard, with no electricity; you crouch over a deep, smelly hole in the ground. The Ovitzes had the same type of toilet sixty years ago. In the absence of plumbing or a sewage system, the *primar*'s secretary is patiently waiting outside with a glass of water and a towel.

The 7,200 inhabitants of Rozavlea have had electricity since 1960 and automatic dialling since 1994; but in 2000 only half the population had running water. The other half continues drawing water from stone wells that are dug in their yards. As in the old days, the clean water of the Iza River is preferred for laundry. Daily life in Rozavlea is hard by modern standards and the economic conditions are harsh – so harsh that they have caused a steep decline in the birth rate. In the Ovitzes' time, every family had eight to ten children; now most families have only two or three. 'We cannot afford big families – simply cannot feed them,' says the *primar*, a father of two.

Young people cannot find work in Rozavlea; their greatest dream is to leave the country. Twenty Rozavleans who have done 'guest work' in Israel are the envy of the village. After just two years on the sun-scorched scaffolding, they returned to build the most beautiful villas in the village – for themselves. Visovan Gheorghe enjoys an extraordinarily high salary by Romanian standards, 150 dollars a month, but is prepared to forsake it all if we can get him a work permit as a builder in Israel, where, he says, he could earn 600 dollars in a month. And could we tell all ex-Rozavleans in Israel that they are invited to the Roza Rozalina, the Festival of Giants, celebrated every August?

Most of the houses in Rozavlea have been built along the main road. Perla's precise description leads us to the spot where the Ovitz family's big wooden house once stood. There is still no pavement and the pedestrians share the street with the traffic – occasional cars and, more often, horses and carriages. Wooden fences shield the houses from the street and – as in the old days – each family has a bench outside, where it can sit and watch the world go by. The Ovitz house was demolished in 1969; some of its planks have been used to build a new shed in what was its yard. Even the synagogue next door, which had been refurbished with the Lilliputs' money, has been razed and two houses have been built with wood stripped from the holy site. Ion and Maria Timis know that their house stands on the foundations of the Ovitz house. Timis is a former *primar*. He takes us to a row of plum trees in the yard and points out the two oldest – they were planted by the Ovitzes. His wife gives us a jar of her special plum marmalade, a gift for Perla.

'I remember their car,' Timis says as we follow him to the spot where the garage once stood. 'I was a child when they left and for years the abandoned car was our Disneyland. Gradually it was dismantled piece by piece.' Not much has changed over the years: the stone well still stands at the entrance; fragrant flower beds still brighten the front of the house; there are still vegetables growing in the back yard, two rows of beehives, cows in the shed.

A gate of climbing vines leads to the new house. The interior not only resembles Perla's description of the old one, but virtually mirrors her current house in Haifa today! The Ovitz and Timis families are strangers to each other yet, like twins split by a twist of fate, they share an uncannily similar taste for plastic flowers, decorated cups displayed in glass cabinets, little china animals and dolls, huge family photos hanging on the walls, embroidered red table cloths. Only the tiny chairs and stools in Perla's Haifa flat mark a difference.

Of the hundred Jewish families living in Rozavlea on the eve of the war, only five returned after it, and the last of them left in 1964. Most surviving Rozavlean Jews now live in Israel. A few of them, those willing to forgive the hurt and put aside their anger over their expulsion from their birthplace, keep in touch with a former neighbour or schoolmate. Economically the Israeli Rozavleans fare incomparably better than their Romanian counterparts; before we leave for Romania, they give us parcels of instant coffee, bubble gum, cigarettes, stockings and sweets, which we distribute on their behalf.

The cemetery is the village's only sign of a former Jewish existence. At an early-eighteenth-century wooden church – the pride of the village – we turn right. After warily treading the planks of a rocking, fragile, narrow wooden bridge slung across the Iza River, we pass a corn field, and then an apple orchard. The ground is muddy and slippery.

Then we see the stones standing erect at the foot of a green hill. The cemetery plot is enclosed by a wire fence and Rozka Gamber, who lives nearby, has a key to the gate. Our driver and guide happily stay with her, in order to fill cotton sacks with ripe red apples to take to their wives. There are about a hundred tombstones. The graves of the prominent rabbis and leaders of the community are marked by solid monuments of white marble, which have fared well in the rough weather. Many of the more modest stones have simply crumbled away, their inscriptions now beyond recognition. We try to concentrate on our search for the name Ovitz, but find ourselves lingering by each tombstone. We read aloud the Hebrew names and epitaphs, as if we were holding a private memorial service for each of the deceased. For it has been decades since these graves were last visited, and decades may well pass before the silence here is broken again. We reach the outer edge of what is left of the cemetery. Among the profuse weeds and the withered headstones sinking into the soft earth, we spot the moss-covered tombstones of the Lilliputs' parents.

The Jewish community of Rozavlea was so pious that it buried men and women in separate rows. Even married couples were not interred next to each other. But the Ovitz children had managed to purchase a place for their mother in the women's row directly behind their father (then seven years dead) in the men's row. The Hebrew inscriptions, 'an honest, decent man' and 'the modest woman', bespeak a secret code that only we can decipher. From the back of the tombstones we carefully peel a splinter of each stone for Perla – Shimshon Eizik's dark grey granite; Batia's light grey.

All that is left in Rozavlea of the Ovitz family's vibrant eighty years here are two tombstones, two plum trees and a smile on the faces of the old people at the mention of the once-famous Lilliputs.

It is only a ten-minute drive to pastoral Dragomireşti in Berciu Petru's Delta but, six decades ago, it took the convoy of weary Rozavlean Jews, loaded down with their belongings, half a day to walk the eight miles to the ghetto. Today, the sound of a solitary violin from a late-afternoon music class spills from a window as we stroll through the huge, empty schoolyard – and conjures up the ghostly presence of 3,500 terrified people clinging to life and their belongings.

●

We continue following the route that the deportees took into remote Poland. The Iza flows calmly along the road as we wind through the hilly terrain. We edge past carts struggling under mountains of hay. Peasant women dressed in black stare at us from their yards, just as they might have stared at the ragged convoy on that hot day in May 1944. It is late afternoon, just as it was then. We get to the railway station of Vişeu de Sus and a stairway leads to a large waiting room with wooden benches; the walls are painted beige in a flowery pattern. The line for tickets is on the left. But this is not the way the deportees entered. They were led around the back of the building and pushed up towards the rails. There was no platform.

We step outside. The seemingly endless freight train standing in the station seems chillingly unreal, nightmarish, like a hallucination. We measure our height against that of a cattle car: the floor is over one metre high – for us, a strenuous climb; for the dwarfs, an impossible one.

You can't cross the border from this station. If you want to go to Auschwitz there's a train to Cluj, six sluggish hours away, twice a day. There you change to Oradea for an even longer, bumpier trip. A third train gets you to Budapest, and from there you take a night train to Kraków. For ten hours we are confined to a comfortable, cushioned sleeping compartment, grumbling about the unending clatter of the wheels, the tasteless coffee, the bad odour coming from our private toilet. It's impossible to imagine the conditions in the stuffy cattle car. The soft beds of the night train to Kraków somehow make us feel guilty of comfort and we sleep under the burden of history.

There are endless police and customs checks all along the way. We give up trying to tell the uniformed guards one from the other; they make themselves known with brisk commands and barking dogs. Repeatedly they wake us up by banging on our door, and every little delay in returning our passports speeds up the beats of our hearts.

●

The train from Budapest to Kraków passes through Oświęcim. A rather nice hostel now stands at the site of the death camp but, as practical as it would be, we find it too eerie even to consider sleeping under the same once-burning sky. We feel it would be sacrilege to say 'we stayed a week in Auschwitz'. We also rule out several hotels in town. The Oświęcim tourist board will never be able to tempt visitors with slogans like 'come and enjoy our facilities' or 'you'll have the time of your life in Oświęcim'. As hard as it tries, the town cannot shed its ignominious history: its name is permanently contaminated. 'Dyskoteka System', with its weekend soft-porn performances, just two kilometres away from the former death camp, sparked international denunciation: 'So near ... so soon.' In Oświęcim, time and distance will always be pedantically, austerely, morally measured.

We decide to stay in Kraków. The receptionist at the Europejski Hotel recommends the convenient one-hour train ride to Oświęcim, but we recoil at the idea of arriving by rail and decide to rent a car. For a week we shuttle between Kraków and Auschwitz, but somehow it always takes us twice the time to arrive there than it does to make the journey back.

It's free to pass under the sign *Arbeit macht frei* (Work Makes [you] Free) but you are charged at the parking lot. The visitors' centre is like any such centre anywhere in the world: a smiling hostess at the information desk, an auditorium, souvenir and book shops, public telephones, money exchanger, automatic drink machines and Bar Smak – a self-service cafeteria. Each day we arrive early in the morning and leave in the late afternoon. We skip the cafeteria, which is always packed with famished tourist groups. We cannot bear the thought of standing in line for a bowl of soup in Auschwitz; we're afraid we might even find it palatable.

Among the half-million annual visitors to Auschwitz is a steady stream of Polish high school students. They do not hide their delight at having the day off. Their exuberant puberty is incongruously highlighted when they cavort next to the barbed wire. On a screen in the auditorium, in an endless loop every thirty minutes, exhausted, tiny Ludovit Feld and Mengele's twins again plod out of the camp gates on liberation day.

When you enter the barracks area, ambiguity assails you. Several tourist groups move through the site simultaneously; the languages – Polish, German, English – dissolve as they intermingle with each other. So that you don't lose your group, you are issued a special coloured badge – ours is orange – to stick on your clothes; a disturbing echo of Nazi rules for classifying humans.

Auschwitz, as opposed to Birkenau, is where the Lilliputs underwent special medical tests. In 1942, wooden shutters were installed on the windows of the notorious block 10 to prevent observation of the criminal experiments, mainly castrations and sterilisations. The shutters remain closed to this day, and block 10 is out of bounds to visitors.

Block 24 now hosts the camp archives. On the first floor the inmate-cards in the wooden boxes are all standing in *Appell*. These cards represent the lucky ones, since 90 per cent of those who arrived to Auschwitz were extinguished immediately – their names unregistered, their arms not tattooed. For the many who were admitted but later sent to the gas chambers, these registration cards are their only tombstones.

In an austere reading room on the second floor, the archivist allows us to handle the original medical documents regarding the Ovitz family. The information on the small pieces of paper is neatly typed or gracefully handwritten in ink by prisoners who hoped their clerical skills would save their lives.

Whenever a new calligraphic style appears, we cannot help wondering why the previous prisoner-clerk was replaced and what became of him. The forms carry Mengele's extravagant signature. The banality of clinical paperwork permanently renders our Perla an inmate-patient in Auschwitz.

Many of the archive's rooms are decorated with reproductions of Dina Gottlieb-Babbitt's portraits of Gypsies and in block 12 four of her original paintings are on display. There are seven souvenir shops on the site but none sells her prints, removed when she began her legal dispute with the museum.

It is a short drive from Auschwitz to Birkenau, where over a million Jews were murdered and the Lilliput group was imprisoned. We enter by the same gates that the hundreds of trains from all over Europe passed through with their human cargo. The clean air is the first thing that strikes us. Perla and all the other survivors we interviewed spoke of the smell – always present, smoky, nauseating – of burning flesh. The second thing you notice is the green sweep of the grounds – the blades of grass and small flowers now covering the muddy marshlands that once pervaded the camp.

Nature has managed to heal itself or to restore to the land its innocence. Then we are struck by the emptiness of the place. Of the 198 barracks that once stood in Birkenau BII, just twenty remain today. All the others were levelled. The only traces left of them are the foundations and the forest of chimneys that rise like grim headstones in a horrific graveyard.

We peep into one of the remaining barracks. Slogans on the wall in Gothic German letters read 'Cleanliness is your Duty!'; 'Quiet in the Barrack!'; 'Forbidden to Drink this Water – Dangerous for Health.' The signs might have been painted by Dina Gottlieb, as such work was one of her first artistic assignments in Auschwitz.

Inside the barrack we verify the details of Perla's descriptions: the small room, like the one the Ovitz group shared at the entrance to the barrack; the wooden bunks in three tiers; the mouldy darkness. We see it all, but we don't grasp any better how on earth they ever got through it.

A guide stops by with her group. 'The lower bunk is the worst because of the cat-size rats swarming on the floor,' she explains, but her recitation sounds more like a tip for potential victims than a matter of historical fact. The huge toilet barrack has no partitions; it is made up of three long concrete banks with 174 toilet holes spaced so closely that the occupants were forced to sit next to each other, buttock to buttock, back to back.

On the ramp, you can stand on the exact spot where Mengele stood and, with the flick of a finger, determined fates. At the side of the ramp, for those who cannot visualise easily, the museum has placed blown-up prints of black-and-white photos that were taken in the summer of 1944: columns of cattle trucks, rows of dazed human beings, lines of impassive guards. One of the photographs sums up the horror and the pity of it all. It shows a desperate old woman, her face wrinkled, her body stooped, as she hurries towards the gas chamber with her three grandchildren. Afraid to lose them, she holds the youngest two tight, while the third grandchild, a girl no more than eight, trails behind, her head bowed down.

You see it all.

You understand nothing.

•

We are navigating with a plan of the camp that we bought at the book shop. Like devoted postmen, we call at every address the Ovitz group occupied: barrack 30 at the Czechoslovakian

'Family Camp', barrack 14 at the male prisoners' hospital, barrack 9 at the women's camp, then the yard where the concert was held. Near the kitchen is parked a bread cart, similar to the one in which the Ovitzes and the Slomowitzes made their way to freedom. With our legs we measure the long and, for the Lilliputs, arduous distance from their barrack to Mengele's clinic; with our eyes we assess the height of the electrified barbed wire fence and the watchtowers. We slide into the deep, muddy ditches that were dug to separate the camp sections. It's amazing the extent of security precautions that were taken by the Nazis against people so helpless and feeble.

We see it all, and understand nothing.

As if we were archaeologists exploring an excavation site, we search the ground of a block where Perla once lived. Among the rubble we find a rusty, punctured white enamel soup bowl and a tin cup without a handle. We bend down to examine the artefacts more closely, but refrain from touching these skeletons of memory.

Then, suddenly, we spot it. Something familiar: a large brown coat button.

We remember that Perla's sheepskin coat had buttons just like this, and we allow ourselves to pick it up. Tenderly, we rub the dust from it.

For a moment, we consider taking it with us and returning it to Perla.

For a moment. Then we lay it back down on the ground, to remain forever in the place where it belongs.

●

Perla Ovitz, the last of the Lilliput Troupe, died peacefully in Haifa on 9 September 2001.

SOURCES

ARCHIVES

World Center for Documentation, Research, Education and
    Commemoration of the Holocaust, Jerusalem, Israel
Auschwitz-Birkenau State Museum, Poland
Bundesarchiv, Ludwigsburg, Germany
International Tracing Service of the Red Cross, Bad Arolsen,
    Germany
The public prosecutor's office in Frankfurt am Main, Germany
US Holocaust Memorial Museum, Washington DC, USA

BOOKS

Adelsberger, Lucie, *Auschwitz: a Doctor's Story*, Northeastern UP,
    Boston, 1995
Astor, Gerald, *The Last Nazi: the Life and Times of Joseph Mengele*,
    Donald Fine, New York, 1985
Braham, Randolph L., *Genocide and Retribution*, Martinus Nighoff
    Publishing, Boston, 1983
Czech, Danuta (ed.), *Auschwitz Chronicle 1939–1945*, Henry Holt,
    New York, 1990
Enderle, Alfred, Meyerhofer, Dietrich and Unverfehrt, Gerard (eds),
    *Small People, Great Art: Restrictred Growth from an Artistic and
    Medical Viewpoint*, Artcolour Verlag, Hamburg, 1994
Fenélon, Fania, *Playing for Time*, Atheneum, New York, 1977

Gutman, Israel and Berenbaum, Michael (eds), *Anatomy of Auschwitz Death Camp*, Indiana UP, Bloomington, 1994

Hoedeman, Paul, *Hitler or Hippocrates: Medical Experiments and Euthanasia in the Third Reich*, Book Guild, Sussex, 1991

Klee, Ernest, *Auschwitz, Die NS-Medizin und ihre Opfer*, Fischer, Frankfurt, 1997

Kraus, Ota and Kulka, Erich, *The Death Factory: Documents on Auschwitz*, Franklin Books co., New York, 1966

Lengyel, Olga, *Five Chimneys: a Woman Survivor's True Story of Auschwitz*, Academy Chicago Publishers, Chicago 1995

Lifton, Robert J. *The Nazi Doctors: Medical Killing and the Psychology of Genocide*, Basic Books, New York, 1986

Lingens-Reiner, Ella, *Prisoners of Fear*, Victor Gollanz, London, 1948

Mannix, Daniel P., *Freaks: We Who Are Not as Others*, Pocket Books, New York, 1976

Matalon-Lagnado, Lucette and Cohn-Dekel, Sheila, *Children of the Flames: Dr Josef Mengele and the untold story of the twins of Auschwitz*, William Morrow, New York, 1991

Moskowitz, Elizabeth, *By Grace of the Satan: the story of the dwarves family in Auschwitz and Dr Mengele's experiments*, Rotem Publications, Ramat-Gan, Israel 1987

Müller-Hill, Benno, *Murderous Science: Elimination by Scientific Selection of Jews, Gypsies and Others in Germany, 1933–1945*, Cold Spring Harbor Laboratory Press, Plainview, New York, 1988

Nomberg-Przytyk, Sara, *Auschwitz: True Tales from a Grotesque Land*, The University of North Carolina Press, North Carolina, 1985

Nyiszli, Miklós, *Auschwitz: A Doctor's Eyewitness Account*, Fawcett Crest, New York, 1961

Perl, Gisella, *I Was a Doctor in Auschwitz*, Ayer Co. Publishers, North Stratford, NH, 1948

Piper, Franciszek and Swiebocka, Teresa (eds), *Auschwitz, Nazi Death Camp*, Auschwitz State Museum, Poland, 1996

SOURCES

Posner, Gerald and Ware, John, *Mengele: the Complete Story*, McGraw-Hill, New York, 1986
Samuelson, Benjamin, *Abiding Hope: Bearing Witness to the Holocaust*, Ulyssian Publications, Los Angeles, 2003

SELECTED ARTICLES

Enderle, Alfred and Unverfehrt, Gerd, 'Die historische Bildpostkarte als Zeugnis menschlicher Wachstumsstörungen', *Osteologie*, 1999
Koren, Yehuda, 'Saved by the Devil: an interview with Perla Ovitz', *Daily Telegraph*, 27 February 1999
Müller-Hill, Benno, 'The Blood from Auschwitz and the Silence of the Scholars', *History and Philosophy of Life Sciences* 21, pp.331–65 (1999)
Negev, Eilat, 'They Say I called Mengele "Daddy": an interview with Shimshon Ovitz', *Yedioth Ahronot*, 28 April 2000
Seidelman, William, 'The Professional Origins of Dr Mengele', *Canadian Medicinal Association Journal*, vol. 133, pp. 1169–71, 1 December 1985
Sinonius, L., 'On Behalf of Victims of Pseudo-Medical Experiments', *International Review of the Red Cross*, no. 142, pp. 3–21, January 1973

FILMS

Dood Spoor? – Alexander Katan, a film by Van Gennep, Roest and Scheren, Holland, 2001
Liebe Perla, director: Shahar Rozen, Israel, 1999

INTERVIEWS WITH EYEWITNESSES

We are grateful to Perla Ovitz, Shimshon Ovitz, Batia (Ovitz) Ben Shitrit, Mordechai, Joseph and Judah Slomowitz, Regina Ovitz and Bassie Fischman-Glazer, who agreed to undergo with us the emotionally straining journey to their haunting past.

We are also deeply indebted to the other survivors of Auschwitz, who selflessly put aside their own tormenting experience, to tell the tale of their co-prisoners, the dwarfs: Dina Gottlieb-Babbitt, Kalman Bar-On, Peter Grünfeld, Efraim Reichenberg, Solomon Malik, Abraham Cykiert, Gitta Drettler-Budimsky, Isaac Taub, Eta Tessler, Zvi Klein, Leah Nishri, Ibby Mann, Arie Rubin, Zipora Schaps, Moshe Offer, Sarah Wirzberger, Yona Lachs and Sarah Angel.

Many ex-Rozavleans and inhabitants of Transylvania enriched us with reminiscences about life in the village before the war, and their colourful accounts were vital to rebuild the story: Haim Perl, Abe Glazer, Arie Tessler, Roza Stauber, Shoshana Glazer, Herman Szabo, Efraim Topel, David Giladi, Hanan Akavia, Ben-Zion Tessler, Israel Popowitz, Eliezer Stauber, Malka Solomonowitz, Dvora Pach-Kahana and Miriam Sheinberger.

And we thank Alphons Katan for sharing with us the story of his parents.

INTERVIEWS WITH EXPERTS AND ADVISORS
We are grateful to the historians Professor Israel Gutman, Professor William Seidelman, Dr Daniel Nadav, Professor Isaac Peri, Dr Gideon Greif, Helena Kubica, Professor Bezalel Narkiss, Professor Alex Carmel, Professor Michael Har Segor, Amnon Weinstein and Tuvia Friedman.

The geneticists Professor Benno Müller-Hill, Professor Raphael Falk, Professor Zvi Borochovitz, Professor Avner Yayon and the biochemist Alexander Sharon.

RESEARCHERS AND TRANSLATORS
Our researchers, Professor Ladisau Gyemant and Maria Ujvari in Romania, Gjorgi Szilagyi in Hungary, and Joseph Rosen, Miriam Shkedi and Inbal Berner in Israel, furnished us with invaluable findings.

SOURCES

We could not make our way in the Babel of tongues without our small army of dedicated translators: From Romanian: Yehuda Gur-Arie and Joseph Tennenbaum. German: Miriam Ron, Michael S. Englard and Nurit Carmel. Dutch: Effie Weiss. Polish: Michael Ben Avraham. Hungarian: Judith Berner. Russian: Haim Dobolpolsky.

We enjoyed the good assistance of Hannelore Witkofski, Moritz Terfloth, Mihai Armenia, Hari Markus, Eva Kor, Sylvain Brachfeld, Haviva Peled-Carmeli, Ferenc Katona, Shahar Rosen, Benoit Massin, Dr Ute Deichmann, John Dollar, Debbie Perman-Brukman and Professor Gustav Spann.

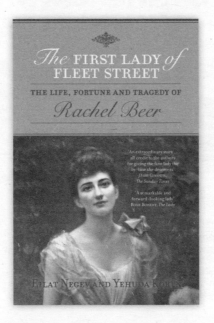